I0639761

SWORN

BOUND TRILOGY BOOK THREE

KATE SPARKES

SPARROW & CAT PRESS

For the readers~
The ones who believe in fairy tales, who carry the magic of stories in your hearts, and who bring worlds to life in your imaginations.

Thank you.

1

ROWAN

The fairy tales that once fed my hunger for adventure made it all seem so simple. After the heroes overcame their challenges, the happily-ever-after followed just as dawn follows the darkest night. Small losses led to greater gains, love overcame all, and those with the purest intentions were certain to win in the end.

My own recent adventures had turned my thoughts away from those stories, but I longed to inhabit them again as I struggled to calm my pounding heart and the magic within me. Never had I felt so far from living the fairy tale I'd once dreamed of.

My prince had rescued me, and I had personally vanquished my greatest enemy. But instead of riding off into my happy ending, I found myself surrounded by enemies—a band of disheveled and tough-looking thieves who had stopped us on this dark forest road and taken our weapons. The ever-after I so hoped for seemed to be retreating as quickly as my dear friend Florizel. I'd told her to flee when enemies came, and the flying horse was now no more than a dark speck against the blue sky that showed between the branches overhead.

Florizel's departure didn't leave me without allies. I had Aren by my side, a man I once feared and now loved more than I loved the magic and the freedom he'd helped me discover. Counting him, myself, and Ulric, the deposed king of Tyrea, we had three powerful magic users in our little party.

Added to that we had Aren's sister Nox, a gifted Potioner who, even without channeling magic, could hold her own in a fight. Flanking her were the merfolk, Kel and Cassia, appearing to be nothing more than beautiful, bronze-skinned humans as they sat astride their horses and shot glares as cold as the ocean's depths at our would-be captors.

Thirteen thieves surrounded us in a neat circle. The thief standing next to Ulric was needle-thin and sharp as a blade. He let his eyes wander from face to face, then down over my body. I pulled my ragged, filthy skirt a little lower over my legs and wished we'd found time to stop in a town to pick up a change of clothes. My comfort was a minor concern, but I had a history finding myself in inappropriate clothing when I needed to flee. I had no doubt we would be doing just that as soon as Ulric gave the order. They had taken our blades, but we still had our power.

I glanced at the king, who had ordered us not to identify him, and found I couldn't read anything in his expression. He was as hard and inaccessible as the first time I'd seen him in a lonely prison cell, if somewhat more fearsome now that I knew who he was and what he was capable of.

The leader of our enemies, a fellow in a jaunty cap completely out of place on a rogue thief, released my horse and Aren's as the others closed the circle around us and finished distributing our few weapons among themselves. He shifted his attention back to the dirty, pale-haired girl who had burst in moments before to leap to our defense.

"They're not coming with us," the thief said.

She crossed her arms. "They have to."

Patience had spoken for us after the thieves attacked, but I still didn't know whether she counted as friend or foe. She'd been friendly once, when her family of Wanderers had sheltered me and Aren on a rainy night, hiding us from enemies. Much had changed since then. My stomach clenched as the sunlight illuminated scars on her face that hadn't been there the last time we met. Back in the autumn, Patience had been bright, cheerful, strong-willed and ready to command the world. She'd been whole, and running through a fire-warmed tent with her friends. Now she walked with a limp, and her left eye was gone, replaced by a scarred mess of shiny skin.

Her remaining eye, blue as the sky, never left me as she spoke to the thief. "They can help us, I know it. Jevan, please. Just bring them back, and let Goff and Laelana decide what to do with them."

"This is foolishness," interjected a broad-shouldered brute who stood near Ulric, gesturing with his newly-stolen sword as he spoke. "Cut their throats or toss them on their asses and take the horses. I don't care either way, but we've been standing here too long. We should be gone as ghosts by now."

This Jevan fellow had stated their mission clearly enough. *Death to the monarchy.* He clearly had no idea he'd announced this to the rightful king of Tyrea and his son, that his words should have been justification for the Sorcerers killing him where he stood. To these thieves, we were a small band of travelers unfortunate enough to have been caught in their trap. Powerless.

The urge to release my magic's destructive potential grew stronger as Jevan eyed his weapons and the others gripped their mismatched daggers and clubs tighter, eager for a fight. The familiar tingling of magic flowed through me as I struggled to hold back, to obey orders. My horse shuffled nervously, and Ulric shot me a sharp look. His gray hair, peppered with brown now that his magic was recovering after years in prison, hung over his eyes and gave him a savage look.

Aren watched my struggle as well, guarded and concerned. "Better control that," he muttered.

The thieves would think he meant the horse. I knew better. Aren hadn't seen the flooding I'd caused back in the city, but he knew what my magic could do if unleashed, its potential to harm friends as well as foes. His dark eyes never left me, even as a thief stepped closer to his horse.

I looked to Ulric again, and he shook his head.

To not act now when we were so able seemed cowardly. Aren could have reached out and broken the leader's mind, or transformed into an eagle and attacked while his father called an earthquake, blinded them, or stole their strength. And I—

Could kill by drawing water, a dark voice within me offered.

That did it. My magic quieted instantly as Dorset Langley's face appeared in my memory, full of life at first, then drawing in on itself as my magic—as *I*—pulled the water from his body until he was little more than a bony husk on the ground. Relief came with surrender, and I despised myself for being happy to let go. Even after everything I'd accomplished in the past week, my fear was strong enough to turn me into a mouse when I should have been a roaring mountain lion.

And I was glad of it, if it meant not killing again.

Coward.

Ulric turned to Patience. "I don't think your friends are inclined to listen to you, my dear."

Patience spit on the ground. "Jevan, take 'em back and I promise I won't follow you any more. And I won't pester about helping with the hunt."

Jevan's pale brows drew together, and a hint of a smile turned the corner of his lips. "This is that important to you, little savage?"

She crossed her arms. "Not just to me. They have something to do with all of the big things going on in this country. It would be stupid to kill them without letting Laelana get some answers."

Jevan scratched at his neck. His men looked at him, at each other, at us. Clearly they weren't about to make a move without his say-so.

"Very well," he said at last. "But this is on you, girl. We'll take them with us, but when Goff doesn't like the look of them and their heads end up in the dirt, that'll be your fault. I'm happy to leave them here and let them live." The casual words about what he obviously considered our inevitable deaths sent a chill over me.

Ulric's lip twitched. *He must be insane,* I thought. Trading fair odds of escape for what could turn out to be an army and a bloodthirsty leader, perhaps one with magic we knew nothing about...

Patience nodded. "Fair enough."

Jevan rolled his eyes. "Gods, Patience. You're going to be the one with an axe at your throat one of these days."

She looked over our party again. She obviously didn't recognize the deposed king, and she'd never met Kel, Cassia, or Nox. She only knew me and Aren, and not by our real names. We'd been rain-soaked and exhausted travelers when she met us. She had no idea what she was getting herself into if she brought us back into her life.

"Nah," she said quietly. "Goff won't like them. Laelana won't either, but she'll see reason."

Something besides the fresh scars troubled me, but it took me a moment to figure it out. The child seemed to have aged incredibly in just a few months. She'd struck me as a charming little girl of perhaps eight when we'd met, spirited but well-meaning, precocious and playful. She'd obviously been an educated child before, but now spoke like an adult, and appeared to carry the weight of the world on her thin shoulders.

What happened to you?

Questions would have to wait. "Off your horses, three of you," Jevan ordered us. "Double up. Timmin, take a horse and we'll lead them. Everyone else surround and keep up."

Aren frowned and glanced at his father. Surely now we'd act. Patience may have meant well, but this detour would delay our mission. Ulric only stared straight ahead, and Aren's jaw clenched tight. He obeyed, though, and kept his silence.

Perhaps he trusted that Ulric had a plan. I certainly hoped so. I couldn't seem to get a handle on the man at all. Not since we'd gained our freedom and he suddenly lost whatever respect and affection he might have had for me when we were imprisoned together. I'd received a pat on the back for killing a man Ulric hated. Since then, I might as well have been invisible to him. No more encouragement, no kind words, no suggestion that I might be helpful in the upcoming struggle to regain his throne from his eldest son.

It pained me to be discarded so easily, and with no reason given. All he'd put me through in his attempts to shape me into something he could use to escape prison, the work I'd done and everything I'd accomplished, seemed to mean nothing. I flushed with anger at the memory of the cruelty he'd thought necessary to train me, but it cooled quickly. I'd seen what he was capable of. Stealing an enemy's strength, confusing them with moments of invisibility, shaking the earth and causing it to swallow soldiers whole. Even without his magic he was dangerous, a strong and capable fighter. I could hardly afford to make an enemy of him.

So I will obey. For now.

I climbed up behind Aren on his horse, and Patience took mine. She sighed as she settled into the saddle, taking weight off her feet. Kel rode with Nox, leaving Cassia with Ulric. He maintained his stony expression as she found her seating and put her hands gingerly on his arms to steady herself. The pair didn't let their discomfort show, but acted as though a human king and a mer woman were the most natural companions imaginable.

And that, I realized, was how we had to present ourselves. Unified. No sign of the tension between Aren and Ulric, left over from years of neglect and cruelty. None between Nox and her father after his abandonment twenty years ago. No visible uncertainty in me as I struggled to understand my place in the group, in the world. Certainly no clue that the merfolk had a neutral yet tenuous relationship with Ulric, and only wanted him back on the throne because he was less of a threat to them than Severn, the son who deposed him.

No problem at all.

Jevan rode ahead of Nox and Kel, their horse's reins secured to his saddle to keep them from bolting. He didn't seem to notice Nox's icy blue eyes glaring at the back of his neck, or the way her fingers twitched as though longing to reach for the dagger they'd taken from her. Kel put an arm around her waist, and she leaned back against him.

They made for a strange couple. Nox was every bit as cold and hard as Kel was kind and warm. Human and mer. Land and sea. For the life of me I couldn't figure out what he saw in her, but he was obviously smitten.

Another of the thieves rode Cassia's horse and tied Aren's to it, preventing escape unless we wanted to attempt an awkward dismount and flight on foot. Ulric rode slightly ahead of us, flanked by men with swords and knives drawn, and another on foot leading the horse by the reins. I doubted Ulric would have submitted to such an indignity under other circumstances, and wondered again why he wouldn't allow us to act.

Aren tensed as his father glanced back at us. I squeezed my arms tighter around his waist, and he brushed his fingers over mine.

I relaxed slightly. We were together. That was the important thing. We'd almost lost each other only days before. Aren had nearly lost his magic and his life. But now we were together, and we would be fine. His magic was strong. His wounds were nearly healed. I had control over my power, at least in theory, even if the memory of what I'd done with it gave me nightmares. We would face whatever came, together, stronger as a team. I could overcome anything as long as I had him.

Ulric's glare focused on me, and his brows gathered into a deep scowl. My heart skipped. A week before, that expression had been saved for the prison guards and times when Ulric spoke of the Darmish king or Dorset Langley.

And I killed one of them, I thought. *I saved us. How does that make me your enemy?*

We rode on through the spring forest, leaving the road behind. Yellowish mosses covered the trunks that surrounded us, and the horses' hooves crunched over last autumn's foliage. The forest here was less lush than what we'd encountered days before at the border. Spring was stunted. The sun shone warm enough, but something else felt wrong. I closed my eyes and loosened my hold on my magic slightly—not to attack, but to feel. The lack of water quickly became obvious. Even if I'd wanted to use my skills, I wouldn't have been able to call much to me from these woods.

Still, the forest canopy came alive with birds tweeting to each other as we passed, their voices masked beneath the mumbled conversations of the men around us. Our group kept silent until

Cassia whispered something into Ulric's ear. The fellow walking beside them slapped her hard on the leg.

The look she shot him should have had him writhing on the forest floor, but he just grinned up at her. She lifted her chin, paying him no more attention than she would a nipping fly.

Do something, old man, I thought. Nothing I'd heard about the king of Tyrea had led me to believe he'd put up with such disrespect, even if he believed Cassia capable of taking care of things herself. But he remained as he had been, unconcerned.

Patience glanced back over her shoulder at them, but said nothing.

Nox snapped her fingers, and Aren and I turned around. She didn't speak, but stared pointedly at her twin brother. His shoulders tightened, and he shook his head. She nodded and closed her eyes, and I realized that she was trying to communicate with him. As a Potioner, she lacked the magic that protected me from Aren invading my thoughts. I'd assumed he was barred from trying that with her, but a moment later she opened her eyes and raised her brows, questioning. Aren shook his head slightly and turned to face forward.

"You could have a full conversation with her, couldn't you?" I murmured.

"Not easily, and not without them noticing," Aren said quietly, speaking back over his shoulder. "That Jevan has a little magic in him. He'll notice if I try to use any more."

Even with that quick exchange, Jevan looked suspicious. If Ulric wanted our power to remain hidden, we'd have to act like average people, giving up every advantage until he said otherwise.

"I hope your father knows what he's doing," I said.

"Me, too." Even at that low volume I picked up on the concern in Aren's voice. The thief leading our horse glanced back, and I didn't dare ask more.

We rode on until I lost track of time and forgot to be frightened. My stomach grumbled, and my thoughts wandered to dark places I only wanted to leave behind. I longed to get down and walk to ease the ache in my backside, or to reach some place interesting.

Be careful what you wish for, I reminded myself.

At least the sun was warm on my back. Nights were still cold, and our blankets too few. The deep chill in my bones felt like it had moved in permanently.

The man who had slapped Cassia touched her leg again, brushing his fingers over the outside pocket on her thigh. It seemed he'd spent some time working up his nerve. "You from around here?"

"No." Ice dripped from Cassia's voice, but the idiot kept grinning.

"Just passing through? Too bad about all this. I'm sure we can make you comfortable for the night. I have a lovely—"

"No."

Ulric looked down his nose at the man. "The lady's not interested, friend. And as much as I'd enjoy seeing her hand you your stones on a platter, I would advise leaving her alone. We don't want trouble."

A smarter man would have cowered under the look in Ulric's eyes, and the tone of his voice would have sent him running. As it was, he merely snatched his hand away from Cassia's leg and stepped back. He chuckled nervously. "Feisty one, eh?"

"Shut up, Morgan," Jevan barked. He'd lost his jovial attitude over the afternoon, and if he wasn't fearsome, he at least looked like someone to be taken seriously. I tried to sense his magic, and couldn't. Years of being cut off from my own power had left me without an instinctive feel for it. I'd need to practice that.

Aren stretched his back and rolled his left shoulder forward. He'd done an incredible amount of healing since our return to Tyrea, but the deep knife-wound he'd taken back in Darmid still troubled him. The scar would fade. His always did, save for the strangely patterned one that his brother Severn had left on the other side of his back when Aren was a child. I reached over and absently scratched at my left arm, where I'd taken a nasty injury only days before. Magic had held me together and Nox had offered a salve to speed things up, and the scar was healing well.

But something about my magic felt wrong, something that went deeper than my horror at what I'd done.

Patience let out a high-pitched whistle as we reached the top of a low rise in the forest floor. An answering whistle came from high in the trees, and a young woman dropped to the ground, landing in a crouch well ahead of the horses.

She stood and looked the group over.

"I don't think this were the plan," she observed, and sucked air through the gap between her front teeth.

"They're friends," Patience said. She looked back again and made eye contact with me for the first time since we'd left the road.

The young woman looked us over again and walked away, dirt-brown ponytail swinging behind her. Aren's horse plodded forward. We came closer to Ulric and Cassia, and Aren leaned over to speak to his friend.

"You all right?" he asked her.

She brushed her thick, dark hair back over her shoulder and shrugged. "Fair enough. The old man might need a rest, though. He's slumping."

Ulric grunted.

"Is that so, old man?" Aren asked.

Ulric shot him a dark look. "Not too old to whip you, boy."

I couldn't tell how much of the conversation was for the benefit of the thieves.

Patience slowed to ride beside us. "We're almost there now. You'll all be able to rest."

"Almost where?" I asked.

"I guess I'd call it home." She certainly didn't sound excited to be there.

"Are the others here?" I asked. "The Wanderers?" It would be good to see them again, to know that they were safer than Patience's appearance might indicate.

She closed her eye and drew in a long breath. "Those who are left are here." She leaned forward to address the man who led Ulric's horse. "Mind if I speak to them privately?"

He frowned and turned to Jevan, who nodded. The thieves

released the horses and rode ahead, though others still surrounded us.

Now, I thought, expecting Ulric to make his move. He only accepted the reins and kept his eyes forward as though this were all part of his plan.

"It was the king's men," Patience said.

"Severn's?" Ulric asked.

Patience raised her eyebrows. "Only king we've got. He found out that we were harboring fugitives. Guess he didn't care for that much." No accusation in her voice, but I felt her words like a knife to the heart. Patience squeezed her eye closed, and a tear trickled from between her whitish lashes. "Same ones that got us the first time, before we met you two. When that demon horse screamed and I saw the torches, I thought I was having a nightmare. They..." She shook her head, hard. "Mama's dead. And Papa. And Frans. And—"

I squeezed Aren's hand as the girl took a deep, shuddering breath. I wanted to reach out to her, and didn't know how.

"I'm sorry, Patience," Aren said, and I sensed that this was one of his rare, genuine apologies rather than an expression of condolence. "Your mother was a great woman, and wise. I only knew her briefly, but..." His voice trailed off.

What else was there to say? Without us, the Wanderers might have been left alone to make a new life somewhere. Because they'd given us shelter, Jein and her husband were dead, and Patience was a half-blind shadow of the girl she'd once been. They'd helped us, and Severn had made them pay for their disloyalty.

The Aren I'd met back in the autumn wouldn't have cared, or wouldn't have allowed himself to acknowledge it if he had. Not so now. "I'm sorry," he said again.

During our time in prison, I'd become familiar with the strain of displeasure that showed around Ulric's eyes as he listened to Patience's story. He'd worn that expression while calculating escape plans and plotting his revenge on the people who held him captive. I remembered what Aren had told me about Ulric, that he was a bad father and a good king. It seemed he wouldn't leave this debt unpaid when he took his throne back.

One more item in Severn's ledger, written in blood-red ink. At least that was one thing we could all agree on.

We rode through a section of forest where the trees grew so close together that the horses had to pass through single-file, flecking their coats with sharp-scented pine sap. On the other side, an encampment of wooden huts came into view, nestled amongst shallow dips and hollows in the land. The village blended into the forest and stretched so far back into the trees that I couldn't see where it ended. The buildings were cobbled together from a combination of wood, stone, and metal that might have been plucked from a garbage pile, but they looked sturdy enough. Peak-roofed canvas tents dotted the spaces between.

People walked about, talking and laughing. Light flashed from the only stone building in view, accompanied by the hammering sounds of a blacksmith's shop. Several adults sparred with swords in a makeshift village square, dressed in simple leather armor and cheered on by a flock of small children. A chicken squawked, and an axe bit into wood. Somewhere nearby a baby cried, and a horse whinnied in the distance.

Patience's lips set into a firm line as she took in the sight.

"Welcome to Rebel's Glen."

2

AREN

Over the course of my life, I'd used my power for many things. To keep secrets, to gain trust, to twist minds and challenge foes, and to defend those I learned to love. I overcame challenges that would have destroyed a lesser Sorcerer, fought my way past great dangers, and set a lost king free.

I thought I'd freed myself, as well, but all it had taken was a nod from my father to tell me I was back to following orders and being used for my family's benefit. Our humiliating capture had left me with plenty of time to think things through, and I didn't like any of the conclusions I reached.

"Dismount," Jevan ordered as we entered the village. Ulric offered Cassia a hand to help her down, allowing her to ignore a less-appealing offer for assistance, then swung his leg over the horse and eased himself to the ground. The thief who had led their horse through the woods took it away, along with their bags. My father had recovered well from his prison ordeal, and from his unexpected collapse in the mountains after he used up the last great burst of the excess magic he and Rowan had gained after their escape. He looked none the worse for the day's adventure.

I looked closer. He glanced around with narrowed eyes, but

not an unpleasant expression. People were already gathering at a safe distance to look at us, and he nodded to those who offered a friendly expression or a warm smile. He looked as though he already ruled the place. He did, in theory, at least until time ran out for him to reclaim the throne that Severn was technically still only minding for him. I couldn't remember exactly when he'd been declared missing, but it was in the summer. Time was running short.

So why are we here, I wondered again, *instead of on our way to him reclaiming what's his?*

We both turned at the sound of Nox's voice, grumbling and cussing out the apprehensive-looking young flagpole of a man who had claimed the horse she and Kel had been riding. I felt a sort of sympathy for the poor fellow as he ducked his head and fled under a near-physical barrage of muttered "Son of a—" and "Does your mother know you're—" and "Worm-eating, pasty-skinned, arse-kissing—"

"Nox," Ulric warned. She turned her glare on him, but quieted.

While he was distracted by her, I opened myself to him. He wasn't using any magic, but its presence felt strong. At least that was reassuring. I'd wondered when he refused to use it whether he was weak, in spite of his physical recovery. I probed deeper. The magic would protect him from my skills, but if I could catch a glimpse of anything…

I caught only the faintest sense of his analytical interest in our surroundings before he turned to glare at me. I stopped prodding.

"Enjoying yourself?" he asked.

"Furthest thing from it."

Ulric walked a few paces away, and the people watching took matching steps back. He didn't seem to have any desire to speak with them, but had no fear of them, either. That fact should have made me feel more confident about our situation, but his actions that day were still all wrong.

We could have escaped. Had I been leading us, we'd have left the thieves bleeding into the dirt and been on our way before Patience showed herself. They deserved no better.

Patience, though. She was different. The girl now paced in slow circles around our little group, and I couldn't tell whether she imagined herself to be containing us or warning off the others. I reached out to her, letting my magic take in what she held near the surface of her mind. Not prying—she would notice that, sharp as she was. But the girl had no magic that I could sense, and would be easy to read without digging too hard. Not as easy as a drunk or someone who was emotionally excited, but I would take what I could.

The air around the girl darkened, and the grief she carried with her wrenched at my gut. She hid the depths of it well. Just opening myself to a sense of it weighed me down so that I wondered how she found the strength to take each step as she circled us.

This was why I'd tried for so long to shield myself from my own emotions and to ignore them in others as best I could. Feeling meant pain, and showing pain meant showing weakness. Though she hid the worst of it, Patience still wore her broken heart like a heavy cloak wrapped tight around her. If she knew what was good for her, she'd turn it into armor. The weight of it was too much for someone so small to have to bear, but that fact hadn't protected me when I was far younger than her.

Grief and loneliness don't play by the rules of common decency.

Nox muttered again, and I turned. She stood with Kel, fingers entwined with his as he rested a hand on her waist—presumably to keep her from charging after the man who was walking across the camp with the bag containing her collection of magical herbs.

"Honestly," she said. "It's not as though anyone here will know what to do with them."

Kel bit back a smile. "That's your greatest concern? We've been taken prisoner by people who seem set on killing off your family, and you're worried that someone will misuse your carefully preserved and curated collection of plants."

"Yes."

The smile broke over his face. "I do like you."

Nox sighed and quirked an eyebrow at me as she nodded her head in Ulric's direction. It was the same gesture she'd made back on the road, obviously wanting to communicate. Back there I'd caught her question—*What's wrong with Ulric?*

I wished I could answer. Even if I'd been free to use my magic to put my thoughts into her mind, and even if my doing so wouldn't have frightened and disgusted her, I had no answer to give.

I stepped closer to them. "You really want to try that?" I asked. "Thus far you haven't seemed too enthusiastic about me invading your thoughts."

Nox frowned and brushed her black hair out of her face. The afternoon had grown warm, and strands stuck to her cheek, tracing the curve of a faint scar. "Not really. It's unpleasant, and I'd prefer to never have anyone mucking about in there. But if it could help..." She shivered. "I'm willing to do what it takes."

"Thank you. But you're safe for now."

"I wish you could promise that we all were," Kel said, and glanced at our surroundings. "Not from you. From all of this."

"I know. Try to be ready for anything."

Nox reached for the dagger at her waist, then flinched as she remembered that it was gone. "I feel distinctly unprepared."

"Ulric seems to think he has things under control." I didn't bother hiding the hint of irritation in my voice.

She scowled. "Very reassuring."

Seeking our father had been an act of desperation on my part. I disliked the man, and had felt no sense of personal loss when he went missing years before. He'd ignored me through most of my childhood, passing me over in favor of more promising children. He'd allowed Severn to mold me, to use me, to turn me into a heartless monster in his own image. I wanted to have faith in my father, to trust that he would take his throne back and finally give me the respect I deserved and the freedom I desired, but things were never so simple in my family.

Nox's lips disappeared into a tight line as she watched Ulric, who stood near Jevan—not speaking, not moving, not appearing at all concerned. Kel leaned in to whisper something to Nox, and she relaxed. She said something back, and he chuckled.

"What's so funny?" I asked.

"Nothing," he said. "It does help to find humor where we can, though. Sometimes it's all that gets me through."

Cassia came closer, joined by Rowan. "I'm afraid I don't see anything amusing here," Cassia said.

"You're just not looking hard enough," Kel answered, and gave his sister a forced smile. "We'll get through this. You'll be home soon."

Her lips tightened. "We'll see."

Cassia and Kel had been invaluable in saving Ulric and Rowan, but the journey had taken a toll on them. Though Nox was able to treat the cough that came with a mer spending too much time on land, Cassia lost more of her energy and her usual shine every day. If Kel still had his, I suspected it was only because he had Nox to keep him interested in life on land.

"What are you thinking, Aren?" Rowan asked. She'd been taking everything in as we entered the strange village, and though she had to be as uncertain as any of us, she didn't show it. Quite the change from the first time I'd seen her abducted.

"I just want to know where we stand," I replied, aiming for a reassuring tone that did nothing to settle my own nerves.

Jevan stepped into our circle. "You'll know soon enough. Who speaks for your group?"

Before I could answer, Ulric spoke up. "I do." He gave me a warning look, as though he knew I'd been about to speak.

Rowan looked from him to me, eyes narrowed.

He's the rightful king, I reminded myself, *and my father.* He had every right to take command. It rankled me, though. I had no desire for his position, but I'd led this group for longer than he had, and no one had asked him to take over. *Get through until he's back in Luid and Severn's gone, and then leave all of this behind.*

The thought calmed me. I could suffer his insults, his contempt, even his attempts to control me until then. As long as the end was in sight—an end that, Goddess and gods willing, would involve me and Rowan leaving my family behind forever

—I could make it through. He wouldn't control me or change me.

We all followed Jevan to a hut slightly larger than the rest. A pair of burly men stopped us outside the door.

"What's this, Jev?" asked the one on the left, a bald man with a deep scar cut across his right cheek and over his nose. His fingers played over the hilt of a sword that was little better than a clumsy iron rod. Dangerous enough in the hands of a fellow as big as this, but if that was the best these people could offer their guards, they might not pose as much of a threat as I'd anticipated.

Jevan removed his cap and brushed thinning hair away from his forehead. "Visitors," he said. "Patience thought Laelana and Goff should see them."

The other guard snorted. "Ye're gonna get it." His left eye looked toward us, moving independent of the right. "Or they are."

When the cockeyed guard stepped into the building, I leaned closer to Ulric. "You're going in there?"

"It would seem so," he said, quite calmly.

"Why? We could be gone already. We could have escaped back on the road, and no doubt should have."

He frowned but said nothing, as though my concerns meant nothing to him.

You will take me seriously, I thought, but held my tongue. He needed me, needed all of us. If this was the price I'd have to pay to get my brother off the throne, so be it. I'd suffered worse indignities than a king's dismissal.

The guard returned and motioned for Ulric to enter. "You and one other. The rest stay outside."

Ulric turned to look us over. His gaze rested on Rowan, considering her. This Laelana was a woman, and from the way people spoke I thought she was in charge. Showing a strong female presence wouldn't hurt. It would be a smart move for him to take Rowan inside.

He turned away from her and nodded to me, then strode into the hut. I caught Rowan's wince at the slight I'd hoped she wouldn't pick up on, but there was no time for reassurances. I followed my father.

It took a few moments for my eyes to adjust to the darkness inside the windowless building. A few lamps burned on the walls, set mid-way up and sending out smoke that darkened the roof and thickened the air. My eyes watered. Two figures sat at one end of a long table, both wrapped in furs that turned them into indistinct lumps. They rose as we approached, followed by the scar-faced guard.

"Good day, strangers." A woman's voice, clear and musical. She stepped forward and lowered her hood—bear-skin, unless I was mistaken.

Ulric smiled at her. "It certainly was until your men decided to relieve us of our horses and belongings. I'm afraid our situation has become somewhat bleak since then. I don't suppose you could suggest a way we might rectify that?"

Her wide lips returned his smile, but her eyes remained distant as they took him in, then turned to me. She radiated strength and self-assurance, but not magic. I opened myself and sensed no immediate threat. If anything, she was confused about what to do with us. As her gaze traveled over me, taking in my face, my body, and the travel-worn shirt that clung to my chest, I sensed that she was getting ideas. Nothing that would get us to Luid any faster, though.

"I don't think you really expect to get your horses back," she said, and turned to her companion. "Goff, what shall we do with our guests?"

He grunted. "Too late to kill 'em, I suppose."

"Indeed. Or to abandon them on the road, as Jevan should have done. Where is Patience?"

The guard ducked out and closed the door behind him.

Laelana shed her furs and laid them over the table, revealing a lean body and long, blonde hair that glowed in the lamplight. "Where were you bound, strangers?"

Goff drew a long dagger and tapped it against the table. He kept his hood up, but the ugly expression on his heavy-jawed face showed clearly enough.

"Home, my lady," Ulric said. He made no effort to hide his cultured accent, as though he'd forgotten that these people's explicitly stated mission was to kill us on sight. Perhaps Jevan had said that for show. He seemed like he was probably full of shit. Still, exposing our identities, even our origin, would be a mistake.

"Tell me," Ulric continued, "is it true that you work against the usurper?"

Laelana narrowed her eyes. "It's good that you call him that. Every person in this village has been harmed by him in some way. We've seen Sorcerers in our towns taken to Luid under threat of violence, or killed for refusal. We've lost family members, friends, and important members of our communities. We've fled our homes to escape the punishments for trying to hide the people he wanted to take in." She gritted her teeth. "Some have lost children, or parents. If you're friends of his, tread carefully and make peace with your gods now. My husband's knife is liable to slip." Malice swirled around the woman, directed at Severn but ready to push her to action against us at the slightest provocation.

Careful, old man.

Ulric raised his hands in front of his chest, open-palmed. "Not at all, dear lady. In fact, we may be interested in aiding you. You'll not find any among us who would wish to see Severn remain on the throne."

Goff and Laelana exchanged another glance. "Who are you?" he demanded.

Ulric turned to me, and I shook my head. We couldn't trust them. Their goals may have been the same as ours, but there was a chance that their animosity extended back further than Severn's rule. I couldn't know without probing deeper into their thoughts, and that would alert them to what we were if they had their wits about them. My muscles tensed, ready to flee or to fight.

A slow smile crept across my father's face, and he turned back to them.

"I am Ulric, the rightful king of Tyrea."

Goff's dagger was at Ulric's throat in an instant.

"Aren, don't," my father ordered, before I had a chance to transform and rip the man's face off.

Laelana stepped in and placed her hand over Goff's. "Don't be stupid. Hear him out."

Goff snarled and held his hand steady.

"Goff!"

The knife dropped, and the brute stepped back. Laelana moved closer again. Her green eyes studied Ulric's face. "It may be that our interests align, at least temporarily. Tell me, how does sparing your lives benefit us?"

"I can take the throne back," Ulric said. "But I suspect my son won't give it up easily. We need support. An army. People who recognize me."

"Still don't see what we get out of it," Goff said.

My father's smile was somehow both savage and horribly appealing. "Revenge. Your enemy removed from power." He spoke to Goff, but his attention kept returning to Laelana. "Power and wealth and security, if you earn it. I take care of those who are loyal to me. You may remember."

Laelana nodded. "Your enemies were never too fond of you, though."

Ulric shrugged. "As one would expect. But I'm sure I never hurt you as Severn has, and I promise he'll pay for what he's done."

It made no sense that Ulric should seek help here, but I had no way of asking him what he was thinking. For the moment, I acted as though we were in full agreement—or at least, I didn't let my incredulity show.

Laelana tapped a ragged fingernail against her front teeth. "So the old king lives after all. But we have no army to offer. We have men, women, children. Regular folk."

Goff rubbed his chin. "Imagine if they trained, though. Imagine them fighting. That bastard in his lovely little city falling."

Laelana glared at him. "Severn has a proper army under his command. We can't hope to fight them."

"Then what kind of rebels are you?" Ulric asked. "Is robbing folks on the road helping depose my son?"

Goff scowled.

"A fair point," Laelana said, amused by the jab rather than offended. Though Goff seemed open to the idea of fighting, my father would need to win her over if that was truly his plan.

"I will say that we're grateful for the provisions and the occasional weapons that we acquire," she continued. "Goff and I will discuss this further." I reached out to sense her surface thoughts and emotions. She held them close, but I picked up her self-interest. If she helped us, it wouldn't be for our sake. The keen glint of her eyes revealed something deeper, the seed of a scheme she wasn't prepared to think through until we were gone. "In the meantime, we'll find tents for you and your companions. You will be comfortable here." She glanced at me. "This one doesn't say much."

"No," Ulric said. "But he's useful."

The corners of her lips curled upward as she looked me over again. "I bet."

With a wave of her hand she dismissed us. The guard returned as we headed for the door, hauling Patience into the room by one arm. I looked back to make sure they weren't going to hurt her, and the girl reassured me with a cocky grin.

At least someone feels confident about all of this.

We stepped out into the sunlight and left Goff's grumbling behind us.

"That was an interesting approach," I said.

Ulric rolled his shoulders back and took a deep breath. "One must be adaptable, Aren. On the road it made sense to hide our identities and not use magic to defend ourselves. Even if we'd escaped—and we would have—Severn would have found out and known where we were. But now there's an advantage to having people behind us, to surround us and take up arms if needed to protect our interests, which align with theirs. Think of it. They're here, plotting against Severn in their ineffectual way, many of them wanted criminals, and no one has come for them. They're perfectly hidden. Where would we be safer while we make our plans?"

"I see that." I chose my words carefully, remembering that my father would not appreciate being contradicted. "But I wouldn't have trusted those people. They're desperate and powerless, and Laelana is already making her own plans. It's a bad combination, and there's no guarantee of their loyalty."

My father shook his head. "I wonder if your skills don't let you see too much sometimes. But you'll learn." He frowned, lost in thoughts I didn't dare interrupt. "We'll give these people a few days, see what they're made of, how they feel about me. There may be time to get back and take the throne by law and without a fight, but we must consider other approaches. This is a start."

"That time must be growing short," I said. I stopped as an older man approached, cautiously and unthreateningly. Without a word he moved closer, took a hard look at Ulric's face, and smiled with toothless joy. He reached out with both trembling hands, and Ulric offered one of his own to be clasped tight.

"You've returned," the old man said. "They said you were gone, but I knew you wouldn't leave us to him."

Without another word, he left us.

Ulric smiled after him, far more kindly than he ever had at me. That was his way. Beloved king of so many of his people. Ruthless with his enemies. Detached with his family, at best. Strict priorities, never violated.

I decided it didn't matter. All the better for us if he had support. I cleared my throat to get his attention again. "Surely if we left now and went straight to Luid, informed the right people of your return—"

"Aren." His voice carried a deep warning, and something else. A hint of anxiety broke through his defenses, faint and sharp as the scent of pine on the breeze. "Not now."

My chest tightened, and a chill came over my skin as I realized this was about far more than taking advantage of a bad situation, putting potential enemies at ease, or finding his supporters in an unlikely place.

He wants to hide here. But why?

Even if he thought Severn would put up a fight, he still should have felt ready to challenge his oldest son to single magical combat for the throne. Ulric was undefeated against challengers. His ability to drain and use their strength against them meant no one had ever stood a chance, except when he'd been taken by surprise. He should have been charging to Luid, not scurrying for a dark corner.

He had lost his confidence. I just didn't know why.

I was about to ask him outright about it when Rowan hurried over, followed by the others. "Well?"

"We have a place to sleep, food to eat, and folk willing to join our cause," Ulric said. "For what any of that is worth. No promises on getting the horses back."

Nox raised a dark eyebrow. "You don't think Severn's going to race out the front gates of the palace and leap into Daddy's arms when you get back to Luid?"

Ulric gave her a cold, though not disapproving smile. "Not likely. If we can rally these people, I may have an easier time of it. But we need to get them well and truly on our side, and their leaders won't be much help with that. We have a lot of work ahead of us." He looked us over. "Aren, I need you with me as much as possible. I need to know what kind of people I'm inter-acting with, whether they're liars or flatterers or hollow brag-garts. I need their strengths and their weaknesses, and you can feel that out. Use your skills, get deep into their minds."

"I'll see what I can do."

How many times had I heard similar words from Severn? I ignored the feeling of an invisible collar slipping around my neck, ready to direct and control me.

He nodded. "I doubt there's much magic in the people here, or many who would oppose you as long as you're subtle about it. Practice your magic in free moments, build any skill you can use against Severn or in battle. And if there's an opportunity to get close to Laelana, you take it." His eyes narrowed. "Understand?"

He looked to Rowan, waiting for some objection. Her jaw hardened, and she said nothing.

"I'll try to be friendly," was all I promised. This was one order I would not obey, no matter what it cost us.

Ulric turned to Nox. "Your skills will be useful here. Heal them. Help them if you can. Stitch their wounds, remind them that my leadership brings good things. Build them up, make them strong. Share your hatred for Severn."

Nox squeezed her eyes closed, possibly to keep from rolling them. "I'll do what I can."

To the merfolk he said, "Are you with us? You are of course permitted to leave, and you'll go with my gratitude. But we could use your help."

Kel didn't hesitate. "I'm staying," he said. "We told Aren that we'd see this through. Our elders want Severn deposed as soon as possible."

And if that's only the half of it, I thought as he looked to Nox, *we'll still take it.*

Cassia sighed. "He's right. We'll stay until it's more of a benefit to go."

"And I thank you," Ulric said. "I've never had the honor of fighting beside a mer, but I've heard tales of your people's bravery and ability. Do you think you can transfer your battle skills from underwater to land?"

Nox opened her mouth to object, but Cassia nodded. "It will take practice, but we've found our footing. The rest will follow."

Ulric nodded his thanks. "We'll try to keep you out of battle, but it's best to be prepared. I'll ask your opinions should we need to plan an attack on the harbor. Also, you know how irresistible your sort can be to humans."

Kel beamed. Cassia sighed.

"I'm not asking you to do anything unsavory," he said to them, and I couldn't hold back a sneer of irritation. *Oh, to be an ally instead of his offspring.* "But the more you can become a part of this village, the more likely the people will be to support me. They may find me and Aren intimidating when they learn who we are, but you can overcome that."

"No doubt," Kel said. "Should be interesting." He actually

seemed keen on the prospect, though Cassia clearly didn't share his enthusiasm.

Ulric turned to Rowan next. She looked up and squared her shoulders, ready for whatever assignment he might give her, whatever training he might challenge her new power with. "Yes?"

"You're friendly." He didn't say it as though it were a compliment. "Get in among the people. Find out what they need, what I can promise in return for their help, what they hate most about Severn." His voice could have been carved from stone for all the warmth it carried, a sharp turn from the tone he'd taken with the merfolk. "Do whatever they ask of you. Work in the kitchen. Mind their brats. Clean up the stable, if they have one in this godsforsaken place. Try not to draw attention to yourself. It will make them suspicious if they know what you're capable of. Be who you were before we met. It shouldn't be difficult."

She took a step back. A flash of anger crossed her face in the creasing of her brow and tightening of her lips, but she quickly smoothed it away. "Is that all?"

"That's all."

She hesitated, and her gaze flickered from him to me. "If it will help."

I flinched inwardly, but didn't let it show. It was for the best that she understood what my father was. I suspected she'd seen a kinder side of him when they were imprisoned together. He'd have shown her what she needed to see in order to trust him and work with him, but that wasn't the Ulric I knew. He would use her as readily as he would me if it meant getting his throne back. For now, he'd decided she needed to be put in her place, and there would be no arguing with him.

Something tugged at my sleeve, and I looked down to find Patience holding a stack of blankets, with our bags slung over her arms.

It was good that I had so much practice at hiding my emotions and reactions, given the shock I felt when I looked at her. It would take a while to get used to the sight of her missing eye, and to the dark fog of sorrow that surrounded her even when she smiled. Strange that I hadn't felt her coming, though. She had a quiet presence.

"We're moving some things around, making room for you," she said. "Guess you're my guests now. Penelope and Doug and friends.... But those aren't really your names, are they?"

That surprised me. "Your mother told you who we are?"

"She said you weren't who you told us you were, but that it was okay. That you were friends. Wouldn't say your real names, if she knew them. Gimme a hand with this stuff?"

Wonderful friends we turned out to be. I didn't normally feel guilty over things that weren't directly my fault. Until recently, I hadn't felt much guilt over things that were. Still, my gut wrenched at the thought of what had happened to Patience's family as a result of our presence among them.

We'd make things right some day. We had to.

"I'm Aren," I said as I took the blankets from her and the others relieved her of our bags, which looked far lighter than they'd been when we arrived. "That's Rowan."

The girl nodded. "I like those names better. Come on. Rowan, I've got real clothes for you. Pants and stuff. We get a lot from people on the road, so you all can use what you need." She gave Rowan's torn-off skirt a once-over and shook her head in a way that made her look like a tiny, disapproving grandmother. "Don't worry, I'll take care of you."

Rowan hid a smile behind her hand and thanked the girl.

We followed her past the space where a pair of strong young fellows continued their clumsy sparring. Ulric held me back as the others went on.

"Watch," he said. "Watch all of these people, but start here."

It was a sad display, all told. I'd never had much enthusiasm for swords, preferring to fight with my magic, but had trained for physical combat. These men had obviously not had the same advantage. Their clumsy motions would have made my old teachers cringe. One lashed out in an uncontrolled swat that landed on his opponent's arm, thanks more to the other's incompetence than the attacker's skill.

The grins on the young men's faces revealed how they

enjoyed the action, and their minds shouted their excitement to me. They'd already become legends in their imaginations, thinking themselves brave knights in the heat of battle, assured of victory. If Ulric told them they would be great warriors, they would surely follow him anywhere.

All I could picture was these heroes lying dead on a field, victims of Severn's forces and their own incompetence.

We had a lot of work to do if they were going to stand any chance at all.

3

NOX

The girl Rowan had introduced as Patience stood still as the birches behind her, watching as we dropped our bags in the tent. A pair of boys about her age ran past, yelling and kicking up dust. They swerved to avoid her as one reached out to pull another girl into their game. If Patience noticed that they overlooked her, she didn't react.

I tried not to stare at the girl's injuries, knowing well how sensitive she probably was about them. My own faint scars always set me on edge around unfamiliar people, made me wonder what they were imagining about my past. Her remaining eye was sharp and clear, but carried a distant look even as she focused on the needs at hand. That paired with her dour expression told me all I needed to know about her. That eye had seen things that didn't bear speaking of. She was bold enough, though. No shy little flower there. She already struck me as the kind of child who would grow up to accomplish great things, as long as no one held her down along the way.

"This all right?" she asked. "I know it's not much."

Cassia looked around the peak-roofed tent. Made of stained canvas, it was at least well constructed, with poles in the corners to give the space a bit of height. The space was empty, with a packed-dirt floor. The warm afternoon outside had made the air inside stuffy. "It's a little tight, but we'll be fine. At least our bedding will be out of the rain, right?"

Patience wrinkled her nose. "We haven't seen much of that around here lately."

A frown twitched at Cassia's brow. Lack of water was never good news for a mer, but she and Kel chose not to let on what they were to people who couldn't guess, and she said nothing more about it. "We're not putting anyone out, are we?"

"Nah." Patience stepped into the tent. "A couple of the hunters were using it, but they've all gone south to look for game. You'll have to use your own bedrolls, but the space is all yours for now."

Kel set his bag down and turned around slowly, broad shoulders scraping the sloped roof of the tent as he tried not to bump into Rowan. He looked like a bull trapped in a tiny pen, but he'd make the best of it. We all would. No sense complaining.

"It's great," he said, and smiled. Patience blushed. I couldn't blame the kid if she was already infatuated with him. Though I'd fought hard to ignore it, I'd been attracted to Kel from the first moment he turned that casual grin on me. It had taken longer for me to admit that I was drawn to his mind as much as his body . . . to his kindness, his humor, and the way he accepted me even though he saw straight through to all of my dark places.

I watched the muscles in his arms flexing as he spread out our bedding, the bend of his spine that was far more graceful than should have been allowed for such a broad form.

Gods, that body. Something I hadn't yet allowed myself, and a temptation that I thought might drive me mad. But that would just be another step toward being his completely, another knot to tie me to someone I had to be prepared to let go of.

Patience's whitish eyebrows pulled together, drawing the scar tissue on the left side in tight.

"You guys aren't going to have enough room for all your beds in here," she said. "There's another tent, if someone wants to help me move some boxes out of it. It's just tiny, room for one bed, but it would make more space in here if someone wants it."

"Sounds perfect," Rowan said. She grabbed her bag and Aren's, and followed the girl out the door. I tried not to be jealous of the fact that they'd have privacy. *Better to have supervision to curb temptation,* I told myself.

"Two down," Kel said quietly.

Cassia shot her brother an irritated look. "I'm sorry, am I intruding?"

"No," he said. "You are entirely welcome. But his highness will be an awkward roommate."

She grimaced. "True enough. Maybe Ulric will talk that Lala woman into finding him a private room."

"Laelana," I corrected, and set a few more blankets on top of Kel's. The bedroll they'd bought for me on our journey had been commandeered by the old man, but thus far Kel had had no problem with me sharing his space. In spite of my conflicted reluctance to move things further, spending nights with our bodies fitted together like puzzle pieces had been both lovely and surprisingly restful.

I fell harder for Kel every day, thawing under his attention. He made me feel warm. Wanted. And I wanted nothing more than to make him feel the same. But I'd been hurt before. I couldn't give myself over completely only to find myself broken again, and couldn't risk breaking his heart if I had to sacrifice myself in my personal quest to destroy Severn.

Cassia coughed into the crook of her arm. I'd need to get my supplies back and fix something for her soon. "We'll fit the three of us in here, but barely," she said. "Where did Ulric and Aren go, anyway?"

"Probably very important Sorcerer things to do," I muttered.

Kel snorted. "I know you're not jealous that Aren gets to spend time with him."

I gave a dramatic shudder. "Hardly. But it would be nice to be included in whatever's happening. A few days ago we were all working together. Ever since we added Ulric and Rowan to the group, it seems Aren's always talking to them."

Cassia stopped smoothing her thin blanket and sat back on her haunches. "I know," she said. "Believe me. At least you two have each other now. I'm sort of wondering where I fit into all of this."

Kel laid a hand on his sister's shoulder. "Sorry, Cass."

She smiled sadly. "Don't be. I'm glad we went with Aren to Darmid. It feels like that part of the journey was meant to be. But much as I agree with what you said earlier, how much good can we really do here?"

Guilt prickled at me deep in my stomach. "You're not leaving us, are you?" I asked.

In spite of the fact that we'd only known each other for a short time, Cassia was the first real friend I'd had in years. Or ever. Kel was a friend of sorts, but that was complicated. With Cassia, it was just... good. She was nearly as guarded about her emotions as I was, but I trusted her, and I enjoyed her company. I couldn't say that about many people.

But as I looked down at my things resting right next to Kel's, and hers spread out on the other side of the tent, I could see why she'd feel left out. She had explained mer ways to me more fully than Kel had, how they weren't supposed to want the emotional web that Kel and I were weaving, but that didn't mean she wasn't lonely.

"We'll see," she said. "I need to do what's best for our people, not for me, and right now getting Ulric back to Luid seems to be what we need to do. Mariana and Arnav will be happier once things are settled. But someone is going to have to report back to them some time and let them know what's happening in regards to Severn. Maybe there's even a chance that they'll help if I ask."

Kel sighed.

"What?" I asked. He just looked sadly at Cassia.

"I don't have to say anything about this," she said softly, and gestured toward our bed. "But they're going to find out some time, especially if this goes on as I think it will."

"There's nothing here you'd have to report about us, right?" I asked. By mer standards of physical affection, Kel and I were barely friends.

Kel stepped into the patch of sunlight that fell through the tent flaps. "There's more than I'd like the elders to know. They wouldn't have much of a problem with it if I was tumbling you or any other human in the hay. Even regularly and exclusively."

Cassia's lips pulled into a cat-like smile. "No. They would dismiss that as Kel being Kel."

He narrowed his eyes at his sister. "As if you haven't had humans in your past."

She flashed a coy smile, and I remembered that she and Aren had once had a very different sort of relationship from what they currently enjoyed. Even if she had no desire for that now, seeing him with Rowan couldn't possibly help her feel less like an outsider in the group.

"No," Kel continued, speaking to me, "it's the fact that we're involved in that other way that's the issue. They won't be pleased." He turned toward the doorway. "It's dry in here. Think there's anywhere around to swim?"

That was how it always went, especially in recent days on the road. We'd get close to talking about something deeper than our current situation, and one of us would change the subject. We never talked about the future, about him going home, or what would come after our mission was done. I assumed this was because there was nothing to say. Even if he did love me, even if I ever admitted to myself or to him that I felt the same, I couldn't imagine a future for us.

"There has to be a place to swim nearby," Cass said. "They wouldn't have set up a village too far from a water source, right?" We'd managed a few quick dips along the way, but the mers needed far more. She stood and stretched. "Nox, you coming?"

Much as I disliked swimming, joining them would be far better than waiting here for Ulric to come back and order me around. And there were definitely worse ways to spend my time than watching Kel in his natural form. On land, he was indistinguishable from a human man, if a distractingly attractive one, and with better manners than most. I'd been surprised when he first showed me his mer form, and continued to be astounded by how engrossing I found that body when he changed to swim— grayish skin, smooth tail, gill slits and all. Either way, he was Kel, and he was perfect in ways I'd never realized existed.

Cassia stopped a young woman as we stepped out of the tent. "Excuse me, but could you tell me where we might find a lake?"

The woman pursed her lips and looked each of us over in turn. "Nope," she said, and gave us a strange look. "You let us know if you find one, though."

Cassia thanked her, and we moved on. Rowan joined us near the kitchen tent. "What's going on?"

"Nothing so far," Kel said. "Looking for somewhere to swim."

"Oh, perfect," Rowan said. "I have something I need to practice, but I need water. A lot of it. And preferably away from people, just in case." She looked down at her hands, and a pinched expression came over her face.

She was a strange person. Too innocent, too trusting, too eager to please. She hadn't complained about the insulting task Ulric had set for her, and her lack of spine didn't warm me to her. And yet she'd been kind to me even after I stated outright that I didn't like her, offering help, thanking me for the potions and ointments that had helped heal her injuries and Aren's, asking me questions about my work. She'd saved our lives when we escaped from the city, and that was a mark in her favor. She obviously cared deeply for my brother. That was another. But in spite of the great things she'd done so recently, she seemed unsure of herself. Seeing a person in that state made me uncomfortable. Where I came from, hesitation and doubt made one a victim, as did seeking the approval of others.

I would know.

"Your magic is fully recovered and under control?" I asked.

She turned to me, eyes wide. Probably surprised I was speaking to her. "I think so. But I need to practice. I learned control in that cell, but I haven't had many chances to practice at full power since the pushback effect wore off. I don't want anyone to get hurt if it turns out I still need help containing it."

I was about to point out that her joining us might not be the best idea if she could injure us, but didn't. Kel caught the tightness of my expression, and watched the two of us carefully.

Rowan noted it, too, and took a step back. "I'll ask in the kitchen where we can find water."

"I'll come," Cassia added, and they left us.

"That was pleasant," Kel observed.

I sighed. "I'm trying to be nice, but what was I supposed to say? She rubs me backwards, that's all."

Kel laughed. "Pardon?"

"It's an expression. If you pet a cat the wrong way, back to front, they hate it. It ruffles them."

I waited for the *I'd like to ruffle you* comment that was clearly waiting behind his smile, but he held back this time. "I'm not going to tell you what to do, Nox. You can't force these things. But you might think about why you don't get along with her. See where that takes you."

I frowned, but couldn't put my heart into it. "Not everyone can be friends."

"I know. But tolerance wouldn't be a bad thing, right?" He pulled me close and kissed the top of my head.

Rowan's shoulders slumped with disappointment when she returned. Cassia looked absolutely devastated.

"There's no water."

"What?" Kel released me and placed his hands on Cassia's arms. She just shook her head.

Rowan stepped closer. "We talked to a woman in the meal tent. They used to get their water from a lake nearby—nothing impressive, but it provided enough for drinking and bathing, and was clean and clear when they got here. It's almost dried up now, just since the autumn, and everything in it was dead before that. They were collecting snow through the winter, and now they're using rainwater." She gestured to a set of wooden barrels outside the tent. "Even that's running low. It hasn't rained properly in weeks. A lot of the people want to move on, but Goff and Laelana won't have it. I suppose they feel safe here."

I scraped at the ground with the scuffed leather toe of my boot. Beneath a layer of dust, the soil was hard and cracked. "You can call water though, right? That's your magic thing?"

Rowan paled. "I... I have, when it's available. I could try now, but—"

"Never mind." I sighed and tried not to blame her for being nervous about it. She'd just killed a man with her magic a few days ago, something I wouldn't have thought her capable of. I'd try not to judge her for shying away from it now.

That's progress, I thought. I was clearly spending too much time with nice people.

Kel rubbed a hand over his face. "So there's nothing?"

Rowan glanced back at the tent again. "I don't think they'd be too happy if you stuffed yourselves into their barrels of drinking water. But we could look for what's left of the lake, and I could try to get something for you. Might get us in good with the people, too, and that's what Ulric wants."

Cassia leaned into her brother, and Kel stroked her hair. "It'll be okay, Cass."

"It's just so dry," she said, her voice muffled by his shirt.

I tried to think of something comforting to say. I didn't get a chance.

"You!" An old woman in a dirty brown dress hobbled quickly toward us, pointing a bony finger at me. A young man stumbled out of the way as she shoved past him. "You, black-haired girl! You're a Potioner?"

"I—yes," I stammered, and stepped back. The woman was tiny, but moved with the force of a hurricane.

She shoved past the others and squinted up at me with sharp green eyes framed by wrinkles like the cracks in the earth at our feet. "You're to come with me. I need help, and nobody around here knows anything."

"But I was just going to—"

She crossed her arms. "I was told you were all here to help us. This is how you're going to do it."

I gritted my teeth. *Damn you, Ulric.* "You all go, I'll see you later. Good luck with the water."

Kel nodded, and he and Cassia followed Rowan in the direction she'd indicated when she spoke of the lake.

"Now," the old woman said as she looked me over. She didn't seem impressed. "You come back to my cabin. We'll see whether you're any more useful than the rest of these ninnies."

The woman spoke quickly, and trying to keep up with her left me feeling three steps behind. I had no choice but to obey if I was going to help Ulric's mission, but I couldn't say I was pleased about it. I'd just begun to find my freedom, out from under the watchful gaze of my old teacher and then my husband. I'd had a year to make something of myself, and suddenly this crone thought she was going to use me as her new helper.

Perfect. Fantastic, really.

I remembered what Kel had said about tolerance, and told myself that cooperation would help us reach our goal of dethroning Severn faster. Perhaps I'd find something of interest to me in the old woman's supplies. *Maybe even my own confiscated ingredients.*

I followed her to a wood hut that looked to have been constructed in stages. Half had been built of logs, the other section planks, and the covered porch on the front could have been slapped on as an afterthought. A man with a bandage wrapped around his head waited outside.

"Mama Bunn," he groaned, "it hurts."

The old woman spat on the ground. "What'd you do? Horsing around again?"

"Training, Mama Bunn." He spoke respectfully, and I thought affectionately, in spite of the old woman's harsh tone.

He bent over and let the tiny woman unwrap the bandage, revealing a lump covered in cracked skin. "Looks fine," she said. "Wait here, I'll put something on it after I deal with this one." She jerked her thumb over her shoulder at me.

I followed her into the building, which was well lit by large windows, the only proper ones I'd noticed in the camp. A narrow bed sat to one side of a large room, and a curtained door covered the way into the back, which I assumed was her work area.

There could be something to learn here, I decided. I'd made the best of bad situations before, and would dig something of value out of this mudpit as well. And she might be a better Potioner than my old teacher. Odds were she didn't have my natural skill. Few did, but I could stomach a partner for a time. Perhaps we'd come up with something to lessen the people's need for water, or to expand the food supply. *I could show her what I've worked out for my own injuries, and...*

The thoughts died as she pushed a curtain aside and ushered me into her workspace. Equipment covered the rough wood counter, every piece of it filthy. The glass jars on the shelf sat un-labeled and almost empty.

"Can't get out much to forage these days," the old woman said, and sniffed. "Not as spry as I once was. But you're my assistant now. You can do it."

A deep, throbbing pain blossomed in my temples, and I real-ized I was clenching my jaw muscles tight.

"Of course," I said, eager to leave. "I'll head out now and collect—"

"No. First, you clean up. Then we'll see what comes next."

She grabbed a glass jar half-filled with creamy ointment from the shelf and marched out the door with a lopsided limp.

I set my hands on my hips and took in the mess. A large tin basin in the corner had an oil heater beneath, which I lit with a flint I found among the items on the counter. In spite of the drought, someone had filled the water barrel in the corner. I added water and soap flakes to the basin, but it would take time for things to warm.

I closed my eyes and took a deep breath. I would need hours to organize everything to my liking, but the place had the right feel for a Potioner's workshop. Sad as the supplies may have been, I felt their potential calling to me.

"I'll make this work," I told myself, and rolled up my sleeves.

~

I LOST TRACK OF TIME, pulled into the silent world of Mama Bunn's collection. The plants, dry and dull though they were after a long winter in storage, spoke to me, whispering their secrets and their potential. She'd left a brown sprig of death's light lying out—a beautiful and innocent-looking vine, but fatal even at the brush of a finger. I wondered whether that was care-lessness, or a test to see if I was a worthy assistant. I couldn't help smiling as I searched for forceps to pick it up, and decided that the old woman might be fun after all.

The light outside the windows was fading when the door creaked and soft footsteps approached.

"She's not here," I called, and dunked a gunk-covered mortar and pestle into the soapy water in the basin.

"I'm not looking for her."

Kel's voice sent a pleasant tingle through my body. I glanced over my shoulder and tucked my hair behind my ear, leaving a trail of bubbles across my temple. "Sorry, I got busy. Did you find the lake?"

"Such as it is, yes." He leaned back against the workbench and crossed his arms over his chest. "Not deep enough for us to bother with changing, and absolutely filthy. We didn't even try to wet our hands."

"I'm so sorry. Rowan couldn't help call more?"

"No. It's as if she—I don't know. She tried, then said she couldn't feel anything to draw from, anyway. She seemed relieved about it. What do you make of that?

"I have no idea what goes on in a Sorceress' head." I still suspected she was dealing with a case of nerves, or lingering shock. I might find something to help if she decided to speak to me about it.

"Watch what you touch over there," I told Kel. "I haven't finished cataloging it all."

He pushed off from the counter and wandered around the room. I turned my attention back to my work, but listened as he took the lone book off the shelf and flipped through it, moved a few clay bowls around, and went to look out the window. Always curious. I kept myself from watching him, but couldn't turn my mind away.

I was lost in my thoughts when I sensed his gaze on me. He moved closer, and the hairs on the back of my neck prickled.

"Everything good with you?" he asked.

"Of course. Why?"

"You've been washing that same bit of equipment since I got here." He looked over my shoulder and watched me rubbing bits of leaf matter off of the dark stone pestle. "Actually, you're not even washing it. More like stroking. Seductively."

I pulled a hand from the basin and flicked a handful of water at his face.

He laughed. "No, it's good. This is working for me. Maybe not so much for the rest of the dishes, though."

I resisted the urge to thunk him over the head with the club-like instrument, which still had bits of false clover stuck to it. He pressed his body against my back and sank his hands into the water next to mine.

"It *is* working for you, isn't it?" I teased.

"It's not the dishes, believe me." He brushed my hair back over my shoulder with one wet hand and kissed behind my ear, then down my neck. I tilted my head away, leaving more room for his lips to explore.

"I know," I whispered. Kel always managed to steal my voice away. "Kel, if it seems like I've been evasive about—"

"Shh."

His fingers found mine under the water, and he massaged the palm of my right hand. A tiny gasp escaped me.

It's just your hand, you silly girl, I thought, *and in filthy dishwater, at that.* But damned if it didn't make me think of all the other places I wanted him to touch me, no matter the consequences. *Perhaps a little kiss or three wouldn't hurt...*

I turned around. He was standing so close that I had to lean back and put my arms around his neck to hold myself up. "Kiss me," I said.

He did, long and deep, and wrapped his arms around my waist, pulling me even closer. His lips trailed down over my jaw and across the scar on my cheek. My hands seemed to have minds of their own as they wandered over his back, then explored the hard curves of his chest under his shirt.

"Nox, wait." A hint of regret tinged his voice.

"What?"

He pulled away. "Nothing bad. I've been thinking, and it seems important that we talk again about—"

The door in the front room slammed open, and Kel jumped back.

"You still not done?" Mama Bunn threw open the curtain. Her eyes widened. "What is this? You have men in here already?"

"Just the one," I said, biting back my irritation at the interruption.

She didn't seem impressed. "It's supper time. They've been roasting the damn pigs all day, but it won't take that long for them to be eaten. Get out of here."

We weren't going to be able to enjoy any more privacy in the cabin. I grabbed Kel's hand and pulled him out before she could change her mind and make him leave without me.

The carcasses were half-demolished before we arrived, and the line for food snaked back from the cooking pit. The crowd living in the village was larger than I'd thought, and they were all hungry.

Cassia sauntered over carrying three plates of food. She handed one to each of us and picked at the stringy meat with her fingers. I dug in as well, but Kel hesitated.

"It's not bad," Cassia said. "Really."

Kel's normally lovely skin had gone ashen. "I'm sure," he said.

"You don't like pig?" I asked.

"We're just not used to eating them," Cassia explained. "Fish makes up most of our diet underwater. Raw, but we enjoy it cooked if we're on land or at the Grotto. Fowl is fine, and we've had small animals recently. Kel, you didn't mind those rabbits."

"Does pig taste like rabbit?"

"No, but you should try it."

"I don't think I have much choice." He poked at the meat. "We're out of luck for fish around here. Or vegetables, at least for now."

There was bread, though, and I offered my share to Kel. He thanked me, and refused. "It's all about necessity, isn't it?" He pinched a bit of pork between his finger and thumb, tipped his head back, and chewed carefully.

"It's different," he said.

"Bad different?" I asked.

"No. Just different. I could get used to it."

As with so many other things in life, I thought as Cassia left us to get back in line for seconds.

"She's always been more adventurous than me," Kel said.

"I think you balance each other well."

"We do work well together when we're not bickering."

After the food was gone and the carcasses carted off for soup, the party started. Several members of the community produced instruments from their homes, drums and stringed things and flutes. Kel brightened as they began a light, lilting song.

"Now this is *good* different," he said.

"Actually, it's not." We both turned toward Aren, who wore a pained expression. "Their timing and tuning are both off."

Kel turned his nose up, but he smiled. "Don't spoil it, it's better than nothing. And look how much fun they're having."

They were, indeed. The fellow playing the tin pipe bounced on his toes, and the drummers nodded their heads to the out-of-sync beat. The children were the first from among the crowd to start dancing, but as the sun set more adults joined in. They built up the fire that lit the clearing and sent quivering shadows up onto the trees.

"You want to join them?" Kel asked me, sounding only halfway hopeful.

"No. Thank you." I looked at the ground, where his heels and toes bounced alternately. "But you go. Have fun. Just make sure you come back to me."

He grinned, kissed me hard, and shot off into the crowd.

"So you don't like swimming," Aren said. "And you don't like dancing."

"Correct."

"I'm not going to ask what you have in common."

I crossed my arms. "That remains to be seen."

Aren's lips twisted in a half-smile. "Ah. I'm sure you'll find something."

My cheeks grew warm. I had no doubt he was right, but I wasn't comfortable with that insinuation, especially from him. I scrambled to change the subject. "Where's Rowan?"

"She decided to go finish setting up our space in the tent. I don't think she really enjoys crowds and noise any more than you do."

"And you love them?"

He rubbed the back of his neck. "No, but I'm supposed to be visible." He nodded toward the other side of the fire, where Ulric sat deep in conversation with Goff, Laelana, and Jevan. "I never realized how fortunate I was that Severn let me avoid this kind of thing in the past."

"He wanted you in the shadows, didn't he?"

"He did. I think—"

Someone screamed, and the crowd surged away from the fire, headed toward us. Most of them seemed uncertain about what was happening, but were eager to get away from whatever the trouble was. They picked up speed as people closer to the fire shoved from behind. We pushed past the confused and drunken crowd to see flames crackling on the ground, outside of the fire pit and spreading at an alarming pace.

I looked around at the wood huts, the canvas tents, and the dry trees. "This whole place is going to go up."

"No, it won't." Aren's voice was confident, but something in his eyes betrayed uncertainty even as he stepped toward the flames. Ulric did the same from the other side, where Laelana remained seated, observing him carefully instead of fleeing from the danger. The fire surged up toward the wood pile near the fire pit, and from there toward the lower branches of a tree.

A massive man, stinking of sweat and bad wine, crashed into my side and knocked me down. Several pairs of feet trampled over me, and I curled into a ball with my hands protecting my head and neck. Someone kicked my lower back, and I let out a stream of curses that went unheard.

When I got to my feet again, Aren was gone.

The crowd continued to move away, though a few had turned back to see what was happening at the fire. Someone cried out. A gasp, murmurs, and then a child squealed and clapped. I couldn't see anything around the pair of tall men that stood in front of me.

A cheer went up. I shouldered my way to the front and found that the flames had disappeared completely. Ulric raised his hands to the crowd, and they hurried forward to thank him. An older woman who had clearly had too much of whatever they were drinking threw her arms around his waist and hugged him tight. Ulric patted her on the back and smiled, waving off other people's thanks as though nothing serious had happened.

Aren nodded politely at anyone who spoke to him, but moved swiftly back to where we'd been sitting. He cradled his right hand in his left, and as he came nearer the pain he was trying to hide became clear.

"What happened?" I asked.

He grimaced and held the injured limb out to me. The skin was burned red and blistering from fingertips to forearm, his shirt sleeve singed. "I'm not used to putting out fires I didn't start," he explained, "and I'm not even well-practiced at that yet. And Ulric didn't—" He frowned, hesitated, and looked back at the crowd. "These things happen when you have to try new magic. And at least the people are happy."

"Come on," I said, deciding I'd ask later what he'd been about to say about our father. "Let's get you fixed up."

I took him by his good hand and led him back toward Mama Bunn's hut.

The place was dark, and resonant snores drifted out the open window. I placed a finger to my lips and eased the door open. We tiptoed through the main room toward the curtain, making not a sound. Still, the snoring stopped and the old woman sat upright in bed.

"Who's that?"

"It's me. Nox."

"Who?"

"Your new assistant. I just need something from the back. I didn't mean to wake you."

Fumbling sounds, and the strike of a flint as she lit the lamp. She narrowed her eyes at us, and I realized I was still gripping Aren's wrist. Mama Bunn's mouth opened, then snapped shut. "Another one? Really?"

"It's not like that, Mama. He's my brother."

Her jaw dropped again, and she shook her head slowly. "I don't know how they do things where you come from, young miss, but—"

"No, Mama. Look!"

Aren held out his injured hand.

Mama Bunn sighed and swung her legs out of bed. She poked at the red, blistered skin, and Aren hissed through his teeth. "It's bad," she said. "But I have something. Come."

"I can get it," I said. "Really, we didn't mean to wake you."

The old woman's eyes disappeared into wrinkled slits. "Fine. You go ahead. Impress me. Your bag is on the table."

I forced the tension out of my shoulders as I entered the back room, lit the lamp, and discovered my things spread out on the workbench that I had so recently cleaned up. I didn't care about the mess, as long as everything was still there.

Something to cool the skin and stop the burning, I thought as I found my ice grass and combined it with the small portion of dimbleberry leaf Mama had on her shelf. I added oil from a half-empty bottle.

Mama grunted. I ignored her.

Next to promote healing, then something for the pain. Aren's magic would do most of the work on the former, but I was out to impress her as much as to help him. I deserved better than to be used as a housekeeper.

Minutes later, I had a thick ointment made up. Mama took the bowl from me, sniffed, and nodded. "Not bad. Maybe you're not useless." I smiled to myself as she turned to Aren. "You, here."

Aren stepped closer, and she slapped the salve on his burns. He winced, but didn't seem like he dared complain. She bandaged his hand more efficiently than I could have, gnarled fingers flying.

And then we found ourselves out the door. Moments later, the snoring started up again.

"So that's Mama Bunn," I said.

"I got that." Aren leaned closer, as though there were someone nearby who might overhear him speaking. "Listen, we need to talk about Ulric. We shouldn't be wasting our time here. He's stalling, and I think there's something wrong with his magic. I was only burned because he left controlling the fire entirely to me. He didn't even—"

"Aren!" Ulric appeared from the direction of the fire. He crossed his arms and gave us a dark look. "I thought we'd lost you."

Aren's features smoothed into a neutral expression. "Thought I'd wandered off?"

Even in the shadows the displeasure that flashed over Ulric's face was clear. "Just wondered whether you were planning to re-join us. Everyone was so pleased that we saved them. Might as well make the most of it while we have their attention."

"Good thing *we* did that," Aren responded.

Ulric frowned. "Let's go, then." He nodded politely to me, then led the way back toward the flickering light. Aren followed.

We do need to talk, I thought, and followed at a slower pace to give them their space. Something was very wrong, and Ulric couldn't keep me out of it forever.

4

ROWAN

The first shriek sounded like a terrified animal, and was quickly joined by more human shouts and cries. By the time I poked my head out of the tent, a stampede had started. A slow one, granted, a jumble of confusion and uncertainty, but the herd had picked up on the idea that something was wrong.

"What's happening?" I asked a young woman as she passed, hauling a child under one arm.

She didn't answer, but she didn't need to. The tent I was to share with Aren sat far enough from the fire pit that though the music had been overwhelmingly audible, the only light in the tent had come from the oil lanterns set up on the roughly sketched street outside. The bonfire now flared high enough that it lit the area, and when I squinted toward it, I caught a glimpse of flames licking at tree branches.

I ducked back into the tent and stuffed everything I had so carefully unpacked back into my bag.

Someone cheered as the light faded, and the crowd responded with happier shouts. I didn't bother stopping anyone this time as they passed by, but stepped out and headed toward the fire pit. When the crowd became too dense to pass through, I climbed into the lower branches of an accommodating old oak to get a better view. Ulric stood to the left of the fire pit, shaking hands with the people who crowded around him.

Aren was nowhere to be seen, nor were any of my friends.

I supposed I couldn't count Ulric among that group anymore.

Stop it, I ordered myself as I went back to the tent to unpack again. *Aren told you exactly what his father was. How he used people, how cold he could be. Well, he used you to escape, and it worked, and now it's Aren's turn. It's not personal.*

But it was. I'd known the sting of rejection before. I'd felt it first when my parents sent me to live with my aunt and uncle, rarely visiting. Victoria and Ches and their servants had done much to help with that, and I'd moved past the pain and learned to thrive at Stone Ridge. But lately it seemed everyone was turning on me. Callum, who I'd once planned to marry, had lured me back to Darmid and imprisonment. Felicia, my dearest friend, had offered to shelter me and had instead turned me in. And now Ulric, who had comforted me after my death sentence and had taught me to control my magic, apparently wished I'd just disappear.

Well, I won't.

I finished re-arranging blankets on top of a pair of large, flat crates and considered climbing into bed. I could have gone back to the party. Judging by the resumed music and hearty laughter, it was going on like nothing had happened. But I'd had a long after-noon of failed attempts at making friends, I'd made the leather-and-dirt scented tent feel as comfortable as I could, and I was ready to rest. I had no desire to dance or mingle, or to see Laelana leaning in too close when she spoke to Aren, resting her hands on his arm and laughing deep in her throat.

And sleep would make for such a lovely respite from the world. Ever since our escape from Ardare I'd felt off. Flat, some-how, and far more exhausted than I should have. The return to Tyrea and its magic had improved my mood and allowed me time to recover, and I was grateful to be back with Aren and our friends. Still, I felt myself slipping.

I just didn't know into what.

That afternoon, I'd tried to use my magic to call water at the lake. Former lake, really, and now a rotten mud pit. I'd searched hard for water, sending out my magic in an attempt to feel it as I had so easily when we passed under the river in Ardare. There had been a little, deep undergound, and I'd tried to call it up. It hadn't answered, though I couldn't say why. I'd expended a great deal of magical energy in the attempt.

Magic that hadn't replenished. At least, not right away, as it should have from the rich magic of Tyrea. The loss had left a gaping hole in me.

The magic had returned within hours, leaving me feeling as normal as I ever did anymore. I decided I'd try again instead of going to sleep, to see what would happen. There was a good chance, I reasoned, that this was related to my new-found aversion. My fear.

I couldn't ask Ulric for advice, not with the way he was treating me. Aren would want to know, but I didn't want to worry him until I was sure there was good reason for it. I thought Nox might have some ideas, but she always looked at me like I was something horrid stuck to her boot.

I will ask, though, if it turns out it wasn't a fluke. Maybe my magic is just as exhausted as I am.

Maybe if I worked at it...

My stomach turned at the thought. It had been the same since we'd crossed the border. I was fine as long as I let my magic lie. It was when it reared its head and when I thought about using it that fear flashed through me like frozen lightning, along with memories.

But I wouldn't let fear rule me. I'd come too far, faced too much. I had controlled my magic once, and saved us all. I would master it. Prove myself.

I closed my eyes and tried to let my magic fill me as my teacher Griselda Beaumage had taught me back at the school on Belleisle. No pressure. No thought. The familiar warmth came, and I tried to accept it instead of analyzing it. It felt good. Natural. Not as strong as the overwhelming power that filled me when we escaped the city. Or after.

Dorset Langley's face appeared in my mind, setting my heart

pounding and my skin crawling. *A handsome face, drawn into a snarl, slowly pulling taut as the water left it, forming a puddle at his feet.*

Me. I did that.

My magic quieted without me having to tell it to settle and retreated until I barely felt it. A month before I'd have considered that kind of control a miracle, but it felt wrong. Like my power was running from me—or worse, I from it.

I let out a long, slow breath. *The bastard deserved it. You know that, right?*

No one deserves that, I answered myself. *That's not how I want to use my power.*

A shadow appeared against the side of the tent, becoming smaller and disappearing as someone moved out of the lamplight of the path and approached the flaps at the entrance. "Penelo—I mean, Rowan?"

Patience stood outside, holding aside the thin blanket I'd rigged up to cover the gap in the tent flaps. She hesitated, reluctant to step from the lamplight into the dim interior.

I motioned for her to come in. She hung back at the entrance, shifting her weight from foot to foot.

She looked around, squinting, and took in the hard bed. "You could stuff a mattress tomorrow," she said. "We might have empty sacks around. Lots of last year's grass still out there. It'd be more comfortable."

"That's an excellent idea. Maybe you could help?"

She came in and hopped up to sit on the crates, apparently comfortable now that she'd invested herself. "Probably. I'm a really good woodsman. Actually, I'm good at a lot of things."

I smiled at her easy confidence. She looked brighter than she had earlier. Perhaps seeing us then had brought on bad memories that dragged her down. "I bet you are. I remember what a wonderful performer you were, too."

I immediately wished I could take those words back. The girl hardly needed me to remind her of better times, even if those good times had seemed difficult back then. When we met them, her family had recently been attacked and evicted from their home, but at least those who remained had been together.

I couldn't take the silence, or the slump of the girl's shoulders. I sat beside her and struggled to find something better to say. "It's good to see you again. Have you made friends here? I noticed there are a lot of children."

"Kind of. Some of the littler ones were scared of me when they got here because of how I look. I just don't get along with the older ones. Most of them still have their parents to take care of them." She shrugged one shoulder. "I take care of myself, mostly. I kind of have a new mother, but she's busy."

Someone outside hit a sour note on a flute, and others laughed. There hadn't been much in the way of drinks to go around, but it sounded like they were well into the small supply. I hoped they wouldn't be up late. The private tent was nice, but too close to the party for my liking.

And much too close to Ulric's.

"How long have you been here?" I asked.

"Not long. It was winter when the king's men found us again. Mama and the others were doing their thing to protect us, but it didn't work. And it was just like the first time, except that there weren't as many of us, and... well, and not so many of us got away this time. Just me, and Keela—she's the only lady that got out, the one I'm staying with. And there's Devlin, Drover, Jimmy. I guess that's it. No other kids. We joined Goff and Laelana when we met them and their folks."

"I'm sorry." It was a great loss of life. Talented children, and adults who had welcomed and sheltered us when we had nothing to offer in return. So much life and potential and worth. This was how the world repaid them.

I thought about my own family then. Not all had abandoned me. My aunt and uncle and their servants Matthew and Della had all loved me like a daughter, but I'd had no word at all from them since my disappearance. I worried often about them and about my parents. I wished I could sort things out with my mother. I missed my brother Ashe, who had been my only ally in my family after I moved back home. Nox had given my mother medicine to treat his recent illness, but I knew nothing about his current condition.

At least they're alive. That's more than Patience has.

Patience pulled a thin black scarf from her pocket and tied it over her hair, draping it so that it covered the scar where her eye once was. "What do you think of this?"

"Hmm." I tilted my head, taking in the effect. I reached out and she flinched slightly, but allowed me to tighten the knot. I adjusted the angle of the scarf to free more of her hair. The fabric covered the damage to her face, and made her look a little more like the girl I remembered. I tucked her hair behind her ear, and this time she relaxed into my touch.

"It looks good," I said. "Very mysterious. Like you might save the day. Or rob someone."

She giggled. "I guess that's pretty close to what I did earlier. Sorry about those guys."

"It's not your fault. If you hadn't been there, we'd have been left with nothing, wouldn't we? But now we've found you, and maybe we can all help each other."

"Yeah." She stood and turned to leave, then came back and wrapped her arms around me. I hugged her back, and she sniffled. "I'm just so glad you guys remember my mama," she whispered. "Sometimes I think I'm starting to forget her face already."

She dashed out of the tent.

"Whoa," Aren said outside. The dancing lamplight cast their faint shadows on the wall of the tent, his tall and lean, hers tiny and thin. "You okay?"

"Good. Thanks." She ran off, back toward the fire.

"What happened?" I asked as he stepped into the tent. "It sounded like we were being attacked, and then it was all laughter and music again."

"The fire got a little out of control," he said. "We took care of it. At least the people seem impressed, which should be helpful."

I nodded at the thin white bandage wrapped around his right hand. "Was that part of taking care of it?"

"It's nothing." He held up his hand to wiggle his fingers, as though that proved the point. "You've seen how Nox fusses. I would have been fine." I narrowed my eyes at him, and he smiled. "Nice to see that Patience is still your friend even now that you're using your real name."

"Oh, yes. She's going to be my source of information, you know. I have to get in good with the locals."

Aren smirked at my facetious tone. "Your big assignment. Are you disappointed?"

I shrugged. I didn't want to admit to him how being over-looked undercut my confidence. "Should I be?"

"No. You should be glad you don't have to sit with him at meals. Come here."

I stood and shuffled sideways to the door in two steps, and he pulled me close. He smelled of heavy smoke and something herbal that reminded me of Nox's potions the night after we'd escaped Ardare. "I've missed you," he whispered.

"What, since you saw me at supper?"

"Mmm-hmm. It's been far too long. I'd have come here with you earlier, but my father—"

"I know." The situation left much to be desired, but at least I had him for the moment, and everyone else was safe. Well, everyone I knew about.

"Not to change the subject," I said, "but you haven't seen Florizel around yet, have you?"

"No. I wouldn't expect to."

I leaned back. "Do you think she's gone for good? I told her to escape, but..."

"She's a flying horse, and flight is in her nature in more ways than one. Her instinct is to rely on her herd, and she'd be trained to flee at the first sign of danger. It's incredible that she fought that off for long enough to get you out of the city, but to ask her to spend her days with this many ignorant humans and their weapons would be cruel. She's probably suffering from the after-effects of your escape just as much as you are."

I crossed my arms. "I'm not suffering anything."

"Liar," he muttered, though not unpleasantly, perhaps remembering all of the times he'd said similar things to me. He didn't press the issue. We'd talk when I was ready.

Gods, I love you, I thought as a familiar, pleasant ache spread through my chest. We had our differences, but the deeper ways in which we understood each other covered the gaps.

"I hope Florizel will come back," he continued, "but she'll be better off away from camp and our problems here." He released me and looked around the tent. "Not bad. Are we alone?"

I grinned. "Taking the smaller tent was a terrible hardship, but I volunteered even though it means I have to be alone with you all night."

"How horrid," he agreed as I ran a hand down his arm.

"I'm sure the others will have much more fun together in their—"

He pulled me into a kiss that turned my knees to clay. One of his arms wrapped around my waist as I tangled the fingers of both my hands in his dark hair, drawing him closer, urging him on as his lips brushed over my jaw, my throat, and my collarbone. I moaned softly as his free hand grazed my breast. He pulled the hem of my shirt out of my pants, and I raised my arms over my head to pull them out of the sleeves.

He slipped out of his shirt and reached for the laces on my pants.

"We can't lock that door," I said.

"No. Do you care?"

I took in the dim outline of his body, and tingling heat spread through my own. Instead of answering, I pushed his hands away and undid the knots myself, hooked my thumbs into the waist-line of my pants, and slipped them down over my hips.

He took in a sharp breath and pushed me back on the crate bed. With only a few blankets covering the wood it was hardly comfortable, but I was beyond caring. This was the first time we'd had alone together since he'd left Belleisle to search for his father. Not a day had gone by since then when I hadn't craved his touch. I'd thought I lost him forever when they threw me in a Darmish prison, and still wondered every time I looked at him how it was possible that he'd found me.

We'd spent the nights since then sleeping next to each other as our health and his magic recovered, separated only when it was time for each of us to take watch, but it wasn't enough. Not by far.

This... this is what I need.

The fire outside dimmed as people made their way past our tent to their own meager homes, some singing, some shouting, others shushing them. Aren leaned closer to the door and listened, then shed the rest of his clothes as the tent grew dark.

"Try to get some sleep, children!" Kel called as he passed. A slapping noise and a laughed "ow" indicated that Nox was still out there with him, or possibly Cassia.

I shivered. Though the days were growing warmer as we traveled south and the calendar moved toward spring, the nights were still cold.

Aren's hands weren't, though, or his body as he laid it over mine. He propped himself up on one forearm and with his other hand he brushed my hair away from my face, then placed a kiss between my eyes.

"Rowan," he murmured. My fingertips pressed into the skin on his back, tracing the faint ridges of the scar that spread out from his right shoulder. My breath caught in my throat as he kissed me again.

The camp grew silent around us, leaving us as good as alone. The morning would bring duties and demands that neither of us could escape, but in that moment there was only us, only our bodies and our magic, warm breath and whispered promises that it would be us, together, always.

I only hoped the pounding of my heart wouldn't keep the rest of the camp awake.

5

ROWAN

A rooster crowed, ordering the sun and the community out of bed, and the heavy thump of wood landing in the fire pit signaled that at least one person had obeyed. He called out to someone who shouted back from the other end of camp, and with that, the place swarmed to life.

Inside the tent, I struggled to get moving. Even with Aren's arm to rest my head on and a few wool blankets beneath us, my back had grown stiff and my muscles tender overnight. My breath came out in a plume of white as I climbed over him and collected my clothes from the floor.

Aren yawned. "Come back," he mumbled. "I'm not ready to start the day."

I sighed. "I'm supposed to be making friends."

"*I'm* your friend. Get over here."

He held the blanket up, and I slipped underneath. Aren pulled me close and rested his chin on the top of my head, and I molded my body to his, trying to steal his warmth. *Just for a minute,* I told myself. We wouldn't get on anyone's good side by being lazy and letting them do all of the work. Aren might be able to command their respect because of his power and status, but...

But nothing. I'm powerful, too, even if I'm not a princess.

So where did that leave me? I wasn't going to be the sort of person who lorded my power over others, who expected special treatment. Aren had been raised that way, and he was trying to get past it. I had the advantage of growing up thinking I was perfectly average. No point letting magic go to my head.

I would volunteer for breakfast duty, be friendly, gather information. I told myself that the idea of not using magic wasn't a relief, but the tension flowed from my shoulders as I considered a day with no worries about hurting anyone, and maybe no horrid memories sneaking up on me.

I'll get back to it, I promised myself. Aren and I would find time to work on it, somehow.

Aren's hand moved over my back, tracing circles on my skin, moving lower. "Don't start," I said, my voice muffled by his shoulder.

"We have a lot of time to make up, Miss Greenwood. Belleisle, your time in prison..."

I tilted my head up and placed a kiss where the soft skin of his throat met the hard line of his jaw. "Mister Tiernal, I—"

Footsteps approached outside, crunching over the dead leaves on the ground. I waited for them to pass, but the tent flap flew open, flooding the space with light.

"Knock it off," Kel said. I gasped and sat up, clutching the blanket to my chest. He leaned in and smirked as he sipped something from a steaming tin mug. "Fun time's over, friends."

Aren glared at him. "You jealous?"

Kel shrugged. "It's not my business, but I wouldn't keep the king waiting if I were you."

He left, and Aren sighed. "Guess it's time to go, then."

I kissed him again. "Told you so."

We dressed quickly and stepped outside, squinting in the bright sunlight. Nox handed us each a cup. "Drink," she ordered. "It'll wake you up. You both look exhausted."

Nox rarely spoke to me unless it was absolutely necessary. I'd tried to adopt Aren's confidence, his assurance that his value didn't depend on being liked, but it didn't work. It hurt to be disliked, made me feel small. I thanked Nox for the drink, and she nodded. At least she was making an effort. The dark, bitter tea burned my tongue, but I drank it anyway.

Not that I care what she thinks of me, right?

I shouldn't have. She obviously didn't care what anyone's opinion was of her. Nor did Kel and Cassia. Though they were by nature perceptive and frequently tried to accommodate people, they didn't go out of their way to gain anyone's approval. They just accepted it.

I shook my head to chase the thoughts away. In less than five months I'd gone from good—if slightly rebellious—Darmish girl, to inept Sorceress, to a powerful one still afraid to use her magic. It was far too early in the morning to decide yet again who I wanted to be.

Aren looked into his cup. "Interesting flavor. What is it?"

"Are you asking because you're really interested, or are you just making conversation?" Nox asked.

"Both."

Before she could answer, she caught sight of Ulric striding toward us. "Excuse me," she said. "I believe I'm needed elsewhere." She spun on her heel and hurried toward Kel, who was listening as several men and women showed off their makeshift weapons.

Aren drained his cup as though the contents would fortify him.

"Everyone well-rested?" Ulric asked. Demanded, really. Every question that came out of the man was an interrogation, every statement an order.

"Well enough," Aren said. "Did you sleep well?"

"Well enough," Ulric echoed. "Rowan, anything to report?"

"No. Patience told me a little more about what happened to her family, but I think we already knew that your sons are among the most horrible people alive." I nodded toward Aren. "Present company excepted."

Ulric didn't seem amused. Didn't even look at me. "I suppose we won't learn anything more with you here, will we? Best you get back to it."

I held out my hand to take Aren's cup, refusing to be stung

again by the dismissal. "I'll be off to see what's cooking for breakfast, then."

"Wait," Aren said. A boy of about thirteen walked past, and Aren motioned him closer. He took my cup and passed both to the boy. "Take those back to wherever they belong, will you?" The boy nodded and scurried off.

Ulric raised his thick eyebrows. "Aren?"

"Rowan should stay with us so she knows what's going on. If we need to fight, you'll want her magic on your side." Though he spoke calmly and reasonably, I knew it couldn't be easy for him to stand up to his father.

"She has no experience with these things," Ulric answered, his voice sharp enough to cut. "She's not Tyrean."

Aren's expression hardened. "She's had different experiences. She sees things I don't."

I felt invisible as the two stood eye to eye, locked in their battle of wills. I wanted to step in, to say that it didn't matter and I was fine in the kitchen, but Aren was right. If only I could find my voice and say so.

"Very well," Ulric said, drawing out the words. "Rowan, please come with us." He gave Aren one last, hard look, and turned away.

Aren let out his breath.

"You didn't have to do that," I said. "I can slap boiled oats into bowls if it will help."

"I appreciate that. The truth is, I didn't do it to save you from breakfast duty." He looked at me and tried to smile. He almost succeeded. "I truly do think we need your help, but it's not only that. I need you near me. My father makes me feel like the person I used to be. That may be helpful, especially if it comes to war, but I need balance. I need a reminder that my life isn't about trying to gain his approval, that I'm not the old me anymore."

"Well, thank you either way." I gave his hand a quick squeeze, then let go. It wouldn't look right for the king's son to be seen walking around holding hands with his—what? There didn't seem to be a word for it. And now that I thought of it, our future might not be—

"You coming?" Aren asked.

"Yeah. Of course. Just thinking."

We caught up to Ulric, who stood watching the sparring in the square. "Goff said they do this every day," he said, just loud enough for us to hear. "Volunteers only, but many of them enthusiastic. They have exactly two people in this community with any proper training. There's a former militia member, and one who apparently used to work for me. So I suppose we would have been recognized even if I hadn't revealed who we were yesterday."

Aren nodded, but his lips tightened as though holding back a response. If I had to guess, I'd say he'd just been put in his place.

"Those two train the others when they can," Ulric continued. "These men and women are not an army, but it seems that Goff has had it in his mind for some time that they should be. In spite of what I said yesterday, I don't wish to see them go into battle and die." Aren seemed to relax a little at that. "The appearance of an army might get us past the city gates, though, or at least gain us the support of people outside who might otherwise stay neutral. They could be the rich soil that causes other citizens' confidence to blossom."

"They're shit, if that's what you mean," Aren said under his breath.

Ulric ignored that. "We could persuade more to train with them, just in case. We need the defenses, if nothing else. If Severn doesn't know we're here yet, he will soon enough, and he will attack."

"How many might we have?" Aren asked.

"Three hundred people in this community total. Removing children under the age of thirteen from the equation—"

"Thirteen?" Both turned toward me when I spoke. "That seems young."

"Old enough to pick up a sword," Ulric said, not sounding pleased about the prospect. "Gods willing, it won't come to battle, and we'll keep the more experienced ones at the fore. As I was saying, excluding children and those who care for the younger ones, the elderly who can't fight, and a few who are lame, injured, or ill, we have a little over a hundred and fifty."

"I'd have expected Laelana to keep better track of her population than that," Aren said.

Ulric grunted his agreement. "She's a decent leader, but I don't think she was expecting that her people would be called for something like this."

"So what do we do next?" Aren asked.

"Train those who are available. We'll have your friends help with that."

Aren frowned. "They'll need their own training first. They might help with physical conditioning, though."

Ulric watched Cassia walk past the other side of the sparring field. "They are in excellent physical condition, aren't they?"

Aren's shoulders tensed visibly. I wondered what Ulric knew about Aren and Cassia's history.

"So you'll train the troops, such as they are," I said, just to break the silence and the feeling that maybe I really wasn't needed. "What then?"

"That's what we need to figure out." Ulric kept a close watch on the fighters. One of them swung and thumped the other lightly on the head, and they both laughed. "Find some way to make them take this seriously. Pray to the gods that it doesn't come to battle."

"Any magic users among them?" Aren asked. "Besides Jevan."

"Nothing significant, as far as I know, and little that's useful. Jevan has some skill with tracking. He leads hunting parties and has been training a few scouts, as well as those he takes when they're on their supply-gathering missions. That could be quite useful. Otherwise, no. Most of these people are here because Severn took away the Sorcerers and lower-level magic-users who lived in their communities. They heard about this group and came looking for help. Leaves us with very little, other than bodies to make a statement with."

"Hmm. Not that many of them, though."

Not since we first met had I had so much trouble reading Aren. He was guarding himself, being the person his father expected him to be. I reminded myself that it was a mask, an act. Still, my throat tightened uncomfortably at the thought of him slipping away, changing back to what he was when we first met.

"What about Albion?" I asked. "If Severn may be a threat to Belleisle, it would be worth their while to assist us."

Ulric's lip curled in distaste. "We don't look to Belleisle for help. Albion has never been involved in anything important. Power, politics, war, none of it. The people of Belleisle will wish to be left alone, believing their defenses are sound, and Ernis Albion is no particular friend of mine. I'm sure Aren has explained that."

He had. Ulric had married Albion's daughter against the gentle Sorcerer's wishes. Ulric sent her away several years after Aren and Nox were born, when her life was in danger. She'd taken Nox with her and left everyone else—Aren included—thinking she was dead.

"Perhaps if you told him you didn't have his daughter killed after all?" I suggested, and fought the urge to flee from the sharp look Ulric shot me. "Might warm him to you."

Aren looked at his father. "Yes, sending her to die in a frozen dragon-land was much better." His words drew out in a derisive drawl that surprised me.

"Watch your tone," Ulric warned. "I'm still your father and your king, no matter what you think I owe you."

My heart fluttered in my throat as magic thickened the air. I didn't think Ulric would hurt Aren, or Aren his father, but I could never stand watching people argue.

Aren held his gaze. "The latter position will be in question if we don't figure out how to get you back to Luid and prove you're still alive, and soon. We're wasting time here."

Ulric didn't answer, and neither of them moved.

"Are you magical types beyond eating, now?" We all turned toward Nox, who gestured back over her shoulder. "There's grain porridge back that way, but you'll want to get there soon. Lots of hungry people about."

"Thank you, Nox," Ulric said. "Have you eaten already?"

"Yes. I'll be assisting in the infirmary tent if anyone needs me."

"Nox?" Aren asked. "I need to speak to you later."

She nodded and walked away, shoulders hunched forward against a strong breeze that blew through the woods, kicking up dust.

"We should eat while there's still something left," I said. An approaching group of villagers drowned my voice out, but Aren nodded.

The people fell silent as they came near us—all except the children, who didn't know to be afraid of our power.

We fell in behind the sparring partners and followed the river of bodies to a black tent. I joined the end of the line at the entrance, but Aren motioned for me to follow him and Ulric to where Laelana stood near a bubbling pot of gruel inside the massive canvas structure, speaking to a hunch-backed old woman. The volume of the voices from the crowd inside kept me from hearing their conversation, but the old woman seemed pleased by whatever her leader said.

Laelana had shed the heavy fur cloak she'd worn to the party the night before, but looked no less imposing in her fitted pants and loose tunic. She'd pulled her mane of hair into a long braid that swung over her shoulder as she turned to us.

"Good morning, my lady," Ulric said, and offered a tiny bow. "I thank you again for the accommodations."

"I trust everything was adequate?" she asked. Her gaze drifted to Aren. "We might be able to make you more comfortable, if there was any problem."

I gritted my teeth and held my tongue.

"Everything was perfect, thank you," he responded evenly.

The woman's eyes turned to me, considered something, and then looked back to the Sorcerers, apparently dismissing me in less than a second. I unclenched my teeth and forced my shoulders to relax.

"I'll see about getting your breakfast," she said.

To her credit, she returned with three bowls balanced in her hands, and offered one to me.

"My grandfather was a Sorcerer," she said. "Derk Dimning.

Able to communicate with animals, if they were intelligent enough. Had a great deal of skill with plants, too."

Ulric paused with the spoon half-way to his mouth. "I remember him. I asked him to come to Luid to work for me. He refused. Said he had too many obligations at home. Very impressive skills."

Laelana lifted her chin. "Indeed. But he had no desire for city life, or to consort with nobility."

"It's a shame he's not here to help us today. Having someone around who could grow a crop of vegetables would be ideal."

Laelana's expression hardened. "He refused to join your son's cause. It didn't end well for him. For any of us."

"A great loss to you and to us," Ulric said, sounding as sympathetic and sincere as I'd ever heard him. But I knew how quickly that could change.

"It certainly is." She looked me and Aren over again. "This is all the magic you have on your side? Not much to speak of."

The corner of Ulric's mouth twitched in a half-smile, taking pleasure in her baiting.

He approves of her, I realized. He didn't respect her, but he was having fun. As much as I thought he could, anyway.

"I believe I have more with me than you do."

Laelana's smile widened, showing off one long and crooked side-tooth that gave her a predatory look. "For now."

Ulric appeared unimpressed. "Are you expecting company?"

I forced myself to eat as I listened, though I hardly tasted the mush. Aren kept a sharp eye on Laelana, monitoring her, ready for any thoughts that came close enough to the surface that he could catch them without prying.

She grinned wider still and looked over Ulric's shoulder as someone shouted outside of the tent. "I *have* company," she corrected, and moved in long strides toward the door.

"Well?" Ulric asked, turning to his son. "What did you learn?"

Aren scraped his spoon against the bottom of his bowl and licked it clean. "She has a plan. She's pleased about it. Feels she has leverage to use against you if you try to take over her people."

"Pah. I could have told you that."

"She's guarded. Not by magic, but she's heard rumors of what I can do, and she's waiting for me to try something. I'm not going to use my magic in any way that will turn our allies against us."

"Seeing thoughts is not the same as changing them. You'd do no harm."

"She'd know I was looking."

Ulric snorted. "I guarantee she wants you to. I'm sure she'd show you a few things. Do try harder next time."

"Or," I said, and they both looked at me. I got the feeling they kept forgetting I was there. *Speak up, dummy.* "Or we could just go out there and see what's happening. I don't think it's much of a secret anymore, and it'll be more useful than speculating."

Ulric strode toward the door.

"He's a lovely fellow to work with," I said as we followed.

"Even better than I remembered."

We dropped our dishes in the woven baskets near the door with the others, and were greeted by a wall of bodies outside the tent. People closest to us craned their necks to see over the ones in front. Aren took my hand and picked his way through the crowd, which parted before him though no one noticed us until we'd passed.

Five riders on sturdy horses had stopped at the other side of the square. Their leader had her head down, speaking with Laelana, who was grinning like a cat that had caught a bird.

A beautiful, olive-skinned, blonde bird.

I gasped. "Griselda!"

Aren looked at me with raised eyebrows. "You know her?"

"She came back to Belleisle just after you left. It was her idea for me to work on illusions. I didn't mention that?"

He arranged his features into their usual neutral mask. "No, I don't think you did." He hesitated. "She didn't say anything about me, did she?"

"She said it wouldn't be right to talk about you when—Oh." Suddenly her desire to not talk about what Aren had been like in Luid made more sense.

He grimaced. "It was before I met you."

"Of course. It's just a little...it's fine. This isn't weird."

"It's not. Trust me." He offered a warm smile, which I couldn't help returning. It didn't change anything. His history with Cassia hadn't caused problems, and this wouldn't either. And Griselda would be a great help to us.

I ignored the jealousy that twisted at my gut.

Ulric reached them before Aren or I did. Griselda spotted him and sat up straight, her mouth opening in surprise. She swung to the ground, revealing a small, furry, black lump seated on the saddle behind her. The lump—a cat, as it turned out—arched its back in a high stretch and spread its feathered wings, which were also black as soot. It shot us a haughty glance and flew up to perch on a low tree branch.

"Your Highness," Griselda said with a delighted grin. "This is a wonderful surprise."

Before he could respond, she looked past him toward me and Aren. Her hand flew to her mouth. "Laelana, you didn't say."

Griselda took a step toward us, but caught the narrowing of Ulric's eyes and paused. She had enough experience with the man to read him better than I was able to.

"They only arrived yesterday," Laelana said. "Looking for help to get the king back to his throne."

Griselda grinned again and turned back to her companions, three men who looked utterly bewildered. "Gentlemen, we've had a change in plans."

Aren stepped closer to Ulric. "What was that about Albion not caring enough to send help?"

Ulric frowned. "Help for these rebels. Not for us."

"It works out to be the same now," Aren replied.

Ulric crossed his arms. "We'll see."

"Hold on," Laelana shot a glare at Ulric. "Ms. Beaumage, we need to discuss this before we involve him. I haven't yet decided what's happening with this lot."

The ground beneath us shifted. A subtle tremor, to be sure, but the people fell silent at the deep rumbling, and a small child cried out as he lost his balance and fell on his bottom. The crowd dispersed, suddenly remembering things they needed to do elsewhere.

Laelana's lips pulled back in a silent hiss, unappreciative of Ulric's reminder of his power. Though I hadn't seen further evidence of it since he'd opened the earth to swallow several men at the border, I suspected he could level Laelana's village if he so chose.

She had strength of numbers. He had strength of magic, especially if the Belleisle folk joined us.

Griselda laid a hand on Laelana's arm. "Of course, we must speak privately." She offered an apologetic glance to me and Aren, then spoke to Ulric. "I'm so pleased to see you are well, sire. The governor and Albion sent us to assess the situation here and see what could be done about the threat Severn presents to the island, as well as to the people of Tyrea."

"With the promise of more magic-users to come." Laelana grinned.

"With the *possibility* of more," Griselda said gently. "If you'll excuse me, sire, I'll speak to you after I've met with Laelana and Goff."

I wondered whether he would try to stop her. She wasn't his subject, but this was still technically his land, even if Severn was ruling it. And what of the rebels? His subjects, but Laelana seemed comfortable testing him, knowing that the power balance in the village still favored her. I knew so little about politics and how things worked in Tyrea.

But I could listen, and I could learn. Aren would answer my questions when we were alone, when I wouldn't feel foolish asking them in front of Ulric.

"Aren, come," Ulric ordered, and stalked back through camp. Aren followed at a more casual pace, but Griselda held onto my shirtsleeve and kept me back.

"Good luck with those two, Sorchere," she said with a wink, and released me. "You and I will talk, as well. We've been so worried about you and Aren. You must tell me everything."

"I will," I said, and wondered whether that was the right response. Ulric already didn't trust me. I was fond of Griselda. She was my favourite teacher by far, and I trusted her. But maybe *everything* wasn't exactly what I should share. I no longer knew who I should trust.

She turned to the trees and made a puckering noise, and the flying cat soared down to perch on her shoulder. "I don't believe you met Gwyn back at the school. She tends to keep to herself."

I held out a hand and smiled at the cat, but didn't make eye contact in case she didn't like it. She sniffed my fingers, tickling them with her long whiskers, then sat and began washing her face.

"We'll talk later," I told Griselda. "The others are waiting for me."

"Of course." I couldn't tell whether her tight smile was amused, or whether that was a hint of suspicion I spotted. "Later."

I turned and hurried after Ulric and Aren, determined to not be forgotten.

6

AREN

"Catch anything useful that time?" my father asked, speaking over his shoulder as we moved away from the crowd. His skin had gone pale, and a faint sheen of sweat coated his forehead. I pretended I didn't notice, and didn't answer until he stopped and I caught up, just as Rowan joined us.

"Laelana has little interest in seeing you back on the throne," I said. She'd been more open in her excitement, and I'd slipped deeper into her thoughts. "Her chief goal is to see Severn deposed, but putting you back on the throne isn't the resolution she had planned."

"Obviously. Everyone thought I was dead. But even now, knowing I'm alive and capable?"

"She's considering her options. She thinks you're better than Severn, but not necessarily ideal."

Ulric's lips pressed together into a tight line. "And is that your opinion as well?"

I chose not to answer that. "I don't think Laelana knows what she wants, exactly. Just that Severn's not it."

"And that's why she doesn't deserve to lead these people," Ulric said, speaking to himself as much as to me, and I thought not at all to Rowan. "Clear goals and an unwavering path toward them are what's needed. No faltering. No distractions."

He turned to Rowan with a stony glare, then nodded slightly as though confirming something to himself. "I'll speak to Aren alone now. Go about your assignment."

She held his gaze for a moment, then looked away. "I'll be making friends in the kitchen." She left us, and Ulric turned to walk in the opposite direction.

"You're cutting off a potentially powerful ally," I reminded him.

He turned to watch her disappear into the kitchen tent, wearing a far less pleasant expression than I ever did when I watched her leave.

"At least she has the sense to respect me," he said, ignoring my words completely.

"She doesn't respect you," I said quietly, and he turned. "She fears you."

"Is that so?"

"She saw the joy you found in killing a handful of prison guards with nothing more than a wave of your hand, how you fought your way through a dozen more in the city. She knows what you can do to people. I'd say her caution is warranted."

He turned to me with narrowed eyes. "Yet you suddenly find it in yourself to speak disrespectfully and second-guess my every decision. Why is that?"

I pushed down the instinctive, childish fear that his glare still called up when he turned it on me. "Things have changed. Besides, you taught me that to show fear is to show weakness. I'd say you should be pleased."

He snorted derisively. "At least you learned one of the lessons I tried to teach you. Not the most important one, though."

I didn't have to ask what he meant. My father had virtually ignored me throughout my youth, but he'd taught me a few things. Fear, regret, and love were all weakness, and if we couldn't keep from experiencing them, we could at least keep them to ourselves. I'd known my relationship with Rowan would horrify him. I just hadn't particularly cared.

"Aren, part of wisdom is understanding the difference between immediate and important." He paused to take a shuddering breath, then continued as though nothing had happened. "Right now, Rowan could be an asset. She could train, learn to control her magic better, fight with us. But if she survives that, she'll be a threat. The effect she'll have on your life will be disastrous, and that's only the barest beginnings of the problem."

I followed him into the woods, leaving the sounds and smells of camp behind us. "Rowan is nothing if not loyal. If you'd just—"

The toe of Ulric's boot caught on a log as he stepped over it, and he lurched forward. Without thinking, I reached out to steady him.

"Leave me," he snapped, and ripped his arm from my grasp. He leaned back against an ancient oak and turned his face to the sky.

I watched from a distance—out of his arm's reach, if not his magic's. He caught his breath and recovered quickly, but not quickly enough to hide much from me. He looked ill. Worse, he looked *normal.*

This was why he hadn't helped me extinguish the fire. I flexed the fingers of my left hand, where the skin had healed but remained stiff and tight. My skin prickled at the realization that this went far deeper than I'd suspected. He wanted us to think we'd kept our magic hidden in order to win the trust of these people, that everything had played into his hands, but that was a lie. He'd disguised it well, but Ulric's magic was either failing or hurting him. And a man with weak magic couldn't rule Tyrea. Not for long, rightful king or no.

If his magic was weak, our plan had already failed.

"Are you going to tell me what's wrong now?" I asked, offering no sympathy in my voice.

"There's nothing wrong with me," he snapped, then took a deep breath to regain his composure. "Just been a little off since prison. I'm still recovering. I shouldn't have let my temper loose back there." He pushed away from the tree, straightened his clothing, and squared his shoulders. "You're going to end things with her now. I've arranged for you to move into a tent next to mine."

My shoulders tensed, and I fought the urge to clench my hands into fists. His order didn't trouble me. There was no question of me obeying him, not when losing her would cost me so much. What angered me was the assumption that I would slip back into my old habits of obedience so easily, that I would follow his orders as I had Severn's for so long.

"I will do no such thing," I said, keeping my voice low. I crossed my arms and hoped I was projecting confidence rather than the cold fear that filled me when he stepped toward me, his magic thick in the air, ready to strike. Even pale and ill, the man carried an air of danger and destructive power with him.

"Don't defy me, Aren. Not now. Not with so much at stake, with the fates of three countries at risk if Severn keeps the throne. Now is not the time to question me."

"No?" I refused to step back, even as he glared at me, lip curled. "Someone has to question you. Nothing about what we're doing here makes sense. If you feel so much is at stake, why are we wasting our time with these people? We could be on our way to Luid. You could challenge him, steal his strength, and be done with it. The only reason he didn't just challenge you in the first place is because he knew he couldn't overcome that. Give me a reason for your hesitation. Tell me why we need these people, and why you're so concerned with my personal affairs."

He folded his arms over his chest, mirroring me. "You'll know my mind when you've earned the right to answers. For now you will obey me because I am your king. Prove to me you deserve more consideration than that."

I fought the urge to look away from his cold, dark eyes. "With respect, father, you need me. Without me, you'd still be locked in a Darmish prison cell without magic or hope of escape."

He sneered. "Is that a threat? If I don't change my mind, will you flee like you did when Severn's demands became too much for you? Run away as you always do?" He spat on the ground. "The scar on your back marks you as a coward."

Heat flashed into my cheeks, brought by shame as much as

anger. An echo of pain cut into my right shoulder, and the ache spread across my back. Severn had nearly killed me. Worse, his magic had worked its way into my body, and he used the pain to control me as he made me his servant.

"I was a child," I said as clearly as I could with my jaw clenched tight. "Should I have stood and fought, and died? Fleeing seemed prudent at the time."

"Perhaps you would have died. Severn's older siblings did. But at least you'd have fought."

I kept my shock from registering on my face even as my heart stilled. "His older what?"

I'd suspected my father had other children, but he'd never spoken of them. No one did. They'd been erased from written records. But then, so had Nox, if she'd ever been recorded at all.

The corners of his lips twisted downward. "There's nothing to be gained by speaking of them now. Severn may be a traitor and a power-hungry fool, but he knows how to do what's necessary to secure his future. Can you say the same?"

"I don't know." The words were out before I'd considered them. "I don't know what future I'm securing."

"You are my only heir, Aren." A pained expression crossed his face that cut me deeper than his accusation of cowardice. "Severn will die for his crimes. Wardrel and Dan have supported him, and they will suffer the same fate. Nox has no magic, and the others are all dead by Severn's hand. You will be king some day."

"No."

His cold smile didn't reach his eyes. "You think you're the first who's wished to ignore this responsibility? I tried to escape, once, in a small way. Your grandmother did, too, and both of us for the same stupid reason as you."

"A desire for freedom?"

He shook his head. "Love. And the idea that it's anything but folly, that it brings anything but pain and defeat."

"And how would you know?" I asked. As if he had any idea. I suspected he'd felt more for my mother than he'd ever admitted to anyone, and knew he'd risked everything when he spared her life and sent her into anonymous exile instead of having her killed as a traitor. But the Ulric I knew was incapable of feeling true affection, or of putting anything or anyone ahead of his position and power.

He almost smiled at that, but whatever he was thinking turned it into a rueful smirk. "I know more than you'd think. You know how it ended, how that relationship nearly cost me everything. I only wish you were clever enough to learn from my mistakes instead of repeating them."

"I'm not you."

"How well I know it." I didn't respond to the implied insult, and he frowned. "I don't want to talk about this. Not now. But if it's the only way to make you understand, so be it."

I waited.

He rubbed a hand over his jaw, then looked away. I let my arms relax, but kept my guard up. This wasn't a friendly conversation, and I'd be a fool to believe he was opening up to me for my benefit. But the magic that tightened the air surrounding us lessened, withdrawing that threat.

The creases in his forehead deepened. "I made it many years, ruled for a century without letting my guard down. I held my throne, increased my power, maintained peace and nurtured my people—occasionally with a firm hand, but they were ultimately grateful for it. When I felt my position was secure enough to take a queen and my magic strong enough to risk an heir who might some day challenge me, I made that decision based entirely on the potential of our children to keep the crown in the Tiernal line. She seemed like a worthy match. I cared for her as one might a fine brood mare, I suppose. She did not disappoint me in that, even if she did in everything else later. Nor did my other wives, though only two of their children could stand up to Severn. The others…" He shrugged.

Ice pooled in my stomach. "How many?"

He raised an eyebrow. "Enough that you should be amazed by your own survival, but that's completely beside the point. I met your mother when I was vulnerable, feeling weary and longing for—" He shook his head and looked away. "It doesn't matter. The fact is that she made me weak. I allowed affection to cloud my judgement, my passion for her to overcome reason. And though I've never forgiven Severn for what he did to your mother, or myself for not being able to prevent it, he wasn't wrong. He saw weakness that should never be visible in a king, and he used it to challenge me." My father lifted his gaze to meet mine again, and it had become hard as I knew his heart to be. "This is why I taught you that love is dangerous. You can't begin to imagine what my foolishness cost me, or what the loss of her did to me."

I tried to imagine doing what he had—banishing Rowan, letting people think I'd had her killed, never seeing her again— and felt the briefest moment of sympathy for my father. "You overcame his challenge, though," I said when it seemed he'd finished speaking.

He nodded absently. "After that incident, I knew I needed to keep a closer eye on Severn and his ambitions, and for years I did. Things were going well in Tyrea. Severn seemed to have regained his respect for me, and he'd turned his attention to you, among other things. Yet I developed an empty ache inside. I dreamed of your mother, wondered what happened to her, whether she'd fared well and found a place for herself. I knew my orders and her desire to protect her family had kept her from returning to Belleisle, but I knew nothing else. She never tried to contact me." He swallowed hard. "From the day she left, every time I looked at you it reminded me of her, of how stupid and blind I was to marry her. I hardened myself to you, shut you and everyone else out, and still she haunted me."

My father sat on a boulder and rested his elbows on his knees. I had so many questions, but held them back. He had never opened up to me. Though I thought I knew where this conversation was headed, I wasn't in a rush to see it end. Much as part of me hated my father, decades of desiring his approval and attention were hard to let go of when that desire was being rewarded. My guard slipped.

"I made a foolish decision," he continued. "I went to look for her. I kept it quiet. Didn't tell my governor in Cressia that I was coming, though I'd have paid him a surprise visit to discuss some displeasing matters. We were attacked along the way by magic I'd never felt before. Confusion and disorientation that made it impossible to fight. I was down before I could use my magic, and woke in a Darmish prison cell."

Probably the greatest embarrassment of his life, even if no one but him had survived to talk about it.

"You're certain Severn was responsible for that?" I asked.

"I am, though I still don't know why he didn't just have me killed." He stood and stalked toward me, expression closed, invading my space, forcing me to step back. It seemed our friendly chat was over.

"Severn betrayed me, but he only had the opportunity because of my weakness. Love is every bit as dangerous and foolish as I raised you to believe it is. Had I walked away after I met your mother, I might never have lost my keen edge. I kept my distance from my other wives. Caring for Magdalena put the ridiculous notion in my head that I should search for her after she was probably long dead."

"She wasn't," I said quietly. "She is now." My sympathy for my father's struggles only went so far, and I wanted to see how much truth there was to his admission of weakness. "She was alive when you set out to look for her. You might have found her if you hadn't been captured."

He drew in a sharp breath, and for a moment his pain and grief were written clearly on his face before he forced them back. He wasn't lying. He'd loved her, and he had sacrificed her for the sake of his power and his people, and the shame and pain of it had made him the Ulric I knew and despised.

The knowledge changed nothing for me.

"Listen well, Aren," he said when he'd regained his composure. He spoke softly and reasonably, almost pleading. "We aren't like regular folk. We have privileges. We have wealth and power. We also have a great and terrible responsibility, and it needs to come before anything else. I will have my kingdom again, but some day it will be yours. And you know as well as I do that a king cannot marry a Sorceress. It's never been possible for two people with strong magic to produce an heir, and our laws will not bend to allow such a union. Not even if a king wishes it. Rowan is jeopardizing your future. She's making you weak, distracting you, and will become a powerful enemy when you leave her for someone better suited. And she—" He thrust a finger toward camp, and his expression closed in anger. "She is the worst match you possibly could have chosen."

I took another step back, creating space between us. I couldn't think with him so close. "You know nothing about her. About either of us." He wasn't wrong about the laws, or about the fact that Rowan and I could never have children. He was wrong if he thought that I gave a damn, though.

His shoulders tensed. "Think with your damned brain for a minute. She's a powerful Sorceress. With training and time, she could be as powerful as you. And she's from Darmid."

"So you know about that problem?" Severn certainly did, and was planning to go to war with them to release the magic that should have been flowing freely in their land.

He snorted sharply. "Know about it? I was the first person to notice that their killing off of magic was having an effect on ours. I have no doubt that Severn is blowing it out of proportion, using it as proof that I'm an unfit king. He'll march an army over those mountains to prove himself, I suppose."

"He's said almost as much."

"He's a fool. It is a problem, and Darmid will pay for it." He pressed his lips together and clenched his fists. "They have so much more to answer for now. But it's a problem we had time to approach by other methods."

"He seemed so certain that he had to act now," I said.

Ulric scowled. "If he had to act, it was to secure his position, not for the good of magic or the people. But listen carefully. Even if I take the throne back and dismantle Severn's plans, the time will come when we must face this problem in Darmid, and there will be war. Think about what happens with Rowan when I have to act. Or gods forbid it, if I die and you take the throne and have to deal with it yourself." He watched me carefully as he spoke. "Will she sit idly by and allow you to take her people's land? Watch them die under our swords if they resist? Will you do what must be done to save Tyrea and our magic, or will you have mercy on them for her sake? Or will she fight you, take the throne for herself if she has to? She might, if she's as strong as I suspect she is, and if she learns to channel her power properly." He looked deep into my eyes. "End it with her now, before you get in any deeper and lose yourself completely."

"Or what?"

For the briefest moment, I felt something from him. Not the rage he projected with his body and movements, but fear. He recovered quickly, but the chill remained on my skin after I'd lost access to his mind—access I never should have been able to gain.

"Or we fail in this." No anger in his voice now. "I can't use you to win this fight if you don't respect me and obey my orders. In spite of your insistence otherwise, you will follow me as king." I caught the fear again, like a scent on the breeze. "But we won't make it that far if you run from your responsibilities now. Severn will keep the throne, though he's nowhere near ready for it. He'll let his ideas about magic and power ruin Tyrea as he strives to claim more of both, and he'll take Belleisle down as soon as he's finished with Darmid. Or perhaps before, if he sees an advantage in that."

Belleisle. The beautiful island. My grandfather's home—and my mother's, before she left it behind for the love of a king. Had my life gone differently I might have been at Severn's side as he attacked, might have been his greatest weapon against the island. Instead, I would fight against my brother to save it.

"Tyrea needs me," Ulric said. "They need a king who will watch over them—all of them, not just those with power, those who Severn considers important." He stepped back and looked me over. His forehead wrinkled, but the confident expression he usually wore returned quickly. "You won't walk away from your responsibilities or your rightful place. Prove to me that you deserve answers beyond *because I'm your king*, and you'll have them. Prove to me that you're not a coward, that you deserve to rule Tyrea after me. Let go of this dangerous infatuation and learn from my mistakes."

I couldn't find words to answer. He wanted to mold me, to

shape me to his image as he hadn't been able to do with Severn. My own desires and plans didn't matter. Not compared to the fate of Tyrea.

But that was his battle, not mine. He wouldn't control me.

Before I could speak again, he strode back toward camp. "Move your things now," he ordered over his shoulder, then turned back. "If you fight me on this, if you keep on with her, I will have her imprisoned for defying my orders and tortured until she begs for death. Don't think I won't. If you won't end this for the sake of our people or to save your own sorry future, do it for her."

He walked away, moving with as much strength and confidence as he had before his magic weakened him.

I fought my anger down, pushing it deep beneath a layer of false indifference.

He wouldn't dare. He can't do this without me.

I sat on the boulder and considered my options as rationally as I could. He was wrong about Rowan, surely. If he knew her better, he'd see that. She'd left her family behind, and knew better than to return to Darmid again. She would never betray me, never let magic die for the sake of people who hated her.

Are you certain of that? whispered a dark voice in my mind. *Certain enough to stake the fate of a nation and your own survival on it? Are you sure loving her and wanting to protect her hasn't made you weak?*

I shook the thought away.

I had several options. We could leave and abandon Ulric to whatever fate he'd chosen by driving us away, but then Severn would win. I didn't know what was wrong with my father or his magic, but it had to be serious to shake his confidence in his power. He seemed desperate now, and not entirely rational. He couldn't win this fight in that state.

Or I could listen to him, trust that the man knew what he was talking about after his long life and great losses, and break Rowan's heart as well as my own for the sake of Tyrea's future. I could resign myself to the same fate as him, cold and lonely, chained to the throne, a powerful slave.

Or I had a third option. Rowan and I could separate to keep Ulric happy, to appease whatever it was in his mind that made him so mistrustful of her and uncertain of his own future, just until the winds shifted. I would earn his trust and find out exactly what was wrong with him. Rowan would prove that she was no traitor, and she would help us win the battle. Nox would find a way to heal whatever was wrong with our father, and we would see him back on the throne.

And then Rowan and I would leave all of it behind forever.

It was the only sane solution. Surely she'd understand that.

~

"Are you crazy?" Rowan asked, managing somehow to whisper and yell all at once.

I'd pulled her out of the kitchen and told her we needed to separate. Given her reaction to the news of my father's order, I decided our little tent might be a better place for further discussion. I didn't answer, but led her toward something resembling privacy.

"I just got you back," she continued as she followed me in.

"It's temporary."

"It's ridiculous."

I turned to find her standing with her arms crossed, blocking the door. I gathered the few belongings that weren't still stuffed in my bag, hoisted the pack onto my shoulders, and waited. She didn't move.

I sighed. "What else would you have me do?" I'd told her what Ulric wanted, though not everything he'd said about her and threatened her with. It seemed too hurtful, too ridiculous to mention.

It's not a lie, I told myself. *It's simply not important. And it's not because there's any chance he may be right.*

I silently cursed my father. He was wrong, but I couldn't forget his warnings.

She sat on the bed. I sensed taking my chance to leave and

avoid this conversation would be a bad idea in the long term, and I sat beside her on the hard edge.

Rowan rubbed her fingers over her forehead in a gesture I was familiar with from the days when headaches plagued her. She looked at me, apparently choosing her words carefully. "Are you sure this is the best thing to do? You say he called you a coward. Is rolling over like this going to earn you his respect?"

My entire body tensed. "You think the same of me as he does?" The faint suggestion from her stung a thousand times worse than the outright insult from my father.

She held up her hands in surrender and leaned back. "I didn't say that. It's just..." She shrugged. "This seems wrong. After standing up to Severn the way you did, after how hard you've fought for us to be together, and with you wanting to earn your father's respect, I just don't understand this. How does us hiding help anything?"

I forced my jaw to unclench, my shoulders to relax. "It's complicated with him. He says I need to prove myself, but I don't think that's what he really wants. I'm not the only one who's changed since he disappeared. He's afraid, and I've never seen him scared before."

"Of what?"

"That's what I'm trying to figure out. I think he's afraid he's lost the support of his people, and that taking the throne back may be impossible. That may be part of the reason we're staying here—he needs to know his people still want him. But there's far more to it, and that's what he's keeping secret. He needs to see that I respect him and will obey him, and that will help me earn his trust. Or at least I might get close enough to figure it out myself. I already have an idea." I almost told her about my suspicions of his magical weakness, but held back.

Damn him.

She reached for my hand. "And if you disobey him now?"

I closed my eyes and tried to picture the logical progression of events, given my suspicions about my father. "He can't defeat Severn without me. So he fails, and Severn hunts us down. That, or I challenge him myself."

"Putting us right back where we were before you got your father back." She squeezed my fingers tight in hers. "So I pretend to lose you for a while, or I risk losing you forever?"

"There's a risk of loss either way. Nothing about this is certain." I tried not to consider my odds of survival if I challenged the person who had shaped my talents, who knew most of my strengths and all of my weaknesses and could turn them against me with barely a thought.

She watched me carefully, obviously reading more on my face than I'd intended to show.

"I know," she said. "That's why I wish I could at least have you safe by my side every night." She straightened her shoulders and brushed her hair back from her face, then forced a smile. "Maybe once things calm down, Ulric will realize I'm not the worst thing that could happen to you." The smile faltered. "Is that the problem? Did he even trouble himself to explain why he doesn't want us together? Why he hates me now? Why he doesn't seem to want to use or develop my skills?"

My stomach sank at the hurt and uncertainty in her eyes. I wouldn't make it worse, but we'd need to talk about at least part of it. "He has questions about your loyalty, given your past."

Her lips narrowed into a tight line, and she nodded for me to go on.

"Even without that, there's the question of succession. He thinks I'm planning to take the throne after him. I think I've explained to you his thoughts on love."

"You have."

"Right. So he's troubled by that, and thinks he's saving me from myself." I hesitated to go on, but remembered that I'd promised not to lie to her. "But he's more concerned with the fact that a king can't legally marry a Sorceress."

Her brow creased. "You told me that once, didn't you? That night when I took too much heartleaf. I remembered that Sorcerers and Sorceresses aren't able to have children together, but I'd forgotten about your father having to marry women without magic of their own."

"That law has nothing to do with me if I'm not going to be

king," I said. "And I'm not. I tried to correct him on that point, but he wouldn't listen."

She nodded, but her skin had gone pale, making the faint freckles on her nose stand out. "You're sure about that?"

"As sure as I am about anything. I never expected it. Never wanted it. I've worked too hard to get away from that life to want to go back to it."

She twisted her hair between her fingers, lost in thought. "You don't think we could at least clear up the misunderstanding about my loyalties? He's wrong."

"I know. And I tried. He seems unusually on edge about everything right now. I'm probably fortunate he's still trusting me, at least to some extent. So I think it's best for now that we play along, let him think he's getting what he wants, give him time to cool down."

Her dark gray eyes searched mine, and she seemed satisfied with what she found. "That's that, then." She nodded to herself. "Make him happy so we can finish this and you can get away from him. Please."

"So you'll release me?" I tried to ask with good humor, but the attempt fell flat.

She gave me a wry smile that faded as voices approached the tent. "We'll need to make it convincing, won't we?"

"Unfortunately, yes. It's not a game to him. No one can know how desperate I already am to be with you again." I could only imagine his anger if he learned I'd deceived him.

"Likewise." She jumped to her feet and pointed at the door as the voices came nearer. "Go, then," she ordered, raising her voice. "If that's all I mean to you, I don't want you here anyway." The voices stopped, and footsteps hurried away.

I got to my feet and shuffled past her, reminding myself that she was acting. For some reason, the words still bit into me.

"Too much," I whispered. "But good effort."

She stood on her toes and pulled me into a kiss that was over almost before I realized it was happening. "I love you," she whispered. "Be careful. I don't trust your father."

"Nor do I. As soon as this is over—"

She touched a finger to my lips. "Don't talk about that. Worry about now, and we'll deal with later when we get to it." She rubbed her fingers over her dragon scale necklace and sighed. "You'd better get out of here before anyone wonders about the long goodbye."

I wanted to promise her something, but that was unnecessary. We would be together again when it was safe.

I turned and left without another word and went to find my new place next to my father.

7

NOX

The afternoon sun turned Mama Bunn's little cabin into an oven, but I kept on with my work. I had just finished cataloguing the last of her unidentified plants when a knock sounded at the window. I rearranged my sweaty hair and hurried over expecting Kel, who had been banished that morning after Mama deemed him an ongoing distraction. Instead I found Aren, looking concerned.

"Is this about your hand?" I asked. "She'll let you in the front door for that."

He held it up and wiggled his fingers. He'd removed the bandage already, and the skin was barely pinker than normal. "Can we talk now? I don't know how long I have before Ulric wants me back."

I listened for the sound of Mama's snores coming from the other room. The old woman napped as hard as she worked. It was almost admirable, in a way.

"I'll try," I said. "Can't promise anything."

I left my work and crept through the outer room, eased the front door open, and winced as the rusted hinge squeaked a protest. Mama snorted and twitched in her chair, but didn't wake. I slipped out onto the porch and motioned for Aren to join me well away from the cabin.

I breathed in the cool breeze that lifted my hair off my hot neck and took in the sight of the forest, a relief after hours within the walls of the stuffy cabin. There was still life in these woods in spite of the drought. Not much that would help me or Mama Bunn in our work, but that would come with rain and the growing season.

"What's the fuss about?" I asked.

"The old man." Neither of us liked to call Ulric our father, though Aren was more comfortable with the idea than I. I'd as good as dismissed him from my life as soon as I'd learned how he'd banished me and my mother to Cressia, the barren dragon-lands of the north. I was glad to be helping him depose Severn, but aside from his potential in that area I wasn't impressed with the man so far. I'd expected a raging tyrant who would stop at nothing to reclaim his throne as soon as possible. Instead we sat in a rebel camp. Hiding.

At least he was leaving me alone.

Rumors traveled fast in this community, even when one was practically a slave to the local Potioner, and I'd heard all about Aren and Rowan's spat. "Do you need a hand moving your things? Someone said you looked angry, and that she sounded madder than a wet cat. I assume this was Ulric's doing and not just Rowan kicking you out."

He scowled. "I've already got my things moved. Rowan wasn't happy about it, but..." A look of distress came over him and was quickly smoothed away. "That's not what I wanted to speak to you about. Ulric is having problems with his magic."

I'd been watching a robin in the branches behind him—we saw so little wildlife near the camp—but snapped my attention back at his words. "Explain."

"You saw how I almost lost my magic back in Darmid. He was imprisoned there for three years, with them doing gods only know what to his magic to keep him controlled. There's something wrong with him now. He's weak." He held up his burned hand. "This wouldn't have happened if he'd been helping me control that fire."

"You mentioned that." I held back the scowl that threatened to twist my face. "He was all too happy to take credit for saving the camp though, wasn't he? Seemed to be enjoying all of the glory when we left."

Aren shrugged, obviously not concerned with being applauded for his work. In that we couldn't have been more different. I craved recognition. Always had. I was proud of my skills and wanted everyone to know my abilities. Part of my anger at Severn was the fact that he'd stolen that from me. In Luid I'd have learned to be one of the great ones, would have accomplished so much. But now—

"Nox?"

"Sorry, what?"

"You've got that distant, angry look again. Did you have any thoughts that might help Ulric? Because if he's weak, I'll have to..." His already pale skin went ashen. "It'll be up to me."

"Right. Does he know you know?"

"The less he thinks I know, the better. He already seems defensive and mistrustful."

"I understand. That doesn't get us many answers, though." I leaned against a maple tree while I sorted through my thoughts. "I'll give it some thought, but I don't know what I can do to help you right now." I gestured to the woods. "Even if it weren't so barren here, it's only spring. There are grasses and roots, but I'd need mature, powerful, possibly rare plants to come up with something to get him better, assuming you could find out what was wrong. And the equipment here isn't exactly what I'd need to work with, either."

"I thought as much." He frowned. "Laelana mentioned her grandfather earlier. She said he was able to work with plants, make them grow. Someone like that would be helpful, wouldn't he?"

I perked up. "Is he available? Gods, that would be perfect. If someone could speed up the—"

"He's dead."

I blew a stray strand of hair out of my face. "Helpful in theory, but definitely not in practice."

He looked away, considering something. "I'll keep my ears

open for another to assist you," he said, though I suspected he already had ideas that went deeper than that.

My thoughts returned to Luid, though not to imagined glory or fame. I thought of Severn, and how Aren had said his Potioners helped him recover after Rowan's attack. Not the same kind of injury at all, but it made me wonder what resources they might have in the city that I'd never encountered. Plants from foreign lands, perhaps, that I'd never dreamed of.

Not that they'd do us much good now. Someone would have to get into the city to seek that out, and she'd have to be crazy to try it. *But then, if she were in the city, that crazy someone might be in a perfect position to see her enemy suffer for everything he'd done to her...* I shook that thought off.

"How bad is it?" I asked.

"Bad enough that he's hiding like a wounded dog. The Ulric I remember would have charged straight to Luid and made Severn pay for his betrayal a hundred times over, without hesitation."

That sounded more like what I'd heard. "I'll see what I can figure out. But in the meantime, speaking of your abilities..." My stomach turned at the mere thought of what he could do—what I'd felt him do more than once. *But if someone did need to do something crazy, and she wanted to be prepared...*

"I want you to teach me how to defend myself from you," I said quickly, before I could change my mind. I knew I should get back. Mama would make my life miserable if she woke and found me missing, and Ulric would be displeased if I put her off. But this was far more important than an irritated old Potioner. I'd already done her work. I'd take time to do my own.

He gave me a blank look. "Weren't you recently trying to communicate with me using that horrid skill of mine? And now you want to shut me out?"

I shrugged. "You said that wouldn't work, anyway."

He glanced away, clearly uncomfortable. "For me to put my voice or my words into your mind would take a great deal of invasion. I would essentially be changing your thoughts to make them mine. Controlling you, even if it never affected you beyond that. And if I went deep enough to do that, your thoughts would all be open to me. Your doubts, your fears, your desires. Your hate."

His analysis wounded me more than the idea of invasion troubled me. I stood straighter, ready to defend myself. "Is that all you see in me?"

He smiled, more kindly than he usually did. "It used to be. Nox, I respect you and admire you for your skills, your will, and your passion. I'm grateful for everything you've done for me, for Kel and Cassia, even for Rowan's brother. But it took a long time for me to see that because it's hidden under such a thick layer of mean. You're a bit of a harpy, honestly."

I glared at him, but my anger eased. "You're one to talk."

His smile faded only slightly. "I know. For a long time, I thought that was all I was, too. Anger. Pain. A tool to be used by Severn. I killed, and sometimes enjoyed it. I used my gifts to hurt people, and did so with little regret." His head tilted slightly as he looked deeper into my eyes. "I let my anger drive me, and it nearly made me miss out on things in life that are far better."

I narrowed my eyes. "Did Kel tell you to talk to me about this?"

"No." He looked away. "I've changed a lot since the autumn, and everything I've gained from it is threatened now, especially if Ulric's magic fails. But even if I lose it all, I don't regret anything." His voice broke. "Nox, don't let your anger and your need for revenge keep you from being the person Kel sees behind the walls you've built. There's so much more to life than protecting yourself from hurt. I know it's hard, but..." He trailed off and shrugged.

I'd been thinking much the same thing myself, but hadn't wanted to admit it to anyone. To let go of the pain and bitterness, to open myself to using my skills to help people rather than seeking revenge, to stop hiding for fear of getting hurt... it seemed impossible, but it was something to think on.

Later.

"Fine," I said. "You being in my mind is unpleasant for both of us, but I think this is something I should work on."

He swatted a massive black fly off the back of his neck and

frowned at the blood smear on his hand. "We can try, as long as you won't storm off into the woods again when I get in. I could really use the practice right now, anyway. Having no enemies around leaves me with nothing to challenge me."

My throat tightened with apprehension, but I nodded. "Deal."

He looked uncertain. "This could go horribly wrong."

"Just try it." I squared my shoulders. "I'm ready."

"If you say so."

Before I could consider my defense, the familiar sensation came at me. A little niggling feeling at first, similar to what I felt when I wanted to use a word but couldn't quite think of it. Then my thoughts became jumbled, as though Aren had dumped them out. Images of Kel, of my old home, of my dead husband in his drunken anger, of my mother and a flaking painting on a temple wall, all scattered like filthy laundry on the floor of my mind.

"Stop!" I cried, and the images vanished. "I wasn't ready!"

He watched me evenly, untroubled by what he'd seen. "Why is the ability to defend yourself suddenly so important to you? You don't trust me?"

Not hurt, I noted. Just curious.

"No, I trust you not to use your magic on me," I said, surprised to find it was the truth. *We've come a long way.* "But others might use theirs, and I need to learn to protect myself. Didn't you once tell me that Severn has a way of knowing things?"

"It's different, but yes." His answer came slowly as he sorted through the meaning behind my question. "I hope you're not thinking of confronting him yourself. The best protection would be to stay well clear."

"No." I spoke softly. "There was a time not so long ago when I wanted to. I wanted to storm the palace, to make him feel my pain."

"He'd kill you before you so much as thought of moving against him. Even I can't challenge him that way."

I ignored the note of arrogance there, the lingering implication that he was better than me. Stronger because of what he was.

"But I think," I continued, "that you're right about what you were saying before. Maybe I can't stop being a total harpy right away."

He snorted.

"But there is more to life than vengeance," I continued, thinking aloud. "Much as I want Severn to pay for what he did to me, and more for what he did to our mother, maybe it doesn't have to be by my hand. My role might be to strengthen Ulric so he can make Severn suffer. But I still feel like I should be prepared."

Some deep part of me rebelled at the idea of giving up my glorious revenge, but another warmed at the thought of being part of a team instead of throwing my life away by acting alone. Perhaps my name wouldn't go into the history books as the one who destroyed the evil usurper, and perhaps that was all right in the end. Aren was right. There was more to live for.

I shoved the bloodthirsty part of myself aside. *I'll deal with you later.*

Aren's hands flexed at his sides as he smiled slightly, seeming to understand. I wondered whether he was catching something of my thoughts, even though I couldn't feel him in my mind. He appeared pleased.

"You're not going to hug me, are you?" I asked.

"Wasn't even thinking of it. Shall we try again?"

"Give me a minute." I imagined a heavy stone wall in my mind, blocking my thoughts and emotions in, presenting a blank facade to Aren. "Go."

My wall shattered, and my thoughts scattered again. "Gods damn it, Aren." I fought back disappointment as I collected myself.

He raised his hands, palms forward, mockingly defensive. "No one else will hold back when they attack you. If you're going to learn this, you're going to do it properly. There was some resistance there, though. It was a good try."

I glared at him, though without real ill will. "Don't patronize me, you condescending ass."

He grinned wider than before. "Then don't complain when I treat you as an equal, you vile, heartless shrew."

I snorted. Having a brother wasn't so bad. "So what should I do?"

"Let me think." He paced around our small section of forest, head down, absently slapping flies away. They seemed to quite like him. Perhaps not all of the effects of magic were pleasant.

"I want you to try something like what I do to keep Severn from finding me," he said. "It might work, it might not, but it's something."

"Fair enough."

He frowned as he searched for the right words. I imagined it wasn't easy to explain, especially if there was magic involved for him that I couldn't use.

"Make your mind a fortress," he said.

"I tried that."

"No, you imagined a wall. I saw it because you were picturing it. You can't imagine your defenses, they just have to exist. And you can't be on the outside looking in, picturing your wall. You need to be in there, closed off, impenetrable. And you need a roof. Walls won't get you far."

"How about a cave?"

He smiled, I suspected at some memory. "That will work well, I think."

I squeezed my eyes closed and drew into myself. The walls formed around me this time, leagues thick, as though I were trapped in an air bubble within a mountain. I tried not to think, but to stay quiet and focus on my breath, nothing more.

"Better," Aren said. "Now think of something that's important to you."

Kel appeared beside me, smiling and holding out a hand.

The mountain crumbled, and I opened my eyes.

"That was better," Aren said. "Much better than I expected from someone without magic. I didn't realize what you just did was possible to that extent." He frowned, then shook his head. "In any case, that was a fine effort, but you need to work on a few things."

I sighed. I'd asked for help. I just hadn't wanted it to be this much work. "Such as?"

"For one, as soon as you had a conscious thought, I saw it. This means that if you're trying to hide something, it may not be enough to keep it behind a wall. You need to keep it completely out of your mind if you can."

"Got it. What else?"

"You can't stand there frozen forever. You need to work out a way to build and maintain that protection while still having thoughts that seem natural, speaking easily. Any Sorcerer will think it odd if he tries to see your thoughts and there's nothing there, or if you can't function because you're so focused on protection."

I groaned. "It's so much. You think I can do it?"

"I do. You may not have magic, but you're stubborn as a mule. If you want to figure this out, I have no doubt that you will. We'll practice when we can, but my time may be limited." He glanced over his shoulder.

"Thank you." He seemed to want to say something else. "What?"

"There's one other thing that might give you away."

"Go ahead."

He smirked. "When you're concentrating, you look like you haven't moved your bowels in a month."

He jumped back as I swatted at him. "This isn't easy, you know."

"I know. Shall we try again?"

I shook out my arms, worked the kinks out of my shoulders, and nodded. "Damn right we should."

I would think on Ulric's problem, on my own shifting priorities, and on the murky future later. For now, I was spending time with the brother I was growing to accept and care for, learning something interesting, and finding a way to feel safe in an uncertain world.

I tried to shut out thoughts of Kel and Cassia, of my work and the life I might live someday. Aren's magic made the walls of my cave tremble and crack over and over, but eventually they held.

There are good things in life, I thought, *more than I ever knew.*

May we all survive to enjoy them.

8

ROWAN

"Psst."

I looked up from my work wiping down the wooden tables in the meal tent. After a few days, I hadn't accomplished much other than cleaning crumbs and becoming impervious to the glares of the other women. Never had I failed so badly at a task, and I wasn't sure whether I was more irritated with myself, the people of the camp, or with Ulric for forcing me into such an awkward position.

"Rowan, over here."

Aren stood outside in the mid-day sunshine, beckoning. It was the first time I'd seen him since he'd had to leave our tent. In spite of the camp's small population, we'd managed to give Ulric the complete separation he demanded. My heart gave a little skip at the sight of him, and I set my damp rag down and ducked outside. We stood in the shadows behind the massive canvas structure. I ached to hug him, to pull him into a stolen kiss. Instead, I tucked my hands into my pockets and kept my distance in case anyone passed by and spotted us.

"How've you been?" he asked.

"Fine," I said. "Cold at night. Lonely, but I'm getting by. I haven't learned much."

He just nodded.

You agreed to this, I reminded myself. This separation was vastly preferable to having Ulric glaring at me every time I went near Aren. We could pick up where we'd left off later. And if that meant I faced uncomfortable nights alone with the nightmares that plagued me no matter how many times I reminded myself that I'd been right to kill Dorset Langley, that was something I'd deal with on my own. Aren had enough to worry about.

"How have you been sleeping?" I asked in return, remembering his difficulty relaxing in times of danger.

"As an eagle, actually," he said. "I have my own tent, but Ulric asked me to keep watch outside."

"That's horrible! You never get enough rest that way."

"It's not so bad. Nights aren't as cold as they were. By summer it might actually be preferable." He reached out to brush my hair back from my cheek. "It does mean fewer dreams, though. I'd hoped we might share a few, if we couldn't actually be together. Maybe I'll stay human tonight."

I blushed. I'd never got much rest on nights when we shared dreams back at the school, but if I couldn't have Aren with me, they were the next best thing.

"We'll be fine," I said, sounding more optimistic than I felt. "It's all temporary, right?"

His smile tightened. "It is if I have any say in it."

I frowned. "What does that mean?"

He swallowed hard and looked back over his shoulder. "Just that things are complicated. But as long as I can leave my family behind when this is over, we can be together. No one will stop us. Not even the king himself." His expression warmed, melting me as the corners of his eyes creased. He leaned in closer, until his lips brushed mine. I sensed his magic, cold and dark, and felt I might drown in it as easily as I could in the depths of his green-flecked eyes.

"I want you," he whispered. "And I swear I will do whatever it takes for us to be together."

I pressed my mouth to his, trying to make the moment last,

then stepped back and looked more closely at him. He was wearing his mask. Unreadable, and still keeping something from me. I was reluctant to ruin things by pressing harder. He'd promised not to keep secrets to protect me, and I'd try to trust that promise.

"You'd better get out of here before your father sees us," I said. "Neither of us needs any more trouble."

He nodded and left without another word. After a moment to calm myself, I stepped back into the cooking tent. All was quiet, save for a few women sweeping scraps of food off the hard-packed dirt floor.

"Can I help with anything else?" I asked the old woman in charge.

She shot me a suspicious glare. "No, no. You go on and report back to the royals. Tell them what we're up to."

"That's not what I—"

She waved off my explanation. "We don't need your help. If you want to be useful, do it somewhere else."

I tried to catch the attention of the others, hoping for at least a sympathetic shrug, but they looked away.

I am useful, I told myself as I stepped out into the sunlight and headed away from the camp. *Or I will be once I get in control of my mind and my magic.* Practice was what I needed. Instruction would be better, but if I sat around and waited for Ulric to assign someone to do that, I'd be dead and rotted to the ground first. I'd tried to ask Griselda for help, but Laelana refused to let me near. The Sorcerers would have been a great help to me had they been free. Qurwin Black and Griselda were both teachers at Albion's school, and the others surely had skills they might teach me about.

I would find a way. In the meantime I would test myself, see what I could do now that my magic levels were back to normal and I was well away from the confinement of the cell walls in Ardare. I'd already spent too much time avoiding what I feared.

I will live up to my potential, I told myself. *Damned if I won't. Dorset Langley took so much from me. He won't have this.*

My magic surged in me as I passed the last ramshackle cabin, and a wave of nausea soon followed. "You're not going to kill anyone," I muttered. "Relax."

No one stopped me as I made my way farther into the woods. Leaf-buds dotted the branches of the trees in this area, which I supposed meant there was water somewhere in the ground. If I could just sense what was far below, bring it up...

I closed my eyes and listened with my magic instead of my ears, and got nothing—no connection to whatever water might be there.

Control your expectations, I reminded myself. I tried to enjoy the peace of the forest and the lack of pressure. My time imprisoned with Ulric had been non-stop work, constant evaluation, and the knowledge that my success might be the difference between death and freedom for both of us. It had kept me focused, and I'd learned to use my emotions to direct my power.

So what's wrong now?

For one thing, I didn't like using rage and fear to drive my magic. Effective as it may have been, it felt wrong, as though I were encouraging those emotions as I used them. I wanted to let go of them and let my magic flow through me as Griselda had taught me, but I couldn't. Everything felt wrong. Not just the fear, not just the memories that attacked me when I thought about drawing water, but something deeper. I felt broken and disconnected, and didn't know why.

I continued my walk, careful to note landmarks and to stick to my northerly course so I'd be able to get back. Comforting as it was to know that I would have an airborne search party if I got lost, I preferred that Aren not have to do that.

I climbed exposed tree roots that stuck out from an eroded cliff. I still felt nothing. The people weren't lying when they said there had been a dry spell.

If I couldn't work with water, I would try something else. Seeing Griselda had reminded me that I hadn't so much as attempted an illusion since the morning we left Ardare, when I'd used my surplus magic after our escape to create the illusion of a herd of flying horses and riders, all of them exact copies of me and Florizel. It had been enough of a diversion to allow the others time to escape. Florizel and I had made it out, too, though just barely.

The ground leveled out, and I found a small patch of thin, sickly-looking grass. I remembered Griselda's advice. Inanimate copies were supposed to be the easiest thing, and it would be best to start small until I figured out where I truly stood.

I pictured a second clump of grass beside the first.

A faint green shadow appeared and slowly solidified until it was almost convincing.

It should have pleased me. It wasn't much compared to what other people could do, or even compared to what I had done before, but it was there. I also wasn't experiencing any backlash, the unintended and unpredictable consequences of using magic. That meant that I had learned control, at least enough to not endanger people. But when I reached out to sense my magic, to feel that warmth within me, it had lessened. Only a small amount, but enough to set anxious wings beating in my throat.

I stood quietly, surrounded by the sounds of branches rustling in the breeze, and felt it slowly return.

The high-pitched nervous feeling eased, but I still didn't like it. *Maybe I just need to practice more, get my strength up.* I'd been avoiding using magic since the incident at the border, and had used it so hard before that. I would keep working, and would become useful. That was the important thing. Start small, work up, hope that the horrible feelings I now associated with working huge and dangerous magic would fade.

I walked away. When I looked back, the illusion had disappeared.

Time for something a little harder, then a long rest to see if the magic came back more quickly. I closed my eyes and remembered our escape from Ardare. The magic had been so strong then. It had been in control of me as much as I of it, but it had followed my commands. I let that feeling come over me again, allowed myself to be swept away by the memory.

You can do it again, I told myself. *You are a Sorceress. And the magic will return. It is yours.*

I pictured Florizel, my loyal friend. Aren had said that flying horses couldn't help their fearful instincts, but she had shown incredible bravery back in the city. She had once defied her herd's leadmare to attempt to rescue the stallion Severn had taken captive. She'd stayed with me when magic hunters captured me, and had followed us to the city. That had allowed her to tell Aren where to find me. And though she'd confessed to wanting to flee after Aren, Nox, Kel and Cassia went into the fortress to get me, she had come when she heard danger. Maybe she didn't think of herself as brave. Maybe she didn't like acting that way. But she could be.

I hoped she was doing well, wherever she had gone.

She took shape in my mind. A fine-boned horse with a cloudy gray coat, darker on her nose and stockings, with cream-colored mane and tail. Her wings were that same creamy, cloudy white, big and powerful. I pictured her gentle brown eyes, the dappled pattern of her coat.

Something crunched through the dry, leaf-littered forest.

I opened my eyes and there she was, standing still as a rock not twenty paces away, every detail perfect. Far too perfect for it to be my work. A fly landed on her flank, and she flicked it away with her tail.

I squinted. "Florizel?"

"Rowan?" She stepped forward. I held a hand out, and she snuffled at it with her warm nose. "Thank goodness!" she whinnied. "I was beginning to think I'd never catch you away from those horrible people. Is everyone all right?"

I wrapped my arms around her neck and laughed. "Everyone's fine for now. I thought you had left us."

"I couldn't. But people are not always so kind to my sort as you've been, and I didn't want to come into the camp."

"Well, your timing is impeccable. Where have you been?"

She tossed her head, nodding to the north. "About a day's journey that way, by your reckoning. I came to tell you to find me there if you need me. You go straight that way until you come to a deep ravine. There's a giant tree on the far side, and you go toward the mountains from there. I've found a place to stay. Lots of grass, and there's a spring beneath. It's not much, but I'm eating well. Lonely, though."

"I'm so glad you came. I've missed you."

She hugged my shoulder with her chin and stepped back.

A spring. I might be able to do something with that. If even a little water came to the surface, I could try to summon more. Ulric might widen the opening if that were a problem, crack the earth to give us access to more. I'd seen him split the rocks over a cave and open a hole in the earth to swallow enemies. Surely he could do this, too. *And then, if we could get the people of the village to move—*

Florizel snorted, and her eyes widened at something behind me.

"Hello, Florizel."

I winced. It seemed just thinking of people could summon them now. I turned to see Ulric picking his way over some fallen logs and making his way closer.

"Hello," Florizel murmured. She rarely spoke around him. I couldn't blame her. The man gave off an air of danger that made me wonder how he'd ever managed to secure the good will of his people. Of course, he'd gained my trust, once. And the people in the village seemed pleased to have him back.

A chill crawled over my skin as he fixed his icy stare on me, and I wanted nothing more at that moment than to sink into the shadows of the forest and disappear.

"Rowan," he said. "I need to speak to you. Alone."

Florizel shuffled sideways, obviously unsure of what to do. "You can go, I'm fine," I told her, and hoped that was true. "I'll remember where to find you."

She nodded and trotted through the trees until she reached a clear place where she could take off without hitting branches on her way up. A moment later, she was gone.

I watched her go, keenly aware that Ulric's attention remained fixed on me. When I turned back, I found his expression disconcertingly unreadable. Calm, yet with the sharpness of a hunter fixing on its next kill. And, I thought, a hint of wariness.

He doesn't know about my problems, I realized. Aren had said that Ulric questioned my loyalty. I didn't know whether things would be better or worse for me if he knew I was less capable now than I'd been before. I swallowed around the lump in my throat and pretended I had nothing to be worried about.

"Where's Aren?" I asked.

His eyes narrowed. Calculating. Judging. "Why do you ask?"

"I never see you without him anymore. I wonder why you came alone."

The corners of his lips turned up, though I couldn't call it a smile. "He's making friends with the leadership. Doing the work I asked him to do. Makes me wonder why you're not doing yours, why you've wandered so very far from camp all alone."

My stomach turned to stone, but I refused to let my fear show. "I'll get back soon. The others had no more work for me, and no interest in friendship. I thought it would be better for all of us for me to use my time working on my magic."

"Alone?"

"You've made sure there was no one to help me." I bit my tongue too late to hold the response back. Still, I couldn't regret my harsh tone. Perhaps if Aren wasn't going to stand up to him, it would fall to me. I needed to gain the man's respect somehow, and it seemed my magic wasn't the way to do it. "I want to help," I continued, my voice surprisingly calm and even. "If you'd just let me."

His expression didn't change. "And how will you do that? Are you in full control of your magic now? Are you no longer a danger to anyone?" He stepped closer. "Do you no longer fear what you will become if you accept it?"

I gritted my teeth. "I saved your life and everyone else's back in the city. Does that mean nothing?"

He nodded skyward. "You're as fearful as that horse. Yes, you saved us. You acted when you had to. You killed a man who would have killed you, and what has it done to you?" His eyebrows drew together in a mockery of sympathy. "You haven't changed, and training you now would be a waste of time."

"Then let me help some other way." Magic wasn't the only way to gain his respect. Laelana had done it with her strong will and her refusal to let him control her. Lying belly-up in the dirt like a beaten dog wouldn't do anything for me.

"Go on," he said. His voice sounded disinterested, but that sharp gaze never wavered.

"Did you hear what Florizel was saying about water? She found a source just a day's journey from here, back toward the mountains. Longer if we had to take the people around by roads, but still. If we could convince them to move the village, surely that would get you further on Laelana's good side."

His eyes narrowed again. "You would tell them to move farther from Luid?"

My heart quivered, but I pressed on. "They need this. The merfolk need this. And—" My words dried up.

"Laelana is well aware that there is water elsewhere, if not so close," he said evenly. "She feels they're safe here. They'll move when it's in my best interest for them to move, and not before."

I swallowed hard. "Another idea, then. Griselda Beaumage was my teacher for a time. She knows me, and seems willing to speak with me. Laelana has been cautious, but isn't as wary of me as she is of you. She must have picked up by now on the fact that you have no use for me."

"And?"

"Let me get close to Griselda and ask her to train me. If I have her alone, we can make plans that don't involve Laelana, if that's what you want."

His jaw muscles flexed. "My plans, or yours?" He moved closer again, and I took three steps back. His magic filled the air around us, ready to crush me, to steal my strength, or to destroy me with a wave of his hand.

I stumbled back, and only a helping hand from a solid branch kept me from falling. *Don't show him that you're afraid.*

"Why do you hate me now?" I asked. "When we were in prison, you seemed to trust me. You were horrible to me, but when they sentenced me to death, you cared. You comforted me."

He opened his mouth, then paused. The heaviness of magic abated, if only slightly, as a hint of confusion crossed his features. It was gone a moment later, replaced with the cold glare I was coming to know so well. "Everything was different then," he said quietly. "You were a tool I needed to use to gain my freedom. And yes, I felt for you. I'm not as evil as Aren might have led you to believe. I feel empathy, and I'd have felt sadness if you'd died in our escape as I expected you to. I pitied you, believing you were exaggerating your relationship with Aren. I didn't think he'd be so stupid as to… Well."

I didn't answer.

He raked a hand through his long hair and backed off a pace. "And then you lived, and I realized exactly what you could be if you had the training. And I saw you with Aren, saw the hold you have on him, saw exactly what you could do to him and to Tyrea." The muscles around his eyes tightened, and his lips narrowed. If I hadn't known better, I'd have said he was afraid.

I realized then what a grave mistake I'd made in offering my suggestions. He may have despised me for being weak and afraid, but that was how he wanted me. A powerless enemy with no friends is hardly a threat. But if he thought I was plotting to turn Aren against him, or Griselda and all of Belleisle, I would find myself with a powerful enemy.

His eyes widened, showing the whites all around the iris.

I pressed my back against the tree and fought the urge to close my eyes and brace myself for whatever he threw at me. "Aren won't be pleased if you kill me," I said. My voice came out in a rasp, but the words reached him.

He sneered. "And why should it matter to him now?"

I pushed away from the tree and stood straight. Ulric still towered over me, but I felt stronger. "People don't stop caring about one another just because you rip them apart. Do you want to risk losing him over this?"

For a moment, he said nothing. His shoulders relaxed, but he still glared at me. "I know that all too well," he said, almost to himself. "And you're right. Aren's a fool." His expression softened slightly. "You remind me of someone I once knew. I can't say I care for it."

He turned to leave, and my knees trembled with relief.

And then he turned back.

"Stay away from Aren. I assume he was gentle with you when he explained the situation, so I'll do you the kindness of being honest. You have no future with him, even if you think he still cares for you, and no matter what he says about it."

I didn't let my expression give anything away.

"Even if he weren't heir to the throne, even if he turned his back on it, or even if you somehow proved yourself to not be a danger, you would not have what you want from him." The look of sincere pity he gave me came as a shock after the anger he'd displayed moments before. "You will both live long lives, and he would tire of you soon enough. The responsibilities of ruling are great, but so are the pleasures. You'd be asking a king to live on a pauper's meals for the rest of his long life if you wished to be his only love." He paused, watching my reactions carefully. "But it doesn't matter. He will be king, and you will not be queen. Aren will see the error of his past decision."

I took a long breath. "You consider that kindness?"

"Is sparing you pain unkind?" He glared at me again. Keeping up with his shifts in tone and conversation left me dizzy.

"Ask Griselda for training if you wish," he said. "You're not wrong that you might get her alone where Aren and I can't, and perhaps we will find a way to make you useful. But remember that I will be watching and listening. Always. If I catch you acting against me in any way, including continuing your relationship with Aren, I will consider it an act of treason. You will be punished accordingly. And Rowan?"

I looked at him, but couldn't answer.

He covered the distance between us in a few quick steps, forcing me back against the tree. "You will not tell anyone I was here. You will not tell anyone about the water. Not the merfolk. Not Laelana. Certainly not Aren. This conversation did not happen."

He turned and left me, covering the distance back toward camp in long strides until he disappeared among the trees again.

I broke then. Sank to my knees on the forest floor, shaking. *He's mad,* I thought. *He's losing his mind.* The Ulric I'd met in

Ardare had been cold and hard, but not this terrifying, confusing monster.

I'd have to tell Aren, somehow. If Ulric wasn't fit to rule, Aren's problems and mine were about to get far worse than anything we'd imagined.

9

ROWAN

A rushing river sparkled in the bright sunlight, surrounded by long, green grasses and blooming flowers. It may have been a dry, cold spring in Tyrea, but in my dreams it was summer, and better times.

"Where are we?" Aren asked.

"I don't know. Somewhere nice." I reached for his hand, and enjoyed being able to do so without worrying about who might be watching. We had so much we needed to discuss while we had time, but I wanted just a few moments to enjoy him, first. The sensation of his skin on mine wasn't exactly the same in dreams as in waking life, but it was close enough that I felt the warmth of his touch. "I'm glad you're here."

Aren released my hand and stepped toward the river. "Your dreams are more vivid than mine. More detailed."

"You like it?"

He closed his eyes and turned toward the sun. "It's nice. Not much happening, though."

"Hmm. What can we do about that?"

He reached for me.

And then he was gone.

The sky darkened as clouds rolled in. The flowers around me

closed and shriveled, and a cold wind blew in from behind me, whipping my hair around my face.

"Aren?" I called. There was no answer.

Voices echoed through the woods, arguing. I hurried toward the sound, drawn to voices that sounded familiar even if they were too distant to be identifiable. I was relieved to find this wasn't one of those dreams where it felt like I was running through mud. The forest floor beneath my feet felt solid and real as I pushed against it.

The voices grew louder as I realized I was in the forest near Stone Ridge, the house where I grew up under my aunt and uncle's care. I recognized my aunt Victoria's voice, loud and strong in my ear, but speaking nonsense sounds. My mother's chimed in, crying in pain. I gasped.

And then the voices faded away.

My heart raced, drowning out the muffled sound of my footsteps on what had become a hard dirt road beneath my feet. I made it over the rise in the land and came to a stop.

The iron gates were closed. Never in all my years at Stone Ridge had I seen them like that. They'd always been open, welcoming, a reminder that I wasn't a prisoner there after my parents sent me away. Given the sad state of the walls, closing them for security would have been an absurd token gesture. I hurried toward them and pushed, but though no chain or lock held them closed, the gates wouldn't move.

Something crashed through the underbrush to my left.

"Aren?" I called again. My voice came out in a squeak.

Another cry of pain, this one deep and masculine. Matthew, who worked for my aunt and uncle and had been as good as another father to me in my years there.

I ran for the wall and vaulted over a low spot in the crumbling granite.

There was nothing on the other side. The fall into darkness ripped a feeble scream from my throat as I reached out to feel for something to grab onto.

The fall slowed until I found myself floating. A light appeared, revealing a room holding my family. My parents, Aunt Victoria and Uncle Ches, Matthew and Della, my brother Ashe and my sisters. I could no longer hear them, but the pain and terror on their faces tore me apart.

Dorset Langley stood over them. The man who hunted magic, who had hunted me. A man of no scruples, willing to do anything to complete his mission of destroying magic.

And he's dead, I reminded myself. *You killed him. This is a dream.*

With that thought, Langley's face tightened and distorted. Every moment of his horrible death played out slowly until he was a husk of a body, shriveled and hideous.

And yet he kept moving as though nothing had happened. He raised his sword, ready to bring it down on my aunt.

"No!" I screamed. He turned to me, and I suspected he would have grinned had his mouth not already been twisted open, teeth bared.

The floor appeared under my feet as dream logic dropped me into the scene. "Rowan," my mother gasped.

My magic roared to life as Langley brought the sword down, just as it had the night it broke the binding that had held it inside me for so long. *Wait*, I thought, but the magic wouldn't hold back. It flooded from me in a blinding flash of light.

When my vision cleared, I realized what I'd done. My family's bodies lay in a pile, broken and lifeless.

It's just a dream. It's just a dream.

But so real. I let out a long, low wail.

Dorset Langley still stood, and a laugh as dry as the wind through the rebel camp echoed from his throat. He stepped toward me, covering the distance with inhuman speed.

His bony hands clamped on my arms, and I screamed into the darkness that descended over us.

~

THE GRIP on my arms didn't release even as I opened my eyes in darkness. I struggled, and the hands let go.

"Rowan, it's me." Aren's voice, concerned but calm. "You're dreaming. It's all right."

I sucked in a deep, rasping breath and rolled onto my side in a ball. Aren sat and ran a hand over my back until the shaking stopped.

I forced my body to straighten, my eyes to open against the darkness of the tent. I sat up and shifted to lie with my head on Aren's lap, then reached up to touch his face and trail my hand down over his chest. His loose shirt was unlaced at the collar, probably thrown on quickly when he rushed to my tent. I pressed my cheek to the rough cloth covering his thigh, savoring the solid realness of him.

"I'm fine," I said. "It was just a nightmare."

"That wasn't just anything," he said, and dragged his fingers through my hair. "I woke up when you disappeared from our dream. I didn't want to risk coming to check on you, but you sounded like someone was killing you."

"Thank you. I guess I needed help to get out of that one." I sat up and reached for my sweater. I forced a smile, though he wouldn't see it.

"Do you want to tell me about it?"

I didn't answer until I'd played the dream back in my mind. It felt less real now that I was safe, but the horror of what I'd seen—of what I'd done—held my heart tight in its icy grip.

I relayed the events of the dream to Aren, and tried to convey the strange foreboding I'd felt at the sight of the closed gates, even before I'd been pulled into the other part of the dream. Words failed me. "It was just... horrible." I took a few deep breaths and wished the lamps outside were still burning. The utter blackness that surrounded us made it harder to shake the feeling of the dream. "I'm used to dreaming about him," I added, unwilling to say Langley's name. "But what about the rest of it? Why would I be pulled from a dream with you to see *that*?"

His fingers drew slow circles on my back as he thought. "Are you still concerned about your magic hurting your family? Or anyone?"

"No," I said, surprised to find it was true. "I have better control. I'm not scared of that happening again."

"Then perhaps it's simply that you're worried about your family." He put an arm over my shoulders, pulling me close. "Are you worried about the magic hunters going after them? About your magic harming them indirectly in that way? You haven't said much about them since we left Darmid."

"No. I thought..." What? That he wouldn't want to talk about them? He'd told me about his meeting with my mother, said he'd told them to get out of town. He'd cared enough to do that, and would have listened if I wanted to talk. "I am worried," I admitted, "but I feel as though I'm supposed to forget about them. Now that I'm free, after going back was such a disaster, and if in theory they're safe after your warning, I should be able to move on. My life is here now."

"But you're still concerned about them."

Tears pricked at my eyes. "What if Ashe didn't get better? What if they didn't get out before the king sent magic hunters to interrogate them?" The dream images flashed back into my mind, and I shivered. "And the people at Stone Ridge. They're not safe, are they?"

"No. You're not the only one in your family with talent, are you?"

I drew in a long breath and leaned into him. "Victoria has the same gift as Laelana's grandfather, doesn't she? Or she did, before the boys died. Everything changed after that."

"Your aunt and uncle's children were killed for their magic. It stands to reason that it came from somewhere."

I nodded, a motion that he had to feel rather than see in the blackness of the tent.

Matthew had convinced me when I was a child that the trees' constant flowering and fruiting, the longevity of the garden blossoms, and the vegetable garden's incredible bounty were the product of a skilled gardener's care and nothing more. But of course, that couldn't be true.

"I want to tell you that they're probably safe," Aren said.

"But that would be a lie."

"Yes."

"The king's hunters won't leave them alone, will they?"

"I don't think so. Not after your escape. They may have bigger things to worry about for now, but they're not going to let it go."

I leaned forward and rested my forehead in my hands. "So what do I do? Do I go back to collect them? Fight for them? Bring Victoria here to feed the village?"

"I think that would be unwise, though I can't say I hadn't thought about how useful skills like hers could be." He was silent for a few moments. "It's too dangerous for you to go back there again, especially alone. We barely made it out. I can only imagine trying it again after what just happened in the city."

My chest tightened. "I can't just abandon them, Aren. I know you don't care for them, and you disapprove of what they did to me. But they're my family. I love them. I can't let this go, because —" I stopped. *I should be able to.* Aren would. He'd turned his back on his family for me, once.

He lay on the bed and gently pulled me down next to him. I wrapped my arms around him, a little ashamed of how much I'd missed this after just a few nights of separation. "Rowan, you wouldn't be you if you just let this go. You have so much love and loyalty in you. I used to think that was weakness, but it's not. Not in you. It's what made you go back to Darmid the last time."

"Not the smartest thing I've ever done."

"No." He brushed my hair away from my face and planted a gentle kiss on my forehead. "You think too much with your heart. It rules you. But though it causes problems, I admire that about you. It's one of the things I love about you." He still hesitated over that word. "I know my father hasn't been kind or respectful toward you, but he doesn't see what I see. You're not like us, and that's where your strength lies. Don't turn your back on it."

I snuggled closer to him. "So where does that leave me?"

"In a bit of a bind, I'm afraid. It's your choice, but I'd prefer not to lose you again. Please don't go back alone. We'll find a way later, somehow." He tipped my chin up and kissed me, then pushed up to sit on the edge of the crates. "I have to go. I don't know whether my father heard you earlier, but if he's awake, he'll be watching for me."

I'll be watching you, Ulric's voice echoed in my mind. *We did not have this conversation.*

Treason.

"He will be," I said softly. "He told me he would."

Damn the warnings, Aren deserved to know.

He sat up straighter. "When did he say this?"

"He followed me into the woods today. Told me to stay away from you. He..." The memory of the maniacal flash of his eyes made me shiver. "Aren, I think he's a little crazy. He seemed sane most of the time we were talking, just excessively angry. But these things he thinks about me... He's seeing threats that aren't there. He thinks I'm going to betray him, or turn you against him." I ran through the conversation in my head, and realized how much worse it would make things if I so much as mentioned the possibility of me going to Darmid again. "He said not to tell you we'd spoken, but I'm worried."

Aren sighed. "I am, too. And I appreciate you letting me know."

"Please don't mention this to him. Not my dream, not my family, not that we talked about this. If he knew, I think he'd kill me."

I expected a big reaction to that. Instead, Aren stood. "I won't say a thing. Try to stay away from him from here out. I'm going to try to get him to speak to Nox. Maybe there's a simple solution for all of this." I heard rather than saw him move through the tent. "He'll get past it."

I very much doubt that, I thought as Aren opened the tent flap and slipped back out into the night. I hoped he'd have a good sleep.

I was certain that I wouldn't.

∽

"SWING." Griselda ordered. "No, with control. It's a sword, not an axe!"

I dropped my weapon to the ground and wiped the sweat from my brow. "I'm sorry, I'm not used to this."

"Obviously. You're sure you don't want to try magic instead?"

"I'm sure." Laelana had decided not to tag along when I suggested that my teacher help me with combat training, but I suspected she'd take more of an interest in the proceedings if magic was involved. More than that, though, I remembered Ulric's face when he thought he realized I was a true threat to him. If he was watching, I didn't want him to see anything that might reinforce that. "Magic another day," I continued, and meant it. I would build my skills up again, and I would ask Griselda to help, but only after Laelana and Ulric lost interest in what we were up to.

Besides, if it came to battle, I planned to be fighting beside Aren. I'd need to learn to do it properly, and time was running out.

I'd told Griselda what happened during the weeks after I'd left the island, about the control I'd learned in prison, the incredible power that had filled me after I was free of the prison cell and the shackles that held my magic in, the illusions I'd used to escape the city.

I hadn't told her that using it now made me feel like vomiting. That was still my own business, and I would figure it out soon enough.

Griselda frowned and nudged the sword with the toe of her boot. "Piece of garbage, this, but it might one day be the only thing between you and an enemy. Pick it up."

I groaned, but complied. My arms ached, and we'd only been working for an hour. I rolled my shoulders forward. The leather armor was sitting wrong again, digging into my waist and under my arms.

"Slowly this time," she said. "Start at the left, come down across your body. Lift your arm. No, the other one."

She swung her own sword over her head with a flourish that clearly impressed the few folk who had gathered to watch.

A moment later, she disarmed me.

"You seem distracted, Sorchere."

I smiled at the nickname. We hadn't spent much time together at Belleisle, but Griselda had helped me find my talents, and I considered her a friend as well as a teacher. "I am, sorry. I have a lot on my mind."

"Ah. Well, best that we get through this, then, so you can focus on your own problems after we get the old king back on the throne."

"Young enough to take you on, Griselda Beaumage," said a low, cultured voice behind me.

A grin spread across Griselda's face at Ulric's words. She bowed theatrically. "It would be an honor to spar with the king, if you'd care to join me."

Ulric narrowed his eyes. "Later, perhaps." He watched us, but I refused to move until he left.

Griselda didn't speak again until he was gone. "Is this what's on your mind?"

"Partly." I swung, and she blocked me easily. "We got along fine when it was just the two of us in that cell. But now he's watching me, waiting to catch me slipping up. He thinks I'll betray him. And he's chasing me away from Aren." I kept my voice low enough that only she would hear.

"Hmm. Pay attention, now. Widen your stance, you're going to topple over as soon as I hit you."

I complied, and she swung. I blocked her and stumbled backward. "You don't think Ulric hating me is a problem? He's trying to control Aren, and I don't think Aren's enjoying it much."

Griselda looked back toward Ulric and shook her head. "This is life in the Tyrean royal family, I'm afraid. I think you're fortunate to be allowed to stay out of it. Perhaps a little space isn't a bad thing."

"That doesn't help Aren."

She smiled sadly. "No, it doesn't. But neither does us talking about it, really." Her voice dropped to a murmur as she stepped closer. "Perhaps Aren is doing as I am. Complying, biding his time, watching and learning, feeling out the options."

I wanted to ask more, to know why she and the others had come and what they hoped to achieve, but she held up a finger to stop me. She waved to someone, and I turned. Laelana stood a good distance off, watching carefully.

"Now," Griselda continued, loud enough for anyone nearby to hear and not mistake our training for anything else. "Have you ever tried archery?"

"I did well enough with it when I was younger. I never liked hunting, but shooting wasn't a problem."

Cassia approached from the side of the sparring ring, tying her thick hair back as she walked. "May I try?"

I handed her my sword and shrugged out of the armor. "Please do. I'll watch and catch my breath."

In truth, I wasn't out of breath, and my muscles were recovering more quickly than they once would have. Months on the road and doing physical work at Belleisle had made me stronger, but I felt discouraged and even more useless than I usually did. I couldn't make friends. Hadn't found time to work on my magic. Couldn't even swing a sword properly.

"I can help!" a young voice shouted. Patience dashed up next to Griselda and Cassia. Her limp was less pronounced when she ran, but as she slowed it became obvious. "I can fight."

Griselda considered the girl, took in her missing eye, her limp, her tiny frame. "Why don't you let me and miss Cassia work for now, eh? Children shouldn't have to worry about these things. No one is going to send you into battle."

Patience nodded and backed away, chin held high, as Griselda explained movements that Cassia copied almost perfectly the first time she tried. Patience sat beside me on the ground.

"She meant I won't fight because of this, didn't she?" She gestured toward the scarf that covered part of her face. "Not because I'm a child. Peter's learning, and Jon. They're not much older than me."

I didn't point out that the boys also dwarfed her. "You'll get your chance."

She sighed. "Will I? Nobody wants me around here. They feel sorry for me, but I could be a hero. I could learn to fight."

"If it comes to war, most of the people who are learning how to fight right now will die."

"I know. It's just because of my mother, you know?" She wrapped her arms around her knees, making herself impossibly small.

"Not exactly. Do you want to talk about it?"

She was silent for a while, watching as Cassia and Griselda moved into slow and gracefully staged combat. I told myself that Cassia only took to it so naturally because she was a warrior at home, underwater. She was figuring out how to transfer her skills, not learning new ones. It didn't help.

"My mother died a hero," Patience said. "When those men came after us the second time, she told us to run. She and some of the others tried to hold the men back so we could escape, but it was too much. There was so much screaming and smoke. Crying. I hid, then tried to find her, but the big man found me first."

Wardrel, I thought. One of Aren's brothers, and one I hoped I never had the displeasure of meeting.

"He got one of his men to help hold me down," she continued. "Most of their work was done by then, I guess. He took a torch and held it under my bare feet, and he laughed when I screamed." She closed her eye and squeezed her hands into tight balls that she pressed against her thighs. "I heard my mother calling for me, trying to find me. Maybe if I'd stayed quiet she would have got away, but I couldn't. I was so scared, and it hurt so bad."

I didn't speak. The lump in my throat would have prevented it even if I'd tried.

Patience's voice remained steady as she continued. "He got tired of that pretty quick, and he... he grabbed my head like he was gonna kiss me. And he squeezed, and his thumb went in my eye. And he kept pushing. Slow. And then the torch came again..."

My stomach twisted. I could only imagine her pain. Her fear. Her confusion.

"I thought it would kill me. I don't really remember what happened after that. Something hit him, he let me go. Mother was screaming, but I couldn't see anything but the hem of her nightgown as she ran. They followed her, and I crawled away. Point is, they killed her. But she saved me. Or what's left of me. I want to be like that. I want to be brave, and fight, and save people. Do dangerous things or sneaky things and take big chances and change everything. But no one will let me."

I forced back the tears that stung my eyes. The last thing the girl wanted was pity. "It's a noble goal," I said when my throat cleared. "I'll do whatever I can to help. I'm afraid I won't be much help with your training, though."

She turned and smiled. *Incredible.* "Yeah, I saw. You're not very good with a sword."

I gave her a light punch on the arm. "Watch it, kid."

She thumped me back. "I could take you."

I laughed. "You probably could. And I have no doubt you'll be a hero some day."

She put a hand on my knee and pushed herself up to stand. "We'll both show them what we're worth."

She watched Griselda and Cassia. A crowd had formed, most of them likely appreciating things other than the Sorceress and the mer woman's battle skills.

"Hey, Patience?"

"Yeah?"

"Do you know how to handle a bow and arrow?"

She grinned. "Do I? I used to get more rabbits than Papa when we went hunting. My aim's a little off now that I've lost an eye, but I'm getting better every day."

"Perfect. I could use some help. I'm really out of practice."

Her grin widened, and she grabbed my hand. I smiled, too, and waved to Aren as we passed them. Aren nodded back. Ulric turned away, as though he hadn't seen me.

No matter. Somehow, Patience and I would both find our places.

I watched Rowan and Patience disappear in the direction of the supply sheds. When I turned back to my father, his cold gaze was focused on me.

"How much of a problem is this going to be?"

I decided that playing ignorant would only work against me. "It's not. Rowan and I are no longer so much as speaking, I assure you."

He smiled and nodded at a dumpy middle-aged woman as she passed, then turned to me. Though his overall expression remained pleasant for the sake of the people, anger burned in his eyes. "I know you went to her last night."

Of course he was watching. I felt one step closer to being back at home, under Severn's constant, suspicious surveillance.

"Did you think I wouldn't notice that you two were sneaking around?" he asked. "That I wouldn't expect it? You gave up far too easily for me to believe you'd given up at all."

"She had a nightmare and needed me. Nothing else. What would you have had me do?" I matched my expression to his. Just a father and son engaged in pleasant contemplation over royal business. "I've tried to act according to your wishes, which I still don't fully understand. You won't listen to me when I try to explain—"

"There is no acceptable explanation for your disobedience."

I kept my voice even, though his bull-headed insistence on blind loyalty made me want to lash out, or to turn and walk away from him. "Very well. We lied to you. I lied when I said I would end things with her, and I did it to keep you happy."

He gave me no answer save for a dark look that said he'd never trusted me.

"I see no reason why I should give up the only thing keeping me sane right now amidst—" I stopped myself, but too late.

My father glowered. "Amidst the shit I'm putting you through? Get used to it. This is far bigger than you or your petty troubles, and always has been."

He walked beside me through the village, nodding to people who greeted him, keeping an eye on those who didn't. When an older woman dropped into an awkward curtsey, he replied with a slight, formal bow and a smile. He would win them over.

He turned toward the woods and motioned for me to follow. I resigned myself to the conversation, if not to my fate.

"You're allowing yourself to be manipulated," he snapped, "sneaking around like a whipped dog, disobeying me because you're too selfish to see beyond your own needs. It's only going to get worse. If you'd listened to a damned word I said to you when you were younger—"

"I listened," I growled through gritted teeth, then forced myself to be calm. He wanted to get a reaction from me, and I wouldn't let him have it. "I tried to fight it. Every time I felt something for her, I fought."

"I find that hard to believe. You've always been desperate for approval and acceptance, ever since you lost your mother. I saw that, even from a distance." His face twisted as though he'd smelled something foul. "Severn saw it, and used it. And now it's got you into this mess."

The words cut as deep as if he'd accused me of betraying him to Darmid. The fact that I was beginning to think he was right only made it hurt more. I'd been starved for so many things, and become a glutton when Rowan offered them.

Nothing would change my mind about her, or about my

future. My resistance seemed childish, but the thought of the alternative made my throat close as though a noose had tightened around my neck. *Tied to the throne. No Rowan. No freedom. The weight of a kingdom on my shoulders.*

"Say something," he barked, eyes wide. I saw a glimmer then of what Rowan had described—mistrust that went beyond reason, a sideways slip of his mind into irrational fear.

I pressed harder against his defenses, not caring whether he sensed it. His anger at my betrayal washed over me, and beneath that I uncovered shame at his capture and his mistrust of every person in camp. Before I could dig deeper his magic pushed back, closing the chinks in his mental armor, pushing me out. The last thing I felt was his rage at the invasion.

My father stepped closer, lips curled into a snarl. The air pulsed with his magic, dark and cold as my own.

That's the father I remember, I thought, almost relieved to feel strength from him.

"Gods, you're worse than I thought all these years," he snarled. He took another step, forcing me back. His shoulders tensed as he raised his loosely clenched fists. "Not only weak, but disloyal and completely unfit to be king. If I had any other choice in my heir—"

The raw power he held within him became nearly palpable as he drew on it, preparing to attack. I ducked out of the way as he released a blast of magic that narrowly missed me and sent a tree behind me crashing to the ground, splintered where the magic had turned the middle into sawdust with its sheer force.

I glanced back at the tree and pretended my heart wasn't pounding as memories of Severn's first attack on me flashed through my mind. The pain, the fear. Magic breaking bones, tearing flesh.

Ulric's expression went blank, and his breath wheezed as he inhaled. He collapsed as though he'd taken a hit to the gut. Bent double, he rested his hands on his knees as tremors overtook him. Barking coughs racked his body until he fell to his knees and spit out blood that soaked into the dry dirt. I started forward, more from concern for protecting my own future than from compassion for the man who had just tried to kill me, but he waved me off.

He wiped his mouth on his sleeve. "I bit my tongue," he said.

"Is that so?"

He searched my eyes as he looked up at me, and found nothing. No concern for his well-being. No fear. I wouldn't give him the satisfaction of either. In that moment of openness, though, I felt his confusion, and how he hated himself for being so weak as to lose control of his emotions. He regretted his action, but I had no expectation that he would apologize.

His skin had lost all of its color, and he'd aged years in only moments. I'd been at least halfway right about his condition, and it was far worse than I'd suspected.

"This is why you're so concerned with my situation, isn't it?" I asked. "Your magic is failing. You can't win this fight."

He climbed to his feet, and any trace of openness disappeared. "Not failing. It's as strong as it's ever been, but when I use it, I feel it might kill me. The Darmish didn't destroy my magic, but I believe they broke whatever it is that protects us from the damage it might cause us. Gods damn them. They may not have intended it specifically, but this is their doing." He brushed the dirt from his pants.

"Then what do we do about it?"

"I am recovering. It's nothing for you to concern yourself with."

You're not, I thought, *and it is*. "You need to tell someone else. Someone who can help."

He shook his head. "This is one more thing you must learn. Strength is important, but even before that comes the appearance of strength. You never show weakness or fear, never let your people doubt you. If I go to Nox and the old Potioner figures out what she's up to, she'll tell Laelana and Goff. We'll lose our support." He wheezed again. "I'll get my strength back. You know the power of our healers in Luid."

The noose tightened again. "And if you don't, what then? Even if you manage to take the throne back by law, even if Severn steps down, the first person who challenges you will take the throne."

"And so you must be prepared to take it from me first. You are strong enough to hold it. It's simply a matter of training you in the proper skills."

My chest constricted. "I'm not ready for that. Even if I wanted it."

My father smiled bitterly. "I know you're not. And it's good that you know it, too. I will get through this."

I watched as he leaned against a tree, gathering his strength. "Nox wouldn't tell anyone."

His jaw tightened. "She's inexperienced."

"She's good. She could at least try."

"But would she?" A hint of sadness touched his voice—or perhaps it was only the lingering effects of his collapse.

"Not for your sake. But if it meant removing Severn from power, absolutely. That's why all of us are here. Rowan included."

He leaned against a tree and closed his eyes. "I haven't changed your mind on anything, have I?"

"No. I'll ask Nox to help you find your strength, and do what I can to help you. I will respect your wishes for the time it takes to return you to Luid. But you're wrong about Rowan."

He opened his eyes, and for once he dropped his act. He looked pained, uncertain. "Maybe Rowan is smart. Maybe she's clever. Maybe we even need her. But make no mistake." He coughed again and cleared his throat. "She is a threat. You can't do what's best for Tyrea when a Darmish Sorceress rules your heart, and you can't be king if you don't follow the laws of marriage and succession. Don't fail in this. You're Tyrea's only hope."

I was about to assure him I wouldn't fail him when he added, "Gods help us all."

Words like a knife in the back. I'd almost forgotten how effortlessly he wounded those closest to him.

I turned and left the sick old man in the woods. He'd find his way back. The bastard always did.

"Aren!" he called after me.

I turned back.

"Laelana agrees that the people need to move, even if it means giving up the safety they've found here. She's instructing them now to pack up for the journey to somewhere with more water."

"Toward Luid?"

He nodded. "I've had to make her many promises, but I think we have her support. I need you to make sure we have it from the people your grandfather sent from Belleisle. They trust you more than they do me. Convince them of the fact that our victory is theirs. If Severn's got Tyrea's strongest magic-users inside the city walls, we'll need support outside."

I bowed slightly. Formally. "I'll see what I can do."

He sat down hard on a rock, and I left him. If I spent one more moment with the man, I was going to lose my mind. As I made my way back to camp, I couldn't help thinking about what he'd said before. He was wrong about Rowan being a threat. He was right about her potential, but she didn't want to rule a country any more than I did.

No, but you will if it's the only way to save your people, won't you? whispered a slick, silky voice at the back of my mind. *Who's to say she wouldn't make the same sacrifice, or greater, for hers?*

I shook the thoughts off before my father's carefully-chosen words could sow doubts.

I needed to talk to Nox again. There had to be something she could do.

If there wasn't, an entire nation's problems were about to become mine.

Mama Bunn wasn't especially warm, and didn't go out of her way to make me like her.

Fortunately, I didn't care about that.

The only real teacher I'd ever had was an arrogant horse's arse who thought he was the greatest Potioner in the land because he had memorized the four books on his shelf and had a decent knack for feeling a substance's potential. He knocked me to the floor when I tried to be better at it than him, dismissed my ideas if they didn't line up with what he knew so well from his leatherbound tomes, and expected me to sit and listen like a good student even when I knew he was wrong. It wasn't until I married, moved away, and started working on my own that I discovered what I was truly capable of.

Mama Bunn may have been hard on me, but she respected my gifts. She'd allowed me to assist with preparing potions, and had taken my suggestion of adding a simple mix of pine and griproot extracts to her healing potion to dull her patients' pain. It was an unusual natural reaction and not well-known, one I'd sensed out myself, and she'd seemed pleased.

"It's obvious that you have sharp instincts," she said to me as she sorted through the herbs I'd picked up that morning. There hadn't been many to find, and there was plenty of room for her to spread them out over the work table. "That doesn't mean you have nothing left to learn."

I held back a sigh. "I know that, Mama."

When she narrowed her eyes, they disappeared in folds of wrinkled flesh. "Do you? You seem pretty damn cocky to me."

I continued stringing up stems and hanging them from a high shelf. "I apologize if I've offended you. You have far more experience than I have." I couldn't guess how much more. The woman had seen many years pass, but it was hard to tell exactly how old she was. Potioners didn't experience the life-extending benefits of magic as Sorcerers did, but we had ways of maintaining health and beauty. Either Mama Bunn had rejected these completely, or she'd lived so long that even her potions couldn't keep up.

"Indeed," she said, not sounding like she believed my false humility. "Instincts are important, but so is living. Reading. Learning from the mistakes others have made, and making our own. If you do all of this, you have potential to become one of the great ones. And with your connections, perhaps to change things for us. Get Potioners the respect we deserve from Sorcerers."

I remembered Aren's attitude when we first met, his ideas that a Sorcerer's power was far more important than anything I could do. "That seems an ambitious dream," I observed.

She shrugged. "I'm old and tired. Dreams and my memories are what get me through the day."

Her knife flashed so quickly it became invisible, slashing through tender leaves and tough stems with equal ease.

"Can you teach me how to do that?" I asked.

She smiled, and her eyes disappeared again. "There you go."

She demonstrated more slowly, and I mimicked the angle of her knife on my own subjects. Still, I couldn't match her. She watched for a few minutes before she took a jar off of the shelf. "Try this."

I opened the jar and sniffed at the odorless blue substance inside. "What is it?"

"Dip your knife, rub it in with the cloth. Yes, there you go. Rub harder, don't leave the blade wet. Now try."

The knife slipped through a woody branch as though it were a blade of grass. "Incredible," I whispered. I'd never seen anything like it.

"It took me twenty years to perfect this. You don't want to use these knives on food now, at least not on anything you'll be consuming in the next few days. No good on meat, it'll rot it immediately. But for herbs to store, this is perfect." She watched me work. "Good. I'll teach this formula to you. But you still could use some work on your cutting technique. You just crushed the juice right out of that one."

"Thank you, Mama."

I spoke respectfully. If there was one thing I knew, it was how to hide the way my pride objected to correction. Hiding my irritation had saved me from beatings on more than one occasion.

A knock sounded from the front room. Mama Bunn glared at the door—or rather, at whoever had disturbed us. "Come in!"

Aren stepped inside. "Nox? Might I speak to you?"

Mama Bunn continued to glare. "You again." She turned to me. "Was this the brother, or the other one?"

"My brother. His name is Aren. King Ulric's son?"

She waved a hand in his direction. "Go, then. I've learned not to stand in the way of a Sorcerer's business, or the king's. While you're gone, find me a catalyst that will make oak bark react with gemflower root."

"Oak doesn't react with—"

"Go!"

I dipped my hands in the basin and wiped them clean on my apron, then went to Aren. "We should talk somewhere else."

He appeared relieved. "Thank you, Mama Bunn," he said. She nodded, and we stepped out onto the porch.

We headed to the shade behind a storage building. He looked around, listened, and seemed satisfied that we were alone. "How's your new job going?"

"It's fine." I narrowed my eyes at him and leaned back against the wall. "But you didn't come here to talk to me about that, did you?"

"No." He hesitated. "It's about Ulric."

"I haven't had any brilliant ideas on that. There's nothing here to work with, and believe me when I say I've looked. I foraged for hours this morning, and nothing spoke to me. It's not the right season for anything useful to be blooming."

"I have more information." From the look on his face, I took it that the news wasn't good. "It turns out that his magic isn't weak, as I'd thought. It's strong as it's ever been. He's not using it because it hurts him to do so. Just a few minutes ago he was angry with me, lost his temper. He threw a blast of magic at me, and he started coughing up blood."

I stood up straighter. "He did what to you?"

Aren waved the question off. "My point is, he's suffering ill-effects from magic he's been able to control most of his life. Physical and mental effects. And I'm quite concerned."

I chewed my thumbnail as I thought it through. "You've said something about learning new magic, how it can hurt people. That's why Rowan's been so reluctant to test her abilities here, isn't it?"

He looked away. "That may be a small part of it. I think whatever she's dealing with is different, though."

"Is he experiencing those effects, though?"

Aren frowned. "He could be, I suppose. I've never heard of it happening to someone as experienced as he is, or of it being entirely confined to a person's body..." He seemed lost deep in his memories. I didn't interrupt. "It happened to people who tried to break bindings placed on their magic. The mer elders said that when Rowan wanted to try to free herself."

"But he's not bound."

"No. But he almost was."

I nodded. "We need to know what the walls in that cell were made of, and what the guards in that city were using to suppress his magic."

"Rowan said they were the same substance, or at least closely related."

"I said what?" Rowan appeared from around the corner of a building, carrying a squirming baby of maybe ten months. She stepped into the shadows and glanced nervously over her shoulder.

I couldn't read Aren's expression when he saw her, but hers was clear enough when she turned back. Glad to see him, and at the same time afraid. She didn't try to touch him, and stood at a distance. Aren motioned for us to follow him back into the woods behind Mama Bunn's cabin. Rowan's eyes didn't leave him as we walked.

Gods, but she had to be lonely. I had Mama Bunn to keep my mind occupied during the day, and Kel and Cassia to talk and laugh with in the evening. Aren might not have enjoyed his time with our father, but at least he had an interesting problem to work on and people around. She had no one—ignored by the villagers, forced to be apart from Aren. I'd seen her talking to Cassia, but even she and Kel were busy with their assignment. She got to be with Griselda, but only while training.

An outcast in the middle of a teeming community.

I know that feeling, I thought, and felt a little warmer toward her. *Maybe being pretty and powerful doesn't get you everything.*

She held the baby out to Aren. "You want this? He's getting heavy."

He stepped back and grimaced. "No, thanks. Who does that belong to?"

She moved the baby to her other arm and tucked a stray lock of bright red hair behind her ear. "I have no idea. It's kind of a family free-for-all around here. Somebody asked me to watch him. I'm being helpful, as instructed." She rolled her eyes, and Aren smiled. "What are you talking about?"

The baby grabbed at her hair. Rowan grimaced and leaned her head away.

"It's nothing," Aren told her, and shot me a quick glance, warning me not to say anything.

The baby let out a crowing sound, and Rowan winced. "That takes me back. You sound like my niece. Gods help your poor mother."

I caught Rowan's eye. "Do you know what they were giving you at the prison to control your magic?" Aren clearly didn't want her to know about Ulric's condition, but we needed this information.

She frowned slightly. "Only that whatever they stuck us with inhibited our magic temporarily. If we weren't in the cell, or if we didn't have those shackles on, our magic overcame it. And they said they were working on something that would take care of the magic completely. Kind of like a binding, but I think it removed magic rather than suppressing it."

"Thank you," I said, and her pinched expression softened.

She shifted the baby to the other side. "Aren, didn't those Dragonfreed fellows give you something to put a temporary damper on your magic? Might have been similar, if Nox is interested in that sort of thing."

A guarded look came over him, and left just as quickly. "They did. I don't know what was in that, either. Phelun mentioned dragon egg, but that was in the one he used to shield himself from me, not the one that kept my magic quiet. What?"

He'd caught the widening of my eyes. "You didn't think of mentioning that to me when we talked about blocking you?" I asked.

His shoulders tensed. "You have a ready supply of dragon egg?"

"Still might have been useful information."

"You're right," he said, and relaxed. "The truth is, I don't care to think about what happened there, and offering that information didn't cross my mind. Does it help you?"

I sucked air through my teeth. "Not without a dragon egg."

Aren threw his hands up in a *why do I bother* gesture, and Rowan looked at me and smiled. I couldn't help thinking this was what family should feel like.

The idea made sense. Dragon eggs were notoriously hard to find in the wild, in part because it was impossible to use magic to locate them. They protected themselves. Perhaps they could protect a person's mind.

The baby squealed, and the most horrible odor filled the air.

Rowan grimaced. "I think it's time to figure out who this belongs to. Lovely to see you both. We'll have to do this again some time." She held the baby out at arm's length as she hurried away, though it had to weigh twenty pounds. I smiled at her awkwardness. At least we had one thing in common. Babies were fine, but I'd never had any desire to bring a child into the world—especially not when my world had been confined to a cruel husband and a cold, unforgiving landscape.

Aren watched them go, looking like he wanted nothing more than to chase after her. He sighed and turned away.

"What was that about?" I asked.

He rubbed the back of his neck. "The less she knows, the safer she is at this point," he said. "I hate to keep secrets, but if Ulric knew that she knew he was weak..." He shook his head. "I don't know what to do about any of this, but I know she's the last person he wants involved, and for now I'll respect that." Something strange came into his voice then, something regretful and cold.

"I wish I could do more to help."

"You're going to have to talk to him," he said as we walked back toward the village. "You'll be the one to figure out what's wrong and what to do about it, not me."

"I can't talk to him. I can barely say three words to the man without losing my temper." Besides that, I had no desire to. Never had. I'd only joined in on Aren's mission because it seemed the fastest way to get Severn off the throne.

"Someone has to," he said. "He's angry with me. I think I've thrown away any chance of him telling me everything."

"Maybe Mama Bunn will help. If she's there to back me up, give another opinion, maybe he won't look down on me like—"

He held up a hand to stop me. "Nox, no. No one can know about this except us. No one can doubt his power, or his ability to see this through. Not even the old woman. Not Griselda Beaumage, who I'd have thought he might listen to under other circumstances. It's all over if anyone finds out. Severn wins."

Hatred pushed up in me at the mention of his name, and I shoved it back down. Ulric had sent me and my mother away, condemned us to a life of hardship, but it had been Severn who forced him to do it. He'd been making life miserable for people in my province and elsewhere since he took the throne, and had sent soldiers to abduct me so he could use my gifts.

This is my role, I realized. *I fix the king, he takes the throne back, I find something other than revenge to live for.* Not an unappealing thought at all, especially if Kel decided to stick around. Less glorious than what I'd imagined, but I could do it.

"Fine," I said. "Tell him I want to speak to him in his tent tonight. I need you there, though."

"Of course. Thank you."

He left me then. I turned toward Mama Bunn's cabin, but remembered my assignment. It was probably impossible, something to teach me humility. Or it was a basic skill that I'd never had reason to learn.

Oak's not reactive, or magical, so...

I caught sight of Cassia hurrying across the village, and followed. I would have left her alone, if not for the fact that she was carrying her pack and bedroll. "Cass!" I called. "Wait!"

She stopped and smiled, though it looked forced. "Nox, I was looking for you."

"What's going on?"

"I wanted to say goodbye."

My heart skipped. "What? Why? Where are you going?"

"I can't take it anymore," she said, keeping her voice low. "I'm glad to have been with you for this long, to have met you and helped everyone, but I need to go home. It's so damned dry here. I may go insane if I have to stay in this body much longer." She scratched at her arm and glared at the rough cloth of her shirt-sleeve. "I need to swim, to feel water on my skin. And we haven't had contact with our people in far too long. I'm going to tell them what's happening, ask for help. I spoke to Ulric about it yesterday, and he wouldn't say no to help if I can convince the elders it's in our best interest to keep an eye on things near Luid."

My mouth went dry. "Is..." I cleared my throat. "Does Kel feel the same way about being here?"

She smiled sadly. "He does, and he doesn't. He's not coming with me."

"Oh." My relief at having Kel stay was severely tempered by my concern when I imagined my friend crossing the wilds of Tyrea alone. "You'll be all right?"

"Yes. With the route I have planned, I'll be home soon enough if I go by way of the caves. I can take care of myself. No need to worry."

"I'll miss you." My voice cracked, and I cleared my throat. "A lot."

Don't be a sentimental idiot.

Cassia held my gaze and lowered her chin. "I know it's not easy for you to say that."

"Well, I thought you should know. We didn't get off to the best start, but I don't think I'd have been able to go on this long without strangling Aren if not for you."

She'd hated me at first, and I hadn't been too keen on her, either. She either lacked Kel's perception of some scrap of good-ness in me, or hadn't placed much value on it. In fact, I considered her early opinion of me far more accurate than Kel's, much as I was grateful for his belief in me. But over time I'd discovered that I admired Cassia, and she'd decided I was worth being friends with.

When did that become a possibility? It hadn't been so long ago that I'd been criticizing Aren for being as changeable as the weather. *And now look at me.*

"It's been interesting," she agreed. "You still have Kel here if you need to talk about your brother, though."

"Does he know you're leaving?"

"Kel? Of course. He helped me pack." She smiled gently. "Tried to talk me out of it, of course."

"No," I said quietly. "Aren."

She looked away. "I can't say goodbye to him. Never could." She shifted the weight of her pack on her shoulders. "It's complicated."

I stepped forward and pulled her into a hug. She put her arms around me and squeezed back, and it seemed neither of us wanted to be the first to let go.

"Thanks," she whispered. "I'll miss you, too. Take good care of my foolish brother. He's important to me."

"I will."

"And yourself, too." She pulled back and winked. "I want you to be around to see the mess you're going to cause when Kel tells Mariana and Arnav how he feels about you."

"I'll do my best." Something she'd said before came back to me. "Cassia, back when we first got to this camp, when you mentioned heading home and talking to the elders, you said something about me and Kel. Something like, 'if this is going where I think it is.' What did that mean?"

"Aah. That." She set her pack down and rolled her shoulders. "Kel hasn't mentioned soul-bonds to you, has he?"

"In passing." I tried to remember what he'd told me. "Your elders have that, right? When two merfolk are so much in love that it's like they become one soul, but without losing themselves?"

"You've been paying attention."

I wrinkled my nose. "He mentioned it right after telling me about your thoughts on magic, and death, and other lovely things. I was ready to hear something nice—Oh!" She nodded, and I realized what she was saying. "That can happen with a human?"

"No. But Kel has become incredibly attached to you, and I can see it being something similar. We don't love as easily as you do, but when we do, it's deeper. It's irrevocable, lasts until death and even beyond. It's not fickle like human love. I want you to know what you're getting into before things go too far."

"You mean..." My stomach fluttered.

She smiled. "You're not going to have me around to make things awkward. If you give yourselves to each other completely, body and soul, if you make a conscious decision to love him, that might be it. Is that what you want?"

My mouth went dry. If I weren't so worried about my heart being broken again, or breaking his if I had to leave... if I could truly let go and give myself completely...

Cassia smiled. "It's a lot to think about, I know. I shouldn't have said anything. He may not even be considering that." One eyebrow arched as she watched for my reaction.

I suspected this was what he'd been about to mention before

Mama Bunn interrupted us in her cabin. He hadn't tried to bring it up again, though.

I didn't know whether to be excited or terrified.

"Should I talk to him about it?"

She snorted. "Not if you think he's got a drop of mer blood in him. I could be reading this all wrong. My dear, wonderful, horribly irritating brother has been rather closed off to me lately. The very mention of eternal devotion would send most mers running for the deepest convenient body of water."

Unexpected relief flooded me, and I let out a long breath. "Thanks, Cassia."

"Anything for my loved ones. I'll miss you both. All of you." She picked up her pack, slung it over her shoulders, and walked away. "Until we see each other again," she called back.

I raised my hand to wave, but she had her eyes forward, leaving us all behind.

"Gods keep you," I whispered.

12

ROWAN

That afternoon I learned that while I thought I'd been an outsider before, nothing turns a person so invisible as the act of wandering around, searching for someone to take a smelly baby. Still, I managed to root out the child's mother when we passed her at the stable and he started screaming for her.

No sooner had I relieved myself of that duty than another came. Patience dashed up to me, breathless. "I wondered where you'd gone," she said. "Was I too hard on you before?"

I laughed. "Not even close." Our archery practice had gone well. She was far better than I was at first, but I soon recovered the skills I hadn't practiced in some time. I supposed I should be happy with that, but my lack of further development frustrated me. Magic was supposed to help a person learn things and pick up new skills more easily. That may have been true for many, but it didn't seem to be helping me much.

Patience narrowed her eye at me and nodded. "Good. Because I'm not going easier on you next time."

"But not now, right?" My arms still ached.

"No. Now we pack."

"Sorry?"

She gestured around, and I noticed that the people in the

stable weren't merely cleaning. As we watched, they loaded items into a wooden cart—a pitchfork, a shovel, a few bales of hay that I suspected had been lifted from unwary travelers.

As we left the stable, I nearly ran face-first into Goff.

He glared down at me. "Help at the infirmary," he ordered, and walked away.

"Please and thanks," I added under my breath, and Patience smirked.

"He's always like that," she said as we arrived at our destination. "Probably just passing on orders from Laelana. She'll be with those Sorcerers somewhere, making bigger plans."

A burly fellow with a scraggly black beard handed me a box. Patience climbed into a waiting cart, took the box from me, and set it down.

"You don't see them together much, do you?" I asked.

She shoved several crates aside to make more room, then stood with her hands on her skinny hips, considering. "I think their marriage is more about convenience than anything. He was a community leader before, but she's got the brains."

I laughed. She sounded far too grown-up. "How did you ever get to be so observant? At your age I wouldn't have noticed."

"Different lives I guess. My mama taught us to notice things. She made it a game. We watched people, tried to guess what they'd do next, tried to say why they did the things they did. We had no way of knowing whether we were right most of the time, but it was a good thing to learn. And I can see those things as well with one eye as I could with two."

We continued loading. "How old are you, Patience?"

She paused. "Ten? Eleven? Nine? I don't know. We don't keep track, and our people let children stay young for as long as possible. But you grow up whether you put a number to it or not, right?"

"True." I tried to imagine what that was like, and decided it would be wonderful. No raised eyebrows and, *You're nineteen and not married yet?* Education wouldn't be tied to one's age. If a precocious child wanted to push herself to learn adult things, perhaps no one would stop her. And if one fell behind, no one would judge.

Ideally, of course, I added to myself. *No society is perfect, and surely some folks keep track in their minds. But still—*

I looked up to see Patience grinning down at me from the cart. "You see an idea running past and chase it like a dog after a rabbit. That's my observation on you."

I laughed. "I won't deny it."

"We'd be a good team." She looked around. "Goff's gone. You want to go do something more interesting?"

Before I could reply, Patience's attention snapped away from me. Her gaze fixed on a spot across the camp, and she shielded her eye against the sun to get a better look. "The scouts are back. Come on."

I had a hard time keeping up with her as she dodged between people, her tiny body passing through tight spaces while I was forced to "excuse me, pardon me" through the busy crowd. By the time I caught up, she had already made her way close to a group of riders who dismounted and handed their horses off to a villager.

"Goff! Laelana!" bellowed their leader, a broad-shouldered fellow with light brown hair shorter than I had become accustomed to in Tyrea. He seemed familiar, though I was sure we had never met. "News from the border!"

Laelana emerged from her cabin, and Goff jogged over from the direction of the kitchen. "Spit it out, man," Goff ordered.

"Refugees from Darmid," the man said, and took a long swig from his water skin. "Crossed the border a week ago, give or take."

Laelana frowned. "Why?"

The scout wiped his mouth on his sleeve. "I couldn't get a straight story, but you know how they are over there. Seems the magic hunters are coming down hard on people. Most of 'em seemed confused. People were being accused who had never showed any signs of magic. Some said people were being executed without trial, but I doubt any king's foolish enough to allow that. I mean, theirs is clearly not all there." The man knocked on his skull with a fist. "But that'd be suicide."

I pressed my palms against my thighs to keep my hands from trembling. They'd been hunting magic for generations, but I couldn't help thinking that this new pressure was my fault. I'd escaped. I'd killed the king's top hunter, and several others were dead because of my rescuers. We'd stolen the king's prized captive. And now other people were suffering for it.

Laelana didn't seem impressed with the story. "I hoped you'd have something useful for me, Hank. What am I supposed to do with this?"

"Dunno. You said to bring news. I didn't hear anything else that we hadn't heard before." He turned in a full circle, watching the people returning to their work. "What's happening?"

"We're leaving. You almost missed us."

Hank scratched at his sun-reddened face. "I thought you wanted allies. These Darmish people have none here. They have nowhere to go except the town they're in now. If you took them in, I'm sure they'd be grateful. They're hungry, a few of 'em hurt. Some might actually have magic."

"And no skill in it," she added. "They're useless to us. They won't fight. It's just more mouths to feed, and right now, we can't afford that."

True enough, given the way things were going in the camp, but the way she said it made me want to slap her. *Those are my people, not empty, needy stomachs.*

Hank rested his fists on his hips and watched her leave.

I stepped closer. "Excuse me?"

Hank turned. "You're new."

"New here, yes. Could you tell me where those people were?"

He crossed his arms. "That accent. You're Darmish?"

"I was. I'm not quite sure what I am now. My family might have been in trouble with the hunters, and with the king. It's possible that they're there. You didn't hear where those people were from, did you?"

Now that I was closer to him, I realized why he seemed familiar. He reminded me strongly of Callum Langley. This man was more worn out, with a few streaks of gray speckling his hair. Still, the similarity was uncanny enough that I couldn't help feeling like a mouse before a barn cat when he looked down at me.

Surely you're not thinking of going back there, to those people and that danger, I thought.

No. Not that far. But perhaps to a Tyrean border town....

"Can't say I paid close attention," he said. "They might've mentioned a few towns, I think. Um... Ramsull?"

"Ramsdale," I whispered. Just an hour's journey from my hometown of Lowdell.

"Sure," he said. "Lowdown, maybe."

My heart jumped to my throat. *This doesn't mean your family's there.* "Where are they?"

"I can tell you they were in Durgin's Post when we were there about three days ago."

"So three days' journey west?"

"About that. We didn't take a direct route back."

"Thank you."

Hank nodded and stalked away. With him out of the way, I saw Aren standing not far off. My stomach twisted as I waited to see whether he'd come to me, or move on to keep his father happy. He moved as though to leave, but he must have caught something in my expression. He approached with a concerned look.

"What was that about?" he asked.

"Darmish refugees in Tyrea. Some from my hometown, maybe."

"Must be bad for them to come here." He spoke without apparent concern or emotion, and seemed to be feeling out my reaction to the news.

"That's what I'm thinking." I stepped into the dimly lit space between two buildings and sat on the ground. Aren crouched next to me with his back against the wall, and Patience stood in front of us. "I can't decide whether I should be worried that my family is there and among the injured and hungry, or that they aren't." I swallowed back the lump in my throat. At least I wasn't crying.

Aren took one of my hands in his and squeezed. Though I couldn't be grateful for the circumstances, I couldn't help relishing the feel of his skin on mine.

Get a hold of yourself. It's only been a few days.

"They'll be fine," he said. "Even if they're not out yet, there's obviously a way through. They'll make it to safety." But he didn't sound certain.

"You could find out," Patience said. Aren gave her a look that said she shouldn't say any more, but she didn't seem intimidated. "It's only a few days, right? You could catch up with us later."

"A dangerous few days," Aren said. He released my hand and rested his forehead in his hands. "I won't stop you if you want to go look, but I don't know what good can come of it. Either they're there and safe now, or they're not. And what then? Are you going to go back into that gods-forsaken country again to look for them?"

The hard edge to his voice surprised me. "Are you still mad at me for last time?"

Patience backed away. "I think I should let you guys talk alone." She turned and hurried off.

"Rowan, I could have lost you last time you went back there," he said. "Do you have any idea how frightened I was when I found out they had you? Or how much I hate feeling that way?" He sank the rest of the way to the ground. "I need you. And if you go back again... I can't stand the idea of something happening and me never knowing what became of you. You can't expect your luck to hold out if you go back a second time. And if I'm going toward Luid with my father, that's only taking me farther from you."

"What about what you said before, about not letting go of what makes me who I am? I can't help worrying about them. They're in danger."

"That's not your fault."

"Isn't it?"

We didn't say anything for a few minutes.

"The fact is," he said slowly, "that there could be benefit in you finding your family. If your aunt were with them, if she were willing to help us, it would be a great help to Nox in her work."

"Not to mention feeding people," I added. "What's Nox working on that's so important?"

He shook his head, and my chest tightened as I felt the invisible chasm between us widening. There were secrets now, when we'd promised there wouldn't be. Our separation was supposed to be a show for Ulric's benefit, but the distance was becoming real.

"It's nothing you need to worry about," he said. "Just something for my father. But the fact is, you can't go alone. At least, I'd prefer that you didn't, and I can't come with you."

I almost mentioned Florizel then, but remembered the threat in Ulric's voice. I'd told Aren about the conversation, but wasn't sure I could stomach revealing that I'd held that information back for fear of Ulric finding out we'd spoken.

It seemed the king had us both keeping secrets.

"What if we both went after everything else is settled?" he asked. "We could go to Luid, see my father back where he belongs, and then find your family."

My stomach clenched. "How long will that take?"

"I don't know. But I don't know what else we can do. It kills me to say it, but I can't do this without you. If you disappear again, I—" He smiled sadly, and there was something else in his expression I couldn't read.

"What's wrong?"

"Nothing. I think I'd forgotten how hard my father could be to deal with, that's all. Even if we're not supposed to be talking, it helps to have you around. I still think you have a part to play in all of this, even if my father disagrees."

"What aren't you telling me?"

There was pain in his eyes then, deep as I'd ever seen it. "We'll talk about it later, I promise."

Voices drifted toward us, and my blood froze as I recognized one of them as Ulric's.

"You should go," I said. "It won't be good for either of us if he catches you with me."

He frowned. "It won't always be like this," he said gently, and reached out to touch my cheek. I leaned into it, even as the doubt in his eyes made me want to pull back. "We'll get away. I swear he won't control us forever."

"Sure we will," I said, and made myself smile.

Aren darted out the other end of the alley. I didn't move until his voice and Ulric's reached me. I crept away in the other direction.

I returned to my tent alone, left to chase my thoughts through a rabbit-warren of possibilities, each less pleasant than the one before.

13

AREN

Nox met me as the sunlight faded, and we walked together toward Ulric's tent. He had begged off afternoon work and supper, saying he had things to do before we left for Luid, and I couldn't say I'd missed his presence. His near-intrusion on my conversation with Rowan had been one more grain of salt in freshly re-opened wounds. I had no desire to speak to him, but we had no choice.

Though we'd all tried to help the community prepare to leave their dying village, Nox and I got a few guarded, nasty looks as we passed. In spite of their low food stores and dwindling water supply, the people obviously blamed us for the uprooting.

"I hope he had a lovely and restful afternoon," Nox muttered.

"I hope so, too. Maybe he'll be in a better mood than he was earlier."

She stopped me. "What was he so angry about that he had a temper tantrum and tried to murder you?"

"If he'd wanted to kill me, I'd be dead. It was nothing important." And nothing I cared to talk about. He was wrong about Rowan being a threat, I knew that. But she still carried her family in her heart. They were a distraction now that they might be in Tyrea, and could indeed be an obstacle later. And as for the marriage issue, and my father apparently wishing to shape me in his own image... *No, nothing important at all.*

Nox frowned. "Why tell me, right?"

"It has nothing to do with Ulric's situation."

We passed Rowan's tent and then mine, and came to a sheltered spot where Laelana had made space for Ulric in a private tent. He met us at the entrance.

"I heard you coming," he said.

"It wasn't a secret," Nox answered, an edge to her voice.

"Is that how you speak to a king?"

She set her jaw and didn't answer him.

He stepped aside to let us in. The interior of the tent was simple and far from luxurious, but better than what the rest of us had, and probably more comfortable than most of the homes in the community. His bed had a properly stuffed mattress resting on a simple wooden frame, a thick quilt, and a thin pillow. An oil lamp burned on a desk made from crates, and he had papers spread across it. Someone had found him ink and a quill.

He actually had been working.

"What is it?" he asked, and sat on a folding stool next to the desk. Nox and I remained standing, and he didn't indicate that we should do otherwise.

Nox motioned for me to speak first.

"The same issue we spoke of earlier. We're concerned about your health and your magic."

He leaned forward so that his elbows rested on his knees, looking sharp as a hungry wolf. "Is that so? Well, I appreciate your concern, but I feel fine now."

"You weren't fine in the woods earlier. Sir. And with due respect, it would be to everyone's benefit if we spoke openly and made our plans based on the reality of your situation rather than what you want everyone to believe."

Ulric leaned back on his seat and crossed his left ankle over the other leg. "Is anyone nearby to listen?"

I reached out with my magic, and sensed no one. "No."

He cleared his throat and looked to Nox. "Unusual things

have been happening. Aren thinks you might have ideas on how to improve my condition."

"If you tell me exactly what you're experiencing, I may. I've come up with potions that sped healing before, and that bolstered physical strength. It might be possible for magic." She didn't make eye contact with him, but sounded confident enough.

He gave her a condescending look. "I know you have a gift for this. Your mother's mother was a great Potioner. You've inherited that, and Aren has told me how helpful your skills were when you traveled to Darmid. But this is different. I'm not sure it's something anyone has encountered before, and you lack the range of experience we'll need."

Now her gaze flicked up to meet his as her shoulders tensed with irritation that radiated from her in waves. "You're broken. All I have to do is protect you from your magic if it's hurting you. It's a form of healing, and that's what I do best."

The tent was silent while he thought it through. It seemed odd to me that he should resist this when there could be no harm in trying.

"All right," he said at last. "How do we begin?"

She relaxed slightly. "I have questions. You'll have to be honest with me, even if you don't want to."

He nodded. "Aren, a little privacy."

I slipped out of the tent without any objection to the order. He would hold back if he thought I was listening. I'd step in if I had to, but time alone would be good for them. If I had to deal with the old man on my own, so did she.

Kel stepped out of the shadows. "Nox in there?"

"She is securing the future of the Tyrean monarchy as we speak," I said dryly, hoping it was true.

"Hmm. I thought you were that future."

I shot him a dark glare. "Don't talk about it, please."

He just grinned, white teeth flashing in the gloom. "Might as well face facts, my friend. Maybe there was a time when you thought you'd got out from under all that, but not now. You're back in, and it's your own fault."

I stepped farther away from the tent so our conversation wouldn't disturb Nox's work. "I know. Though I still don't know what else I could have done, save for abandoning the country to Severn."

"That's why you're going to be a good king," he said, more serious now. "You don't want this because it's your right, or because you crave power. This is actually a selfless act on your part. Mostly."

"Who'd have thought we'd see the day?"

Kel frowned at my facetious tone. "Admittedly, you went through a bad time there. You didn't help Severn because it was the best thing for Tyrea. You did it to cover your own ass, to make a good place for yourself, to... whatever. You didn't care who you hurt, as long as you were safe."

I winced. "True, and a lovely summary of my character. Thank you."

"But now." He paused. "Actually, you're still seven measures of asshole in a five-measure pot, but you're getting there. And at least you're doing things for better reasons now."

I sighed. "Thanks. But I still don't want this. Or rather, what comes after our victory." I tried to sound certain of that part, at least.

"Why?"

I walked in a small circle as I tried to sort my thoughts out. "I like my freedom. Not that it's ever perfect or complete, but I've had a taste of it now. And there are other issues." I motioned for him to come closer. "Problems concerning a king's duties. Lineage. Marriage. And that not involving Sorceresses."

Kel raised his eyebrows. "Right. I'd forgotten about that."

"Any brilliant suggestions?"

"Sorry. I don't know anything about this mess. I'm just figuring out the whole love part, never mind the complications you people add on to it."

The mumblings from the tent grew louder, both voices fighting to be heard. "Sit down!" Nox demanded. Silence followed.

Kel sighed. "I do like that woman."

"I'd noticed. Speaking of futures..."

His brow furrowed as he sat on a rickety wooden bench, abandoned in the rush to get things packed. "We'll figure it out. All I know right now is that I have to be with her. It's not rational. We make no sense. We're from different worlds. I'm miserable here, away from water and my people. Nox is the only thing that's keeping me going, but she can't join me at home."

I sat beside him. "There's the Grotto."

"She'd be lonely there. I know she acts standoffish, but she really enjoys helping people once she lets herself feel something for them. She needs human contact as much as anyone, and I can't be everything for her. And I can't say the elders would approve of our relationship." He leaned his shoulder against mine, as though I might carry some of the weight for him. "Why did I want this, again?"

I snorted. "Damned if I can tell you that. You're a fool."

"If I am, you are too."

A lone cricket chirped in the bushes, and from inside the tent came the continued mumblings of muted conversation. One by one the stars appeared in the darkening sky. In the morning there would be chaos as everyone finished packing and moved out. It wouldn't be an easy journey, but I'd flown out and scouted a route earlier that day that would get the group to roads leading east. They'd be close to Luid in just a few weeks, if they kept moving at a steady pace.

Peaceful as the night looked, hopeful as the outcome of all of this seemed, it was an illusion. Nothing was certain, least of all victory.

"Where's Cass?" I asked.

Kel sat up straight. "She didn't...? No. Of course she didn't."

"What?"

"She's gone. She went home."

"What?" I repeated. A sense of betrayal stabbed at me. "Why didn't she tell me? Are things so bad here?"

"She needed to get home, back to the water. She doesn't have a Nox to keep her happy here, you know? Not that she wants one. She's mer through and through." The corners of his lips twisted downward. "She's been going through a dry spell in more ways than one. She'll be better off at home. And she's going to ask for help, so that's something."

"But still." I hoped it was too dark to see the wounded expression I surely wore.

"I know. She should've said goodbye to you. It was hard for her to go, though."

Cassia and I had been friends for years, more than friends for a summer, absent from each other's lives for seven years following that, and had picked up our friendship again just a few months before, when she and Kel helped me and Rowan escape from our enemies. Such a small portion of my life, and yet the loss pained me.

Kel watched me as well as he could in the darkness. "It's hard, right? Attachment?"

"I'd forgotten what it's like to have friends." I shot him a good-natured scowl. "You're more trouble than you're worth."

"Aren't we, though? But she'll be fine. You'll see her again."

There didn't seem to be anything else to say about that, and we returned to silently watching the stars come out. Under their ageless and impassive eyes time seemed to collapse, bringing the past into sharp focus.

"Kel?"

"Yeah?"

"Thank you. If I haven't said it before, or even if I have, thank you. For everything." I allowed long-buried memories to wash over me, and with them an understanding of how the merfolk had changed my life. "Remember when we met?"

"How could I forget? It's not every day you come across a human child lost in the caves, about to be devoured by an earthwyrm."

"Gods, that thing could have swallowed either of us whole. I never asked why you saved me. You didn't know me. Shouldn't have cared."

He shrugged one shoulder. "Some of us can't help being heroes, I guess."

I snorted. "That's you all over, isn't it? Thank you for that, and for not renouncing our friendship when you found out about my magic. For introducing me to your people. For helping me and Rowan when you had no reason to so much as speak to me. For joining me to help find my father. I couldn't have done that without you and Cass."

"And Nox," he added.

"Her, too. But she never would have stayed with me if not for you."

"True. And you're welcome."

"I wish I could repay you somehow."

He chuckled quietly. "You seem to think you're the only one who's benefited from this friendship. You taught me about humans. I blame you, in part, for my stupid desire to find out about the kind of love you people experience, even if you never wanted it. I've seen more of the world than I would have without knowing you."

"I suppose."

"You don't see everything there is to mer culture. It's good, and in many ways we have a lot of freedom, but it can be closed-off and restrictive. You got me out of that, at least a little, and I appreciate it. Even if you are still twenty pounds of asshole—"

I smiled in spite of myself. "Yeah, I get it."

The tent flap opened, flooding the ground with lamplight as Nox peered out into the night.

"Aren? Oh, Kel." She smiled. "I was looking for you earlier."

Kel ducked as a night fairy buzzed over his head. "I was making nice with the people, but now my time is yours, fair lady."

She grinned slyly. "Just your time?"

He tried not to smile, but couldn't help it. Kel was never good at hiding his feelings. "Anything you desire."

She smiled mysteriously and disappeared back into the tent. I followed, and found Ulric seated on his bed, scowling.

"She wouldn't tell me anything until you came back in," he said.

"Didn't make much sense to say it twice," she retorted.

At least they'd warmed to each other in my absence.

"Aren, I think you were right," she said. "Being in that cell for so long, being exposed to whatever potions they were using or testing on him, has somehow changed his magic. It's not broken exactly, but they weakened him. From what he's told me, I agree that his defenses against the harm magic naturally causes are damaged."

Ulric said nothing, but nodded.

"We should ask Griselda Beaumage," I said.

The king shook his head. "No one outside of this small circle can know."

"She's been studying magic her entire life, traveled all over the world to do it. If anyone would know, it would be her."

"Absolutely not. We can't trust her not to report back to Albion. That flying cat she has with her is trained to carry messages between her and the island."

"And so what?" I asked. "He won't take advantage of your weakness, even if you would of his."

"You're so sure of that, aren't you?" Ulric scowled and turned away, effectively ending the conversation.

There had been a time when I hadn't known that there were people like my grandfather, that a Sorcerer could be powerful and kind, could gain respect without hurting people. I had seen it, though, and with each closed-minded statement from my father, my need to escape grew.

I crammed the increasing pressure deep inside, as I always had.

"So what can you do?" I asked Nox.

"Experiment."

Ulric rolled his eyes. "When I get back to Luid, I have Potioners and doctors there. Experienced ones."

Nox rubbed the back of her neck. "But as you said, they're in Luid. You're stuck with me for now, unless you want me to talk it over with Mama Bunn. And it's not like I have no experience." The volume and emotion in her voice increased with every word. She stopped for a moment before she spoke again, more quietly if not less passionately. "This isn't going to be me throwing random ingredients in a pot and hoping I don't blow anything up. I know what I'm doing. I'll work this out."

Ulric looked up at her. "Very well. And I thank you, Nox."

She chewed on her lower lip. "It's a bad time of year for this. Most of what I'll need isn't blooming, or is underdeveloped." She nodded to herself. "But I will make this work."

She didn't sound entirely certain, but the barest hint of a smile creased the corner of Ulric's eyes. Nox didn't seem to notice, but I did. He'd wanted her help from the start, but knew she wouldn't do it if he demanded it. She needed to be opposed to him, to prove herself, to show him he was wrong.

I couldn't help admiring his manipulative skills, much as I resented it when he tried to use them on me. I still had much to learn.

"Aren, is everything under control with your situation?" he asked.

"Everything is fine."

"I've been thinking about the refugees," Ulric said.

I narrowed my eyes. I had no idea where he might go with this. We hadn't spoken much about them earlier, save for me passing on the information. "Have you?"

"Perhaps Rowan should go see to them. If there's magical talent there, we might make use of it. They're her people. They might listen to her."

He watched me intently, waiting to see how I'd interpret the idea. Everything was a test. Always had been, and I'd failed many times.

"It could be a dangerous journey," I said, allowing only the barest hint of displeasure into my voice.

He raised his heavy eyebrows. "I thought she wanted to be helpful. This is potentially beneficial to our cause if she succeeds."

"And to you personally if she fails." I couldn't hide the disgust in my voice.

His lips curled. "I won't deny that it would make things easier for me. And for you, Aren. Long-term thinking. There's no way we lose." I didn't need to pry into his thoughts to know where he was going with this. He would use this to test her, to see whether she'd run back to them as soon as she had the chance. He had no desire to have help from untrained Darmish magic-users. He just wanted her gone, and justification for his mistrust.

I allowed my mouth to widen into a smile. "You know, you're right. She should go. After all, it's for the good of Tyrea."

The creases on his brow deepened as his smile faded. "Indeed."

He didn't trust me. *Good.*

"I'll speak to her. Goodnight, Father."

I stepped out of the tent and Nox followed, taking quick steps to keep up with me. Kel fell in beside her.

"Aren, what's going on?" she asked.

"I'm going with her."

"What?" Nox asked. "You can't leave us."

I turned to face her. "You'll be fine. Stay with the group, try to fix Ulric's magic. Rowan and I will catch up. We'll move much more quickly than these people."

She crossed her arms and frowned. "You can't leave me with that horrible man."

I put my hands on my sister's shoulders. "This is for Ulric's benefit, and yours in helping him. If Rowan's aunt is among them, I suspect that she and Rowan will be a great asset in feeding these people, especially if it comes to a siege. Victoria is gifted in botanical magic—think what that will mean for you if we can convince her to join us."

"Botanical magic? Like Laelana's unfortunately deceased grandfather?"

"It's a guess, but based on good information," I said, becoming more excited now that the plan was made. I wouldn't let Ulric sabotage himself and destroy my future. Better to defy him now, help Rowan, and perhaps secure our future and his. And a few days with Rowan might help release the pressure I felt to become my old self, help me focus on our true goals rather than on appeasing my father.

I offered Nox my most convincing smile. "You could have all the ingredients your heart desires by the time the people reach Luid. My reasons aren't entirely selfish, I promise."

"Just mostly selfish. But I guess we won't get far without

something of that kind of help." She sighed. "Fine, go. Leave us. Have fun. Who needs you, anyway?"

I squeezed her arm. "Thanks, Nox."

"Yeah." She stared up at the sky, deep in thought. "Let me give you some potions in case anyone gets hurt. And bring me some dragon eggshell if you come across any. It might not help Ulric, but I'd like to test some things out for myself."

My skin turned cold at the thought. "I'm hoping we won't meet any dragons this time, but I'll keep that in mind."

Worry creased her brow. "Please do. And be careful. Ulric's acting like he can do this without you, but I'll tell you truthfully that he can't. It's not just his body. You're right. He seems to be losing control of his thoughts, becoming overly suspicious and mistrustful. I didn't know him well before, but I heard plenty about him. This isn't the fair and decent ruler Tyrea lost several years ago."

I wondered whether it was prison or his current affliction that had done it, and hoped Nox could help either way.

"If you die out there," she continued, "or decide not to come back, this is over."

"I'll be back. I promise. I wouldn't be going if it wasn't important." Her mentioning the dragon egg made me remember something else. "You should talk to Patience and Jevan about blocking while I'm gone. The Wanderers and his crew both seemed adept at it."

She nodded, but looked uncertain.

Kel frowned and looked toward the east. "I don't like you and Rowan leaving. I have a bad feeling about this."

I shivered. "Me, too. But what choice do we have?"

14

AREN

"Rowan, wake up."

Her eyes snapped open, barely visible in the thin light of a lamp that had been left burning outside. "What?"

"We need to go."

"It's morning?" She sat up and rubbed her eyes, then looked at me again as though remembering I wasn't supposed to be there. "What's going on?"

I sat next to her. "If you still want to, we're going back toward the border to look for your family."

That woke her up. "You... we're... what?"

Seeing her expression brighten made me even more certain that this was the right thing to do. "Just you and me, while everyone else is traveling toward Luid. We'll find the people who crossed the border, see if your family is there, or if there's anyone else who will help us."

She slipped silently from the bed and pulled on her pants, sweater, and jacket, then wrapped a long, knit scarf around her neck. She stuffed a few more items of clothing that she'd picked up from the supply tent into her pack and turned to help me roll up the bedding. Her over-cloak went into the already bulging pack next, and a broken comb. She paused.

"Your father didn't give you permission to leave, did he?" She asked warily. "He needs you here."

"Not as much as we need someone like your aunt to help feed these people, or as much as we need to hope that she's among those who crossed the border." It was a long shot, and we both knew it, but it was a chance we needed to take.

Rowan's movements slowed. "I hesitate to mention this," she said, "because all I want is to go with you to get my family. But even if we find Victoria, she hasn't been herself for years. You saw her that night in the garden."

"I did, I just don't have any better ideas. There's a chance she can recover. Perhaps the magic of Tyrea will help."

She smiled. "You don't have to convince me. Let's go."

I tied her bedding to the bottom of her pack. "We'll talk more while we travel, okay? If I recall correctly, you're good at that."

She gave me a wry smile. "You recall correctly. I will have all of your secrets, Mister Tiernal."

"All of my everything, fair lady, in time. We should go before someone sees us, though."

The camp was asleep as we crept through the darkness, our path lit only by the stars and a full moon. "Isn't anyone keeping watch?" Rowan whispered.

"Yes. But it won't be a problem."

I appreciated the fact that she didn't ask the obvious question. The last time we'd spoken about my talents, I'd said I would continue to manipulate people's minds if I had to, but I would be more careful than I'd been in the past, use my skills judiciously and with minimal harm to innocent people. I still wasn't sure exactly how that would work, though. Would it be acceptable to make a person forget he'd seen us? There was a time I'd have done it without a second thought.

I sent my awareness out into the night, trying to sense human presences coming closer.

I wrapped a hand around Rowan's wrist and guided her gently into the shadows. A young woman in black clothes passed us a few moments later, completely unaware of our presence. It wouldn't always be that easy to avoid trouble, but I'd take it while it lasted.

We left the village behind us, and Rowan glanced over her shoulder.

"They'll be fine," I said.

"I thought I heard something."

I concentrated harder. Nothing felt out of place as it had before Jevan stopped us on the road, and I sensed no magic aside from hers. "Probably just an animal, but we'll be careful. That town the scouts mentioned was due west. We should head that way, and go as quickly as we can." I hadn't wanted to take horses from the village, knowing they were all needed for the journey, but was already regretting the decision.

Rowan slowed, then said, "We need to go north first. We'll move a lot faster if we find Florizel and you fly."

I stopped. "You didn't say you'd seen her."

She smiled sadly. "We haven't had much time to talk. It was just before my pleasant little chat with your father, actually. She's found a good place to stay, and gave me directions. Follow me. We'll find it."

She walked close beside me until we reached a steep incline, and then took the lead. Sparse trees dotted the land at the top, and moonlight flooded the ground. Our boots crunched over the dirt and scattered stones. Though we paused frequently to listen, we didn't hear anyone following.

In spite of what we'd said earlier, we walked through the night without conversation. Rowan had changed so much since our first journey together. Then, she'd been afraid of me, and ignorant of everything around us that was so much more of a danger to her than I was. She'd experienced much in recent months that had forced her to change, to grow beyond her sheltered upbringing—and apparently quieted her.

When we reached a deep gorge, we climbed down. "Florizel said to look for a tree. There." In the faint pre-dawn light, the massive pine stood like the silhouette of a twisted giant atop the opposite bank. "Then we head toward the mountains."

She climbed ahead to the top of the chasm, slipping in the dry dirt that cascaded down onto me with each step. I let her get ahead, and then followed. By the time I reached the top, she had set her pack on the ground.

"Getting warm," she commented, and slipped out of her jacket.

"You need a rest?"

She frowned. "Of course not."

She seemed distant, and had since we'd left camp. "What's wrong? You've been so quiet."

"I don't want to bother you with it. Or anyone. But you should know." She sounded frightened, and so much more alone than I'd realized. "It's about my magic. I can't use it like I did after you rescued us."

"That's to be expected," I offered.

"I know." She squeezed her eyes closed. "And maybe that's all it is, me not knowing what normal is supposed to feel like, what my normal abilities should be. It just… it feels like I'm chasing my magic, but I keep missing it. Or something. I don't even know."

I had no idea what she was talking about. Magic was inherent, a part of her as much as it was of me. It was a matter of learning to use it and increase it, not capturing it. But I nodded for her to go on.

"And it's not coming back when I use it. I mean, it is," she added when she saw the horrified expression on my face, "just not immediately. It's taking its time." Concern filled her eyes as they met mine. "It's bad, isn't it?"

"Why didn't you tell me?"

She sighed. "You have so much to worry about right now. Everyone does. I don't want to be a burden. My troubles can wait."

"No," I said quietly. An owl hooted back from the forest. "They can't. Not if you're going to help us bring Severn down."

She grimaced. "Ulric doesn't want my help. I think he'd be happy to know I'm struggling, but I don't want him to see that I'm weak."

I couldn't argue with that. "We'll figure it out," I said. "We can both practice along the way. See what we can learn about your situation, and how we can help each other prepare for whatever is coming. Don't let Ulric's dismissal make you feel less important. We need everyone's help if we're going to get through this."

I tried not to let the depths of my concern come out in my voice. If whatever they did to them in Ardare was hurting Ulric, perhaps Rowan was suffering lasting complications as well. Nox might have more challenges on her hands than we'd realized, and this only made the need to find help more urgent.

"Is it hurting you?" I asked. "Are you feeling ill when you use it?"

"A little," she said, "but that's because every time I do, I remember how I used it to kill. Maybe that's why I'm not feeling it as much. Why it doesn't come back to me. I just don't know."

Not quite the same as Ulric, then. That was a relief, but the apprehension didn't leave me.

She looked like she wanted to say something else, but didn't. Her jaw set in a firm line, and she looked west. "I'll get past it. We should keep going."

"Should we talk about it?"

"I'd rather not."

We adjusted our course toward distant mountains that were beginning to look far too familiar to me.

The silence weighed on me. I wanted to tell her everything, but my father's warnings came back to me. If he knew I'd told her about his illness, that would be the end of any chance I had of gaining his trust. And if just speaking with her caused him to lash out...

No, I decided. *I won't let him do that to me.* I would trust her, at least with the parts she might help with or that might help her. I couldn't afford to shut her out. More than that, I didn't want to. I'd promised to stop keeping secrets from her, and I wouldn't let this be an exception.

"Ulric is being harmed by his magic," I said. She slowed and looked back.

"What do you mean?"

"When he uses it, it harms him physically. Perhaps his mind, too, which I'm hoping explains some of the way he's been treating you."

She stopped walking and stared at me for a few moments, and I watched her expression change as she reached the obvious conclusion. "He can't face Severn like that. That's why he's kept you so close, why he's been so obsessed with the idea of you being prepared to take his place."

"It won't come to that."

She nodded, but something in her eyes said she didn't quite believe me.

"Nox is working on healing him," I added. "Protecting him from the damage his magic is doing to him. But she needs help, and ingredients. That's why this mission of ours is so urgent. It's not just about feeding the people. If Nox can fix him, Ulric will take the throne again."

Rowan smiled sadly. "No one can fix everything that's wrong with your father, I'm sure. But I hope we can get Nox some help."

"And she might be able to do something for you, as well," I added.

She brightened a little at that. "Here's hoping. But Ulric first. For our sake more than his. Maybe things will be more pleasant for me once he's feeling less threatened."

I sometimes forgot how perceptive she was, even without the benefit of my magical skills.

When we reached the shores of a green, grassy field, Rowan dropped her pack.

"Is this it?" I asked.

"I think so. What do we do if she's not here?"

"Keep walking."

The sun broke over the horizon behind us, turning the land to gold. Bright flashes between stalks of grass indicated that the lower parts of the land were covered in water. It was a remarkable spot, quiet and completely uninhabited.

"The people could have come here," I observed.

Rowan winced. "Yeah."

She stood at the edge of the wet land and held her hands up, beckoning. A ripple passed over the water, pushing it closer to her and moving the grasses as it came, and then lay still. She scowled and gritted her teeth. Water rose in a wave that washed over her feet, then calmed again. Her hands dropped to her sides.

"I know I can do this," she said softly. "And yet I can't."

"Why?"

She sighed. "It's there. I want to use it, and I don't know what's stopping me. I get there, right to the edge, and a door slams shut."

I considered the problem. It wasn't like anything I'd experienced. But then, I'd grown up with my magic, chasing after every bit of progress without the fear she'd had instilled in her from birth or the guilt she felt over her actions. "Is it the pressure?" I asked. "Perhaps if you didn't feel you had to repeat what happened in the city. If you could just enjoy your magic as the gift it is."

She nodded. "I'm trying."

"But I still think the connection between your problem and Ulric's is worth exploring with Nox when we get back."

Her posture relaxed. "You really think I can master this?"

"In time? Absolutely. You're meant for greatness, but it doesn't have to happen today."

I reached out to touch her hair, which the early morning light had lit like a fire. She turned to me and smiled, and the warmth in her gray eyes spoke to something deep inside of me. I felt myself opening. Relaxing. Letting go of the pressure I'd been under since my father's rescue.

"This is perfect." The words were out of my mouth before I realized they were coming.

She wrinkled her nose. "You think so?"

"I do. Not your problems, of course. But look at what we have right now. No Ulric. No pressure, no looking to the future."

It couldn't last, but we could make the most of it while it did.

A smile curled the edges of Rowan's lips, as though she were reading my thoughts, and she stepped closer. "We might have to wait a while for Florizel."

She gasped as my fingers tangled in her hair and I pulled her toward me. She grabbed the front of my jacket and drew me into a deep kiss that lit my body on fire as the world around us faded to insignificance.

Even if I live a thousand years, I will never wish for anything but this.

"Excuse me?" inquired a small voice.

I released Rowan, and she jumped back. I turned, instantly defensive, magic ready to attack. The interruption angered me almost as much as the fact that someone had managed to sneak up on me in my moment of distraction.

The sight of a small, scarred girl did little to take the edge off of my irritation.

Rowan's eyes widened. "Patience, what are you doing here?"

The child winced. "Are you angry?"

Rowan glanced quickly at me, then back to the girl. "No, we're not angry. A little confused, though."

Speak for yourself.

Patience adjusted the small pack she carried on her shoulders. "I heard Aren talking to the others last night. You need my help."

"You might have brought it up then instead of listening in on private conversations, sneaking around, and following us all night without announcing your presence," I said through clenched teeth. I wanted to ask how she'd tracked us without me knowing, but didn't care to bring up that weakness. I'd find out soon enough, somehow.

The girl stared at her feet. "I could have. And you'd have told me not to come, or sent me back."

"Yes, we would have," Rowan said. "Patience, I know you want to help, but you belong at camp. They'll be frantic with worry by now."

"They probably haven't even noticed I left." Tears shone in Patience's eye when she looked up, but she kept her jaw firmly set. "I want to go with you. I want to help do something important. Something big. Don't tell me you don't need another eye keeping a lookout."

Rowan sighed. "Give us a minute to talk this over."

We stepped to the edge of the water. "What are we going to do now?" I asked. "Send her back alone? Have Florizel take her?"

Rowan looked back at Patience. "Or we let her come, if Florizel can carry both of us. We're going to have to come back on foot if we find Victoria, but maybe we could still fly there with Patience."

I turned around. The girl was still watching, but the defiance had left her expression.

"Please," she said, just loud enough for us to hear. "I know I can help."

I walked farther along the edge of the water, and Rowan followed. "She needs to feel useful," she said.

"I understand that, but this isn't a game. As excited as I was to be alone with you, happy as I was to get away from my father, this is important. We need to find those people, hopefully your aunt among them, and get back before the rebels get too far away. Having a child around is going to slow us down, and if there's trouble we're going to be responsible for her."

She smiled. "You've kept me alive all this time."

I snorted. "Don't pretend you haven't done as much for me as I have for you."

"Between the two of us we should be able to handle one little girl for a few days, right? And she's already proved she can be sneaky. Might come in handy."

"Why is this important to you?"

She lifted her hands helplessly. "I don't know. I just feel for her. She's lost her family even more permanently than I've lost mine. All she wants to do is help, and no one lets her because they think she's useless and broken. I know how that feels."

I turned back and looked at Patience, who watched us carefully. I wanted nothing more than to be rid of her, but I had questions about her real reasons for following us. There was more to it than she was saying, but when I opened myself to her thoughts, I found a blank space.

Who taught you that? I wondered. Her family had some skill in hiding themselves, and perhaps the answer was as simple as that. But they'd had magic on their side.

I'd keep the girl close, and I'd have answers one way or another.

"We'll see what Florizel says," I told Rowan. "If she can carry both of you, I suppose Patience can come. If not, Florizel takes her as close to the villagers as she's willing to, then comes back for us."

Rowan stepped closer as though she were going to kiss me, then glanced back over her shoulder. "I'll thank you later."

"No you won't." I scowled as though that were the only thing on my mind. "Not properly. Not if she's here."

"We'll figure something out."

As Rowan went back to talk to Patience a shadow passed over us, broad wings and lean body distorted by the dips in the land. Florizel landed at the edge of the marshland and walked toward me.

"Aren," she called, and trotted closer. "I thought it was you, and then I saw the girl, and I wasn't sure."

"It's us," I said, and ran a hand over her neck to reassure her. "Are you well?"

"Very well. The grass is good here. I thought you would come with the people and I'd have to move on, but all has been peaceful."

Rowan and Patience hurried over. Patience's face lit up in a grin, and as she came to a stop her hands flexed at her sides as though desperate to reach out and touch the lovely horse.

Rowan quickly explained our plan, and Florizel looked the child over.

"She's small," she said cautiously. "It may work if she can keep from squirming, and if you all don't have too much to carry. Let me try her."

Rowan gave Patience a boost onto the horse's back, and the girl bit back an excited squeal.

"You'll be riding in front of me," she told Patience. "I can't risk you letting go and falling off if you're behind. Florizel, can you fly with Patience's legs in front of your wings?"

"I don't think so. You'll have to sit farther back this time if you want another passenger."

A nervous look passed over Rowan's face, but she nodded.

"We'll work it out. Can you take Patience for a trot around the field, just to get used to each other?"

Florizel went through various paces, stops and starts while Rowan and I sorted through the bags to see what we could leave behind. Rowan would have to carry my things and hers if I was flying, and there would already be added weight. We needed two sets of bedding now, even if I slept in eagle form, but we only took the barest minimum for warmth rather than comfort. I hadn't packed much food, and Patience had brought none, but we took what little I'd lifted from the kitchens on my way from Ulric's tent to Rowan's. We reluctantly left our spare clothes, but Rowan would wear both of our coats as long as it didn't become too heavy for Florizel. We kept the thick, healing ointment Nox had sent, tucked deep in the bottom of Rowan's bag, and a few smaller items we thought would be useful later.

"Are we ready to try this?" Florizel asked. Patience grinned and bounced up and down, and Florizel's ears went back. "Ouch. Human child, please."

"Sorry."

Rowan followed me to a thick patch of trees, where I took off my clothes and handed them to her.

"You know," she said with a sly smile, "you could have just changed. I would have picked your things up for you." She reached out to trail her fingers over my chest and down my stomach.

I shivered and flashed her a lazy grin. "Just wanted to remind you of what you're going to be missing now that your little friend is joining us."

"You're evil."

"I know."

I stepped back and transformed. Rowan crouched and ran her hand over the feathers of my head and back. I arched my neck under her touch.

"Safe flight," she said, and I realized I'd forgotten to wish her the same.

I took off and glided in slow circles overhead as they sorted out how two humans and their bags were going to fit on the back of one smallish flying horse. They eventually ended up with Patience sitting in front of Rowan, wearing her pack on her front while Rowan kept hers on her back.

Rowan reached around Patience to hold onto Florizel's long mane, but the arrangement looked far from secure to me. For this reason and many others, I wished again that Patience hadn't followed us. It wasn't only the danger, or the distraction, or the fact that this brief journey might have been my last chance to be alone with Rowan before we had to make hard decisions about our future—or futures, if my father was right. I also didn't trust the girl.

I'd decide later what to do about her.

Florizel went through her earthbound paces again, faster this time, getting used to the extra bulk. The flight should have been impossible, but then, so should a flying horse. She had magic on her side, and I hoped it would be enough.

She took a long running start and pushed off the ground, then landed again in what I imagined was a teeth-jarring thud for her passengers. She circled around and tried again, leaping higher this time, neck muscles straining as she stretched her head forward, wings flapping hard. She made it, but just barely, and fought for every bit of altitude she slowly gained.

"Come on, then," she gasped as she passed me. "Haven't got all day. Lead on."

And so I did, back toward the western mountains for what I could only hope would be the last time.

15

NOX

I set a jar of calembella petals into a small crate next to one full of heartleaf bark strands, packed straw between them, and made a note of both on Mama Bunn's list. Her own handwriting was so shaky as to be illegible, so I had taken over the note taking as well as the packing. The old woman sat on a spare crate and leaned back against the wall, leafing through her potions book and fanning herself with a folded paper while directing my actions.

"Mind you keep the swamp-grasses away from the starflower," she said absently.

"I know, Mama." I held back the irritation in my voice—or at least, I thought I did.

She snapped the book shut. "You know a lot, don't you?"

I took a slow, deep breath and wished for a nip of the distilled barley that still sat on the top shelf. I'd never get to it without her noticing, though. "As I've said, I'm happy to learn more from someone as experienced as yourself."

She cackled. "Your false humility is always entertaining. Tell me, have you figured out how to make the oak reaction?"

I thought she'd forgotten about that little riddle. "No, Mama."

She opened her book again, apparently satisfied that she'd put me in my place. "You talk to me again when you've got that figured out." She hummed to herself as she traced her fingers over the scribbled notes and drawings on the pages before her.

I got back to work. It was past time for us to be on the road, but everyone was moving slowly. We all should have been eager to leave. The gardens were dead, there was no sign of rain, and every animal save for the horses and the hunting dogs were dead and eaten. We'd starve if we stayed, and certain members of the community had been encouraging their leaders to move on to greener spaces for months. But to move on meant uncertainty. Maybe riches lay ahead for those who supported Ulric, or maybe war and death. There was no knowing.

At least starvation was a quiet certainty.

I picked up a dusty paper packet marked in a scribble that said something like "yrbex mimsy" and opened it. Powdery pink petals crumbled as the light hit them. They didn't give off any energy. I turned to ask Mama what they were, but found that she'd dozed off. The crone's ability to flip between sleep and complete awareness was incredible.

I noted "yrbex mimsy, ask later" on the paper and tucked the envelope into the crate, then reached for the bottle of barley. I mixed a half-portion with essence of sun-lily and a drop of pine-sap, careful not to let the spoon clink against the side of the chipped teacup.

The potion burned as it went down, but immediately relaxed me. I finished packing and carried the last crate out to the wagon, then returned to make sure I hadn't missed anything.

"You ready to go?"

The rough edge to Kel's voice made it unrecognizable until I turned to see him standing just inside the doorway.

We hadn't spoken much the previous night. Hadn't done much of anything else either, in spite of finally having the tent all to ourselves. When his hands had roamed, I'd tensed. Said I was tired. He hadn't objected, and certainly hadn't tried to talk about our relationship again.

What the hell is wrong with me? I looked him over, and felt ashamed for hesitating. Anyone would be a fool to not be climbing all over him the moment they were alone with with him. And yet I'd frozen. I thought I loved him, but I'd been wrong about that before. I knew I wanted him, but giving in to that would finalize things in a way that made me want to flee for the mountains. I'd always known that sex and love weren't the same thing, but it felt like for us, they might be.

Should have jumped on him before it came to this.

I knew what I wanted, and was still afraid to embrace it. Choices I'd made in the past and diverging paths for my future crowded my mind, as they had as I lay awake the night before with his arm draped over my waist. My sleep had been filled with frightening dreams of abandonment and loneliness, death and monsters in dark woods. Morning's light had been a relief, though I rose feeling no more rested than when I'd lain down.

Kel cleared his throat. He sounded worse off than I felt, and as flat as his eyes looked.

"Kel, what's wrong?" *Gods, say it's not me. Say my hesitation hasn't crushed your pride or your will to live, or—*

He forced a smile. "Just the usual. The dryness is hitting me hard today. Do you need a hand with anything there?"

I smiled back and pretended I didn't notice the dark circles under his eyes. "Not unless you want to carry the old woman out."

"Bah!" Mama Bunn vacated her crate, stepped onto the porch and climbed into the front of the wagon without any assistance, taking up the reins attached to a bony gray nag that dozed in the sunshine. It snorted as the old woman twitched the reins and whistled, and heaved its weight into the collar.

"Best be off," Mama called back over her shoulder.

"Guess we're walking," Kel said.

"I could try to fix you something," I said, though my lack of optimism came out in my voice.

Kel smiled and shook his head. "Really, it's nothing. We're moving toward water, right? That's all I need to know to keep me going."

I didn't bother looking back as we joined the moving column of people, horses, carts, and makeshift sleds that filled the forest and then the road when we reached it. This wasn't my home. Whatever came next had to be better.

Well, perhaps not better. But it would be something.

Kel didn't seem to want to talk, so I used the next hours to consider Ulric's problem. Nothing I'd found among Mama's supplies had given me any hope, but I'd find the answer even if it killed me. Getting his magical strength back up was the surest way of getting Severn off of the throne, and that had been my goal since the day I'd left my old life behind.

I tried to focus on the idea of creating something to help protect one's mind from magic—an interesting problem, even if there was no immediate need for it, and I did love a good challenge. My thoughts kept drifting to Severn, to Luid, to everything I'd lost. And from there they turned to my mother, to the loveliness of her face even as life carved lines into her skin, to the love she'd found to give me even when crushed under her own heartbreak. Her determination to go on after she'd lost everything had been an example for me, shaming me when I wanted to collapse under my own struggles.

"What's on your mind?"

Kel's voice snapped me back to the road. "Nothing. My childhood."

"In Cressia?"

"Silly, right? I should leave the past in the past." I said it as a defense, putting myself down before someone else could, but the truth of it struck me. I had decided to look to the future, but the habit of ruminating on old hurts anchored me.

"I'd like to hear about it," Kel said. "I'd appreciate something to keep my thoughts occupied, if you're willing to tell me."

"You haven't told me much about your childhood, either." I'd have loved to know more. To hear about how mer children lived, how Kel became the person he was.

"We're not allowed to talk to humans about our lives." He sounded apologetic. "I can defy my elders when it won't harm them personally, but the wall we've built between our culture and yours isn't meant to be breached."

How promising for our future, I thought, but couldn't fault him for his loyalty. *Well, not much.* Being rebuffed, even gently, still stung.

"How old were you when your mother was banished?" he asked.

"Four."

Thanks to the plodding pace of Mama Bunn's ancient horse, the rest of the group had passed us. Kel and I slowed further, leaving us alone with my story. I spoke words I'd thought many times, until they'd become something like a story in my mind. I'd never told it to anyone else.

"We nearly starved that first winter," I began. "Whatever money Ulric sent with us disappeared along the way, though my mother never told me how. I had this constant, gnawing ache in my belly. In time, I stopped noticing it so much, started sleeping more. The people in town tried to help us, but had so little to eat themselves that there wasn't much to spare. They gave what they could."

I paused, and Kel nodded for me to go on.

"They let us stay in an abandoned temple after we arrived. Mother said it was good luck to shelter under the gaze of the white dragon. He frightened me. The paint on his eyes was peeling off." If I closed my eyes, I could still see the image as vividly as if I were a child again. White paint on old wooden wall, with a chipped and flaking forest in the background. A fearsome monster, but flat and powerless.

"The what?" Kel asked.

"The white dragon—the diamond dragon, actually. I found out later that he was supposed to be either the Goddess's pet or her earthly aspect. Or something. People weren't too sure by then. Whatever he was, he didn't bring us any luck. Just stood there painted on the wall and watched us waste away."

Kel reached for my hand. "No luck at all? You survived somehow."

"My gift saved us, not the dragon. I was looking out the window on a sunny day during the winter, watching the red birds in the trees, wondering what they'd found to eat out there, imagining I was one of them."

As I spoke, I was transported back in time, existing in both the present and the past.

"My mother was sleeping again. She always was those days. Suddenly something outside called to my heart like music. Or like a delicious smell, though the only scents in that temple were dust, rotting wood, and wet ground. I wandered out to see what it was." A remembered chill came over me, prickling my skin. "I was afraid of the dark forest, but felt certain that I needed to find whatever it was that was calling me. My skin was all goosebumps, my teeth chattered. And I just kept walking." I remembered it all so clearly now that I was speaking about it—every detail down to the long, ragged tear in my too-small red skirt.

"The day stretched on, the shadows grew long. I decided I'd imagined the lovely thing. I imagined a lot that winter, when I had the energy for it. But this had been so real. I laid down, and the snow soaked through my clothing. I didn't care. I was just so sleepy. I opened my eyes to see the last of the sunlight, and caught a glimpse of something bright in the shadows beside a boulder. I crawled toward it, just to see, and that feeling grew stronger."

Kel waited, then asked, "What was it?"

I smiled at the memory. "Lichen. Orange and purple lichen. It glowed, and the closer I got to it, the brighter it seemed. I touched it, and it felt warm. I tasted it, and I grew stronger. Like the glow was in me. So I ate more, until I thought I could fly."

Kel smiled too, just a little. "Did you take off and soar back to the temple?"

"Not quite. I gathered as much food as I could in my pockets. By then it was getting dark, though, and I realized I was lost. But suddenly the woods were full of voices, calling out for me. Mother had roused herself, panicked, and begged the townspeople to help."

Kel let out a low whistle, and Mama Bunn looked back over her shoulder.

"Lucky thing that they found you," he said. "You must have been nearly frozen by then."

"I was. And my mother was upset, but relieved to have found

me. When we got back to the temple and the other people left us, I shared the food from my pockets."

"Just with your mother?"

I pulled my hand away from Kel's, hurt by the implied judgement. "They'd have taken it. My mother and I had nothing. The lichen I collected kept us alive over the winter."

He held his hands up as though to defend himself. "Nox, I'm not saying it was wrong. It's just interesting that a four year-old had that kind of foresight."

"That's one word for it." I supposed others would call it selfishness. I'd been accused of worse.

"And that's how your mother figured out you were a Potioner?"

"Yes. Her mother was a great one, so she knew my gift when she saw it. After that she dedicated herself to trying to get me an education so that I could make a place for myself someday."

"Maybe the Goddess's dragon was smiling on you, after all." Kel stopped and sat down next to the road. "I just need a minute. I'm not used to being on my feet all the time. Or to having feet all the time."

Mama's cart creaked to a stop, and she climbed down to the road. "Problem?"

"No, we'll catch up," I said.

Mama Bunn grunted and rooted through the boxes in the back. She returned carrying a dark bottle and a paper box in one hand, and her teacup in the other. "Pondsquinch three parts, dusty blarch two. Stir and drink, repeat an hour later." She passed the items to me and shook her head sadly. "Foolish merfolk think you're invincible, don't you?"

Kel raised his eyebrows. "I didn't know you knew. I appreciate you not saying anything to everyone else."

Mama Bunn scratched at her chin. "I've lived enough years to have seen a great many things and to know what's what. You're too beautiful to be a human if you're not a Sorcerer, and the only men I've known built like you were clam-divers and merfolk." She patted his shoulder. "Keep on, young man. We'll find water soon." She hobbled back to the cart, clucked her tongue, and started off again.

"She's not so bad," I mused as I mixed the simple potion. The combination hadn't occurred to me, but now that I held the ingredients together, I felt their incredible potential. One item from the land, one from a lake, combined to create a reaction that would bolster a mer's resistance to this dry world.

I do have a lot to learn.

Kel gagged at the taste of the potion, which smelled like rotting meat, but drank it down. We followed well behind the cart and didn't speak more. I kept thinking, though. I'd spent years focusing on the bad things that had happened because of Severn. From the moment I'd learned my true birth story, I'd been filled with resentment—for the opportunities I'd lost, for the fear that surrounded us for years, for the fact that my mother had to offer her services as housekeeper to a Potioner in order to secure me an education, and the fact that she'd had to share his bed. I'd seethed over having to hide my talents so as not to upset my teacher.

I never thought about the bright spots, never recaptured the gratitude I now remembered feeling as a child for a warm hearth, for a mother who could teach me to read, for my small bed under the rafters that was so much better than the old temple floor.

True, my life hadn't been easy, and my mother's had been harder. We had few friends in that suspicious town, little time for recreation, and plenty of hard work to keep our backs bent. But at least we weren't freezing, and we hadn't starved under the baleful gaze of the diamond dragon.

I found my attention drifting back to Kel, who walked with his head down, watching the road ahead. Would I have met him if my life had gone differently? Might I have become spoiled and lazy in Luid? Aren had called me a harpy, and I couldn't disagree, but perhaps my obstinate, prickly nature wasn't entirely the fault of my upbringing in Cressia. And Aren had said I should be grateful for not growing up under Ulric's thumb, for never having to know Severn.

I won't thank Severn for what he did, I decided, *especially for how he destroyed my mother. I will continue to do everything in my power to bring him down. But then maybe I can let go. Move on. Be free....*

The tightness I always carried in my chest loosened a little. When a warm breeze blew up behind us, I turned and let it blow my hair back from my face.

"It'll be time for that second dose soon," I told Kel.

"Do you know what I should expect? I don't feel anything yet."

"No. I'm interested to find out what comes of that horrid goop, myself."

He gagged again at the memory. "It'll be worth it if it makes me feel better." His broad shoulders drooped and his feet dragged, but he didn't stop again.

"Do you want to talk about it?" I asked.

"I doubt it will help."

"Try. I've been doing all the talking, and it's helping me feel better."

He sighed. "I just feel dried out. Used up. Like I'm going to blow away at the next strong gust of wind. I've always enjoyed visiting land. It's different, and there's this strange feeling of absolute solidity that you get when you step out of the water. But it's been too long. I'm not myself. The weight is dragging me down. I want to swim for the surface, but there is no surface. And there's no depth below me to dive into. Everything is flat, and I find myself becoming flat, too."

"Not entirely flat," I said, and cast an appreciative glance over his body, noting the way his shirt clung to the muscles of his chest and shoulders.

A week before, that would have earned me a laugh and a deep, long kiss that said I could explore that body further when I was ready to. Now all I got was a silent half-smile. He was right. He was slipping away.

"Is it just being here?" I asked.

"Mostly. I'm also worried about Cass, and hoping she's safe. And now that Aren and Rowan are gone, I feel like my heart is split in too many pieces. I know I made the right decision staying here with you, though."

"Why?"

"Because it keeps me with the biggest piece of my heart."

His words filled me with a warm glow as I mixed the second dose of Mama's recipe, and for a while I forgot about my bitterness. "Drink up, big guy."

He did, and by the time the group stopped to make camp, he had brightened considerably. Mama noticed right away.

"Feeling better, my friend?"

"I am. It's not home, but I feel more myself. Thank you, Mama."

The old woman beamed. "If I were fifty years younger I'd make you feel even better."

Kel chuckled as she shimmied away, and laughed harder when he saw how my jaw had dropped. "I like her," he said.

I pressed my lips together, holding back a smile. "She's a treat, all right."

Mama Bunn looked back. "Bring the box with the finished potions in it," she called to us. "We need to try to stretch out the stew. The folks who stopped first should have something heating up by now."

"Nox!" A tall fellow approached, one of Goff and Laelana's former lackeys who had been spending time around Ulric lately. "The king needs you immediately."

I sighed and handed the heavy box to Kel. "Make sure the old woman gets that, will you? I don't think I'm going to get anything to eat."

"The king will, though," the lanky man said. His pompous tone irritated me, but ignored it. "Told me to tell you to bring him some food when you come."

"Might as well make myself useful," I muttered.

I made my way toward the scent of the meal that the first arrivals had started cooking and scooped two servings of thin stew from the massive iron pot. Ulric's messenger marched ahead and led me toward wherever the king was holding court. Ulric would miss out on whatever beneficial things Mama Bunn tossed into the stew later, but that was his own fault.

Impatient old sod.

We found him with his small tent already set up. No bed

this time, but his bedroll looked far more comfortable than mine, and he was out of the sun. He sat on a folding stool where he'd just finished shaving the stubble from his jaw. He set his razor-edged knife aside as I entered alone and handed him his meal.

"Any progress?" He tasted his meal and grimaced, but ate it anyway.

"No. I've been somewhat occupied with helping Mama Bunn pack her things. She's a necessity right now, and so are her supplies if we're all going to make it to Luid alive."

"Agreed. But I need your mind on my problem at all times."

"Are you certain I shouldn't ask her for her opinion? She has more experience than I."

He frowned. "You know we can't let anyone else know."

"If I start slacking off my work to ponder on potions for you, she'll know there's something going on." I rubbed my temples to ease the tension that crept up whenever I spoke to my father. "She looks older than boots, but she's sharp."

Ulric glanced down at the cracked leather that covered my feet. "Indeed. Well, if you would be so kind as to turn your attention to this minor detail when you get a chance, I'd be ever so grateful."

I took a deep breath. "Is that all? This has been lovely, but I should get back out there."

He set his bowl on the ground. "You know, I've had people's tongues cut out for less insolence than you show me."

"My apologies. I'm hardly accustomed to addressing royalty. Sir." The ice in my voice matched the chill in his eyes as he continued to look me over.

"Tell me everything you know about where Aren has gone. And about Rowan, and their relationship."

I shot him a suspicious glare. "Are you going to have my tongue cut out if it displeases you?"

He smiled at that. His smile never made him look happy. "No."

"I don't know much. Probably no more than you."

"Let's find out, shall we?"

This was surely a test. He knew something, and wanted to see if he could trust me to tell him. Fine. No harm telling him what he already knew. But not too much. I wouldn't betray Aren.

"They went west to find the Darmish refugees."

"How?"

"I don't know. They left on foot. I didn't ask a lot of questions. He said they'd catch up with us before we reached Luid. He hasn't abandoned you, if that's what you think."

The king grunted at that. "That wasn't my concern, but thank you for the reassurance. And what about Rowan?"

I shrugged. "I don't know her well. She's a Sorceress, but you knew that. Dead loyal to Aren, but you knew that, too."

"And is he to her?"

"Loyal? I'd say so. He didn't go to Ardare looking for you, remember. He wanted her back, and would have torn that fortress down to get to her if he'd had to. You were a lucky coincidence."

Ulric rubbed a hand over his jaw. "Thank you for your honesty."

"If we're through—"

The tent flap behind me snapped open, and Goff stepped in. I moved aside. The man was little more than Laelana's assistant , but I still didn't need to be on his bad side.

"You need to do something," he said to Ulric, jabbing a finger in his direction.

Ulric ignored the bad manners, but he surely noted every insolent word and gesture. "I'm doing many things. What, specifically, would you have me add to the list?"

Goff glowered. "We're nearly starving. Everything we had left just went into the pot."

"Shall I snap my fingers and create a feast?"

"You're the king! We've passed two distant farms already. If you ordered it, they'd be forced to share their stores with us. They couldn't say no."

"Hmm." Ulric stroked his chin. "And you think they have any more than we have, after the long winter?"

"They must have something. The fields are green enough out this way."

"So you'd have us rob them to feed you, is that it?"

Goff's mouth pulled back in a disbelieving sneer. "We're on the king's business. Surely that's more important than them."

Ulric turned his eyes toward the roof. "Thank the gods you're not king and never will be. I'll not turn my people against me before I've regained the throne. Or after, for that matter."

Laelana joined us in the tent. "Goff, enough."

"I told you to wait outside," he snarled.

Interesting. I'd always thought that Laelana wore the crown in their relationship, but it seemed Goff had some fight in him when he got worked up.

She turned to Ulric and made a short bow. "My apologies. Goff does get cranky when he's on tight rations." She glanced sideways at Goff. He stepped back, glowering. "In spite of his poor manners, Goff is correct. We are out of food. With your permission, sire, I'll send some of our trained fighters out to hunt. It will be good practice for them. " She frowned. "Perhaps if we detoured to a river or a lake and found fish. It wouldn't put us off by more than a day, I'd guess." Laelana tried to speak well and sound educated, but her backwoods accent crept into her voice.

Ulric's mouth twitched. "Use what and whom you need, but we stay on course. Perhaps we'll find something when we start passing through towns, but for now it's down to what we can hunt and forage on our route."

She bowed again and left the tent.

Goff continued to glare at Ulric. *Idiot,* I thought. *Were he at full strength, you'd be dead by now.*

"You promised us wealth and power if we helped you," Goff said. "Glory. Fame."

"All these things will be yours," Ulric said in a calm tone that offered no room for disagreement. "But not until they are mine."

Goff turned and stalked out of the tent.

Ulric leaned forward on his stool and rested his head in his hands. "I'm quickly remembering why I left Luid."

"People like him?"

"Like all of them. Demanding special treatment, trying to order me around. Me, the king and the most powerful Sorcerer ever to rule Tyrea. At least he's open about it, though his continued desire to see his people sent to war troubles me. The liars and the schemers are worse, and they're everywhere in Luid. I suppose when I set out to find your mother, I was hoping to bring back a bit of peace and sanity to my life."

My breath caught in my throat. "You were looking for us? Aren had heard you might be, but you never came."

"No, I was waylaid, wasn't I?" He paused before he spoke again. "Nox, I do regret everything that happened to you and to your mother. I don't suppose you'll ever understand why I had to send you away, but it was that or kill her." He appeared troubled. "Perhaps that would have saved you if I'd gone through with it. If Magdalena had died..." His voice broke, but he regained his composure quickly. "If I'd had her executed, you could have gone to the nursemaid who pretended you were hers. No one would have known any different. But I couldn't do it." Regret and helplessness weighed his voice down, and softened him in a way that surprised me to the point of discomfort.

"Of course not," I whispered. I couldn't say I felt compassion for him, but my shell of hatred softened. In spite of everything, I wanted to comfort the man who had once cared for my mother, who obviously still did. "You did what you thought would save her, and you tried to get her back."

When he looked up, his expression was hard. The instant change shook me, and I stepped back. "I was a fool. No good came of my compassion, of my... my weakness."

He'd been about to say love, I knew he had. And he couldn't, even now. Still, it was something. I'd never expected such honesty from him, and such vulnerability.

Perhaps there is more there than I thought. He's struggling.

"You both fared poorly in Cressia," he continued. "She died in the end, anyway, and my household lost a potentially powerful Potioner. We could have done great things with you, Nox. And in the end, knowing she was still out there gave me false hope of a return to the way I felt when she was around. I acted foolishly, and look what's happened. Severn stole my throne, and removing him from it may prove impossible. I'm broken. Aren is gone."

"You'll have your position back," I said, more for my benefit than for his. "You'll take it, and Severn will pay for what he's done."

"He certainly will."

I warmed again. *We are sworn to the same purpose*, I thought. *I don't like you, but—*

He shook his head, angry. "I should have just had her killed. We'd all have been better off if I'd been stronger."

My shell hardened again, immediately and completely. My sympathy had stretched past its limit, and the backlash of it snapping stung me hard. "If you'll excuse me," I said flatly, "I think I hear Mama Bunn calling."

"I'm not going to let Aren make the same mistake I did," Ulric said. He was talking to himself, though. It was like I had never been there at all.

16

ROWAN

I've heard that if a person falls from a great height, she'll die before she hits the ground. I spent almost as much energy during our long flight hoping that was true as I did trying to keep from finding out. A mid-air death sounded far more pleasant than a hard landing at the bottom.

As comfortable as I'd become on Florizel's back during our previous journeys, this was hardly the same thing. With Patience seated ahead of me, I constantly slipped back on Florizel's haunches. I clamped my thighs against her and threaded my fingers tight into her mane, pulling myself forward with my arms and pressing as close as I could against Patience's back, but nothing made me feel secure.

As the sun reached its highest point and began its descent toward our destination, my legs began to numb.

At least I could keep my eyes open now, not like when Florizel and I first started flying together. I looked to my right, where Aren glided easily under his own power and in complete control of his flight. I decided then that if I survived this journey, and when I had a better grasp of my magic, I'd see about trying that transformation thing. Heights might not be so bad if I weren't afraid of falling from them.

He flew ahead, scouting, then led us off-course to the south.

He had no way of telling us what he'd seen, but Florizel followed willingly.

Each time he flew ahead or disappeared into the clouds, I felt the distance between us, and couldn't help feeling that some day —not on this journey, but some day—he wouldn't be back.

I didn't want to think about it, but I had nothing else to do. *It's this, or back to thinking about falling.*

Aren it is.

I ducked my head down behind Patience's to block the wind and watched him through the pale hair that whipped back against my face. The sun glinted off his feathers, making it easy to track him even with my eyes squinted half-shut. There had been a time when I called the eagle Aquila, until I found out who he really was. It seemed I still had much to learn about him. Every time I pulled back a layer, there were a hundred more beneath.

Aren had made it clear that he didn't want to be king, but if what he said about Ulric being weak were true, what choice would he have? *And maybe it's what he wants after all,* I realized, even if Ulric recovered and took his throne back. Maybe Aren had only convinced himself he didn't want it because it wasn't a possibility before. With Severn out of the way he'd be Ulric's heir. He could have everything—the world at his feet, and all the recognition and respect he'd been denied all his life. I wouldn't hold him back from that, especially if it was the only way to save the people of three countries from Severn.

And maybe he didn't want to tell me until he figured out how not to hurt me with it.

The thought made my chest tighten painfully.

Just ask him about it, you idiot, and then you can stop worrying.

Patience's weight shifted in front of me as she brushed her hair away from her face. "Aren's going down!" she yelled over her shoulder.

I crouched lower, and my heart leapt into my throat as we dropped. We rushed toward the ground, and I wrapped one arm around Patience's waist to hold her steady. Florizel landed hard and stumbled over the uneven ground. She went down on her knees, pitching forward and sending me and Patience tumbling forward over her head. I shoved Patience out of the way so I wouldn't land on her and tucked my chin to my chest, landing on my right shoulder with a grunt. The grass provided a softer landing than I'd expected, and I was able to catch my breath and stand as soon as I'd stopped rolling.

I turned to see Patience lying flat on her back, not moving. Aren landed beside her and looked at me, obviously uncertain as to whether he should change and try to help, or wait until he could put some clothes on.

I knelt beside the girl.

She opened her eye, looked around, and laughed. "That was amazing!"

I gave her arm a shove and went to see about Florizel, who stood with her head hung low, long mane hiding her face. "Patience is fine," I said. "We all are. You did well."

She snorted and shook her head. "I'm sorry. Landing was just too much."

Aren's sharp shriek pierced the air. I looked for danger, but saw nothing. Not even the town we were supposed to be looking for. I turned to Aren, and he nodded toward me. No—toward the pack on my back.

"Right, hang on." I looked for a sheltered spot for him to change, but the only things close by were the thin, wind-stunted trees that dotted the grasslands. "Patience, don't look."

The girl clapped her hands over her face.

I took Aren's clothes out of the bag and set them on Florizel's back. "Do you mind?" I asked her.

"Not at all." She spread her wings out to the side, and Aren hopped around behind her. He dressed while I applied Nox's ointment to Florizel's knees, and brushed past me as he walked over to where Patience still lay in the grass. He nudged her side with his boot, and she giggled.

He gave her a thin smile. "You going to live, kid?"

"Probably." She sat up. "Where are we?"

Aren looked around, getting his bearings again. "If the directions Jevan gave me last night were accurate, we should be a few hours away from the town we're looking for. My wings were getting tired."

That was a lie. I'd seen him fly farther before, and for longer. He knew Florizel needed a rest, even if she wouldn't ask for it, and didn't want her to think she was holding us back. He patted the horse's neck as she passed him on her way to graze on the fat green grass next to a boggy place, and it was all I could do to stop myself from kissing him again.

We'd talk as soon as we could get away from Patience for a few minutes. I needed to know whether I should start ignoring the way my heart swelled when he insisted on being amazing.

We ate some of the food from my pack. "I should have hunted before I changed back," Aren said. "But I thought we should talk about our plans."

"Definitely," I replied. "What we do next, but I also wanted to talk about—" I cut myself off as I saw Patience listening. "Well, the other things can wait. What do you think we'll find when we reach this town?"

It might have been my imagination, but I thought Aren looked relieved when I only asked about the near future.

"I don't know," he said. "A lot of it will depend on how this town is operating right now, whether they were prepared for an influx of strangers in need of aid. It will also depend on how the people who came from Darmid are handling all of this, whether they're opposed to magic. They might not have run into much of it yet, if Severn has taken magic-users from the area back to Luid. If all goes well, we'll get to town, find your family, make sure they're safe for now, and ask your aunt to accompany us back if she's with them."

I frowned. "Yes, but since when has all gone well for us?"

He gave me a dark look that should have been frightening, but that sent pleasant tingles through my body instead. *Down, girl.*

Patience dug through her pack and sighed. "I forgot a hair brush."

"Hang on," I said, and found the broken comb I'd picked up after the stables were packed. I motioned for her to come closer, and she scooted over to sit in front of me. "Why so concerned with appearances?"

"We'll want to make a good impression. They're not going to welcome us if we show up looking like a tiny band of thieves, right?"

Aren watched as I pulled the comb through the wind-tangled ends of Patience's hair and worked my way up. "Good thinking," he said. "Did your mother teach you that?"

Patience looked down and picked at the sleeve of her sweater. "It was just the way we operated when we traveled. Best foot forward and all of that."

Aren's gaze moved to me, to my face, and he smirked. "You might want to give that thing a run through your own hair."

I tried to pull my fingers through my hair, but couldn't get far. The wind had pulled much of it free from the tail I'd had it in when we took off. I glowered at him as I untied the rest and shook out the strands. "Fine. You don't have to look so smug about it, feather brain."

Patience giggled as Aren flashed me the most self-satisfied grin I'd ever seen and shook out his own hair, which had suffered absolutely no ill effects from a trip taken in eagle form. If he was as confused about things as I was, he did a good job hiding it.

I finished brushing Patience's long hair out and helped her adjust her scarf, and she stood.

"I have to go... you know," she said.

"Come with me, child," Florizel said. "We'll find a place, or I'll make one." Patience hesitated, looked at me and Aren, and then followed the horse away.

Aren held out a hand. "Give me that."

I passed the comb over, turned my back to him, and he went to work on my hair. I winced as he pulled through the tangles. Once he was past those, it was heaven. He dragged the tines of the comb over my scalp, sending waves of pleasurable shivers down my back. His fingers followed, pulling freely through my hair then pushing it forward over one shoulder. He leaned in close on the other side and rested his face against the side of my neck.

"Much better," he whispered. His hand crept around my waist and pressed against my stomach. I turned and moved closer, resting my shoulder against the solid support of his chest, and he caught my lips with his own as I turned my face toward him. So gentle, such a contrast to the rough treatment he'd given my hair moments before. I lost myself, until Patience hollered and brought me back.

"Hey! We going?"

Aren sighed. "Yes."

He stood and changed, leaving me to pick up his clothes this time. I stuffed them in my bag and stood on legs that had grown stiff while we rested. I braided my hair behind my neck with a ribbon, tucked it down the back of my jacket, and tied my scarf over my head. I did the same for Patience. When I was done, the poor girl's head looked like a bundle of rags.

"You're sure you're all right?" I asked Florizel. "We can walk, if it's too hard."

"No, I feel refreshed. Thank you."

We climbed onto the trunk of a hunched-over tree and mounted from there, and after another few false starts Florizel had us in the air. My thighs ached with the effort of holding on, but I couldn't force them to relax. *Just a few more hours.*

I imagined that the pain and exhaustion I was feeling couldn't be anything compared to how Florizel's wings felt, and decided not to complain.

The sun moved ahead of us, the wind grew colder, and I lost track of time as we flew. Patience tipped forward, then snapped her head back up.

I leaned in closer. "Don't fall asleep, now."

She nodded and hunched forward, holding her body parallel to Florizel's neck. Florizel's wings continued to beat in their hypnotic rhythm, and I too had to be careful not to fall asleep. I forced my eyes to remain open and watched as Aren flew ahead of us, catching updrafts and spiraling off-course as the wind lifted him, but always returning to us. Later on, he pushed farther ahead before returning and dropping below us, indicating that we should land. Not near the town, I noted. I could only imagine the stir we'd cause if anyone saw us.

Florizel landed with a little more grace this time, at least managing to keep us on her back, though I slipped to one side as she slowed to a walk. We dismounted and Florizel stood still, wings hanging toward the ground, muscles trembling.

"It was too much, wasn't it?" Patience asked.

I ran a hand from Florizel's forelock down her nose. "Poor thing. You need to rest."

Florizel's eyes rolled up to look at us without lifting her face. "I am a little tired. Perhaps a snack, and I'll sleep while you all go to town. We... we won't be flying back with another person, will we?"

"No, I think two is our limit," I said. "Do you need a rub-down?"

"Thank you. If you have time, that would be lovely."

I left Aren's things in a patch of trees near a burbling stream and grabbed a handful of fragrant leaves to wipe the sweat from Florizel's coat. She sighed as I worked the knots out of her muscles. I retrieved Nox's ointment from my pack, and rubbed more on the scrapes where she'd gone down on her knees earlier.

"Rest well," I told her.

"I will." She lifted her head and sniffed the breeze that came toward us from the mountains that now loomed ahead of us. "Smells like home."

"You'll get there," I told her. "If we go to Luid, we'll find Murad." She'd said that if she ever succeeded in rescuing her stallion from Severn, they might try to go back home.

She sighed. "I know. I keep reminding myself that helping you folks is helping him, but it takes so long." Her ears flicked forward and back. "Not that I wouldn't want to help my friends, anyway. I think you are my family now."

The tears that burned my eyes shouldn't have surprised me. *Once a sentimental fool, always a sentimental fool.* I couldn't help it. I'd once dreamed of having adventures and interesting friends, and it was all far more incredible than I'd dreamed.

"Of course we are," I said. "And we'll be back soon. Rest while you can, please."

Aren stood at the top of a rise in the land, looking beyond it. I climbed up to join him and found a pretty little town in the distance, much like one we'd once stayed in before. The white-washed buildings and peaceful farms were surrounded by ploughed fields that hugged the curves in the land.

"Is that it?"

"If the name you got from the scout back at camp was correct, it is. Seems quiet enough."

Patience appeared beside me. She shook out her hair and adjusted the scarf over her missing eye. "Best foot forward, remember."

She started down the hill, and Aren and I followed.

17

ROWAN

"Can't we walk on the road?" Patience asked as we neared the town. "My feet are getting wet."

"No," Aren said. "In fact, I'd like to stick closer to that ravine." He waited for her to catch up, and we made ourselves disappear as well as we could into the thin forest that grew at the top of the broad cut in the land.

"What's wrong?" I asked.

"I'm not sure. The town seems perfectly normal, doesn't it? Maybe that's the problem." He stopped walking, and appeared to be listening for something. "I don't know what it is. Let's find a place near the road to watch from for a while, get a sense of what's happening. I don't trust that there's no one following us just because I can't feel them. There seem to be a few people slipping past that lately."

He didn't look at Patience as he said it, but she ducked her head and stepped away from him.

I wasn't about to argue. Much as I wanted to hurry up and find my family, and much as my grumbling stomach yearned for a hot meal at an inn or a tavern, I trusted Aren's instincts. His cautiousness balanced my own tendency to see only the possibilities in a situation. Trusting people had got me in trouble too often lately for me to object to taking things slowly here.

We stopped at a bend in the ravine, as close as we could get to the town without revealing ourselves. The road met the curve of the forest there, giving us a good view in both directions and allowing us to watch the town, which sat on the downslope of a slight rise in the land.

"Do we have any more food?" Patience asked.

"Later," Aren replied.

She sighed and sat on the ground with her knees tucked up against her chest.

I crouched beside her and offered a sympathetic smile. "Were you expecting this to be fun when you decided to follow us?"

Her mouth opened and closed, and her gaze flicked to the side. "Not exactly. I'm not that hungry, really."

Aren glanced at her with narrowed eyes.

I mouthed, *What?*

He shook his head and turned back to the town.

I gave Patience's knee a reassuring squeeze and went back to stand with Aren. I found myself distracted, but managed to limit myself to only sneaking glances at him every few minutes. He didn't seem to notice. If he had anything other than our mission on his mind, it was well hidden.

A flash of movement caught my eye far up the road, but when I turned to look, it was gone. A moment later it came again, a blotch of red and white coming over a rise in the road. I nudged Aren with my elbow and pointed. When they came into view a third time, he pulled me back into the trees until a thin screen of leaves covered us.

Six riders in red uniforms on white horses, coming quickly but not riding as though it were any sort of emergency. They passed by close enough that I picked out the flame insignia branded on their horses' hindquarters.

"What do you think?" I asked after they passed.

Aren frowned. "I didn't get much. There was no sense of urgency among them, so I doubt they're here because someone spotted and recognized us. They're here on Severn's business, but I don't think any of them were focusing on that. I couldn't get anything else."

"That's plenty."

He expected so much of himself. The fact that he'd caught anything while they were riding past and paying him no attention was impressive, but it would never be enough for him.

"I suppose we should eat now," he said. "Wait until dark to get closer to town." He pointed at a weather-beaten barn that stood a short distance from a newer, larger, red-painted one. "We can take shelter there. I haven't seen anyone go near it yet."

Patience grabbed my bag and dug through it, pulling out anything remotely edible she found. It wasn't much. A little bread, dried apples, a cube of cheese that needed to have the mold scraped off. She looked up at me. "That's it?"

"I couldn't take more than that," Aren answered. "And I wasn't expecting another mouth to feed." Patience flinched at his short tone. "We can't risk a fire to cook meat, but I can hunt and eat as an eagle. You two share what's there, and we'll figure something else out for breakfast."

And then he was gone, transformed and flapping toward the tops of the trees.

"Be careful," I said, but it was too late for him to hear me. I supposed an eagle wouldn't be a strange sight this close to the mountains, but local farmers wouldn't be pleased to see one.

He can take care of himself.

Still, I couldn't help watching the sky instead of the town and the road.

Patience ate without speaking, and we went our separate ways to take care of other business in the woods. I thought she'd have something to say when we came back to our lookout spot, but she remained silent.

"You okay?" I asked.

"Yes. I am sorry for causing trouble, though. Aren's mad, right?"

I hesitated. "He's not pleased, but he'll get past it. You have nothing to worry about. I'm going to take a better look at the town, if that's all right with you."

She nodded and picked at the cuffs of her sweater.

I climbed a sturdy oak tree that offered a decent view into the village. I watched as four of the soldiers, red dots at that distance, walked through the square, occasionally stopping to speak to people.

I climbed back down.

"Patience," I said, "you might be exactly what we need."

She perked up at that. "Really?"

"Absolutely. There are soldiers in town, and Aren can't go and ask questions with them there. If Severn is taking an interest in these Darmish people, he probably knows we might be here. I shouldn't risk it, either. They'll know what I look like. But you..."

Patience chewed her lower lip for a moment, then smiled. "I'll do it."

I smiled back, but my stomach tightened. This was a dangerous mission for someone so young. "Can you think of a good story as to why you're there?"

She looked insulted. "Please. Did I not grow up with actors? Am I not one myself?"

I laughed quietly. "Just be careful. We have no idea what's actually going on down there."

Aren emerged from the trees, buttoning his shirt as he walked. I tried not to stare. The distance between us, real or imagined, only made me want him more.

I explained the plan.

"Good enough," he said. "We should get closer first, and wait for morning. If there's trouble, we need to be able to get her out of there."

Patience seemed pleased that he was concerned about her safety, but I noticed that Aren wasn't speaking directly to her.

We waited until after dark, then crept toward the old barn. The sky had clouded over in patches, providing occasional cover from the moonlight, but the near-total darkness and unfamiliar terrain made for slow going. By the time we reached the decrepit structure it felt like we'd been moving for hours.

We slipped in through the half-open double doors and climbed straight up to the loft, though my legs screamed in protest. The barn was empty save for a few bats nesting among the rafters. I suspected there would be more returning by morning, and shuddered. We found a relatively clean corner and set our things down.

I had a hard time containing a groan as I sat and stretched my legs out in front of me.

"You all right?" Aren asked, and sat beside me.

"Just sore from trying not to fall off a flying horse."

"Anything I can do?"

Patience mumbled something, and I looked to the corner where she'd already set her bed up in a patch of faint moonlight. She yawned and rolled over, turning her back to us.

I spread my blankets out and lay on my back. "My legs are really stiff."

Aren moved through the darkness, and a moment later his hands were on my thighs, pressing hard. I gasped. "Ouch."

"You want me to go easier on you?" The slight challenge in his voice made me shiver.

"No. It's fine."

He worked in silence, pressing and kneading. I gritted my teeth through the sore spots, and my muscles relaxed even as my heartbeat insisted on doing the opposite. He bent my knee and pressed it to my chest, stretching out the stiffness in my backside, first on one side and then the other.

"Better?"

I nodded, then remembered he couldn't see that in the dark. "Yes. Thank you. Anything I can do for you?"

He chuckled, and the sound made my heart jump. He lay down beside me and ran his fingers over the outside of my jacket, then opened the buttons and slipped his hand inside. I bit back a gasp.

"Nothing I'd want Patience to wake up in the middle of."

I shifted to face him and ran my fingertips lightly over his face, picturing every beautiful feature in my mind. I moved closer, placing my mouth next to his ear. "I wish we were alone."

"It's no accident that we're not."

"What do you mean?"

He pushed himself up on his elbow and leaned toward

Patience's corner, where she snored softly. "It doesn't make sense that she just decided to follow us."

"Have you... you know. Peeked?"

He laid his head down again, and I tucked my head under his chin. Though human now, he still carried the scent of the sky with him, and I inhaled deeply. "I've been struggling with that," he admitted. "She's no enemy, and I said I wouldn't use my skills against allies. But I couldn't help thinking that there was more to this than she'd said. I tried earlier, just to see if she was telling the truth."

"And?"

"You're not angry?"

"I trust your judgment."

He squeezed me tight. "Thank you. And to answer your question, I couldn't tell."

"What do you mean? It's not magic. She doesn't have any." If she had, she might not have suffered such permanent effects from Wardrel's attack. No magic that I knew of could have regenerated a missing eye, but her burns would have healed better. Magic would have interfered with Aren's ability to see her thoughts, but otherwise...

"Someone told her to guard her mind against me, and I have a good idea who. I could break through the wall if I tried, and easily, but I don't want to do that to her without good reason."

I kissed the stubbled skin at his jaw. "Thank you for that. So who would have—oh. Your father."

"Right. And if Patience is working for him now..."

"You make it sound like she's a traitor. She would never do that." But when I thought back on how badly she wanted to be useful and save the world, and how gullible I'd been at her age, I felt less certain.

He didn't answer.

"Aren, she's only a child."

He sighed. "I know. And she seems to mean well. But if he's using her against us, against me, what am I supposed to do? She's lying to us. Spying on us. That is betrayal, Rowan, especially when she's supposed to be your friend. She's a child, but that doesn't mean she's innocent."

My heart went cold. "You wouldn't hurt her, right?"

"I don't want to. She deserves it, or at least to have the fear of the gods put into her. It's far less punishment than I'd have had for betraying my family at her age. I've seen people beaten within an inch of their lives for less and thrown into a cell to rot after they gave up their secrets." He was silent for a few moments, then sighed. "We'll see what happens when she comes back tomorrow. One way or another, I'll have the truth from her."

Anger radiated from him, evident in his tense muscles and overly-controlled breathing.

"Are you more angry with her, or your father?"

His breath came out in a long, slow rush. "My father. I wish I knew why he did this. It might be a test to see what I'll do with her, to find out how soft I've become. It may also be to keep me on a leash. He doesn't want me wandering too far."

"Not with me, right?"

Aren's fingers traced circles over my back beneath my jacket. "No. Not with you."

My eyes had already fallen closed, though I wanted nothing more than to stay awake with him while I had the chance. I wanted to ask whether he was thinking about following his father, accepting the life that was being offered to him. I wanted to voice my objection to him marrying and having children with a bunch of other women, and found I couldn't. Thinking it was bad enough. I was too tired to speak it, and too afraid to hear the answer.

We'd sworn we would do everything in our power to be together, that nothing would separate us. But perhaps fate or the gods didn't care what we wanted. What were the promises of two people when compared with the needs of the entire world?

He sat up. "I should change so I can keep my ears open tonight."

That meant no shared dreams, and no conversation in them. *Probably for the best*, I decided. I never got much rest when we dreamed together, and I did need it. I just hoped I wouldn't be interrupted by nightmares again.

I woke every time Patience snorted or rolled over, every time returning bats scrambled in through the cracks in the walls, every time the wind whistled. Half-way through the night it started to rain, just a soft pattering of droplets on the roof. The sound lulled me into a deeper sleep, but only until the roof sprung a leak that soaked my head. I dragged my damp bedding to a drier spot, but didn't get much sleep after that.

By sunrise, such as it was in the cloudy sky, I was more exhausted than I'd been when I laid down.

Patience woke before me, and made her way slowly down the ladder. She returned a few minutes later. "I'll go now," she said. "Sneak out, get some distance, come back to town by the road. Let them think I was walking all night. That way nobody will come poking around here. I'll see if I can bring anything back for you to eat later."

I watched through a crack in the wall as she made her way through the fields, occasionally bending over and then touching her hand to her mouth.

"Berries," Aren said. I hadn't heard him land, or change and dress. "You could go out and get some."

"Probably best if I don't risk it," I said. "If she's spotted, she can come up with a story. If someone sees me and figures out who I am, it won't be good for any of us." My stomach objected with a loud grumble, but I ignored it. I'd been hungry before and survived it. "What are you going to do?"

He looked out at the gray sky. "I don't know. I could scout, keep an eye on things, but they might be watching for me. I think we're stuck."

"Good." I took a deep breath and prepared myself to ask the questions I couldn't put off any longer. "Tell me everything your father doesn't want me to know. No holding back this time. Everything about your laws, about exactly what your father fears from me and from our relationship, how bad things are for him, and for you now that he can't hold the throne. All of it. No secrets."

Deep lines creased his forehead. "I'm not sure that's a good idea. If he knew you knew everything, it would be dangerous for you. It's bad enough that I've told you a little."

"Would he believe you if you claimed we hadn't talked about it after you disobeyed his orders and stole off into the sunrise with me?"

"True enough."

So he told me. It was worse than I had suspected, and went far beyond me getting in the way of Aren taking his place in his family or a small concern over my loyalties. He told me what Ulric had said about me aspiring to take the throne to protect my people. It sounded ridiculous when Aren said it, but I imagined the words coming from Ulric's mouth, the conviction with which he always spoke, and heard how believable it could be. I also remembered the look in the king's eyes when he'd thought I might scheme against him with Griselda, and how he'd dissuaded me from practicing my skills since we crossed the border.

And Ulric's problem was far more concerning than I'd thought when Aren said he was having troubles and that Nox was working on a cure. His problem was nothing like mine. I felt an aversion to my magic, and it was replenishing slowly. One of those was a problem I would have to face on my own, and the other I could work around until Nox had time to help me. His problem sounded like it could lose him his crown forever, or even kill him if he attempted too much.

Though I tried to focus on Ulric's magic and his problems with me, my mind kept returning to one thing.

When Aren finished speaking, I said, "Just to be sure I have this straight. You can either be king, or be with me. Even if I prove I'm not a traitor, even if I make your father like me once he's completely sane again, it doesn't make any difference. It's the law, and unbreakable."

"That's how it looks."

I swallowed hard and took a deep breath to keep my voice steady. "So our temporary separation really isn't, is it? Assuming there's no miraculous cure for Ulric, you have to take his place.

And that means there's no room for me, no matter whether I overcome my own problems or not."

He didn't look at me. "You could stay in Luid if I were king. I can't imagine my life without you. I'd keep you on as advisor if you were willing, or you'd be free to do as you please and leave, if you wanted. But we couldn't... Well."

I pressed the heels of my hands to my eyes. *We said we'd figure it out. That we'd be together. That—*

I forced those thoughts away. Things had changed.

He went to a tiny, dusty window and stared out, lost in his thoughts. "I would turn my back on anything for you, were it my choice," he said, so quietly I barely heard him. "I don't want to rule. I don't understand why anyone would want it. But the fact is that if Ulric doesn't recover, it's going to be me or Severn. If Severn keeps the throne he'll go to war with Darmid, and he'll turn on Belleisle if he can manage it. He won't stop until all of the human power on the continent is his to control. You and I will never be safe. Nor will the merfolk, if he ever finds out they helped us. He claims lofty ideals, says he only wants to preserve magic, but it's about power. It always has been. That's why he got rid of Ulric instead of trying to help him."

"So you don't have much choice, do you?"

The resignation written on his face when he glanced back at me nearly broke my heart. "No. But I keep telling myself this could all work out. My father's magic might recover. He might announce that he's alive and well, and the people will welcome him back and support him. Severn will see the error of his ways, beg for forgiveness, hand power back. Or fall when Ulric challenges him."

"And you'd still be next in line, which I suspect would put a damper on things for us. Your responsibilities would just be delayed." I swallowed back the lump that filled my throat. No fairy tale had ever prepared me for this part of a relationship with a prince.

He looked out the window again. "My father's not too old to have more children. There are other Sorcerers out there. Not as strong as me, and even less prepared for the job. But there's a chance someone could…" His words trailed off, and he leaned his forehead against the window frame.

I stood behind him and wrapped my arms around his waist. I only meant it to be a supportive gesture, but couldn't help noticing the way his shirt hugged his lean muscles. I closed my eyes and pressed my face against his back, and ran my hands over his stomach and chest. His body tensed.

"Rowan," he whispered, voice thick and heavy, as he turned toward me. "I know what I have to do, but I can't end this. I can't—"

"Shh. Not yet."

I pushed him against the wall and kissed him. My hands roamed over his body, taking in each familiar curve and hollow and burning bright new memories into my mind.

He brushed a tear from my face. I hadn't realized I was crying.

I would never be ready to give him up, but it didn't seem we had any choice. Still, we were together for the moment, and no one could take that from us. I took his hand and led him toward my bed.

We didn't speak. There was no place now for words, only for warm bodies pressed together against the chill in the air, for the swirl of intertwined magics, dark and bright. For a while there was no worry, no future. There was only Aren, the perfect way we fit together, and pleasure so bright it became unbearable. When the world came back into focus, my tears had dried.

Aren kissed my eyelids and held me close. "I'm not going to lose you. We're going to find a way."

I didn't answer, only held him tighter while I had the chance. I wasn't going to have him sacrifice his future and his people if that was what it took for us to be together. I would find my own way. And maybe some day…

The barn door below creaked. We both jumped up, scrambling to get our clothes back on. Aren didn't realize his shirt was inside out until he started fumbling with the buttons. He gave up and left it open. I didn't like the way he stood absolutely still, as though waiting for a fight.

Waiting for the traitor's return.

Patience dragged herself up to the loft and looked around, taking in the blankets on the floor and our disheveled appearances. "I found them," she said casually, and dropped her bag. She sat and removed her boots. "It's so wet out there."

"What's going on?" Aren asked. His eyes tracked her every movement, but still he didn't move.

"Hang on." She worked a paper package out of her coat pocket and tossed it to me. Inside was a wedge of cheese, a bit of cold roast, and a wrinkled apple.

"Thanks," I said. I offered some to Aren, but he refused.

"You found the refugees?" he asked.

"Yeah." She leaned back against the wall. "I didn't want to seem too interested in them, but I think things are going really well here. The people who came from Darmid are staying at the inn, pretty comfortable."

Aren frowned. "Who's paying for that?"

"That's the funny thing. Your brother is." She smiled, obviously pleased with herself for doing her job well. "Everyone's on about how generous Lord Severn is, how the soldiers came with supplies and gold and said to make these people comfortable."

Aren paced the floor, still watching Patience. "He wants something from them, then. He's watching for magical talent."

Patience shrugged. "Probably. But it sounds like people here in town were pretty happy with how things were going even before that. It's strange, right? From what I'd experienced and what Laelana said, I thought everyone in the country was mad at Severn."

Aren ran his hands through his hair. "It's never that simple. Overall, yes, I think he's hurting people. But he'll make sure he has support where it counts, and the borderlands are going to be important to him soon."

She tucked her stockinged feet close to her body and took them in her hands, rubbing her thumbs in practiced motions over the scarred soles. "Aren, is Ulric going to be better than Severn?"

He looked down at her. "I hope so. Did he tell you he would be when he spoke to you?"

Patience's eye widened and her lips moved silently as she struggled to choose her words. "I never..." she squeaked. "I didn't talk to him."

Aren's jaw clenched and he squared his shoulders, then closed his eyes briefly as though searching for strength. When they opened again, I couldn't read his expression. A chill crept over me, but I couldn't move.

He stalked toward Patience and crouched in front of her. She looked away. A bird cried outside, but it sounded far off, as though we three occupied an insulated world of our own.

"He told me a lot of things," she whispered, chin trembling.

Aren's brow furrowed. "He does that. It's hard to say no to him, isn't it?"

She sniffled, and met Aren's hard gaze. "He said he needed my help, that no one else could do it, that he was worried about... And that if you found out, you'd..." She inched away, making herself small as she moved. "Please don't hurt me. Please."

"No." He reached out to touch her arm, and she pulled back again. He let her go. "I won't. But I need to know exactly what he said to you, why you're here."

He could have broken her so easily then, pushed into her mind and stolen the memories. The Aren I'd met months before would have done it without a second thought. Instead, he waited and watched her. He knew his father as well as anyone, and knew well how the man might have used this child's pain to win her over.

The chill in his eyes faded.

"I can't tell you," Patience whispered. She wiped a tear from her cheek. "I guess it's all ruined now, anyway. He said if I did good, he'd make sure the people who hurt my family would pay, that once Severn was gone he'd make sure that..." She sobbed and buried her face in her arms.

Aren placed a hand on her shoulder, and this time she let him. "I don't know what it will be like when Severn is gone. But no matter what else happens, I promise that things will be better for you. The people who hurt you and your family will pay for what they did. Nothing can give your people back to you, but I'll make sure my brothers don't get away with this, and that it doesn't happen to anyone else. And that doesn't depend on you doing anything for me, or for my father. I can't fix everything, but I'll do what I can." He patted her back, obviously uncomfortable.

She looked up and met my eyes. "I'm sorry," she whispered, so softly I barely heard. "I just wanted to help."

"Can you tell me now what Ulric said?" he asked.

She shook her head.

"You could show me what happened, if that's easier. Just think hard about it, push it right to the top. But I think Rowan would like to hear, as well." He glanced back at me.

"I would," I said softly.

Patience took a few heavy breaths.

"He said he was worried about you." Her eyes searched mine, then returned to Aren. "Both of you. He thought Rowan was going to leave us when she found her family, and he worried that neither of you would come back if that happened. He said he needed someone reliable, someone with a strong mind who could keep secrets even from you, and he needed that someone to —" She hesitated.

"To what?" Aren asked.

Patience wrinkled her nose. "It sounds silly now. He said he needed this person to make sure you didn't lead Rowan astray in your desire to keep her around. He said he knew of my family, and how we kept ourselves separate from others and hidden. Thought he saw strength in me, and said I'd been overlooked for too long. It felt really good." She chewed her bottom lip and sighed. "I was just supposed to follow you, join you if it seemed safe, and never let on why I had come. And if you decided not to come back at all, I was supposed to get myself back, find them somehow, and make a report. He didn't want me to hurt you or anything."

"So you lied to us?" I asked. Not with anger, but the idea she'd betray a friend so easily didn't sit well with me.

A flush crept into her cheeks, and she looked down to study the scuffed toes of her too-large boots. "He said horrible things about Aren, and it made me frightened for you." She looked back to Aren. "He said if you figured out I was spying, you'd break my mind, take away my memories, and make me think I was living in a nightmare for the rest of my life. I'd heard people talking about you, saying something about that, so I believed him. And I thought that if you would do something like that to me, Rowan must be in danger, too. That she had to be crazy to love you." A few tears leaked out and slipped down her cheeks, and she wiped her nose on her sleeve. "I know it was stupid, but he made it sound so important. Like I might save the whole world just by going on a little adventure."

"Thank you," Aren said. "I think I understand. He's lived a long time, known many people, and figured out how to get them to do what he wants. What you did isn't acceptable. But you know better now." He sat cross-legged on the floor in front of her.

I relaxed. We were going to be fine.

"So you're not going to break me?" she asked.

Aren smiled sadly. "No. Perhaps I should make you think you're a chicken for a few minutes, just to teach you a lesson? If it would make you feel better."

She smiled back, suddenly shy. "No, thank you."

"We're friends," he said. "At least, I hope we can be now. And I wouldn't hurt you."

She swallowed hard and nodded. "I'm glad we are. I didn't like keeping secrets. I thought this would all be exciting, but it was horrible."

How well I knew that feeling.

"I'm glad you're here," Aren said. "I'm not pleased that you lied to us, but you are turning out to be rather useful. Now, tell me more about the Darmish folk you found."

I moved closer, no longer feeling I was interrupting something important. As Patience spoke, Aren reached for my hand. I squeezed his fingers tight.

The hell of it was that he was going to be a fantastic king.

18

AREN

Rowan pulled her hood up over her hair and peered out from the alleyway, squinting against the afternoon sunlight. "I don't see her."

Patience had gone to the inn to see if there were any soldiers about, and had been away longer than we'd expected. "She probably got talking to someone," I said. "You know how friendly she is."

"I know." She stretched up on her toes and leaned farther out.

"Feeling a little impatient?"

She flashed a sheepish grin. "A little. Aren, my family might be in there. I've been so worried. I still am. What if some of them made it out, but not others? What if they're hurt?"

"Patience said the townspeople are taking good care of them, right?"

She took a deep breath. "Right. Do I look okay?"

"You look beautiful. Better than the last time they saw you."

It was true. Even in dirty clothes and a ragged coat, with a smudge of dirt streaking one cheek, she was fascinating. I wondered if noticing such things so regularly made me a shallow person, and decided I didn't care. I loved her for her courage, her curiosity, her compassion. I couldn't help it if her wild red hair and the freckles on her nose captivated me, as well.

I wiped the dirt away with my sleeve.

"Thanks," she said, and went back to watching the inn. "Tell me again about what my mother said to you?"

I thought back to the strange meeting in a town garden in Darmid, trying to remember whether I'd forgotten anything, choosing the words Rowan needed to hear to calm her nerves. "She said she loves you. She said she's sorry for the pain the binding caused you, and that she wanted to tell you the truth before you—" I stopped myself. I couldn't talk about Rowan marrying that monster. "Before. She just never found the right time. She said Ashe missed you, and never gave up hope that you'd come back."

Rowan nodded and chewed on her lower lip. "Thanks. It's too much to hope they're here, isn't it? My father would never come."

I hadn't mentioned the fact that Kel and Cassia had said her father wanted nothing to do with his strange and shameful daughter anymore. It was too hurtful, and until that moment hadn't seemed to matter. *Perhaps the magic hunters' actions have changed his mind...*

"Anything is possible," I said, "but it might be best to keep expectations low."

She took a long, deep breath, and wrinkled her nose as she glanced at a pile of refuse behind us. "I'm trying. So we're sure that Patience is on our side now?"

"Absolutely." I was glad I hadn't followed my training and forced my way into the girl's mind to find answers. She was a victim in this. If she'd lied to us, she'd done it thinking she was helping. Her remorse had been genuine, once she saw that my father had lied about me—or at least, she thought he had.

I still wasn't so sure.

Rowan was watching me. "You okay?"

"Just thinking. See anything?"

"I do now."

Patience strolled casually past the alley, then ducked back in at the last moment.

"Subtle," I noted.

She stuck her tongue out at me. "The soldiers are gone. They left again early this morning."

Rowan arched an eyebrow. "That's all you've got after all that time?"

Parience smirked. "Almost all." She produced an apple from her pocket and handed it over. "People here are pretty nice. But be careful, okay?"

"We will," I told her as Rowan took a bite of the apple and handed the rest to me.

The soldiers may have left, but if the townsfolk were friendly toward Severn they'd be watching for us, too. Perhaps there was no way for us to get in and out unrecognized, especially if we took Rowan's aunt, but we could try to be away before anyone notified the authorities.

"While we're gone, I need you to do one more thing." I handed Patience the few coins I had in my pocket. It wasn't much, but probably more than the girl had ever had for herself, and her jaw dropped. "Hold on to this for me. Buy yourself some more food now. If we don't come back, find Florizel and get help. But this shouldn't take long."

"I'll meet you back at the barn later." She darted out of the alley at the far end, tucking the coins in her pocket as she went.

I took the heavy pack off my back and stowed it behind a dirty wooden crate, hoping we'd have a chance to come back for it. It would be too much trouble to carry with us now, especially if we needed to fight our way out. "Ready?"

"As close as I'm going to get." Rowan closed her eyes. "Why am I so nervous? They'll be happy to see me, right?"

"Absolutely." My voice held more confidence than I felt.

She grinned. "Let's go."

I pulled up my hood to shadow my face, and we moved into the street. A few people glanced our way, but most were too busy to take real notice of strangers. They probably saw enough of those around there that it wasn't remarkable. We passed by the front door of the red-brick inn and made our way to the back, where willow trees shadowed several wooden doors and curtained windows.

Voices drifted to us from around the side of the building, coming closer. Rowan glanced back over her shoulder as she tried the handle on the closest door. Locked. We hurried farther along the wall, and found the next one open. We stepped in without looking at where we were going, and I closed the door behind us.

A short hallway led to a sharp turn to the left. Down that way we found more doors, and dim lamps lighting the space between them.

"Any ideas?" I asked. I tried to sense whether a trap might be waiting, but all I got from behind the closed doors were muffled voices and a sense that there were people around. Nothing we didn't already know.

She turned and knocked at the door next to us, then glanced up at me. "Better than asking the staff, right?"

"Certainly." She could handle the talking. I'd step in with a different approach if things got out of hand.

A little boy opened the door, watched by a brown-haired woman standing behind him. The boy looked us over, then stepped back to hide behind the woman's skirts.

"Hello," Rowan said, and gave them a friendly smile. "I'm looking for someone, and wondered if you might help." She seemed about to say something else, but stopped and leaned back.

The woman's head tilted slightly to one side. "Have we met?"

Rowan quickly recovered her composure. "I don't think so. Are there many here with you from Lowdell?"

A familiar face, then. No wonder she'd been flustered if this woman might have recognized her.

"No. Just a few came after the... Well, you know. The messiness." She reached behind her and pried the boy's hands from her skirt, then motioned for him to go away. He stepped back, stuck a thumb in his mouth, and watched us with solemn eyes.

"I'm looking for the Greenwood family," Rowan said. "Are they here?"

The woman didn't catch the slight tremble in Rowan's voice that betrayed how important this was to her. Her already narrow lips tightened. "Can't say they are. Don't imagine most of us would so much as have broken bread with them if they did come."

"Thank you." Rowan hid her disappointment only a little better than she had her excitement. "Horrible about that business, isn't it?"

The woman tucked her hair behind one ear and rested a hand on her jutted-out hip. "Unbelievable. First the mess with the girl, and then we got news about some trouble in Ardare. Magic hunters died."

"I heard. And then in town..." Rowan shook her head as though in disbelief, leaving the air open for the eager woman to fill it with her words. I tried not to smile even as I appreciated her developing ability to manipulate a person without magic, letting the woman's obvious inclinations and assumptions carry things forward.

"Oh, my. That was just the worst thing." The woman had obviously switched to gossip mode. She leaned in closer, then shooed the child away. "The hunters took my husband. We all swore up and down that he never had nothing to do with magic, but you couldn't tell them that." I opened my mind to this excessively forthcoming woman and found that she didn't much care in theory about losing her layabout husband, but seeing him dragged away had shaken her badly.

She didn't notice my intrusion, and I closed myself to her. The private thoughts streaming behind her words weren't mine to see. "Folks said that if he was convicted they'd be back for the children," she continued, "so we lit out as soon as we could. Same story as everyone here, I suppose." Her lips tightened. "None of them would've paid any attention to Lowdell if not for those Greenwoods. So no, I don't know where they are. I suppose they either left town or the hunters took them." Rowan's brow creased at that, but the woman was too wrapped up in her own words to notice. "I'd say they didn't find help from anyone I know."

"Thank you, ma'am. I hope your husband gets out safely."

The woman leaned out into the hallway as we retreated. "You sure I don't know you?"

Rowan smiled sadly back at her. "Sorry. You must be thinking of someone else."

We exited through the same door as we'd entered by. There would be little point in asking around further. When we were sure there were no people about, Rowan sat on the grass under one of the willows.

"That was Mrs. Dasmel," she said. "She used to come into the library when I was working. She didn't even recognize me. She looked right at me, we were talking *about* me... and nothing."

"That's good, if she's angry with your family."

Rowan looked up, dazed. "I know. It's strange, though. Like the person I used to be doesn't exist anymore."

I held out a hand and pulled her to her feet. "She exists. I knew her. She's still there, under the magic and the new experiences."

"And the new hair color."

I ran a thumb over the arch of one of her dark eyebrows, which only did a mostly decent job of hiding the wild red shade. "That, too. Are you all right?"

"Other than the fact that I'm now convinced my family is in danger? Sure. But we can talk about that at the barn. We should get out of here."

We picked up the pack and headed out of town, taking a circuitous route through the fields, approaching the barn from the rear.

"Guys!" Patience popped up from the long grass well away from the farm, waved us over, and disappeared. She was gone when we reached the spot where she'd been, but it was easy to follow her dark clothing through the mix of dead yellow and new green grasses, over a hillock to an open field populated by a few sheep and a massive, dead tree.

"There are people working in the yard," she explained.

"Thanks, Patience." I would have sensed them before we entered, but this was better. No one had seen us, or at least they weren't following yet.

"So what now?" she asked. "Where's your aunt?"

Rowan appeared lost. "I don't know. And I don't know. I guess we go back empty-handed. Or you two do." She squared her shoulders and looked toward the mountains. "I can't just leave them now. If they got away, I think I know where they are. But you two should go back before the group gets too far ahead. I'll be fine."

Her announcement didn't surprise me. I'd have been shocked if she hadn't insisted on going. "Will you take Florizel?" I asked.

Rowan raised her eyebrows. She'd probably expected me to tell her to stay with us. To stay safe. "Flying will be faster, if she agrees to come with me."

"It will. For both of us."

Rowan's eyes widened. "You don't have to come. It's better for you if you don't."

"I know." My instincts rioted against the idea of going with her, as did a deep sense of family loyalty bred deep into my bones no matter how hard I fought against it. Going back, supporting my father, and doing what was best for Tyrea was absolutely the right thing to do.

But I couldn't let her go alone. Not this time. Maybe my father was right, and there had never been any chance of us being together. We'd been racing against a ticking clock since the moment we met, whether the threat was from Severn, her countrymen, or my destiny. But time hadn't run out yet, and I wasn't done fighting.

I turned to Patience. "What story did you give the people when you came to town this morning?"

"I said my family lived in the foothills of the mountains, and they died over the winter from a bad sickness. Just made my way down and came to the first town I found."

"And you think they believed you?"

"Sure. I'm believable, if not as adorable as I used to be. The farmer lady I talked to here was really sweet. Gave me pie." Her shoulders drooped. "You want me to stay with them, don't you?"

I crouched to speak to her face to face. "We'll come back for you. Darmid is far more dangerous than this place is. Rowan and I can get in and out more easily if we can both fly, and it'll be too hard on Florizel to carry you over the mountains. If you're careful not to expose yourself, you could get more information here. See whether any of these people have useful magic, find out what else Severn has been up to."

The girl nodded, though my words didn't seem to comfort her any. "Be careful. And don't take too long. Our people are going to get to Luid soon, and your father needs you."

Interesting. "Did he say that?"

She shook her head and hoisted her pack onto her back. "He just seemed pretty concerned about you not coming back."

Patience shook our hands, then made her way slowly toward the white farmhouse.

"You don't have to do this," Rowan said to me. She turned to walk away from town, back toward where we'd left Florizel. "I don't know how long it will take, and your father does need you. You can't worry about my family when your entire country's future is in danger. Not to mention yours, personally."

I hid my surprise. I wasn't accustomed to her pushing me away. "I'm not worried about your family, but I am about you. I won't be able to focus on anything else if I don't know where you are or whether you're coming back. And don't forget how important your aunt could be to Ulric's recovery. Let's go, try to find out what happened to them, and then decide what we're going to do. Once we're back in Tyrea, I can fly ahead if need be and meet up with my father."

She gave me a relieved smile. "How long do we have?"

"A week at least before they get near Luid."

"Then what happens?"

"I wish I knew. I don't understand anything my father is doing anymore."

We found Florizel grazing by a pond. She trotted toward us, ears pricked forward. "What is it? Where's the girl? What's happening?"

"She's fine," Rowan said. "We've had a change of plans. My family's not here, and I'm going back over the border to find them. You don't have to come, but I would certainly appreciate it if you did."

Florizel lowered her head and thought for several minutes. "Are we going to the city again? I didn't care for that at all."

"No," Rowan said, and smiled kindly. "No cities. Just an old house in the country. If they're not there, we'll come right back. Does that sound like something you could do?"

The horse nodded.

"So on to Stone Ridge?" I asked, and undressed.

Rowan turned around so I could put my things in her pack, but watched me over her shoulder. "It's the most logical place to look. If they're not there, we're not going farther. We'll never get out alive if we get in too deep." She settled the straps more comfortably on her shoulders and twisted her hair into a knot behind her neck. "How long do you expect it will take to get there?"

"We could camp near the mountains tonight and go over tomorrow. We'd reach Stone Ridge the next day, easily."

She turned and wrapped her arms around my neck. "Thank you."

I kissed her, then transformed before my body could get any other ideas that might stall our departure. I took off and circled until Rowan had mounted Florizel. Their take-off was smooth this time, Florizel's wing-beats strong and sure with only her single, familiar passenger. Rowan squeezed her eyes closed as they climbed, but this time she was smiling.

19

NOX

P rogress along the road was slow, at best. Far from the hard-marching army that Ulric might have wished for, we were a large and motley band of men, women, and children, and not all in good health. The group could only move at the pace of its slowest members, and even when we stuck those on horses, our movement could best be described as glacial. But Ulric seemed to think he still needed them. People to prove his identity, to spread the word of his return. Perhaps he hoped to avoid challenging Severn. As long as he still had time to take the throne back by law, I supposed it wasn't the worst plan.

But gods, was it painfully slow.

We would never have made it as far as we did without Mama Bunn. She insisted on having access to her potions and her equipment in the evening when we stopped, and went straight to work. Kel kept busy with the tasks Ulric gave him, and Mama pushed me hard as travel-weary folk showed up at her tent.

Keeping on top of her demands and my own work for Ulric exhausted me quickly after a long day of walking. The first night on the road, I'd closed my eyes for just a moment in her tent— and opened them as the sun rose. We'd packed up quickly the next day, and when we stopped for the evening Mama hurried off to tend to people while Kel and I set up her things again.

I had already learned much from Mama Bunn, though nothing I could apply to my own assignment. The woman worked true miracles in potions and more practical matters. She'd been quite serious about stretching the stew. She enlisted a group of energetic children to collect bulbous catweed roots along the way and bash them to mush, then combined that with what meat the hunters brought in to feed the community. Her potions kept the ill on their feet, and her treatments kept minor injuries from becoming infected. She strengthened the elderly and built up the weak, and beneath her intimidating exterior, her love for her people shone through.

As for me, I assisted, I watched, and I learned—and while my teacher was off ministering to the worthy folk she loved, I skulked about her tent and tried to concoct something that would heal a powerful man whom I hated. Though her work was harder than mine, I envied Mama Bunn. I longed to work more directly on a cause close to my heart. True, curing Ulric's condition would get Severn off the throne. But still, it wasn't enough to satisfy me.

Mama Bunn entered the tent just after supper. "Everything set up?"

I glanced up from the notes I'd scribbled the night before. "Hmm? Oh, yes. I was thinking about foraging tonight. We're getting low on supplies." I also hoped I might find something new that would inspire me. I wasn't making much progress with what we had.

She sighed and sank into her chair, the first thing we'd unloaded. "We won't have a chance to prepare most of it properly until we stop."

"Might as well gather when we can, though. There's no telling what we're passing by out there."

"What are you working on?"

"Oh, nothing."

She closed her eyes. "Coming up with something for your mer friend?"

"Yes." I wasn't. I should have been. We'd run out of the ingredients for that nasty drink, and had no way of collecting more until we passed a lake with healthy plant life in it. If we found that, Kel's problem would be fixed without potions. I might have been able to create an alternative, had I not been under so much pressure to work on Ulric's problem.

I told myself that as soon as I came up with something for Ulric, I would be free to help Kel. It felt like that was the only thing that kept me from giving up entirely. No matter how many angles I looked at Ulric's problem from, no matter how late I stayed up working it out in my mind, I simply didn't have what I needed to even get a sense of how to move toward finding a cure.

Mama shuffled her feet around to rest them on a box. "Oh, that's good."

"Is there anything I can do for you?" I hesitated to ask, in case she wanted me to rub her feet. None of us had bathed in far too long for that to be an appealing prospect.

"No. Rest time is already over. That Rhina girl needs me to check to see if the baby's coming early, and I have to try to keep him in there if he is. I just wanted peace for a moment." She pushed herself up and hobbled to the table we'd made from crates and a wooden board. She reached for a thick sheep-oil base and several floral ingredients. "Where's the wortweed?"

I found the bottle and passed it to her. "I can do that for you, if you tell me what you're aiming for."

"I don't think you can." She smiled secretively. She hummed as she worked, moving a dollop of oil to her bowl, adding this and that, seemingly at random. The sound didn't match her appearance, or even her speech. Usually rough and earthy, her voice took on an ethereal tone when she focused on her work.

I watched over her shoulder. The powdered rose-thorns should have reacted with the wortweed to turn the whole thing green and lumpy, but under Mama's experienced hands the mixture remained smooth and cream-colored, glowing slightly.

I found myself mesmerized by her skill, and stepped closer without thought. She was right. I knew absolutely nothing about this art.

She tapped her knife on the edge of the bowl. "Give it a test."

I used the knife to smear a touch of the stuff on the back of my hand. The skin tightened, pulling my fingers straight and stiff. I gasped and shook the creeping numbness out of my fingers.

Mama Bunn chuckled. "That won't last long. Just let it dry out and it'll become less potent. Should do for my purposes, though."

When I looked back at the bowl, the potion had stopped glowing, but retained its beautiful color.

"Mama, how did you do that? I never would have expected that reaction."

She winked. "Haven't you figured out the oak riddle yet?"

"No." And suddenly, I had. A chill raced over my back and stood my hair on end. "Your humming. You're changing the reactions somehow. Controlling them."

"Just influencing them. Using my intentions to gently convince my ingredients to behave themselves." The wrinkles around her eyes deepened as she looked over the array of jars and bottles on the table. "This is what you still need to learn, Nox, and what few Potioners ever do. There are natural reactions, and you have a good sense for those. You can predict with great accuracy what will happen with ingredients, even unfamiliar ones."

I stiffened, sensing the *but* that had to be coming. "I believe I can."

"But what many don't know, and what most Sorcerers won't acknowledge, is that we don't only facilitate natural reactions. We, the greatest Potioners, can influence as well."

My mouth went dry. "That's not how our magic works."

"Tell that to miss Rhina when I put this up her womanly bits and start humming." She cackled. "It won't hurt, but by the gods, she'll feel it. The baby might, too, and he'll give her a restless night. Clean up here, will you?"

I nodded, struck dumb. But before she left the tent, I found my voice. "Mama, are you sure it's a boy? Rhina was calling it a girl when she visited yesterday. Said she wants another one."

Mama Bunn smiled. "It's a boy, and a little magic in him. I get a feeling about these things. I'm never wrong."

I filled the big washbasin and added soap, then lit the fire underneath. Though we'd managed to refill our supplies at a few small streams and to collect large amounts of the dew that had been notably absent back at camp, the continuing lack of a solid rainfall meant no one was allowed to use our drinking water freely. Still, Mama Bunn's services were essential, and this equipment needed to be washed even when everyone was slurping stew off of bark plates to save on dish-washing.

I swished my hands through the cool water and relaxed slightly. Water alone was good for so many ills. *And for some more than others.*

I left the water behind and went out to find Kel. I didn't have to go far. He sat outside of the tent with our bedroll spread out next to him.

"Are we sleeping under the stars tonight?" I asked.

"I don't know. Do you plan on sleeping at all?" The strain around his eyes and the edge in his voice caught me off-guard.

"I'm sorry. I thought I had a good idea about Ulric last night. It didn't work out, but Mama just told me something that might, if I can make it work. But right now, I have something just for you." I reached for his hands and pulled him to his feet, and he followed me obediently into the tent.

He grimaced. "Is it another potion? I'm not sure I can take that."

"No. Look." I led him to the basin and placed his hands in the water. He drew in a long, deep breath and swished his hands around as a smile touched his lips.

"You want me to do the dishes?" he asked. "How alluring."

I unbuttoned his shirt and pulled it off his broad shoulders. "Let the dishes wait. You're more important." I offered him a dry sponge and stepped back.

"You're not going to help?"

I laughed. "You're on your own, friend. I don't need more trouble than we'll already have if Mama comes back."

He dipped the sponge in the water and rubbed over his shoulders, sending thick streams over the hills and valleys of his chest and arms that dripped to the floor. It reminded me of the night he'd revealed his true nature to me, the way I'd felt seeing his mer form for the first time.

I shivered in spite of the warmth that radiated through me.

"You sure this is okay?" he asked, even as he continued to spread water over his skin like it might drink the precious liquid in. "I don't want to waste it."

"I don't think anyone will notice if we use a little extra, just this once. Get yourself clean. It might make you feel more like yourself." I took a step toward him without meaning to. "I'll keep watch outside."

He grinned over his shoulder as he unlaced his pants. "You sure you don't want to stay and help?"

I took in the sight of his warm brown skin, and wanted nothing more than to give him a hand. Both of them. Instead I took a backward step toward the door. "I can't."

He turned back to the basin and dunked his head into the water.

I re-directed a few people who came by looking for Mama Bunn, and a few minutes later, Kel whistled from inside the tent.

"Didn't think I should go out with wet hair," he said.

I moved closer and inhaled. "They're going to be jealous when they smell you. I am."

"What's stopping you? There's water left. Too hot for my liking now, but you could use it."

I hesitated, then placed my hands back in the water. Warm. Soapy. Perfect. I peeked back at Kel and watched him slip back into his shirt, which clung to his still-damp skin. I'd been spending far too much energy lately resisting that temptation. I had no will power left to spend on resisting a stupid bath.

"I'm going to wash now," I said.

"Good." He made no move to leave, and grinned at what must have been my obvious discomfort. "Come on. You saw me naked when we barely even knew each other."

"That was different! You had a tail. I couldn't see your man stuff."

His grin widened. "I don't have to look."

My cheeks flushed. "You can look. Just control yourself, mister."

I turned away and pulled my shirts over my head, then untied my pants and let them fall to the floor. Kel took a sharp breath behind me, but I didn't turn. Instead I closed my eyes and enjoyed the feeling of bubbles on my skin, washing away a week's worth of stale sweat and dirt. I didn't wash my hair, but made sure everything else got a thorough cleaning. When I was done, I felt renewed. The ground under my feet was dark with the water that had dripped down my legs, but that evidence would disappear soon enough. I dumped out what was left in the basin and re-filled it, then dropped the dishes in to soak while the water heated up again.

Kel sat in Mama Bunn's chair and watched me put my dirty clothes back on. "You are the most beautiful thing I've ever seen," he said.

I almost laughed at the awestruck sincerity in his voice. "I find that hard to believe, considering where you come from. I've seen your sister. I've heard that all merfolk are like you two."

"Perfection is overrated."

I went to him and placed a kiss on his forehead. "Do you feel better?"

"In some ways." His hand on the back of my neck pulled my face lower, and he pressed his warm lips to mine. Though his motions were gentle, he was obviously struggling to keep them that way. "Don't work tonight. We can sneak away from camp, just the two of us."

I placed a hand on his shoulder to keep myself from collapsing into him. "Kel, I can't."

"Why?" Even as we spoke, his lips caressed mine, then continued the trail of kisses down my neck. I gripped his shirt tight in my fist, and he paused. "Is it because I'm not human?"

"No. Kel, it's not that I don't want you." A flash of heat climbed through my torso, my body's agreement with that statement. "It's just that everything is so complicated. I was talking to Cassia about how things are with merfolk. About how for you, love is a forever thing in a way it's not for humans."

He nodded. "I do love you. I thought humans considered this a part of—"

"We do. And that's the problem." I pulled away, and he released his hold on me. I tried to pull my thoughts together, forcing myself to face things head-on. "This would be a big step for me, even without you being who you are. Cassia explained that this could go quite a bit deeper than I'd be risking with a human, emotionally speaking."

He let out a long breath. "I'm glad she said it before I had to. I don't know whether it would. Does it get deeper than this? It seems impossible."

I looked away from the intensity of his gaze. "I don't know. I feel like I'm hanging by my fingertips on the edge of a bottomless chasm. I'm afraid. Before you, I only had my husband, and a few other clumsy encounters before him. None of that ended well at all, and rarely meant anything. I know this is more important than any of that, and will be so much better, that *you* are so much better..." *Goddess and gods, am I going to cry?* "I don't know why I'm afraid of something so good except that maybe I do believe that we could have that forever kind of love, and it feels like this—" I gestured between our bodies. "Like this really would seal some kind of contract between us."

He leaned back in the chair. "I know. It's an exciting thought, and I'd be lying if I said it wasn't terrifying. But I still want to find out." He stood to leave, and smiled down at me. "I'm ready whenever you are." He brushed his lips against my forehead and walked slowly away.

"Kel?"

He turned back. "Yeah?"

"We have time to work this out. When we reach Luid, we'll stay back." I took a moment to think, to finalize my decision. "I'm not going into the city. Not going after Severn. Someone else will take care of him."

The smile that broke over his face covered any lingering hint of exhaustion. "So you've chosen?"

I grinned back, and felt the armor I'd spent years building crack. I'd start letting people see beneath it. Start opening myself as Mama Bunn did. Start caring and being a part of the world again.

"I have. And I want you. We'll get there."

Mama Bunn shuffled back into the tent and dunked her wrinkled hands in the dishwater. "Where are you going?"

"Nowhere, Mama," I said as Kel winked and ducked out. "Nowhere at all."

20

ROWAN

Flying made everything easier. A quick flight into the sunset, a night of rest, and then we were on our way again over a broad and wild section of mountains too remote to be populated or guarded by humans. Florizel had no trouble soaring so high with only one human on board, though she faltered a little as the air became thin, and we stopped to rest once on the way up. When I looked back, Tyrea stretched out below us, bright and beautiful.

By midday we'd reached the western downslope. The forest spread out wild and untouched below us, a green blanket cut through by a silver river flowing into Darmid. We dropped low over the trees, so close that Florizel could have reached out and brushed her hooves over the tops. I sat up a little and enjoyed the air flowing over my skin and through my hair. It had been a little hard to breathe at the top, but now—

Aren shrieked. I turned just in time to see him flying straight at me, hard and fast. I ducked as he passed so close that a few strands of my hair tangled around his outstretched talons. An answering scream echoed over the forest, and I turned to see a dark-brown gryphon, nearly as large as Florizel, streaking toward us.

Florizel glanced back, and the whites of her eyes appeared. I leaned in closer to her neck and held on tight as she beat her wings harder, pulling away. I should have held still, but couldn't help looking back when another piercing cry cut through the air. Aren and the gryphon rolled, locked together, but I couldn't tell who was holding whom. The gryphon was far larger, and equipped with a sharp eagle's beak and fore-talons, with a mountain lion's claws at the back. All four of those limbs scrambled to grab at the lighter brown form attacking its face. Aren broke away, but the gryphon followed.

I lost sight of them as Florizel found an open patch of forest and landed, pulling up short on her stop so as not to run straight into the river.

"We have to go back!" I cried. "We have to help!"

"How?" she asked. "That was a gryphon. You don't run to them. You flee, if you live long enough to be able to." Her sides heaved beneath me, and I slipped off her back. Her body was slick with sweat now, panic evident in every twitching muscle.

"You came into the city to get me before," I said. "You were so brave."

She snorted. "I did what I had to, and it was horrid. I can't again. Please, Rowan."

I gave her a quick pat on the neck. "Rest here. I'll come back."

"You won't!" she whinnied, but I was already running back up the slope beside the river, struggling to listen for Aren over the sounds of my pounding heart and gasping breath. I had no idea what I was going to do to help, but I couldn't let him fight alone.

I didn't dare call out in case there were more of them around. My steps slowed, and I caught my breath. *I should have left the bag,* I thought. It was too heavy, but I knew I might need its contents. I pulled it higher on my shoulders and walked on, though the sudden exertion had made me light-headed.

I picked up a few decent-sized rocks from beside the river and carried them with me. A cliff loomed to my right. As I passed into its shadows an eagle shrieked, and I ran toward the noise. Aren, still in his familiar avian form, lay chest-down on the rocks. A few paces away the gryphon crouched on the ground, head held low at an awkward angle, gaze fixed on Aren.

"No!" I yelled. The beast didn't change its position. I threw one of the rocks. It bounced off the gryphon's feathered skull with a dull thunk, but still the creature didn't move.

I stepped closer. Its eyes were closed under the heavy feathers, and its massive talons curved uselessly beneath it. The animal I'd so heroically attacked was already dead.

Aren let out a softer noise, calling for my attention. His left wing stretched out over the rocks, dripping blood. He stood and shuffled forward, head held high, apparently uninjured otherwise.

"Well, this looks familiar," I observed.

He snapped his beak at me.

I set my bag on the ground and pulled out the few bandages I'd brought, and Nox's ointment. "Can you transform without making it worse?"

A moment later it was done, and he sat beside the river in human form with blood streaming down his arm from a row of three gashes that cut deep into the muscle. I tossed him his pants, and he sat next to the river while I examined the injury. "Not far off the last one," I said. "Deeper, but no bones broken this time." The scar from that injury was long gone, but I remembered it well.

"I do aim for consistency."

I studied the wounds, remembering. "I could try it again," I said. "Maybe healing isn't a natural skill, but if I've done it before, I might be able to pick it up."

"All right," he said, but he tensed. "Not too much, though. Remember the last time."

We'd tried it during our time at the school, after I lost that ability. He'd come out of the experience badly burned. A complete failure on my part.

"Maybe I shouldn't," I said. "It was a silly idea."

"No." He took my hand and placed it on his arm just below the wounds. "Nothing is going to get better if you don't try. We're going to work together, remember? Consider it part of our practice."

"We'll need to be careful about the magic in this country," I reminded him. Even if I weren't having trouble replenishing mine, we'd both be in danger of running out once we reached the inhabited parts of Darmid, where the magic hunters had done their destructive work.

I closed my eyes and remembered how my magic had flowed out of me through a weakness in the binding, performing healings I'd never have thought possible at the time. The way it seemed to be pulled from me, the rush of it leaving. My magic stirred at the memory.

"Rowan, stop."

I looked, and pulled my hand away from the frosted-over skin of his arm.

"Did it get any better?" I asked, already knowing the answer. Blood coursed from the slashes in his skin, worse than before.

"No. But at least you didn't burn me."

I hid my disappointment by turning to reach for the bag and Nox's potion. "I liked the idea of being a healer," I said, surprised by how hurt I sounded. As though my magic had betrayed me. "I didn't want to hurt people."

"I know. The gift suited you, and would have been useful. That doesn't take anything away from what you can do. Perhaps you should look at the lives you've saved rather than the ones you've taken." He winced as I spread the slimy pink goo over the cuts.

"You're right. I know." I popped the lid back on the jar and set it down so I could wrap bandages tight around the ugly wounds, holding them closed until his magic could knit the flesh back together. I tucked the end of the cloth strip under the bulk to hold it in place, then sat down hard, suddenly light-headed. I'd tried to joke earlier to lighten the mood, to turn away from the horror we'd so narrowly avoided, but it took my breath as it finally came crashing in.

"I thought that was the end for you when that thing attacked," I said.

"Me, too." He rubbed the gooseflesh from his arms. "I think it was more luck than skill that saved me that time. I blinded him, and he broke his neck when I pulled him down. I've never fought anything like that alone, or as an eagle."

I closed my eyes and leaned against him. There didn't seem to be anything else to say about it. Promises to be careful were well and fine, but we both knew he'd risk his life for me again if he had to, as I would for him.

"Thanks for coming back for me. That was an impressive throw." He nodded toward the dead gryphon and the smooth river rock lying amongst the jagged stones at the bottom of the cliff.

I snorted. "It would have been a lot more impressive if you hadn't already killed him."

"You didn't know that." He pulled his socks and boots on, then his shirt. I stood and offered a hand to help him up. "Where's Florizel?"

"Here." Her voice drifted up from the forest downhill. "I came. I was afraid, but I thought you might need to escape." She stepped into view, looked at the gryphon, and shuffled sideways to get farther from it. "I see that everything is under control."

Aren stepped closer to the gryphon. "I wonder what these taste like. Probably not great, but we don't have many options at the moment."

Rocks shifted and clinked under Florizel's hooves as she backed away. "You don't want to do that. Bigger and worse things will be along soon to take care of the body. We don't want to be in their way when they come."

"We have to eat. Rowan, do you have a knife?"

A few minutes later we had chunks of bloody meat wrapped in large leaves. Aren carried those, and I took the pack. Florizel led the way downstream, and none of us spoke until she slowed her pace late in the afternoon.

"That's better," she said. She lifted her nose to sniff the air. "We can stop now, if you want. I know I'm feeling a little worn out."

We made camp on the banks of the river, in a sheltered spot where we could build a fire on the rocky ground without setting the entire forest ablaze. Florizel went deeper into the woods to find her meal—and, I suspected, to get away from the smell of ours as it cooked.

"Is it strange that I'm sort of enjoying this?" Aren asked.

"Definitely strange," I replied, "but I know what you mean. Not that being attacked by wild animals is fun, and neither is everything we have to go back to. But this, being together, traveling again."

He smiled contentedly. "And actually liking each other this time. It's nice."

Darkness enclosed the world around us, but the fire burned bright and warm. Half of the meat separated and fell into the fire when it was cooked through, but I speared it on a stick and took that part for myself. The outside had burned black in spots, but it smelled fine, and the meat looked palatable.

Aren bit into his and grimaced.

"Is it that good?"

"It's simply delicious," he mumbled.

The flavor was unlike any meat I'd tried before, tart and overpowering. Still, once I'd forced the first bite down, the rest followed easily enough. "I won't be recommending it to anyone," I said after it was gone, "but it did its job."

"Assuming it stays down."

I lay beside the fire, full and sleepy. "What'll we do now? I assume you can't fly with your arm injured. I mean, wing."

"Not yet. We're going to have to—"

Something crashed through the trees, and Florizel screamed. Aren and I jumped to our feet as she burst out from the forest.

"Run!" she yelled.

We left the fire, abandoned our things, and took off.

The river curved left ahead of us, and we followed it. As we rounded the corner, we slid to a stop together. The river banks widened there, but not one of us wanted to risk passing the dragon.

The thing wasn't huge by dragon standards, at least in my experience, but was larger than Florizel and could have killed any one of us with a single bite, or knocked us flat with a lash of its serpentine tail. Moonlight glinted off its whitish scales as it lowered its horned head and bared its dagger-sharp teeth.

The dragon peeped.

Aren and I looked at each other. "It's a baby," he said, voice calm and quiet.

"Does that help us?"

"Not at all. You're not going to be able to reason with this one. Back away slowly. I'll try to grab its attention and run."

The dragon lurched forward, then paused and peeped again.

"Peep?" A low, inhuman voice behind us asked. I didn't dare turn my back on the dragonling, but a chill ran up my back. "No. Like this." The voice growled, and the growl became a roar that made a nearby tree shed several leaves.

I winced, and Florizel let out a weak whinny of terror.

The baby dragon tilted its head until it was on completely sideways and let out a high-pitched whistle, then planted its scaled butt in the water.

I glanced back to see a massive form straddling the river behind us. She looked even larger outdoors than she had the first time we'd met, and she'd been more than imposing then. Standing, the arch of her blood-red back rose higher than some of the trees next to the river. Forefeet with fingers nearly as long as I was tall settled into the riverside stones as she stepped forward, and her massive head swung low to sniff at me.

"Good evening, Ruby," I said, and was surprised by how calm I sounded.

"Human girl." If I wasn't mistaken, there was a hint of a smile in her voice. "Fancy meeting you here. Again."

"We weren't looking for you," Aren said. "Again."

"And yet here we are."

Aren looked back at the baby dragon. "They've grown, just in the past few weeks. Quite remarkable."

Ruby shrugged, a gesture that flowed from her shoulders to her tail. "We don't waste time. They've eaten well, and my cave was well-stocked with treasure. They were nearly ready to grow the first time you saw them, and now they have. It's not complicated."

"You did say they'd be out on their own in a few weeks," Aren replied. "I just didn't think they'd be so... impressive."

Florizel whinnied as the dragonling crouched, eyes fixed on her. Ruby raised her head. "Enough," she said. "Leave it." The dragonling continued to advance, and Ruby let out a warning growl. That got its attention. The smaller dragon stepped back.

"You can't talk to them at this age," Ruby sighed. "I do try. At least she listens better than her brother."

Florizel's head whipped around to search the dark for another dragon.

Ruby chuckled, a rumbling sound like an avalanche. "He's gone," she said. "You only have the two of us to contend with right now. This one listens better, but her brother was the more accomplished hunter. He left us several days ago." Ruby stretched, digging her claws into the stone-strewn river banks as though they were made of garden soil, arching her sinuous back toward the stars. "This one's smarter, too. She recognized you, human prince. Lucky thing she's more curious than hungry."

"Lucky, indeed," Aren said, sounding uncomfortable. "If it's food you're looking for, we left a dead gryphon upstream a ways."

Ruby's long nose wrinkled. "I know. She smelled blood and I let her track it this far, but I don't think she'll be pleased with what she finds. If she wants to be a scavenger, though, she'll have to learn to take what comes." She turned her eyes on Florizel. "I prefer fresh meat."

"Not this one, please," Aren said. "She's a friend."

Ruby snorted her disappointment. "I guessed as much."

"We left a fire burning," I said. "I don't suppose you'd let us go back to it?"

"Oh, of course. Let's do that."

I couldn't say no if she wanted to join us. We were lucky we weren't a meal yet. I led the way, with Aren and Florizel walking behind and Ruby after them, just close enough to make us all uncomfortable. The dragonling trailed behind her, making a racket as she bounced over the shore and kicked rocks into the water.

"Can't imagine why she's a poor hunter," Aren said quietly.

Ruby growled. "I heard that."

When we reached the fire the dragonling continued on, sniffing the air and the ground.

"Go," Ruby called, and waved toward the cliffs. "Find your prize."

Her child darted upstream.

Ruby made herself comfortable on the rocks. The firelight flickered off the glow of her red scales, a mesmerizing sight. Her appearance was as horrible and as beautiful as I remembered, and now that my fear had abated somewhat, I was able to appreciate it. It wouldn't do to get too comfortable, but perhaps I could be one of few people to ever truly enjoy the company of a dragon.

Yes, before she decides to eat you.

"You're far from home," Aren observed.

"Home no longer," she said, "though I intend to return for my treasure some day. It's mostly gold now that the young have devoured the best of it, but still. I'd hate to see it fall into someone else's claws."

"Or hands," I added, remembering that it was cursed. I'd done more reading on that subject in the school library at Belleisle, and had become even more glad that I hadn't taken any for myself when Ruby offered. It would have turned me into the worst version of myself. I didn't wish to consider where that might have led.

Ruby grinned. "I wonder how that would have worked out for you."

"Me, too," I admitted. "Not that I want to see. I just wonder what it would look like."

"If I may say," Aren said, "you seem more contented than last time we met, Ruby."

"Hmm. I feel better, too. Since we left the cave behind, I've felt more alive. I thought I belonged there with my young and my treasure. That's all a dragon should want. That and fresh meat once in a while, and I'd filled up on that before the wee ones hatched. That cave served me well on previous clutches, and I was confused as to why I felt discontented this time. It became a little better once I was in the open air and able to stretch my wings. And then the hunters came and killed one of my young, and I felt despair. I hated it, and I hid away." She glared at me. "What?"

I realized I wore an expression of something between amazement and confusion, and tried to smooth it away. "I just... You've never spoken this much to us. Been so open..." I struggled to find something to say that wouldn't anger her. "It's nice."

She inched her face closer to the flames and let her eyes fall half-closed. "I'm changing as I age, and I don't care for it. I was happier when I was younger, when I didn't have so many thoughts and words in my mind, when I knew nothing but hunger, rage, greed, pain in my muscles after a mating or a fight. Or both. The great pleasures of life."

She seemed to expect an answer to this. "All wonderful things for a dragon, I'm sure," I said.

Her scaly lips pulled into a smile. "Don't pretend you don't know those urges, little human. In any case, life was simpler when that's all there was. But now I think about things that have nothing to do with survival. I have questions, I want to share my thoughts, be a part of the world. This is pleasant, what we're doing now, but it's shameful to me as a dragon." Her wings rustled. "I need to accept it, or do the right thing and put an end to my life. I haven't decided yet. Now, girl. Your prince told me more of your story, but he did a terrible job of it. It's your turn. Tell me what happened after you left me last time, up until when we just met by the river."

I couldn't say no, even though conversation was the last thing my tired brain needed. I'd made a promise when she let us go that first time. I tried to keep my eyes open and my yawns in check, and to make things as interesting as I could.

Ruby rested her chin on the ground and relaxed, but kept her green eyes on me as I spoke. They crinkled in the corners when she caught me glossing over details I wasn't comfortable discussing in front of Aren, but she didn't interrupt me or demand more. I thought Aren would fall asleep, but at the end of the story he was as awake and attentive as Ruby.

"Better," the dragon said. "Much better, thank you. This was quite entertaining, and clears up a few things I've wondered about humans. This love situation in particular is strange and fascinating."

Aren smiled. "I probably did a bad job of conveying certain aspects of the experience."

"You tried," Ruby said, and let out a hot breath. "Listen to me, offering reassurances. I'm a sad shadow of a dragon."

"At least you're not asking for them yet," Aren offered. "So what happens now? You have your story, and to your satisfaction, but I'm not sure we're done with it yet. If you'd consent to once again not eating us..."

Ruby turned her gaze on him without moving her head. "I think we can dispense with that pretense now. We all know I'm not going to eat you."

Florizel lifted her head. "I didn't know."

"Best stay light on your feet, tender morsel," Ruby muttered.

Florizel moved farther away and laid down behind the thick line of trees.

"So what, then?" I asked. "Are you and your young one going to Tyrea? I suspect you'll be safer from humans over there. We heard that the magic hunters are taking an interest in the border-lands these days."

"We're well away from human habitations now," Ruby said. She yawned, revealing sword-like teeth and filling the air with smoky breath. "This is a good area for hunting."

Somewhere in the woods, Florizel moved farther away.

Ruby lifted her head as a long shape descended from the moonlit sky. The dragonling landed in the shallow river and splashed toward us. Ruby pushed herself up and shifted her front half into the water, grabbed the young dragon, and dunked its head under.

"Clean your face after you eat," she said when it popped back up, sputtering. "Go to sleep."

She settled back down, but the dragonling remained in the river, pacing back and forth, flapping its wings. Ruby watched the performance and sighed. "You don't need my permission. Go, if you think you're ready. I'll not stop you. Be safe, little fool." She snapped her teeth at her child, apparently a dismissal.

The young dragon darted in and head-butted Ruby under the chin, then raced downstream, picking up speed until she spread her wings and lifted off to spiral into the night sky.

"Will she be all right?" I asked.

Ruby watched the fire with heavy eyes. "She will, or she won't. I doubt she'll let me know. I didn't see my own mother after I left the nest. Don't even remember what she looked like." She yawned again. "This is why I find it so interesting that you're going back to yours, Rowan."

For some reason, that voice speaking my name set the skin on the back of my neck crawling.

"I desire to know more about this," she said. "About your attachments. It's fascinating."

"Would you like to join us?" I asked.

Aren had been taking a sip from the water-skin, and choked on it at my words.

Ruby shifted her forelegs to rest her chin on her wrists. "You wish it?"

"Rowan," Aren whispered, as though that would keep the dragon from listening in. "We should talk about this."

Ruby smiled, and her ivory teeth glinted. "I'll leave you for tonight. I think your horse friend will sleep better without me here, anyway."

A snort sounded from the forest.

Ruby lifted her bulk onto four feet, turned, and started downstream. "I'll think on it," she called over her shoulder. "You do the same. This could be entertaining."

I looked back at Aren, who didn't seem impressed. "Entertaining?" he repeated. "This is a terrible idea. We can't trust her. She's just going to draw attention as we get near civilization. And—"

"And she can fly. You can't go far when you're injured, right? If Florizel carried you…"

His jaw dropped. "You can't ride the dragon. You noticed the spines on her back, right? I can't imagine that would be pleasant or comfortable."

"We'll see. It's something to think about, at least. This will get us to Stone Ridge more quickly." I was excited by my idea now. "If Ruby carries me somehow, Florizel could take you, or you could fly and give Florizel a break once you're able. Ruby's not going to turn on us."

"You can't know that." He spread blankets out to make one bed, but I suspected there wouldn't be many affectionate touches this night. "You've had some crazy ideas before, but this one might be the worst."

I crossed my arms and resisted the urge to scowl. "Everything has worked out so far."

He glared at me. "Would meeting up with Callum Langley have worked out so well for you if Florizel hadn't found me, and if Nox, Kel, and Cassia hadn't agreed to help rescue you?"

My stomach tightened as his words sank in. "I thought you'd forgiven me for that."

He didn't say anything.

"Gods, Aren. I said I was sorry."

"I wish you'd talk to me before you do something crazy."

"You weren't there to talk to when I left Belleisle."

He laid down on the blankets and made space for me in front of him. "Let's not fight."

"Why, because you don't want a crazy person mad at you?"

He closed his eyes. "I didn't say you were crazy. I said your ideas were. And I think we're both too tired to talk rationally about this. Can we just get some sleep?"

At least I couldn't argue with that. I lay down beside him, and was surprised when he wrapped one arm around my waist.

"You're a strange person, Aren."

"So are you. Go to sleep."

21

ROWAN

A night's rest mellowed Aren's opinions on the subject— or at least gave him the distance he needed to see that we really had little choice. His arm was better in the morning, but the gryphon had clawed deep into muscles that remained too stiff to attempt flight. It left us with little choice. A dragon's assistance, or extra days of walking. When Ruby returned, Aren agreed that we should at least discuss the idea.

Her laugh at the notion of carrying me to my family didn't help my confidence, but I thought she'd see the journey through as a form of entertainment, if nothing else. Aren said a dragon couldn't be trusted, but she hadn't betrayed us thus far. If it meant helping my family, I'd take that chance.

"So how will we do this?" I asked, and adjusted the pack on my shoulders. Aren stood next to Florizel, looking pale and tight-eyed and more nervous than I'd ever seen him. I ignored it.

"I'll carry you in my claws, if it suits you," Ruby replied, and demonstrated by cupping one long-fingered forepaw with the deadly sharp talons curving back toward her chest. "If I use both, it should be more than enough room for you. Terribly cozy."

"That will be fine," I squeaked. It seemed incredible that I managed to speak at all with my mouth so dry. This idea suddenly seemed exactly as terrible as Aren thought it was. Worse, maybe.

Ruby rested the back of her paw against the ground, and I sat on the palm. She smelled of smoke, and something hard and metallic. Not unpleasant, exactly, but some deep instinct begged me to flee.

She sat up on her haunches and cupped the other forepaw around me. I drew in a sharp gasp at the sudden movement as she lifted me, but felt secure enough. The world around me shifted to a dizzying angle, and I pushed myself to a more comfortable position in the cage of her claws.

"Just try to remember not to squeeze, please," I called.

"Hold on, Ruby," Aren said. I thought he was going to call the whole thing off. I half-hoped he would. Instead, he said, "Do you have any egg shells left from your last hatching?"

"No," she said, not sounding amused. "I fed them to the young ones to fuel their growth and offer protection. Why?"

I shot Aren a warning look. The shells were obviously important to dragons, and I doubted she'd want to hear that we used them for potions. "I don't know," he said. "Someone else was curious, and I said we'd ask."

"Fair enough. You asked. Let's go."

The dragon held me close and pushed off the ground with her powerful hind legs. White spots appeared in front of my eyes as we shot into the sky. When they cleared, I chanced a glance downward from between Ruby's thick, scaled fingers and found the forest already far below. Aren had mounted Florizel, and they were gaining on us. Aren made eye contact as they passed. I waved to show I was okay, then wrapped my arms around a finger and held tight. He shook his head in disbelief, and they went ahead to lead us in the right direction.

We flew high in the clouds through the morning. Once I made myself comfortable, I found that the regular beating of Ruby's wings and the slight rise and fall of her body in the air were quite relaxing. The cold mist gradually soaked my clothes and made me shiver, and Ruby pulled me closer to the warmth of her body. I smiled and patted the palm of her hand.

I didn't feel myself drifting off. When I woke, we were descending toward a misty forest. I shifted to try to see more, and pushed at a claw. Ruby spread her fingers slightly so I could peer out, then twisted her neck to speak to me.

"I need one hand for landing," she said. "Just trust me."

Easier said than done. One paw released me, suddenly exposing me to the cold air and rushing wind. I clung to Ruby's fingers as we dropped, and ducked as a sharp claw tightened over my head. No matter how small I made myself or how tight I held on, I felt I was going to slip out of her grasp.

We landed on a familiar road. Aren and Florizel waited next to the dark ridge of stone jutting from the ground. Ruby set me down and chuckled as I ran toward Aren on trembling legs.

He held me for a moment, until the shaking stopped. "You survived," he observed.

"So did you. Guess it all worked out. Should we keep going?"

"Did you have a pleasant flight, little horse?" Ruby asked.

Florizel's eyes widened. "Fine. Thank you," she whispered, and flicked her ears back as she moved to walk on Aren's other side.

We walked down the road and turned off when we reached the long drive that led to my aunt and uncle's house. As we approached the small hill that hid the gates from view, unease crept over me. I slowed.

"What's wrong?" Aren asked.

"I don't know." In truth, a sense of deep foreboding had filled me. We might find my family, but there was no guarantee what condition we'd find them in. "I'm nervous."

"Only one way to get past that," he said.

We topped the rise, and I stopped in my tracks. I blinked hard to clear my eyes, but the vision didn't disappear. The gates were closed, as they'd been in my dream. The roofline beyond sagged in the middle, dropping out completely where vines and branches had pulled it in.

I ran forward and veered toward the crumbled wall at the last moment, knowing that there was no point trying the gates. They would be stuck tight, just as they'd been in the dream. I leaped over the break in the wall, though Aren yelled for me to stop.

I had to see what lay beyond.

Aren caught up with me as I stepped back onto the drive inside the gate. Florizel vaulted the gap, but Ruby stopped short.

"I'll wait here," the dragon said. "I dislike walls. And I'd hate to frighten anyone." She sounded uncertain about that last part.

"Much appreciated," I said, but my mind was already on what lay before me.

Matthew and Della's apartment had collapsed, leaving wooden beams and pieces of the slate roof strewn around the ground-level carriage shed. My skin turned cold, and my heart-beat quickened as I turned to the main house.

The lanterns beside the front door were green with moss that grew thick inside the glass. The front door hung off its hinges like a drunk stumbling home after a long night, and at least half of the windows were shattered. The grass between the flagstones on the walkway grew higher than I'd ever seen it, and new honeysuckle plants trailed over the walls, blooming larger and brighter than they had any right to early in the season.

"This is impossible," I whispered, afraid to shatter the eerie silence. "This kind of damage should take a hundred years, not a season."

"Agreed." We approached the crooked front door slowly. Aren paused. "Should we knock?"

My throat tightened. "I don't think there's much point. Do you think there's anyone in the house?"

He stepped back and looked the decaying building over. "Not in there, as far as I can tell. Should we look around the grounds?"

"No, let's go in. I'd like to see if there's any clue as to where they went." I wanted to collapse into tears, but there was no time for that. Not if there was still any hope.

Florizel lifted her nose and sniffed the breeze. "I'll look around the garden. I'm feeling hungry."

I nodded absently, and she hurried away from the dirt and decay of the house.

I forced myself to forget that Aren sensed living minds, not dead bodies, and tried not to imagine what I might find when we entered. What I really wanted was to back away, to forget the whole thing. Instead, I pushed the door fully open. It fell completely off its hinges and slammed to the floor in a puff of dust, and I coughed as I stepped over the threshold.

The house was better-preserved inside. A thick layer of dust coated the front stairway from steps to curved bannister, and my boots left dark footprints on the floor. But the walls stood strong, and the floral wallpaper that Aunt Vic had loved so much was only peeling a little.

I turned back to Aren, who wore a tight expression as he took in our surroundings. "I'm going upstairs," I said. "Can you look around down here?"

"Sure," he said absently, already focused elsewhere. "I'll meet you in your rooms."

I ascended slowly, careful to test the stairs in case they'd rotted beneath the once-shiny paint. The upper hallway stretched out on either side of me when I reached the top, and I turned right. With the doors closed and the lanterns unlit, the space was all shadows, with only faint light coming in the small window at one end of the house. My heart, my breath, and the near-silent scuff of my boots accompanied me into the silence.

"Hello?" I called, knowing no one would answer. I pushed open the door to Aunt Vic's rooms at the end of the hall. They'd once belonged to both her and Uncle Ches, but since the twins' deaths she'd preferred to be alone most of the time, lost in her dreams and her memories, tended to by Della. Uncle Ches was gone much of the time, and kept a bedroom just down the hall when he came home.

She could have left it an hour ago for all the elements had touched it. The windows here were intact, and the dust hadn't taken over. The blankets had been carelessly tossed over the bed, the pillows scattered over the mattress and the floor. Balls of bright red wool filled a basket next to the chair, and a child's sweater rested half-finished on the table.

I took a slow walk around the room, but found nothing to indicate where they'd gone. All I could tell was that they'd left in a hurry, and that didn't bode well. I only hoped they'd fled, and not been taken to the city.

I'd been to Ardare. If the magic hunters had arrested them, there wasn't much I'd be able to do now.

I made my way through the rest of the rooms, and found no further clues. At the end of the hallway I came to the narrow doorway that led to the back staircase, and slipped through. Going down would lead to the kitchen, while going up would lead to my rooms in what had once been the servant's quarters, back when this was a larger and wealthier household. I went up, feeling like a stranger in my own home.

Cloud-filtered sunlight flooded the space. Half of the roof up here was gone. I picked my way through the shingles and wood beams scattered across the floor and made my way to the window in the bedroom. Florizel stood in the garden below, nosing at the roses.

The door opened behind me, and Aren's footsteps crossed the floor. "Nothing?" he asked.

I swallowed the lump in my throat and pushed aside the disappointment that made me want to crawl under the mildewed blankets on my old bed. "No. Did you find anything?"

"Nothing. A few places are relatively clean where plants haven't taken over, especially the kitchen, but there are a lot of broken windows in other areas. It's a mess. Do you suppose your aunt had something to do with this?"

"It would make sense, but I hate to think what it would have taken to make her do this." In my own experience, my magic came to my aid when I was in great danger. If Vic hadn't even been aware of hers, what trauma might have wakened it?

I looked around the bedroom one more time, then headed back toward the stairs, past my empty bookshelves and my armchair, which now lay on its back with one leg snapped off.

It wasn't only the destruction and emptiness that made the house wrong. I suspected that even if I'd come home to find my family alive and well, the house intact, and a hot meal on the stove, I'd still have felt out of place here. I'd grown up in this house, but it didn't fit anymore. I'd outgrown it, as I had my old life.

I was about to say as much to Aren when Florizel's scream ripped through the air.

We took off down the stairs, Aren slightly ahead of me. I passed him as we entered the garden, and ran ahead.

A man with blond hair and ragged clothing had Florizel backed under a tree. He was speaking to her, but I couldn't make out the words.

"Hey!" I yelled, and ran toward him.

He turned toward me and I stumbled over my feet. Shock registered on his face. "Rowan?"

"Ashe!" Instead of attacking, I leaped into my brother's arms. He caught me and held me tight. He was strong and well.

May the Goddess bless you forever, Nox.

I didn't hold back my tears of joy and relief.

"My God," he said. For the longest time, he wouldn't let go. I had no problem with that. "I thought I'd never see you again." When he pulled back, his eyes shone with tears, too. "You smell smoky."

"Well, yes," I laughed. "There are a few things I should tell you about."

A snort echoed off the house behind me. Ashe dropped me to the ground and pushed me behind him. "Rowan, run."

I turned back to see Ruby's head and neck arched over the wall. Smoke trailed upward from her nostrils, and her teeth were bared in a silent snarl.

"It's fine, both of you!" I yelled. Ashe turned to me, eyes wide.

"You brought a dragon." Not a question, but a bemused statement of fact.

"Well, yes. A lot has happened since I saw you last, Ashe."

Aren stepped out of the shadows at the back of the house, but came no closer. Florizel trotted toward him, and he reached out to pat her twitching hide. His expression was completely unreadable, stern and hard.

Ashe took a shaky breath. "Will the dragon hurt me?"

"I don't think so." I looked to Ruby, who snorted and pulled back to rest her chin on top of the wall, watching with great interest.

"Good," Ashe said, still looking wary. "Is that him? The one who took you?"

"Yes, but it's not—"

He strode forward, gaining speed as he approached. Aren didn't move.

"Ashe, wait!"

His momentum gave weight to his fist as he slugged Aren in the face.

"Ashe!" I cried.

Aren stepped back from the force of the blow, but didn't move to strike back. He rubbed his jaw and glared at Ashe.

"I promised my father I'd deliver that if I ever met you," Ashe explained. He stepped back, but still looked ready for a fight.

"Decent of you to follow through on a promise," Aren replied evenly.

Ashe crossed his arms. "Some of it was just from me."

"Should I expect more of that," Aren asked, sounding a little exasperated, "or are we even now?"

Ashe tucked his hands in his pockets. "Not quite."

Ruby grinned. "This is interesting!"

I took a deep breath. "Aren, are you okay?"

"Yes. I saw what he intended to do and thought it would be easier to just let him get it over with." He opened his mouth and moved his jaw from side to side. "Didn't expect it to be that hard, though."

"Come on, Rowan," Ashe said, and started down the path toward the back of the garden. "The others will want to see you."

"The others?" My heart leaped, and I dashed after him. Aren followed at a distance. "Who's here? And what happened? Are you completely better? Did mother and father get out of town? I heard the hunters came."

"You'll have answers over supper," he said. "As soon as we get back in the house and prepare something." He pulled open the door to the garden shed and leaned in. "It's all right," he said. "You can come out. No danger, but we have some interesting visitors. And I've got a surprise for you."

I stepped back, suddenly nervous. I ran my fingers through my hair, straightened my clothes, corrected my posture.

My mother stepped out of the shed and froze, one hand in the middle of tucking her silvering blonde hair behind her ear. She looked me over from head to foot, taking everything in.

My stomach clenched as I remembered our last months, the arguments while I'd lived under my parents' roof. "Mother, I—"

She pulled me into a hug fiercer than I remembered her ever giving me before. "My girl. You came home."

I relaxed and squeezed her tight.

She wiped her eyes and turned to Aren. "You did it. You got her out."

"We did," he said.

Matthew was next out of the shed, silvery gray hair an absolute mess and his moustache grown far too long, but his mouth open wide in a disbelieving grin.

"By every god in every land," he said, a little too loudly. "The lost lamb has returned!" He gathered me up into a hug that lifted my feet off the ground, and laughed until tears rolled down his cheeks.

A lump filled my throat, and I couldn't respond. It was too much, too fast. But I smiled as my heart swelled at the sight of my family. Every one of them was a feast for my eyes and my heart, both of which were nearly bursting.

I turned toward a soft noise from the shed.

Aunt Victoria stepped into her garden, and my breath caught in my throat. She stood straight and strong, and her eyes were clear and alert. A gentle smile I hadn't seen in years broke over her face. "Rowan!"

"Vic, you're..."

"I'm back, yes." Her embrace was more gentle than Matthew's or my mother's, but longer.

I breathed in the wild garden scent of her long, golden hair that I remembered from my childhood. She'd only smelled like dust and soap when I left.

"We have so much to discuss," she told me.

The next few minutes were an overwhelming blur of introductions. No one was thrilled to have a dragon visiting. None of them had ever seen one before, but they'd heard stories.

"I give you all my word that she won't set us all alight tonight and snack on our bones in the morning," I said jokingly, hoping the exaggeration of their quite reasonable fears would ease the tension. Victoria laughed at that, and Ruby scowled.

"Shameful," the dragon muttered, "but true."

Though I hated to abandon Aren with strangers, I wanted to speak to Ashe privately. We sat down on one of the stone benches near the rose garden.

"Where's father?" I asked. "And Della? What happened to Willow and Laurel?"

I caught his pained expression before he looked away. "Our sisters fled with their families before the magic hunters came," he said. "Father didn't join us when mother and I said we were leaving. He denied all knowledge of your situation and turned himself in. Said he had nothing to hide, and no reason to fear the magic hunters."

My stomach sank. I'd once thought that, too. I hoped he was right. "So he's as good as disowned me?"

"And me, for not standing with him. And mother for... well, for everything. For using magic to try to protect you when you were a baby, for not telling him about the herbs that healed me." He looked back at the group. "She's not here, is she? The potion lady? I'd like to thank her."

"No, she's occupied elsewhere. It's just me and Aren as far as humans go. Ashe, I'm so sorry for all of this."

He twisted his fingers together between his knees and stared at them. "I've come to realize it's not your fault you are what you are. It was a shock to us when you disappeared, and the things we found out after came as a surprise to everyone but Mother. But I understand, or at least I'm trying to. It's hard to believe that everything we've been taught about magic was a lie, though."

"I know. I remember how strongly you felt about it."

He smiled sadly. "I'm still working through it. It's slow going some days."

"So Father went to Ardare?"

"And Willow. Laurel's still holed up with her husband some- where smaller, keeping her head down. Or she was, last I heard. Mother and I fled before the magic hunters could come for us. We found Stone Ridge like this—or about half-way to being this, I guess."

"Victoria made it happen?"

He nodded. "Another surprise, to all of us. She'll be able to explain that better than I can. It's magic, of course, done to make it seem like there couldn't possibly be anyone living here. She's helping me a lot with accepting magic. Her skills have kept us alive."

I looked around the lush garden and noticed the tempting selection of ripe fruits and vegetables. "I'd say. And what about Uncle Ches and Della?"

His cheeks paled. "Uncle Ches was fine when we last saw him. We decided after we arrived that we'd need to get out of the country. This is a great place to hide, but it'll become a prison eventually. He went to get valuables he had stored at banks in a few different towns, things we might sell for Tyrean gold over the border."

"That's smart."

"I thought so. We haven't heard from him since he left, though, and he said he'd be back two days ago. And Della..."

Matthew walked closer, drawing hard at his pipe. "My dear girl is no longer with us." A tear trickled down his face and caught in his thick mustache. "That was before Ashe and Lucilla came. The hunters showed up. Della stalled them while I took Victoria and hid her in the garden so they wouldn't see what she was. I don't know what happened. Della was just supposed to say that the master and mistress were gone out to town. I didn't hear anything save for one bark from Micah. When I went back, the hunters were gone, and she and the dog were..." He squeezed his eyes shut, and several more tears fell.

"I'm so sorry, Matthew." My chest filled with a deep, physical ache. She was gone, and again I couldn't help thinking that it was my fault.

But all Matthew seemed to take from my "sorry" was sorrow, not the apology I intended. He squeezed between me and Ashe on the broad bench, and Ashe shifted to accommodate him.

"I am too," Matthew said. "We miss her. I miss her. And it'll be hard for us to leave. She's buried with your cousins out beyond the wall. Suppose your aunt and I will say our goodbyes there when we go collect the horses. We should leave soon, whether your uncle returns or not."

I couldn't hold the tears back any longer. I buried my face in my hands and sobbed until empty exhaustion displaced the throbbing misery inside of me.

When I looked up, Aren was there. I expected a comment about me always crying in this garden, but none came. Instead, he offered me a sympathetic glance, then turned to Matthew. "I'm sad to hear of your loss," he said. "Rowan told me so much about you and your wife. All good things. I'd have liked to have known her."

Matthew nodded and sucked at his pipe.

"We should see about getting something to eat," Ashe said, and went into the house through the kitchen door.

Aren took his place, and Matthew muttered something about finding spots for everyone to sleep. When he'd left, I said, "This must be awkward for you."

"It's fine," Aren said quietly. "Things are bound to be tense between me and your family. No doubt they've been thinking of me as their worst enemy, on a personal level as well as national. And there's the magic. It's easier for them to accept yours now that they see you're still you, and because they've seen Victoria embrace hers. She's fantastic, by the way, and more talented than I'd dreamed."

"She is amazing."

"But it's different with me. I'm the monster who invaded your life and stole you away, revealed what you are. Stirred everything up. I'm sure they blame me for this, at least in part."

"Funny, I was just blaming myself."

He rested a hand on my shoulder. "It's not your fault that your people are what they are. At least some of your family is trying to do better now, right?"

I leaned in and kissed his cheek. "They are. And they'll come around when they get to know you, I promise."

Half of his mouth turned up in a shallow smile. "It doesn't matter. As long as you still like me, I'll be fine. For now."

My mother called to us and we followed her into the house. Matthew and Victoria sat at the kitchen table chopping vegetables. I still couldn't believe how bright her eyes were. She smiled at us as we passed by on our way to the back staircase, which wasn't nearly as dusty as the front.

"You can't stay in your old rooms," Mother said as we reached the second floor. "The hole in the roof makes a convincing argument for the place being abandoned, but it didn't do much for your mattress. There are still plenty of empty rooms down here. We'll get a few set up for you two."

The firm tone of her voice made it clear that we were not to argue about having separate rooms. It grated on me. If things were different, if I were still her normal daughter and it was Callum staying over before our wedding, there would have been no problem with us sharing a bed. But Aren was no respectable prospective son-in-law, and though he'd saved my life as he'd promised her, it was clear that my mother still couldn't stomach our relationship.

Remembering that it might not matter in the end brought another dark cloud over a joyful day.

At least our rooms were next to each other, the only two in the north wing that had intact windows and walls. After Mother went back to the kitchen, Aren slipped into my room. He sat on the bed and tapped the headboard. "Mine's right on the other side."

I smiled. "I'll knock if I need you." I flopped on the bed, and he did the same. "Did anyone say when we're leaving?"

"Your aunt said tomorrow. Apparently Ches made them promise to leave if he didn't make it back, but they waited. Now that we're here to help them leave the country, she agrees that it's best to go. Still hoping for his return, though." He rolled onto his side and propped himself up on one elbow. "Did you notice the magic here?"

"Not especially. But now that you mention it, it feels a lot stronger than it did in Ardare, or even outside of it."

"I think so, too. I noticed it the first time I was here, when I was able to keep transforming without overly depleting my power. It was still thin, and I was relieved to get back to Tyrea where things are normal, but it is better here than elsewhere. And I think it's stronger now than it was before."

"Victoria."

He grinned. "Her presence preserved the magic on this land."

My thoughts raced to catch up. "After the boys died, she hid it. I don't think she wanted to acknowledge that it was in her, that it had caused their deaths."

"Right, but it still lingered in the garden, and that's what I was able to channel. Now that she's using it again, it's becoming stronger."

I grinned, as much at his enthusiasm as at the discovery. "That's interesting."

"To put it mildly." He sat up, then stood, unable to stay still. "This means that even if Severn is right, it shouldn't be too difficult to bring magic back to this land. Even before the plants regrow and before the magical creatures return, we could try to have Sorcerers settle here."

"Right. And the king here will be fine with that."

He shrugged, but that grin didn't leave his face. "We'll get there. If there are pockets of magic around..."

Someone knocked at the door and Aren answered, pulling the door open with a bit more enthusiasm than he'd probably intended. "Victoria," he said, and stepped back.

"Soup's ready, darlings." I'd forgotten how musical her voice was. "I wish I could offer you a hot bath after, but we've been having some trouble with the well water."

Aren stepped out into the hall. "You should have Rowan look into that," he said. "She has a gift."

I glared after him, but he disappeared from sight.

Victoria and I linked arms and walked down to the kitchen. "He seems nice," she said.

"That's one word for him."

She smiled. "It's good to see you happy."

"You, too. Or if not happy, at least to have you back."

She took a deep breath and pulled her hair forward over one shoulder. Last time I'd seen her, she looked twenty years older. Now, we could have passed for sisters.

"It hurt so much to be present," she said. "I built a world in my mind where my life could carry on as I thought it was meant to. But it wasn't real. With your disappearance and everything that was happening around us, the real world crashed in on me no matter how I struggled to shut it out. Then Della died, and I found that the world still needed me. I found purpose. Life was still painful, but not as unendurable as I'd thought it to be. I missed so much, didn't I? I should have been there for you."

She stopped me before we entered the kitchen. "I should have told you, Rowan. I knew what you were. Your mother wasn't open about it, but I guessed what had happened. I asked her about it once, and she made me promise not to say anything, as the binding couldn't be reversed. And you were always happy enough."

"You did what you thought was best." She always had, for me.

"I did. And at the time, I thought..."

"What?"

"I thought that I had accidentally invited the magic into myself. I felt guilty about it, and eventually convinced myself that I was just a talented gardener when the apple trees bore fruit almost year-round. I forced myself to become ignorant of my power. And I ignored it in the children until it was too late to save them from the people who saw it better than I did."

It seemed I wasn't the only one feeling guilty.

"After they passed, I shut it out," she continued. "The magic was still there, but I didn't feel it in me. I felt less alive, but I could ignore the guilt." She sighed. "It's so good to have it back. To be myself again."

We stepped into the kitchen, where everyone else waited. I

wondered whether Victoria spoke so openly about her magic with any of them.

Matthew served bowls of steaming stew, thick with carrots, potatoes, squash and herbs.

"This is fantastic," Aren said. "Quite amazing for this early in the season."

My mother's lips tightened, and Matthew laughed. "Victoria has always had a way with plants."

"If only the well would cooperate," Victoria said.

Aren looked at me expectantly.

I sighed. "What's the problem?"

"Dried up," Ashe said. "We've got plenty of drinking and cooking water stored away, but nothing extra."

I ignored the anxiety that gnawed at my stomach. "I'll see what I can do."

My mother forced a smile. "Here's hoping you can do something. I think we could all use a good wash. Our clothes, too."

"Thank you, Mother." It had to be hard for her to encourage me to use magic. At least she was willing to try.

I slipped out to the garden alone after supper. The sun hung low in the sky, and a chilly breeze blew in from the forest. Florizel approached from the wild tangles of the trees at the back of the yard.

"Where's Ruby?" I asked.

Florizel nodded toward the forest. "Hunting. She promised not to eat any horses she found, but I don't like anyone else's odds." One ear twitched apprehensively. "What are you doing?"

"Just checking something. I might need to do it alone, though, if you don't mind."

"Oh, of course. Please tell your aunt that this garden is delicious."

I laughed. Though Florizel's plant-only diet was more restricted than those of the horses I had grown accustomed to in Tyrea and Belleisle, she ate a far wider variety of things than local horses did. My aunt might be surprised to discover what had been consumed from her flower bed.

"Eat up," I told her. "We're leaving tomorrow."

When I was alone again, I swung my legs over the low, stone edge of the new well and sat peering into its dark depths. "New" was a relative term. Newer than the house, but older than me. It was, indeed, dry. I didn't need to send the bucket down to know that there was only thick mud at the bottom.

"Where are you?" I asked aloud. "We need you."

I closed my eyes and focused on the magic in the garden. Aren was right. It was strong here. I thought about water. Not well-water, but a mighty river. When memories of Dorset Langley tried to intrude, I pushed him aside and replaced him with a beautiful waterfall. A still lake followed, where loons cried and merfolk might be lurking beneath the surface. The images calmed my mind, and I let everything else drift away.

Ulric had taught me to direct my magic using the depths of my anger and frustration, but I couldn't bring myself to summon them in this peaceful place. My old life came back to me here. My innocence and ignorance, love and losses. I'd always felt safe here, blind to the horrors and possibilities of the outside world. If my magic was to work here, it would come on its own, in peace.

Crickets chirped deep in the shadows. An evening-lark called from the treetops, heralding night's coming. My magic flowed in me and out of me, and I didn't try to force anything. I just thought about water, peaceful and life-giving.

The water soaked my boots before I realized it was there. I laughed and pulled them out of the well, which was, for the first time, full to the brim. As I stepped back, the water sank.

"Don't leave," I called down the well. "Just stay where you are." The water level held steady as I waited. "Good." I closed my eyes again and felt for my magic. It had lessened, but this time I felt no panic. I trusted it would return soon enough, drawn from the garden I'd grown up in. There was no danger there. No fear, no pressure.

I dropped the bucket and pulled it up again, full to the brim, then hurried back to the kitchen, slopping more water over my feet in my rush to get inside.

"I did it!" I yelled, far too loud for indoors. "I got it!"

Matthew beamed as he took the bucket, dumped it into the

big pot on the stove, and went back outdoors. Ashe clapped me on the back as he followed Matthew.

"What, no applause?" I asked Aren, who sat by the fire with Victoria. It looked like they'd been deep in conversation, but now both sat silent, looking pleased.

He gave me a half-smile that made my heart turn a somersault. "I had no doubt you could do it. Any ill effects?"

"None. I'm a little weak, but I'll recover."

He gave me an I-told-you-so look that I absolutely deserved, and we went to help bring water in.

It took a lot of trips to the well—and some subtle help from Aren to keep the fire hot—but a few hours later we were all clean, relaxed, and ready to sleep. Aren and I found clothes in the house to wear when Mother offered to wash ours. As anything I'd left behind in my rooms was fairly well destroyed, I ended up in one of aunt Vic's white nightgowns, which covered me from neck to ankles in soft cotton and lace. Not an attractive style by any stretch of the imagination. I tried to sneak back to my room without being seen, but Aren waited for me in the hallway. He stood with one shoulder leaned against the wall, arms crossed.

"Damn." He wiggled his eyebrows and leered at me.

"You're ridiculous."

"No, really. I like it," he said, unable to keep the amusement out of his voice. "Leaves a lot to the imagination."

I mustered what dignity I could and held my chin high as I walked past. "Goodnight, Aren. Have fun with your imagination."

"Goodnight, Rowan. I will."

He'd been joking about the attractiveness of the nightgown, but that didn't stop him turning to watch me as I walked away.

22

AREN

I tried to behave myself. I didn't knock on the wall, didn't enter her dreams. She needed rest, as did I, but the separation irritated me. The added layer of distance, coupled with the nagging idea that she might decide to stay with her family, left me sleepless.

And what after that? What if she never returns to me?

What would become of her magic if she had no one to help her overcome her fears and her challenges? So many talented Sorcerers saw their gifts wasted through lack of education and development. I wanted her to have everything she'd ever dreamed of, but was no longer certain I could hope to give it to her.

I needed to talk to her about it, needed to see her. I waited until I felt certain everyone should be asleep, then went to the door. I opened my perceptions, scowled, and erased the expression before I opened my door.

Ashe sat on the floor of the hallway, holding a steaming mug of something that smelled strongly of cinnamon. One blond eyebrow arched, and waves of smug irritation washed off from him. I closed myself off.

"Shouldn't you be resting?" I asked. My jaw hardly hurt now, but I still wasn't pleased with him.

He shrugged and sipped from his cup. "Couldn't sleep."

"So you decided to spend some time wandering the halls, and happened to stop to rest here outside my door?"

He nodded. "Did you need something? Toilet's down the hall, if you're looking for it."

"I'll remember that. Thank you."

I returned to bed.

Just a few days with her family, I reminded myself.

And then what? Though I wanted Rowan close by, though I thought we had a better chance of success with her power and potential on our side, I wouldn't drag her back to face my father. Not after we'd disobeyed him.

If she came back, we might try harder to keep apart, no matter how it hurt. But for how long? No matter how well she avoided my father, how I tried to please him in other ways to soften his heart, the laws would not change. Not for me.

My thoughts grew cloudy and confused. I imagined us running away, disappearing like one of her illusions. I imagined her leaving, and me watching her embrace her gifts and love the life she made for herself while I sat chained to a throne, surrounded by empty statues and nodding puppets, turned heartless and cold as my father and brother before me.

I woke to a soft knock at my door and opened my eyes to dim sunlight filtering through the curtains. Rowan stood outside when I opened it, looking fresh and ready for anything, already dressed in her traveling clothes and holding mine in a neat pile. "Uncle Ches is back. Everyone's getting ready to go," she said. "There's breakfast on the table, and Mother is packing the rest of the food. I'll be back soon."

"Where are you going?"

Her smile faltered. "To the woods. Matthew, Vic, and I are going to say some goodbyes."

I dressed quickly and headed to the kitchen.

A tall man with graying hair and a full beard sat eating bacon and oatmeal. He stood when I entered the room.

"Well," he said, and wiped his mouth on a napkin. "Victoria told me we were entertaining royalty. I hope you slept well."

"I did, thank you. You must be Rowan's uncle."

"Chester Greenwood. Pleasure to meet you."

Ashe sat in the corner, yawning. Rowan's mother, Lucilla, offered me a wan smile. She looked more tired than the last time I'd seen her, but appeared to be holding up well, given the circumstances. I couldn't help picking up on her sense of obligation to her family, or the continuing distaste for me that she was trying not to acknowledge, even to herself. The others were no better. Much as they were glad to have Rowan alive and well, those I could read wished me gone.

I closed myself off to them as well as I could. These people were so open, as defenseless as anyone I'd attacked in their land.

No wonder they feared people like me.

"Help yourself to breakfast, Aren," Lucilla said, and forced a smile she probably thought was genuine. "Might as well finish what we've cooked. We won't be taking it with us."

"Thank you." I wondered whether I should warn them, teach them to close their minds as I'd been attempting with Nox, as my father had instructed Patience. But drawing attention to it would make them think me more of a monster than they already did. I decided to leave it, and try to ignore anything I picked up from them. I could ignore them as long as emotions didn't run high and no one got drunk. This wouldn't be the first time I'd been surrounded by hostility, and at least they were trying to overcome it for Rowan's sake.

The food was incredible, hot and perfectly seasoned. I hoped the people traveling with my father would soon be eating this well. But that would depend on Victoria and Rowan, if they came back with me.

We'd have to talk. Later. Alone. For now, I'd try to be friendly with everyone, whatever that meant in this situation.

It clearly pained Lucilla to leave a mess behind, but there was no point worrying about the dishes when the house was practically a ruin and no one planned to come back any time soon.

We met the others in the garden, minus Matthew. Everyone stayed well away from Ruby, who had decided to sleep inside the wall after all. Rowan's reassurances had done little to calm anyone's nerves about the massive beast.

"Matthew's gone to collect the horses," Rowan explained before I could ask. "They seem to have wandered off."

Ruby lifted her head from where it had been resting in the crook of a tree. "I didn't eat them. I enjoyed a lovely, strong doe last night, and had a goat for dessert."

"Oh, dear," Victoria murmured. "I'd hoped to take Melvina with us."

The dragon yawned. "All I was told was to not eat the horses." Her eyes brightened and focused on Ches. "What's in the bag, human man?"

He stepped back. "Nothing. Necessities."

"Not gold? No gems?"

Ches held the bag tight. He obviously knew a thing or two about dragons. "Just a few things to barter along the way."

Ruby grinned. "I could help you carry that."

"I'm sure he can handle it," I said, and the dragon pouted. I had to look twice to believe it.

Matthew returned, leading three horses.

"Jigger!" Rowan cried, and threw her arms around a massive chestnut that I remembered from my first visit.

Matthew patted the horse's neck. "Yes, the old boy's still with us. Your mother and Ashe brought him when they came. Let's load the wagon and be off." The man's voice was thick with grief, but his eyes remained dry.

We soon had everything packed—food, extra clothing and blankets, knives and bows and arrows, pots, seedlings, a few books Ches wouldn't leave behind.

"What about us?" Florizel asked. She nodded toward Ruby. "We can't walk with you on the road. We're bound to meet people, aren't we?"

"True," Rowan said. She looked over the horses and the wagon. "You two fly ahead to Tyrea. Ruby, if you need to leave us, I wish you well. Florizel, you are of course free to leave, but if you'll consent to coming the rest of the way, you could wait for us outside the town where we left Patience."

Ruby snorted, sending smoke into the air. "I'm not going to miss the rest of this. Mistress Feathers and I will both be waiting for you in Tyrea."

Florizel didn't look comfortable with the idea, but also didn't object. She nodded goodbyes to all of us. "Be careful," she said, and took off. Ruby didn't bother with goodbyes, though she did take one last, longing look at Ches's bag before she pushed off. The down-drafts from her wings nearly flattened us all.

Lucilla shook her head as she watched them leave. "Rowan, you have made some interesting friends, haven't you?"

Rowan smiled at her mother. "That I have."

A black horse pulled the cart, which Victoria, Ches, and Lucilla made themselves comfortable in. Jigger was large enough to carry me with Rowan riding behind, and Ashe took the smaller, dun-colored mare. Victoria looked back over her shoulder until the house disappeared from sight.

"It'll be okay," Rowan told her. "It's hard to leave it behind, but there are good things waiting beyond the mountains. You'll see."

Victoria's expression brightened, if only a little. "You would know, I suppose." To my surprise, she winked at us.

Perhaps the family wasn't all bad.

The roads around Stone Ridge were blessedly quiet, and for a time we kept it that way. We'd all be holding our breaths until we made it over the border, no matter how smoothly things went before then. There was no laughter, no conversation. There were also no questions, which I considered a good thing. Rowan's mother seemed to be attempting to accept her daughter's new situation, and Victoria to accept her own. Ches and Matthew were pleasant, but guarded enough that I suspected they'd heard of my gifts. Ashe's dislike for me remained clear, but he said nothing about it.

The magic in the air and the land lessened as we moved away from the garden, and I experienced the familiar ache to be home in Tyrea. The people of Darmid had destroyed so much, so quickly and so recklessly. But there was hope, and that was something.

Victoria moved to the side of the cart and leaned over to

speak to me and Rowan. "Do you feel that?" she asked. "The emptiness?"

Rowan nodded. "Most of the country is like this. Ardare is worse, there's hardly any magic there. It gets better in the mountains."

Victoria's eyes sparkled. "I can't wait."

Lucilla looked a little green, though I couldn't tell without intruding whether it was from the rocking of the cart or the conversation. I lowered my voice to a level just loud enough for Victoria to hear over the rumble and creak of the wagon's wheels.

"You caused all of that damage at Stone Ridge?" I asked, and she nodded. "It's quite amazing. You've had no training?"

"None." Her eyes took on a distant look. "It's a gift I've always had. Not that I wanted to admit it was magic, of course, but it's natural. Easy. This was just a case of me pushing myself, embracing what I could do and the fact that I was using magic, and pushing it hard." She frowned. "It exhausted me. Took weeks to do it, and I was ready to collapse every time I worked at it."

"But you kept your family safe," I said, a little louder in case anyone might be listening in.

A natural gift was an incredible thing. Even the greatest Sorcerers usually only had one, and other smaller talents and learned skills along with it. Severn had thought my own natural gift was mind-reading, and he'd instructed me to develop it into mind-control and extended awareness. It had been a small gift, greatly developed, and I suspected that the fact of its humble beginnings kept him from seeing me as a threat.

Is that your gift, though? A dark voice, hollow and threatening. *Is that what's come most naturally to you, what you've picked up without thought or practice?*

I shut that line of thinking down. I was supposed to have forgotten about the other thing.

I was glad when Victoria asked me more about Tyrea and most people's experiences with magic. She was nearly as curious as Rowan had been when I first met her, though the older woman knew more of the history between our countries than Rowan had. Rowan and I took turns answering questions, and it passed the time quite pleasantly.

If the others were listening, they didn't add anything to the conversation. I hoped they were. They all had a lot to learn before they tried to make a life in Tyrea. The people there wouldn't appreciate the pinched look that came over Lucilla's face every time someone brought up magic.

She's trying, I reminded myself.

Ashe was surprisingly comfortable with the idea of magic, considering what Rowan had told me about him. After lunch, he rode beside us and asked Rowan a few questions about how she'd called the water and what else she could do. She answered with more confidence than I knew she felt, saying a little about the illusion that had helped her escape from Ardare. She'd really only discovered the two abilities so far, but it seemed to impress her family.

"So, Aren," Ches said after she'd finished speaking. I cringed inwardly, knowing what was coming. "I'm sure we've all heard the rumors about you. What's the truth about your magic?"

Rowan's arms tightened around my waist. At first I thought it was a warning, but realized the gesture was meant to be reassuring.

Words she'd spoken to me back on Belleisle came to mind. *I like your claws.* I smiled at that, but decided not to share everything. Instead, I held out a hand and produced a flame that danced on my palm for a moment before disappearing into the air. "That's my newest trick," I said. "It comes in handy. I also change into an eagle."

"We'd heard something about that," Ashe said, clearly not pleased.

Awkward silence followed. I wasn't entirely sure what Rowan had said in letters or in recent conversation, but she'd probably let on that I'd entered their lives in that form and spent time at Stone Ridge in secret.

No one asked outright about my ability to bend people's minds, and I didn't offer any information or explanation. Let them think what they wanted.

Tell them the worst thing, whispered the voice in the back of my mind.

No. It's irrelevant. Even Rowan didn't know about that.

"My sister is a Potioner," I said a few minutes later. "Ashe, she's the one who sent those herbs for you. She'll be pleased to know you're doing so well."

"I find that fascinating," Victoria said, helping to change the subject. My shoulders relaxed. "I'd very much like to meet someone who uses plants in that way."

"Your skills would complement hers well," I told her. "Actually, you might be able to meet her, if you'd like. Rowan and I will be meeting up with her and some other people closer to Luid. We could certainly use someone with your abilities, and you could learn a lot."

Ches grunted and glanced back over his shoulder. "Take her back to help fight your battles? I think not."

"She'd be well away from any fighting," Rowan said. "I would never let you get hurt, Vic."

Victoria didn't say anything else. I hoped her silence meant she was considering the offer.

The road curved south, toward where the mountains descended to the ocean. It was a similar route to the one Rowan and I had taken the first time we left the country, but we avoided the little harbor town that would surely be crawling with Darmish soldiers, if not a Tyrean vessel or two in disguise. We climbed the foothills before we reached the sea, forced by the presence of the wagon to stick to an established road. The one Ches pointed out to us was not well-used, and the few people we met didn't give us a second glance as they passed us heading the opposite way. We made camp for the night, and I changed to hunt. We had plenty of food, but I needed to get away from the group for a while, to feel the wind in my feathers. My left wing was only a little stiff now, and that worked itself out as I soared over the forest.

I suspected Rowan would want time alone with her family, but couldn't say for certain. I'd never desired it with mine.

I saw no sign of other travelers on the road until I was well away from our group, and the ones I found were camped for the night. The sea to the south of us sparkled orange in the sunset. I turned that direction to look over the single trading barge that bobbed on the water, then looped back over a small port and flew back for the hills, feeling confident that no one was tracking us.

I didn't like to say it to Rowan, but I was beginning to fear that we'd had too much good fortune lately. It was going to run out sometime, and though I didn't think of myself as superstitious, I felt it was going to run out in a big way when it did.

I returned with a pair of pheasants and dropped them next to the fire before I landed.

Rowan's family stared at me for a moment before anyone spoke.

"Thank you," Ashe said, and took the birds and his knife into the forest.

"How lovely," Victoria said. "Will you change back now? Let us see how it's done?"

Rowan laughed. "I don't think that would be appropriate. His clothes are back in the forest."

I held my wings out in an apologetic gesture.

"I suppose you'd best get back to them, then," Ches said. "Rowan, give me a hand with the fire?"

"But Aren can—"

"I'm sure we can manage it the old-fashioned way while he changes."

Victoria met me after I dressed, out of sight of the rest of them. "I apologize if my husband seems rude." She picked at the hem of her shirt as she spoke. "His relationship with magic has always been a difficult one. He knew about me, more clearly than I ever did, and he did what he had to in order to protect me. Out of love, you know. But we never spoke about it, even after the children, and I can't say he's comfortable with it. He knew about Rowan, I think, but again..."

"You never spoke about it."

"No. He's a historian. He's aware of where our people came from, how our ancestors overthrew the Sorcerers who oppressed us and how they made this new land. I don't say that our forefathers' methods were right, or even that Ches agrees with all of our people's beliefs. I know he's against what the king is up to now, this new push to destroy magic. But he's rooted deeply in our culture. We all are. Or once were."

"I understand. I hope that doesn't make things difficult for you wherever you settle." It would, I had no doubt. But people could change.

She took a deep breath and looked up at the now star-filled sky. "You don't think there's hope we'll come back?"

"Not for a long time. It could be sooner, if my father takes his throne back." I explained the situation to her, and how we needed her help to feed the people who were traveling with my father and friends, who would in turn help him get back into the city to take back the throne peacefully. I left out the part about Ulric's failing magic, but mentioned potions again, as it had interested her earlier.

"It does sound like your sister and I could be a good combination there," she mused, "especially with Rowan's help. I can't make things grow spontaneously, though, and I have to be careful about the soil and water."

"Just speeding up what's already growing would be enough," I assured her. "Imagine the growth you brought about at Stone Ridge, but used to feed people, or to grow medicinal plants."

She smiled. "That does sound lovely. I've been cut off from the world for so long, and I would like to get back out and contribute something meaningful. But my family needs me, too. Much as I want to come with you, learn more, see more of the world, I don't know whether that's possible." She let out a little sigh. "I might be too old for adventure."

"It's certainly something for you to consider, anyway."

Victoria closed her eyes, face still turned toward the sky. "I will. Thank you."

Rowan raced uphill from camp. "Aren, I'm—Oh, Vic. Hello. Everything all right?"

Victoria's eyes sparkled as she turned to her niece. Hard to believe this was the same woman who had seemed a ghost when she walked the gardens months before. "Just fine, dear. Aren was telling me about this situation in Tyrea."

A strange expression crossed Rowan's features, tense and sorrowful and uncertain. "Quite the mess, isn't it?"

"Sounds like it. And yet Aren has mentioned the possibility of me joining you."

Rowan bit her lip. "Right. You know, it's really not so bad…"

Victoria laughed. "No, I'm sure."

We all walked back to the camp and waited for the meal to finish cooking. Ashe had done an expert job preparing the meat, and there were plenty of fresh greens to go along with it.

Victoria had brought along potted plants, and she settled in for the night among them in the wagon as the others set up their bedrolls on the ground. I'd packed one at the house, but offered my blankets to Rowan.

"Changing?" she asked.

"It's easier. Less awkward."

She only nodded.

I made the fire burn low, careful not to let the flames lash back at me, and transformed again. A branch not far from where Rowan had settled served as a reasonably comfortable perch. I watched Rowan after she fell asleep. She looked contented enough, pleased to be back with what remained of her family. She was safer with them now, or would be once we crossed the border. She'd be loved freely, and she'd find purpose in helping them settle in Tyrea—purpose my father was trying to deny her.

It's the best thing for almost everyone, I decided, and fluffed my feathers, *if that is her choice.*

If only I could make myself understand that in human form as well as eagle. Though my emotions in that form were stronger than they once were, it still gave a small bit of distance.

Not enough, though.

Not nearly enough.

23

AREN

The night passed without incident, and we were awake and moving on before the sun came into view. The horses, as well-fed as the rest of us, gave us no trouble about the early start. They were good horses, for all that they were Darmish beasts with no magical blood in them. Not the most intelligent, swiftest, or strongest animals, but they got the job done.

I scouted the road ahead several times and didn't see any threats. Being an eagle had the advantage of speed and mobility, but it did make it difficult for me to sense human presences, and I had to rely on my keen eyesight. I found a path that appeared to be an abandoned road. It would be difficult to get the wagon to it, but the one we were on now would take us straight past a huddled bunch of huts. Not a town, but a fenced-in compound, likely housing border guards. Perhaps magic hunters, as well.

Not a good time to take chances for the sake of convenience. We'd have to get the wagon through the woods and onto the path somehow.

When I re-joined the group, no one argued with the plan. We rigged the tracings so that two horses could pull, but we had to lift the cart several times when it became mired in mud or the wheels caught on rocks as we travelled through the thin forest.

"Levitating things isn't one of your skills, then?" Ashe grunted, and threw his shoulder against the back of the wagon.

"Doesn't look that way, does it?" I added my own weight to the push, and the wagon jolted forward.

Rowan wiped sweat from her brow, gave Ashe a dark look, and walked ahead. He followed and spoke to her. I hoped she would give him hell, but suspected she was attempting to be a bit more diplomatic than that with her much-loved brother. He put an arm around her shoulders, and she leaned in briefly before she broke away. Ashe returned to the cart and helped me push again as Rowan led us onto our new path and turned toward the border. The cart jolted and caught one more time, and we gave it another hard shove to get it into the thin wheel ruts leading through the woods.

Distracted as I was by physical exertion and my irritation with Ashe, I almost missed the feeling that something was wrong. I opened myself, and sensed danger. Human presences. Before I could call out a warning to Rowan, three burly men stepped in front of her from a thicket of trees.

"Border's closed," the one in the center of their line said. All three had their weapons drawn, two swords and one set of daggers.

Rowan took a step back. "Is that where this leads? We're a little lost."

The man who had spoken sneered as he looked back into the forest from which we'd just emerged. "Staying on the main road might have prevented that."

She retreated farther. "We'll go back the way we came, then, thank you."

"I don't think so," the one on the right said.

Ashe stepped forward, but I placed a hand on his arm to hold him back. He shot me an indignant glance, which I ignored.

"Let us handle this," I said quietly.

Ashe's jaw muscles flexed in irritation, but he stepped back.

I took in our surroundings. Trees pressed in close on both sides of the path, leaving little room for me to maneuver if I transformed and attacked.

"Gentlemen!" I called in a relaxed, friendly voice. There was no time to dig out a weapon, but that didn't leave me helpless. "Surely this is a simple misunderstanding. We don't want trouble."

Except that I did. We'd been avoiding trouble, but when an enemy appeared I found myself eager to meet the challenge. Three men, and likely not one of them with magic, but better armed than we were. I stepped out from behind the cart and walked forward.

At the sound of my voice, they all looked at me. The one on the left was already focused on Rowan, and I didn't like where his thoughts were taking him. His distraction left him open, and I reached into his mind and snapped it. No false memories, no gentle dissuasions or attempts to convince him he had business elsewhere. He screamed, dropped his sword, and raced into the woods, running head-first into an oak trunk. He lay at the base, twitching and moaning.

The fellow on the right watched him go. He tried to guard his mind—they'd been warned about me at some point, perhaps back when Rowan had been in Ardare. He couldn't do it. His thoughts rushed out, and I grabbed them and twisted, sending his mind into a cyclone of confusion. It wasn't something I'd tried before, but it came naturally enough. Magic flowed through me and outward, depleting my stores. The man's face went blank, and he dropped to his knees. A trickle of blood ran from his nose.

In just moments, I'd destroyed the minds of two enemies. My heart raced, and a mad grin came over my face.

I kept moving forward. The one remaining, the ringleader, was ready for me. Fear pulsed from him, but he was better prepared. I'd been wrong in my assumptions about him. He may not have been aware of it—and certainly his superiors didn't know—but his mind hummed with a trace of magic that made my job more difficult than I'd anticipated. I struggled to push my way into his mind, but it resisted. He grinned, thinking he was thwarting me all on his own.

He raised his daggers and crouched, ready for a fight.

Very well.

He flinched as I disappeared, stumbled back as I reappeared in eagle form and launched myself at him. I'd have had a hard time getting past those knives if I hadn't had the element of surprise on my side. As it was, his confusion made him drop his guard. Only for a moment, but it was enough. I relished the strength in my wings as they battered about his head, further confusing him. He slashed at the air with his knives, but his aim was off, his movements suddenly stiff and slow.

One more moment and I'd have his throat out.

He dropped the knives and grabbed me, taking fistfuls of body feathers and one wing. My bones strained under the pressure, and I screamed in his ear. He dropped to his knees, tucked his chin down, and kept squeezing.

I had only moments to make my decision. Would I change back, break his grip, and fight as a stronger-boned but decidedly unclothed human? Or keep trying this?

He ripped a fistful of flight feathers from my wing and reared his head back with a roar. Searing pain ripped through my body, blinding me with a flash of white light. Rowan yelled behind me, the sound followed closely by a thump and a series of crashes. Something whistled by me, and a moment later the man's terrible grip released. He pitched over and landed next to his broken-minded comrade. When my vision cleared, I saw the red-fletched arrow protruding from his eye. I turned.

Rowan lowered the bow and set it back in the cart. Baskets and pots littered the ground at her feet.

"Sorry," she muttered, and wiped her brow with her jacket sleeve. "Someone packed this under a lot of other stuff." She looked down at the ground. "I tried to draw his water, but I..." Her voice trailed off. "I'm sorry."

Had I been able to speak, I'd have told her not to apologize, pointed out that I was alive. She'd slowed him, at least.

A fresh wave of pain from my wing cut off those thoughts, and I opened my beak to breathe through it and clear my head.

Rowan's family stood by, faces as expressionless and shocked as the only one of our attackers who remained semi-conscious.

"So that's magic, is it?" Ches demanded. "That's how it's done in Tyrea?"

"They would have killed us, Ches," Victoria said. She stepped toward me. "Are you all right?"

Blood dripped from torn skin on the back of my wing. I honestly didn't know whether I was all right or not. I grew light-headed from the pain, and angry from the feeling that this body had betrayed me. *I should have won.*

"I'll take care of that," Rowan said, and reached for her pack. "Aren, come with me. Everyone else can clean up." She grabbed my clothes as she passed.

I hobbled after her into the woods, trying not to bump my wing on the ground but finding it hard to hold it up. We reached a clear spot out of sight of the rest of the group, and she set my things down.

She pressed the heels of her hands to her eyes and took a shaky breath, then turned to me. "Are you going to change, or do you want me to bandage you like this?"

I'd expected her voice to be flat. Instead, there was a brittle edge to it.

I transformed, and found my muscles still trembling from the exertion and continued pain.

"You seem angry," I said quietly. "Should I have tried harder to negotiate?"

"Damn it, Aren." She took my injured right arm in her hands. "I mean, at least it's the other side this time, but look at this."

The skin had been ripped away, leaving a deep, bloody wound surrounded by red marks that covered the remaining skin to my shoulder. I looked away.

"I'm not mad at you," she said more softly. "I just wish you'd have waited for help. The rest of us didn't even have time to react. You broke those first two before I realized what was happening."

"Before they did, too. It's better that way."

"I know, but I was scared. I didn't know how to help." She smoothed ointment onto my arm, and I let out a sound some-where between a growl and a whimper. The stuff burned as it entered the open flesh of my arm, and the pain radiated out from there. "I'm not *that* good an archer. I could have shot you just as easily as I did him, but I didn't know what else to do." She wrapped her arms around herself. "I started drawing his water. He slowed down, and it seemed to be working, and I just froze. It wasn't like calling water at the well, where it was peaceful. This was battle, and killing, and... and he got away from me. I couldn't let my fear get you killed, so I grabbed the bow instead." She rubbed her forehead with one hand. "I'm a coward."

"No, you're human. You did fine. You thought quickly and saved my life." She didn't say anything. "Are you okay with what you did there?"

"Yes," she said, with only slight hesitation. "I mean, I hate it. But he would have killed you."

"So how is that different from using magic to do it?"

She shook her head. "I don't know. Because it seems like an unfair advantage? Because I still feel guilty about it? Especially with my family there, maybe. I don't even know. But you're right. I'll try to remember that." She squeezed her eyes closed. "I almost let him kill you."

"But you didn't." She looked up, and I caught her eye. "Maybe the arrow was a good idea," I said. "At least if you'd hit me you'd have ended my pain."

I smiled to show her that I was only teasing, but she wasn't having it. She stepped back and smacked me in the ribs. Tears filled her eyes. "That's not funny." She wrapped her arms around me and rested her face against my chest.

"I..." The words didn't come easily for me. "Rowan, I'm sorry. I shouldn't joke. Kel was right, though. It does help a little."

"You can joke when I stop having nightmares about it." She bandaged my arm, though the ointment had already slowed the bleeding. "That's the last of the bandages, and of that stuff Nox gave you. Be careful. You're on your own now." She waited for me to dress, and we re-joined the group.

"Two are dead," Ashe said. "What do we do with the other?"

I observed the third, who remained on his knees off to the side of the path, dazed. "He'll be fine," I lied. "Leave him. Let him find his way back. Unless you have a better idea of what to do with him?"

"No, I can live with that," Ashe said. "Will we have time to get away before he sends people after us?"

The man reached up to touch his face, and stared in blank wonder at the blood on his fingers.

"I'd say we'll have time, yes." I re-mounted Jigger, who someone had already released from the cart, and Rowan climbed up behind me. "But we should move on."

I couldn't force myself to feel guilty about leaving him there. Every one of those men would happily have done the same to all of us. A part of me wished the last to go down had lived long enough to find out about his tiny power and suffer with the knowledge, but that didn't matter now.

Nothing in this gods-forsaken country did. All that mattered was getting to Tyrea and meeting up with the others. I wasn't entirely sure the family would follow when Rowan and I rode on down the path, but they did. Victoria and Ches had a hushed argument in the front of the cart while Lucilla rode in the back, but I didn't try to listen in. Whatever it was would work itself out, or not.

We crossed the border without further incident and reached a familiar town that evening. If not for the spring buds on the flowers instead of orange leaves on the trees, it could have been only a few days since Rowan and I had last visited. I led the way down a side street to the white inn and dismounted. I'd never expected to return here, and certainly not with Rowan.

"You should see about rooms," I told Ches. "I don't know whether they'll take your treasure here or not, but this will be a good place for you to stay while you decide what to do next."

He nodded and went in through the front door without another word, with Victoria following. Ashe hugged Rowan somewhat less enthusiastically than I'd seen him do before, and followed.

"We're not ready to be on our own here yet," Lucilla said. "Rowan, if you could just stay with us for a while. Help us get to know the customs and find a place to live. You belong with us. Please."

A look of intense sorrow came over Rowan's eyes as she looked at me. "Aren."

"It's fine." I made myself smile at both of them, though my heart felt as though it were trying to detach itself from my body. "You stay. I'll get back to my father. It's probably best if you help them get settled, stay out of Ulric's way until I smooth things over…" I trailed off. There was no point lying. I wanted her with me.

Rowan chewed her lower lip. "I need to speak to my family alone, if you don't mind."

My chest tightened. *This is the end.* "Of course."

I walked to the corner of the building and was surprised to find Victoria waiting there.

"I'm coming with you," she said. "Ches isn't happy about it, and Lucilla won't be when he tells her, but this is my decision."

I smiled. At least something was going right. "Fine by me. But why?"

She set her hands on her hips. "I feel like it's the right thing. Maybe it's because I owe it to Rowan after being absent for so long when she needed me. Maybe it's because it makes no sense for me to have come back to life as I have, only to waste whatever gifts I have here when I could be with your people, learning how to use them better." Her voice dropped. "Maybe it's because Ches won't fully accept who and what I am until he's had some time to adjust to life in this country, and I don't want to be around for his growing pains. Or Lucilla's, for that matter."

I couldn't help smiling at that. "I don't imagine it will be pretty. You are, of course, welcome. We'll leave right away, meet up with our friends, and then we'll make our way east."

Her smile turned nervous. "I'll just need to get my things. Are we going to meet your father, then? The king?"

My own smile disappeared. "We are."

"I see. Be right back." She hurried into the inn.

Rowan appeared from the shadows, carrying what had been Ashe's pack and bedroll. "So that's good news."

My heart leapt at the sight of her bringing her things. "It is. Not as good as having you with me."

She turned her chin up and gave me a surprised look. "You thought I'd abandon you?"

"I wouldn't have thought of it that way." I sat down on a bench, and motioned for her to do the same. We had a lot of walking ahead of us that night. "You should do what's best for you. I don't know what we're going to find when we get back. My father's not going to be pleased with either of us, but at least he acknowledges that he needs me around. Unless Nox has fixed everything, he can't get the throne back without me. But you... he might send you away. Or worse."

"He might not."

"Even if he doesn't, he won't let us be together. Much as I hate it, the law is the law. I don't think I can pretend it doesn't affect me anymore. I need to grow up and accept my responsibilities." The word tasted bitter in my mouth.

"I know." She pulled her feet up onto the seat of the bench and rested her arms on her knees. She didn't speak for a moment. "I think this is where it ends."

Numbness spread through me. "When all of this business is over—"

She took my hand in one of hers. "Is it ever going to be over, though?"

I swallowed down the tightness in my throat. "No. Not for me."

She nodded. Not agreement. Confirmation. "I don't want to lose you, but maybe us being together isn't what the world needs." Her voice wavered, but she pressed on. "I can't be selfish. I can't let Tyrea fall apart because I love you. You have a bigger purpose right now, and it doesn't look like it includes me. At least, not as I imagined it would. Even after Severn is defeated..." She took a shuddering breath and wiped the back of one hand over her eyes. "I guess we never really made sense together, did we? I love you in a way I thought was only possible in books and fairy tales. More than anything I've ever known. But we can't be together if you're going to be king some day, and I won't let you give that up for me. You have a great destiny that you can't ignore for one person."

I rested my face in my hands and willed myself to think clearly. She was doing what I should have, and I felt like a coward for not being able to make the right decision myself. Even when I could speak, I found I couldn't look directly at her. Sorrow closed around my heart and squeezed until I had to fight for breath.

"I still don't regret any of this," I said. "Do you?"

She let out a hollow, hopeless chuckle, and sniffled. "Never. Maybe if I'd known how much this would hurt, I would have avoided it. I'm glad I didn't."

"It would be easier for you if you stayed here. You could avoid my father's anger, stay safe. Help your family."

She rested a hand on my forearm and squeezed. "I know. And I'm tempted to, but I can't. I have a larger purpose, too, even though I don't understand it yet. If I had my way I'd be by your side through any battle. I need to help. I belong with you, with Kel and Nox and Griselda. Not here. I need to be there to learn to use my talents, to fight against Severn, to find out what my place is in this world. And even if that place is without you, forever—" Her voice caught in her throat. "Even then, this is what I have to do."

I wanted to tell her we'd get through, that we'd find a way to be together, but we had an agreement. No more lying to preserve each other's illusions or emotions.

I sat up and took her hand, unsure of what else to do. Tempted as I was to start pushing her away, to pretend that this didn't hurt and that she'd never meant as much to me as I'd thought, I wouldn't. Pain like I hadn't felt since before I could properly remember swelled within me until I thought I would burst. Or crack. Or simply cease to be. I had never wanted this, and yet losing her felt like losing a part of myself I hadn't know existed until she came into my life.

She sat back against the bench and nodded to herself. "I have to figure out what my life is going to look like, what I want to be. Maybe someday I'll help fix things in Darmid, who knows?"

My heart ached at the resignation and powerful determination in her voice. Gods, how I adored her. "Maybe you will."

"If I stay here now, my family will drive me insane, as will not knowing what's happening in Luid. What's happening to you, Kel, Nox. Now Victoria too. No, I'm coming."

I placed a kiss on the filthy shoulder of her shirt, knowing that even that was more than I had any right to now. I couldn't help myself.

She rested her head against me, just for a moment. There was nothing left to say.

Victoria returned with her pack and bedroll. "Shall we?" Tear tracks marked her cheeks, but her voice was calm and certain.

We left the horses. They wouldn't be able to keep up if any of us ended up flying. As the sky darkened over us, the two Sorceresses and I set out to the north, where I hoped we'd find a dragon, a flying horse, and a half-blind little girl waiting.

A strange fairy tale, indeed. If only we could all find the happy ending we were all searching for.

The sky clouded over as we passed through a series of small towns. At his request, I had been riding near Ulric at the head of our procession, but this morning Laelana had insisted on speaking to him privately, giving the rest of us a bit more distance. It suited me well enough. I preferred to speak to him as little as possible, as I hadn't forgiven him for what he said about my mother.

I couldn't get too far away, though. Ulric didn't like to have to search for me.

He made no grand proclamations of his return as we passed through towns, but also didn't deny his identity when folk were brave enough to approach and ask. I suspected he was assessing their reactions, deciding whether he could expect support when he did declare that the rightful king had returned.

Or I might have been completely wrong. If Aren had been there, I could have asked him. He knew how all this worked far better than I. But there had been no sign of him for four days, and no word that anyone else had seen or heard from him.

Damn him, leaving me to deal with the old man on my own.

The people seemed glad enough to see their king returned to them, which gave me a good feeling about our prospects. Less than a week and we'd be at the city gates. I wondered what would happen if Severn chose to respect the law. Would he still be executed? I hoped so. He would always be a threat. A man so cruel and power-hungry would never give up, not even after a hundred years in prison.

Ulric motioned for me to come closer and sent Laelana away, apparently done with her for now. "Any news?"

I looked back over my shoulder, but no one was close enough to listen in. "I'm making progress. I found some interesting notes in Mama Bunn's books about controlling magic—old stuff on the bindings they used to perform, and ways to block the effects of magic."

He narrowed his eyes. "You'll have to enlighten me. I don't see how reducing magic helps my problem."

My shoulders stiffened at his condescending tone. "Sometimes when you can't solve a problem by approaching it head-on, you need to go around the back way. By looking at the ingredients and techniques that lessen magic, I'm getting ideas on how to protect you from it while you recover. Great ideas."

Making those ideas a reality was the issue.

The stone-serious line of his mouth didn't change, but I thought I detected a slight lift at the corner of his eye. Amusement? Pride? I couldn't tell.

Laelana returned. "We have nothing left to spend."

"Then barter," Ulric said without favoring her with a glance. "Surely among your people you have some who have services to offer in exchange for food and clean water."

She sneered. "When you showed up, I thought our fortunes had turned. I promised you my people's support because I thought we'd benefit from it. And what have we seen from you? We're displaced, hungry, dirty, exhausted."

"All things in time, Laelana. You're starting to sound like your beloved husband."

"I defended you when he said we were fools to follow you to Luid. I'm beginning to think he was right."

I didn't need Aren's gifts to see that the king wanted no more of this conversation. Still, he didn't order her away. "You would have had to leave that encampment anyway, in search of water," he said, speaking with only the barest hint of irritation in his voice. "And tell me, how have I benefited from having your people come with me? You slow me down and pester me for food, as though I can pull it from my own body to feed you. In spite of the training we've offered, I doubt you could defend us if Severn came after us. Your people's support is appreciated, but don't overestimate your value. You'll benefit more than I will in the end."

He looked up at the dark clouds. Thus far the results of their appearance had been unimpressive, just enough of a sprinkle to tease us and leave a small offering in the rain barrels before the clouds disappeared, only to return later to taunt us. The draught had been localized to the rebel camp's area. The lack of rain on our journey was a simple matter of bad timing or bad luck.

Lightning flashed so far in the distance that I almost missed it.

"Better get ready to collect water," Ulric said. He looked back at the people. "You're right, they do look exhausted. Let them rest now. I'm going to take a few people and scout farther ahead. Nox, you stay with me. Laelana, please find Nox's friend Kel and send him along."

Laclana's mouth drew back in an irritated snarl. She dug her heel into her horse's side and wheeled it around, nearly trampling Kel as he approached on foot.

"The king wants you," she spat.

"Thanks," he said, and looked to us. "I was just looking for an update on our plans."

Exhausted though he was, he preferred walking to riding when possible. I supposed riding an animal felt strange when one was accustomed to getting around by one's own flukes, and walking gave him plenty of opportunity to associate with the people. He seemed to mind spending time with them far less than Ulric did, enjoying the chance to see the world with people who were unlike him.

"You'll come with us. We need another set of eyes." Ulric snapped his fingers and motioned for a young man to fetch another horse, and didn't speak again until Kel had mounted.

Kel and I exchanged a glance. If he was irritated by the order or Ulric's short tone, he didn't show it.

Ulric looked once more at his people, and took the lead as we picked up our pace and left them behind.

"More like a stone around your neck than an army, aren't they?" I observed.

Ulric kept his eyes on the road ahead. "They're my people. I usually try to avoid being this close to them, but they are my responsibility. Severn forgets that, I think. The dissenters are our responsibility as much as the sycophants and the flatterers in Luid. Severn seems to think he can show favor to the people who please him and let the rest rot. He would see these people dead before he fed them, I'm sure."

"You wouldn't, if they opposed you?"

"I might have when I was younger. I hardly remember. But I know better now, and I won't have Severn ruin everything I've worked so hard to build."

I wasn't sure what to say to that, so I let my frustration simmer in silence. How could this man be so infuriating and cruel to his family, and yet sound so noble when it came to his people? It didn't strike me as a deception. He apparently felt genuinely justified on both sides.

He glanced sideways at me. "I feel that. Your anger."

"Do you?" I tried not to feel like a child caught with her hand in the cookie jar.

"I don't have Aren's talents, but I have always been able to read people better than most. When you focus so hard on your hatred, especially when it's directed toward me and you're in such close proximity, I know it."

I leaned in closer. "Are you using magic, then? Is it making you ill?"

"I'm fine. I'll let you know if that changes." He shot me an appraising glance. "You have a lot of anger, don't you?"

"Yes. Most of it's not directed at you, but you piss me off. Frequently."

He smiled then, but it faded a moment later. "That's no surprise. And I understand, of course."

"Do you?"

"You think I'm a bad father."

I gritted my teeth. "That's not even a portion of it. I'm glad you know it, though."

He laughed. "Nox. One of my children had me locked away in an enemy land and stole my throne, and several others are dead because of him. Two support him, one of whom is a monster who takes pleasure in causing others pain. One son stands with me, but reluctantly and with much rebellion in his heart, and even he's run away. My only living daughter was exiled to the dragon lands at my order, and now hates me. I know I'm not the victim of a massive misunderstanding."

"And yet you won't change."

His expression hardened. "No. I'm the king. Country before family and before self. If Aren hates me but becomes a better king some day because of what I've put him through, I'll have done my job. If—"

Griselda Beaumage rode up beside him, followed by another Sorcerer. Qurwin, if I remembered correctly, a dark-haired fellow with a strong jaw and sharp eyes. I'd hardly seen any of them since their arrival. Laelana was careful to keep the Belleisle Sorcerers close to her and away from Ulric as much as possible, and Griselda had not objected thus far.

"Your Majesty, I apologize most sincerely for the interruption."

Ulric turned back to me. "That, my dear, is how one addresses a king." Then to Griselda he said, "Always a pleasure to speak with you. Is there a problem?"

"I'm not sure. I asked Maks to ride ahead, and he's reported a building staffed with soldiers just down the road. It wasn't on my maps."

Ulric frowned. "Thank you. Would you care to ride with us?"

"We would."

They spoke quietly about the people. Ulric never asked directly about Laelana and Goff or their private plans, but I sensed he and Griselda were communicating something about that amongst their words about concerns over food, the weather and the poor spring, and a missing child. She asked after Aren, and Ulric said he hadn't had any news.

"We'll need him soon, won't we?" she asked.

Ulric's mouth tightened. "We'll manage without him if we have to."

"Of course," she replied, but something in her tone said she suspected more about Ulric's situation than she was supposed to.

Tell her, I thought, hoping he might pick up on it, but he was right. He didn't have that gift.

We rounded a wide curve in the road. On the other side we found a building that looked like a small stone fortress with few windows and an imposing wooden door, shut tight. A soldier in a red uniform appeared on the roof, shielded behind a stomach-high wall. Four more joined him in a row.

The first to appear was also the first to speak. Tall and thin-shouldered as he was, his wide beard gave him a comically unbalanced appearance.

"Hold, travelers. Where are you headed?" His voice boomed out, rich and deep.

"Is this not a free road?" Ulric called back to him.

"This is the king's road, as are they all. State your business."

Ulric took in the sight of the soldiers wearing the usurper's colors. *Back away,* I thought. *We'll go around.*

He stood his ground. "I am Ulric, king of Tyrea. Lord Severn will no doubt be overjoyed to hear of my return. Perhaps you'd be so kind as to send a messenger and let him know that as of this moment, he is relieved of his duties. I thank him for governing in my absence, but he's free to step down now."

The soldiers looked apprehensively from Ulric to their leader, who showed no such uncertainty.

"Oh, he'll be interested to hear that the whispers are true," he called down to us. "You should tell him yourself, though. I'm sure he'll be eagerly awaiting your return."

Ulric's jaw muscles tightened as he glared upward. "What's your name, soldier?"

The bearded fellow jerked his head toward us, and two of his men picked up bows and arrows to take careful aim.

"They call me Hal. Hairy Hal to my friends."

"Do you consider Lord Severn your friend?"

"No, I consider him my king as of yesterday's proclamation. Step back. Ulric is dead."

He knew as well as I did that the rightful king stood before him. It was evident in his arrogance, and the nervousness that showed on his men's faces. They all knew. But they had orders, and they had clearly sworn loyalty to Severn.

Ulric showed no sign that this news surprised him. He backed his horse up, and the rest of us did the same. "I'll remember your name, Hairy Hal, and I promise I won't forget that face. Pray we don't meet again."

Hal spit over the edge of the roof. "I don't think we will. Gentlemen?"

We didn't waste any time in turning the horses. Kel's was last to obey, and took an arrow to the chest and one to the neck. It crashed to the ground, thrashing, with Kel's leg trapped under it. "Go!" Kel yelled.

I turned back and put my horse between him and the arrows, which now arced over our heads toward the king. "Come on!"

He grunted as he pulled his leg free and climbed to his feet. I offered a hand up and had the horse in motion before he was properly seated.

Griselda's horse shrieked as he took an arrow in the rump, but kept running.

We didn't stop until we were far from the building and it became clear that they weren't following us.

"So there it is," Ulric said, and dragged his hands through his hair.

The gesture would have been commonplace on anyone else. On him, always so composed and controlled, it shouted his distress.

"You expected otherwise?" I asked.

"No, but there was the possibility that he would respect our traditions and laws. I expected a little more time, at least."

"How can he do that?" I asked. "Aren was certain you had until summer."

Ulric's brow creased. "If he has convinced his council that they're facing war or a great threat, they may have moved to solidify his power early. It's a security measure."

"So there's no way to reverse that?" Kel asked, and rubbed a knot out of his thigh.

"I think not," Ulric said. "Not while Severn lives. The only thing I'm certain of is that Laelana's people are no longer needed. Their recognition and support mean nothing if I can't assert my legal right to the throne. From here out, they're a danger and a distraction."

Griselda dismounted and looked over her horse. "We'll come with you. There must be a way the true king can return, especially after what Severn did to you. Some law—"

Ulric sighed. "Beaumage, you seem convinced that the letter of the law is the only way I'll reclaim my throne."

She looked evenly at him. "Your power's not what it was, sire. I can't say I knew you well when I stayed in Luid, but I met you enough times to know your behavior has changed. I would appreciate complete honesty in this, if I'm to be a part of your temporary council." She spoke respectfully, but her expression said she was in no mood for an argument.

"You can be on it permanently if you help me get my throne back," he said. "Very well, we carry on without the others. I can't say what Severn will throw at us when we arrive, but it's nothing they're prepared to fight against. Beaumage, if you would be so kind as to gather your men to join us. Tell Laelana I thank her for their service, and their rewards will come."

I wondered about that. They'd done nothing of practical value, except to bolster Ulric's confidence slightly after he'd lost everything. Perhaps, to him, that was enough.

Apparently deciding her horse was fit to ride in spite of the arrow sticking out of his wide arse, Griselda re-mounted and rode off.

Thunder rumbled overhead like the hoofbeats of a thousand war horses.

"Aren will be back soon," I said. "He can challenge Severn if you can't."

Kel's hands tightened at my waist.

Ulric sighed. "He can't. No matter what angle I look at this from, I keep reaching the conclusion that Severn has planned this too well. He's now within his legal rights to refuse challengers, as security and stability are considered paramount in times of war. It's how my grandfather held power for so long."

"Something tells me Severn will want to have it out with Aren," I said. "End that threat once and for all, if he has a chance. Aren is strong enough to fight him." The thought nauseated me, knowing how badly Aren didn't want that. *But he could.*

"I know," Ulric said. "But, and I admit that this is partially my fault, Aren allowed Severn to direct his gifts and his schooling. Severn made him focus on mind-control, even though it may have cost Aren in the development of other skills. But he didn't give that order until he knew he was safe from it. He made Aren into a weapon that couldn't be turned against its master."

"What about Aren's other skills?" I asked.

"If Severn knows of them, he'll have found ways to defend himself," Ulric replied. "I'd wager he's been training against eagles for as long as he's known about that trick. And if he used that, Aren would put himself at a disadvantage if he wanted to change back. Anything else he can do is a minor gift. That, or unpracticed and therefore as much a threat to him as it would be to Severn. If he had years to practice, yes, he would have a good chance. It's not strength he's lacking, it's breadth of skill. There's a reason most kings don't take the throne when we're young. It might take a century to master skills that don't come naturally to us."

"And there's the pain," Kel offered, speaking softly.

"Pardon?"

Kel took a deep breath before speaking again. "I think it shames Aren. He doesn't often speak of it. You knew how badly Severn once injured him?"

"I do," Ulric said. "He nearly died. Most would have."

"Well, the scar runs deeper than what shows on his flesh. Severn can bring him pain—deep, physical pain that goes far beyond what most of us have ever felt. There's some connection there that I don't quite understand. All I know is that Aren hasn't found a way to stop it. I don't even know whether there's a limit to it, whether it might kill him."

Ulric nodded. "Thank you. That seals it. It's down to me."

Kel looked away, apparently ashamed for sharing a secret to protect his friend.

We got the horses moving toward the town as a light drizzle misted over the road. "I might be able to help him block the pain," I said. "With the right ingredients, and with Mama Bunn's help—"

"No." Ulric spoke firmly, but not unkindly. "I have no doubt that you could, but the law strictly prohibits outside interference in a confrontation for the throne, if Severn even allowed Aren to challenge him. It's Sorcerer against Sorcerer, bound by strict rules and observed by many witnesses. May the strongest win."

"But Severn already cheated!" I spoke louder than I'd meant to. A crow squawked back from the trees beside us. "He had outside help getting rid of you. He's denying you your right as current and living king to take the throne back, and is therefore breaking the law. He's obviously willing to use force if he has to. How is it wrong for you to use the advantages you have? Or for Aren to use his? For that matter, what's to stop us simply attempting an assassination?"

Kel placed a calming hand against my ribs. I slowed my breathing, and my heartbeat followed.

"The law means nothing if we disregard it," Ulric said.

"Damn the law! We're in the right, here."

Ulric's jaw tightened. "We will consider your offer, Nox. Thank you." He rode ahead of us to meet the Sorcerers as they approached.

I leaned back against Kel. "He doubts his right to the throne," Kel said, speaking so softly that I had to strain to hear even with his mouth next to my ear.

"He can't."

"He does. I might not see into people like Aren does, but I do have my skills." I remembered how he'd judged me worthwhile when anyone else would have walked away, and nodded. "What I sensed in him didn't add up until he started talking about the law. According to it, the strongest Sorcerer is entitled to the throne. He isn't the strongest anymore."

I sat up straight and urged the horse forward. We followed the others off the road and into the woods.

"Then we build him back up so he is," I said through gritted teeth, "or we find another way. If he won't cheat, I will."

25

NOX

After Griselda returned with uninjured horses for Kel and herself, our small group left Laelana's people behind quickly. It sounded like Goff hadn't been too pleased about losing his chance at glory, but we couldn't worry about that. We rode without speaking, making our way through the thick, dark forest. Gwyn, the little winged cat, alternated between soaring overhead and perching on the saddle behind her mistress.

Qurwin was an accomplished scout and woodsman who used magic to choose our route, avoiding natural obstacles. The ground beneath the horses' hooves remained uneven and they couldn't move much faster than a quick walk, but with no false steps and no need to detour around unexpected obstacles, we might as well have been on the open road.

All of the Sorcerers carried their camp gear with them, as they had for the entire journey. They'd insisted from the beginning on keeping their food and gear separate from everyone else's, and had not accepted offers to lighten their loads by letting others carry their packs in the carts.

"It wasn't anything against those people," Griselda explained to me. "We just needed to be able to get away quickly should the need arise."

"As it did," I said, and she smiled.

"This is not the first time we've done something like this. Our governor has sent many of us out on diplomatic missions before, usually to Tyrea, but occasionally overseas. We behave ourselves, respect customs, try to learn what we can, and fit in with cultures and species that are not our own. But we do not become a part of them. Our first loyalty is always to Belleisle."

Ulric fell back to ride beside Griselda. "You did well enough in Tyrea when I held the throne."

"You made us comfortable and never threatened our safety," she said. "I can't say quite the same for Severn. I went back alone the last time. He followed customs, never made me feel that I was a prisoner, spoke respectfully when we met." Her eyes took on a distant look. "But I always felt threatened in his presence, though I couldn't say why. I left when he sailed for Belleisle. He took only his personal vessel, and wasn't planning an attack. But his presence near the island was a threat, and I didn't trust that I was safe in Luid. If I'd stayed—"

"Then you wouldn't be able to help us," Ulric said. "I suspect you would be a prisoner by now, in practical terms if not officially."

"Perhaps."

"Were you there when Aren detected?" I asked. He'd never said much about leaving, but I knew Severn's reaction hadn't been pretty.

"I was," she said softly. "Aren was almost never around before then, always doing one thing or another for Severn. Him disappearing was nothing new, or cause for concern. And Severn never let me in on what was happening. We rarely spoke." She looked up into the treetops, deep in thought. "I heard things, of course. That Aren had really disappeared this time, that Severn feared him captured or dead, and seemed to be losing his mind over it."

"He was that worried about Aren?" I asked. "I didn't realize he cared."

Ulric snorted. "If he'd sent Aren to Darmid, I'd say he was

more concerned that they'd captured him and Aren had found me in the prisons. That would have been dangerous."

"Indeed," Griselda agreed. "So then people claimed to have seen Aren, and said he and Severn left with a few men but no word of where they had gone. A few days later the entire palace was living in fear of Severn's temper. Not that it was level at the best of times, but in those days the servants feared beheadings if his tea was cold, and his advisers dreaded banishment if they spoke too loudly in his presence. Severn disappeared frequently on that flying horse of his, and apparently wouldn't even tell Dan where he was going."

"Dan?" I asked.

Ulric chuckled. "One of your brothers, Nox. Never one to draw attention to himself. I suspect that's how he's survived this long with Severn."

"He's Severn's second now," Griselda added. "He should know absolutely everything. He acts like he does, but I had my doubts. No one ever seemed entirely clear on what had happened. They held Aren's trial in secret and convicted him of treason, and orders went out that if anyone saw him they were to turn him in."

"Rewards?" I asked.

"Rewards, and threats against anyone who didn't comply. And then one day we stopped seeing Severn. He was there, but only Dan, his Potioner Sara, and a handful of doctors were allowed to see him. The curtains to his rooms were always drawn, and everyone was afraid to even speak of him. I don't know whether he's appeared in public since then. I learned later from Ernis Albion what happened when Severn caught Aren and Rowan, and she released her magic. I don't know how Severn survived that. She's a powerful force, that one."

Ulric nodded, but looked troubled.

"Shame that he did survive," I muttered, and wondered how bad things might still be. Was Severn hiding because he was weak and didn't want word to get out? Aren had said our brother looked ghastly when he last saw him, but that Severn had claimed to be recovering quickly.

Maybe that means Ulric might...

No. That had only been Severn's physical appearance. Aren had felt his magic and found it effective, if not fully recovered.

I wondered about this Sara person. How was she aiding his recovery?

That set me to rifling through the ideas I'd scribbled in my mind, thoughts on the angles, the possibilities, the ways I might make a potion work to help Ulric. I kept returning to the fact that a Potioner in Luid would have access to far more ingredients, information, and resources. If only I could have those, just for a day.

It was hours before I realized that Kel had hardly spoken.

"You okay?" I asked.

"Not great," he admitted. "Surviving. Holding out hope that we're going to find a lake or a good river soon."

I left him and rode up next to Qurwin. "Any water near here?" I asked.

He slowed his horse and looked around. "Not directly on our route, but there's something to the west a ways. A little too far out to camp there, though."

No, Ulric wouldn't be pleased if we strayed from the path he'd set in his mind, or if Kel and I went off on our own when we might lose them.

I went back offered Kel the water skin, but he refused. "Save it for later," he said. "I don't want to be the weak spot in the group."

"You're not." I looked back at Qurwin. *Maybe after we stop...* "You want to help me forage later? I might have a surprise for you."

He raised his eyebrows. "Of course."

The sky remained cloudy, providing a respite from the sun but offering no rain. *Tease,* I thought, and glared upward. *Just a little rain. Please.*

The sky rumbled again, but nothing changed.

Nothing changes unless we make it happen, I realized. I couldn't make the sky give up the rain, but I could renew my efforts to change Ulric's situation. If Aren were truly incapable of defeating Severn, I had to find a way to make sure Ulric could do it.

We made camp late in the afternoon, when Qurwin said we'd

reached the last reasonable safe stopping place for many hours. After some tense discussion with Ulric, Griselda sent Gwyn off to Belleisle with a cryptic message tied to one of her back legs. Ulric seemed entirely uncomfortable with the idea of exposing his need for help, but the time for pride had passed.

"I need to collect some things," I told Ulric after Griselda left him. "I don't have Mama Bunn or her equipment now, but I want to see what ingredients might be available in this area to help you." In truth, I thought I had a far better shot of finding something to help Kel, but doubted Ulric would let me wander off just for that.

He nodded, dismissing me.

I found Qurwin setting up his tent. "Where did you say the water was?"

He smiled kindly. "Your friend having problems?"

"You could say that. And I've been lacking in aquatic ingredients for my potions. I thought if I could reach it without too much trouble, I should take a look."

He pointed to my left. "Go straight that way. North by north-west, if you know your directions. If you take a horse, you'll get there in an hour or so. Lake. That's all I can tell from here."

I could have hugged him. "That's an amazing skill. Thank you."

His smile tightened. "I had a mer once. Couldn't get her to stay, but damn. Best week of my life."

I borrowed Ulric's horse. He always claimed the finest ones, and the strong animal would carry us easily. Kel mounted behind me. It took more than the hour Qurwin had suggested, but after a hard ride through pine forest and a detour around a wide ravine, we found it.

I sighed. "Not much of a lake, really."

Kel's arms snaked around my waist and he kissed my hair as thunder rumbled again. "It'll do. Thank you."

It was really more of a bog, a huge area of rocky mud with a flat circle of silvery gray water in the center that looked deeper. Kel and I dismounted, and the horse set to finding something to eat. The air crackled and hummed, and a light sprinkle of rain began to fall.

Kel closed his eyes and turned his face up. I did the same, and he laughed as I tried to catch the rain on my tongue.

We waited for it to stop again, to disappoint us, but the rain only came harder as the droplets grew heavier. Kel looked like he might cry as it became clear that we were in for a real storm. Water soaked our clothes and our hair, and Kel came alive under it. His hands trembled as he fumbled with his shirt. "Nox, help."

My fingers flicked over the buttons as though I'd undressed him a hundred times. He lifted his arms into the downpour and took deep, heaving breaths. Water slicked his body, rippling over his skin.

"It's incredible!" He had to yell to be heard over the fat raindrops that slapped down on the thirsty ground.

"It is," I agreed, and stripped my own shirts off over my head to let my bare skin drink in the glorious rain.

Lightning flashed across the sky from west to east, with a crash of thunder on its heels that shook my bones. Drawing in a breath became difficult under the downpour, which now crashed over us as though we stood under a waterfall. My heart leapt as sheets of rain soaked my hair and chilled my skin, washing away the dirt and the cares of the past weeks, melting the stony armor that I'd built up to protect me from the world.

I tilted my face up and closed my eyes. Before I could open them again, Kel's lips were pressed to mine. Water sluiced between my fingers as my hands slid over his body, unable to get the grip on him that I wanted so desperately. I tangled the fingers of one hand in his hair, anchoring myself to him, afraid I might wash away otherwise. His mouth was hot against my rain-chilled skin as he worked at the waterlogged laces of my trousers, then allowed his hands to stray upward, apparently trying to cover every bit of exposed skin with his touch.

I understood. I couldn't stop doing the same, though my smaller hands covered far less area than his did on me. Unable to open my eyes against the downpour, I was left to focus on the sensations that flooded my body, driving all other thoughts from my mind. The chill of the rain, the warmth of his hands, his lips. All I knew was that I wanted him, completely and without reservation.

No more holding back. The past would not anchor me to my fears and doubts, and the worries of the future could wait. If such a thing as soul-mates existed, Kel was mine. No more running from love, from connection, from hope.

Our clothes landed in the mud and were quickly trampled under our feet as we moved to a grassy area farther from the pond. Kel scooped me up. I wrapped my legs around his waist and my arms around his neck to keep from slipping, pressing myself to the warmth of his skin as cool rain washed down my back.

"Kel, you're sure this is what you want? I mean, if this is forever..."

His lips curved into a familiar grin. "I've never been so certain of anything. Are you?"

My breath caught in my throat, and I laughed. "Yes."

He dropped to his knees and set me on the grass, shielding me from the worst of the downpour with his body even as he pulled back.

"What's wrong?"

He chewed his lower lip. "I'm actually a little nervous."

I laughed and pulled him closer to plant a tender kiss between his eyebrows. "You have no reason to be. You're already the best thing that's ever happened to me. And I—"

He covered my mouth with his. "I love you, Nox," he whispered.

I tried to say I loved him, too, but couldn't speak the words. Instead, I let my body answer, hoping it could express the affection, the passion, the admiration I felt for him.

The rain pounded down on us as the storm raged. I thought I might drown in Kel if not in the deluge, and yet I wished the storm would never cease.

But all things end, no matter how hard we wish it could be otherwise. The thunder moved off into the distance, and all too soon the early evening sun broke through the clouds. It found us wrapped in each other's arms and lying under the open sky, drenched, exhausted, and completely at peace.

"It is different this way," Kel whispered as he brushed my rain-sodden hair away from my face.

"Better?"

"So much. I've never known anything like it before."

"Me, either." I sat up slowly and reoriented myself. "The lake looks a little more promising now, if you want to go for a swim. If we stay out too much longer they're going to send a search party."

He stretched his arms over his head and stood. "I think you mean a roll in the mud, not a swim. It's probably shallow and filthy, but I don't know when I'll get another chance."

I took a moment to appreciate the view as he walked away, then called for him to rinse our clothes out if he could. He didn't reply, but scooped the muddy items out of the muck on his way by. He walked out into the water, which covered his ankles, then his legs to the knees.

Not much of a lake, indeed.

Then he grinned back at me over his shoulder and dove, disappearing completely.

I hurried to the edge of the lake, hopping from rock to rock instead of letting the mud squelch between my toes. At the spot where Kel had disappeared, the murky water became clear and deep. I held my breath and stepped forward, plunging toes-first into icy water that took my breath from me. Strong hands closed around my waist, and our heads broke the surface together. I laughed. When my hand strayed downward, I found that his body below the hips had become a smooth, muscular tail that moved gently, bearing us up.

"We're going to make this work," he said. I smiled at the certainty in his voice. "I've just figured it out. A house by the sea, right on the beach. We can live together there, I can take to the water whenever I want, gather food and whatever ingredients you want to experiment with. If we're near enough to a town, you can do your work for those people. When word gets out about your talents, they'll come from all over the country to see you. Maybe farther. Or you can tell them to flick off, and it can just be the two of us." He grinned.

"That sounds amazing." I still had trouble imagining such loveliness in my future, but I tried. "Will your elders be happy with that?"

He planted a solid kiss under my jaw. "No, but I don't care. They can banish me if they won't accept this, and I'll be free to be with you."

His words surprised me. His loyalty to them had always been unshakable. "Kel, you love your people."

"I do. But I can't let them confine me."

I sighed and held him close. "I want that future, so much."

"We could just ride off, right now."

"And abandon everyone here?" I ran my fingers through his wet hair, brushing it back from his face. "If I leave now, Ulric loses the throne. Aren is bull-headed enough to try to take Severn down even though it's a fight he can't win without my help, and then what?"

He slipped his arms more fully around my waist. "I know. I suppose our future will keep, at least for a while."

He helped me out of the water and dove to retrieve the clothing he'd dropped.

I wrung the lake water out of each item. "I'll spread these out to dry a little, but I think we're going back to camp wet."

"Suits me. Just gives me few minutes to swim."

When Kel emerged from the lake, he brought an armload of plants with him. I sorted through and selected three that felt promising, and sent him back for more.

"See how well this works?" he asked when he returned.

"I do," I said. "And look, there's pondsquinch. If I pick some dusty blarch along the way, you can have that lovely potion again that Mama Bunn came up with."

He made a gagging noise. "Better than drying up and blowing away. I suppose."

I dressed as he went back for more of the pondsquinch. Something warm still burned within me even as my damp clothing chilled my skin. It took me a few moments to realize it was hope. This was what had been growing in me since my conversation with Aren, since I'd decided to look to the future instead of the past. I couldn't remember ever feeling it before. The thought of living a life with more meaning than mere survival, of finding peace when the need to fight was past, was completely foreign to me. Thinking of it was like trying to look at the sun, so bright it was blinding.

The immediate future was uncertain, but if we could just get through that...

"Kel?"

"Hmm?"

I slipped my foot into a boot that squelched with rainwater. "Let's make it a plan. Officially. As soon as we're free to leave, as soon as all of this mess is on its way to being cleaned up and everyone can do without us, let's find that house by the sea. Let's buy a big, warm bed and spend days on end in it. Just us."

His grin undid my heart. "It's a deal."

26

ROWAN

We walked through the night. Aren and I didn't speak more about our situation. Even if Victoria hadn't been with us, there still wouldn't have been anything left to say. We loved each other. We couldn't be together. It wasn't the first time my expectations or plans for my life had gone off the road.

It just hurt more this time.

As the sun broke over the forest we found Florizel in the field outside of the town where we'd left Patience.

"Where's Ruby?" I asked. "Did she go on?"

"No," Florizel said. "She took shelter in the wilder parts of the forest so as not to frighten the townsfolk."

Aren raised an eyebrow. "That was decent of her."

Florizel snorted. "She wanted to head straight into town and demand a tribute in exchange for not razing the place to the dirt, but I convinced her that the people here are probably richer in pointy weapons than they are in jewels."

"Thank you," I said, and tried not to laugh.

I left Aren and Victoria with her while I went to look for Patience. I crossed the fields, careful not to trample the new sprouts, and found her in a dusty yard playing with a pair of boys about her own age, perhaps a little older.

"Avast!" she yelled, and brandished a wooden sword at the side of the new barn. "Board her and pillage, men!"

The boys obliged, climbing a stack of crates and throwing themselves in through an upper window. Moments later they scrambled back down, arms loaded with small burlap sacks.

"Well done," she said.

"I don't think pirates are so free with praise," I said as I approached.

Patience's face lit up in a broad grin, and she ran toward me with open arms. I squeezed her tight, and my heart swelled. I'd missed the kid.

"I'm not a mean captain," she said.

"Deadeye, watch out! That traitorous wench may be skleevin' ye!" hollered one of the boys, a mop-haired thing with a healthy belly under his brown overalls.

I laughed. "Deadeye? Really?"

The boy nodded solemnly. "Only it's not 'cause of her you-know." He motioned to his own face and squinted one eye closed. "Pa took us all hunting and she killt more rabbits than any of us."

His brother, a slightly taller fellow with an impressively freckled face, kicked at the dirt. "She was lucky."

"Was not!" Patience released me and punched her pirate friend in the arm. He winced. "Your Pa said by rights I shouldn't be able to shoot with one eye. That makes me even *better*." She turned back to me. "He said it must be a blessing from the Goddess, if I don't do it by magic."

I smiled. "Maybe it is." The poor girl certainly deserved something for her suffering—not that any gods I knew operated that way. "Are you coming back with us? If you want to stay here, that's fine. We'll miss you, but—"

"Naw, I'm coming." She handed her sword to the fat kid. "You're captain now, Mister Tubbs, but only until I come back. Don't make me whup you again."

"Godspeed, Deadeye," he said. I had to cover my mouth to hide my smile.

"Rowan, you should go ahead," Patience told me. "I need to get my stuff and say goodbye to their Ma and Pa. Don't want them to worry if I just disappear."

"By all means." She ran off, and I waved to the boys. "It was lovely to meet you, gentlemen. I hope to never meet you on the high seas. Do you mind if I borrow this?" I picked up a large, heavy tarp from the ground, one that was stiff and dusty enough that I thought it hadn't been needed in a while.

After a whispered discussion, they said I could take it. "But beware, ye're indebted to pirates now," said the taller boy.

"I won't forget. Thank you."

I walked slowly, and Patience caught up with me before I reached our friends.

"See that?" She grinned. "See how I can move?"

She had indeed made good time. "I did notice. Most impressive."

"Their Ma gave me these new boots that hold my feet tight, and soft socks for inside. Running doesn't hurt so much."

She still limped a little, but Patience's gait was smoother than it had been. Such a simple solution. I ruffled her hair. "Thank the gods for Ma."

By the time we returned, Florizel had flown to the forest and retrieved Ruby, who waited under the shelter of the tree line. She looked over the group. "How will this work?"

I dropped the tarp on the ground. "I think you might need to carry me and Patience, and we'll have Victoria on Florizel. Will this help?" I knew she could carry one of us in each forepaw, but couldn't shake the mental image of her dropping one of us while landing.

"Might be more than just the two of you," Aren said. "My arm's still not healed from having the feathers ripped out, and I'm not sure I'll be able to fly."

"I can take two smaller humans," Florizel said. "I've rested."

Victoria looked nervously from the horse to the dragon. "If it's all the same, I'd prefer to ride with Florizel. I can't say the thought isn't terrifying, but it's more like what I'm accustomed to on land."

Aren closed his eyes. "Fine. Victoria, you and Patience ride on Florizel."

"I'll be careful," the horse promised. "This lady's more slender, anyway."

It was true. She appeared healthier than I'd seen her in ages, but Vic still hadn't put back on the weight she lost after the children's deaths. She'd have to hold on tight so as not to blow away.

"Guess we're flying together this time," I said to Aren, and took Patience and Victoria's bags from them. They mounted Florizel, and she took them through her paces around the field. Without bags to bulk them up, they looked secure enough.

Ruby's scaled lips opened into a grin, and Aren pulled me a few paces away.

"I need to say this aloud," he said quietly, "just so I understand. We're about to entrust our lives to a dragon and the tensile strength of a bedsheet?"

"No. A sheet of thick canvas."

He paled. "I see. That makes me feel much better."

We spread the tarp out on the ground and loaded the bags into the middle. "How would you like to do this?" I asked Ruby.

"Sit on the bags. I'll bundle you in the cloth and carry you that way. If my claws poke or you can't breathe, just yell."

Aren and I did as she instructed, and massive claws picked up the corners of the tarp. Ruby gathered them at the top, leaving plenty of space overhead, even if we did get squished at the sides. She held the top of the huge package tight and lifted us gently. The bundle swayed, unsupported from beneath.

"Wait," Aren said. "How do we yell if we can't breathe?"

There was no time to ask Ruby. As soon as the words were out of his mouth, we were thrown together and jerked upward as Ruby shot into the sky. A moment later Ruby's other forepaw cupped the canvas and the bags beneath us.

"Rowan?"

"Yes?"

"Your elbow's in my—"

"Sorry."

We shifted around, trying to get comfortable, and settled for

Aren being squashed between the bags with me sitting sideways, legs across his. I leaned against him and rested my head on his shoulder, pressed in tight by the side of the makeshift bag we now occupied. "Is that comfortable for you?"

He yawned. "No. But it's good."

Neither of us kept our eyes open for long. We'd been walking all night, we were emotionally exhausted, and the air in our little bundle was warm and relaxing. The light filtering through the canvas and the colder air coming through the gaps overhead weren't enough to keep us awake. Aren's body relaxed, and his breathing slowed. I felt myself drifting off soon after.

I woke to the sound of a woman screaming, followed by several people shouting. Ruby's grip beneath us disappeared, leaving us swinging in the air. My stomach leapt into my throat and refused to leave until she touched down and set us on the ground.

"Quiet!" she roared.

I pushed my way out of the bundle and into the afternoon sunlight, and Aren followed as soon as he'd extricated himself from the straps of our bags. "It's fine!" I yelled. "She's not going to hurt you!"

Florizel shuffled nervously nearby, with her passengers still mounted. "This is the right herd, isn't it?"

I spotted a few familiar faces among the crowd. This was our group, no doubt. "The dragon's not here to eat you!" I shouted. "She's a... a friend."

Ruby snorted, but said nothing. I hoped I hadn't just insulted her.

Goff strode forward with his sword raised. "You won't find Ulric here," he said. "Nor his daughter, nor the turncoats from Belleisle. I'd suggest taking your dragon and going now, if you don't want trouble. They weren't welcome here, and neither are you. I don't need more useless mouths to feed."

I looked beyond him. They'd set up their camp again, this time outside of a small town in a farmer's field.

"So you kicked them out because they weren't contributing?" Aren asked, unable or unwilling to hide the disbelief in his voice.

If there had been a split, Ulric had certainly left them behind. Goff was obviously hurt.

"Aye," he growled. "So piss off."

"Patience!" A woman's voice called out from the crowd. Victoria helped the girl to the ground, and she ran to the young woman who had spoken. "I was so worried!" She looked to us, and her lips narrowed until they disappeared completely. "Patience belongs here. Not where you're going."

Patience shook herself free and ran back to me. "I can fight," she said.

Aren placed a hand on her hair. "You can, but you don't have to. Stay here. These people need you to watch out for them." The words would have sounded like a shallow attempt at placating the girl but for the sincerity in his voice and expression.

"But you need me," Patience said, almost pleading.

"You've done plenty," I told her, and crouched to speak more quietly. "If Ulric has left these people, they'll need you again. Your work isn't finished. Besides, do you really want to see that old bastard again?"

She smiled at the word, but only for a moment. "I guess you're right," she said. "You'll find me when it's all over, though?"

"I will." I hoped I'd be able to.

Patience nodded and stepped back. "Then I'll stay."

Victoria dismounted and spoke quietly to Aren. He nodded.

"We'll leave," he said to Goff. "We just need a short rest." He turned and followed Victoria farther out into the fields. I jogged to catch up, leaving Ruby grinning at the villagers and blowing an impressive amount of smoke out of her nostrils.

"Will this do?" Aren asked, and Victoria nodded. "I'm going to step aside, just in case."

He took my hand and pulled me a good distance away as Victoria walked ahead.

"Is she using magic?" I asked.

"She's going to try. See what she can do here, away from her familiar source."

Victoria looked back at us, then out over the fields. She

reached up to untie the knot she kept her long hair in, letting it blow free in the wind.

I took a lock of mine and twisted it between my fingers. "She's done this before. She should be able to control it. Right?"

A warm breeze passed over us as Victoria stooped to touch the plants at her feet.

"No good?" Aren called. She shook her head. "Try again," he said. "Less force this time. Go easy."

She walked to a new patch of ground, leaving a broad swath of wilted plants behind her.

"She'll be fine," Aren said. "But the magic here may be of a slightly different quality from what's in her garden, and stronger."

Green shoots sprouted around my aunt. Her feet disappeared in a mass of vines covered in broad leaves.

"Rowan?" she called. "Help?"

It took me a moment to realize she needed more water. I closed my eyes. It must have rained recently. The earth felt heavy with it when I reached out with my mind.

I reached for the peaceful feeling of Victoria's garden, and the magic flowed, if somewhat hesitantly. I pulled water a little at a time from the nearby forest instead of the fields. This was more difficult than it had been at the well. There, the ground water had been available but low. Here it was a matter of drawing it out of sodden patches of mud and out of tree moss that held it like a sponge. Sweat broke out on my forehead, and the effort pulled my breath from me.

No hurry, I reminded myself. *Just let it come.* The depletion came, too, but I refused to fear it. Instead, a bright spark of hope lit up within me.

I can work with this. Given a peaceful place to practice and enough time to recover between attempts, I thought I might learn to perform great magic.

If only either of those things seemed guaranteed once we caught up with Ulric.

A tiny stream snaked over the field, shimmering in the sunlight. It broadened slightly, never much more than a trickle, but it was enough. When it reached Victoria I released it, and even from a distance felt it soak into the ground.

The plants grew again and produced fat squash in several varieties as the growth spread in an even and expanding circle of green around the Sorceress. Victoria spun and clapped her hands together. "It worked!" she called.

Aren followed me as I walked to meet her. "Nicely done," he told me quietly.

"Difficult, though. I don't think I could pull it from the trees themselves, or try—" I shrugged. I'd been about to mention using my power against enemies, but had no desire to bring back those associations. "I'll get there."

We moved on to the orchard, passing fields where the plants were still developing in an ever-widening circle. Victoria's magic left a lingering trail of influence behind her, just as it had in her garden after she stopped visiting. She seemed to have none of the hang-ups I'd struggled with after I left Darmid. She'd been through all of that already, and now accepted her power fully. If only it had been that natural for me. Even after all the work I'd been doing, it seemed to come easier for her.

"It probably helps that she has more life experience than you," Aren said, and rested a hand on my waist before pulling it quickly away. "She likely knew that the Darmish were wrong about magic long ago, and just had to accept it."

"I thought you couldn't read my thoughts."

His lips pulled up at one corner. "They're written on your face. You've never been good at keeping a secret."

A balding man in work clothes approached from the direction of the farm house, hat in hand, but kept a respectful distance as he watched the magic unfold. His eyes widened as ripe peaches, plums, apples and gorganfruits appeared on the trees. I plucked a fat peach and bit into it. Absolute perfection. Juicy, sweet, firm. The insects and elements hadn't had a chance to interfere with its growth. I picked another and carried it to the farmer.

"I hope you don't mind," I said, and offered it to him.

"No, no," he said, and accepted the fruit as gently and wonderingly as if I were handing him a newborn child. "It's just that my grandfather did this sort of thing, and I used to love to watch him. I think the land still carries the blessing of his magic. We do better than other farms, though I don't use magic myself. Thank you."

Victoria approached, dazed and stumbling. "I think I overdid it."

Aren took her by the arm and led her to a shady spot to sit.

"You're welcome," I told the farmer on her behalf. "If it's not too much trouble, do you think you might share some of this food with the people camped in your back field? They're friends of ours."

He bit into the peach and closed his eyes as he savored it. "I will, though these would fetch a fine price at market in Luid." He looked down at the fruit. "Or would have, if the city were open. The high-born and gifted do love treats like this."

"It's closed off, then?"

"Oh, yes. Lord Severn ordered supplies brought in a month ago, from all over the country. Just yesterday they closed the gates. No one in or out save for soldiers, as I've heard it."

That didn't bode well for Ulric. "I hope he paid you well for your goods," I said.

"Well enough. But he took much of what we had stored away, and harvest is a long way off. A man can't eat gold coin. Please thank your friend for me, and tell the others that if they help me with this first harvest, I'll share all I'm able with them. I could use a few extra hands around here through the summer, anyway. We've lost a lot of good workers since they started ordering magic-users to the city."

I thanked him, and started back to the encampment with Aren and Victoria. Vic walked with shaky steps. "I definitely overdid it," she said, but smiled.

"You'll find your balance," Aren said. "Yours is an impressive and useful gift, but please try not to give so much of yourself that it hurts you."

She nodded. "It's coming back to me now. The magic. Some-times I still catch myself resisting, pushing it away. Old habits are tough."

"Do you think that, given seedlings or seeds, you could feed people as needed?" Aren asked.

She crouched and brushed her fingertips over the plants closest to her. "Depends on the soil, I think. I can aid growth, but the plants need more than water and magic to grow. I'm only speeding things up. I think if I tried it too much without replenishing the ground, it would kill the soil. We'd need to rotate crops, fertilize... but yes, I think we could do quite well, given time and the right set-up."

"Excellent." Aren helped her to her feet again, and we headed back to the others.

Laelana waited for us on our return. A dark, angry bruise covered half her face. She glared at us.

"Goff told you to leave. The dragon is scaring the children, and we have no need for you here."

I glanced toward Ruby. The great dragon lay with her eyes closed, chin resting on her crossed wrists. The children approached, led by Patience. When they got close, Ruby's eyes snapped open. The children screamed and ran away, giggling and tumbling over each other. Ruby chuckled.

Laelana frowned. "Well. Doesn't do to have them think all dragons are like that. And you never know when she'll snap."

I refrained from rolling my eyes. With most dragons, she'd be absolutely correct. "We'll go, then. Patience can stay with you?"

"She's one of our own. She stays."

I explained the arrangement with the farmer, and Laelana nodded. "I'll send some people over later." She spun on her heel and stalked away.

Aren frowned after her, but didn't seem too upset over us not having to stay with them.

No one else spoke to us. "I think we're dismissed," Victoria said. "And I think I'm glad."

Victoria rode Florizel alone, and Aren and I packed ourselves back into the canvas bundle. "I'd give everything I have for some more healing balm so I can fly under my own power," Aren muttered as we lifted off.

I relaxed against him, glad for one last chance to do so. "Just enjoy this while it lasts. Gods know what we'll meet when we get back to your father."

His arms closed around me. "I haven't forgotten. I'm glad we had this last bit of time together. My life is certainly more interesting when you're around."

I laughed, though the resignation in his voice, the indication that he had accepted our fate, sent a tear slipping down my nose. At least he couldn't see it. "More interesting than de-throning a king? I doubt that."

"More pleasant, then. Dangerous at times. Occasionally terrifying. But at least you're there."

"What's Ulric going to do now that we've disobeyed him like this?"

"I don't know. I won't let him hurt you."

I shivered in spite of the warmth surrounding us.

We dropped, and then dropped again. Ruby set us on the ground, and sunlight flooded over us.

"That didn't take long," Aren said.

"They weren't hard to find," Ruby said quietly. "But listen. I have no desire to meet your human king, or any of these people. I don't fear them, but I don't think they'll welcome me either. I leave you here. I may stay close by, though."

"Too curious to leave?" Aren asked.

She snorted. "Just want to make sure I've seen the end of all of this before I choose my own end. It's past time for me to die. I'm an embarrassment to my species already."

I knew better than to try to talk her out of dying if that was what her ancient mind had decided on. "Thank you, Ruby." My heart thudded as I stepped closer and placed a hand on her snout, as I'd done once before. That first meeting felt like a lifetime ago. "Thank you for everything. For your scale that saved my life. For not eating us any of the times you could have. For indulging your curiosity."

"You're welcome, human girl. Fare well. You too, prince."

Aren smiled and nodded.

I kissed Ruby's nose. Her hot scales burned my lips. "I'll miss you when you're gone."

She laughed. "I doubt anyone's ever said that to a dragon before."

Aren took my hand and pulled me away. "No one who's lived to tell of it, certainly."

Ruby chuckled, then took off, quickly disappearing over the trees.

I was losing everyone. My family. Patience. Ruby. I couldn't look at Aren. *Not yet. Please. One more kiss, one more night, one more—*

"We should move on," he said softly. Fingers entwined, we walked through the forest. Victoria remained seated on Florizel, who showed no desire to have her gone. None of us spoke as we moved toward the sound of voices.

The full weight of what Aren and I had done settled onto me. The king himself hadn't wanted us to go, and he'd been angry with me even before that.

Two people stepped into our path. Aren dropped my hand as Kel wrapped his arms around him.

"You're back!" He released Aren and scooped me up. I held onto Kel's strong neck and hugged him back. He set me down and turned to Victoria. "Hellooooo."

Nox slapped his arm. "No."

Kel grinned at her. She rolled her eyes and surprised me my throwing her arms around her brother. She'd never acted affectionately toward him before. "You are in so much trouble right now," she murmured, and released him.

"Is he angry, then?" Aren asked.

"Just a bit. Tell me what happened—quickly, before he has you hanged."

I hoped she was joking. The quick smile she flashed me was surprisingly welcoming, but not exactly reassuring.

Aren filled Nox and Kel in as we walked on. Nox was interested in Victoria's gifts, and asked a flurry of questions. When Victoria decided she felt strong enough to walk, Nox took her arm and walked ahead with her.

We reached a camp comprised of five tents set up in a circle with an unused firepit in the center. They must have set up camp for the night just before our arrival.

"Rowan, Aren," Griselda said. She smiled cautiously, but didn't come closer.

Ulric came out of a green tent at full speed, headed straight for us. He drew up when he saw Victoria, and nodded politely to her. Victoria dropped into a shaky curtsy.

"Nox, please make our new guest comfortable." Ulric's voice was low and calm on the surface, but a storm brewed beneath.

Nox complied without question, and Kel followed her and Victoria into the largest of the tents. Ulric motioned for us to walk ahead of him into the woods, out of sight of the others. I trembled with fear, but didn't dare reach for the comfort of Aren's touch.

"Stop," Ulric ordered, and we turned to face him. He didn't speak for several moments, only looked back and forth between us. A vein throbbed in his left temple, and I stared at it. Better than looking into his eyes, which burned with rage.

He seemed to expect me to speak. I said nothing. His gaze snapped back to Aren. "Where's the little girl?"

"I killed her when I found out you'd sent her. Cut her throat and threw her body into a ravine."

Ulric's jaw tightened. "Did you, now?"

"No."

Ulric's hand lashed out, quick as a snake, and struck Aren across the face. "I'm tired of your insolence."

Aren didn't offer a reply, and Ulric turned back to me. "Did you find what you were looking for? Are you satisfied?"

I opened my mouth, but it took me a few seconds to find my voice. "We brought Victoria back to feed your troops and help Nox with her potions."

"You left without my permission, took my son with you when I needed him here."

The cowardly part of me wanted to tell him that it had been Aren who came to me, it had been his idea, I was a good girl and please, sir, don't hurt me. I looked to Aren, who nodded. This time it was his thoughts that were clearly visible. *Tell him.*

My breath caught in my throat. Aren would take his punishment, and wouldn't fault me for telling the truth that would save me a beating, if not banishment or death.

"Answer me!" Ulric roared.

"It was wrong of me," I said, my voice hardly above a squeaky whisper. "I needed to see whether my family was safe, and wanted to help. I was afraid to go alone."

Aren stepped closer, and Ulric held out a hand to stop him. "It was my decision, Father," Aren said. "Rowan wanted to go, but she would have stayed. I said we should do it and not tell you, as you would never let me go. We need Victoria. Nox needs her, and therefore you do."

Ulric's expression didn't change, and he didn't look away from me. "So you're a liar as well?"

I closed my eyes and tensed, expecting pain that didn't come.

"I propose we leave off discussing this," Aren said quietly, "at least until we calm down. You're better than this, Father. You're a fair judge when you can be dispassionate, but right now there's no answer Rowan can give that will satisfy you. If she tells half-truths, it's to protect me. This is my fault."

I looked up. Ulric faced Aren with clenched fists. "Or you're saying that because you think I'll punish you less harshly than I will her." He forced his hands to relax. "I should have you both tried for treason. Don't think I'll forget before this is over. For now, you work for me."

"Yes, Father." He lowered his head, as though a great weight had settled on his shoulders. "Whatever you need."

"Rowan," Ulric said without looking at me. "You help Nox. Do anything she asks. And stay out of my sight."

"Yes, sir."

I walked away, but slowly. The last thing I heard before I was out of earshot was, "Aren, you're going away for a while."

27

AREN

I didn't let my gaze follow Rowan as she left.

"Well?" Ulric asked.

"It's over."

He turned to watch her go, then studied me. "You ended it?"

I felt no anger now. Only sorrow, and I wouldn't let him see that. "She did. She wants to help, and doesn't want to hold me back. She understands what my future will be if we win."

"And do you?"

I swallowed hard. "I do, now. I don't like it, but I accept it. Where are you sending me?"

Ulric stepped back. If he was pleased with our decision, he didn't say. At least he believed me this time. "To take a message to my brother. You'll leave first thing in the morning. Fly as hard and fast as you can, come back with his reply."

"Xaven?"

"Have I any other brothers left?"

Subtle threat, Father. "I'll do it."

"Very good."

The evening was beyond uncomfortable. Maks and Qurwin went hunting, and we all ate in silence. Even Kel didn't try to lighten the mood that evening. He assisted Nox with whatever potion she was working on in her tent, and Rowan and Victoria joined them. I let the others work out their own sleeping arrangements, and settled for a branch outside my father's tent.

He seemed pleased with that.

When I entered Ulric's tent in the morning, he was already awake and dressed, writing out a letter for Xaven. He rolled the page into a tight scroll. "I don't need to tell you this, but that should go to no one save for Xaven himself. If he's not there, destroy it and return to me. No heroics."

"I wouldn't dream of that. Sir." I controlled my tone, holding back the anger that welled up every time I looked at him. I'd told Rowan his pushing her away wasn't personal. He didn't write the laws, and he was doing what he thought best for his people. Perhaps even for me.

Such thoughts did nothing to lessen my dislike of him.

"You know where to go?" he asked.

"Show me where we are now, and I'll find it."

He tapped a finger on his map, indicating that I'd need to head north to find my uncle's home, then handed me the scroll. I wanted to ask what would happen to Rowan in my absence, but sensed that would only make things worse for her.

It's really over, I reminded myself, though thinking it tore at my heart like dragon's claws. *That path is finished. It was always a detour, if the most pleasant one possible. Look back to the road now. Grow up.*

I left my clothing in Ulric's tent and transformed, gripped the scroll in my talons, and took off. At one time, this had been the the safest way for kings to send important messages. Those rare Sorcerers with the ability to fly in bird form were far more reliable and secure than the enchanted birds of the non-human variety that might otherwise be used, faster and less conspicuous than riders.

I tried to clear my mind, focus on the mission, and enjoy the sun on my feathers, but even my eagle mind was now unable to let go of human concerns. If I pushed thoughts of family from my mind, Rowan took over. When I tried to think instead of my future, I saw myself bound to a throne, sworn to follow in my father's footsteps, to put my country before all else. Before myself, before family or friendship. I would become like him, afraid to love in case it came to a choice between that and Tyrea. A good king, and a shell of a human.

Try as I might, I still couldn't understand why anyone would scheme, fight, and kill for the privilege of being a powerful slave. *Give me my freedom, the wind in my feathers. Give me Rowan.*

So much to ask.

The wilds of Tyrea stretched beneath me as I flew, forests broken by shining rivers, hills and valleys, deep ravines and towering rock formations that looked like they'd be more at home by the sea. Vast tracts of the land had thus far been left untouched by humans, and with good reason. The creatures of Tyrea had as much claim to this place as we had, and everyone benefited if we humans kept to ourselves and let the dragons, the fairies, the elves, the mer, the Aeyer, the gryphons, and all of the others live as they saw fit. It made for long travels when we had to go around these forests—or dangerous ones, if we chose to cut through—but that was a small price to pay.

A flash of shining white caught my eye as I passed over a clearing in a particularly lush patch of forest. I circled over, careful to keep my distance, but I needed something interesting to distract me.

It was gone. Nothing there but a clear pool and a few flowers.

I adjusted my wings to carry me away, and caught sight of it again from the corner of my vision. I circled once more, and when the white thing didn't disappear, I looked down.

It was similar to a horse in appearance, as the stories said, and yet not. Even without the shining, pearlescent horn that twisted from the center of its forehead, one would never mistake this for a common beast. Its coat shone like sunshine on waves—even its mane and tail, which hung in thick, matted ropes nearly to the ground.

Had I been human, the sight of the near-mythical beast would have left me breathless. Even in eagle form, I felt myself drawn in by its power and strength. Never had I imagined that a unicorn would live up to the legends, but there it was.

I dropped closer, and the unicorn reared on his hind legs. His forelegs paddled at the air, balancing him. He kept his eyes on me, as well as his horn, which looked as though it could run a dragon through with little difficulty.

Green leaves tangled in the unicorn's mane and the long hair that covered his lower legs, but he seemed to repel all other dirt. Even his dark golden hooves remained spotless as he lowered himself to the ground and paced around the muddy perimeter of the pond. He shook his mane and made another threatening gesture with his horn.

I won't hurt you, I thought, and wondered how the creature seemed to know what I was. After one last, long glance, I climbed to the clouds. When I looked down again, he was gone.

People like me weren't supposed to see unicorns. I'd always suspected the "pure of heart" bit was mere fable, something to enchant the minds of good little children and keep them in line, just in case they might happen upon a unicorn one day. He hadn't appeared happy to see me, but he hadn't run, either.

So much for fairy tales.

Still, the sight of him made my heart soar higher than my wings could ever carry me. His beauty and strength were surely a part of it, but there was more to it. His wildness had taken me by surprise. He looked nothing like the clean, groomed, nearly domesticated creatures from story books. And his warrior spirit, the certainty he'd projected that he could and would run me through without hesitation, had pleased me. You couldn't cage such a creature, couldn't chain it to a life it didn't want or make it become something it wasn't.

Not one person in ten thousand found a unicorn by chance. I wasn't superstitious enough to think of it as an omen, but I still couldn't help being pleased about it. It would be my secret. No one would understand what I'd felt—or if they did, they'd think less of me for it, and speaking about the unicorn would diminish it in my mind somehow.

Perhaps I would tell Rowan, if the chance arose, but even her questions would make the memory too solid, to earthly.

I flew on, and soon found patches of forest cut away to make room for fields and roads. I passed over farms, and then a quiet town. Too quiet. A child played in a tiny, fenced garden, and a few adults moved with hurried purpose from building to building, but considering the beautiful spring day and the size of the town, the streets should have been bustling. No carts moving over the roads, no one out tending gardens... even the farm fields were deserted.

Springtime should have meant the people leaving their homes, preparing their fields, opening the earth and encouraging growth that would feed them through next winter. Something serious had to have happened to make them ignore those duties.

My unease grew as I flew over more towns, more farms, all of them quiet as graveyards. This was Xaven's province, and his people. If Severn had found out that Xaven helped me find my father, if he'd suffered the same fate as the Wanderers, I wouldn't get a chance to deliver the message.

The only other sign of human life visible before I reached Xaven's home was a group of travelers who I took to be farmers on their way to Luid. They moved at a good pace, but didn't seem to be fleeing, and their carts appeared to be filled with early harvest and last year's goods, not their belongings. I took that as a good sign, but couldn't shake the feeling that something was off.

No smoke from the chimneys at Xaven's house, no servants working outside. I flew closer, but there was nowhere on the steep roof I could land to look inside.

Had my luck been better, I'd have found Xaven outside and been able to give him the message without need of explanation. The limitations of this form meant I couldn't communicate with a servant, should one answer the door, and changing in front of them would be awkward for all involved. I remembered my cousin Morea, who I'd met on my last visit, and the pretty blue-skinned maid who had served us tea, and hoped everyone was safe inside, or well away from whatever trouble might be brewing.

I needed another plan, but none presented itself. How had the old messengers done it? Perhaps they'd been as skilled as my grandfather, who could change from human to fox and back, taking his clothes with him. Or they'd worked out speech in animal form, something I hoped to achieve some day. But for now...

I landed on the porch railing—or rather, I tried to. My landings had improved greatly over the past months, but I'd never had to do it with one foot. I slowed correctly in my approach, reached out, grabbed the railing, and promptly tipped forward. Hard as I flapped, I couldn't stop my descent, and I crashed headfirst into the oak boards beneath me.

Well done, Aren. Most impressive.

I only let myself rest for a moment as the white fairy-lights faded from my vision, then righted myself. At least no one had seen me. I hobbled to the door and rapped at it with my beak three times.

No answer, and no sounds from within. I tried again.

Still nothing.

I glared at the door and hopped away, trying to balance on one flat foot and the clenched toes of the other, and made my way around to the back of the house. The scroll was being crushed by my talons, but there was little I could do about that. I found the kitchen door and repeated my knock there. When no one answered, I shrieked. Knocking with my face gave me a headache.

A faint shuffling noise. I backed away from the door, ready to fly, to destroy the message if someone other than Xaven tried to take it from me, to attack if one of Severn's soldiers answered.

The door opened a crack and an eye squinted out, taking in the sight of an eagle crouched in the grass. I held up the scroll, and my uncle opened the door farther.

"Who're you?"

I shrieked again, more quietly this time. He grabbed a heavy overcoat from somewhere behind the door and tossed it to me. "I'll not let you in if you can't state your business."

Better him than Morea. I changed and wrapped the coat around me as I stood, scroll in hand. "Good afternoon, Uncle. I hope you're well."

His expression tightened, and his gaze darted behind me, to the sides, to the service road that ran behind the barns. "Get in," he whispered, and held the door wide. As soon as I'd stepped through, he slammed it and twisted the lock.

In the fading light from the windows and the flickering flame of his oil lamp, my uncle's appearance became ghastly. In mere weeks the lines on his face had deepened, and the skin on his face hung looser than it had when I last saw him. I hoped it was a trick of the light that made him appear ill. The sight unsettled me more than the empty fields and roads had.

"Aren, I wasn't expecting you. Come upstairs, we'll talk. Is that for me?"

I handed him the letter, and he carried it upstairs with him. As we walked, I slipped into the coat and filled him in briefly on what had happened since our last visit, when he'd given me information that changed everything. He listened without comment or question.

"I can't say I envy you," he said as he opened a door to his rooms. All of the furniture save for the bed and the wardrobe were draped with white dust sheets, which he moved off of a pair of chairs so we could sit.

"You're looking well," I said. "As is your home."

A rueful smile pulled at his lips at the obvious lie. "Aren't we, though? I'm afraid my age is catching up with me now that Morea's not here to keep up with my potions. I'm down to dried teas. Feels like it's about time to go find my daughter."

I was about to ask more when he held up a finger and opened the letter. He sipped from the teacup on the covered table next to him as he read, then set the letter on his knees and closed his eyes.

"What do you think?" I asked.

That smile again. "I think I know your father too well. Shall I write out my response, or trust you with it?"

"I'm fairly trustworthy."

"Good. Should this information fall into the wrong hands, it would put many lives at risk. Your father has asked me for troops, and you can tell him that they're ready and waiting in Wildwood."

"I'm sorry?" Wildwood was only a short distance from Luid.

Xaven smiled, pleased with himself. "Some time ago, we received word that we should increase goods already being shipped to the city. I suspected Severn was nervous after he lost you. The request became a demand a few weeks ago, which interested me. I hoped it meant you'd been successful in your mission and were returning, but no one could tell me anything."

"So Severn is preparing for siege."

Xaven nodded. "I believe so. I sent the goods as Severn requested, and extra items as a sign of my support. I had supplies left in Wildwood, weapons and armor and such, but I hope Severn never knew that. Certainly more than enough reached Luid. I sent my people to make the deliveries, and when they had done that I told them to stay in Wildwood instead of coming home. And then I sent more. And more. So instead of twenty people making the trip six times..."

"You have a hundred and twenty in Wildwood now." I spoke quietly, almost superstitiously, as though saying it out loud might shatter the truth behind the words.

He nodded again. "More than that, actually, but that's the idea. It's hard on those left behind to care for the farms and the shops, but they've pulled together, and thus far no one there or here has let information slip." He rested his head in his hands. "The people I sent aren't warriors, though I did send some militiamen, and a few with magic who we managed to hide from Severn. Kept a few here, just in case. It doesn't do to leave folks unprotected, you know. But we're spread thin, all of us."

"So why are you hiding here? And where's Morea?"

Xaven stretched his legs out in front of him and clasped his hands over his belly, which was only slightly less impressive than it had once been. "My dear Morea insisted on being one of the first to go. I presume she's safe in Wildwood, but can't be sure."

"She won't be fighting, I hope?" I remembered her as pleasant, kind, and well-mannered, but hardly the warrior type. More the refined sort of Potioner one found working for the wealthier families of the city.

"I don't know," he said, and stared at the ceiling. "The girl knows her mind, and she'll do as she sees fit, whether it's tending to the wounded or picking up a sword. Don't think I haven't had her trained to defend herself, and to attack if need be. She'd have insisted if I hadn't, I'm sure."

I smiled. "Of course." I hardly knew my cousin, but she sounded like someone it would be good to have on our side.

He grunted, sat up, and drained his teacup. "It's time for me to go, too. I was going to leave it a few more days, but if your father is on his way, I'd like to be there to greet him." He glanced out the window at the late afternoon sunlight. "Bad time to set out, but I can't stay now that you may have been seen here." He left the dirty cup and saucer on the table, reached behind his chair, and pulled out a leather suitcase with brass buckles. "Not ideal for a long trek, I know, but I'm accustomed to traveling in comfort. My servants took the more practical luggage when they left. Walk me down?"

I followed him to the small barn behind the house, where a black horse waited, already hitched to a cart. "You know my mind better than I know it myself, Stanwold," he called into the shadows.

A lean figure stepped out and nodded. "When your visitor arrived, I suspected it might be time to go."

Xaven hoisted his suitcase into the cart and rearranged boxes and sacks to cover it.

"You'd be safer here, Uncle," I said. "I don't think my father wished for you to join the battle."

"I'm sure he didn't," Xaven sighed. He climbed onto the seat of the cart, and Stanwold joined him. "But the fact is that I'd rather die doing something worthwhile than stay here, hiding under my bed until Severn sends his soldiers for me."

"He won't send them if we win."

Xaven took a deep breath of hay-scented air. "And I'm going to help make sure you do. Be safe, Aren, and fly carefully. We'll see you soon enough."

I watched them ride off into the dusky evening, then changed again and flew back toward my father. I'd have to stop for the night, but I could make some progress now and find something to eat before I settled in.

I'd caught my uncle before he left, delivered the message and received good news. Perhaps the unicorn had been a good omen after all. But I still couldn't rid myself of the certainty that every bit of good fortune was an illusion, and it would soon come crashing down.

28

NOX

The same instincts that had once led a starving child to food now brought me to my best chance for finding a cure for a king, and perhaps preventing a war.

A sad, sickly thing, in fact, struggling to grow in a patch of rocky earth. Had the seed fallen a few paces in any direction, the wild barbarose would have flourished. This area had water, rich forest soil, and warm spring breezes, and yet this stunted little plant wouldn't have one blossom this year.

So much depends on the soil, I thought as I crouched to rub a thin leaf between my fingers.

"Well?" Rowan asked.

Ulric had ordered her to help me in any way I asked, and as far as I knew, he hadn't spoken to her since. She carried a basket over one arm, full of plants that were useful, but not quite what I needed. Kel stood behind her, watching me work.

"This is it," I said, and shook my head. "The plant is right, but I need petals. Victoria?"

Rowan's aunt stepped closer, hesitant. "Is that the only one?"

"I think so." I dug up the roots with my knife—a simple task, given the thin soil and shallow root depth, but I took great care not to bruise anything. Moments later I'd moved the tiny shrub to a more likely spot in a patch of dappled sunlight. "It's the only one I feel that might help, anyway. There must be more around, but the seed may have been carried from far off. Why?"

"I just don't want to kill it by trying to help, that's all."

Rowan gave her aunt a reassuring smile, but rubbed the back of her neck nervously. "You won't know if you don't try. Just remember how it felt in that orchard. Take it slow. You can always do more, but not less, right?"

Victoria swallowed hard and nodded as Rowan and Kel backed away. I stayed with the plant. I couldn't protect it if this Darmish woman found she couldn't control the magic here in Tyrea, but I might pluck a blossom before things went too far. I hated to think that this little shrub might be our only hope, but I'd found nothing else this promising in our travels.

"Rowan?" Victoria asked. "A little water?"

Rowan seemed confident enough in her power now, at least in small things, and I wondered what had happened on her travels to change the situation. She breathed deep, relaxed her shoulders, and her fingers out in front of her. At first, nothing happened. Then a hint of a smile touched her lips, and a stream of water trickled over the freshly dug soil, soaking in. "Good enough?"

"Thank you," Victoria said, and looked to me again.

I nodded, and she closed her eyes.

The air trembled with magic I could barely sense, and the plant grew. New shoots unfurled from the ends of nearly dead stems, and bright green leaves appeared all over. I held my breath as buds the color of midnight formed along the thickening stems. Victoria opened an eye to check her progress.

"Keep going," I whispered.

Five blooms opened, deep blue with turquoise hearts, fresh and perfect as anything a queen might wish to find decorating her chambers.

"Stop!" I ordered, and the blooms held as they were, open to just short of losing their first petals.

Rowan bounced on her toes and reached out to hug Victoria, who couldn't seem to quite believe she'd done it.

I cut the blossoms and placed them carefully in the basket,

then added a few leaves and stems in case they might be useful later. Kel scooped one bloom into the palm of his hand and studied it, then raised it to his nose.

"Incredible," he said. "Much as I miss the sea, land does have some things to recommend it."

I snorted. "It took a rose to make you realize that?"

He winked and inhaled again, then put the flower back in the basket and took my arm. "We'll have those at our cabin by the sea, won't we?"

My heart skipped. "Climbing every wall if you want them," I promised. "And a field of everything else out back."

Rowan hung back as we neared camp, saying she wanted to check on Florizel. I suspected she'd heard Ulric's voice, and didn't wish to offend him by being present.

Stupid man, I thought. Much as I'd once disliked Rowan, she'd proved herself useful many times over, and I had to admit that there was nothing truly objectionable about her. Nothing offensive about her presence or her mannerisms. No excessive pride in her skills, which I'd expected when I met her. Without her and Aren's unauthorized trip to Darmid, I wouldn't have these roses now.

So make them count. Fix him, get this over with, and maybe we'll all find peace.

I ducked into my little tent. Underequipped though I was, I thought I could make something. Kel took his position next to my bag, ready to assist, as I took out the few bowls, knives, and the rough cutting board I'd made from a slice of firewood the evening before. I set everything on the ground.

"Hand me the swampweed," I said. "No, that's elvesfoot. I need the soggy one you got from that pond."

Kel passed me a handful of dark green leaves that I'd wrapped in cloth. He gagged. "Smells delicious."

"It's not the smell I care about. Hush for a second." I breathed deep to calm the tremor of uncertainty in my heart and focused on the items before me. My knife slipped through the swamp-weed, then a small handful of the rose petals and the only starflower plant we'd been able to find.

This had better work.

I silenced the inner voice and concentrated harder as I hummed over the ingredients, passing my hands over them, placing them into the large bowl with greater care than I normally took. With every movement and sound I projected my influence over them, controlling each reaction. Normally I wouldn't have tried this particular combination, and would have expected it to be a waste of components. But I'd been working it out in my mind, using every spare minute to practice with less-potent ingredients, making reactions that should have been impossible....

The trance-like state was familiar to me from my years of experimenting, but this went deeper than I'd experienced before. I saw deeper into the plants, understood them better, found more possibility than they showed me when I only looked at the surface of things. Working on instinct, I crushed the leaves, used my knife to cut the shredded petals in rather than mixing them, sprinkled salt only into the left-hand side of the bowl before mixing it all together, added more water than my educated mind said I should and watched it all come together into a glowing purple liquid that the plant pieces melted into. It would need to set for a few hours, but it felt promising.

I didn't notice my hands shaking until I'd pulled my mind back to my body, and the world came into focus. I stood, stepped back, and stumbled. Kel grabbed onto me. I turned, and we sank back to the floor together with me leaning against him.

"That was amazing," he whispered. "I felt the magic. Do you think it worked?"

"We'll see. And then I'm going to sleep for about a week, if that's all right with you."

"I think safe in our bed would be my first choice of places to see you while the Sorcerers and warriors battle this out." A hint of uncertainty tainted the tenderness and slight teasing tone of his voice.

"Mine, too."

Please, I begged the painted white dragon who haunted my dreams, the one who'd perhaps brought more good fortune than I'd ever realized. I didn't know who else to pray to, and he'd watched over me once. *Let the healing be miraculous, let my part in all of this be over. Let me and Kel have our forever. Let this work.*

~

MY PRAYERS WENT UNANSWERED. There was no immediate effect on Ulric's magic. We decided to give it time, to wait and see.

A few hours after Ulric sampled the finished potion, he sat on the edge of his bed, ready to be tested again. "What shall it be?" he asked with a wry smile. "Shall I draw your strength to test myself, Kel?"

Kel looked up from where he sat in a corner and returned the expression. "Though it would be an honor to assist, I'm afraid I'll have to decline."

"And no earthquakes," I added. "What about the light you made in the prison? Or making yourself disappear?"

Ulric nodded, and raised one hand. A white light filled the tent, then dimmed slightly, leaving a pleasant glow that he maintained seemingly without effort.

My heart skipped. "Better?"

"We'll see," he said. "This is a small thing. Simple, and requiring little magic." He let the light fade. "But I feel only slightly weak."

He shouldn't have felt at all weak, but I didn't want to discourage him. "It may take time for the effects to accumulate," I said. "More doses." It was a possibility, at least.

He glanced up at me, and then he was gone. A moment later he reappeared, gasping for air. I hurried to help him lie down and pressed a hand to his chest. His heart beat hard, as though he'd just run from danger or had the greatest fright of his life, and his breath came hard and ragged.

He waved me off. "I'll recover in a moment," he gasped.

I looked to Kel, who appeared as disappointed as I felt. He wiped the expression away before he stood to speak to Ulric.

"Perhaps you'll need to build up to that," he said. "Nox will figure this out."

"Keep taking the potion twice a day," I added. "We'll keep scouting for ingredients." I forced myself to smile, to not reveal the disappointment that turned my stomach into a hard, knotted pit. "There was some improvement?"

Ulric nodded. "Whatever you did, that was better than I've managed since the border. And look. I'm awake. Not coughing up blood. Keep on with what you're doing." He reached for the potion, and I took it from him and set it aside.

"Not too much," I cautioned him. "I wouldn't try it more than one dose at a time, at least not until your magic has recovered more. That swampweed will do horrible things to your digestion."

He set the bowl on the ground next to his bed and sat up. "Perhaps you could work something into the next batch to counteract that."

"We'll see."

It seemed I'd made a good start, but we weren't going to see the full recovery that he needed. Not without ingredients I still believed existed, but that I couldn't access even with Victoria's help.

I thought again of the Potioner in Luid who had brought Severn back from the brink of death, about what I could do with what she had available to her. A new plan formed in my mind. One I didn't like the thought of, one that was almost too dangerous to consider. *But if it's the only way...*

I sat on the edge of the bed. "Kel, could I have a moment alone with him?"

"Of course." Kel ducked out of the tent.

Ulric rested his folded hands on his chest. "I'm listening."

"Tell me truthfully," I said. "If this doesn't work, if your cure isn't anywhere in these forests, what happens then?"

He looked up to meet my gaze, level and calm. "I don't know. I can't fight Severn if I'm incapacitated. I can't imagine what would happen to me if I actually tried to steal someone's strength. His, especially."

"Maybe that would help you."

"Maybe, if it were my power failing and not my natural protection from it." He frowned at his hands. "I suppose we'll find out soon enough."

"And you're sure Aren can't defeat him."

He didn't answer, which was answer enough.

My breath trembled, and I didn't speak until I was sure my voice would be still. *You wanted this once,* I reminded myself. *Danger, glory, a chance to be an active part of Severn's downfall.*

I pushed thoughts of Kel from my mind. *Be strong. Be brave.*

"You have great faith in your Potioners and healers in Luid, don't you?" I asked.

"I do," he said, speaking slowly, watching me carefully. "They have centuries of knowledge behind them, and all the world's potion ingredients at their fingertips."

"I think the answers are there," I said. "This potion may help you more over time, but it won't be enough. I could find something, though, either in the libraries or with your people, or in my instincts once I have access to those supplies. And then—"

"No."

"I haven't told you my plan."

He chuckled under his breath, though there was no joy or mirth in it. "You want to sneak into the city."

"Not sneak." The plan I'd been considering after I left my home in the north came back to me, though the outcome I desired was far different now. "They wanted me before. The soldiers came for me. I can offer my services, get into the city, into the palace. I can find you a cure, and information that will help in other ways."

"I think not." He didn't sound angry. He simply dismissed the idea, which was far worse.

"I'm not rushing into anything." I added, determined to be heard. "We'll try this potion until we reach Luid. If it's not working by then, if you're not strong, I don't see what choice we have."

He coughed into his hand. "They'll see right through you. You don't know Severn."

I chose my words carefully, unwilling to lose the argument because I lost my temper. "Aren is helping me block interference with my mind. Once I get the hang of that—"

"No. You can't. I know you better than you think, Nox. You may get in. You may make progress. But your need for revenge will cause you to stumble."

My cheeks grew warm. "That's not what this is about. Not at all. That may have been true before, but I have a greater purpose now."

Ulric pushed himself to sit up, putting us eye to eye. "Believe that all you want, but this is personal for you, and that will make you careless. You'll take any chance you get to do him in. Knowing Severn, he'll survive. But you won't. You'll be dead and no good to anyone, and if anything you'll have compromised our plans. No, you'll stay here and keep working on my problem."

"What plans? What will I compromise? As far as I can see, you don't have a chance without me. And I'm not going in to kill him. I'll find your cure and a way back out. That's all."

He waved me off. "My word is final, Nox. Go to bed. In the morning we'll move on again, so you'll need to be up early to pack your things."

I stormed out of the tent and ran directly into someone's chest.

"Good talk with Daddy?" Aren asked.

I glowered at him. "Fantastic. Thank you. How was your trip?"

"Fine. What just happened?"

I was about to tell him, but stopped myself. Something told me that this time, Aren and Ulric might be in complete agreement. He wouldn't want me to put my life in danger to spare his.

"Just the same old things," I said. "I thought I had a cure for him, but it's not working as I'd hoped. I need better supplies. Better equipment."

Aren's brow creased. "I sincerely wish things were working out better for you."

"Likewise. Have you seen Rowan?"

"No." He almost whispered it. "And it's probably best if I don't."

"So this is really it?" The genuine remorse I felt at the idea surprised me. I'd had my differences with both of them, but Aren and Rowan together had been a fact. He'd been willing to risk his life to save hers, and she for him.

And I wanted that kind of love to be possible.

He shrugged, apparently trying to make it hurt less by acting as though it didn't matter. Faced now with the idea of leaving Kel, I found that my sympathy for Aren and Rowan's situation had only grown.

"How was she yesterday?" he asked.

"Fine. Helpful. Quiet."

He nodded and didn't say another word, but stepped into Ulric's tent.

Better luck to you, I thought.

It was difficult to pick my indignant stride up after I'd dropped it, but I managed to carry it through until I reached my own tent.

Kel had cleaned my knives and was setting up our bed. Victoria and Rowan were sharing Griselda's space, leaving us alone again. "Hope you don't mind that I cleaned up," he yawned, and climbed under the blankets. It was early yet, just past sunset, but we were all exhausted. "I assumed you were finished for tonight."

"I'm done. There's nothing more I can do here."

Kel held the blankets up and I slipped out of my shirt and pants and into bed. The night air was cold and the ground hard, but somehow lying there with him was the most comfortable place in the world.

He pulled me closer and kissed the back of my neck. "You're leaving, aren't you?"

I sighed and tried to enjoy the sensual tickle of his lips on my skin, but my mind was racing too quickly for my body to keep up. "Unless some miracle happens and that potion heals Ulric, I don't see what choice I have." Tears squeezed out from between my closed eyelashes for the first time in as long as I could remember.

"I wanted this," I whispered. "I was so angry when you all

stopped me from going to Luid on my own after we met. I didn't want to love you because I thought it would interfere with my plans, and now all I want is to let go of all of that and stay with you." I sniffled, and Kel held me tighter. "I didn't have anything to lose before."

"You won't try to kill Severn now, though. Will you?"

"No. I'll be a ghost in their halls, and avoid him completely."

Images filled my mind, ones that had once kept me going—Severn begging me for his life, Severn choking to death on poison, Severn with his head on a chopping block after a truth serum forced him to confess his crimes. All of that faded as Kel's hands roamed over my body, as though he were memorizing every curve. I imagined never feeling this again, saw myself captured, chained and beaten, executed without trial, without ever seeing Kel's beautiful eyes again.

Deep, piercing pain wracked my chest. I rolled over and hid my face against him as the tears fell. "I'm so scared."

"Me, too." His fingers tugged gently at my hair, lifting my face. He kissed my tear-stained cheeks. "If anything happens to you, I don't know what will become of me."

"I don't want to leave you."

"Just tell me you'll be careful."

"I promise."

"Come back to me, and we'll make a home together."

I sniffled, and smiled as his lips brushed over mine. "And find a bed that's more comfortable than this one, right?"

"Anything you desire."

I only desired one thing, and he was right there with me. I decided that I could put other concerns aside, after all, and make some pleasant memories to take with me to Luid.

Something told me I would need them.

29

NOX

We traveled two more days through the forest. Though he continued to improve in magical strength and stamina, it became clearer that the potion I'd made was still not the cure Ulric needed. He went off into the woods at every chance to test it, and never returned with good news. By the second day he seemed to have reached a plateau—impressive abilities for a regular man, but attempts at magic that would do him any good against Severn left him weak and ill.

Victoria was a great help when I wanted ingredients to experiment more, but she could only work her magic on existing plants, and the ones I needed weren't easy to come by in the forest. We had interesting conversations, though, and her calm presence kept my mind off my worries.

Rowan and Kel joined us in excursions. I wondered whether Ulric had ordered Rowan to keep an eye on me in case I tried to run off. If he wanted someone guarding me she would have been an unlikely choice, and therefore just the person I thought he might use. Still, I found I didn't mind having her around. She asked a lot of questions, and it was nice to have someone with that sort of magic taking an interest in my work. I had a few spaces left on the pages of notes I'd started back in the rebels' village, and she added beautiful sketches to them for me. We didn't speak of personal things, and perhaps because of that, I found myself warming to her.

"Is there anything I can do to help?" I asked. I'd just caught her staring at the clouds after she'd done a respectable job of locating and unearthing a clump of bright pink bramblebush roots I'd asked for.

She looked at me as if waking from a dream and shook her head. "I'm fine. If my headaches taught me anything, it's that some pain just has to be lived through. It always gets better in the end. I'll survive."

There was nothing to say to that. A headache I might have helped with. Fixing the feeling of being ripped from security and love was still a little beyond my reach.

"I am sorry," I said. "But I'm glad you came back, in spite of everything."

She made herself smile, if awkwardly. "There is something you might help me with," she said, "but later. After Ulric's taken care of."

Kel was listening, and grinned at me as Rowan left us to carry my plants back to camp.

"What?" I asked, though I already knew.

"You like her."

"I don't know if I'd go that fa—"

"You're *friends* with her."

I slapped his arm. "Don't push it."

His smile faded as we reached camp in time to see Ulric pull Rowan aside. She didn't make eye contact as he spoke. At least he wasn't yelling now.

Aren approached us, but said nothing.

"What's going on there?" I asked.

"I don't know anymore. He doesn't say anything to me about her. Only speaks to her when I'm not around, and otherwise..."

He didn't have to finish. The 'otherwise' was that he constantly had work to do, and no chance to speak to Rowan even if he wanted to. Aren rode with Ulric during the day, and they planned. The Sorcerers from Belleisle rode with them, and presumably knew what was going on. Victoria, Kel and I rode behind, and Rowan brought up the rear, riding Florizel.

Ulric sent Aren ahead to scout every evening when we stopped, and Aren slept in eagle form outside of Ulric's tent. Any free time Aren had he spent alone, working on his magic, or with me, working on my blocking skills. I was making progress, if slowly. Much as I hated taking Aren away from his time developing skills he could use against Severn, I increasingly felt that my own practice might become just as important.

I forced my thoughts back to the present. Thinking of future possibilities was still too much. *Nothing is decided yet*, I reminded myself.

"Ulric has you on a short leash," Kel observed to Aren. "We miss you."

"I'd rather not talk about it." My brother had changed since his return from Darmid. He didn't laugh now, and hardly smiled save for a cold little thing that didn't reach his eyes. The worst of it was that Ulric finally seemed pleased with his youngest son. I'd seen him nodding when Aren spoke, clapping him on the arm when Aren brought back reports after his flights. Aren had told me how he'd once craved our father's attention. He certainly didn't seem to be enjoying it now that he had it.

We watched as Rowan and Griselda headed for the woods. Kel excused himself and followed.

"Having any further success with your potion?" Aren asked, and seated himself on a boulder.

I sat next to him. "I wish for everyone's sakes that I could say yes."

"It's not your fault. You've done more than anyone expected." He rested his head in his hands, hiding his face. "So that's it for Ulric. And for me."

I reached out and gave his shoulder an awkward pat. "Everything is going to be fine," I told him. "We're going to make it, you'll see."

His shoulders shook, and I thought he was crying. Moments later, I realized he was laughing.

"What's so funny?"

He wiped his eyes. "It's not funny at all. None of it. It was just you trying so hard to sound optimistic. Nox, Tyrea's dark princess, never one to look on the bright side of anything in the time I've known you. And yet we've apparently found a situation so dire that even you can muster a pitiful cheer for the troops."

I smacked his arm. "Yeah, that's hilarious. Listen to you, Aren, Tyrea's daft prince—"

He hit me back, and a high-pitched yelp of a laugh escaped me. We'd missed so many years of this. I supposed we were too old for it now, but it felt good to be teasing my brother. Tensions were too high, and we all needed a release. If I didn't laugh, I'd cry again, and I couldn't have that.

A sharp look from Ulric shut us up, but I still felt better for having laughed.

We reached a small town called Wildwood the next afternoon. An old man with gray hair rode out to meet us. He and Ulric clasped hands, and he greeted Aren warmly. I couldn't hear their voices from my position at the rear of the group, but watched Ulric making introductions between the man and the Sorcerers. The mayor, perhaps, or someone who had worked for Ulric in Luid and had escaped the city.

I didn't expect them to make their way to the rear of the group, but after they'd finished speaking to Griselda, Ulric motioned for the man to follow as he rode closer to us.

"This is Nox," he said. I offered my hand and a polite nod. "My daughter. She's one of the most talented Potioners in Tyrea. Nox, this is my brother Xaven."

My uncle beamed at me. "Such a pleasure, my dear. I'm sure you and my daughter Morea will have much to discuss. She's a Potioner, as well."

I nodded again, feeling a bit like a pigeon with all the head-bobbing, but unsure what else to do. I hadn't expected to have more family thrown at me until Luid, and hadn't expected such warmth from anyone.

Xaven looked at his brother. "Ulric, I've never heard you speak with such fatherly pride."

I snorted, and tried to pretend it had been a sneeze.

Ulric nearly succeeded at holding back a smile. "I'll admit, I'm proud to have such a gift in the family, but Nox takes all of the credit for the development of her skill."

I looked to Aren, who rode beside Xaven. His eyebrows crept toward his hairline in surprise, but he seemed pleased to hear our father recognizing my talent. He mouthed something to me behind Ulric's back that looked like *Remember this day.*

"This is Kel," Ulric continued, "Rowan, and Victoria. And Florizel."

Xaven's eyes widened slightly at Rowan's name. "We meet at last," he said, and offered no further explanation. He turned back to Ulric. "If you're ready to move closer to the city, we are as well. Some of the people from here in Wildwood have offered to join us."

"Have they?" Ulric asked.

Xaven nodded. "You have supporters, Ulric. People don't forget so easily."

"Some do," Ulric muttered. "Yes, I think we should get as close to the city as is feasible without risking attack."

"There's going to be a risk no matter where we are," Aren said.

"Out of range for them to fall on us without warning in the night, then," Ulric said.

"We've just the place." Xaven turned his horse around, waved and nodded to a young man standing outside of a shop, and continued down the road. "I'll bring my best people now, and the others will come later with supplies."

"If they can bring seeds or fresh cuttings of plants, that would be helpful," Victoria offered.

Xaven squared his shoulders. "I'll see that they do, though I hope we're not planning to be camped there for long enough to grow crops."

"We'll see." Ulric's voice became grim. "They're well stocked in there, and have the advantage as long as they don't run out of food."

"Little farmland to speak of inside the walls," Xaven said. "Though I'd say they'll work around that."

Aren cleared his throat. "Severn has been collecting magical talent, remember. If there's anyone who can conjure food from outside, he's in there right now. And they do have the port for deliveries, unless you have a navy up your sleeve."

Such dire conversation made for an unpleasant ride, but soon enough we reached a place where the road and the land sloped sharply downward, leveled into a long, flat area, then dropped again. There at the top, we had a fine view of everything below. The ocean sparkled to the south, stretching from a sheltered harbor and spreading to cover the world to the horizon in a dark, rippling blanket.

Kel will be pleased, I thought, and turned back to the land. In the distance, beyond a cleared plain cut through by a dry riverbed, a dark shape stood silhouetted against the early evening sky.

Luid.

I'd dreamed of the city many times after my mother revealed who we really were. In my imagination it shifted between being a city of delights and a place of dark horrors and evil kings. Seeing it now from a distance, I supposed it was probably both, and neither. Still, I'd never visited the city before, and its presence made me shiver for reasons I didn't understand.

The others moved far off into the woods to make camp, but I stayed and watched as lights appeared in the city. Night covered the land surrounding them, leaving them adrift as the land became indistinguishable from the sea. Kel rode up beside me and motioned for me to follow him away from the road.

"This is as close as the group is going to get, isn't it?" I asked. "At least until the battle starts. They won't dare camp closer."

"That's the plan."

"It's not so far. I could make it overnight. Right?"

He didn't say anything as we made our way into the camp, which was well-hidden far from the road. Thirty or more people were there already, setting up tiny sleeping tents, erecting the larger structures we had been using, setting up a place for the cookfire, and unloading piles of battle gear: leather armor, weapons that ranged from excellent to only slightly better than what Laelana's crew had used for sparring, light saddles, and smaller necessities. I dismounted and led my horse until we found our tent, where Victoria was directing the unloading of our supplies.

"Do you want your things set up?" she asked. "The people from town brought out a table, some extra bowls, a few other things. I grabbed what I could for you."

Don't bother, I thought, but said, "Please. I'm tired now, but I'll want to work in the morning."

She called Rowan over and we got to work, and soon had everything set up in my tent. Rowan gave me a strange look as she passed on her way out.

"Did you say something to her?" I asked Kel.

"No. Nor to Aren, as promised."

Rowan came back a moment later. "Just so you know, they're setting up a heavy rotation of guards around the outside of the camp."

My heart skipped. "That's interesting."

"I thought you'd want to know in case they ask you to take watch at some point." She reached up to gather her hair into a knot at the back of her head, and frowned. "I think most of us are going to bed early, just in case. I'm not sure when Aren's watch is, but I heard Ulric say something to him about a stream at the northern end of camp."

Kel put his arm around me. "Thank you, Rowan."

She shifted her weight from foot to foot. "I don't... ugh, never mind." She opened her arms and pulled me into an awkward hug. "Thanks for not killing me these past few days," she whispered. "I know I probably irritated you horribly. Take care."

I watched her leave, then ducked into the tent. My heart seemed to be fluttering in my throat. "How did she know? No one should."

Kel shrugged. "You've obviously had something on your mind. You've been muttering about the lack of ingredients available to you, and she knows about Ulric's problem. You just spent an hour watching the city. Maybe she saw you and Aren working on your mind-blocking thing. She's observant. Give her some credit."

"I suppose." I tried to relax. "She won't say anything to Aren, will she?"

"I don't think she'd dare get close to him even if she wanted to tattle."

I changed into my dirtiest, rattiest clothes and packed just a few items into my bag. My story would be more convincing if I arrived with nothing except what I would have needed to survive on the road, and I suspected they'd confiscate anything I took with me when I reached the city.

The hours slipped away as I considered and calculated. I knew I should be feeling more. Fear, certainly, at the unknown future awaiting me in Luid. Sorrow at leaving Kel and making him worry, though I had every intention of returning alive. Loneliness at the prospect of losing the strange, cobbled-together family I'd found here. But I felt nothing. My heart had hardened itself as I'd trained it to do when I was young, when feeling things was too much of a risk.

Kel held my hand as we sat on his bed and waited for the rest of the camp to go to sleep. It took longer than I'd expected, and I guessed it was past midnight before they finished setting up the camp.

"I'm coming back," I said.

"I know you are. I'm scared for you, for what will happen there, but you're going to make it." He paused, then pulled me into his arms and kissed the top of my head. "You're my hero, Nox."

I wanted to laugh at the simple, childish statement, but couldn't. He was too serious. Instead I said, "I'll try to live up to that."

He watched me for a minute with intensity I'd begun to take for granted. "You once asked me what I saw when I looked at you."

"You sort of told me."

"I know. Here's the rest. I saw what you've been showing me for the past week, the potential for openness, for hope, for letting someone through your defenses. But I saw something else, too. Bravery. A heart of warm steel, loyal and strong."

"I wish I felt brave." My voice broke, and I kept it quiet so it wouldn't sound like I was about to cry. "I talked big about wanting revenge, and I meant it. But I'd be happier saving my own skin. Running off with you."

"And I hope you will, after." His eyes never left me, even as the light faded. "But the part of you that does what's necessary to survive, the part that will do what it takes to see this thing through and save everyone else... I love that as much as I do the softer bits. Just be careful. Please."

"I wish I could promise more," I whispered.

"I know," he said.

And we waited.

At last, the camp fell silent. I opened the tent flap and stepped out into the moonlit darkness. Kel followed.

"Don't," I whispered, and laid a hand on his chest. His heart pounded under my palm, and for a brief moment it all flooded in —everything I was risking, the pain I might cause. Tears burned my eyes, but I held them back. I reached up to touch his cheek, to brush the hair out of his eyes. "Let me go now, or it'll be too hard."

His eyebrows pulled together. "I love you."

Such words from a mer, and spoken with such sincerity. "I love you, too. I'll see you soon."

I thought he'd call me back, beg me not to go, but he just stood outside the tent until I was out of sight. I shoved my sorrow down again. I'd need my wits about me if getting out of camp was going to be as difficult as Rowan had warned. I darted from shadow to shadow, but saw and heard no one awake inside the camp, which had grown larger in the hours I'd been in my tent. I made it to the trees without being stopped and picked my way through slowly, though a deep part of my mind screamed for me to hurry.

A thump to my left was followed by a whispered curse. I moved to the right. If I knew where one was, perhaps I could avoid the rest of the line.

A dark shape appeared in front of me, and a big hand clasped my arm.

"Let go of me!"

Instead of answering, he dragged me to a sheltered spot where the moon filtered down through the trees, revealing his face.

Aren.

Shit.

"I can explain," I said.

"Please do." He didn't sound amused.

"I need to forage at night so I can see the moon's effect on certain plants I need for Ulric's potion."

He released me and crossed his arms. "Fascinating. Tell me where you're really going, or I'll escort you back to camp."

Please do, my more cowardly self begged. *Send me back to bed.*

I could have lied again, and kept lying until he let me go or sent me back. But I realized I didn't want to. And I needed his help.

"I'm going to Luid," I said, and explained my plan.

Aren listened without interruption. When I finished, he rubbed a hand over his face. "Nox, do you know how much trouble this is going to cause me if I let you go?"

"Do you have a better idea of how we can win this if I don't?"

"No," he admitted. "That doesn't mean I approve of it, but I won't stop you." He paused, then sighed. "We need this. I wish you had a more solid plan, or that you'd told me sooner. I might have helped. But if you feel you need to do this... Come on, I'll walk you closer to the plain."

Irrational anger flared in me at the idea he would be willing to sacrifice me so easily. He could have tried to stop me, as Kel and even Ulric had.

"I can feel that," he said softly. "Walls up now, and keep them there."

I recaptured the feeling I'd had during our last practice session, safe inside of myself and looking out. "Thanks."

"It's not that I don't care," he added as we continued through the forest. He held a branch aside so it wouldn't whip back in my face. "I wouldn't choose to send you into danger. I would prefer not to lose you."

I smiled, though he wouldn't see it. "Understood."

He stopped. "What about Morea? She's a Potioner, too. Maybe if you worked together, you could come up with something better for Ulric."

"He'd never let me explain the situation to her."

"He's getting better," Aren said, though he sounded uncertain. "Whatever your current potion is doing for him seems to be making him at least a little more rational. Less fearful."

I chewed my thumbnail as I thought. I wanted to jump at the idea that something miraculous might come of collaboration, to know that I didn't have to leave after all. But it wasn't knowledge or instinct I was lacking.

"We still wouldn't have what we needed to fix him," I said. "I know it can be done. There's always an answer. I just need more pieces to the puzzle, and if they exist, they're in that city. If I go back now, I won't get into Luid later. I have to try before Severn knows we're here."

We continued through the forest, away from camp and toward the downslope of the hill. Along the way, Aren told me a little about the city and the layout of the palace. He was right. I should have spoken to him sooner, but I'd been certain he wouldn't let me go.

"Just so you know, and so your pride's not too damaged," he said as we reached the edge of the lower slope of the hill, "I'm tempted to stop you. I don't want to let you do this, but it's not a bad plan. If there were any other way you thought you could cure Ulric..."

"I know. And this was my idea."

"This is as far as I go," he said. "Stick to the cover of the trees for as long as you can, then approach by the road so it doesn't look like you're sneaking up on them. When you get in, show them a good portion of your talent, but hide your intelligence. Don't let anyone feel threatened by you."

I felt him attempting to get into my mind, and did as we'd practiced. I became a fortress, an impenetrable cave, safe against the storm raging outside my walls.

"Speak to me," he ordered.

I smiled pleasantly and thought of nothing but the world in front of me, of the words I spoke, and the forest around us. "Good evening, mister guard," I said. "I'm but a poor, innocent Potioner in search of work..."

He winced. "I sincerely hope you're trying to be amusing."

My smile became genuine. "You can't tell?"

"Don't get over-confident. But no. I can barely read you. You seem like a perfectly thoughtless idiot." He touched my shoulder. "I wish we'd had more time to work on this."

My teeth chattered, as much from nerves as from night's chill. I squared my shoulders and offered my hand for him to shake. Instead, he pulled me into a tight squeeze. "Thank you," he whispered. "And be careful."

I pulled back and cleared my throat. "Anything for the cause, right?" I forced a smile. "Keep an eye on Kel for me. He might be fine, but if anything should happen to me—"

"I will. Remember to make up a blocking potion as soon as you have access to the ingredients. Even with that, try not to think of us at all while you're in there. Focus on whatever they have you working on, let them think you really are on their side. I still don't think Severn can read thoughts the way I can, but..." He paused. "Just stay alive. Keep away from Severn if you don't want to be found out. And watch out for Sara. She's a good Potioner, but very much under Severn's influence."

"I will. Try to keep Ulric calm. If your cousin is a decent Potioner, have her keep making my potion. The notes are in my tent, Kel will find them for you. And tell Ulric I'll bring something better. Once I get that to him, he'll be able to handle Severn. He just needs to be patient and wait for me."

"Giving orders to our father? Wish me luck with that." Aren started away, but turned back. "One other thing. When you lie, put as much truth into it as you can. It makes for less confusion when you have to remember your story later. Fewer chances to forget, and it will be more believable. Trust me, I learned the hard way."

And then he disappeared into the forest. It was as I'd imagined it, once. Just me against Severn, armed with my wits and my skills. Whether it was by my hand or another, he was going to end up paying for what he did. The idea didn't fill me with rabid anticipation as it once had.

I thought about praying, and decided against it. It hadn't worked for me so far. Perhaps one needed to make a sacrifice if one wanted to get the attention of the Goddess or her representative.

I only hoped I wouldn't end up being the sacrifice, myself.

30

ROWAN

C ome on. Just a little. Give me something.

I squeezed my eyes closed.

Focus harder. Want it more. You've done it before, you can do it again.

I'd left camp at dawn after a restless night. Thoughts of Nox and where she might have gone had made falling asleep difficult, and even when I managed to push that aside, the guilt took over. Ulric had once accused me of wasting my talents by not taking advantage of them. He may have changed his mind about that, but it didn't make him wrong. Every day I spent avoiding my problems only made it harder to face them. I was finally comfortable with drawing small amounts of water to help Victoria, but it wasn't enough.

Not with time running out and our enemies just a short ride away. I needed to do more. To *be* more, even if it frightened me.

I'd found a place well away from camp, a shadowy forest glade bursting with life. The earthy scent of moss and the sharp sting of pine hung heavy in the air, an irritated squirrel scolded me with a stream of high-pitched chatter, and a flash of blue feathers overhead told me the little rodent wasn't the only one keeping an eye on things. The forest here was so different from the stunted brown we'd been surrounded by back at the rebel camp. This place was lush, green and deliriously alive.

And under that, holding it up and flowing through every part of it, there was water. I felt it in my bones, sensed it as clearly as I ever had. That part of my magic was working quite well, an undemanding current of awareness that flowed through me like an added sense when I chose to pay attention to it. The water was there in the trees, in the animals—and, more interestingly for me, in the earth beneath me. Not just in the rocky soil, but in springs beneath it, in deep caves and potential wells, a world of dark and wet.

We needed that. Victoria could grow plants to feed the troops and to help Morea keep up on Ulric's potion, but she needed more water. We all needed to drink, to wash. A spring brought to the surface would be just the thing, if only I could access it. So much easier than me having to call it and drain myself each time we needed some.

Of course, that would have been easier had I felt able to approach Ulric to ask him for help with cracking the hard earth.

And I will, I told myself. *I just want to try, first.*

I located a dip in the earth where I felt the pull of water more strongly than elsewhere—a spot where the underground lake or river had weakened the ground. I searched for the peace I'd felt at Stone Ridge. I pictured Glass Lake, and the ocean at home lapping gently at the hulls of fishing boats.

My magic stirred.

That's it.

I forced myself to relax into it. *Let it flow through you*, I reminded myself. *Let it happen. It is your gift.*

I'd learned to claim the peace when I tried small things. But anything larger had thus far proved a challenge, one that still made no sense to me.

My chest tightened, and a wave of cold washed over me from my face to my toes, accompanied by a soft tremor coursing through my body. Dark panic flooded my mind, and a strange feeling like grief. I opened my eyes, and the warm sensation of my magic disappeared. Nothing had changed.

The squirrel let out a stream of what I assumed were profanities.

"Go stuff yourself with a nut," I muttered, and sat on a mossy boulder.

I turned toward the sound of approaching footsteps, half-hoping to see Aren appear among the trees. Instead, Griselda pushed between the overlapping branches of a pair of pines. She set her hands on her hips and looked down at me.

"Having troubles?"

I smiled and held out a hand to let her help me back to my feet. "You could say that. Just feeling blocked, that's all." I brushed the pine needles off the back of my pants. "Did Ulric send you?"

"No. Aren did, actually. He saw you leave and wanted me to see if you needed help."

I ignored how pleasant that made me feel. "Will Ulric be angry if you help me?"

She shrugged. "Perhaps. But he has charged me, and all of us, with working in his best interests. I believe you and your magic have a part to play in returning him to the throne, so really, I'm following orders."

"I like how you think."

She gave me an appraising look. "Perspective is the secret to many things in this life. So tell me, what's happening with you? You've seemed frustrated and upset. I suspect this has something to do with the situation with Aren, but also your magic."

"Among other things. I'm trying to focus on developing my skills."

"Hmm. And how's that coming?" She had her teacher demeanor on, serious and focused. It was something of a relief to fall back into my role as student, learning from a powerful and experienced Sorceress.

"Not so well," I admitted. "I had a few breakthroughs when Ulric and I were in prison, and right after our escape I had this overwhelming abundance of magic at my disposal. That plus the control I learned in the cell allowed me to do incredible things. I made illusions to distract enemies, called water to crush them..." My throat closed, and I swallowed hard. "I killed one when he attacked me. But now it feels impossible. I know I've done these things before, but every illusion I create is a shadow of what I did in the city, and though I'm learning to push through my fear when I call water, I can only manage to draw small amounts from easy sources. I want it to be like it was before. I want to call a river to me if I need it."

Griselda rubbed her slender fingers over her jaw. Her eyebrows drew together as she thought. "Tell me, why is this so important to you? You know how long it takes most people, even those with great power, to master a skill. You've said you know that what you did before was aided by many things—an excess of magic, the pressure of a life-and-death situation. Ulric has as good as excused you from battle. Why not relax?"

I chewed my lip and dug below the obvious answer. Clearly, I wanted to help remove Severn from power. But she was right. I was asking so much of myself. Everything I'd accomplished, even something as simple as drawing up water in an established well, was more than I'd dreamed possible back in the autumn. I considered what would happen if I failed, if I stopped pushing and let the skills come when they wished, if I stayed well away from this battle.

I thought of an eagle trapped in an enemy's hands.

"It's for Aren," I admitted. "A few days ago he was badly hurt because I couldn't use my magic to save him. He didn't blame me for it, but I do. I blame myself. And I can't let it happen again. I want to be there, wherever he's going during this battle. And I want to fight. I don't want to hide, or be a burden. I want to be able to protect myself and everyone else."

"I see." Griselda paced between the trees, and I left her to it. "And your magic. What exactly is the problem there?"

"I don't know. For a time, I was afraid. I panicked every time I tried to use it, especially to call water. I saw the face of the man I killed, and it was horrifying. I had nightmares about hurting people with it."

"And now?"

I drew a deep breath. "And now I'm forcing myself past that. I think I've accepted that I did what I had to. I saved myself and my friends from someone who would have killed us. But the feeling is still there. I can do small magic when I work through the tightness in my chest and the feeling that something terrible is about to happen. But when I attempt something big, I panic. It's like I'm trying to force myself to jump off a cliff. I know I have to. I know I'll land safely. But I freeze." The words poured out of me unconsidered, but horribly truthful. I twisted a lock of hair between my fingers and pulled it tight, enjoying the physical solidity of the minor pain it caused. "Does that help?"

She raked her hands through her thick hair and nodded. "You mentioned Aren. Not yourself. Not the greater good or justice or peace between three nations."

Heat rose in my cheeks. "Those things are also important."

Griselda chuckled. "I'm not doubting that they are to you. But he was first on your mind."

"It happened so recently. I failed him twice on our journey. Once in not defending him, and once before that in not being able to heal him. I accept that second part. Healing isn't my gift. But yes, I want to use the skills I have to help him."

"You love him."

I nodded without hesitation. "I do. He's not mine anymore. He can't be. But that doesn't change anything." My chest tightened, but I forced myself to remain calm.

"Why is that? What keeps you apart?"

"My magic." I winced. "I mean, the law. And Ulric."

She smiled gently. "But those things would not be a problem if not for your magic?"

My shoulders slumped. I didn't answer.

"I don't blame my magic," I said. "But it's hard when I think about the hurt I've caused since I found out about it. My family had to flee Darmid, and my old community is shattered. People are dead because of me."

"Enemies?"

"Some. But that's not where it ends." I sighed. "My father has disowned me and anyone who wouldn't join him in renouncing me."

Griselda winced. "That must hurt."

My eyes burned. "It kills me. Della is dead. She was a mother to me, and she's... she's just gone." A hot tear slipped out. "Maybe I'd have died if my magic had never showed itself, but maybe that would have been better. She'd be safe. So many people would still be alive. My family wouldn't be displaced. Maybe the Wanderers would be alive, too, if Aren and I hadn't stayed with them."

The woods had gone silent.

"Good," Griselda whispered.

I laughed, sharp and quick. "Good? What I'm saying is horrible." I sniffled and wiped my nose on my sleeve. "I didn't even know I thought all of this." The thoughts seemed to have come from nowhere, yet felt intimately familiar.

She patted my arm. "Exactly. As I said, thoughts and perspective are the secret to many things in life. If we know them, we can change them. Follow it through. Say your magic had remained hidden. Say your family was safe. Say you had died. What else?"

A soft breeze rustled through the trees, and I breathed in the heady forest scents. "I suppose that would require me not finding Aren. So he'd be dead at the hands of Dorset Langley and Callum." My heart froze at the thought. "Even if he did escape them, he'd still be working with Severn if he hadn't met me. Ulric would still be in prison. Aren would never have found Nox, or returned to the lake and met with Kel, so Nox and Kel wouldn't have met." I dried the last of my foolish tears. "Severn would keep the throne. He'd attack Darmid."

"And Belleisle, in time," Griselda added softly.

I nodded. "Aren breaking away from Severn changed everything, didn't it?"

"And you changed him."

"Because of my magic."

She smiled. "Not just your magic, I think. But it was the catalyst for everything that came after. And he's not the only one who has changed."

I leaned against the trunk of a birch and leaned forward to rest my hands on my knees. It was a lot to think about all at once. I looked up at her. "So you think I've played my part? I'm done?"

"No." Griselda paced and stretched again. "You'll accomplish far more than this, once you find your purpose. What do you think of your magic now?"

"I think…" I hesitated, searching for what I felt to be true rather than what I thought I was supposed to say. With everything laid out, it became clearer. "I think I've been pushing it away. I've known in my head that I should want it, that it was everything I'd always dreamed of, but it brought so much pain for so many people, it caused so much destruction, and I wasn't prepared for that. But I see that it's not bad. It's not good. It is what I make of it. Isn't it?"

My teacher flashed a mysterious smile. "If that's what you believe of it."

I sat and leaned against the tree and closed my eyes. With my most prominent sense closed off, the awareness of the water in the land and the trees flooded in. *Magic is like water,* I realized. *Absolutely necessary. Beautiful. Life-giving. But if you fight it, it will drown you.*

And how I used it was my choice.

A slow smile spread across my face. There would still be fear and lingering doubts. Perhaps my anxieties wouldn't disappear overnight. *But if I can let go of the guilt and the blame, and swim with the current…*

Tingling warmth swept through me and settled into my body. When I opened my eyes, Griselda was smiling down at me.

"It will come," she said. "You've made a good start. I do think you have more work to do on letting go of other things. It will help you let go of any lingering doubts."

I sighed. "Aren? I know. It will just take some time."

She gave my arm a comforting pat. "Good. Now, let's see what you were working on."

I climbed to my feet, dusted off again, and focused on the water beneath the ground. It responded, drawing upward. The chill of habitual fear came over me, but I gently pushed it aside. *Irrelevant. Carry on.*

Magic flowed from me, sure and strong. The water came nearer, pushing and filtering through the soil until it hit the hard-packed layer beneath the forest floor.

I resisted the urge to force it, and ignored the thought that I should wait, that I should convince Ulric to come and crack the ground to make it easier. *Water is as strong as the earth,* I told myself. *It's just a question of pressure, and what will break first.*

One big pull...

I gritted my teeth, but not in pain or anger or fear. The effort was thrilling and exhausting all at once, an incredible feeling. Water broke through the ground, soaking the dirt and driving upward, eroding its path as the underground flow diverted up. A sinkhole opened and a new spring bubbled up, glinting clear and fresh in the tree-filtered sunlight.

I stopped. I let go. The water continued to flow.

Griselda stepped up behind me and rested her hands on my shoulders. "Now, that is something. You've changed so much here with your magic. And now we have water." The smile in her voice was warm and approving. "A little shift in thinking is powerful, isn't it?"

I couldn't speak. It wasn't the greatest feat of magic ever performed. It wasn't even the greatest thing I'd done with water, in no way comparable to building up a wall of it, holding back the accumulated current of a river and releasing it over enemies. But I'd done it with my power and nothing more. And without fear.

My power.

I gasped. The warmth of my magic had faded, and I'd been too caught up on the results of it to notice. "Griselda? There's one other problem."

"Hmm?"

"My magic isn't returning to me as quickly as it should. It's taking its time. It always returns, but right now I feel quite depleted."

The creases between her eyebrows deepened. "This is concerning. Not a question of perception. Do you think—"

A musical trill interrupted her. I stepped back as Gwyn descended and pulled up just in time to land on Griselda's shoulder. My teacher reached up to scratch behind the little cat's ears, and a loud, rumbling purr filled the air. Griselda glanced back toward camp.

"You've returned alone?"

Gwyn just purred.

"If they're coming, you'd best finish the job. I'll meet you in camp." She reached into the pouch on her belt and produced a bit of dried meat that the cat wolfed down. "Go on, now."

Gwyn spread her wings and leapt upward, then was gone.

"That was fast," I said. "How did they come so quickly?"

"They'll have been ready and waiting," she said. "Albion never intended to not send help. He just needed to know where and when. We should get back." She frowned at me, concerned. "Are you feeling weak?"

"Not at all. Just a little deflated, really." I made myself smile. A little of the now-familiar warmth returned. "It will come in time. Hasn't abandoned me yet."

She didn't seem comforted by that. Perhaps it only troubled me less because I hardly knew better. "Remember, you were in that prison with Ulric," she cautioned. "Not for as long, but you had the same treatment as he did, and a binding before that. We're still trying to figure out what has happened to him. Don't break yourself before we find time to treat you. Agreed?"

I nodded. "I'll be careful. I'll practice small things once I've recovered, and see how it goes."

"Good." The creases on her forehead faded. "Now let's go. Whatever happens, I don't think we're going to want to miss this."

I took one last look at my spring, then chased after her.

31

AREN

Harder. Brighter. Hotter.

Though I didn't consciously formulate the commands, the idea was there. My power responded, and magic flowed through me. My stolen moments of practice were paying off. A minute here. A fire lit, encouraged, and extinguished there. No marathon training sessions like I'd had under Severn, exhausting and overwhelming, enough to break me down so he could rebuild me. This was another kind of strength and control I was building, tackled in the moments when there was no other work for me to do.

The flames before me danced, consuming a pile of brush, contained only because I said they were. They leapt higher, licking the underside of a dead pine's high branches, but I didn't give them permission to ignite it. The sweat on my forehead came as much from my effort as from the incredible heat. My concentration was absolute. Nothing existed outside of my body, the fire, and its fuel, which should have been burned up long ago. I was learning to control that, too, and though I was nowhere near as skilled as Severn at production or control, I was at least beginning to feel that this was a skill I could use when the time came.

Now, the challenge.

I released my control. The heat from my fire ignited the wood and needles above until the entire tree was bathed in natural flame.

I drew my magic in and released it, blanketing the fire to douse it. It roared higher. I narrowed my focus, closing my eyes to work by feel rather than sight. I imagined my magic absorbing the heat and the air that fueled the flames, cutting them off.

The fire I'd created obeyed. The new one did not, and raged on.

"Gods damn it."

This wasn't unexpected, after the trouble I'd had controlling the fire back at the rebels' village. My muscles trembled with exhaustion and effort as I drew on my magic again. I had a theory, and for the sake of the camp and the forest, I hoped it worked.

I drew on my magic again, which had already replenished from the land and the air—a blessing I did not take for granted after too many trips to Darmid. I created my own fire, hotter and brighter than that which naturally consumed the tree, and let it cover the old pine. I felt it as my fire overpowered the other, stealing its energy. If my magic couldn't dampen the flames effectively, I would drown them out with my own fire.

I pulled back, drawing my fire away and extinguishing it.

Smoke rose from the tree's bare and blackened branches, but the fire was gone.

"Impressive."

I turned toward my father's voice. "I'm glad you think so."

"Perhaps not the best use of your time or skills, though." He didn't sound angry. Perhaps disappointed. "Severn doesn't fear flames."

"I know." I wiped my brow with the sleeve of my shirt. "It seemed that having a better understanding of the skill might be helpful, though. And there are worse ideas than fighting an enemy with his own weapons. I've made great progress."

"It's still not enough." Ulric's brow furrowed. "What else are you working on?"

I gave the tree one last look, but the danger seemed to be past.

No smoke. No heat. I started back toward camp. "I've made progress with seeing thoughts in people when I don't have their attention, and I've been working on finding ways around some non-magical defenses. It won't help against Severn, but might be useful in getting us into the city. And I've been keeping myself open to people in camp, making sure everyone is sincere in their desire to help us." He didn't say anything. "You know well enough what I'm trained to do. Right now I'm trying to come up with anything that will help, or surprise him, or defeat him. Flames are all I have at the moment."

"It's a good skill," he said, and I had to glance back to make sure I'd heard correctly. It was too close to praise. He gave me a tight smile. "It may not be enough to overcome him, but you're learning to protect yourself as you direct it, aren't you?"

"I seem to be."

"So that's something."

I looked up at the sentry sitting high in an oak tree. He nodded down at me and went back to scanning the forest for threats.

The camp was alive with the morning's work—Food preparation, weapon organization, caring for the horses and the livestock that Xaven's people had brought with them. Even with most of them still back in Wildwood, it all made a lot of noise, and I wondered whether we should set lookouts farther out in the forest for the inevitable attack that would come when Severn noticed us.

I was about to ask how my father's own skills and strength were coming along when a high-pitched whistle went up beyond the far end of camp. Not a warning of attack, but an alert nonetheless. I ran toward the noise, and found a crowd gathering.

A group of weary-looking riders emerged from the woods, led by Griselda Beaumage on foot. Rowan walked beside her, practically bouncing with excitement.

Please, gods...

My heart leapt as I recognized several of the teachers from Ernis Albion's school, as well as less-familiar faces from the nearby town. All of them Sorcerers. All of them talented. Twenty of them in all, and behind them came others. Another dozen men without magic, and at least as many women, all of them riding horses loaded with supplies, weapons, and armor.

It had been far too long since I'd seen such a welcome sight.

Griselda said something to Rowan, who darted off toward the other end of camp, presumably to see about making room for more tents.

I scanned the faces. They'd obviously been traveling hard, and had to have been making good time to have come so far so quickly. A few looked grim, but most seemed pleased to have reached their destination, whatever might lay beyond it. Griselda's companions hurried to greet their countrymen and to assist with unloading horses.

I sighed, realizing the most important one wasn't among them. *Of course he wouldn't have been able to leave the island. And sending these people was more than—*

"Aren!" Griselda called, and motioned for me to follow her toward the back of the group. She glanced over her shoulder and grinned as she cut through the crowd. When I caught up to her, I saw why.

Ernis Albion, my grandfather and one of the greatest Sorcerers of our age, stood next to a docile white horse. Gwyn lay on her back in his arms, wings drooping toward the ground, purring contentedly as he rubbed her belly. She turned for long enough to narrow her eyes at me, then closed them again.

I placed a hand over my mouth to hold back my surprised laugh, then decided it didn't matter. Albion returned my grin and released the cat, and reached out to shake my hand. He pulled me into a one-armed hug, which I returned, if somewhat awkwardly.

"What are you doing here?" I asked as he released me. "I hoped you'd come, but didn't expect it. Is everything all right at the island?"

"A few Tyrean ships on our waters. Nothing we can't handle for now," he said. "Still, we thought it best that I come here and see if we can't cut the threat off at the roots before they figure out a way to breach our defenses."

"Which will be fine without you there to maintain them?"

He waved that off. "Not to worry. It took decades to set up the shield, and it won't disappear overnight. The island is in good hands."

"And Emalda was happy to let you go?"

He chuckled. "Not happy, but understanding. She said she hoped I'd find you and Rowan well."

I raised an eyebrow. "Did she?"

He shrugged. "You never can tell with that woman. Fascinating person." His expression tightened. "She knows as well as I do that, personal differences aside, having Ulric on the throne was far better for Belleisle than Severn is or ever will be. So here I am, if I'm welcome."

I glanced back toward the rest of the camp, but didn't see my father. "You'll be welcome," I said. "We need you. All of you. And perhaps personal differences could be set aside."

"Or worked through," Griselda added, and chewed her lip. "I don't know how it will go with his current state of mind, but it's worth a try."

My grandfather's expression darkened. "There are some bridges that aren't meant to be rebuilt."

"There's much you don't know," she said.

I nodded. "He has a lot to answer for, but it would be worth the two of you setting things straight. At least enough that you can work together." I wanted to tell him that Ulric hadn't had my mother killed as we had all thought for so long. I wanted him to know that Ulric had loved her, at least as well as he could, that their marriage hadn't been a slight against Belleisle or Albion himself, even if it had been a bad idea and doomed from the start. But that wasn't my story to tell. I only hoped my father would find himself ready to share it.

Gwyn settled on the horse's saddle as we walked into camp. I was about to ask Griselda to go ahead and find Ulric to share the news when I spotted him, and he us. His eyes widened, and his lips pulled back slightly to bare his teeth. A sting of pain, perhaps, or a wave of suspicion.

Not that, I pleaded. *Not now.* His mental state had seemed much more stable since he'd been taking his potion and become more careful about not using his magic, but there was still a chance he remained too mistrustful, that he'd make another enemy out of someone who should have been an ally.

Ulric's expression smoothed, and if it didn't become pleasant it at least became less hostile.

I opened myself to him, and got nothing. Instead, I tried to imagine what might be going through his mind.

If I were weak, unable to use my magic and uncertain about my worthiness to take back my throne, if I saw enemies everywhere I looked and had no certain path to victory, and a great Sorcerer who had hated me for decades or more showed up when the throne of my country was ready to go to the worthiest challenger...

A chill passed over me. I could see well why Ulric would feel vulnerable. Though he knew as well as I did that Ernis Albion had never shown any inclination toward taking any throne, let alone that of Tyrea, the threat was there. And to Ulric, wounded as he was, every threat was a disaster.

I stepped forward. "Isn't this wonderful?" I asked before he could say anything. "Who could have imagined that Belleisle would offer this much help?"

Ulric smiled thinly. "Indeed. A great and selfless gift. Griselda must have been quite persuasive in her letter." He answered me, but addressed my grandfather.

"Not at all selfless," Albion said, his voice firm but not threatening. "We wish to be left alone. Severn will not let us be, so we wish to see him removed from power." He grimaced slightly. "It seems you may be Belleisle's best hope."

Ulric nodded. "I certainly hope to restore the peace we've enjoyed for so long."

Enjoyed seemed like a stretch, but if quiet and bitter tolerance could be called peace, I supposed that was true. I wondered whether things would have been different if Albion had ruled Belleisle, whether there would have been a war, or at least a fight between kings.

Perhaps that was why he chose not to rule. Not lack of ambition, but an abundance of self-knowledge.

"Aren tells me we should speak privately," Albion said, and

removed his glasses. He polished them on his sleeve, gave them a long look, and sighed as he tucked them into his pocket.

Ulric paled, but nodded. "I suppose we should. But first, I suppose your granddaughter will want to meet you." He turned to me. "Where's Nox? I haven't seen her all morning."

The hard edge to his voice told me he had a very good idea of where she was, that I was lucky he hadn't brought it up earlier. When I didn't answer, the curved-lipped snarl returned.

"Please excuse us for a moment," he said to Albion. "Your grandson and I need to speak, first."

I followed him to his tent, and he held the flap open for me to enter, then let it fall closed behind us. "Well? Where is she?"

I didn't answer. I didn't know how to. The air grew thick with his magic, pulsing and churning. "What would you have me say?" I asked.

"The truth would be quite acceptable," he growled. "Or will I need to bring Rowan in to ask her? Would she know better? Would she be more willing to spill her secrets if I persuaded her strongly enough?"

I gasped as his magic reached out to me. The dark energy wrapped around my heart, and I felt myself weakening. Ulric flashed a grim smile as sweat beaded his face. "Think that would do it?"

"Enough," I spat. I fought to control my legs, which trembled as he slowly pulled my physical strength. Not my magic, I noted. That would cost him more.

Nox will be in the city by now if she's going to make it. No point keeping secrets.

I looked into his eyes. "You know where she is."

He released me, and my strength flooded back. I drew a sharp breath as it settled back into my muscles.

"The city," he whispered, and leaned forward to rest his hands on his knees as he caught his breath. "You made her go."

"I let her go. I wasn't any happier about it than you are. But how could I not? Look at you. Nox is right. You need a cure, and she's never going to find it in these woods."

His magic gathered again, heavy with threat.

"What are you going to do?" I asked. "Blast me to pieces? Take my power? Blind me?"

"Don't tempt me," he snarled, and spat on the ground.

"Is this how you treat your allies, now?" I asked, no longer caring what he did. I allowed my pent-up anger to bubble to the surface. Letting him have his way wasn't working. "Is this the king we're all supporting? I'm all you have. I saved your life. I got you out of Darmid. I made you look good at the rebel camp, and you know as well as I do that Ernis Albion is here as much for me as for you. I have disobeyed you, but everything I've done since I left Belleisle has been to bring down Severn or to get you back on the throne." *Mostly true*, I thought. For him, or for Rowan, who was as much a part of this as I was. "And all you've done is belittle me, punish me, push me away. I let Nox go because it was the best thing for you and the best thing for Tyrea."

He glared at me, but I was too angry to feel fear, or to stop speaking. "This is not the Ulric I remember. I've never cared for you any more than you did for me, but there was a time when I respected you. You were a good king, once. Generous with those who supported you, even if those people were nobles you hated or the governors of distant provinces who you didn't fully trust. You were fair, you cared for your people."

"And what do you see now?" he demanded. He sat on his bedroll and let out a stream of barking coughs that left him slumped over and gasping. At least there was no blood this time. "Go on. You've obviously been waiting to say it."

"Now you make enemies of people who should be the opposite," I said. "You demand respect, to be obeyed without question, as though you still sit on the throne and control the fates of your subjects. But you don't. You have no power, aside from what your allies bring with them." I thought back over the past weeks. He'd bent himself backward to please the rebels and his former subjects, but turned on anyone with real power. Anyone who might be a threat.

"You can't keep this up forever," I continued. "Rowan isn't afraid of you anymore, and has no respect for you. She only supports you because she would rather see you on the throne than see me take it, and because she wants Severn gone as much as any of us. She's here of her own free will, supporting and helping you, and you repay her with disrespect, threats, isolation, and a flat-out refusal to develop her obvious skills because you're afraid of them."

He grimaced. "I know."

I paused, surprised. "You know what, exactly?"

"That I'm losing everything." He clenched his fists, then relaxed them. "I had it all, once. Political power. Magic. Respect. I worked hard to gain all of them, but in a sense they were also handed to me. I've lost every advantage, now. I feel as though I'm clinging to the top of a cliff by my fingernails, and I'm slipping." His voice grew weak.

"Perhaps if you treated your allies better, they'd pull you up and help you stand until you're well enough to do it on your own."

He shook his head slowly. "Do you know what it's like to have no one near who you can trust?"

"I remember. I found that life became easier when I learned to gain respect through decency rather than fear. I have friends who would give their lives for me, but it's because they know I would do the same for them. I thought that was the kind of king you were, once."

"I was," he said softly. "But everything around me has changed. How can I not?" He frowned. "I thought I could finally trust you, and Nox as well. Yet here we are."

I sat next to him as as the chill of his magic retreated. "I want what's best for us, and for Tyrea," I said. "If Nox gets into Luid, she might find your cure. If not, she might still better our chances of entering the city. What were our other options?"

"And you felt that disobedience was the answer?"

I considered my words carefully. He wanted honesty, and I was done pandering to his sensitivities. Still, the feeling of having my strength stolen lingered, and I had no desire to provoke him further. "Had Nox come to me sooner, had I known of her plans, I would have spoken to you and tried to help you see that letting her go was the only way. Had you told me yourself what she was planning, we might have discussed it. As it was, I needed to make a quick decision last night, and I did. I think denying her this was a mistake on your part. I regret that we didn't have time to better discuss it."

"She'll die," he said, and I realized that though he may have told himself he was only angered by our lack of respect, it went deeper. He cared for his daughter, perhaps enough that he'd let it cloud his judgement. He'd tried to keep her safe, even if it cost him dearly.

"She's clever, and as prepared as she can be," I said. I wasn't going to offer false reassurances, but he needed something. "We've been working on keeping people out of her thoughts, and if she makes it to the Potioners' workroom, she'll be able to do more to protect herself."

He rested his forehead in his hands. "Severn bested me, Aren. He'll defeat you, if it comes to it. He'll see through her."

I tried to harden my heart and think like he always wanted me to. "And then what have we lost? Severn surely knows we're here already. Sending in a spy won't seem out of place. Nox won't reveal your weakness."

His lips tightened as he looked up. "Not even if he has her tortured?"

I pushed away the images that flooded my mind, memories of what Severn was capable of. "This was her decision. She knew the risks. If she thinks she's been found out, she won't let it come to that. She'll make sure she can't talk."

"You think she's strong enough to do it?"

"I do. She won't let herself betray us."

He gritted his teeth and pushed himself back to stand, and I got to my feet as well.

"And what of everything else?" he asked. "Pretend you're the king's advisor. You did it so well for Severn, you can for me. What should I do now?"

At least he was listening. "I would suggest you go out there and make amends. Much as I know it kills you to admit you were wrong, Ernis Albion is not the one who owes an apology here. Tell him the truth of what happened to his daughter. Embrace

those who support you. You have people out there who are interested in seeing Severn defeated, and more back in Wildwood." I
waited until he looked at me again before I continued. "And in
seeing you back on the throne. Severn may have strategic allies,
but I think most Tyreans want their old king back. Not one who
will rule by fear, as Severn does. Accept the fact that for now, you
need our help. Be grateful for the people who are here with you.
Be the king they remember."

"Are you finished?"

"I think so."

He grunted. "At least you know how to make a speech. That
should come in handy some day."

"So you'll talk to Albion?"

He nodded. "Give us some space. We'll work it out."

He left before I could say anything else.

I remembered my promise to Nox, and searched the camp for
Kel. He'd looked terrible when I saw him earlier. I found him
outside of camp, sitting on a fallen log and drinking something
from a dark bottle, looking almost exactly the way I felt. I sat
next to him, in spite of the damp bark.

"One of Nox's potions?" I asked.

He pulled the bottle away from his lips and studied it. "No, it's
something one of Xaven's men gave me. Said it's the traditional
human cure for heartbreak. Something fermented. Like wine, but
far stronger. Decent fellow."

I took the bottle from him and sniffed, and wrinkled my nose
at the astringent scent of the alcohol. Strong, low-quality stuff,
sharp enough to peel paint with fumes alone. Kel's eyes were
already unfocused.

"Is it working?"

"I don't know. It still hurts." He set the bottle down and leaned
his head against my shoulder. "I miss her. More than that, I'm
frightened for her. What will Severn do if he figures out who
she is?"

"He won't." I put an arm around my oldest friend to steady
him. "She's a survivor, right?"

"She is that. It's not that I think she needs me so much as I just want to be there with her if she can't be here safe with me. Even though I know she's safer if I'm not... Am I rambling?"

"I understand. I'm sorry, Kel."

He pushed himself up straight. "I sort of knew that this was a part of the experience of this kind of love. Most mers know about it, intellectually, and are thankful to not deal with it. I just didn't think it would hurt this much. It's as if my heart—my physical, beating heart—is consuming itself."

"I suspect that's why it's called heartbreak."

He picked the bottle up and pointed it at me. "Yeah. You'd know, right?" He nodded sagely. "You know."

I accepted the bottle and took a long drink. It tasted terrible, and burned all the way down. My magic would lessen any ill effects, but the stuff was potent.

Potent, and almost gone.

"Kel, did you drink all of this?"

"It hurts a lot. He said it would help."

"Come on."

I stood, and Kel followed. When he stumbled, I pulled one of his arms around my shoulders and held him up by his waist. "Don't make me carry you," I warned. "You'll embarrass both of us."

The bedroll he'd shared with Nox was unmade, the blankets tossed back. I set him down on it and got him a cup of water from among Nox's things, then on second thought took the jug and placed it beside the bed. The dehydration brought on by consumption of alcohol would be worse for him than it would for a human, and anyone would feel it after the amount he'd had.

"Listen," I told him.

He opened his eyes. "I'm going to sleep."

"Drink this. All of it."

"Let me die." He closed his eyes.

"Don't be dramatic. Come on, wake up." I made him sit up and drink the first cup of water, then poured another. "You should sleep this off, but after you drink the water."

"Will I feel better then?"

"No. Drink."

"This is a stupid cure," he muttered.

I sat with him until the water was gone, and after as he stared at the roof, lost in his thoughts.

"Aren?" His eyes grew bleary with tears, which held a strange golden color in the light of the tent. "You're a good friend. Best I've ever had. Nobody back home would understand this, or care."

"You're going to get through it. You have a bigger, stronger heart than anyone I know. It's not going to be broken forever. She'll come back."

"Yeah. We're going to get through this. You and me." He patted my arm and laid down again. "I just need to sleep for a minute."

"Take your time. I'd say we'll need you soon enough."

I left him and walked around camp. People gave me my space, and no one asked for help as they set up their tents and got the horses settled. Victoria offered a smile as she carried seed packets off into the woods, where Rowan waited. I raised my hand to wave at Rowan, and she smiled back. Then they were gone. I hoped that meant they were both making progress in their connected gifts. We'd need more food, and soon.

I tried not to think too much on how natural it already felt to see her at a distance. *Distance is good,* I told myself. If I was going to have to face Severn—and Ulric's continued poor health seemed to indicate that I would—she would be better off far from me.

I looped back around to my father's tent and arrived in time to see him and Albion emerging. Both looked shaken, but at least it seemed that their discussion hadn't come to a fight. Though I didn't want to look too closely or be caught staring, I thought I spotted a hint of red in my grandfather's eyes. If he'd shed tears, Ulric didn't appear to think less of him for it. The two shook hands, and Albion strode off toward his people.

I followed.

"What's next?" I asked.

"Defenses," he answered, his voice lower and rougher than I was accustomed to hearing it. "It will take a few days to set up, and using this much magic may draw Severn's attention before we can repel it, but it needs to be done. I'll set up something similar to what we have surrounding Belleisle, on a much smaller scale."

"And then?"

He stopped walking and took a deep breath. "That will be up to your father, and whoever he'll allow to help. This is his challenge, but you're the one he seems to trust the most."

I couldn't decide whether that was promising or horrifying, given how little he trusted me.

"He told you everything?"

Albion gave me a sad half smile. "As much as needed to be said about old wounds, and more about recent concerns. Enough for me to understand what we're up against."

"And what do you think of it?"

He shook his head. "I don't know. We'll have some hard decisions to make in the coming days. For now, we've agreed that it's best we dig in here and defend ourselves until the winds shift. I hope your sister is as good as he thinks she is."

"She is." My stomach churned. "I just hope she's all right."

32

NOX

The road was quiet as I made my way toward Luid, which in the darkness had become a floating island of light, crowned by stars. I forced my mind to clear, free of memories, speculation, and plans. In time there was only the plodding of my feet, the almost nonexistent weight of my pack, and the wind at my back that pushed me onward even when I hesitated. I ran through my story over and over, seeking holes, solidifying everything so my answers would be ready.

As of that moment, Kel, Aren and Cassia had not saved me after I left my home town with those soldiers. Dragons had freed me when they'd attacked our party. I'd taken a dead soldier's horse and belongings after the poor man was eaten. I'd been sentenced to death at home, so I had decided to take Lord Severn's offer to come to Luid, though I'd been reluctant to do so at first.

Best to stick as close to the truth as I could, as Aren had said.

The city was farther off than I'd thought, or my legs more reluctant. I crossed the bridge over a wide, dry gully as the stars began to fade. The sun broke over the city before I reached it, blinding me as it sparkled off the ocean to the south in a dazzling display that would have been absolutely breathtaking on another day. I held my arm up to shield my eyes and kept walking, fighting to remain calm as I drew nearer to the city and my fate.

I came to the outer city first, a handful of buildings spaced out on either side of the wide road, dotted with the skeletons of dead oak trees. This had been part of the dark ocean on which the city's lights had floated. A strange feeling crept over me, and it took a minute for me to realize it was an absence. I felt nothing here, no plants, no life, no potential. This place was dead and empty, and the thought that it might also be haunted crossed my mind. Tempted though I was to stop and peek in windows, I decided against it.

The sun continued to rise, and I took a good look at the city walls, which rose high above me, all gray stone with narrow window-slits cut into it at regular intervals. I stepped into the long shadows that seemed to reach toward me. This area, too, seemed far too quiet. Surely the city wouldn't still be asleep. Though I liked to tell myself that the people of Luid were spoiled and useless, there had to be some up and about.

I glanced up. A soldier in a red uniform topped with a gleaming golden helmet looked down at me, but said nothing. I kept walking. Voices and clattering noises drifted from beyond the wall, but they sounded impossibly distant.

The road led straight to a massive gate built of iron scroll-work, backed by panels of solid wood that blocked my view of whatever lay beyond. Smaller doors constructed of the same ironwork on a smaller scale flanked the gate, leading into stone tunnels through the wall. I stepped closer to one and rested my weight on one aching foot to give the other a break.

Please don't kill me, please don't kill me.

"Hello?" I called, and didn't have to try too hard to sound uncertain and lost. "I'm here because Lord Severn sent for me?"

Better that they thought I was a little stupid than be suspicious of me. Maybe they'd take pity.

A tall, broad-chested guard in scarlet clothing topped by a gold-toned breastplate stepped up to the left-hand door, and I moved a little closer. He squinted at me. "State your business."

I just did. "Hello. I'm a Potioner from Cressia. Lord Severn ordered me to come here, and the soldiers who were escorting me... well, they died."

"Sorry. No one in or out without authorization."

"But I've been walking for weeks! Could be longer, I lost track." At least that wasn't a lie. "Please, I have nowhere else to go."

He narrowed his eyes at me. "What's your name?"

Had the soldiers known my name when they came for me? If they had, I couldn't very well lie. Better to be safe. "Nox," I said. "Nox Dunfee." It left a bad taste in my mouth to use my dead husband's last name, but if they knew of me, that's how I would most likely be recorded.

"Hold on."

He disappeared, and several minutes later a similarly-uniformed and significantly smaller woman replaced him. She looked me over, clearly unimpressed. The gate creaked as she swung it open. I stepped into a short, dim tunnel, and she locked the gate behind me.

"You really should have gone home," she said in a conversational tone.

"I don't have one."

"Pity."

I matched her long stride, and we stepped out into sunlight. I didn't have to feign my surprise at the sight and sounds of the city. Nothing Aren told me had prepared me for the majestic stone buildings, the clean cobblestone roads, the bright windows, and the bustle of the people in the streets. Hard to imagine they were preparing for war. A group of women in beautiful dresses sauntered down the street, parasols blocking their fair skin from the sun. Each of them wore an elaborate hairstyle. I wondered how early they had to get up in the morning to achieve that.

A great, black horse plodded by, pulling a wheeled puppet show that performed as he walked. Children followed behind, laughing, carrying candied apples on sticks. A moment later they were swallowed by the crowds.

This is where I was supposed to grow up.

My guide turned and signaled to someone behind me. Before

I could turn, a forearm snaked around my throat, catching my windpipe in the crook of the elbow and pressing tight. White spots bloomed before my eyes, covering the wonder of the city. I didn't dare struggle, even when another set of hands slipped a dark hood over my head.

"Told her she should have gone home," the female guard said, and a man laughed.

Pain exploded in the back of my head, and I heard no more.

∼

I WOKE SLUMPED in a hard chair with my wrists tied behind me, back and arms aching. My mouth felt parched and my brain wooly, and I wondered how much time had passed. Gentle hands pulled my hair back from my face as I struggled to sit up straighter, though I couldn't see who they belonged to thanks to the bright light blinding me.

"Turn that down," an unfamiliar voice said from behind me. An order, and one that was immediately obeyed, but spoken in soft tones. As the light faded I saw that it came from a man's hand. Not a lantern in his hand, as I thought at first, but from his skin.

"That'll do," said the soft voice. "Actually, a little more."

The hand brightened. My eyes adjusted, and I looked around as much as my tied-up state would allow, turning only my aching neck, straining against the ropes. The fellow with the light in his hand was small and thin, clean-shaven from scalp to throat, with a blank expression on his face. He didn't move. If not for his light's responses to the voice, he might have been a statue. He wore dark clothes, which only made his inhumanly white skin and the purple circles beneath his eyes stand out more.

"Perfect." The man who had spoken stepped around from behind me, standing next to the light so I couldn't look at him without blinding myself. "Are you comfortable?"

I twisted my head to see where he'd come from. A fire burned low and hot in a grate behind me—sufficient light, which made me think the other was only there to throw me off.

Not promising.

A long table to my right held a set of tools and a few papers. Other than that it was me, the two men, the chair, and a single wooden door.

"Not exactly comfortable," I said. "Who are you? What's going on? I thought I was wanted here. Lord Severn sent for me."

"King Severn," the speaker corrected. He moved closer, out of the light and into view. "People are having such difficulty with the change."

Unassuming was the first word that came to mind, and nothing else followed. Brown hair, long but tied neatly back. Thin mustache, pale-brown eyes I suspected I'd forget as soon as one of us left the room. Dressed in a shade of green that did little for his pasty complexion. Middling in height and weight.

Middling in everything, in fact. Forgettable. Nearly invisible.

"We'll have you out of here soon enough," he said. "Terrible business, this. We're waiting on confirmation of your story. In the meantime, I thought we might talk. We aren't getting many guileless visitors to the city these days. We should become better acquainted. Might I offer you a sip of water?"

Smooth voice, reassuring tone, friendly offer. And yet my heart pounded and sweat dripped over my brow. How he expected me to warm to him when ropes bound my wrists, I couldn't guess. But then, I'd never cared for being tied up. Maybe the clean water and kind words worked to put other people's minds at ease.

I started to wish I'd never come, and shut the thoughts away before Kel and everyone else could come to mind. I didn't know what this fellow was capable of. Damned if I'd let him catch me that easily.

He held a cup to my lips, though I hadn't accepted the offer. Cool water passed like silk over my dry lips and throat. He pulled a handkerchief from his pocket and wiped a dribble from the corner of my mouth.

"How clumsy of me," he said. I shivered as his gaze met mine.

"You can untie me," I said, sounding as innocent and confused as I could. "I really didn't mean any harm by coming here."

"Hmm? Oh, no, I'm sure you didn't, but we do need to be certain. I'm charged with many things, and ensuring the security of the palace and our king is one of them. If anyone tries to get too close, or arrives without anyone here knowing who she is... you understand, I'm sure."

"I just want to help. I'm a Potioner. A good one."

He poured another glass of water and sipped from it. "I'm sure you are."

"What was your name again?"

"You can call me Dan."

I didn't allow my face to register my surprise. This was another of my half-brothers, and one I'd rarely heard spoken of, even when I was with Ulric and Aren. I could understand why. This man was a lukewarm shadow, lacking the charisma his younger brother possessed, and which I'd heard Severn practically embodied. Still, I didn't doubt that he was good at whatever job Severn had selected for him.

A knock at the door. Dan answered, spoke softly to someone outside, closed the door, and turned to stare at me. "Bimby, I think it's time to fetch Wardrel."

I'd nearly forgotten about lamp man. He doused his light and shuffled from the room without looking at me.

Dan didn't speak while we waited. The minutes stretched out, each longer than the last, but I didn't dare break the silence.

The door slammed open and a monster of a man strode in, grinning. His eyes widened at the sight of me, and his tongue snaked out over broad lips. I held back a scream, but my entire body trembled.

This one, I had heard about. I remembered Patience's burned feet, her missing eye, the way Aren wouldn't talk about this brother unless he had to. But I couldn't let these people know any of that. I ground my teeth together to stop their chattering and pressed my arms against the chair to slow the shakes.

Certainly a show of fear was justified, though, when faced with a man like this. Cut-off sleeves revealed rippling muscles and scars that would have faded if his magic had been stronger— or perhaps they'd been injuries that would have killed someone else. Something like lust burned in his eyes, but I thought that wasn't quite right. What had Aren said?

He brings pain. That's what he lives on.

With Bimby gone, only the hearth's flickering flames lit the room. Dan went to the table and leafed through a few papers. "It seems nobody's heard of you," he muttered. "Quite a problem. Nox... Dumfry?"

"Dunfee," I rasped, and spelled it for him.

Wardrel chuckled, though I didn't see what was so funny.

Dan frowned, made a note on the paper, and passed it out the door. "We'll see whether anyone remembers sending for you by that name, then. In the meantime, I just have a few more questions. Who sent you?"

I feigned confusion. "I... I sent me. I mean, the soldiers came to get me, but then they died, so I—"

"Wardrel?"

The monster stepped forward and grabbed my hair one massive hand, snapping my head back. With the other he reached for the water pitcher and dumped it over my face. Water burned down my throat and into my chest, but with my head tilted as it was I couldn't cough hard enough to expel it. He released me, and I keeled as far forward as my bonds would allow, hacking until tears poured from my eyes. My breath returned in harsh, sobbing gasps.

I hadn't thought I trusted Dan enough to feel betrayed if he turned on me. It seemed I was wrong.

"Tell me again who sent you?" Dan asked. His tone hadn't changed. He'd ordered the attack, but still spoke levelly, calm and soft as before.

"Please," I moaned. "I don't know what else to tell you. I'll leave, I shouldn't have come. I'd heard there were opportunities here. I didn't want to leave home at first, but—"

"Wardrel?"

"No!"

Wardrel reached behind the chair, grabbed my left wrist in

one hand and my index finger in the other, and twisted the finger until the longest bone snapped. I screamed as pain shot up my arm.

"Who?" Dan repeated, voice as conversational as it had been when he offered me water.

House by the sea, I thought before I could shut the thought out. *Survive this.*

I moaned in response, as I assumed someone with no other answer to give would.

"Do you believe her, Wardrel?"

I looked up, ready to plead my innocence, and quickly realized that it made no difference to Wardrel. He wanted my tears, my pain. I calmed my mind. I wouldn't give him the satisfaction of begging. Not unless I had to.

"I think she's lying," Wardrel said.

I barely caught the distaste-filled twist of Dan's upper lip before it disappeared. "Of course you do. Try again." Wardrel disappeared behind me, and Dan crouched in front of my knees so that I had to look at him. "Miss Dunfee, please. I don't like this any more than you do. If there's something you want to share with us, this will be a lot easier for everyone. He can go for hours. I can make it quick."

"Why don't you believe me?" I whispered.

"Because it's my job not to."

He backed away and Wardrel stepped into view, this time holding a red-hot fireplace poker. He tapped it against my forearm. Just a taste. I'd been burned worse before, but in my already-panicked state the pain was heightened. My heart slammed against my ribcage, my breath caught in my throat, and I struggled against the ropes. My broken finger screamed in protest.

Wardrel returned the poker to the fire. "Not hot enough," he muttered. "Dan, get me more flesh."

Dan's lips narrowed into a thin line. Perhaps this wasn't the job he'd signed up for. His fingers flicked delicately over the buttons on my shirt and he pushed the fabric back over my shoulders, leaving me covered only by my undershirt, which left far too much of my skin exposed to air and iron.

I made eye contact with Dan. "Please. Tell me what you want me to say to make him stop."

He sighed. "The truth, my dear, is all we ask."

"I'm telling the truth. Please. You have to—"

Someone knocked at the door. "Excuse me," Dan said, and answered it.

Something moved near the back of my head, and I smelled burning hair.

"That's better," Wardrel mumbled, and held the hot metal before my face. "Last chance." I leaned back against the chair, but the poker followed. "What do you think, Dan?" The poker hovered over my chest, so close it warmed my skin. "Start here? Or..." It moved, now nearly pressed against my cheek. "Not so pretty anymore if we do that. Or here." He pulled my shirt up and aimed the hot steel at my belly like a sword, ready to stab. "If it burns hot enough, that might not kill you too fast. We could still have hours of fun."

Tears I couldn't stop streamed down my face, but I didn't answer. *They're guessing. They can't know.*

"Fine, I'll choose." The poker returned to my face. "Not so hot now. But it'll do."

His eyes glowed with anticipation as he brought the iron closer to my right eye, inch by inch, drawing it out, savoring my fear.

"Hold on," Dan said.

Wardrel scowled and gave my cheek a quick slash with the poker before stepping back. Pain seared into my skin, sharp and bright. I gasped, and broke down sobbing as the shock opened the dam of emotion I'd been holding back. Dan stepped behind me and cut the rope. "She actually is who she says she is, or at least her story holds. They couldn't find Dumfry in the records, but Dunfee's there." He stepped in front of me and shook his head. "I keep telling them that it's essential to be precise in one's paperwork, but they never listen. Now look what's happened."

The scowl didn't leave Wardrel's face as Dan helped me to my feet and quickly passed me into the waiting arms of a soldier.

I drew in a long, shaky breath and cradled my injured hand against my stomach.

"I still don't trust her," Wardrel said.

Dan studied my face. "No? We'll see what happens. You two may meet again."

Wardrel rammed the poker back into the coals. "I look forward to it."

Dan escorted me and the soldier down the hall, around a dizzying number of corners, and into a small room containing a simple wardrobe, a washbasin, a table and chair, and a narrow bed with white blankets. The soldier set me down on the bed.

"I'll have someone come in now to speak to you about starting work as soon as you've recovered," Dan said, and left.

The soldier stood watch by the door. I didn't bother speaking to him. A while later a beautiful young woman with hair the rich gold of honey stepped into the room carrying an array of bottles in her apron skirt. She dismissed the soldier and pulled up the chair beside the bed.

"My name is Sara," she said, and her voice was as honey-like as her hair, sweet and smooth. I didn't react to the name, or show I'd heard of her. She brushed my hair back from my face, and her hand was cool and comforting. "Look what they've done to you, poor thing. Let me see to that. We'll talk about your skills tomorrow, after you've rested."

She applied a sweet-smelling ointment to the burn on my face. She pulled hard on my finger to set the bone, and a few more tears squeezed out of my eyes.

"Sorry. Had to be done."

"I know." I immediately wanted to like Sara for her competent efficiency, but remembered Aren's warning.

She applied another potion to the finger, this one a liquid that seemed to flow right through my skin and into the bone, burning as it went. "That'll be uncomfortable, but it will make things heal better and faster."

"Fyreflower?" I searched my mind for the correct ingredients, and found that it distanced me from the pain and panic. "Wortroot?"

She smiled. "And a hint of toad's skin for added potency, plus a few more exotic items. You're good at that."

I forced a smile. "I have some experience."

She pulled my eyelids back and frowned. "So red. Crying, or strain?" She didn't wait for an answer. "That won't cause permanent damage either way, but I can give you something to clear it up." I nodded, and she placed drops of a cool substance in my eyes. "I'm so sorry this happened. I would have remembered your name, but I was with our king and couldn't be excused. My assistant was left to sort through months-old paperwork."

"Do they torture everyone who comes in?"

She smiled sadly. "Torture? That was just Wardrel getting warmed up. I suggest staying out of his way. Out of all of their ways, if you want to stay in one piece. Sleep now."

My eyelids grew heavy as if on command, and I struggled against fog that crowded my thoughts. "Is it safe to?"

She smoothed my hair again. "It is. I'll have my personal guard posted outside your door, and no one will trouble you. Rest, please. If you're as talented as you claim, we'll find a good place for you. All of this will be a nasty memory soon enough."

The door's lock clicked shut behind her. I was a prisoner, even if it seemed I'd be well cared for.

At least I'm in, I thought, and drifted to sleep before I had a chance to do more than wonder why, exactly, sleep was coming so easily.

33

ROWAN

T he camp was only truly silent in the smallest hours of the morning. After the arrival of the Belleisle folk, more had come from Wildwood. People had been up well into the night, talking or planning or setting up tents. It took hours for the night's depths to subdue the last of us, for the gentle stars to drain the excitement and nerves, and for the chill of the air to send everyone retreating to their beds.

Yet even with the silence, even with the warmth of a heavy blanket and the comfort of knowing how many competent people surrounded me, I couldn't sleep. My thoughts refused to settle, and instead of resting they chased their own tails through my mind, repeating the same questions and worries until I thought I'd go mad.

My family was safe. Things were settled with Aren, if not as I'd have wished, and I was learning to let go. My magic was coming along. But every step in getting those concerns settled was a step closer to the precipice of the future. Toward battle, perhaps. Certainly toward danger, and all of it shrouded in the fog of secrecy. No one seemed to know what the plan was, except to settle in and protect ourselves until Nox's return or a break-through on Ulric's part.

I punched the sweater I was using as a pillow, attempting to soften it and knowing it wouldn't help me rest. After a few more minutes of blinking up into the darkness, I threw off the blankets, slipped into the sweater, laced my boots up to my knees, and stepped out into the night.

With all of the lights in camp doused, the stars overhead were fully visible, spilling across the sky so thick and bright that they looked like grains of sand on a beach. I imagined they were diamonds, and smiled at the thought of Ruby flying up to catch them to feed to her next clutch of dragonlings.

But there won't be a next, I remembered. *She wants to end it.* I couldn't be sad about not having more dragonlings to contend with, but I also knew the world would lose something with Ruby's death, however she chose to go. A wealth of knowledge, centuries of experience, a different way of thinking and seeing the world.

I walked toward the paddock, a rough enclosure of cut wooden boards and tree branches that held the camp's horses. We had a good number now. Not enough for everyone to ride into battle if it came to that, but a good-sized herd. The challenge in the coming days would be feeding them. Victoria was already growing vegetables to feed the people, but the horses needed more. Taking them out to forage had already become a massive job for a few of Xaven's people, and would only become more challenging if Ulric ordered us to stay within Ernis Albion's defenses once they were finished.

I found Florizel beside the paddock, as I'd expected. She enjoyed the company of horses, even though they couldn't speak to her, but disliked the business of large groups of humans. She watched over the mostly-sleeping animals now, seeming to draw in their calm and peace. I admired the starlight on her pale wings, which seemed to glow in the darkness.

She looked up as I came nearer.

"Is all well?" she asked.

"As good as it can be," I said. "I can't sleep, though."

She glanced up at the sky. "Morning will be here soon." She looked back at the horses. "I do miss that. Sleeping peacefully, knowing a leadmare was watching over me. I feel I must always be alert now, waiting for sunrise."

We stood together for a while, and waited. The stars began to fade, and the chill of the early morning crept into my muscles. "Care for a walk?" I asked.

She fell in beside me, and we moved away from the crowd of tents. Florizel leaned in close, and her breath tickled my ear. "Are our walls up yet?"

"Not quite."

She looked away and snorted. "The illusions are, though. I had to find the camp by memory. Couldn't see a thing from above."

"That's good."

Griselda and Maks, one of the Sorcerers from Belleisle, were in charge of that. We'd have Albion's defenses up soon enough—a wall of magic that would shock and hold off anyone who tried to enter the area with ill-intent while letting our own people pass through unharmed. But until he was able to build that up and solidify it, Griselda had proposed a cloak of illusion to make the camp look like just another part of the forest. Setting up something so enormous had exhausted her, and maintaining it seemed to be causing some strain for both her and Maks, but watching her work had been an incredible experience for me. It made me realize what I might be capable of once I was fully in control of my power.

The illusion wouldn't keep anyone out, but we hoped it would at least throw off scouts when Severn sent them out.

"This should be it," I said as we approached the spot where I'd stood as Griselda wove her half of the dome-shaped illusion. It was invisible from within camp, leaving us with a clear view of the forest beyond—a fact which had only added to the challenge for Griselda, who had never before attempted such a thing. The only people permitted to step beyond were our sentries and watch-keepers, and anyone taking the horses out. Still, I stepped as close to the invisible barrier as I dared, and motioned for Florizel to stay back. Though sunrise was still a ways off, the sky had brightened while we walked, revealing the hulking shapes of the forest against a purple sky.

I looked up at the massive elm that marked this border of the illusion. The lookout posted up in the branches wouldn't be able to see me, but I felt safer knowing there was someone up there.

The tree was empty.

I glanced down and bit back a gasp at the sight of a crumpled body lying at the tree's roots, cloaked in dark clothing and only visible when I knew to look. I scanned the forest, but saw nothing.

And then I did.

Silent as a shadow, he approached. Bow at the ready, sword on his hip, dressed all in black and nearly invisible in the dark forest. He crept toward me, cat-like in the elegance of his movements. Another shadow moved behind him, deeper in the trees.

I slowed my breath, but didn't dare move. He hadn't seen me behind the illusion, but he would surely hear me. He stepped closer, until we stood almost nose-to-nose. He paused, perhaps sensing the faint magic of the illusion, or feeling a slight sting as he neared the still-weak defensive wall.

He held up a hand and made a soft clicking sound. The person following him stopped.

My body felt frozen, but I forced myself to step back slowly. I turned my head to see Florizel standing motionless save for the twitching of her ears and the swish of her tail. I held a finger to my lips and hoped the gesture made sense to a horse. She nodded.

I turned and walked away as quietly as I could, but the dead leaves on the forest floor rustled under my feet.

"They're here," whispered a voice behind me.

I ran, and Florizel followed. "Fly for help!" I ordered. "Tell Ulric and Albion. Wake everyone!"

Someone cried out behind me. It seemed Albion's defenses were making themselves known, but a little shock wouldn't hold anyone back for long.

I slapped the sides of tents as I passed, hollering for people to wake. We'd been found out, and there was no point trying to hide. Sleepy faces registered shock as people sat up and shook off their slumber, but I had no time to stay and explain the situation.

I abandoned that task as the noise started waking everyone up without my help, and focused on getting to Aren.

He was already gone when I reached his tent, and nowhere to be found. I headed back to my own tent and collected the short blade that was all I could realistically handle. My arrows would be useless in the dark, and enemies wouldn't be the ones carrying torches. Still, I grabbed the bow and arrows and slung the lot over my shoulder as I tucked the blade into my boot. I reached within myself to feel for my other weapon—one that hadn't come to mind until after I'd picked up the physical ones. The magic burned strong and bright, but my heart thundered at the thought of releasing it.

Too bad, I told myself, and ran back toward the outer edges of camp. My hands trembled, and I gripped the bow tighter.

I'd been in fights before, but never in a large group. Never a battle, or so much as a skirmish. I tried not to think about that, only to remember the training I'd had in archery and what Ulric had taught me about defending myself when we were imprisoned.

The sky had lightened enough to outline the bodies that moved around me, crowding and pushing. I didn't see Florizel anywhere, but spotted Aren. Ulric held him back and said something. Aren nodded, but seemed displeased. When he turned and saw me, he hurried over.

"Stay back," he said.

"I can fight."

His brow furrowed, shadowing his eyes. "I know. Try to stay toward the center of camp, though. They're coming from all sides." His frown deepened. "Ulric doesn't want us to lose more powerful magic than we need to, and that includes you. Be careful."

And then he was gone, lost in the crowd.

I climbed onto the tall stump of a tree that stood next to the cook tent and tried to get my bearings. With so many unfamiliar people around I couldn't tell who was friend and who was foe, and wondered how the others were managing it.

Small skirmishes had broken out all around as the

intruders entered camp and met our resistance. To my left, a pair of men in black clothing raced into camp. A Sorceress from Belleisle ran at them, hands empty of weapons. Her slight form hardly seemed threatening, though the determination with which she moved would have given anyone pause. Mid-stride she transformed, human form disappearing, replaced in an instant by the hulking form of a massive blondish-brown bear. She landed on all four fearsomely clawed feet and kept running, letting out a roar that shook the forest. The two men skidded to a stop, but only one escaped the deadly swipe of her paw.

The forest filled with shouts and the sounds of weapons clashing. Still, this was no army that had attacked us.

Not a battle, I realized. *A test.* Severn wanted to see what our defenses were, what magic we had at our disposal and how many fighters.

A mighty gust of wind ripped through the camp, toppling me from my perch. I landed hard on my left elbow as I twisted to protect my weapons, and cried out at the sharp, tingling pain. As soon as it eased, I climbed back up. The wind had died as quickly as it came.

I looked beyond the fighting and spotted a lone figure in black perched half-way up a tree, watching. The others Severn had sent were falling before the weapons and magic of our people, but he seemed unconcerned, and not at all interested in joining the fight. He had another job, I suspected. And if he were allowed to complete it, we'd all be in trouble.

I couldn't harm him with magic at that distance, but that didn't make me useless.

I slowed my breath, strung my bow, pulled an arrow from my quiver, and took aim.

One deep breath to shut out the clamor around me.

Another to steady my tired arms and ground my body.

My magic swirled through me. It would not direct the arrow, but I trusted it to sharpen me, to help my mind and muscles remember the skills I'd already learned.

I released the arrow, and the man in black fell.

I waited for the fear and horror, but they didn't come. Magic had aided me in killing, and the world hadn't crumbled.

"At least that's a step in the right direction," I told myself, and turned to look for more observers in the trees.

If there had been more, they were gone. Hardly any time seemed to have passed since I first spotted the intruders, but the fighting was done. Bodies littered the ground, though in the dim sunrise light it was hard to tell how many were ours. Someone had opened the paddock—an enemy, presumably— and most of the horses were gone. I climbed down from the stump and headed toward the outer ring of tents to see whether I could help.

Aren's cousin Morea stood over the body of one of Severn's men. Half of his face had melted off, exposing the white globe of an eye that stared blankly into the sky.

"Did you do that?" I asked, speaking softly.

She turned to me. "We Potioners have our weapons, too. It's not all healing and tea parties."

"No, of course," I said. "I'm impressed."

She laughed, and clamped a hand over her mouth. "Sorry. I'm a little on edge. I suppose the real work begins now. Please excuse me." She headed back to her tent, presumably to collect her healing supplies.

I moved slowly through the crowd, glad to see that most of our people seemed to have come through unscathed, if rather shaken. I stopped beside a smaller form. The bear Sorceress lay naked on the ground, a knife protruding from her throat.

In the shock of seeing her, in the aftermath of the high emotions of the fight, I didn't feel an urge to cry. Just an over-whelming sense of regret and loss, an emptiness that left me dry-eyed. She'd been a stranger to me, but an ally to our cause, and a brave one. I removed my jacket and covered her as well as I could with it, and drew the long knife from her body.

I dropped it next to the man who lay beside her with his stomach clawed out.

A hand rested on my shoulder, and I jumped.

"Sorry," Aren said. "I didn't mean to startle you. You all right?"

"Better than her." I looked up into his eyes. They were filled with concern, and with sadness when he looked down at the body. "I um…" The tears suddenly threatened, but I held them back. "I didn't know you… that people like you turned back into humans when they died."

He swallowed hard. "We do. I suppose it's a mercy, if a terrible one." He reached out as though he wanted to brush my hair back from my face, but hesitated. His hand fell back to his side. "Thank you for taking care of her."

"Least I could do." I wanted to say more, to tell him how I hated all of this and how glad I was that it wasn't him lying at my feet, and how horrid that thought made me feel. That the gulf between us that was so much more than physical distance was killing me. But I said nothing. No good would come of it.

"How many losses?" I asked.

"I don't know. Not too many on our side. I've seen perhaps a dozen of theirs."

I remembered the watcher. "Think any are headed back to the city to report? That's what they came for, isn't it?"

"I suppose. And I hope none escaped." He reached up to rub the back of his neck. "I should find my father and grandfather. What will you do?"

"Help where I can, I suppose," I said. "Maybe find Florizel and round up the herd."

"Be careful," he said. I sensed there was more that he wanted to say, but I knew he wouldn't. No matter what was still between us, we had started on different paths. Looking back only made it hurt more.

I spotted a flash of cream-coloured feathers and ran to ask Florizel for help with the horses.

If Aren did choose to speak, I wasn't sure I could take hearing what he had to say.

34

AREN

I found my grandfather at the edge of camp, hard at work. He stood with his eyes closed and his hands raised, arms trembling and fingers hooked into claws by the strain in his muscles. His breath came in long, deep waves that lifted his shoulders, and with each inhalation the air grew heavier, weighed down by the magic he wove. I had never realized it was possible to call and control so much at once.

The invisible wall would solidify, built up in layers. I hoped we wouldn't be there long enough for the camp to become as safe as Belleisle, but it would be far more than we'd hoped for before his arrival.

Though I moved almost silently, he heard me coming and glanced back. More footsteps, and my father appeared beside me. I braced myself for accusations, perhaps a fight.

"I should have stayed awake through the night working on it," Albion said. His exhaustion came through in the gravelled tones of his voice. His shoulders slumped, and the magic faded. "I knew we weren't safe yet, but I was so drained. I could have, though. I could have pushed it." He sighed. "How many dead?"

"Perhaps half a dozen of ours. Twice that of Severn's, if it's any consolation." The calm in my father's voice surprised me, and I turned. His long, graying hair hung loose over his shoulders, tangled and wild. His eyes showed the strain of long nights and bearing the burden of deaths, but it didn't appear he'd used his magic. He'd commanded. Others had acted. I wondered how that felt for a man like him.

"It's not," Albion replied. "But thank you."

He didn't ask whether the dead were his people or Xaven's. Perhaps at that point it didn't matter. We were one force, small though we may have been.

"It was a test," Ulric said quietly as we walked away, leaving Albion to his incredible task.

"That's what Rowan thought," I said. Ulric nodded, but said nothing. "We passed, though."

He grunted, displeased. "We defended ourselves, and didn't lose many. But Severn gained information, didn't he? If any of them got away, if they saw anything, Severn will know about our magical defenses and what skills we have available if we attack. And what have we gained?"

"Nothing. But thank the gods Rowan and Florizel were awake and spotted them."

He let out a quick snort of a laugh and shook his head. "I thought I'd finally gone completely mad when I woke to that horse's head popping into my tent and screaming, 'Excuse me?'" He sobered immediately. "It is truly miraculous that we didn't suffer heavier losses."

"I didn't note magic among Severn's people."

"No." Ulric frowned. "No, he didn't send his best. Not this time."

Qurwin Black walked among the dead, half-carrying a wounded woman from Belleisle. A great wildcat, larger than any I'd ever seen, with a tawny coat, a long tail, and massive paws paced beside him, ears twitching and curved fangs bared.

The wildcat prowled closer to us, and a moment later Griselda stood there, fully dressed, though she'd dropped whatever weapons she'd carried before. I studied her clothes. Leather boots and pants, simply constructed. A plain brown shirt, unadorned save for laces holding it closed across the top of her chest. She rarely wore anything else, unless an occasion called for fancier dress. I'd assumed it was an issue of comfort and practicality, but wondered now if it was more of a necessity of her magic.

"Damn it, Maks." She knelt beside a body, and I recognized one of her Sorcerer friends beneath the deep wound that had split his face. The other illusionist, in fact.

Griselda closed his remaining eye and stepped back.

"This is a terrible loss," Ulric said quietly.

She squeezed her eyes closed. "We all knew the dangers when we agreed to come here. He was a good friend, though." A tear slipped down her cheek as she looked back at the body. "I'll miss him."

Ulric nodded. "Aren, we'll need to speak later. For now, do what you can to help them."

A few people were already dragging the dead farther into the woods, outside of our circle of safety. There was no point trying to bury them in the thin soil of the forest, and we needed to get them far from camp before they started to rot or attract animals. I helped carry one and went back to assist with the others.

If we could spare a few people, I'd organize a crew to cover the bodies in stones to at least show respect and keep the animals off. If not—well, war was never pleasant business. I'd hoped I'd never see it myself, but we'd run out of options. We would have to move forward, or be trapped here.

Some time later, I watched as a pair of Xaven's men deposited the last body and started back toward camp.

"You coming, sir?" one asked, and wiped his sleeve across his brow. He held his arm out and looked it over, surprised to see it covered in his own blood. He had no magic, and I couldn't be bothered to shut out his thoughts, which raced and pulsed outward in the wake of the excitement. He'd been too busy taking care of the dead to notice his own wounds.

"Go on ahead, and get that arm looked at. Morea will give you something for the pain," I said. "I'll be back in a few minutes. I want to pay my respects. "

Surprise registered on his face, and in his surface thoughts.

He hadn't thought I cared. None of them did. But he was pleased. "Sure thing," he said.

They left me alone with the pile of bodies. Birds twittered in the trees, and the sun shone down. Nothing in the wider world changed. We humans would go about our business, slaughtering each other, but it hardly mattered to anything else. I couldn't decide whether that was comforting or terrifying.

"It's a damned mess," I told the bodies. With them all laid out as they were, wearing regular clothes rather than uniforms and few of them familiar faces, I couldn't tell which had been our men and which were Severn's.

Soon enough they'd be nothing but bones.

Stupid, senseless loss.

A deep, unsettling calm came over me as I looked at the corpses, and my magic moved. Ready. Excited. A chill passed over my skin.

It probably wouldn't work. I hadn't tried it in years. But the urge to try, to test the idea, was overwhelming.

Darkest magic, whispered a voice I hadn't thought of for weeks. Brother Phelun of the Dragonfreed Brothers, who had nearly convinced me to give up my greatest gifts. I'd decided he was at least half-wrong about the mind control. But this...

The body nearest to my feet twitched, a tremor that jerked his body up in the middle. His left arm, which had been resting across his chest, flopped onto the ground. Next to him, an older man's fingers twitched like a spider's legs, dancing in place as they drummed on his stomach. I focused on his wrinkled face, and blank eyes opened.

"No." I stepped back. Bile rose in my throat. "Sleep now." The eyes closed.

I turned and ran from the power I'd kept hidden for most of my life. My deepest secret.

Gods, but that was easy. A small thing, but so... natural.

I turned and threw up in the bushes as the image of dead, dancing fingers flashed through my mind.

THE EVENING AFTER THE ATTACK, I made my way out to meet my father. I stuck to the woods, walking parallel with the road toward Luid. The camp was on high ground which sloped toward the city before I'd gone far. From the road I'd have had a good, if distant view of Luid, but on my current path it was all trees and tangled vines. The slope continued downward for a good distance, then leveled out again until it reached the next point of descent toward the great plain.

I found Ulric standing with his hands clasped behind his back at the edge of the road on the lip of the hill, keeping silent watch over the heart of what had once been his kingdom. The sight of the city filled me with dread, but he showed nothing but calm.

The plain, an empty stretch of wind-blown grass, stretched toward the handful of buildings outside the wall. From this distance the wall beyond was clearly visible, as was the shape of the massive iron gates, locked tight. I hoped Nox had made it through safely and found her way to the palace. Uneasy as the thought of her there made me, the alternative was far worse.

"Risky place to spend an evening," I said, and Ulric turned.

"They already know where we are if they want us."

I stood an arm's length from him. "Do you think she got in?"

"No reports of her body hanging from the wall over the gate. That's a good sign."

"I suppose so." Gods only knew what might be happening, though. I thought then that perhaps Ulric was right, and I shouldn't have let her go. Too late now, though, and regret was as pointless as worry.

He reached into the pocket of his jacket and handed me a rolled sheet of parchment. "Took a while to get here," he said. "Came via rider, but he had a harder time finding us than Severn did."

I unrolled the paper and my heartbeat quickened as I scanned the words, which ended with Cassia's neat signature at the bottom.

Ulric held out his hand to take the paper back, but I read the words over again, more carefully this time. "The merfolk aren't coming."

He took the paper and rolled it before tucking it into his jacket. "I can't say I'm surprised, but capable troops in the harbor would have been a great help."

"At least we get to keep Kel."

Ulric nodded. "He's getting along well with Xaven's men. Makes for a good bridge between them and us, especially when they see him and you together so much. You and I make them nervous, I think."

I'd have laughed if I thought the understatement was a joke. Even the people who supported Ulric's return treated him with deference and awe. He wasn't one of them, and neither was I. Kel, on the other hand... Well, they'd tried to treat his heartbreak. No one would have dared offer me the same, had they known.

"I'm glad to have him here," Ulric said. "And you. You're doing well, Aren, now that you're focusing on what's important. Connecting us with Xaven's people was a great help."

"And finding someone to feed them, and to help Nox prepare something to sustain you, if not cure you?"

He grunted. "The outcome of that little folly wasn't entirely undesirable. You have a long way to go in terms of learning obedience, but you're not stupid. You have more potential than I thought."

I'd have checked him for fever if I hadn't been afraid he'd take my hand off for it. Such praise, and all it took was losing the things that were most important to me.

"Should anything happen to me," he continued, "you'll be in command. I've already told Xaven and the Belleisle folk. None of them will oppose you. You have Albion's full support, as well as everyone else's."

I knew I should thank him, but couldn't make my lips form the words. Not when I wanted so badly for someone else to take on that responsibility. But Ulric would never pass it to someone outside of our family, especially a non-Tyrean.

"I won't disappoint you," I said instead.

He frowned as he continued to watch the city.

There was more to say, more plans to be made, and yet he remained silent. A few minutes later I cleared my throat and said, "A wise man once told me that worry is pointless, and a waste of energy we could better direct toward other things."

He nodded. "It's good advice. Did I say that?"

"You did. Long after my mother died, when I was anxious that my magic wasn't developing quickly enough to please you."

"You remember my words from that long ago?"

"You spoke to me so rarely."

He winced. "You said a wise man, not a kind one. Not so wise, in the end. I handled my grief badly after I lost your mother."

I had no reply for that, and decided he wasn't looking to offer a heart-felt apology. I wasn't sure I was ready to hear it even if he wanted to. "What are you watching for?" I asked.

"Weakness. What do you see when you look past the plains, Aren?"

"I see Luid. My home, though I haven't seen much of it in recent years. I see the wall. If I were a little closer, I'd likely see armed soldiers moving about on top of it. Beyond the wall, I see the city spread out, rising toward the ocean cliffs in the east, and the palace spires. I see the sea to the south, and no ships coming or going."

"Look to your left, beyond the wall. What there?"

A chill passed over me. I didn't have to look, and didn't care to. "The Despair."

"Hmm." Ulric faced it full on. "How would you describe that?"

I turned to look at it, and a familiar sense of confusion washed over me, even at this distance. Though nothing appeared out of focus or hidden, I couldn't find words to describe the desolate space that spread out from the city's low north wall. All I wanted was to look away and forget the place existed. "I can't say what I see, only what I've heard."

"Good enough."

I continued to stare at it, trying to make it solidify in my mind. "It's barren. I've heard it called the Doldrums, or the Desolation. It's a place that breaks a person's heart and mind with sadness."

"Almost correct," he said, voice barely a whisper. "Did you ever venture into it?"

"No. I visited the northern part of the city on few occasions. Even with the wall's magical protections, I felt it. Each time, I returned to the palace with the feeling that nothing mattered, convinced that my life was worthless no matter what I did, that hope and happiness were lies."

Ulric nodded. "Well remembered. That barely digs below the surface of what it is, but you have the idea."

"What is it?" I asked. "I've heard stories saying that it's the absence of magic, or that someone tried to work magic out there and it backfired in the most spectacular way anything ever has, or that it's a natural phenomenon. No one likes to talk about it, though it's right there."

Ulric continued to watch it, and I wondered whether he saw more clearly than I did. "No one knows for certain. It's from my mother's time as queen. She never spoke of it, and reports from the time are conflicting. It seems to be a created thing, but while one account claims it was intentional, placed as a defense for the city, another states as you said that it was a mistake. But there's strong magic there. Plenty of it, not that anyone dares access it." There was very good reason why there was no gate in that section of the wall, and why that area was less well-guarded. No attacker would be foolish enough to approach that way, whether man or beast. If they did, they wouldn't get within an arrow's shot of the wall. Even plants rarely grew out there.

I looked away from the dusty, brown earth to the north of the city. Now that we'd talked about it, I could see it a little better, but didn't desire to look longer.

The wind picked up, blowing from behind us toward the city. Ulric pulled his jacket tighter against his body.

"We should get back," I said.

"Do you see anything else? Any weak point in Luid's defenses?"

My stomach tightened. "Are we talking about taking the city, then?"

His lips narrowed. "Not with the forces we have now. I'd rather find a way for us to face Severn one on one, as is proper, but he'll never allow us in. We're going to have to find a way through those gates, and past all of his defenses. Let's say we did attack directly. Is there a weakness?"

I looked again. "No. The main gate is well-fortified. You and your ancestors did your job far too well. We have no ships to attack the harbor, and no help from the merfolk."

He nodded. He knew all of it. He wanted to know that I knew. "And to the east is all cliffs to the ocean, and us with no way to scale them or method of aerial attack."

"Florizel might help," I said. "She might fly you in, and I could fly, myself. But Severn would have us cut down as soon as we were spotted."

"I thought the same. We need to get ourselves in, but we also need an attack large enough that it will pull every soldier in the palace away from Severn, leaving him exposed." He pressed his knuckles to his lips. "He's got soldiers. He's got magic, and we have no idea what kind or how much. We have a good deal of power on our side, but I'd prefer not to sacrifice lives if we can avoid it."

An image came to mind, and a memory. The natural gift I'd discovered as a child. *Dark magic. Dancing fingers.*

I shuddered, and not from the cold breeze. "What if our troops—at least, those leading the attack—couldn't be hurt or killed? A human wall, marching through the Despair, drawing the worst of the city's defenses away from those who were vulnerable?"

He gave me a look that said I must be insane. "That would be impressive magic, but unless you know something about Albion's people that I don't, I think it's a dead end."

"Not live soldiers," I said. "Not men who feel pain or faint from blood loss. If they took the brunt of the arrows and magical attacks…"

Dead eyes snapped open in my mind, unseeing and unknowing. I didn't know how well they'd follow any orders from me, whether they'd be obedient and agile enough to do it. There was only one way I might find out.

Ulric's lips parted as though he wanted to speak, but couldn't find words. His mouth closed again and he gave his head a firm shake. "No. Aren, no."

"Had you forgotten?"

He kept shaking his head, as though he might erase the idea. "One doesn't forget that his son can do a thing like that. I hoped that you'd forgotten, though."

"I tried to. I haven't been practicing it."

"Thank the Goddess and all the gods for that."

"But it's still there." The plan was flawed, even if I could make it work. A few dozen bodies were hardly enough of a shield. And yet the idea of using them, the thought of the horror and panic they'd inspire in guards at the gate, would not leave me alone.

"No," Ulric said. "Absolutely not."

"This is how we could get to Severn," I said, the plan taking vague shape as I spoke. "Distractions. You said yourself that we need to get Severn's guards away from him. Corpses attacking would certainly help, and would cost us nothing."

He let out a barking laugh. "Aren, what you're proposing is insanity. You think you have any future as king if the people learn of this? You think I have one if I allow it? It's sacrilege. Offensive to the dead, and the gods, and every human instinct."

"And what if I don't care about offending the gods? I doubt the Goddess herself is going to rain fire down on me for it. As for human concerns, I think the people want their land ruled by a good king. And I think this is worth discussing if we have no other options."

He placed his hands on my shoulders. "Aren, listen to me. I'm glad you're coming up with new ideas. But you can't do this. The laws against that sort of magic are based in religion, but it goes beyond that. There are stories of people raising the dead, and the effect of it on them was horrifying. They turned into walking corpses themselves. That's why people came to believe it offended the gods. Because of the punishments the deities sent on those who played with death."

"So that's a no?" I asked.

He smiled, but his expression remained tight. "We'll call that a definite no. And don't mention it to anyone else. Keep thinking, but for now, we wait for an opportunity to present itself. Nox potion will return to us. Our time will come."

As we walked back to camp, I admitted to myself that I was relieved. Better for that part of me to stay in a locked room forever, that no one know. It might have worked, but at what cost? Brother Phelun told me that there was always a price to magic, either to ourselves or others. Surely the effects of working so closely with death were better left unexplored.

That night I dreamed of convulsing bodies rising from the earth, marching to battle. I dreamed I lost control of them, that they consumed the city and every person in it.

I woke drenched in cold sweat, begging some invisible god for forgiveness, and vowed that nothing would make me entertain the idea again.

B y the end of my second full day in the palace, Sara had me completely healed. She was as good at her job as Aren had said, and though I didn't trust her, I admired her. I'd had trouble gaining respect back home, even when I was the best Potioner around. Here in the city, surrounded by as many kinds of power as there were rooms in the palace, she had climbed her way to the top and become head Potioner for Severn before she turned thirty.

I wondered whether we might have been friends if I'd grown up in Luid, or whether we'd have torn each other down in our race for greatness.

In any case, I was happy to let her have it now. Let her be called to Severn's rooms. Let her deal with his needs. All I wanted now was answers and ingredients. For those, I needed to gain her trust, and so I made myself as friendly and unthreatening as I could, ready to help and to serve in any way necessary.

I hadn't been allowed out of my room while I healed, but Sara had come to bring potions, and to offer theoretical problems for me to solve. Simple things, mostly, from healing toothaches to identifying samples of plants she brought to me. I tried to contain my excitement over unfamiliar ones, and couldn't. At least my enthusiasm pleased her, and the questions kept my mind occupied with something other than what might be happening back at camp, or what would become of me if I crossed paths with Wardrel again.

I woke with the sun on my third day in Luid and dressed in the simple black dress and white apron that I'd found in my closet—my uniform, should they choose to allow me to work. I sat on the edge of the bed with my hands folded in my lap, waiting for the thunk of the lock opening.

Today I'll get out. Today I'll find information. Today I'll become useful.

The lock turned, and I stayed in my place until the door swung open. I smiled at the young guard who stepped cautiously into the room. "Good morning, Myk."

He didn't exactly smile back, but a dimple puckered at the left side of his mouth as he handed me a buttered sweet roll and a small apple. I ate well there, if simply.

He ran a hand over his pulled-back, carrot-orange hair. He wore the red uniform, but no helmet. "Good morning, Nox. You're to start work today. Are you ready to go?"

"I'm so ready to get out of this room, I could burst. Let's go."

Myk had stood guard outside my room the day before, and answered any time I knocked. I hadn't asked too many questions, not wanting to rouse his suspicions, but I'd tried to make friends, pretending I was lonely and frightened. He was a nice enough fellow, and had tried to put me at ease.

"It's so kind of you to escort me," I said as we walked down the hallway—the only one I'd been permitted to see since I'd been dumped in my room, and then only on toilet breaks. I'd memorized the location of every door and side-passage we passed, marked the locations of the few paintings on the stone walls so I'd be able to find my way back if need be, but none of it told me anything useful.

His freckled ears reddened. "I wish it were kindness on my part."

"Will I always be treated like a prisoner?"

"I don't know. The other Potioners have more freedom, but none are allowed to leave without special permission. Everyone's rooms are locked at night."

"Why?"

He shot me a sideways glance. "Why are you so curious?"

I tried to act innocent, and shrugged. "In my town, I was respected. Trusted. Accustomed to going where I pleased. I miss the fresh air."

He looked away. "We all pay a price for the work we do here these days. Times are hard, but they'll get better when the king's nearby enemies have been defeated. Then you'll be safe to enjoy your freedom."

I didn't point out that signs indicated Severn was planning a war against Darmid when this little problem was taken care of, and times would hardly get better for a soldier if that were the case. I certainly wasn't supposed to know that.

"I do hope so," I said instead.

He held the door to the workshop open for me, and I murmured my thanks as I passed—and stopped, still as a statue, to take it all in.

The openness was the first thing that astounded me. I'd been trained in cramped cottages and worked in my own kitchen, then in Mama Bunn's little cabin. This room stretched several stories overhead. The window in the far wall was nearly as tall and twice as wide, spanning the length of the room and offering a stunning view of the city below and the plains beyond, letting in ample sunlight. Every corner of the room, from the smooth marble floors to the upper reaches of the ceiling, was immaculately clean. Smooth stone stretched from floor to ceiling, the pattern of the cut granite broken only by windows, cupboards, and doors. No paintings or tapestries here to distract us, though the room had its own kind of austere beauty.

I was the last to arrive for the day. A dozen Potioners stood at the long, stone-topped tables that spanned the width of the room. Each station was better-equipped than any place I'd ever worked. I stepped closer to the nearest station, ignoring the irritated look its occupant shot me. Sophisticated filtration and distillation systems made of glass and metal took up the rear of the table, along with adjustable flame-lights, a set of razor-sharp metal and duller stone knives, and a few other items I didn't recognize. Underneath each table were stacks of bowls in varying sizes and materials, plus mortars and pestles, spoons, sticks, and other implements.

I turned toward the door and the wall beside it, which was covered in polished wood cupboards. I suspected that if the workstations didn't have something we needed, we'd find it there.

"Incredible," I whispered.

Myk grinned as though he'd had the place set up for me himself. "Not bad, right? Better than back in—where did you say you were from?"

"Cressia." I realized my mouth was hanging open, and closed it. Had my situation not been so dangerous, this would have been paradise. And there—a set of doors in the wall perpendicular to the windows. That had to be where they kept ingredients. Even from this distance and through sturdy doors I felt magic calling to me.

An older woman with steel-gray hair pulled back into a severe bun gave me a curt nod as I took up a position at the empty workstation next to her. She was working on what I took to be a simple healing salve. I hoped Sara had something more challenging for me.

Sara spoke to a nervous-looking girl near the large window, then approached me.

"Did you sleep well, Nox?"

"Very," I lied. "Thank you." In fact, my dreams had been night-mares of fire and burning flesh.

"Excellent. Will you join me in the pantry for a moment?"

Would I? It was all I could do to keep from dancing my way over. *Ulric's cure is in there,* I thought. *I know it.*

Don't think about it. Pay attention to the present. The rest can wait.

I followed Sara through the thick wood-and-iron doors and froze again as the atmosphere and power of the place washed over me. I was accustomed to seeking out magical plants in the woods, where I might find just a few truly useful items in a field or forest glen if I were lucky. Here, the challenge would be to not become overwhelmed by the possibilities.

Rows upon rows of shelves lined the walls and stood on the floors, every one covered in neatly-labeled baskets, jars, canisters, bowls, and boxes. Herbs, most of them unfamiliar to me, hung from drying racks on the ceiling near the door.

Sara placed her hands on her hips, inhaled deeply, and watched my reaction. "Amazing, isn't it? My assistants travel to the ends of the world to collect all of this."

"That must get expensive," I whispered, imagining great ships sailing away and carrying back this precious cargo.

"Our king is more generous with and respectful of Potioners than most Sorcerers are," she said softly, and I got the impression that she took full credit for that. I wondered about the exact nature of her relationship with Severn, but didn't dare ask.

I closed my eyes to take in the feel of the room. Though nearly all of the ingredients were sealed away in jars or wooden boxes they still clamored for my attention, shouting their properties, benefits, and potential dangers. I sensed them as vibrations, as faint lights, as an odd feeling at the back of my throat. It was a delicious sensation to feel such power, and yet I thought I might collapse under it.

When I opened my eyes, Sara was smiling. "You do feel it, don't you?"

"Don't we all?"

"Sadly, no. Not the way you and I do." She reached one delicate hand out and brushed her fingers over a bunch of half-dried flowers I didn't recognize, but thought might have been a minor component of the bone-setting serum. "It's not that the Potioners out there aren't gifted. They certainly are, and I'm glad to have them. They're healers, and can be perceptive about the potential of ingredients. But there are levels, just as there are true Sorcerers and lesser magic-users."

I thought of the differences between Mama Bunn and my first teacher, and nodded. "I've seen it."

"You're obviously gifted, Nox, and your talents were being

wasted up north. I don't know how natural talent like yours came from a place like that, or how it was overlooked for so long. I'm not going to waste it now that you're here. I have a special project for you today. If that works out, we'll see about making you my new personal assistant. The last one didn't work out."

Oh, that sounds promising. My heart fluttered. "A test?"

Her smile widened. "I wasn't going to call it that, but I suppose it is, in a way. I don't think you'll fail, you're a clever woman. Here's the puzzle. Some time ago, Severn was in an altercation of a magical nature. An unexpected attack that should have killed him, but he thought quickly and survived."

First name basis, I noted. "Go on."

"He returned to the palace suffering ill-effects from using his magic in untested ways. He'd transported his mind and body back here, but he was a wreck. Totally destroyed on a physical level. It was only thanks to his determination to live and the efforts of myself and a team of physicians that he pulled through. I want to know what you would have done in my position. Make me one potion that would have saved him."

I looked around the room. "I can use anything I find here?"

"You may." She turned to leave.

"Sara?"

"Hmm?"

"Was his magic affected?" When she frowned, I added, "It affects my theoretical treatment options."

Her expression softened. "Of course it does. I knew I was right about you. Let's say it was affected, just for the sake of this test. Good luck, though I doubt you'll need it." The door clicked shut behind her.

My heart leapt again, this time at the realization that I had just been left alone in any Potioner's dream, surrounded by more powerful ingredients than I'd even imagined when I considered Ulric's problem. I had to bite back a laugh of disbelief. The fear and pain I'd endured to get to that room faded to insignificance as I turned my attention to the substances that called out to me.

A person could become drunk on this, I thought, and wondered how anyone could become as accustomed to it as Sara seemed to be.

I wandered the rows of shelves and realized she hadn't given me a deadline. I'd assume the end of the day, unless she told me otherwise. My fingers trailed along the edges of shelves until I felt something interesting, and then I opened a few jars, just to explore. There wasn't nearly enough time to familiarize myself with everything.

Think, then. My approach was obvious. Improving a Sorcerer's magical strength would help his physical healing. I'd seen it in Aren not long before. When in Darmid and away from a strong source of magic, he'd been unable to heal himself. I'd bridged the gap with potions, and once we got closer to Tyrea, his magic had been restored and he'd healed.

As I took in the potential in this room, a smile spread across my lips. *I can do this.* I would pass this test, and then I'd surely find Ulric's answer once I'd earned a little trust and freedom. Getting that potion out of the city might be a problem, but I could do it.

I *would* do it, by whatever means necessary.

The room was organized by type of ingredient. Flowering plants in one area, whole and in parts. Reeds in another. Magical catalysts. Shelves of null items that held no power themselves, but would assist in reactions—sands, waters, metals, slabs of stone, chunks of wood. Within each section, items were shelved by the region they'd come from, and seemed to be set out roughly in order of how powerful the magic within them was. Simple enough, if one knew what she was looking for. Less helpful for me.

At the rear of the room I came upon the animal ingredients. I'd never liked using them, save for the occasional insect or small rodent, but sometimes it couldn't be avoided if one wanted a specific and reliable result. Eye of newt, though somewhat useless, always impressed folks for some reason when they heard we'd included it. Salamanders were actually far more powerful, though the fiery little buggers were difficult to come by.

Bundles of feathers covered one shelf, labeled with hanging

tags. Red parrot was new to me. Eagle. Robin. Harpy. Aeyer. I shuddered at that last. Ingredients taken from the winged people of the mountains came a little too close to home for my tastes. Though I'd used my own blood in potions when necessary, I generally drew the line at asking people to consume anything remotely human. Besides, where would one get the ingredients save from the dead? And to desecrate them would be unthinkable.

Apparently this wasn't an issue for all Potioners. I pulled back a curtain that covered another section and leaned closer to read the labels, gasped, and let the curtain fall.

A jar of eyeballs had been labeled "human," as had the neatly bunched strips of leathery skin. Vials of dark liquid didn't bear closer scrutiny. I moved on, hoping my answer didn't lie there.

On a higher shelf I found several small jars of gold-tinted liquid labeled "mer tears." In my admittedly limited experience with merfolk I hadn't found them overly keen on giving them up, and didn't like to think how someone had acquired these. At least there were no eyeballs on that shelf.

Focus, Nox.

I passed by those and searched the higher shelves, just over-head, which held dragon scales in a rainbow of hues and scraps of their eggshells. I pocketed a bit of shell, remembering Aren's advice about protecting myself as soon as possible.

Unicorn tail-hairs and horn shavings came next. *Horrid.* A unicorn never shed its horn. The only way to obtain that would be to kill the beast, or somehow trap it, cut the horn off, and release. Either way, that would be the end of the creature.

I turned away, but couldn't help looking back toward a power that called to me, unfamiliar and beautiful. I reached for a dark glass jar of horn shavings.

They would help. A unicorn's deep magic would aid a wounded Sorcerer's power and help open blocked channels, protecting and healing. It was the absolute simplest solution, and I hadn't thought of it before because I'd never had access to the ingredients.

It's here anyway. If the unicorn is dead, it's dead. Just use it. Make the potion, get the position. It's the only way to get a step closer to Severn's defeat.

I reached my fingers into the jar, drawn by the overwhelming power of its contents. Even before I touched the thin slices of nacre-like horn, they glowed softly. The essence of an autumn wood reached my nostrils, thick and rich with the scents of moss and mushroom and rotting leaves. A pleasant aroma, to be sure. There was a wildness to it, and the fragrance of the wind caught while racing along the crest of a mountain ridge in the moonlight, with the world at one's hooves, and all the magic in the world coursing through one's veins....

I snapped the hinged lid of the jar closed, and the images vanished. A tear slipped from my eye. I'd seen a unicorn's memory, felt her magic and her life... and she wasn't a part of the world anymore. A silly thing to cry over, perhaps. Sentimental. And yet I set the jar back on the shelf.

There had to be another way. I searched high and low, feeling the ingredients more than seeing them, grabbing a few items to mix with the dragon eggshell and tucking them deep into the pockets of my apron. Though a few possibilities for my assignment came to mind, nothing jumped out at me the way the unicorn horn had.

"Nox?"

I went back to the door to find Sara poking her head back in.

"Everything okay?" I asked.

"Just checking on you. You've been in here for hours."

Impossible, I thought, but the growl of my stomach said otherwise. "Have I? Just enjoying my explorations. You have some fascinating items."

"We certainly have." She raised an eyebrow, clearly amused by my enthusiasm. "You might want to start working soon, though."

I plastered a confident smile on my face until she was gone, then turned and scowled at the shelves. I'd found a component for my blocking potion, but had made little headway on my test. And if I failed that, we were all finished.

I hummed softly, a tune I vaguely remembered my mother

singing to me when I was a child. My voice wasn't much, but the music calmed me.

Come on. I know you're here. Speak to me.

I tiptoed past each shelf again, arms held out to my sides— humming, feeling foolish, hoping it might somehow help as it had with my work on Ulric's potion. I ignored the obvious power of the unicorn's horn. I would do this my way. I closed my eyes and colors swirled behind my eyelids. A fuchsia light to my right caught my fancy, and I turned toward it. I opened my eyes to find a small jar filled with a quintet of blossoms that appeared fresh in spite of the fact that they'd been enclosed in glass. The broad, flat petals, a rich purple at the edges, faded to the blue of the summer sky in the center. Feathered yellow stamens like moth antennae curled up from the depths. I leaned closer to read the label.

"Enshandris," I said aloud. I'd never seen it, nor heard of it. I took the jar, based more on a vague hunch than any strong understanding. When I opened the jar, I felt the light instead of seeing it, a mid-pitched vibration. This wouldn't heal. It would poison, at least under normal circumstances. But if I could persuade it to behave nicely with barberry roots, they might lessen that effect, allowing the poison to draw magic. *If I combined it with—*

I spun. *There.* Cinnamon, and a spiny vine I had also never encountered. Burbentix. It didn't feel powerful on its own, but maybe...

I dashed through the pantry, collecting jars into my apron pockets. I'd cut them on a soapstone block, prevent magical reactions before I was ready for them. With every step, my certainty grew.

I backed out the door with my arms full and tripped over a foot. I stumbled, but caught myself before anything hit the floor.

"Sorry, sweetie," said my table-mate, who made no attempt to help me with my unbalanced armload of supplies. She looked down her nose at me. "We had orders not to go in until you came out. Been waiting here a while."

I muttered an apology and carried my treasures back to my workstation. I slipped the eggshell under the table, safe until I could figure out what to do with it. I'd have to work on my blocking potion here, but not now. Not when Sara was watching so closely.

At least I didn't have to worry about anyone sensing the shell and finding me out. It would protect itself from detection, as it had once protected its contents.

I tuned out everything around me and got straight to work, following my instincts as I prepared my chosen ingredients. Blue sand from I knew not where, sprinkled into the bottom of the bowl. Slices of papery burbentix, thorns removed and set aside.

Sara appeared and glanced over my table. "Interesting choices. You've used enshandris before?"

"No."

"Hmm." She frowned and went back to her own private workspace.

I sensed that the energy in the flowers would never react well to that in the roots under normal circumstances. But Mama Bunn could have done it, and so would I. Instead of trying to mimic Mama's song, I did as I had when preparing Ulric's potion and hummed my own. I ignored the side-cast glances from the others. It seemed they didn't know the trick. I wondered how many did, whether they'd pick up on it. I lowered my voice, not sure why I felt I should hide it, but certain that I didn't want to draw their attention more than I had to.

I took the enshandris in one hand and the barberry root in the other, warmed them with my body heat and my personal energy, and crushed them together between my palms, working entirely on instinct, gently convincing them to create the reaction I wanted.

Red light glowed between my fingers, then faded to warm pink.

Minutes later I had the ingredients combined and set into a straining cloth to release their juices, which gathered in a glass bowl. I set a low flame beneath and watched as the pink glow returned to the liquid, deepening with every drop added to the bowl.

"Impressive," Sara said, and laid a hand on my arm. I'd been so focused that I hadn't heard her coming.

"Thank you."

"You know that enshandris is poisonous? Instantly fatal?"

"I sensed it. I counteracted it."

Her fingers tightened, and her nails dug in slightly before she released me. "That should be very nearly impossible. Tell me, would you be willing to sample your project for me?"

My breath hitched. I was nearly sure I'd succeeded, but if I'd slipped up, if I'd been wrong about my abilities...

No. I'm sure.

I selected a glass spoon from the rack and dipped it into the bowl. The hot liquid burned my tongue and my throat. I gasped as light filled me, and couldn't help the laugh that bubbled from my throat.

Sara's eyes narrowed. "Well, you're not dead." She dipped a finger into the bowl and licked the potion off. A shudder passed through her body, and she took in a hard, sharp breath. "Beautiful. I can't be completely sure it would work, not without a subject to test it on, but I think you've passed the test."

I looked back at the potion, admiring its beauty. "So you don't need to use this? Lord—I mean, our king has fully recovered?"

Sara laughed, then gasped as a pale hand rested on her shoulder.

I stopped breathing, as though stillness would hide me. I didn't dare look any higher than that hand.

Don't make eye contact. Think only of the present. I checked my mental defenses and tried not to think about them. If they failed now, I'd never have a chance to figure out how dragon egg worked.

The long, elegant fingers tightened, and Sara winced.

"Your king's magic was never as weakened as you might have suspected based on your assignment," said a cold voice. It was strong, not nearly matching what Aren had told me about Severn's physical condition, but I had no doubt about who it was.

The potion's light left me, leaving only fear. "Your Highness," I whispered, and dropped into a curtsy. I looked up enough to meet Sara's gaze. Her face had turned into a blank mask.

"Look at me," he ordered.

And so, for the first time, I laid my eyes on the man who ruined my life and condemned my mother to her slow death.

His eyes grabbed my focus and prevented wider inspection. Glacier blue and filled with confident authority, they cut through me. I let my fear take over to a degree that seemed reasonable given my story and focused on his face, allowing nothing else into my conscious mind. If he could see deeper, there was nothing I could do about it.

He released me and took a moment to glance over the rest of my face, my hair, my body. I did the same to him while I had the chance.

Aren had described him to me as he was before his encounter with Rowan. He'd also told me that Severn as he'd last met him was a shadow of his former self, weak and bent, shuffling and thin. This man was none of those things, and no description of Severn's old appearance had prepared me for this. I saw our father in him, in the strong jaw and straight nose. His mouth was softer than Ulric's, and curved up slightly, pleased at what he saw. He stood tall and straight, slim yet strong, and he radiated power from every part of himself. Had I not known he was my brother...

I shuddered and looked away. I should have been accustomed to being around beautiful people by then. Appearances meant nothing, and I knew that. But his eyes, his voice, his very posture drew a person in with magnetic force that surpassed anyone I'd ever met, and I imagined it would be hard to deny him anything if he ordered it. I wondered how Aren had ever found the strength to defy him.

Severn wore simple but beautiful clothing, pants and a jacket that closed fully across his chest like armor, and his white hair flowed over his shoulders. I imagined that this simple attire was worth more than my old home, my potions, even my life.

"Sara explained the challenge to me," he said, apparently finished with his assessment. "Did you achieve it?"

"I believe I did, Your Highness."

He looked to Sara, and she nodded without meeting his eyes. He picked up the bowl and sipped. His eyes widened, and he chuckled. "Oh, you did. You most certainly did. What's in this?"

Sara answered for me, listing off every ingredient accurately. She'd been watching more closely than I thought.

Severn looked out over the city and set the bowl down. "And she did it without unicorn horn. How incredible."

Sara glared at me, but her expression softened before she finally looked directly at her king. "It is most impressive. I don't know that this could have brought you back from where you started, but if you wished continuing treatment that didn't require—"

He shot her a look that shut her up. "Sara, I wish to speak to your new assistant privately. You may go."

Another scowl for me, shot from behind her hair as she curtseyed. The sudden change in her demeanor confused me until I identified the look. I'd worn it myself enough times to know jealousy when I saw it.

Severn took my arm and led me to the door. His touch made my skin crawl. I hoped any nervousness would seem natural, but wished I'd had more time to improve my blocking or work up a potion before I met him. He didn't seem angry, at least. He hadn't called his guards. I was still alive.

He released his grip on my arm, but I could no more have run away than I could have flown out through a window. He seemed to draw me along by the force of his presence. The influence Aren spoke of went far deeper than that of a regular human. I forced myself to believe my story, finally understanding how this man could break me down even without Aren's gifts.

No one spoke to us as we passed through hallways, up a staircase, and through a glass-ceilinged atrium. In fact, no one spoke at all in Severn's presence. Soldiers looked at their feet, others offered low bows. None made eye contact with me.

A guard opened a heavy door, and we entered a bright, pleasant sitting room with an ornate wood desk in one corner and several comfortable-looking chairs near a fireplace.

"Sit," Severn ordered, and I did. A beautiful plate stacked with tiny sandwiches sat on the table, but I was far too nervous to eat.

"Tea?" he offered, and poured two cups before I could answer.

"Thank you." My world had shifted sideways, and now nothing lined up as it should. Severn the monster, Severn the charming king....

It's a clever mask, and that's all, I decided, and accepted a delicate white cup filled to the brim with purple liquid. I sipped at it so as not to spill onto the saucer, and set it down to cool.

"Sara has been looking for someone as competent as you for years." He sat across from me and rested one ankle on the opposite knee. With a flick of his hand he set a hot fire blazing in the hearth. "I suspect she's now got far more than she wanted, but she'll come around. Unless you think you're a threat to her position, that is."

"No, no. I'm here to help."

His eyes narrowed. "Is that all?"

I took another sip of tea to buy myself time. "If I may be completely honest with you... with Your Majesty, I mean..."

His lips curled in a half-smile of vague amusement at my discomfort. "Don't worry about formalities for the time being. I'll see that you get some etiquette training if you're to remain here. But I do insist on honesty at all times."

"Thank you. In all honesty, I did have selfish reasons for coming here."

"Oh?"

I nodded. If I had to speak to him, I'd try to make a good showing. "I'm from a small town, and have always believed I have significant gifts, but have never had the resources for proper training. I heard that Luid was the greatest city in the world, with libraries and schools and the most powerful Sorcerers and greatest Potioners living here. I know I have much to learn, and I can't learn it at home."

All true. Aren would be pleased.

My humility seemed to disappoint Severn, though I couldn't say why that would be. "True enough, and we'll see that you have the resources you need to bring your skills up to the level of your gifts." Another sip of tea, but his eyes never left me. "There's something different about you, Nox. Something familiar." He set his cup down and leaned forward. "I hope you are being honest with me."

My cup rattled briefly against the saucer before I stilled the tremble in my hands. "I'm sure I'd remember if we'd met."

"I believe I would remember you, as well. There's something special about you. Perhaps that's all it is."

I tried to smile at the compliment, but couldn't find words to answer.

"In any case," he continued, "Sara will tell you what she needs your assistance with, a special project she's been working on for me. I need your full attention on this. If your desire truly is to help, this will be the best way for you to do that."

"Thank you."

The pleasant expression faded from his face, and he turned toward the fire. "You may leave."

I set the cup down, thanked him again, and turned to go. It was hard not to bolt from the room.

"Wait," he said, and my heart stilled.

He rose and stepped toward me, then placed a hand on my face, lifting it so I had no choice but to meet his cold, compelling gaze again. A person could lose herself completely in those eyes.

"Watch out for yourself," he said. "The palace is secure, but not always a safe place for those who aren't familiar with our ways. You'll come to me if there's any problem." His tone was convincing enough that I almost believed he cared. I dared not think of what I knew about his true nature.

My heart pounded. "I will," I whispered.

"Good." He smiled again, and let me continue my slow retreat to the hallway.

When the door closed behind me, I leaned against the solid support of the corridor wall and bent over to rest my head in my hands. Though my opinions on him hadn't altered, confusion over my emotional reactions to his presence and personality overwhelmed me. I couldn't blame Myk or Sara for their willingness to follow him anywhere. Had I not known what I did—

A hand rested on my back, and I straightened so quickly that I bashed my head against the wall behind me.

"Sorry!" Myk said, and stepped back. "I just wondered whether you needed an escort back to your room. They already cleaned up your station for you."

I forced a smile. "Thank you, yes."

He looked back over his shoulder. "A bit intense, right?"

I shook my head. "You have no idea."

NOX

S ara as good as ignored me the next day when we met in the workroom. No questions, no concern, not a reassuring comment.

"I'll explain our main project later," she said. "I have something else I need to take care of. For now, see if you can come up with something to get rid of the smell in the dungeons. Not much we can do about overcrowding, but we can make things more pleasant for the guards who have to deal with those people."

I thanked her, and she left the room. I'd get to her assignment soon enough. First, I needed to do some research of my own.

But I was still under observation, not allowed to roam the halls at will. I looked to the door, where two guards stood watching us without much interest. The Potioners were a quiet bunch, and this had to be the most boring assignment either of the trained soldiers could have taken.

"Myk?" I asked quietly as I approached them. The other guard barely looked at me. "Where's the library? I need to look something up."

"This level, but it's a bit of a walk." He looked around and leaned closer. "I'm supposed to stay here and keep an eye on things."

I gave him my most appealing trying-not-to-be-disappointed

look. "Could you just walk me down? I'll wait there for you if you're needed here."

He frowned and tapped his fingers on his crossed arms. "You won't wander off?"

"I'll be good. Please, Myk." I lowered my eyes as though embarrassed. "I've waited my whole life to see this library."

At least that's not a lie.

His expression relaxed. "Of course. Not like you're going to burn the place down, right?"

I held out my empty hands. "Couldn't if I wanted to."

He escorted me through quiet hallways, and I realized I wouldn't be able to find my way out even if I decided to attempt a quick escape.

He pushed the door open and let me step in first. "It seems no one's working today," he said. "You think you can find what you need? Everything the Potioners use is in this nook."

The library took my breath away. I'd imagined what such a wealth of knowledge might look like, but apparently had done a poor job of it. Though the rows of shelves didn't call to me as the workshop supply room's did, the quiet solemnity of the place drew me in and calmed me, and the weight of hundreds of years of writing seemed to send out its own sort of vibration. Not magic, but something else. Something deep and beautiful, and somehow sad.

I looked over the shelves covered in leather-bound paper and nodded. "It'll take some time, but I think I can manage."

"You have two hours, and then I'll be back for you." His brow furrowed. "Please don't get me in trouble. I'm trusting you."

I laughed softly, respectful of the quiet that surrounded us. "I'd be in as much trouble as you would, and I think I'm more disposable."

He smiled back. "Good enough. Have fun."

An hour later I'd familiarized myself with the layout of that tiny section of the massive, dimly-lit library. Much of it was old journals left behind by Potioners—records of their experiments, not all of them well-organized. At least half of the books were written in languages I didn't understand, or in handwriting too cramped for me to puzzle the words out. Still, by the time Myk returned, I'd found a few pages of notes that looked promising, and had sought out a book on dragons as well.

I hoped that if there were library gods, they'd forgive me for the pages I'd torn out and folded into my pockets. At least I had a good idea of how to move ahead, and I had come up with some ideas for the dragon egg.

The next morning, Sara called me to her private office just down the hall from my bedroom—my cell, as I thought of it. Her space was warmed by an abstract tapestry on one wall, shelves lined with papers and books, comfortable chairs, and a massive wooden desk covered in still more papers. A big orange-and-white cat snoozed in a basket in the corner.

"I should apologize for being so busy and neglecting you," she said, and motioned for me to sit in a comfortable chair next to the desk. The words were civil enough, but her voice remained distant. "I'm still the head Potioner of this palace, and can't neglect my regular duties." Her right hand closed over the upper part of her left arm, and she crossed her legs as she sat. "But the king's needs and requests must come first, naturally, and it's time to get back to work on his project."

"Of course." I smiled as though I believed that was all it was. "No need to apologize."

Her smile seemed forced, but I didn't sense any hostility in it. "I have to say that your success the other day took me off-guard. When you chose unfamiliar ingredients, I thought you might be unusually perceptive. Your choice of a poisonous flower did give me pause, even made me question your motivations. But you made it work. I could have done it, but I've only known a few other Potioners who could. Perhaps the one who married that Sorcerer in Belleisle. I can't think of many others. It takes a special gift."

"I'll take that as high praise, then." I still didn't trust her, but she seemed to be trying to accept me. All I could do was remain as non-threatening as possible, given what she now knew about me.

Sara unfolded her body and tapped a dry feather quill against her desk as she looked deep into my eyes. "Who taught you?"

I silently blessed Aren for telling me to stick to the truth. It made it easy to remember what I'd told Severn. Still, I'd have to improvise as I added to it. "My teacher back home wasn't much good, but a few years ago an old Potioner passed through. She stopped to instruct me for a few weeks in exchange for a place to sleep. She explained about influencing the components, making impossible reactions happen. I think I got the better end of that bargain."

Sara set the quill down and ran her fingers over an array of tiny bottles on a miniature shelf mounted on the wall. "I see. Humming?"

"That's how she showed me. I haven't stumbled on another way yet. Is it odd?"

"It's not a well-known technique." She shook her head as if to clear it. "No mind. I'm happy you came here, Nox. I think your mind will complement mine well."

Something told me those weren't her words. Severn must have given her a gentle reminder about his wishes regarding me. *Not so gentle, perhaps,* I thought as she rubbed her arm again.

"I hope we'll work well together," I said. "I think there's a lot I could learn from you. Severn seems to have great respect for your gifts."

Her smile relaxed as she leaned forward. "He has. He's making better use of Potioners than any king has in the past, and it will enable him to do great things. What we're working on now is strengthening his magic. Not that it's weak. He's fully recovered from his injuries."

"I could sense that."

Sara smiled. "I'm sure. It's awe-inspiring to be close to that kind of power, isn't it?"

I chose my words carefully, sensing it wasn't only her professional position she felt protective of. "Impressive, indeed. I find myself uncomfortable with Sorcerers. I've never really been around them much. I'm more comfortable speaking with you."

Her smile broadened again, and I began to relax. "You'll get used to it," she said, "but I'd say you won't have to worry any more about dealing directly with the king. I'm the only Potioner he typically speaks with."

"That's a relief."

She nodded. "I won't bore you with the details, but our project is to find a way to build his magic up even beyond his full strength, and especially when the ambient magic in the land is low."

In case he has to go to Darmid, I added to myself. Some way of bolstering magic would certainly have helped Aren when he was there.

"What have you got so far?" I asked, and Sara pulled a thick sheaf of papers from the shelf behind her.

"Take a look."

We spent hours poring over the notes and drawings. Her skill was certainly impressive, and the creativity with which she'd approached the problem astounded me. She'd left no avenue unexplored, had tested every ingredient in that pantry to find its full range of properties. At the pages showing her work on human and magical-animal components, I kept my expression neutral and showed as much enthusiasm as I could muster. Some of her methods were beyond questionable, involving pain and fear, things I'd never considered using to influence reactions.

But, I reminded myself, *anything for the king.*

A knock at the door interrupted us, and Sara stood to answer. "You're needed in the king's private chambers," announced a guard.

Sara chewed her lip, then smoothed her skirt. "Is there a problem?"

"As far as I know, it's a personal request rather than professional."

Sara's shoulders relaxed, and a flush crept into her cheeks. "Thank you." She glanced at me. "Nox, I'll be back."

I looked through the notes again when she was gone, searching her results for something that would help Ulric. The potion I'd made for my test might help bring him strength, but it needed far more. We weren't recovering magic. We needed to keep it from hurting him. *But with another technique and different ingredients...*

Hours later, another knock came at the door.

"Sara's not here," I called, and the door opened. The same guard who'd taken her away poked his head in.

"I know. I'm to tell you she's feeling unwell and has retired to her personal chambers for the remainder of the day."

"Oh. Thank you." A feeling of unease swept over me, and I wondered about Sara's apparent mix of affection for and fear of her king.

"And you're wanted in the king's chambers."

My heart leaped into my throat. "Am I in trouble?" I asked, realizing that Sara had asked practically the same thing.

"I don't know," the guard said, expression neutral. "He didn't seem angry."

That meant nothing. Severn was obviously good at projecting whatever mood he pleased. I followed the red uniform up a circular staircase to the room I'd met Severn in before.

The king didn't stand when I entered. He sat in the same chair by the fire, his legs stretched out in front of him, head resting against the back.

"Sit," he ordered, and again I obeyed. His expression and demeanor were calm, even peaceful, and I found my nervousness decreasing.

Watch that, I reminded myself. It was probably exactly what he wanted.

"Find anything?" he asked.

"No, I'm sorry. Sara has been explaining everything, though. I think we can work something out." I thought no such thing, and suspected that we were shooting at a target we could never hit, but that news would not please him.

"That's good to hear." His fingers tented over his stomach and he tapped the tips together as he stared at the ceiling. I wondered whether Sara had drugged him, until his gaze focused sharply on me. "There are things she hasn't told you."

"Oh." I tried not to look too interested.

He sat up and leaned forward, and I wished he'd turn that

intense gaze elsewhere. "Sara and I work well together in many ways, but we disagree on a few things."

He waited for a response.

"Unicorn horn?" I offered, remembering his comment in the workroom.

He nodded. "I appreciate everything Sara does for me. I take most of the credit for my survival, but she certainly deserves some. Her potion got me through the worst days. I was angry when I learned what she'd used in it."

"You care for unicorns so much?"

He smiled. "Not personally, no. But even educated people say that to kill a unicorn brings a curse. To taste a unicorn's blood, to consume it or use its body does the same. I'm not a superstitious man, but magic is enough of a mystery that I'm not prepared to dismiss such things." He rose and walked to the window and looked out at the view of the city and the harbor beyond. "At least she didn't use the damned mer tears, though she wanted to. Harming them is said to be as bad as killing a unicorn, though I do wonder whether the merfolk started that tale themselves."

Not something I'd heard before. But then, we didn't tend to deal with merfolk in Cressia.

"In any case," he continued, "I'd prefer to be safe. Sara doesn't see that. She only feels the magic and the potential, and if she can do something, she will. I generally find this a positive quality in her, but her insistence that there was no other solution troubled me. I thought it laziness on her part, but she told me that unicorn horn was the only solution."

And I'd proved her wrong. No wonder she was angry.

Severn poured himself a glass of wine. "I have a specific goal for my life. I can't have curses getting in the way, unicorn or otherwise."

"Would it be out of place for me to ask about that goal?"

His eyes narrowed. "Why?"

Careful, Nox. I aimed for a tone of casual interest mixed with a little awe at being permitted to ask a great Sorcerer such things. He liked boldness, I could see that. But not too much. "You seem driven. You took charge so quickly after your father left, and you don't seem content with just having the throne. You have larger plans, don't you?"

He smirked over the top of his wine glass, then set it down. "You don't have to be coy. I'm aware of the rumors about me regarding my father's disappearance. You think I did him in?"

"Well, I..." I had no idea what he wanted me to say.

He chuckled. "You're delightful. I do grow tired of the practiced speeches of the city's flatterers. I'll tell you this. If I had killed him, he'd have deserved it." No mirth in his voice now. "My father was a weak man in so many ways. A coward, afraid of his own people."

"People say he was a good king." I hesitated to disagree, but it seemed a natural observation, given my story.

Severn watched me, considering something. "He was, in some ways. But he let so many things go. He let people disrespect him. Not a month went by when he didn't have someone challenge him for his position."

I narrowed my eyes. "But they all failed."

He nodded. "They did. Ulric was strong in magic, no doubt. But he made himself a fool. He'd face these challengers and give every one of them a fair shot. He played by the rules, but it was so much worse than that. He could have crushed any of them easily. He could steal a man's strength, yet he never did that straight off. He always made it a show, gave them a fighting chance when he should have just been done with them as soon as they announced their intentions."

Hearing more about Ulric as king interested me more than I cared to admit to myself. "Why would he encourage them like that?"

Severn glanced back at the wine bottle, but made no move to get more. "Because he wanted his people's respect, of all things. He said the challenges weren't just about defending his position, that the people saw themselves in the challengers just as much as they saw their enemies. They needed to see that their king was capable of defending them, but also that he would deal with them fairly. He didn't want them to see him as a tyrant, capable of crushing rebellion with nothing more than a flick of his wrist. He wanted to be seen as human. Struggling like them, and always prevailing."

He ran his hands through his white hair and moved back toward his chair. "It's ridiculous, yet I find myself constrained by those expectations, and by the laws of magical combat. Threats await just outside the city. I could win a challenge if I allowed it to happen, but I have no wish to meet this particular enemy in front of spectators and those who would judge me for crushing him."

"Who?" I kept my voice soft, not wanting to draw so much attention to myself that he'd stop speaking.

He sank into the armchair. "The old king is back."

I acted surprised. "How? What does that mean?"

"For now, it means nothing. The throne is mine, unless he takes it back by force." His fingers tightened over the ends of the chair arms, digging into the upholstery. "If the people see me destroying him outright, they'll hate me for it. Ulric was weak-willed, and ultimately bad for the people. True, the threat in Darmid isn't as urgent as I may have implied to some when I wished to gain support, but the fact is that he should have dealt with it years ago. Belleisle, too, should fear us far more than they do, and should be part of our territories. I deserve this position. I will have my empire." His voice became agitated, and his hands clenched into fists as a hint of magic even I could feel touched the air. I struggled not to take off running from the room.

And yet, a small part of me wanted to agree with him, to assure him that he was right, that no one could conquer him. How much worse would that be, I wondered, if I wasn't protecting my mind?

"You'll have your empire," I whispered, allowing a hint of that deference into my voice. He'd be expecting it.

His lip curled in a snarl. "I won't have it without the people's support, and I'll lose that if they see how I break the old man. It's almost funny."

"What?"

"I did betray him, in part because of the weakness I saw in him. And now I'm bound by the same laws, the same rules, and if

I break them, I may lose the people's support as he always feared he would. Maybe he was weak, but he was less of a fool than I suspected."

"So what will you do?" I didn't know how I'd get the information to Ulric, but I'd find a way. At least I had time. Ulric wouldn't attempt to attack Severn until he had his strength back, and that meant waiting for my return.

"Don't you worry about it," he said, and nodded to himself. "Thank you, Nox."

"For what?"

"I needed to think this through, and speaking to you has helped immensely. I see now that I have only one choice. I must defeat my enemy, but I can't allow it to happen here." His gaze sharpened. "Why are you looking at me like that?"

I realized I had let my guard down. I turned my gaze toward my feet. "I'm sorry. I've never been treated this way before. Never been allowed to help someone so powerful. I can see why Sara enjoys it, but it overwhelms me a little."

He frowned. "You may go now."

Finish what you were saying.

"Thank you, your highness. If there's any other way I might help..."

"Not now. Sara won't be returning to work today, but you may continue. Use her notes, whatever you need. I'll leave word that you're in charge of the Potioners until her return, and I'll instruct Myk to hand over your room key to you. We'll see what Sara's new assistant does with a little freedom."

"I'll do my best."

He flashed a charming smile that I didn't trust. "I think you will, at that." He stretched his shoulders back and sighed. "Gods, but the crown is heavy."

I went to the door, and though he followed again, he didn't touch me. I was grateful for that.

I turned back. "You said you'd leave word. Are you going somewhere?"

His eyes turned cold. "I said you'd been useful. Beyond that, you'd do best to mind your business and leave everyone else's to them. Understood?"

"Yes," I breathed.

"Good. You have potential, Nox. Don't waste it."

This time I didn't wait for Myk to escort me.

I ran.

"Rowan!" Victoria's voice, calling from near her tent.
"One minute!"

I grunted, and slopped water onto my boot as one of the two buckets I carried bounced off my leg. Apparently my magic did nothing to give me increased strength. *Pity. That would make so many things easier...*

That's not to say that things *weren't* easier. Over the days since my breakthough with Griselda, I'd spent as much time practicing on my own as I had helping in the camp, though I took her advice and was careful not to push myself too hard. I'd found so far that calm surroundings seemed to help my magic replenish faster, but even then it came slowly. The only advantage I had was still being acutely aware of the sensation of it moving through me, so I always had ample warning when it got low.

There was no chance of my flame accidentally burning out.

I'd kept working on fully accepting my magic, focusing on all the good it could bring to the world instead of the destruction it had caused. I'd practiced calling water, and had drawn up another spring closer to camp. I was also doing what I could to keep Victoria's gardens watered. The system wasn't perfect. She was depleting the soil faster than we could replenish it, even with the fertilizer that the horses so generously provided. Still, we were both doing our part, and my skills and control were developing rapidly.

Rapidly, and on my own terms. No using anger to propel my power, as Ulric had suggested. No focus on fighting. At least, not yet.

I dropped the water buckets off at the infirmary tent. Ulric hadn't spoken a word of praise to me for my assistance in keeping the camp going, and I didn't care. I had value, and I knew it. That was all I needed.

Well, I thought as I watched Aren enter his father's tent, shoulders slumped under the weight of whatever he was dealing with. *Almost all I need.*

I'd decided to let myself remain undecided on many things, including what to do with my bruised and battered heart. Every rational thought told me that staying away from Aren was a good idea, and I was trying. I was also working on letting go of my people's ideas of what made a successful life, namely getting married and everything that followed.

The problem was, it wasn't my people's beliefs or my old expectations that made me want him. It was just Aren that I wanted, and my heart wasn't about to give up on him just because my brain and every outward circumstance said it was better to let go. I would, eventually. I had no choice. But I wouldn't deny what I felt, or harden myself to my concern for him. That wasn't me, and I was done denying myself.

No more being who I think other people want me to be. A Sorceress' life is too long to live by anyone's rules but my own.

I met Victoria at her tent, and was surprised to find Griselda, Florizel, and Morea with her. Three of them I knew well, but Morea was still a bit of a mystery to me. She was nice enough, and had offered to work up something that might help my problems. But she was a strange sort of quiet. Not nervous quiet like Florizel, who now stood beside the tent, watching me approach, ears flicking this way and that. Nor did she have Aren's intense, calm quiet. Hers was more like a mystery that she wrapped close around her, a shield that closed the world off even as she worked within it.

I'd decided I liked her for it.

She held out a silver flask. "I feel like I should apologize for the container," she said. "It was all I could find without leaving camp. My others are all in use."

I smiled. "At least it's convenient. What's happening?"

Victoria held up a covered basket. "Griselda suggested it might do us all good to get away for a few minutes. Still within the protections, but we decided we could use a little space. This won't be much of a picnic, and no better than what they'll be serving at the cook tent, but a little quiet might be—"

A resounding belch echoed through the camp, followed by laughter.

"I couldn't agree more," I said. I didn't mind being around people, but the sounds and smells of the place were getting to me. I couldn't imagine what it would be like when we added more to our numbers.

"And I want to see how your magic is coming along," Griselda added. "Better to test you now and give you time to recover. We can try that potion out."

I tried to smile as though that sounded like a wonderful idea, but couldn't. Using magic on easy tasks was one thing. A test was another entirely. The old doubts crept back, and I shoved them aside.

You'll never help Aren defeat Severn if you don't learn to work under pressure, I reminded myself.

We headed out into the woods. Just before we reached the boundary, we stopped. Griselda had found a pleasant spot for us at the top of a high, rounded rock that curved gracefully up from the earth. Without her illusions protecting us we'd have been dangerously visible.

"How are you feeling?" I asked Griselda. She was doing the work of two now that her friend Maks was gone.

She shrugged one shoulder. "The magic isn't a problem, but I'm not used to such continuous usage. Still, it's good experience." She was obviously trying to look for the positive side of the situation, but her voice came out flat, and for the first time since I'd met her, she seemed exhausted.

We finished our meal—dried meat, fresh fruit, and slightly stale bread—in almost no time at all, and Griselda turned to me with an expectant look.

"Water?" I asked. "That's what I've been working on, and it's coming along well."

"Then no. Try the illusions now."

I supposed that made sense. Versatility would be as important as strength in battle.

Morea and Victoria sat in quiet conversation, but I knew they were paying attention.

I'd start with something simple, but not too simple. I focused on a tall pine at the base of the rock and let my magic flow through me. A moment later a duplicate appeared next to Florizel, who shuffled away. The tree was pale and unconvincing, but with additional effort I made it look solid and real, from the hair-like needles to the rough bark.

Griselda bit her lower lip and narrowed her eyes. "Good. Give me more."

I created a second tree exactly like the first, and a third. The last one was paler, no matter how hard I worked on solidifying it. Florizel sniffed at the illusion, then walked through it.

"How does that feel?" Griselda asked.

"It became easier as I went," I said, "and seemed to use less magic."

She nodded. "As it should be when making copies of copies. Go back to the original when you can and work from that. Continued reproductions may be easier, but they'll continue to deteriorate in quality as you go on."

I looked to the live pine again, and reproduced it. I felt the drain on my power more acutely, but she was right. It looked more real. A squirrel leapt onto the branches of the real tree, and after a few minutes I managed to add it to mine. It took far more concentration to form the illusion, but once there it followed the movements of the original exactly, without direction from me.

"Lovely," Victoria said, and laughed as the real squirrel let out a stream of rodent profanities that the illusion could only silently imitate.

"It really is quite good," Griselda said. "Given how short a time you've been doing this, it's amazing." Her brow knit, and I could nearly see the ideas and connections flashing through her mind. "Makes one wonder how much of the early training we do is necessary... But no mind." She shook her head and smiled to herself. "Thoughts for another time. Is your magic depleted?"

"More than I care for." The loss left me feeling cold, and a little sad. I didn't know exactly how deep the well went, but I knew I didn't want it to get too dry.

"Use more," Griselda said. "Drink the potion first, but then I want to really see what you can do." The smile had left her, leaving something more cold and analytical in its place.

Morea stood and came closer. "That may not be wise," she said. "I have no idea whether the potion will work."

"She won't use it all," Griselda said, just loud enough for me to hear. "And she'll recover, either way. This is just to see how long it takes."

I already felt a hint of the warmth returning, but my own experiments had taught me that I never felt exactly right for hours after I used any significant magic. I drank from the flask and hoped Morea was as good at her job as her father seemed to think she was.

I took it slowly, focusing hard on challenging my magic and my skill. More trees appeared, and more squirrels. I pushed harder, drawing on memory to add the slinking form of a red dragon. It wasn't realistic or particularly detailed, but marked a more difficult form of illusion that I'd only attempted once—and that accidentally, propelled by fear.

An empty chill filled me, and I stopped. The dragon had drained me further than I had wished.

"Well?" Morea asked.

I waited. Nothing came back. I turned my attention away from the illusions, which still drew faintly on my power to maintain themselves. That was a little better, but not by much. I shook my head. "I'm sorry. I don't think it's working."

Morea reached out and took the flask back. "At least we know," she said. "I'll see whether I can come up with a different approach." She thought for a moment. "Victoria, would you help me back at camp?"

They left, and Florizel made her way off the rock and into the real forest to forage. Griselda motioned for me to sit.

"Might as well enjoy the quiet while we can," she said. "See how your recovery comes. Let me know when you feel something."

"I will." I let the illusions fade as I sat on the rock and turned my face up to the sun, and felt Griselda watching me.

"Have you thought more about what we talked about?" she asked.

"About accepting my magic? I think it's all coming along well."

She cleared her throat softly. "About Aren. About letting go. Have you thought about what you might like to do when this is over?"

I looked at her with raised eyebrows. "Seems a little silly to make plans at this point, not knowing when or how this will be over." I spoke flippantly, but my insides had turned to a mass of jelly at the mention of Aren.

"Your heart will heal."

"I'd rather not talk about it."

She moved closer and leaned back on her elbows, turning her face to the sunlight that streamed unimpeded through her illusion. "I know. But you must. Your life will be too long to live it with regrets. It took me many years to learn that, and I'd like to spare you some of my pain."

I watched a fluffy cloud pass overhead. "Go ahead," I said, though I knew what she was going to say. "I do appreciate it. This isn't easy, though."

She paused before she spoke. "All I wish to say is this. Don't imagine Aren is the only love you'll ever have."

The words hit me like a punch, but I forced myself to keep listening.

"He's not the only person you'll ever care for this deeply," she continued. "Not the only person who will ever make you see the bright lights while you're enjoying his body."

I blushed. "How did you—oh. You'd know."

She smiled, eyes still closed. "This is what I mean. It's different for us. Though only the king is allowed to have multiple marriages, you won't find many of our kind sticking to only one love our whole lives through. There's a reason I've never married, why Maks left no family behind. He will be mourned, though, as intensely as anyone can be."

Her voice broke, and I realized how important he might have been to her at one time or another. I wondered how many times one had to survive heartbreak when she lived such a long life. How many losses.

"I know your people taught you differently." Her voice was strong again, full of reason instead of emotion. "But there's so much more to life than this one, small aspect. You have great gifts, Rowan. If you learn better how to use them, you will become one of the Sorceresses they'll tell stories about centuries after you're gone. And not because a prince fell in love with you, either. You will do unbelievable things."

I took a deep breath. "So you're saying I should let go? I know. I'm trying." *At least, I think I am.* I ran a hand through my hair, shaking out the red waves. "Love can't just be doused like a flame, and I won't force myself to deny it."

She cleared her throat again. "I'm saying that though you have to let go, this is not the end of your life. Be open to new experiences. This is a good thing for you. I could tell you stories, Rowan. The adventures I've had." She seemed to be far away, reliving those adventures. "I've sailed the seas, visited lands you've never heard of. I met the centaurs and forged relations between them and the people of Belleisle when I was young."

I smiled. "I know you're not going to tell me that one of your many loves was a centaur."

She leaned over and bumped my shoulder with her own. "Take your mind out of the mudpits, young miss. But you see what I mean. There's a big world out there filled with adventure, danger, new lands, and amazing people. There's so much to learn. People here think that they have magic figured out, but we don't have even the slightest idea."

"Ulric seems to think he knows everything about it."

She wrinkled her nose. "The only time you can be sure someone is wrong about magic is when he thinks he's got it all figured out. There's always more to learn, and it grows with us, if we allow it to. If we try to contain it…" She shrugged. "We don't limit magic, but we limit ourselves. Tyreans know much about magic, but they focus on the how, with little concern for why. I think you might enjoy exploring the mysteries."

Eternal mystery, always more to learn. Not a horrible future.

"This is what life is about, Sorchere. Knowing the world, discovering its secrets. There is always more to see."

It sounded wonderful, but I still thought I'd rather see it with Aren by my side—or failing that, to know that at the end of my adventures he'd still be the home I returned to.

She patted my leg. "Develop your skills and your knowledge for yourself, for your own purposes and the good of the world. Make your own contributions. Love fiercely and without reservation, and let go when you have to." Sadness flickered across her features, then disappeared. "I only wish someone had told me the same when I was your age. You have so much more to offer the world than just your love for one Sorcerer."

"Thank you, Griselda." I hoped she was finished. Everything she'd said made perfect sense, and the idea of finding my own path thrilled me. It was all the complete opposite of anything I'd been raised to believe, or anything I'd thought to dream for myself, but I could so easily imagine it.

I could have had that with Aren, I thought. *The adventure and mystery, my own life exploring the world… and him a part of it.* It was too much to wish for, and always had been. But gods, he was hard to let go of.

Voices drifted up from the forest. I stood and shielded my eyes against the sun. Aren and Kel passed by, deep in conversation, headed past the boundary of our defenses and moving toward where the bodies from the attack on camp rested under piles of stone. My heart warmed at the sight of the two of them. Perhaps in a hundred years all of this would seem distant and foolish, but at that moment all I knew was that I needed to see Aren. To speak to him. To let him know I was making progress, that I'd help with the fight, and above all that I would be all right. If he was half as worried about me as I was about him, he'd want to know.

I watched and waited, but saw no sign of Ulric following them.

"Griselda? I'll be right back."

I scrambled down the opposite side of the boulder and raced through the woods in the direction they'd been headed, following the sound of their voices. Before I reached them, Florizel trotted over.

"What's happening?"

"Nothing. Just going to see Aren and Kel. Come on."

She walked next to me, but dropped behind as we caught up to them in a clearing where the stony ground dipped in a wide crater shape, like a massive bowl lined with grasses and low berry bushes. I stopped short when Aren and Kel turned around, unsure of what would be an appropriate greeting now. I clasped my hands behind my back. "Um, hi."

Aren looked me over, expression unreadable.

Things had changed. I'd forgotten that in my excitement. If he was doing a better job of making a clean break than I was...

Don't cry. Please don't cry. "I didn't mean to interrupt anything, I just saw you two and wanted to say hello." I bit the inside of my lip. "And ask whether you'd heard any news."

Aren turned to Kel. "Would you mind giving us a minute? Don't go far."

"Not at all." Kel turned his back to us, and Florizel got the idea and did the same. They walked a ways into the trees, and Kel reached out to scratch behind behind the horse's ear. "Far enough?" he called back.

"Sure." Aren opened his arms, and my heart leapt as my fears fled. I ran to him. He held me tight and rested his face against the top of my head. "I've been so worried about you," he whispered.

"Likewise." He smelled of a campfire, and the wind. I never wanted to let go.

Aren's chest pressed tighter against my face as he took a few slow, deep breaths. "I'm glad you're here."

"Me, too." The need to say anything else passed. Just being together for a moment was enough.

"No news, though," he said, and released me.

I stepped back. "Oh." Not that I'd thought that Ulric might have been miraculously cured without Morea's knowledge, but hearing that we at least had a plan or a way forward that didn't involve Aren stepping up against Severn would have been nice.

"I think we're a bit stuck. Ulric doesn't want to move ahead until he's stronger, and Morea's not making any more progress with that than Nox did. We'll have to wait and see what she comes back from the city with. Retreat might be involved, at least for a time. Kel, you can turn around."

Kel rolled his shoulders back and stretched his arms out ahead of him. "I didn't see anything."

Aren smiled at his friend. "I certainly appreciate that."

He sauntered the few steps back toward us. "I could not see more, if you wanted me to turn around again."

I sighed. "That's fine. Thanks, though. I should get back. I don't want to cause trouble. It's good to talk with you, Aren. You're looking..." *Gorgeous. Incredible. Kissable. I need you.* "You're looking well. I just want you to know that I'm training with Griselda, and things are coming along really well. I'm moving past the things that were holding me back."

"That's wonderful," he said. "Just what I'd hoped for you. No more problems with it replenishing?"

"Well... we're working on that." He frowned, and I hurried to finish my thought. "If you need my help with anything, I'm available," I continued. "I can fight. Sort of. I'm getting better with archery, and my magic is starting to help. I was just practicing illusions and might need a few days to recover now, but..." I trailed off.

Sadness filled Aren's eyes, but he smiled. "I sincerely hope it won't come to that. But thank you."

I turned and embraced Kel, who I hadn't seen much since Nox left. Without her work to keep him busy, he'd become a constant go-between for Ulric and the people.

"I miss you, too," I told him. "We should talk more."

"Everybody misses me when I'm not around," he said. "I'm charming."

"You're certainly something," Aren said.

Kel laughed. "You know it's true."

Florizel shied and nearly stepped on my toes.

"Hey, now—" Kel said, and stopped. "Oh. Aren, I think you're wanted."

Florizel shuffled away, revealing Ulric standing with arms crossed behind her. "Is everyone having fun here?"

Aren's smile faded, and his expression closed off. "I needed to get away for a few minutes. The camp was becoming suffocating."

Ulric tilted his head toward me without actually looking in my direction.

"I wasn't supposed to be here," I told him. "I spotted Kel and Aren coming out here and I wanted to say hello, so I followed them. It's not their fault. I'm not here to cause trouble."

Ulric's upper lip curled, but still he wouldn't turn his eyes on me. He kept them squarely focused on Aren. "Go now. All of you but Aren."

The way Aren and Ulric had each other locked into their wordless standoff, the world might have crumbled around them and neither would have noticed.

I gave the meeting up for lost, mouthed a silent apology that Aren didn't see, and took one last look at him before I turned to go. Something moved behind him in the bushes at the other side of the clearing, and my heart jumped into my throat.

"Aren," I said, but my voice barely registered to my own ears. "Run."

Instead, he spun, pulled a dagger, and placed himself between the rest of us and the figure emerging from the trees.

A white-haired figure, riding a black, winged horse.

38

AREN

S evern slid to the ground, landing silently on the forest floor. The horse stood like a statue. With Severn there, the magnificent animal could do nothing but await his next command.

I only realized at that moment how close I'd come to letting him do the same to me.

I listened for the sound of the others retreating, and heard nothing. The birds had fallen silent. Even the wind had stopped.

Florizel whinnied, low and desolate. "Murad."

"Well," Severn said, and brushed a bit of dirt off his dark pants. "This couldn't have worked out any better, could it?"

"What are you doing here?" Ulric demanded. His shoulders tensed, and the air pulsed with magic.

Careful, I thought, but wouldn't say. To give away his weakness would be the end of him.

Severn's grin struck me as more insane than amused, but his eyes said his mind was all there. "I should ask you the same thing. I might have had them release you some day, you know. Once the throne was mine, once I was sure I had everything under control."

"Why do I doubt that? Aren, step back."

I didn't move. He'd said he was improving, but the old man couldn't hope to take Severn on. Not yet.

Severn stepped away from the horse. "Come now, Aren. You'll all get a turn."

"Is that why you came?" I asked him. "To challenge us? You might have just let us into the city, and we could have done this through the proper channels."

"No. I don't trust either of you." He turned his gaze on Rowan. "Any of you, actually. I'd rather take care of this privately."

I narrowed my eyes, focused my attention, and tried to see what he wasn't saying. His mind, as always, was a blank wall to me. He'd have had the advantage in the city, surely. And then I understood. Severn intended to use every filthy trick in his arsenal to defeat us. No witnesses.

"Very well," Ulric said.

I centered myself, readied my magic. There was no time to be nervous, to consider the pain that was coming. My mind quieted, and I ran through a mental list of Severn's skills—at least, those that I knew about.

Ulric placed a hand on my arm. "Not yet," he said quietly, cold glare still fixed on Severn. "This is my fight, the one he should have challenged me to years ago instead of betraying me."

Severn's mouth twitched. "Believe it or not, Father, part of the reason I did that was to spare you the humiliation."

"You would not have defeated me then," Ulric said. "I'd have whipped you like the disobedient pup you are, taught you how to respect me like you pretended to. If you survived, you'd have been better for it. If not, we all would have been."

"Such words, Father. As though I didn't plan each detail of my taking the throne, didn't wait until my power was sufficient and I had every piece in place." He glared at me. "Almost every piece, at least. But nothing is perfect."

"Father," I said, "I—"

"No. Aren, step aside. Show me that much respect." Ulric squared his shoulders and raised his hands as though about to conduct a grand piece of music, and stepped to the edge of the hollow in the ground. The air hummed with magic. I stepped aside. He knew his strength. Perhaps it was greater than he'd let on. "Usual challenge conventions from here out?"

Severn nodded. "Of course."

I knew better than to trust him. I only hoped Ulric knew it as well as I did.

I stood as far away as I could without disappearing into the woods, and motioned for the others to do the same. Kel pulled Rowan back. Florizel backed up a few paces, but her eyes never left the horse frozen on the far side of the clearing.

Kel tilted his head back toward camp. I was about to nod when Severn said, "No, I wouldn't do that. We're surrounded here. I've instructed my Sorcerers not to interfere. You might wish to keep yours out of it as well, for your sake and theirs."

"Of course," Ulric said, as though this were the most reasonable request imaginable. "Shall we?"

I reached out my awareness, but sensed no one else in the area. Either he was bluffing, or they had strong enough magic that I couldn't sense their presences. I wasn't about to risk anyone's life on a bet that it was the former.

Movement caught my attention, and I turned to see Rowan take Kel's hand. He pulled her closer to him, away from the Sorcerers preparing for their battle, and put an arm around her. She glared at Severn. I fought back the urge to scream at them to run in spite of Severn's instructions.

If Severn took Ulric down, and then me, Rowan would be next. He hadn't forgiven her for what she did to him the last time they met, and she'd said that her magic needed time to replenish. She'd be defenseless.

I won't let that happen. I remembered Rowan's words from the last time we'd met Severn in the woods. *This isn't how it ends.*

Not if I had any say in it.

The two bowed. Before Ulric straightened, Severn swung his arm around and sent a blast of power out. Ulric was ready. He deflected it with some magic unfamiliar to me, which set the air and the earth shaking around us. It was powerful, frightening. *Thank you, Nox,* I thought, as the two squared off again.

And then the former king fell to his hands and knees, gasping for air.

The surprise on Severn's face told me this wasn't some new trick of his. The potion had shored up Ulric's strength, but his magic was still hurting him. His skin turned blue around his lips, and the wrinkles around his eyes deepened, aging him before my eyes.

Severn laughed. "Well. This is interesting." He crouched in front of Ulric, just a little more than an arm's length away. "I think I have something back in the city that would take care of that for you. Pity you won't make it there."

Ulric's sunken eyes burned.

"Go ahead," Severn said. "Take my strength, if you can."

Ulric's already wrinkled forehead creased further as he focused. Severn gasped, and a surge of hope flowed through me. It was dashed as soon as it came. Ulric cried out and released whatever of Severn's magic he'd just drawn, but the damage was done. Blood streamed from his eyes like tears, and he struggled again for breath.

Severn sighed. "I won't say I'm sorry. You taught me not to. You taught me all of this." He leaned in closer and spat on the ground next to Ulric's face. "I hope you're proud."

Ulric's lips were no more able to form words than his lungs were capable of delivering the necessary air. He collapsed face-first into the stony ground. Severn watched for a moment, but Ulric didn't draw another breath.

My own breath stilled for a moment as I processed the idea that he was gone. *But Nox hasn't come back,* I thought, completely irrationally. *It's not time yet.*

I forced my mind to turn back to Severn. If Ulric were dead, everything rested on me. No time for mourning, for mixed feelings, or for fear.

Severn got to his feet and looked to me. "Aren. I do wish this could end differently."

"It's a little late for that, I think."

Kel stepped forward, apparently unafraid. "May I move him?"

"You're the mer, aren't you?" Severn asked, and frowned. "By all means. Take him." He stepped back.

Kel flipped Ulric's body over and rested a hand on his chest. A look of deep sadness came over him. He hadn't cared for Ulric, had never claimed to see goodness hidden deep inside of him, but he understood what we'd lost.

Kel wrapped his hands around Ulric's wrists and dragged him behind a bush. He brushed his hands off on his pants as he returned to stand next to Rowan.

"You're far from home," Severn observed.

Kel's expression remained perfectly neutral. "I have loyalties here."

Severn's lips tightened. "I mean your people no harm, and I have no quarrel with you. It is out of respect for your people that I ask you to leave now. Avoid the camp, speak to no one. Return to where you belong."

Kel didn't answer, but took Rowan's hand again. Cold fingers wrapped around my heart as I watched him pull her back a step. Not far enough. It never would be, as long as Severn lived.

I felt a hint of her magic on the air. Weak, but ready to join mine, to do whatever she could to help. I shook my head. Her magic faded, but she continued to fix an ice-cold glare on our enemy. He ignored it.

"Very well." Severn turned back to me. "Aren, you can't win this any more than the old man could have. You know that."

I stepped to the edge of the dip in the clearing that had become Severn's arena and dropped my knife as required by the rules of magical combat. I blocked everything but Severn and his magic from my awareness. "Are you offering again to let me join you? Nice position in Darmid, perhaps, if I come back to work for you?"

Severn chuckled. "Hardly. You've had your last chance, and I've given you far too many. Tell me, would you take it if I offered you one?"

A strange sense of calm settled over me. "No. You ran out of chances with me long ago."

"Very well."

Without preamble, without ceremony, his magic lashed out at me. Flames erupted from his hands, a wall of fire that covered the space between us in a moment. I sent my own fire out, larger than anything I'd attempted before. It didn't burn as hot as Severn's, but it didn't need to. The power was what mattered. Our magic collided between us. Severn's flames could come no closer, but it took all of my strength to keep them at bay. He pulled his back. I stumbled forward, pulled by the force of my magic, which faded as the flames washed over him without causing harm.

"That's new," he observed, and paced sideways. Considering. No showmanship this time, not so much as a flick of his hand as pain blasted into my shoulder hard and fast, washing the world away in its bright fury.

Fight back, I ordered myself, barely able to hear my own thoughts under the screams of agony that shot through my body. *Block him. Build a wall.*

As I attempted to form a shell around my body as Nox had around her mind, Severn's magic pressed harder. Slowly I became aware of my own breath, coming in gasps. My teeth should have cracked under the pressure of my clenched jaw, which couldn't hold back the animal noises rising from my throat as brighter pain than I'd ever felt before slashed deeper into my body, tearing me apart. Rocky ground dug into my knees and the palms of my hands. I hadn't realized I had fallen.

I forced my magic to act in new ways, to reach its greatest heights and depths to protect me, blocking the pain from my mind, if not my body. The air grew cold. Frost formed on the ground beneath my hands as the undeveloped skill robbed the surrounding air of its energy. I raised my head as the pain receded, if only by a fraction.

More.

The world solidified, though the pain still kept me from moving. Severn's face contorted with effort, and something else. A few breaths later, I realized it was panic.

I forced myself to my feet, though a thousand hot knives of

pain cut into my back. The agony radiated out from there until every part of me screamed that I should beg for death.

Slowly, fighting the searing agony every movement, I commanded my body to stand straight.

"Beg for mercy!" Severn screamed.

"No." Tears coursed down my cheeks and froze there, but I stood with my feet planted firmly.

Severn drew his power back to himself, but the pain lingered. *Change*, I thought, and thought better of it when I remembered my last fight in that form. He would be ready for it, and I would be left without other magic.

"Enough." Severn's voice had become hoarse. "I've been merciful for too long. No more games."

A blast of raw, destructive power shot from his hands. I collapsed, allowing it to pass overhead, and the magic splintered the middle of a pine behind me. The top half of the tree crashed to the ground, sending out the sharp scent of sap from the shattered wood.

Rowan let out a startled cry that barely registered in my mind. Severn snarled. "Don't be a coward, Aren."

The pain tried to return, and I found that this time, I blocked it a little more easily—at least enough that I could keep moving, though every motion made the agony flare. A flame shot toward me, and I sent my own out. I fought to clear my mind, to recapture the way I'd felt when I put out fires before. When our flames met, I allowed them to mingle, wrapping his in mine. He grinned as his fire reached toward me, singeing my skin. The grin faded as my fire encompassed his, and I doused both.

My power sang through me as it never had before, alive and awake and willing to fight, sharpened by my pain and rage. For the first time, I understood that I was strong enough to defeat him.

I stepped closer to Severn, and his eyes widened. "Do you want to see what else I've learned?" I asked, and let him feel my energy building. Panic flashed over his features. He sent out another blast of magic. I moved again, but it caught my left hand,

and pain flared as skin split and several bones cracked under the force.

The pain would have been unbearable had I not just suffered worse, and had I not been so completely focused on what I felt in Severn's magic, which I was so intimately and disastrously connected to.

His magic was weak for the briefest moment, just after the blast and before he drew again on the ambient magic of the land. Taking the only chance that would ever present itself, I pushed my pain aside and slipped into his mind. He was still too strong for me to break him, but he felt me there. I pushed harder, cracking his ever-strengthening defenses as a root breaks a stone wall.

Screams filled my mind. Images of torture, of blood. Panic. Fear. The scent of smoke. He tried to pull away, but I held on. I could have had his heart gripped in my fist for all the power he had against me at that moment.

I pushed harder, willing my way past his surface thoughts. His eyes darted to the side as he searched for something to break my focus and my control.

Toward Rowan.

His thoughts focused on her destruction.

"No!" My voice came without bidding from me, and I struggled to keep my focus on Severn even as he sent out another blast of magic—this time at someone who couldn't defend herself. I might have got deeper then, broken him, but Rowan's scream ripped my focus away from my task. Severn's mind slammed closed, and he shoved me away with another blast of magic, though this was more like a strong wind than raw power.

We stood there, both of us shaking. I wouldn't look away. Not if there might be another opportunity. I could still feel his mind, just out of reach.

Severn's eyes darted to my right, and widened. A flash of terror radiated out through the thin connection that still existed between us.

And then he was gone, body and mind, leaving only an echo

of his magic and a pile of clothing to make it clear that the visit hadn't been a horrible dream.

His horse shook its head, then glanced across the clearing. "Florizel?"

"Murad!" Florizel cried, and raced toward him.

The black horse blinked slowly, and then his eyes widened. "No!" he screamed. "Stay away! He calls to me." His head whipped back and twisted on his neck, forcing him to turn. "Don't follow me there!" he cried, and then stopped, entranced again. In a graceful, unhurried movement his hind muscles bunched, and he launched himself into the air.

Florizel ran after him and took off. Both horses disappeared behind the trees.

Severn was alive, then, but likely weak. *If I follow now I might—*

"Aren." Rowan's voice came out a thick sob, full of agony and fear. "Please, help."

I forgot about Severn, and about my own lingering pain.

Rowan sat on the ground with Kel's head cradled in her lap. Tears streamed down her face as she stroked his hair—as much of it wasn't soaked in blood from the broad gash that revealed the bone beneath, crushed and mangled. Blood soaked his shirt, which had been torn open, revealing another irreparable injury to his chest. He had been shattered by Severn's magic. He lay still, and then his body convulsed, and he groaned.

The injury would have killed a human immediately, and it would have been a mercy. A mer's body was so much stronger. His body trembled, then went stiff as his muscles tightened.

I ran to them and fell to my knees beside Kel. A chill filled the air, and he gasped. His eyes rolled, showing white, and then focused on me. Otherwise, his face had gone slack and expressionless, overtaken by pain.

"I can't—I can't heal him," Rowan sobbed, and pressed a bloodstained hand to his chest. "I can't stop it. I can't fix it. I'm trying, but I can't—"

Kel's breath hitched, and he seemed to return to himself. "Don't," he whispered. "I know you can't—" He cut himself off with a sharp breath. "I'm fine."

"You're not," she said, and brushed away one of her tears that had fallen onto his face. "Don't lie. But merfolk are strong, right? You're going to live. When Nox comes back, or if we could find a healer... Maybe Morea can help."

Kel closed his eyes. His face contorted as another spasm gripped his body, lifting it nearly off the ground.

Rowan looked to me. "I don't think Kel even thought about what he was doing. He pushed me away when Severn threw his magic." She placed her hand back on Kel's face and stroked his eyebrows. The spasm calmed, and his face relaxed.

"Help me." Rowan unbuttoned Kel's shirt, further revealing the gaping wound in his side. His ribs lay exposed and splintered. "We can try to stop the bleeding, get him back to camp." There was little hope in her voice.

"Rowan," Kel said, and reached up to take her hand. "It's no good. Sometimes being strong only means a slower death. Don't chase it off."

Her chin trembled. "You can't leave us."

Kel coughed and drew a hard breath. "I don't think I have much choice. Severn's magic still moves in me. My body's fighting, but I feel it breaking me down. I can't fight this."

As he spoke, a fresh stream of blood coursed from the wound in his side, and he gasped for breath.

"Ulric lives," he said. "I didn't want Severn to know. Rowan, you should take him back to camp. Quickly."

She looked from Kel to me and back. "But I—"

"Please. I need a minute alone with Aren."

Pain more raw than anything Severn could inflict directly on me welled in my heart. Rowan looked at me, eyes wide and red-rimmed. "No," she whispered.

"Please go," I told her.

She lifted his head with trembling hands and placed it gently on the mossy ground, then bent to kiss Kel's forehead. "Thank you," she whispered. "If I could return all of my other gifts in exchange for getting back the ability to heal you—"

"I know."

She turned away and bent to lift Ulric's arm over her shoulder. He stirred and mumbled. Kel watched as she dragged Ulric away. She set him down, and turned back. Without speaking another word, she closed her eyes and raised her hands.

A rumbling arose from the earth where Severn and I had fought. The ground shimmered as water bubbled up from the ground. Rowan's face contorted with the effort, and the bubbling turned to a fountain. The water level rose as it filled the broad indent in the ground, and the air grew thick with the rich, metallic scent of it.

She met my gaze, lowered hers, and stooped to pick up the man who hated her. She dragged him slowly through the woods, and they disappeared.

The water kept coming as though a dam beneath the earth had been opened. It licked at Kel's feet. "Take my boots off," he said. I did. One ankle was clearly broken, but he didn't complain as I pulled the boot off. I poked his leg. No reaction.

Still the water kept rising until it surrounded Kel's body. I pulled him toward the center, where it was deeper.

"Can you change if we get your clothes off?" I asked.

"Are you trying to get me naked?"

I couldn't muster a smile. "I thought you might be more comfortable in your natural body."

He drew in a halting breath and watched the clouds that passed over us. "I don't have the strength to change. But being in the water is good. Bless that woman."

I dropped to my knees so that the water came to my chest, and held him close. "Does it help the pain?"

"A little, I think. But the magic." His body shook, and he flailed until he'd gripped my broken hand in his. I hardly felt the pain as the bones ground together. "Aren, I can't die by magic. I can't."

A lump filled my throat, but I managed to say, "I remember." The merfolk had many beliefs about magic. It had set them against humans long ago, as the mer believed magic should not be used for personal gain or as a weapon. They thought it unnatural, and feared a death by magic more than any other.

Kel's eyes turned to meet mine. "If I die this way, my body will remain and rot. I saw it once. My spirit will be trapped."

Another story I'd heard but never truly considered. Merfolk were supposed to disappear when they died, to leave the world entirely, free and unburdened.

A tear slipped from his left eye. "Don't let me be anchored, Aren. Please. Help me."

My cowardly heart wanted me to run, to deny him this even after everything we'd been through, everything he'd meant to me. We'd lost many years, but even when I'd left the merfolk behind I'd never had to imagine a world without Kel's smart mouth, his laugh, his easy confidence that everything would turn out right in the end.

I leaned back and searched under the water until I'd found the place where I dropped my knife.

"I'm sorry," I said. "Sorry you're here, that this happened. That I let Nox go."

He tried to shake his head, and winced. The water around his head stained deeper red. "I'm glad she won't see me like this. Just tell her I love her. And tell her I'm sorry. Aren, I don't regret any of this. I—"

Another spasm, this one followed by a painful gasp that echoed in my own body.

"Please," he gasped. "Hurry."

I dipped my head and kissed his cheek, and didn't bother to brush away the tear that fell on his skin. "I love you, Kel. And I will miss you always."

I pressed my knife to his throat, and closed my eyes.

39

ROWAN

When Ulric's weight proved too much to drag behind me, I hauled his all-but-lifeless body up so that his chest pressed against my back, and I held his arms over my shoulders. The thick forest made passage difficult, as did the exhaustion that had already drained my arms, and the black sorrow that threatened to overwhelm my heart.

I couldn't think about what had happened, and I couldn't think of anything else. When my mind tried to speculate on what might be happening back at the clearing, I focused on the sound of my feet instead, falling heavy and crashing through the woods like an injured monster. So intense was my focus on our return to camp that I didn't hear the hoofsteps behind me.

"Let me help." Florizel's soft voice pulled me from my stupor. She lowered her forequarters and held her wings aside, and I used the strength that remained in my arms to shove Ulric over her back, arms hanging over one side, legs dangling down the other. I held onto one boot to keep him from falling, but Florizel bore his weight as we moved on.

"Where's Aren?" she asked.

"Back with Kel." My voice sounded far away, and unconnected to me. Even my body felt distant, though it did everything I asked of it. The only thing close to me was emptiness. It should have been horrifying to feel nothing at such a time, but I welcomed it. Feeling just hurt too much.

"Is Kel—?"

My breath hitched. "I think so, by now. They wanted to be alone. To say goodbye." More than that, I knew, but that was between them. I remembered what Cassia had told me about mers dying by magic. The emotions threatened to return then in a swell of agony. Not for Kel, but for Aren. Gods willing, Kel was gone now, released from his pain. Aren's was only beginning, and there was nothing I could do this time to save him.

Crowds gathered as we entered the camp, but no one stepped in to offer assistance or to ask questions. I supposed no one dared touch the old king, even now. I led Florizel to Morea's tent, and when we found it empty I unloaded and dragged Ulric inside.

"Find the Potioner," I said, and Florizel hurried off as I let Ulric slump onto the bedroll. Morea couldn't have gone far. It felt like a lifetime ago that she'd offered me her potion on top of the bald rock. I reached for the flask and sipped again. Perhaps it hadn't helped, but it also hadn't hurt. I'd been strong enough to offer Kel one last gift. I would be grateful for that, even if I now felt dried up. The magic was still there. I would recover.

A pair of bottles clanked together as I knocked one with my boot. The edges of the floor were lined with them, all full of potions and ingredients, none labeled.

Ulric's eyes cracked open, and I couldn't help being thankful that I was too drained to show my shock at his appearance. He'd grown old. Truly old. His eyes had clouded over since his collapse, and his sagging skin had developed dark spots.

Suddenly the mysteries of magic didn't seem so perfectly wonderful.

"What happened?" He tried to sit up, but couldn't so much as raise his body onto his shaking arms. "Where's Aren?"

"He'll be back soon. He's alive. Severn is gone for now." A tear squeezed out of my eye, though I'd been sure they were used up. "Florizel has gone to find Morea. She'll help you."

His eyes narrowed, then softened. "And the other? Kel?"

I pressed my lips together and shook my head.

"I see. Severn's doing?"

I nodded and wrapped my arms around myself, as though that might hold in the flood. *No weakness,* I told myself. *Not in front of him.*

"Is Millie coming, then?"

"Morea?"

He glared at me, then rested his head on the blankets. "That's what I said. Damn beetles can't raise a barn to save their hides."

Before I could answer, Morea stepped in. She wore dirty work clothes, but had a white apron tied over, and her thick hair plaited neatly behind her back. "Good afternoon, Uncle." Her face registered shock at his appearance, then careful scrutiny. "Perhaps a fresh batch of what Nox worked up for you. Victoria's got some barbaroses coming along quite nicely for you, and I think I have a few ideas for additions."

He waved a hand at her, like batting away a fly.

She crouched next to him. "I'm going to help you feel better, but you have to trust me."

I left them, and went to Aren's tent to wait for him.

Everything inside was neat, orderly, and completely without indication that an actual person spent any time in the place. Bedroll made, everything else put away, out of sight. No papers on the wood crates that he might have used as a desk, no clothing left out.

I sat cross-legged on the bedroll and tried not to muss the blankets. I waited. When it became too much to hold my body upright, I lay down and rested my head on the folded blanket that served as his pillow. Outside the tent, people talked and worked. Someone laughed.

To think that someone would laugh. That the world would dare to just go on.

I woke to the rocking sensation of a cold, wet hand shaking my shoulder. Not much time had passed. Bleary afternoon sunlight still shone through the walls of the tent.

"You're soaked," I said.

Aren looked down at his clothes, as though he hadn't noticed.

"Is he... gone?" I asked.

"Completely."

So Aren hadn't let the magic kill him. I reached for Aren's hand, and noticed that at some point the blood stains had disappeared from mine. "I'm so sorry."

"Yeah." His lips pressed together in a hard line, and he squeezed his eyes closed. "He said to thank you for the water. I think..." His voice cracked. "I think he was happy to end it there. Where's Ulric?"

"Morea's tent. She's taking care of him as well as she can." I hesitated to add more to his burden, but he had to know. "He looks his age, gods help him. I think his mind is gone now, too."

Aren sighed. "There must be some magic working if he's alive, but that's it for him. He's done, and we can't afford to wait for Nox to return."

It took a moment for me to find my voice again. "So it happens now, unless you want to call everything off and flee." My voice caught in my throat. We weren't ready. Not one of us, not all of us together. Not even Aren, who had just pulled Severn to the edge of defeat. If we went ahead now, we were as good as dead.

Aren's expression simmered with quiet rage that made my skin prickle. "We're going to get into that city, no matter what the cost," he said, deadly calm. "Severn will suffer for this. If I have to cast my soul into Despair to do it, I'll—" He looked up, away from me, beyond the walls of the tent. A maniacal light came into his eyes. "We will not lose this fight. I need to speak to Albion and Griselda. Can you find them?"

"I can."

"Have them meet me in Ulric's tent at sunset."

I stood and went to the door. "And until then?"

Aren lay on his bed and rested an arm over his eyes. "Send for Morea when she's done with Ulric." He lifted his left hand, and I fought back a shudder at the twisted fingers and half-flayed flesh. "No one else enters this tent. I need time alone to make decisions. This has changed everything."

"Of course." With Ulric completely out of commission, this

was all on Aren's shoulders. He had become our leader in every sense of the word. The absolute last thing he'd wanted.

I supposed the fact that I hadn't been asked to the evening's meeting meant I wasn't in Aren's inner circle anymore. I tried not to be hurt by that.

"Is there anything else I can do?" I asked.

"Let people know what's happened, and keep them away from me for a while. Tell Xaven we need the rest of his people brought in from Wildwood. Keep yourself safe, and make sure no one leaves camp." He rested his arm over his face again. "That's all I need for now."

I wanted to go to him, to put my arms around him and try to take on some of the pain he had to be hiding. It was unfair that he should have to deal with it alone, or that any of us should. But I sensed he didn't want that. Perhaps the emptiness was the best thing for him. Emptiness, or whatever it was that he wouldn't show me.

I left without another word, and didn't turn back at the heart-broken moan that he cut off as soon as it began.

We both had work to do. If we were going to attack the city, we would need more help, and I thought I knew where I might find it.

40

NOX

No one could tell me where Severn had gone.

"He has concerns he tells no one about," Myk told me as I carried Severn's supper to his rooms to await his return—apparently a task that normally fell to Sara. As her new assistant, it was now my job. I hadn't heard a word from her since Severn called for her, as she'd remained locked in her private chambers, saying she needed some privacy.

I couldn't say I minded having her out of the way. Severn's favor had placed me firmly in position over the other Potioners, who hadn't minded when I gave them the afternoon to rest. With them absent I'd been free to experiment for a few hours, and believed I'd come up with an idea to protect Ulric from his own magic as he healed. It would take a few days to test out my theory and make a proper batch of the potion, but I was on my way toward something promising.

As soon as I found a way out of the palace and the city, my part of the mission would be over. Kel and I would remain to see Ulric's victory, which I now felt more certain of than I had at any time before, and then we'd leave Luid behind forever.

Just a few more days, I told myself, and felt a faint surge of hope. With any luck, I'd manage to avoid Severn for the rest of my time in the city. I couldn't stop worrying about where he might have gone, but wanted nothing more to do with him.

Myk unlocked the door to Severn's chambers and held it open. I moved silently over the thick carpet. Without Severn's voice and presence to fill it, the place had the feeling of a temple, solemn and quiet and frightening.

"I didn't realize you worked so closely with the king," I said, and set the tray on the desk in the outer chamber.

Myk squared his shoulders. "Not as closely as I might wish to, but he knows that I'm trustworthy. Like you, I think?"

I smiled as though that pleased me. In fact, my skin crawled. Though I found myself falling under Severn's spell when I was with him, it disappeared when I was alone and returned to my senses. "I think he's beginning to trust me. He's very perceptive."

"He is that. I don't see the king often, but I am allowed these important little tasks. Makes me feel I'm a part of something big. Like I'm making a difference in my own way."

Severn doesn't deserve such loyalty or affection, I thought. Still, I couldn't help smiling. Myk was clearly smitten with the charismatic king. As long as he didn't get too close, my new friend was safe enough.

I poured wine from the bottle on the table into the glass on the tray, then turned to Myk. "Is this all I do? Leave this here?"

Myk's cheeks flushed. "I don't know. I usually get kicked out at this point. But I know Sara adds something to his drink. It used to be a shimmery black liquid, but now it's a glowing pink one." He pulled back a wooden panel on the wall next to the door that I suspected led to Severn's bedroom, revealing a hidden shelf with a few bottles on it. "This is the one he's been having lately. Should I send for Sara?"

My potion. The bottle was still half-full, but he'd been taking it.

Building up the enemy's strength. Just what I came here to do.

I pushed that thought back behind the walls of my mind. Myk couldn't read me, but I wasn't about to let my guard down anywhere. I picked up the bottle and swirled the contents, which seemed to glow even brighter in the dark than they had that first day in the workroom.

"Actually, it would be helpful if you could ask Sara what dose he's accustomed to. I don't want to get it wrong."

Myk grimaced. "No, I suppose that could be bad. Wait here, and don't touch anything. He's very particular."

I made my eyes widen. "I'd say. No, I'll stand right here." I planted my feet on the carpet and shoved my hands into my apron pockets.

Myk smiled and hurried off, leaving the heavy door open.

I waited for a few minutes, only chancing a quick look around, not wanting to be caught snooping. Nothing in the room had changed since my last visit. The fireplace was cold and empty, the room silent.

It might not hurt to look around a little, I thought. *Sara's room is close, but—*

I screamed as Severn appeared directly in front of me, wide-eyed, gasping, and completely naked.

"Sara," he gasped. "Where is she?"

"I don't know—I'll try to find her." But before I could move, he fell forward and grabbed onto my arms to steady himself.

"Myk!" I screamed.

He rushed in, followed a moment later by Sara. A split lip that hadn't been there when I saw her earlier was already three days healed. A talented Potioner indeed, but I understood why she hadn't wanted to be seen for a while.

"Severn!" she cried, and ran to him. Myk followed, but hesitated to touch the king.

"Help us get him to bed," I ordered, and Myk complied, assisting Severn through the door next to the fireplace. The room beyond was dim, the afternoon's sunlight filtered by heavy curtains. Myk deposited Severn gently in the big, wood-framed bed that filled much of the space, and Sara hurried to cover him to his waist with blankets. I stood beside a wooden desk, far less ornate than the one in the outer rooms.

Severn's body trembled, and he gasped for air. No change in

his appearance, I noted. Whatever had happened, he wasn't hurt as badly as he had been after Rowan dealt with him.

Pity.

"Nox, get that potion!" Sara shouted.

I hurried to the outer room and returned with the one I'd concocted. "No, the other. The black one with the unicorn horn."

Severn roared and clutched his stomach as I set my potion down and went to get Sara's. "Not that one! You've cursed me, you idiot."

Sara shook her head and forced his hands away so she could examine his abdomen. "Let me treat you as I did before. You don't know what you're saying. Whatever just happened had nothing to do with unicorn horns, or—"

He still had the strength to slap her across the face hard enough to send her to the floor. "The pink potion. Now."

I took the bottle to him. Severn grabbed it and drank. He collapsed back onto the pile of pillows behind him, laughing maniacally.

"Cursed," he said again. "There's no other explanation. I go to challenge my enemies, certain of my victory."

"I told you not to try transporting yourself that way again," Sara muttered as she stood and straightened her skirt.

Severn ignored her words. "And what happens? Who should get in my way? A gods-be-damned mer in the middle of the forest." He laughed again. "That's not bad luck. That's a curse. I believe it now."

I stepped back into the shadows and forced my heart to quiet, my mind to not imagine the worst.

"A mer stopped you?" Sara asked. Her voice took on a hushed, panicked tone I didn't understand.

Severn took another swig of potion. "He might as well have. I took the old man down, but Aren was stronger than I expected. I tried to pull myself back here and—Well. Something has changed in him, and he held me there. I panicked and threw magic at the Sorceress to distract him, and the mer got in the way."

Don't react. Don't let anyone see. I held my breath, then let it out slowly.

Sara, who could not by any reckoning be called superstitious, paled. "You didn't kill him, did you?"

"I don't know. I might well have, for the damage I sent at him —a blast as large as any I've killed with before."

I forced myself to forget Kel's warm eyes, his smile, the feel of his lips against mine. My face had slipped into an expression of shock and pain, but I forced it to mold itself into concern before anyone could see. My heart became a stone, and I stepped forward again.

Severn looked again at Sara. "What did you say before?"

"Nothing, my king," she said. "I spoke out of turn."

"You said, 'I told you not to try that again,' did you not?"

Sara reached for his hand, and Severn allowed her to take it. "I shouldn't have said it. I was concerned for your safety. The last time you transported yourself like this, you nearly died."

"The last time I did this, it was new to me. And yes, it cost me dearly. Do I look so poorly now?"

Her eyes roamed over as much of his body as wasn't covered by the blankets. Whatever damage had been done to him was invisible. He looked as strong as ever.

"No," she admitted. "You appear to be in proper health, physically. But you're experiencing pain. I was only concerned. Let me make it up to you. I will remember my place next time."

"That you will," he said, and pulled his hand away from hers. "You," he said, and snapped his fingers in Myk's direction. "Take her to her room for the night, or until I have time to decide what to do with her. The bedroom, not her work space, and clear out everything but the bedsheets and the chamber pot. Lock her in."

"You can't!" she cried, and struggled as Myk forced her hands behind her back. "You need me!"

Severn's gaze turned to me as Myk dragged his Potioner away. His eyes burned, and a secretive smile crossed his lips. "I think, perhaps, that I don't."

My heart beat wildly as the desire to be away from him drove me halfway mad. I put my hands in my pockets to hide their trembling.

"Fetch me my robe from the corner," he ordered, and I

retrieved it from a standing rack. He sat up, slipped his arms in, and tied it. It was several moments before he could stand straight, and did so only by holding on to one of the posts at the head of the bed. He pulled on a tasseled cord, and a small man entered the room.

"Did you see the guard who just left?" Severn asked.

"I did."

"See that he doesn't survive long enough to talk about what he's seen here."

"It will be taken care of, sire." The little man bowed and retreated.

My heart's flutter turned to a pounding. Panic beat about my mind like the wings of a great bird. *Don't think. Don't think.*

Severn sat again. "Nox, I need a different potion. Something to strengthen my body."

"The pink potion should help, if it's shoring up your magic."

"Make it stronger."

I dipped my head in a quick bow and backed toward the door. "I'll see what I can come up with, if I'm excused."

He waved me away, and I forced my feet to carry me slowly out the door and through his outer rooms. As soon as I reached the corridor, my emotions threatened to boil over. Rage battled with fear, grief with hope. He didn't see Kel die. *But he said...*

I broke into a run and headed straight for my room. I fumbled to fit the key in the lock, pushed my way in, slammed the door and locked it.

"Kel," I moaned, and pressed my face deep into the pillow as my sorrow poured out in a raging torrent. Kel's face came to mind, his touch. A house by the sea. A life. Love that had threatened to pull me out on its tides.

I should have run away with him as soon as he suggested it.

Surrounded by the cold stone walls of a palace which should have been my home, I let it all out, screamed my loss into the mattress and took my anger out on the feather pillow.

And suddenly my heart stilled. Peace filled me. The scent of the sea came, and the taste of salt on my lips.

A *shhhhh* that could have been the crash of waves or the

comforting noise a mother makes to calm her child filled my ears. The tears continued to flow, but my sobs quieted.

"Kel," I whispered. "Please. I can't do this."

The peaceful feeling passed, but I had regained control of myself. And I would maintain it. If anyone knew about this, it would be the end. I forced my legs to support me, and splashed cold water over my face at the basin in the corner.

There would be time again later for grief, and for memories. For now, I would do the job I'd wanted to come to Luid to do in the first place.

If Ulric was dead, he had no need of my research or my potions. If Kel was gone, I had no reason to return safely to the world outside of the palace. Nothing would stop me from following this path to the end—the one Severn had created the night he'd forced my mother to flee for her life.

I would see him dead, but not before he fully understood my pain.

41

ROWAN

"I think the merfolk deserve to know about this."

Aren turned slowly. I'd caught him alone in his tent, and he'd allowed me to enter. There was no embrace this time, though. Everything about him was cold and hard, closed-off and focused on one goal. He'd had reason to want Severn gone before. Now, he wanted revenge, and nothing would distract him. A night's sleep after the challenge and Kel's death had done nothing to cool his rage.

Or dull my pain.

"It won't change anything," he said. His voice came out flat, either from exhaustion or distraction.

"But they should know. He was one of theirs, and I think one of their best. You can't let them wait for his return. They'll have to find out some time. And maybe this will change things."

His jaw muscles flexed. "It could turn them against us. I let this happen."

I stepped closer, but didn't dare reach out to touch him. "Kel made the decision to stay and fight with us. He whispered to me to not interfere, to not use my magic. He pushed me aside when Severn attacked." I still wondered what might have happened if I had stepped in sooner. Maybe I could have distracted Severn and given Aren an advantage. It would have been a dirty fight, but it hardly seemed to matter now.

Or maybe Severn would have destroyed all of us if Aren was the one thrown off by an illusion, or maybe he'd have had a way to turn my skills on me if I opened myself to that. Aren still didn't know what Severn was capable of. No one did.

That's the problem with 'if only', I thought. You never know what, exactly, you're wishing for.

Aren sat on the folding stool he'd taken from Ulric's tent.

"Please," I said. "I can't help here. I don't know battle strategy or politics, or even as much about magic as any of you. But I can do this. Florizel and I will go back to the cave we left in the autumn. I'll take a message if you'll write it."

He looked up at me. "How's your magic?"

"Full strength, as far as I can tell." It had taken some time to come back. All night, in fact, after the effort of pulling up Kel's spring. "I'll be careful. We'll be in the air most of the journey. Morea's improved her potion for me, and I'll have my weapons."

He paled at that, but nodded. "You'll probably be safer there than here. Just don't go into the caves. Remember how easy it is to get lost in there, and that's the least of the dangers. You're not likely to get out."

Silence followed.

"That's it?" I asked. "No speech about how I'm not ready?"

He smiled sadly. "You are, though. If this is the contribution you wish to make, I won't stop you. I'll worry, but I would no matter what you were doing."

That had been easier than I'd expected. Pride in how far I'd come mixed with fear of what I might find on my return. "I'll be back as soon as I can," I said.

"Good. I'll write the message, and you can leave this morning."

"Good," I echoed.

There seemed to be nothing else to say.

～

FLORIZEL TURNED her head back toward me. "You're certain there was no cave closer?"

"Sorry. There probably is, but with no one to lead us there, this is the best we can do."

She lowered her head to the wind and flapped her wings harder, carrying us forward. Kel's death had shaken her, and she'd vowed to do what she could to help. I suspected that seeing Murad again had only fueled her desire to see Severn taken down.

We were making good progress, flying through fair skies over quiet forests and towns, heading east toward Belleisle. We wouldn't get that far, though. Just to the stone forest, near the first place I'd faced Severn.

He won't escape this time, I told myself. *If we meet, if we fight, if he tries to take what I love...*

The thought was interrupted as a massive shadow passed over us, flying up from behind. Florizel shied sideways, and I gripped her mane tighter to stay seated. We dropped quickly, but my stomach seemed determined to stay aloft. I felt like it had climbed into my throat by the time Florizel's hooves brushed the tops of the trees. I braced myself for landing.

She hit the ground running, darting between trees that sheltered us from whatever was above.

"Wait!" bellowed a voice that echoed through the forest. A great crash followed as a huge body shattered branches and close-set tree trunks, then shook the earth with a graceless landing.

"Skittish creatures," the rough voice muttered.

My heart continued to race even as we stopped and turned. Florizel laid her ears flat and marched back toward the red dragon who sat brushing leaves and bits of shattered wood from her scales. When we reached Ruby, Florizel stretched her neck out and let out a long, irritated whinny.

Ruby raised her eyebrows—or whatever the scaled equivalent of them might be called. "Does that mean you're not pleased to see me?"

Florizel snorted. "It's rude to sneak up like that! You are huge!

You are terrifying! You are..." She shook her head, and the tremor continued down her body. She sighed. "You're not going to eat us, though, so I suppose that's all right."

I held back a laugh. "So glad to see you're still with us, Ruby."

She shrugged. "I didn't want to get too far. I haven't grown bored with watching all of this unfold yet. Where are you going?"

I explained what had happened, and our little mission. I still found it hard to say that Kel was gone, but it came easier every time I spoke the words. It also became more real, a fact that I disliked. Still, I would need to be able to say it calmly if I met a mer. They wouldn't want to see me cry.

Ruby pursed her lips. "I'm sorry to hear it," she said. "I understand what loss is. I may not grieve in the same way as you do, but I know that this is painful. It makes me..." She cocked her head to one side. "I believe it makes me sad. How horrifying."

"You've felt sadness before," I said.

"I have, but for my own losses. This mer meant nothing to me. I didn't know him. Yet I feel it for you. For the human prince." She made a horrid face, filled with disgust. "I really should end things. I'm so far gone."

"You could," I said, and held up a hand as an idea struck me. "But first, perhaps you might join us for a while?"

Florizel snorted again, but didn't seem completely opposed.

"Why?" Ruby asked.

"We need you. Not that you should care, but we do. Aren once told me that dragons help anchor magic in the land, and there are a few of us who might benefit from having you close. You'd get a good seat for what's to come, and maybe you could play a part if they decide to attack the city."

Ruby drummed her fingers on the forest floor. "I suppose it would be terrible to pass up the chance for a feast like that. Soft, tender city folk..."

"Well, maybe not that," I said hastily. "I'm not sure Aren would want all of them killed. But soldiers. City guards. Think of the armor. And if you want a great and glorious end..."

The dragon's lips pulled back in a grin. "I make no guarantees about my appetite. But we'll see what happens."

A few minutes later we were all back in the sky. I felt safer having Ruby with us, though I declined her offer to carry me. I might have made it to the cave faster, but had no desire to be clutched in those terrible claws again if I could avoid it.

Florizel did her best to keep pace with Ruby, and we covered the distance to the stone forest far more quickly than we could have on foot. It took some time for me to find anything that looked familiar. The forest looked so different now, with leaves covering trees in a landscape that had been covered by an early snowfall the last time I passed through. By working back from the river, though, I eventually located the rocky entrance to the cave.

"What now?" Florizel asked.

"Find yourself something to eat," I said, and re-settled my pack on shoulders that had grown tight and stiff after hours hunched over Florizel's neck. "I'll be back as soon as I can. You should eat too, Ruby."

Ruby opened her mouth, but Florizel cut her off. "Don't even joke about it," she said. "I'm not a tender morsel, and I don't believe you're going to eat me."

Ruby sighed. "You used to be fun, horse."

I left them to their semi-friendly argument and climbed into the cave. Moisture dripped down the walls, and the place smelled of the decaying leaves that had drifted into the entrance the previous autumn. The walls still glowed with their eerie light as I moved deeper.

Not too far, remember.

"Hello?" I called, feeling foolish. The merfolk would have no reason to be close to this entrance. I could hope for a fairy, but they could be anywhere. With the way the caves shifted, they could be near the northern mountains one minute and at glass lake the next—or if not that quickly, at least fast enough for it to be dizzyingly confusing.

I looked back at the cave entrance. Late afternoon light still shone in. The caves wouldn't shift around me until I came to what Cassia had called a "changing," something like an intersection of tunnels. As long as I stayed in this one, I could make my way back.

"Jasper?" I called. "Beryl?"

I reached into my pocket and rubbed the smooth paper of the message Aren had sent. It wasn't sealed, but I didn't dare read it. The words there were for the merfolk, not for me, and I didn't know whether it would hurt more to find he'd revealed his pain in his letter or glossed over it.

I kept walking. The air grew colder, and I shivered. The tunnel ended, opening into a round cave with rough walls and three more tunnels exiting from it. I didn't dare step in, lest the tunnel I stood in change. I might never find my way back, and either be expelled somewhere far from my friends or lost. I leaned against the wall. "Beryl?"

A pair of cave fairies buzzed out from another tunnel, flying loops through the open space of the cave. My heart leapt, then calmed as I realized neither were familiar. They had the same round, fuzzy bodies as Jasper and Beryl, the same massive, dark eyes and moth-like wings, but these both had dark edging on their wings and black hair on their tiny heads. They buzzed closer, curious, and beckoned for me to step into the cave.

"I'll have to decline," I said, and retreated further into my own tunnel. They didn't follow, but also didn't leave. Cave fairies didn't speak the common language of most species on the continent of Serat, from the humans in Darmid to the dragons of Tyrea and the merfolk of the surrounding seas. Still, they understood. "I'm looking for friends of mine. Fairies."

The larger of the two fairies, a male with a deeply furrowed brow, chuckled musically.

"Well, acquaintances," I amended. "Jasper and Beryl. They led me here several months ago, and I need their help. Could you find them?"

The two conferred quietly, then flew into separate tunnels.

I sighed and sat on the floor, back leaned against the cold, glowing wall. My options were limited. I could go back and give up, or I could wait to see whether they returned. The thought that they might bring back something terrible crossed my mind

—they'd certainly seemed mischievous enough, wanting me to lose myself in the caves.

But what choice do I have? I'd known this wouldn't be easy.

I yawned. I'd hardly slept the night before as new nightmares invaded every time I let myself drift off. Dorset Langley was no longer the greatest horror in my recent past. Now there was Severn, and Kel's injuries. Even the horrid, empty stare of Murad as Severn controlled his every movement.

I shivered and pulled my jacket tighter around me, then closed my eyes to rest them, just for a moment. When I opened them, a fairy hovered a hand's breadth from my nose. I gasped and leaned back, reacting slowly. My muscles had gone stiff.

I'd been asleep, and I didn't know for how long.

Jasper crossed his arms and frowned at me, apparently completely unimpressed. He buzzed away and returned a moment later, followed by quick footsteps.

I climbed to my feet as Cassia entered the cave, dressed in a warm sweater and a plain skirt in a heavy fabric that hung straight to her bare ankles.

Her beautiful face lit up when she saw me, and it was all I could do not to burst into tears at the thought of that joy being shattered. She and Kel had nagged and picked at each other as much as any pair of siblings I'd ever met, but they'd loved each other fiercely.

And she had no idea he was gone.

I forced a smile as she pulled me into a hug, and held her close. Her thick hair held the salty scent of the ocean, wild and deep. For a moment I couldn't let go.

I'm not ready for this.

She pulled back. "What are you doing here, Rowan? Not that it's an unpleasant surprise." Her brow furrowed. "Is everyone all right?"

I fought to control myself, to not let my face contort. "Not exactly."

"Is it Aren?" She looked ready to take up arms and charge after whatever enemy might have harmed her old friend.

"No. Cass, I—" I pulled the letter from my pocket and handed it to her. Aren would have said it better than I could.

She hesitated, and licked her lips. "I don't want to open this, do I?"

"No," I said softly. "I'm so sorry."

A tear slipped down her cheek before she'd even opened the letter. Her breath hitched as she read, her chin quivered, and she let out a soft groan as she reached the end. No dramatic display of heartbreak. No denial. She folded the letter and tucked it into the pocket of her skirt, and her face crumpled as the tears came harder.

I opened my arms, and she leaned in. I stroked her hair, mumbled something nonsensical but vaguely comforting, and cried with her. I wanted to be the rock she could beat her grief out on, but I couldn't. All I could offer was my own brokenness, so insignificant compared with hers.

I'd lost a friend and someone I admired greatly. She had lost so much more.

She pulled back to wipe her eyes. "We were so different. I always thought him silly for not using his brain, for following his intuition and his heart so strongly, even if it went against my better judgement. He thought I was too distant, too analytical. We listened to each other, though. I kept him out of trouble, and he led me into it in the most wonderful ways. I was his mind." Her voice dropped to a whisper. "And he was my heart." Her nose wrinkled, and she squeezed her eyes closed. "How do I live without my heart?"

I had no answer for that.

She wiped her nose on her sleeve. "I, um... Is Aren all right? Nox?"

My stomach sank. "Nox doesn't know. She's in the city. Aren is planning to attack Severn, though I don't know how. Ulric is half-mad and as good as useless, for all I can tell. We have support from Tyrea and Belleisle now, but I don't think it's nearly enough."

"And you?"

"I'm here." I shrugged. "For what it's worth, I suppose."

"I'm glad you came. It's best to hear it from someone who knew him." She grimaced as a few more tears escaped.

Jasper buzzed closer, clearly agitated. Cassia glanced at him. "I'll explain on the way back," she said. "For now, can we make sure Rowan gets back to her entrance?"

Jasper flew ahead, back toward the surface.

Cassia and I didn't speak until we stepped out into the night. The sky was a blanket of stars that watched over a sleeping horse and the red dragon curled protectively around her. Ruby opened one eye, then closed it again.

"I'll pass the message on to the elders," Cassia said quietly, barely breaking the heavy silence of the forest. "I tried before. I argued. I tried to shame them, much good it did me. Nothing would move them. We never attack, not unless there's a direct and immediate threat against our people." She reached into her pocket. "Maybe this counts. I don't even know. But I'll see what I can do."

I embraced her again, and she disappeared back into the cave.

Ruby yawned and stretched. "We were beginning to think you'd never return. Is it done, then?"

Florizel flexed her wings. "We decided we're ready to leave when you are. There's enough starlight to guide us, and no one will dare attack if we have a dragon watching over us."

All I wanted was a little more rest, but they were right. Better to get back.

I used a boulder to mount Florizel, and we left the cave, the fairies, and the broken-hearted mer woman behind.

I only hoped we hadn't missed too much while we were gone.

42

AREN

My muscles burned. Rough rocks scratched my hands until blood flowed from scrapes on my fingers. Though the morning air was cool, recent days had been warm, and the bodies gave off the sick, gassy odor of rotting meat. Some animal had been at the cairn and had made off with a leg, but otherwise the eighteen corpses were fairly well intact.

Intact, and blessedly still.

I picked up another rock and tossed it away from the bodies.

Hard as I'd tried overnight to escape from the grief that overwhelmed me and the worry that Rowan wouldn't return, sleep hadn't come. Instead I'd lain awake in my tent, grief turning to anger, anger fueling determination.

I'd told no one what I was planning. I would, but only if I had to. I still wasn't entirely sure how I'd use these bodies, but I knew they had a part to play.

At least I had Albion's support for my leadership, and that of the other Sorcerers. I'd spent the evening after Kel's death explaining Ulric's condition and announced my intention to take his place. No one objected. They had expected it. The next day, while Rowan was gone, we'd discussed tactics, ways to get into the city, and how to get me to Severn so I could finish what he had started. He may not have been accepting challengers, but he was bound by law to complete any he issued. If I defeated him, the burden of Tyrea would be mine.

And so I would finish it. I would do anything it took to get in and hunt Severn down while he remained weak. No law, moral or otherwise, would keep me from using every tool at my disposal to do it.

I owed Kel that much. And my mother, and the siblings I'd never known, and every person Severn had destroyed in his quest for power.

A rough chunk of rock snagged on the bandage wrapped around my left hand, pulling me back to the present. I took the wrapping off and flexed my fingers. Morea had done a good job setting the bones, and in the wake of battle my magic seemed even more willing than it normally was to heal me. I'd never felt anything like the power that had flowed through me as I faced Severn. I only hoped it would happen again when I needed it.

I sensed Rowan before I saw her. Relief flooded me, but I maintained my distance. She had been right when she ended things. I couldn't afford to be distracted.

But gods, it was good to know she was safe.

"You're back," I said. "Any trouble?"

She shook her head. "I saw Cassia. Gave her your letter. She's going to speak to the elders again."

"Thank you. Was she…" I sighed. "Of course she was."

Rowan nodded. "Shattered. But glad I went, that you chose to send me."

I picked up another rock and tossed it aside. Focusing on the physical was a relief after a day of thinking, and far more feeling than I had ever desired.

When I looked back at Rowan, a lock of bright hair had fallen over one eye as she looked down at her feet, lost in her thoughts or sadness. I could never bear to see her that way, but fixing it was beyond my power.

"Are you all right?" she asked, and shook her head, answering her own question. "Of course not. You just—you seem different. If you wanted to talk about it, we could." She looked at the bodies, and seemed to be judging how best to approach my apparent insanity. "About anything, I mean."

"I'd rather not. I'm fine." My voice sounded as drained as my muscles felt. Flat and emotionless. It was a relief, really. No shameful tears or outbursts. Just nothing.

She offered a half-hearted smile and let the matter drop. She'd have expected that answer. What else would I have said? That I felt nothing now except a cold determination to see Severn dead, no matter what sacrifices it meant for me or my future? That a part of me had died when I ended Kel's life?

Talking would do nothing to heal that.

Rowan turned her attention back to the bodies, and her nose wrinkled. "Should I ask what you're doing out here, though?"

"I don't know whether you want to know." I let the next rock drop from my hands. "But you should. You should know what's going to happen in the next few days."

She brightened at that. "You can use me?"

I tore my attention away from the bodies. It wasn't easy. My magic was becoming excited, as though it sensed it would have a chance to act soon. I'd never experienced this around a dead body before. Perhaps it was only because my intentions changed. Whatever it was, it horrified me even as it gave me hope.

I wiped my hands on my shirt and wished I'd thought to bring something to wash with. At least I hadn't touched the bodies yet. "Can we sit?"

Rowan chose a spot on a log that left plenty of space for me to join her. I did so, but left room between us. No more closeness. No more stolen touches and awkward smiles.

"I wasn't happy with the idea of you leaving to deliver that message," I said. "But I'm glad you did."

"So am I."

"Not just for Cassia's sake. It helped me realize that you're safer when you're not here. I want you to leave again."

One dark-red eyebrow arched. "Excuse me?"

I shouldn't have sat. I needed to pace, not to be forced to meet her stormy gray eyes. But I did face her. I owed her that. "I need you to leave. Go back to your family near the border if you want to. Belleisle would be better. Take Florizel, go far from Luid. As soon as possible."

Her mouth opened, but she didn't seem to be able to find the words she wanted. She frowned. "No."

I'd known she wouldn't make it easy. I hardened my voice. "It's not a request. Unless you want to swear loyalty to Severn, I'm in charge here. I'm ordering you to go."

She glared at me. "I haven't sworn loyalty to any Tyrean king."

I threw my hands up. "Then go to Darmid. Anywhere but here."

She glared at me, any trace of gentleness gone. "Why are you doing this?"

"Because I need to focus on this battle. I can't be worried about you, about where you are and whether you're hurt."

She narrowed her eyes. "So you think I'm too much of a distraction?"

"It's not that." I rested my forehead in my hands. "I just lost my best friend. Even though I know that you and I aren't supposed to mean as much to each other as we..." Emotion threatened to overcome me, but I held it back. "I can't lose you. You need to be where you're safe."

She was silent for a while, then rested a hand on my shoulder. "We did need to talk. You're right. You can't worry about me."

Relief flooded me, and I looked up. "Thank you."

She smiled sadly. "I'm not leaving, though. I've been training for this. I'm not a warrior, but I can fight. I'm more in control of my magic than I've ever been, and I've learned my limits. You need me here."

I hated how that pleased me. Somewhere beneath my good intentions to keep her safe, I knew I needed her. And wanted her. "You understand how dangerous this is?"

She looked toward the bodies. "I do. When we met, when I agreed to go with you to find a cure for my binding, I told you I wanted adventure. At the time, I didn't know what that meant. I expected it to be exciting and interesting, but didn't realize how much it would cost, or how many mistakes I'd make along the way."

"We both made mistakes," I said quietly.

Her smile was pained. "And then I fell in love with you. I guess that was a mistake, too, but I can't say it's one I regret. I've accepted that our paths aren't taking us in the same direction."

Those words cut deeper than I'd have expected. "Have you?"

Our eyes met. I wondered whether mine were as filled with sadness as hers were. "I'm trying. My mind understands it, even if my heart doesn't. I'm thankful for what we've had, but I don't want to stand in the way of your destiny."

I wish you would.

She nodded as though I'd agreed. "So what I'm asking now is that you offer me the same consideration. I have a gift, Aren. You've said so yourself. It's mine to use as I wish. When this is all over, I'll make my own adventures. But for now, I want to use my gifts to help you. To defeat Severn. To set things right. If you can't let me do that..." Her words trailed off, and she shrugged. "I guess that says a lot, too. What am I to you?"

I looked at her again, trying to forget what I expected to see. A part of me still thought of her as the girl who'd found an injured eagle by the side of the road and nearly killed herself trying to save him. Courageous, but a victim of her circumstances and naive about the world outside her home town. Curious, but afraid. Open-minded, but trapped in her people's beliefs. I'd fallen in love with that person, with her determination and her courage and her willingness to love me in return.

The woman who sat with me now was still Rowan, but she was *more*. Fierce, defiant, certain of her course. She'd saved my life in more ways than she knew, and I'd done my best to return the favor—not because I owed it to her, but because my life wasn't worth much without this strange, generous, often illogical person in it.

"I don't know," I admitted. "What I feel for you terrifies me as nothing else ever has. Love isn't what I expected it to be." For some reason, the unicorn came to mind. Nothing like the stories, but wilder and stronger, a thousand times more real. "If you want to stay and fight, I won't try to stop you. I can't say I know what you are to me now. I know what I want you to be."

She closed her eyes, but not before I saw the tears forming there. "Please don't."

"You should hear this." I took a deep breath. "You would be the perfect queen, Rowan. Not in the ceremonial sense, but as a co-ruler. We balance each other. We could have done great things for Tyrea together."

She took a shaky breath. "If not for my magic, right?"

I laughed, though it wasn't at all amusing. "Without your magic, neither of us would be here." I tucked a lock of her wild hair behind her ear. I never could resist touching it.

"So I stay? Should I report to Albion?"

"No." I resisted the urge to put my arms around her. She would stay. That didn't change anything else. "It would be easier for both of us if you did, but I think if we want to win this, I need you to stay with me."

"For now." Barely a whisper.

"For now," I agreed. "Unless what I need to do bothers you, in which case you are still free to go. I won't have you hunted down as a deserter if you decide to take me up on my first offer and flee entirely." I kept my tone light, but my stomach clenched. She didn't know. I'd never told her. I wouldn't blame her if she turned away, horrified. Everyone else did.

She sat up straight. "Why?"

I'd heard that question from her more times than I could remember, and had never had so much trouble deciding how to answer.

The body closest to us twitched as my magic reached out to it. Rowan turned her head slowly, eyes wide. "Did you see that?"

My power rushed to fill me, and seemed to anticipate my commands. Never had anything come so easily to me, and elation battled with disgust as the body lifted a hand and opened its eyes. Nausea gripped my stomach. A strange effect for magic, but not unheard of.

Rowan froze, but her lips moved. "Please tell me you know what's going on."

"I'm controlling it," I said. "Just wait. I haven't done this in a long time, or on anything this large."

I fixed my full attention to the body. Though my magic followed my directions, it took more effort than I expected to make the rotting flesh obey my command to sit up, and more still to make him stand. The flesh felt heavy, as though rooted to the earth. Rowan gasped as the dead man got his feet under him, then straightened. Sweat broke out on my face from the effort, and a wave of dizziness set white stars blooming at the edges of my vision. Heaviness entered my muscles, dulling external sensation even as a deep ache filled me. I held on. My magic rushed out more quickly than I could replenish it from the ambient magic, and I pulled back.

The body remained standing, but stopped moving. Its jaw hung slack, giving it an expression of bored disbelief. The stomach pushed out, muscles flaccid.

Rowan remained perfectly still.

"It's not going to hurt you," I said, hoping that was her greatest concern.

Her face turned slowly toward me, though her gaze remained fixed on the corpse. "You..."

"Yes." I wiped the sweat from my face. The body was still drawing on my magic, but it seemed to be the raising that made me feel ill.

That made me feel death in my own body, I realized. This had been a small experiment, but what might happen if I tried to raise an army? If the effects compounded, I could see why people thought the gods cursed those who attempted this. It would kill me, I had no doubt. Or worse.

"I see," she said, surprisingly calm. Her brow furrowed. "So it's like a puppet? It's not aware of what's happening to it?"

I nodded. "I would know if there were a mind in there. It's just a body. If his spirit still exists, it's not here." It was flesh, obedient and unaware, and nothing more.

Her shoulders relaxed. "It's still a little unnerving, isn't it?"

I laughed. She looked at me as though I'd lost my mind.

"I'm sorry," I said. "That's the most beautiful understatement I've ever heard." She wasn't going to run. She didn't hate me—at least, not yet. Maybe that would change after she'd had time to think about it.

I pulled my magic back further, and the corpse sagged in the middle. I stood him up again, and a sound like groaning, incoherent speech bubbled from his slack mouth.

Rowan squeaked and scrambled to duck behind the log. "Aren!"

"It's just air escaping. He's not trying to talk." Even my heart had jumped at the noise. This was going to take some getting used to. I could only imagine how it would look to other people.

The corpse's hand fell off. "That was nearly chewed off already," I said. "They're not all going to do that."

The fingers twitched against the forest floor. Rowan turned and threw up.

"Are you still with me?" I asked.

She nodded and wiped her mouth on her sleeve. "I don't understand what the plan is, though."

"Distraction. We're going to attack the city, engage all of Severn's soldiers and get him alone so I can finish his challenge. I just hope others will agree to the plan. These bodies will be a help, once I prove this is possible." I let her think it over as I raised a second body. This one's lips had pulled back in a dreadful sneer, and his left eye had sunk completely into his skull. I'd hoped it would be easier the second time, but found that nothing changed. The ache returned, and a feeling that my blood was turning to muck in my veins, slow and dark.

I could do it though. *This* was my natural gift, not mind-control. I'd just been ignoring it most of my life.

The first body remained standing with very little help from me as I worked on the second, and though the drain on my magic increased, it replenished quickly. *If only it would leap to defend me against the effects of playing with death.*

I set the two bodies walking. They lurched forward, off-balance, arms swaying, but held upright by my will and my power. Memories of the first time it had happened came flooding back. My dog's empty eyes staring into nothing, her body ignoring verbal commands that she'd known when alive, but responding to everything I told her through magic.

Like a puppet. Exactly right.

The bodies kept walking when I slowed the release of magic, and even continued to obey me without draining my magic further. I looked over the remaining corpses. I could manage this many, as long as I took time between to restore my magic and my health. There weren't enough here to make an army, though, or even a distraction on the level I wanted. Certainly not enough to use as a shield.

"What's happening?" Rowan asked. "You look terrible, like I haven't seen you since Darmid."

"It's nothing. Just feeling a little ill."

I let the bodies lie with their companions. I couldn't take them to camp with me, and there was still much to do back there before we could make a solid plan of attack.

She watched them until they lay still, then turned to me. "So what's next?"

"Explain this idea to people who won't want to hear about it. Ask Morea for something to keep me healthy while I do this. Figure out how, exactly, to use fewer than two dozen bodies to divert an entire city guard." I sighed. It was a good idea, but the obstacles were too great. "At least we have this as an option."

I clenched my fists. The answer was there. I just needed more help to find it.

"If it's distraction you want, I know someone else who will help." Rowan nodded back toward camp. "Ruby came back with me, and I already promised she could join us if we attacked. Send her in. She doesn't care if she comes out. You have nothing to lose."

"You're brilliant." If we sent the dragon into the eastern end of the city first, where the nobles lived in their massive homes, they would demand a swift and impressive defense from the palace. It wouldn't be enough on its own, but it would take some of the pressure off of the front gate, and neatly divide Severn's forces.

Rowan picked up a rock and set it down on top of the body I'd raised and stepped quickly away. "I guess we should cover these guys for the night, if you don't want them eaten by morning."

I wanted to kiss her then, in spite of the ghastly surroundings. Never had I expected such acceptance from her, or from anyone.

Instead, I picked up a rock and helped.

～

MOREA MET us before we made it all the way back to camp.

"I was going to send Florizel to find you, but I was afraid the guards would shoot her down if she tried to leave," she said, and I thought I detected a hint of reproach in my cousin's voice. "Your father is awake."

"Is he speaking coherently?" Rowan asked.

"He's better. Demanding his potion, but he insists that I prepare a new batch in front of him each time. He memorized the formula, even if he understands nothing about what's proving to be a difficult reaction. He makes damned sure I only put what he wants in it." She seemed to be trying not to show her irritation. "I think he's wary of me slipping something dangerous in there. He still only took half of it. I tried to get my father in to talk some sense into him, but Ulric won't speak to his own brother. He's ranting about everyone stealing his power."

"I guess sending Albion in isn't an option then," Rowan said, almost to herself.

"He hasn't trusted anyone since his capture," I told Morea, "and now his mind has slipped further."

She frowned. "The damage is terrible. I've never seen magic do this to a person. He's coherent. Convincing. But completely wrong."

This would be problematic. If he could convince people he was fit to command, if not to fight, it would undermine my authority. The others would surely be opposed to my plan to use the bodies. If he offered them an alternative... "I'll speak to him."

Morea twisted the ruby ring she wore on the first finger of her right hand. "I'll wait outside in case you need me."

"I will, too," Rowan added.

I made my way to Ulric's tent and stepped inside. My father opened his eyes, squinting in spite of the dim light. His appearance had improved slightly, but he still reminded me far too much of the bodies in the woods.

"Where've you been?" he demanded.

"I have things to take care of now. Per your orders, I'm in charge. We're going to get into that city as soon as possible. Severn is weak now. We can take him."

"Your friend is dead. Nox's lover."

"I know. I appreciate the reminder, thank you." I wouldn't show emotion. Not now.

He saw through me. "Aren, listen to me. You can't make this personal. Carry on as we have been. Remain calm, rational."

I shot him a look that would have made anyone else quiver. He merely gazed back at me, calm and stern.

"Even after everything you've lost?" I asked. "After my mother, after everything else Severn has taken from you, you can still claim this isn't personal?"

His wrinkled face contorted into an expression of distaste. "It's personal for all of us, but that can't be what drives your actions. When have I let emotion overtake me? When have I let my desire for revenge dictate my next move? Your sister had the same problem, and only the gods know what's happening to her right now."

"She didn't go for revenge. She went for us."

"Still personal." He wiped his nose on the sleeve of his shirt.

"Then what do you propose?" I asked. I couldn't take much more of his hesitation. "We wait? Let him get stronger and attack us again? You're practically dead. We grow weaker every day, not stronger."

Ulric's jaw quivered. "You can't attack the city now."

"I can. And I will, before we lose our chance."

"Aren, this is foolishness."

"I raised bodies." The chill in my voice surprised me. No emotion. No qualms or regrets. "We'll use them, use every bit of magic available to us, and every non-magical person willing to join us."

Ulric's breath hitched, and he pushed his blanket back. "You can't do this. Attacking, yes, but only when we're ready. And not the bodies. Not that."

"I'll ask Morea to help with the ill effects. You weren't wrong about that, but I'll get around it."

"But think of—"

"What, my reputation? I don't care. So the people will hate me. So I won't be king." I crossed my arms across my chest. "There are worse things."

He tried to sit up, and collapsed back onto the bed. "You fool. It's not only that. We're talking about something that is wrong on every level imaginable, and you—"

"Father, please." I crouched so I could speak more quietly. "I refuse to take advice on morals from a man who killed as many as you did on your journey to the throne. I know about your siblings. I know how you've lived your life, how you've treated your family while you let the world think of you as a good man. What I'm doing is no worse. I'm doing this to save Tyrea. I'm just going to be more open about the costs."

"You're acting out of your own anger and grief, not out of anyone else's best interests." His voice rasped out of him, but filled the tent. "At least be honest about that."

I stood again. "Fine. I'm angry. Severn has used me, done harm to me, killed people I cared about and tried to do the same to others. He wants to turn Tyrea into something it was never meant to be, and he'll take down as many other countries and people as he thinks he needs to in his quest for power. He holds my sister captive, he wants Rowan dead, he tried to kill you and nearly did the same to me. Again." My voice remained calm, though my rage threatened to boil to the surface. "And my best friend, who was more family to me than you will ever be, is dead because of him. So yes, I'm far beyond angry. I am going into that city to finish the challenge. He is going to die. And then the throne will be yours, should you be fit to keep it."

"And if I'm not?" His face went slack, and his eyes lost their focus. "I can't... it's so much. The cost of it."

I felt nothing for the wretched old creature next to me. "Drink your damned potion," I told him. "Get strong enough to fake it until Nox finds you a proper cure."

"Aren!" His eyes cleared again. "You are relieved of your duties. You will leave off this plan of yours. You will help me do this the proper way, or you will find yourself imprisoned, and—"

I laughed. "You have no authority. You're not the king anymore, remember? And I'm in charge here. You're certainly not strong enough to stop me. If it comes to it I'll challenge you in the proper way, but that seems a waste of time."

He glared at me. "I've made mistakes. I don't intend to let you repeat them. Tell Morea to bring me my potion. We'll see what happens."

I left without answering and motioned for Morea to follow me to my tent.

"He's not making sense," I told her. "He's getting worked up, and I'm afraid he's not going to recover in this state. Is there any way you can make sure he stays asleep? Just until he's feeling more himself." In truth, it wasn't his recovery I was concerned about.

It was his interference.

She rubbed her thumb over the top of her ring. For the first time I noticed a tiny gold hinge on the side. A Potioner and a poisoner. I wondered what else Xaven hadn't told me about her training.

"I could slip something in there without him seeing," she said, "if that's your order."

"It is. Thank you."

She bowed at the waist.

"You don't have to do that. I'm not the king. I'm not sure what I am."

She smiled, but kept her gaze on the ground. "Knowing as I do how Severn took the throne, I do not acknowledge him as king. No one here in camp does. Your father is not fit to rule. Who does that leave?"

"Thank you, Morea."

After she left, I sat and put my feet up. Ulric had to get better. I was in no way prepared to take this responsibility on permanently. Only until I saw the battle won.

When a shadow appeared against the side of the tent, I thought it might be Rowan coming to check on me. Instead, a man's voice spoke. "Sir, there's someone here to see you. From outside."

I went to the door. "From Luid?"

"No. The other way."

One of the men who had been on guard duty that day stood with one hand clamped around Laelana's arm. I went cold at the sight of her, a ghost I'd hoped we'd left in the past. She wore dirty clothing and no boots on her filthy, scratched-up feet, and trembled with wide-eyed fear. A cut marred her left cheek, shadowed by a bruise. I thanked the guard and stepped aside to let Laelana in.

"Find Griselda," I told the man who had brought her. He dashed off, and I motioned for Rowan to join us in the tent.

I offered Laelana a drink, and she refused. "Later. Listen first." Her voice was frantic, wild as her eyes. "You have to stop them. Or help them. They'll all die."

"Who?" Rowan asked.

"Goff! He got tired of waiting for you people to do something, and he's taken our people toward Luid." She turned as Griselda and Qurwin entered, then looked back at me. "All who were capable of fighting, at least. They're going to try to get into the city."

"Idiot," Qurwin muttered. "We should have seen this coming. He was forever pestering us to act, to move, to share a brilliant plan. He seemed to have latched on to this idea of his people as fighters."

"It's not just that," Laelana said. "Our scouts—"

"Your thieves?" I asked, to clarify.

She nodded. "They had an encounter with travelers we didn't realize were messengers for Severn. When we went through their things, we found a message ordering his troops back from the borderlands. We intercepted that one, but there will be more. Goff decided time was running out."

He wasn't wrong, I thought, and felt as though the earth was tilting beneath me. If Severn's troops made it to the city before us, we were finished.

Griselda turned to me. "What do you want us to do?"

Laelana dropped to her knees. "Please. They'll never get in alive. If you hurry, you can catch them."

I stepped away. "Was this the plan, Laelana? They act, and hope that we'll be forced to jump in?" I couldn't see any other reasoning behind Goff's plan.

"Please," she whispered. "I wouldn't have come if he'd gone alone. But I'm responsible for these people."

"As I am for mine," I said coldly. "Qurwin, have our horses saddled."

He darted out, and Griselda followed.

Laelana slumped further onto the floor. "Thank you. You are too—"

"We're not joining them," I said. "This is Goff's fight, and it will be his loss. I won't sacrifice my forces to save a fool and those who follow him."

Tears streamed down Laelana's cheeks. "You can't just let them die. Save them, and they'll help you, I swear."

There was a time when I might have cared. *Don't let it be personal*, my father had said. *Don't let emotion rule*. This once, I would take his advice. My heart became a stone, and the turbulent thoughts I'd struggled with since Kel's death calmed.

"They're no good to me," I said.

Rowan drew a sharp breath, but said nothing.

More useful dead than alive, whispered a dark, slithering voice that came from the very depths of my mind. I ignored it. I wouldn't allow myself to think that way, even if the truth of it appealed to me on some horrifying level. But I also wouldn't sacrifice my own forces for Goff and his foolish, undertrained and overly-optimistic excuses for warriors. They'd made the choice to follow him instead of Ulric, and they would pay for it.

"We'll head out there and see if we meet them," I continued, "but I'll promise no more than that."

Laelana nodded. "Thank you."

She didn't follow us out of the tent.

Rowan pulled me aside. "Aren, what are you doing? This isn't you. I thought—"

"Please don't," I said. "I'm doing what I have to. Don't complicate it. Not now."

"Should we fly ahead in case we can catch them?" she asked as she mounted Florizel. Her lips pressed into a tight line as she looked down at me.

"No. I won't risk either of you for this. At this point we'll be witnesses to what happens, and if we can't stop them we'll hopefully get some idea of what Severn has in store for us. Gods willing, Goff will come to his senses and retreat before we see anything."

She gave me a hard look, but didn't argue.

I supposed no one would dare.

~

I LEFT Albion behind to watch over the camp and took Rowan, Griselda, and Qurwin with me to the spot where Ulric and I had stood to watch the city, cutting through the woods. Heading straight for the road would have been faster, but I wasn't going to leave my best people exposed for longer than I had to.

Goff's group of around seventy hadn't yet reached the river bridge when we arrived at the top of the hill that overlooked the plain. We hung back in the woods, but had an excellent view of the land below and the city gates at the end of the broad road.

Rowan and Florizel could have caught them if I'd allowed them to fly ahead, though that didn't mean Goff would have listened. I didn't give the order for Rowan to try to reach them now. The sad little band of rebels were too far out into the plain. They'd have been spotted by the city watch already.

Only a few were on horseback. The others marched out of

time, several straggling, others veering off to the side and back. I assumed they were nervous and not drunk, but it could have been either. From what I'd seen of Goff, he would be the sort to let his men drink excessively to life, to battle, to their foolish ideals the night before they marched on the city. Perhaps they drank to him and made him feel like a proper leader, much good it would do him now.

They marched on. Goff rode at the front, unmistakable in his fur cape. They carried no banner, and showed no indication of what their intentions might be.

"What will happen?" Rowan asked. Florizel shuffled nervously.

"They'll be allowed to approach the gate and state their intentions, or we'll see an attack from the city that will stop them before they get there," I said. "Either way, they won't be allowed in."

"There's still time to stop them," Rowan said, her voice stretched thin.

"No," I said as I watched the city wall. "There's not."

The gates opened, and seven riders emerged. All wore silver armor over white, indicating their status as Sorcerers, and rode black horses, save for the one in the middle. He, the largest of the group, wore black and rode a white beast that dwarfed the others. Though they were too far off for us to see details, I knew that his face was scarred, and that the horse's appearance was even more horrifying up close. Great tusks curved up from the creature's mouth, and its eyes burned. I'd spent years avoiding the stables where Wardrel housed the tusker, the one Patience had called the devil horse.

The seven riders flew over the empty road, and in moments had left the outer city's buildings behind them as they charged over the bridge.

"Run, you idiots," I muttered. Curious as I was about what Severn had to throw at them, my only desire at that moment was to see the rebels turn away and flee toward the hills.

A few hesitated and fell behind, but none broke ranks. Goff held both hands up in the air. Calling for peace, but too late.

Florizel's tail swished nervously. "Rowan, there's a child."

Rowan raised a hand to shield her eyes, then turned to me. "Is it Patience? Tell me he wouldn't let her go along for this."

I turned my attention away from Wardrel and back to the rebels. A few smaller figures walked among them. One in a black, hooded coat moved with a slight limp.

My stomach clenched. I hadn't expected Goff to be such a fool as to take children. I should have known better.

"What shall we do, Aren?" Griselda asked.

"We can't go in without giving ourselves away," I said. "I don't know what else is waiting behind those walls."

Rowan's eyes widened, then narrowed into a sharp glare. "You can't let her die," she said.

Before she could dig in her heels to tell Florizel to take off, I leaned over and grabbed her arm. "Don't sacrifice yourself," I told her. She tried to pull away. "Rowan. This is an order." I leaned closer and spoke more quietly. "Not a suggestion from a friend. Not a plea from whatever I once was to you. You wanted to stay and be a part of this. Let me do my job."

She wrenched her arm away, and I let go. She glared at me again. I didn't care. I preferred her angry and alive to what would happen if I let her go.

Wardrel raised his massive sword high over his head and pointed it at the intruders. His tusker reared, and the seven charged. One stopped and raised his hands overhead, then thrust them forward. Nothing seemed to happen, and then Goff fell from his horse. Others lost their hats, their weapons, or their footing in that great blast of wind. Goff staggered to his feet and ran ahead, sword drawn.

Another of Wardrel's Sorcerers hung back and pulled something like a large, round stone from thin air. He threw it, and the object hurtled through the air farther and with greater speed than would have been possible without magic. The Sorcerer to his left appeared to be helping with that, directing with his hands. The item hit Goff in the face. His head snapped back, and he crumpled.

And then the groups met in a clash of weapons and raised

voices. Many of Goff's people tried to flee, only to be taken down by Wardrel's massive sword. Others lost their lives to flying rocks, shocks of energy like lightning, or the jaws of the massive, hairless dog one of the Sorcerers transformed into.

I lost sight of Patience, and only found her again when she ducked under a gust of wind that blew her hood back, revealing her bright, pale hair. She fell to one knee, head down and bow held to her chest. When the wind was gone, she darted forward and grabbed the reins of Goff's confused mount. She climbed into the saddle.

Rowan released a breath as Patience turned the horse toward the road. She, at least, would escape.

Wardrel's white tusker screamed a challenge. Patience's horse broke for the hills, nearly spilling her from the saddle. She held on, though, as it raced toward the road, nearing the bottom of the hill. Patience looked over her shoulder.

She hadn't seen us.

Beyond her, the battle went on. Goff's folk were being slaughtered. I hoped the others were taking note of what magic Severn had at his disposal, because I couldn't tear my attention away from the tiny girl on the big, brown horse. She'd almost reached safety when she glanced back, then hauled on the reins to slow the animal.

She kept her balance as the horse spun and reared, and she clung close to its neck as they raced back into the fray, straight toward the monster who had slain her mother. The sword she carried, narrow but almost as long as one of her legs, bounced as she was nearly unseated. She slipped to one side, and hauled herself back up.

My stomach clenched, and I decided. I would have to fly to get down there quickly enough to do anything, and it would leave me at a disadvantage once I got there. But this was my fault.

If I'd let Rowan go, we could have stopped them.

Griselda placed a hand on my arm before I had a chance to dismount. "Don't, please. We've already lost your father. Don't make this easy for Severn."

Below us, someone put a blade through the dog's throat. One Sorcerer down.

Wardrel continued to go after those who fled, cutting them down like wheat under a threshing blade. If he saw Patience riding toward him, he paid her no mind. When her arrows flew at him, they might have been nothing more than flies buzzing about his head. The girl was a decent shot, but the arrows bounced off of his armor.

Florizel reared. "Rowan, get down." She looked to me. The whites of her eyes showed, but she stood with her hooves planted firmly and confidently. "Aren. You can't let Rowan go, but you can let me."

Rowan slipped to the ground, but said, "We both could, if we can get in and out before—"

Florizel stamped a hoof. "No. I'm so much faster alone, or with just the girl. Aren, please."

She spoke to me as her herd leader. She'd listen if I told her to stay.

I nodded. "Do what you wish."

I offered a hand to pull Rowan up behind me on my horse. She sat stiffly, unwilling to lean into me.

A hard shiver twitched the muscles of Florizel's flanks, and she stamped a forehoof against the ground. "I can be brave again."

Patience continued to loose her arrows against her enemy. One took the tusker in the rump, and it shied. Wardrel held on, but Patience had his attention. He turned on her, bloody-bladed sword at the ready.

He wouldn't recognize her. She was only one of many of his victims. But I imagined his grin, heard his laugh ringing through my mind as he lifted his sword in anticipation of his next kill. He loved this. Killing was fun, and fear was thrilling, but he'd always found a challenger always so much more satisfying than a passive victim. Fighting was his great joy and the course he'd chosen to channel what magic he had.

A small girl as a challenger was far better than none at all.

Florizel pushed off from the ground and flew faster than I'd ever seen her go. Unladen, she moved with the speed and grace of a hawk. She swept down over the hill, climbed, and dove toward Wardrel.

Rowan's fingers gripped the back of my shirt, pulling tight as she watched.

Wardrel's eyes never left Patience as she rode at him. The tusker saw Florizel, though. The beast let out another scream and reared to paw at the air with massive hooves. Florizel turned at the last moment and avoided the horse as Wardrel was thrown. The tusker turned its rear toward Patience's horse and kicked out as it passed. The blow to its barrel sent the smaller creature crashing to the ground, and Patience flew a good distance before she hit the dirt.

Riderless, the tusker continued to rear and scream. Wardrel pushed himself up, but turned his back on the beast. He stalked toward Patience.

I barely felt Rowan's arms as they tightened around my ribs, her anger apparently forgotten for the moment. Though my heart raced and my leg muscles itched to urge my horse forward, my mind was on the battlefield, not with my body.

Florizel landed and danced away from the tusker. She screamed, but not at him. At Patience. The girl looked at her, took a step toward safety, then shook her head.

Wardrel threw his head back, laughing. He spoke, though I couldn't hear his words. Patience drew her blade and ran at him, hair flying behind her. Wardrel grabbed her by the back of her jacket and hauled her high off the ground. The tip of his blade rose toward her, tilted up, ready to catch her the moment he let her fall.

Not yet, though. He was enjoying it too much.

Florizel leaped into the air. The tusker reared and lashed out with his forehooves as she passed over him. He overbalanced and lost his footing, stumbling backward into his master, knocking him over.

"No!" Rowan's cry left my ear ringing. I clamped one hand around her forearms to keep her from slipping to the ground and running into the battle.

Patience twisted to the side and hit the ground, followed by

Wardrel. Florizel landed to deliver a kick to his head. Wardrel slashed out with his blade, and a shower of blood fell from the flying horse's flank. Patience's scream of rage echoed over the field as she turned back toward him. He stood, but slowly. Dazed.

Everything happened almost too quickly for me to follow it. Patience darted into Wardrel's shadow, ducked under his arm as he raised it, and thrust upward with her blade, into the unprotected space under his arm. She fled as he crashed to the ground. Florizel limped toward her, and Patience hauled herself up onto her friend's back. Florizel stumbled away with one hind leg held off the ground and tried to push off. Hard as she flapped her wings, she couldn't get into the air without the strength of her legs. She stumbled again and again, and the tusker charged behind her.

"I'm going," I said, and released Rowan's arms. She slid to the ground and I urged my horse forward before anyone could object. We raced down the hill, faster than was safe. I drew my sword.

They'd nearly reached the hill, but the tusker wasn't going to give up the chase. The ground shook beneath his terrible hooves as he drew nearer to them with every step. The whites of Florizel's eyes showed, and her sides heaved with her breath. Blood streamed from her hindquarters, but still she ran.

At the last moment, the tusker turned his attention from them to me. Too late. I drove my sword forward, into the beast's chest. My horse veered to the side as the vicious tusks threatened to gouge into his side. The tusker ran on, and turned to charge back at us. It was several paces before he noticed the metal that pierced his flesh. He stumbled, but kept coming toward us. My horse backed away. The tusker's front legs went out from under him. He lifted his hideous face toward the sky, and collapsed.

I turned toward Wardrel. He lay on his back, still as the earth beneath him, with the hilt of Patience's sword protruding from under his arm. I waited. He didn't move.

The battle was over. The silver-armored Sorcerers, now a group of four, milled about on their horses. They picked up the dog's body and their other fallen member, and they rode back to the gate.

Apparently Wardrel's body would have to be someone else's problem. I rode past it, just to be sure. His eyes stared up at the sky, and when I reached out I sensed nothing in his mind. He was gone, to wherever people like him went when they died.

Like him, or like us?

I considered following the Sorcerers back to the city, calling Griselda and Qurwin down to chase after them and cut down at least that much of Severn's forces. But he wouldn't have sent his best for the rebels. There would be more waiting, perhaps preparing to come after us even now.

I turned my horse and rode back up the hill toward the others.

Rowan had Patience's coat pressed to Florizel's wounded flank. She glanced up at me. "She'll be all right. There's a lot of blood, but I think it looks worse than it is. Nothing Morea can't handle when we get back."

"Where's Patience?"

Rowan nodded to the shade of the forest, where the girl lay under a tree with Griselda tending to her. I dismounted and crouched beside her.

She looked up at me, wary.

"I told you I'd take care of him for you," I said. "You should have waited and trusted me." Glad as I was to see our mutual tormenter dead, it never should have fallen to her to see it done.

She frowned, then winced as Griselda poured water over a deep gash on her leg. "Wanderers don't trust the word of kings or princes. Besides, this was my fight. I owed him. Not you."

I sighed and stood. "If that were how it worked, I'd have to die a hundred times to satisfy everyone who thought they owed me a blade to the heart."

Patience's eye filled with tears. "It's over now, right?"

"For you, it is."

I walked back to the road and looked out over the field that was now dotted with bodies. For me, it was only beginning.

43

ROWAN

I n stories, they always say "there was a battle." They don't speak of the destruction, the families torn apart and lives lost. Innocent or not, any soul leaves a void when it's ripped from the world.

They make it sound necessary. Noble. It may be the former, but there was nothing noble about what I saw that day.

Well after dark, we approached the battlefield again. Aren had muttered something about it being a sad excuse for a battle, but for me it had been enough to make me hope I would never witness another. Too much blood, too much pain. Too many bodies now for us to clean up.

"It's a shame Ches isn't here," Victoria said. She wrapped her hands around the wrists of a woman's body and dragged it toward the woodcutter's sledge someone had brought us from town.

"Why?" Aren asked. "Is he fond of this sort of work?"

"No, he's a historian. Always has taken an interest in military strategy and such things."

"Magical?"

"No."

Aren rolled the body of a skinny young man so he looked up

at the stars. The boy's face was burned half-off, with further lightning-burns radiating from the wound and disappearing into the charred collar of his shirt. "Then he might not have been prepared for this."

Qurwin lifted a heavy man under the armpits, and I took the feet so as not to drag the body over a stony patch of ground and cause more damage. Aren hadn't told everyone why it was so important that we retrieve the bodies and take them to the forest just outside the city, to the edge of what he called the Despair. They had agreed to help, though, probably thinking we were acting out of respect. Laelana had stayed back at camp, but we had plenty of help.

Griselda gagged. "Does anyone know magic to get rid of the smell?"

Another aspect of battle I'd been unprepared for.

"Let's just get this done before the sun rises," Aren said, and walked toward the bridge and the river. "Rowan, help me?"

I didn't speak until we were well away from the others, surrounded only by the few bodies who had died closest to Luid. "You're going to use them, aren't you?"

"Is that a problem?" he asked, speaking in clipped syllables. He didn't look at me, but at the city.

"I don't know." A middle-aged woman lay at my feet, head caved in. It reminded me too much of Kel. I looked away. "I suppose they're not doing anyone much good if they rot here. And I believe you that their spirits are gone. It's just... it's going to be horrible, isn't it? Especially for anyone who knew them. Even those who didn't are going to object."

He frowned. "And?"

I braced myself for his anger. I didn't want to say it, but someone had to. "And I wonder whether this is why you didn't try to stop them. Because they're more useful to you dead than they are alive."

He turned slowly to face me, and the moonlight falling on his face picked out every aspect of his expression in terrible detail. Sorrow, pain, anger. Perhaps for the first time, I saw all of it. The depths of the darkness in him.

"Is that what you think of me?"

I chose my words carefully. "I would have thought it of the Aren I met last autumn. You've changed since then, but I know how angry you are about Kel's death. Anger makes us do things we wouldn't otherwise. Drives us back to old ways, maybe."

"You have no idea how angry I am."

I wished he sounded angry. It would have made more sense than the ice-calm surface he presented.

"I will do anything to bring Severn down," he said. "You know that. But this was Goff's decision. Not mine. If I can use his mistake for good, is that such a terrible thing?"

"That doesn't answer my question. Aren, I'm with you. I will help you get this done. I also believe you want what's best for all of us, and respect you enough to question you if I see you doing things I think you'll regret." My heart fluttered with anxiety as he stared at me. "I just want to understand what we're doing, here."

He sat on the ground, facing the city. "Come here. Please."

I glanced back, saw that the others were still working, and sat next to him.

"Rowan, you've always known I wasn't like you. I don't care about people the way you do. Since we met, I've discovered that I appreciate kindness as I've seen it in you. I admire you, and there's a part of me deep down that needs you. Most of the time I want to be more like you. But right now, with things as they are and the challenge that's before us, I need to rely on other strengths, ones that got me through the years when there was no kindness or mercy in my life. Severn taught me how to get things done no matter what the cost, and he's about to find out just how well I learned my lessons."

A chill passed over me. There was a time when I'd have begged him not to say more, to hide the ugly truths from me. Now, I only waited for him to continue. I wouldn't look away this time.

He glanced back at the bodies. "I can't weep over every death, but I can make their sacrifice matter. I don't always like who or what I am, but right now that doesn't matter. It doesn't matter whether people are angry with me, or whether they question my motives. Even you. I have to do this."

He seemed so alone then, even with me sitting right there. I wanted to touch him, to tell him everything was okay, that no matter what he said or did, nothing would change. But I couldn't. Everything had already changed, and it wasn't my place to comfort him. My heart broke at the realization of how far we'd drifted apart in such a short time.

"Maybe the thought did cross my mind," he said quietly. "Maybe I knew this was the only way to have enough strong bodies to be of any use to us. But they would have died anyway. If I'd sent our people after them, more would have died, and we'd have lost any advantage we had. Now we know at least something of the magic Severn has available to him. And we have soldiers who can't feel pain."

A cold wind blew toward us from the city, carrying away the smell of death. I closed my eyes. Anger and ruthlessness were as much a part of Aren as were his humor, his passion, and his love for me. Seeing him this way and realizing that fact should have made it easier for me to accept our separation, but I found myself drawn to him again. Though this side of him frightened me, it didn't make me love him less. I wasn't sure what that meant for me, except that he'd changed me as much as I had him.

The world is bigger than we know, I thought, *and life far more complex than I will ever understand.*

"Thank you," I said.

He looked at me, surprised. "For what?"

"For being honest. We should get back and help."

He stood and offered me a hand up. "You're not disappointed? Not going to convince me of how wrong and selfish my motives are?"

"No."

"I just told you I considered letting seventy people die because I'm angry about one death." He followed me as I picked my way through the field of bodies.

I stopped, and he nearly ran me over. "Do you *want* me to fight about it?"

"No. I'm just..." A hint of a smile came to his face. "I'm curious."

"There's a switch." I crossed my arms and looked up at him. "Tell me, if Kel were still alive, would you be collecting bodies right now?"

He looked away. "No. I didn't want to use that talent. Ever. I was glad when my father forbade it just a few nights ago. But things have changed."

"Would you have stopped Goff if Kel were alive?"

He considered that question more carefully. "No. Even if I'd tried, he would have gone on. And I wouldn't have sent our people to join him."

"Fine. If nothing has changed except that we now have a better way to get you into the city, I have no reason to be angry." I turned away, but he grabbed my hand and pulled me back.

"You mean that?"

"A few months ago, I'd have been horrified." I couldn't help reaching out to touch his face. He shivered as my fingers trailed over his cheek, and I let my hand drop to my side. "Back then I'd have wanted you to make decisions based on what I thought was right. And that would have been wrong of me. Aren, I love you. But you're not me, and I'm not you. We have to live our own lives, and I'm not going to judge you for what you do with yours. I know you meant it when you said you want to use your powers more wisely and for the good of Tyrea. Has that changed?"

"No. I think this is the right thing to do. It's just that everyone else I've ever met disagrees."

"They don't know you the way I do."

"Thank you." He almost kissed me then. I saw it in his eyes, the way he leaned forward ever so slightly. But he didn't. Instead, he turned to examine the flat, perfectly round rock that lay on the ground near the woman's body.

"This doesn't mean I'll let you get away with just anything," I added.

"I know. I chose my adviser well."

I joined him in looking at the stone. "Someone was throwing these, right? They did a lot of damage."

"They did." He squinted at it, crouched, and laid a hand on its side. "But this is interesting." He took out his knife and dug into the side of the rock, pulling out a soft, cream-colored chunk.

I smelled it. "Cheese? They killed someone with cheese?"

"It is. And they did." He wiped the knife clean and frowned. "Why might that be?"

"It worked."

"It's more than that, though. These men were sent out to defend the city. Every one of them used magic to do so. If they're not the best Severn could send, they're at least among the most capable. And yet the best this one could come up with was..." He trailed off, but I didn't interrupt his thoughts.

Not until I had one of my own. "You said he was gathering magical talent from all over Tyrea. People from the provinces wouldn't have developed their skills to prepare for battle."

"No. They'd be using their magic for farming, for trades, and caring for their families. They're like Victoria. They might be strong, but they've probably channeled their magic into one skill for so long that they can't learn anything new, and they have to improvise. Conjuring—actually, calling objects from elsewhere— is a rare skill, but this Sorcerer obviously never learned to broaden the skill beyond his work."

"So that's good, right? If this is what Severn has to send against us, we have a better chance of winning."

"Maybe." He started toward the largest body left on the field. No one had yet come for Wardrel.

Armor clanked as he rolled the giant over and pulled a thin sword from beneath one arm, where nothing had protected the massive man from a determined little girl.

Aren's jaw tightened as he observed his dead brother. "Make sure they bring him, but have him set away from the others. I don't want to look at him until I have to." He walked away.

"Where are you going?"

He waited for me to catch up. "I need to talk to Ruby and make space in camp for her. Then to Morea about fixing a potion for me, and about what else we might do for Ulric. We're going to get my father better, and we're going to ride into the city to defeat Severn, find Nox, and put the proper king back on the throne." His eyes turned to look past me, at the city. "I don't want it. Not yet."

44

NOX

Severn's recovery was nothing short of astonishing. With my potion bolstering his magic and his health, his pain eased and he returned to full health within a day. Much as I'd have liked to mess up the formula and have done with him, he called someone in to taste everything that he ate or drank, my potion included. The young man knew what effect the potion was supposed to bring on, and would notice if it were off. So I bided my time and used the correct ingredients when I made a new batch, adding only what would be beneficial.

I found myself with freedom to move around the palace as I pleased, though I always felt as though someone was watching. Not Myk, of course. Another name on the list. Another loss, if a small one, that Severn needed to pay for.

I had freedom to work on my own projects, though finding motivation was difficult now that I knew my journey to the city had been in vain. Still, I wouldn't waste the time and resources I had. And if my path had taken a turn, well, I wouldn't run from that. Not after everything I'd already been through.

I had to keep up appearances during the day following Severn's return, and used the time to test improvements on his potion. The other Potioners stole glances, but seemed generally less interested in me than I'd worried they would be. After they left I worked through the night, and near dawn I finished my potion to block magic from my mind.

I suspected it would work well enough to keep Severn from sensing my grief when we met again, but I'd still need to be extremely cautious. It had the side-effect of making me feel closed off and slow-witted, but it would have to do.

I bottled the translucent, brown dragon-egg potion and left it beneath my workstation. I'd take a dose if Severn requested me. Otherwise, I'd just have to be careful to guard my thoughts as Aren had taught me. Enemies could be lurking anywhere, and I'd need to stay sharp.

Dawn came, turning the sky to the west pink. I tried not to think about the fact that Kel wasn't enjoying that sunrise.

All I wanted was time to sleep, and to grieve. There was more work to be done, though. I forced myself to work when the other Potioners arrived, though I sneaked a nap in my room around mid-day and indulged in another after supper. I returned to the lamp-lit workroom long after the palace slept.

The rest of that night, I planned and experimented until I had my method of attack. Based on what Rowan had told me about her binding, and what she and Ulric had said about whatever they'd been given in Darmid to temporarily quell their magic, I knew I could do something to harm Severn. The problem was that it seemed any permanent solution—either binding or whatever they had offered to Rowan in Darmid—had required submission. A subject had to consent, or be too young to object.

Still, I had my idea. If I couldn't bind his magic, I could keep him from gaining more. And that, I had learned from Aren's experiences in Darmid, could be dangerous indeed.

I very much liked the idea of Severn being vulnerable, whether it be to poison or a blade to the heart. I'd take whatever chance I got. I would have no way to test the potion even to see how it tasted, as several of its components would make it poisonous to anyone without magic to combat those effects. But my deepest instincts told me it would work.

It had to.

Focusing on that made things easier. It kept me from thinking about Kel, or worrying about what might be happening out in the forest. When I was wrapped up in my work, I couldn't think about any of that. There was only the feeling of the plants' powers, my instincts drawing me into the magic as I hummed over my work, the certainty that I was fulfilling my purpose.

The other Potioners filed into the room early in the morning. Still no sign of Sara. I nodded to them, and kept working. No breakfast for me, no conversation. The room and the people in it might as well not have existed. I was so wrapped up in my work that they could have vanished for all I cared.

When I finished, I found that the room had grown brighter. Midday. My stomach groaned and my eyelids drooped.

"Got something good there?" my table-mate asked. "Something for his highness? You look like shit."

"It is for him," I told her, and held back an exhausted chuckle. "This could change everything."

I'd only managed a small dose of the rich blue potion, and lacked ingredients for another. I tucked the tiny bottle into the pocket of my apron, yawned, then moved to the big windows to look out toward where my friends—those who remained— waited. I couldn't see anything of them from the workroom. Just the plain, the bridge, the forest on the hills beyond. I wondered whether they were still waiting for me to return. I hoped Aren would act without me, now that Ulric was dead and no longer in need of my help. I supposed that when I did hear news of them, it likely wouldn't be good, and once again I'd have to hide my feelings, to pretend I was on Severn's side. It had been too close the night he was injured. I'd let my feelings catch me by surprise, and he had almost seen—

"Nox, you're needed in the king's chambers."

I hadn't heard the guard come in, and his voice startled me. "Thank you," I said. "I'll be there in a few minutes."

"Now. You'll come with me now." He spoke calmly. Perhaps I wasn't in trouble. *Yet*.

"Of course."

I took a gulp of the dragon's egg potion to protect my mind.

The guard snorted. "Need a little liquid courage before you face him?"

I smiled bashfully. "You won't tell?"

"Nah. Can't say I blame you. Mind if I have a nip?"

I offered him the bottle. The potion tasted sharp, not entirely unlike something one might buy from a back-alley distillery, and he wouldn't feel ill-effects from it unless it was a little fuzziness in his mind.

"Doesn't pack much punch, does it?" he commented as he handed it back. "You might want another sip. He seemed to be in quite a mood when he passed by me earlier."

I was too tired to think of a reason to refuse that wouldn't arouse suspicion. I took another quick swig.

Might help. A wave of lightheadedness came over me, and a dulling of my perceptions. I no longer felt Severn's potion in my pocket, or the supply pantry's power calling to me.

I followed the guard through the now-familiar passageways to Severn's chambers. The new king didn't seem to care to do business with me anywhere more formal.

The guard left me and closed the door, leaving me in empty and silent rooms. I waited, but Severn didn't come. Perhaps he'd had other, more urgent business come up. He might be back any minute, or I might have had hours to do as I pleased. I had no way of knowing, but I wasn't going to get a better opportunity. I hurried to the table, where the ever-present bottle of wine and glasses sat.

I hesitated. This would certainly poison the tester, who had no magic of his own. I tried to feel the potion and guess its effects, but got nothing from it. I thought it might take some time for the poisons to work, but when they did it would be painful and quite obvious. *I should have tried cutting it with—*

The door opened behind me. I gasped and spun around to face Severn, hands behind my back. I dropped into a quick curtsy. "Sire."

He glared at me. "My mother's dead."

"Oh, I'm so sorry." Severn wasn't taking his eyes off of me. I held my hands at my sides, bottle hidden behind my fingers, trying to look like nothing was amiss. "Terrible loss."

"She was a horrible old harpy," he said. "No one will miss her, least of all me. I'm just telling you why I'm late." He poured a glass of wine that he drank down without testing.

That would have been perfect. I hid my disappointment, and slipped the bottle into my pocket while he wasn't looking.

Someone knocked at the door, Severn went to it and spoke quietly to them. When he returned, he narrowed his eyes at me. "Enemies are attacking the city."

"Who?"

"Rebels. Not the enemies I've been expecting. I've ordered Wardrel out." He leaned his head to one side, stretching his neck muscles. "He doesn't seem to think these people will be much of a challenge, but it's so hard to tell with fanatics."

"Oh?" My heart pounded, but I kept my voice calm. "Should you go?"

Severn watched my reaction, and a slow smile turned the corners of his mouth. "No concern for my dear brother's safety, Nox? No relief that your tormenter may soon suffer or die? No fear that our attackers may harm you if they breach the safe walls of our keep?" He motioned for me to come closer, and I forced my feet to obey. My head still felt like it was floating too high above my shoulders, but thanks to my blocking potion I felt little of his usual influence. "You're a puzzle, Nox. I see how you hide your emotions, how every reaction you give comes only after you've paused to think about it."

My heart fluttered. "I had a hard upbringing, your highness. I'm not accustomed to openly expressing my—"

"But not always," he continued, as though I hadn't spoken. He narrowed his eyes. "There was one time."

His hand shot toward me, and he grabbed my throat. Stars appeared before my eyes as he stepped forward and my head slammed back into the wall. "When I mentioned the mer and said I thought I might have killed him, you reacted. You put your mask on quickly, but even in my pain, I saw it. Shock. Devastation. What was he to you?" I didn't answer, and he squeezed harder. "Answer me!"

"I don't know what you're—"

My head connected with the edge of the fireplace mantel, and he let me crumple to the floor. *If I had my knives, if I wasn't so damned frightened and muddled...*

The hem of my dress burst into flames. I gasped and slapped at the fire, but it continued to burn, searing my skin, creeping higher. "Stop!" I cried. The flames disappeared, but the pain didn't. It washed over me in waves, as though the flames still licked at my skin.

"I can do that again, for as long as you want." He took another drink. "I'm not as skilled in this as Wardrel is, but we can make it work. Did Aren warn you about that?"

Again it took me too long to choose my response. Severn threw his wine glass, and it shattered on the hearth next to my hand. "I knew it. You came to the gate around the same time my scouts reported seeing them in the woods. I was willing to give you a chance because of your immense talent, but something told me you weren't what you claimed. Your story added up, your behavior has been impeccable, but something was off. I felt it, and never trusted you. Yet you passed every test."

"It's just—"

"And then your reaction to the mer dying told me you knew him." He sneered. "You're not worried about these people attacking the city because you know them too. And just now, when I mentioned Aren, you weren't sure how to react." He smiled, and the expression carried something like pity with it. "Just so you know, ignorance would have been a good option. Surprise would have been better. No one but my inner circle knows he's up in those woods."

"I... I passed through a village on my way here, they said they'd seen him." The explanation sounded thin even to me. I didn't know why I bothered.

Severn sighed. "I had hoped I was wrong about you, that we could work together. You have an unusual gift, and your potion has been so helpful. Tell me, who are you really?"

"I told you, I come from Cressia. My mother was a widow. I never knew my father."

He grabbed a handful of my hair and forced me to my feet. His breath smelled of the wine that would never incapacitate him no matter how much he drank, thanks to his magic and my potion that strengthened it. I knew that if I resisted, if I tried to hurt him, the flames would consume me. I couldn't control the way my muscles quaked when he pulled me closer to whisper in my ear, "I don't believe you."

I panicked. My arms pushed out without any conscious order from me, and my hands beat against his chest. He was too close for the blows to have any effect. Before I could raise a knee, he spun me around and twisted my arm behind my back, increasing the pressure until I cried out in pain.

He laughed. "Magic is fun, but we can do this any way you like. Do you want to fight me?"

"No," I sobbed. "Please, just let me go."

He pushed me, and I landed in one of the chairs.

"By all means, let's be civilized about this. Sit and have a nice chat about my challengers. My father's dead now. He was weak even before that. I had wondered what a few years of Darmish hospitality would do to him. I imagine my magic scholars would have had a fine time experimenting on him had he lived long enough. Not that they aren't busy enough as it is." He looked down, presumably toward the prisons, or wherever they held experimental subjects. "It turns out we can learn as much from Tyrean magic-users as we can from the Darmish." He laughed again, but it came out as a mad bark. "Isn't it hilarious? I didn't have to send Aren to Darmid in the first place. None of this would have happened if I'd been willing to experiment on lesser magic users from Tyrea. But no, the laws protected them. And as it turns out, I needn't have rushed so. My father may have been wrong to let it go, but he was right about..." He trailed off again.

He wasn't making any kind of sense.

"It doesn't matter now," he continued. "I will have my answers, and I will still have my victory. Aren made his choice, and he will pay for it."

I pushed myself up in the chair to take my weight off the burned leg that was pinned under me.

The movement caught Severn's eye, and he looked me over. "What were you doing with them? Why did they send you?" His eyes narrowed, and he stepped closer. "You're more than a Potioner, aren't you? Someone trusts you."

There was no answer I could give that would save me. "Obviously I'm not someone they care much for, or they wouldn't have sent me here to be beaten, burned, and nearly killed by your brothers."

"I wonder about that. I'll have the truth from you, Nox. Wardrel's not available, but I think Sara might have ideas on how to open you up. On your feet."

"No." Stupid that I should feel safe in that chair, but all I understood in that moment was that wherever we went next would be worse.

A knock echoed through the room.

"Not one movement," Severn ordered.

He spoke to someone, spat out a string of curses, and returned with a guard. "Take her to the dungeon."

"There's no room, sir."

He swore again and looked to me. "Care to share a cell with someone? I'm sure we could make you comfortable among the criminals and desperate men we're keeping there now."

I forced myself not to reach for the comforting weight of the bottle in my pocket. Instead I kept my gaze locked on his, though it chilled me to my bones.

He leaned in close to whisper to me again. "On second thought, I don't want anyone else to hurt you. Not yet, anyway. I almost like you, and that's always made it more enjoyable. Think as long as you wish about what I might do to you when I get back. I promise that the reality will be worse. You might want to consider giving up your secrets while I'm still giving you a chance."

He hauled me up and pushed me ahead of him into his bedroom, then opened the desk drawer and pulled out a knife and several other sharp implements, a rolled-up leather case like a locksmith's kit, a set of quills, and a letter-opener. "Don't try to arm yourself," he added, and handed the items to the guard. "I'm not foolish enough to leave any other potential weapons lying around in here. Have a pleasant afternoon, Nox. I'll see you soon."

He left, and the lock on the bedroom door turned with a heavy thud. I ran to try the door, though the burned skin on my legs screamed in protest. It didn't move. I moved to the window beside the bookcase, which stretched from the floor to well above my head, the only one large enough for me to fit through. It led to a steep drop-off and a cobblestone courtyard below. Nothing above to reach for, even if I were capable of climbing. The deadly fall might be a way out if it came to that, but I wasn't ready to take the hard way yet.

I looked over the shelves. A full bottle of wine sat on one, next to a stack of scribbled-on papers.

For someone who isn't much affected by it, he sure likes this stuff. I wouldn't complain. Anything to help ease the pain. I took a sip and grimaced at the strong taste. The effect on me was immediate, and my thoughts grew cloudier than my potion had made them.

Not too much. There might still be a chance. Keep looking for answers.

I searched the room for weapons, and found nothing save for the wine bottle. I'd keep that in reserve. Other than that I had pillows at my disposal, and books.

Even the small toilet room was useless, save for the clean well water from the pump that I would use to clean my wounds.

I flipped my fingers over the edges of the loose pages of Severn's notes, then carried them to the desk to look over as I waited for my enemy's return. Physical weapons weren't the only way to harm a person. Information could be deadly, if only one knew how to use it.

I fingered the potion bottle in my pocket and practiced flipping the lid open and closed. I would not hesitate again.

45

AREN

R owan cleared her throat, tearing my attention from the corpses. "Are you going to tell the others what you're doing here?"

"They'll know soon enough. It won't change our plans, other than possibly keeping the living safer." I'd left Griselda, Qurwin, and Albion to finalize their portion of attack plans. After our previous discussion we were close, but there were still so many details to work out. So many lives at risk, but so little time to put every piece in place.

At least these might help with that, I thought.

I turned away from the ten corpses standing among the trees, each of them swaying as though moved by a non-existent breeze. A night in the open hadn't damaged them too badly. They were stronger than the first bodies I'd tried raising, fresher and more willing to respond to me.

Rowan scuffed her boot in the dirt. She'd avoided looking at the bodies since she'd arrived just a few minutes earlier. We'd had our helpers drag them this far, to the woods at the edge of the Despair, where they wouldn't be disturbed by animals or curious humans. I'd started raising bodies at dawn, and would need to increase my pace if we wanted more by the afternoon.

"When does this all begin?" she asked. "The battle. These bodies moving."

"As soon as we have everything else organized. The living troops can be mobilized quickly, and Ruby can do her part at a moment's notice. We'll send her in first to divert as many troops as we can from the gates."

"Should she choose to," Rowan added. She squeezed her eyes closed. "Why do I feel like this is all doomed? Ruby will change her mind, decide that she doesn't want to help humans. The bodies won't make it that far, or you won't get into the palace. Severn will be—" She clamped her lips shut. "Sorry. I don't usually get like this."

"I know. I've had the same thoughts. It's as though Kel was our lucky charm. Everything went wrong until we met him, and since he's been back in my life I've gained so much. I think my luck has run out, and..." I ended with a shrug, not wanting to say more.

"Maybe not." Rowan gestured toward the bodies that still lay on the ground. "I mean, their luck has run out. But not yours."

I wanted to believe that, but the idea of the gods turning on me had crossed my mind more than once. *Silly superstition.* "Did you ask Morea to wake Ulric?"

"I did."

"Good. I'm sure he'd hate to think we planned his return without him."

She frowned. "How will that work? If you finish the challenge and defeat Severn..."

"Then the crown is mine. Nox will fix Ulric, and he'll take it back from me. We'll figure out the details when he can consult with the proper authorities." *If Nox lives,* I added, and closed my mind to thoughts of the alternative.

Rowan sighed. "I always thought kings could make whatever laws they wanted, or change them. I understand why there are limits to power, but it seems like it would be easier sometimes."

She didn't sound like she was only talking about Ulric's situation. I nodded my agreement, having nothing more to add.

I channeled my magic toward the body. Every one of my own muscles clenched painfully as the power flowed through me, and that horrible feeling returned. A taste of decay entered my mouth, seeming to rise from within me, and I spat on the ground to rid myself of it.

I'd asked Morea to work something up that could protect someone from such a thing, should the need arise, and to tell no one I'd asked. She'd given me a horrified look, but said she'd work on it.

She hadn't delivered anything yet.

The body nearest Rowan's feet twitched and sat up so quickly that its upper body pitched forward and its head bounced off its knees. Rowan gasped and jumped back. "Sorry! I think it'll be a while before this seems normal. Or remotely not terrifying."

I focused on getting the corpse to its feet. The fat man's intestines spilled out onto the mossy ground and tangled around his legs as he shuffled forward.

"Gods." Rowan winced, and turned away.

"He can't feel anything."

"I know."

"You don't have to be here if it bothers you," I said, barely holding back the frustration that threatened to make me lash out at her. She wasn't the cause of it, but the irrational temptation was terrible. "I don't like it either, but at least you can leave. I don't have much of a choice. We need more troops, and more fearsome ones. And if these can save lives by taking the brunt of the attack…" I sent the body to stand with the others, and made them all turn away. I couldn't bear to have their blank, unseeing eyes on me. The nausea became almost unbearable, and I turned away to take a few deep breaths. The illness passed, but I still felt heavy and weak. Worse, I felt hopeless. "This can't work."

Rowan didn't answer.

I crouched on the forest floor among bodies laid out like a child's broken dolls. "It's too late. Has been since the beginning. If I had gone to find my father sooner, we might have got him back before time ran out." A dull ache filled my chest as I watched the animated corpses. "No good can come of this. Phelun was right, and the mer elders, and father. What I'm doing here, it's wrong. It's killing me. It's…"

"It's brilliant." Rowan walked to the edge of the woods, just a few paces away. Beyond that, the trees became stunted, then infrequent, and then quickly disappeared. A barren wasteland spread out from there, and beyond it lay the city. When she returned to me, tears streamed down her cheeks, but she forced a smile. "This feeling isn't you. It's not me, either. It's the Despair, isn't it? I don't think I understood it when you explained it before, but I feel it. It would be so easy to lie down and slip away, to let the world fade. Become lost in a fog of dreams, or whatever comes after. To not care anymore. Because none of it matters. There's no hope."

"You do understand."

She looked at the bodies then back toward the Despair. "I feel what you're feeling, yes. But the situation's no more hopeless than it was when you came up with this idea, and what we're feeling is no more real than a nightmare. We're going to wake up from this."

I tried to feel some difference between my true thoughts and what the Despair might be making me feel, but the connection was seamless. "It seems real, doesn't it?"

She nodded. "There's no hope here. Maybe none in your heart right now. But it exists, even if you don't feel it. I remember it. Do you?"

"I suppose." I remembered that I had felt hope before, that I'd believed things worth fighting for. I just couldn't summon it now.

"You have to keep going." She crouched next to me and took my hand. "We have to. Then we'll get away from this horrible place."

"What if I can't? I feel death entering my body with each one I raise. That's not the Despair talking. It's an objective fact, and the same problem as we had when there weren't enough bodies at all. If I can't raise them, they're useless."

"We'll figure it out." She glared at the Despair and raised her voice as though it could hear her. "We'll see this through, what-ever it takes."

The feeling of hopelessness retreated slightly. "Good enough,"

I said quietly, and got to my feet. "Let's say this is possible, then. We should go see whether it's necessary."

I commanded the bodies to remain standing, and hoped they'd obey even after I left them. I took Rowan by the hand and pulled her up, and we walked uphill toward camp. Not hand-in-hand, but still together.

The woman who stood guarding the camp nodded as we passed by, and asked no questions. No one else stopped us as we made our way toward my tent, though Griselda gave us a questioning glance and ducked into Albion's. Behind that, next to Ulric's lodgings, Ruby raised her head to watch us pass.

My mind cleared as we put time and distance between us and the Despair, though its essence clung to my skin like sweat after a bad dream. By the time we reached camp, I felt able to sort things out. Still, the situation looked dire. I turned toward Morea's tent and knocked at the wooden pole.

She answered, and a look of concerned caution came over her. "I have something for you," she said.

"Thank all of the gods and the Goddess herself," I said.

Morea narrowed her eyes. "I can't guarantee this will help that problem of yours that you didn't seem to want to talk about. I've had no time to test it." She rubbed the back of her hand across her forehead and gave me a pained look. "I'm not a healer like your sister is. I mean, I can do it when the need arises, and competently enough. But my strength lies elsewhere, in darker things. Still, I think I've made this work. I'm good with poisons, and I'm good with shielding from them. So here." She handed me a glass bottle filled with a dark green liquid. "It should lessen the effects, if magic were somehow poisoning you. I mixed the potion in a dragon scale for added potency, but that will only matter if it's the right solution." Her lips disappeared in a tight line. "I don't know what's happening to you, exactly, which makes it hard to know how to help."

"I appreciate the effort," I said. "Thank you."

Rowan watched the exchange, and looked more hopeful than I felt.

We entered my tent. I longed to collapse into my bed. Never

before had I felt so drained, so ill and horrid, after using magic. But I couldn't rest. Not yet. I sampled Morea's potion. It certainly tasted like it came from a poisoner.

Griselda and Albion arrived a moment later, followed by Ulric. My father shuffled slowly, but appeared to have recovered some of his strength. His magic was rebuilding him, now that he was resting and not trying to direct it. Perhaps my request to have him kept asleep had done more good than I'd anticipated. He gave me a sharp look.

"I'm back," he said. "Albion will tell you."

My grandfather nodded. "He's as unpleasant as I've ever found him to be, but competent." There was no hostility in his voice, and the glare that Ulric shot him in response was not entirely unfriendly. It seemed that Albion had been choosing his words and his moves carefully enough to not make the old king feel threatened, or Ulric's mind had cleared enough that he now recognized an ally when he saw one.

"You're asking me to step aside?" I asked. "Relinquish command to you?"

Ulric looked at me, his gaze clear and steady. "For now," he said, low and quiet. "Once we get to the palace, Severn will be your business." The lines on his forehead deepened. "It's business I should have taken care of long ago, but I'm not capable now. Are you ready?"

I didn't look at Rowan. I didn't want to see what she might think of all of this. "Ready enough. We can't wait any longer. Not if Severn has troops returning. But command of this group is yours, if you're willing to move forward." I thought of all of the people in camp, of the bodies in the forest whose deaths I was at least partially responsible for. This was why I had never wanted the throne. Too many hard choices, too many scenarios where no one could truly win.

Griselda stepped forward and pulled a rolled-up sheet of parchment from the bag she carried. "Ulric has helped finalize our plan. It will cost us, but we're looking at ways to minimize losses." She unrolled a map of the city, marked in a combination of her handwriting and Ulric's. "The goal is distraction, not destruction. Your father doesn't want to see more of his people killed than necessary, formerly loyal soldiers included, but we'll do what we must."

Ulric grunted.

Griselda smiled faintly. "We agree with you that diverting troops from the palace is your best bet for getting to Severn. The dragon has agreed to help, and seems quite enthusiastic. She'll attack the homes of the wealthy and the nobility in the east end of the city, here." She tapped the map.

Ulric smiled. "I suspect Severn has been working hard to earn their favor, and they'll demand no less than his finest soldiers and Sorcerers to contain the problem. As long as she's in first, he'll have no excuse for denying them."

"That's not great news for Ruby," Rowan said softly.

A snort rang through the tent from outside, and a claw dented the canvas beside Rowan, gently dragging downward. "It's what I want, human girl. A glorious end, remember?"

Rowan sighed.

"Once they're diverted," Griselda continued, "we'll make our move on the front gate. We don't have nearly enough troops to take the city, but it might be enough to draw their attention and leave Severn exposed, or as close to it as he'll ever come."

"Could you add more?" Rowan asked. "At least, the appearance of them?"

"No," Griselda said. "That's the next part of this plan. I won't be with you. I'll have gone into the city, carried by Ruby. Hopefully no one will take too much notice of me in the commotion she'll cause, and I'll open the main gates to let everyone in."

"You know how difficult that will be?" I asked. Opening the gates was no simple operation. It involved a series of levers and complex mechanical operations only performed by those trained to do it.

Griselda nodded. "I had an acquaintance when I was living in Luid. A soldier who frequently manned the front gate overnight."

Rowan bit back a smile.

Griselda caught it, and returned it. "I spent many an evening in the little gate-house inside the wall. I can get the main gates open for you. I've seen it done enough times. Once our people get into the city, they can begin the work of announcing Ulric's return, and hopefully subduing the soldiers. The hope is that most of the rest of the city's residents will stay safely indoors."

I saw what she'd meant about losses. Our troops would have arrows raining down on them as they approached the gates, plus face whatever Sorcerers Severn sent out or had hidden in the walls, ready to attack. Our Sorcerers would fight back, but so many of our people had no magic to rely on. Only whatever armor they'd brought or created.

"What about a shield?" I asked Albion. "I don't suppose your protections here are portable."

"Sadly, no. Entirely fixed. We have Emmet Kyrst from Belleisle, who has developed a remarkable ability to… hold on." He left the tent, and returned moments later with a gangly older man in tow. "Throw something at him. Nothing important."

Griselda stepped outside and returned with a handful of small stones, wound up, and threw them one by one in a steady stream at the Sorcerer, adjusting her aim each time to fling them at his arms, his face, his legs, and off to one side of his body.

Emmet's expression never changed, appearing relaxed and slightly amused as he raised his hands. The air in front of him shimmered in a swirling, translucent vortex no larger than a good-sized shield. He directed it to block the stones, catching each of them in turn.

They disappeared as though they'd never existed.

Impressive.

"Where do they go?" Rowan asked.

Emmet shrugged. "Couldn't tell you. Haven't ever had anything come back. I can't do more than that, but I'm quick. As long as someone's shielding me, I can do as Albion here has suggested and absorb some of the overhead attack. Arrows and the like." He frowned. "My range is limited somewhat, and I can't be everywhere at once. But I'll do what I can."

"Thank you, Emmet," Albion said, and showed him out. "So there's that," he continued. "We have a great deal of magic on our side, but most of it will only be helpful once we're close to the wall or inside the city. Transformation, smaller illusions, wind and fire. A few tricks that could be as harmful to our people as well as the enemy, to be held in reserve." He turned to Ulric. "Have we forgotten anything?"

"We've had people back in Wildwood working on banners to be brought in when the rest of our troops arrive," he said, "which should be soon. Everyone rides or marches under the Tiernal gryphon, which Severn has so completely rejected. If people in the city see us coming, I want them to know it's me returning and not whatever Severn has told them."

"That won't help with the soldiers?" Rowan asked. She sounded like she knew it was a silly question.

"No," said Ulric, not unkindly. "Their loyalty is to their king, as it should be. That's Severn now, however he may have manipulated things to get there. If I still had my claim to the throne…" He shook his head sadly. "I don't know. But there's a chance the Sorcerers he's got in the city may respond. As I hear it, most of them didn't go willingly, and many will have seen those who resisted killed or imprisoned. It depends what he's done to them, or for them, since then."

He sighed. "I've never had qualms about killing enemies when it was necessary, or anyone who stood in my way. But so many of these people were once loyal to me." He looked to Albion, about to say more, but clamped his mouth shut.

I knew what he was thinking, even without seeing into his mind. There may have been a time when he wouldn't have cared how many lives were lost, as long as the end result benefitted Tyrea. Perhaps he still wouldn't let himself care, but the idea was there.

Albion looked to me, unfazed by Ulric's surprisingly compassionate words. "Aren, your part of this is up to you. Much of it will depend on conditions inside the city, but our mission is to get you into the palace. And we'll do whatever we can to get you there."

"Thank you," I said. "I do have one other thing to add, though."

And I told them. Ulric paled with horror as I revealed my secret, and Albion pressed a fist to his lips as though holding back bile or strong words. But they listened. Griselda only seemed interested, and was obviously looking at all the angles.

"So my initial plan," I concluded, "was to use them as a distraction, possibly approaching through the Despair. But I think they'd be better used as a walking shield. They fill in the front ranks and pull the worst of the arrow attacks and whatever else Severn has waiting for our front lines. They're no loss, and seeing what he hits them with will give us time to respond with what magic we have available to us." No one spoke. They all seemed to be processing the information.

Rowan stepped over to stand beside me. "He can do it," she said. "I've seen them. You don't need to worry about the people who once lived in those bodies. They're gone. It's horrible to see, but imagine how that will affect anyone guarding the city who sees them coming."

Griselda smiled, just slightly. "They'll think we're an army of the dead."

Rowan nodded. "These people already died once attacking the city. No reason not to let them finish their job." She turned to me and offered a reassuring smile. At least I had her on my side. In that moment, I didn't feel that I needed much else.

Albion looked a little green, but he nodded. "How are you finding it, Aren?"

"Difficult," I admitted. "The effects of attempting this haven't been exaggerated. I don't doubt it would kill me or turn me into one of them if I made a career of it. But I can do this, especially if Morea's potion helps me."

Ulric looked to Griselda. "Beaumage?"

She closed her eyes and frowned. "My first thought is that it's a brilliant plan, moral qualms and gut-reactions aside. It's like something from an old story, except there it would be the villain using an army of the dead to attack the fair and shining city, not its prince. But it could work. Even if it doesn't, we're not risking any more lives by trying. Except Aren's, I suppose, but he seems confident."

"He's the only one I can't afford to risk at the outset," Ulric grumbled. "No offense to anyone else present." He glowered at me. "You're certain you can do this and still be fit to finish things with Severn?"

No.

"Yes," I said. "Absolutely." I was already feeling better after a bit of space and Morea's potion. If I let the bodies fall at the gate —if they made it that far—I would have time to recover before I reached the palace. The magic in Luid was as strong as anywhere, and I had no fear of running out.

I didn't feel good about it, but I sounded more confident than I felt. Ulric nodded.

A heavy weight compressed the side of the tent. "I think it's a waste of meat," Ruby said. "But I am sorry I won't be there to see it."

Ulric scowled in her direction. "Well, if the dragon thinks it's a good idea…" He turned to me, deadly serious. "I won't stop you. I'll make sure no one else does, either. I can't say I'm comfortable with this risk you're taking, but it should save lives. For that I'll thank you, if it works out."

I tried to hide my surprise. "No fear over the gods judging you for letting it happen?"

"I stopped worrying about them years ago. And while I don't believe the Goddess is as compassionate to the faithful as some would have us believe, I doubt she has time to meddle in our affairs." He looked weary then. "It is abhorrent, what you're doing. But the alternative is worse."

A rousing encouragement, I thought wryly, but nodded. "I'll get started."

We all left the tent. Florizel had joined Ruby outside.

"How long will it take to have everyone ready?" I asked.

"We'll move this afternoon," Ulric said, "and try to keep the fighting as brief as possible. Send Ruby well ahead." He turned to the dragon. "How long can you survive under physical and magical attacks? They'll be considerable."

She snorted, and the air warmed around us. "I'm a dragon. I'll die when I damn well please."

I smiled, and wished Nox were there to see this creature we'd been so afraid of. I looked the dragon over. I'd fought younger ones, though not alone, and seen them fall. Not without a fight, though, and not one of them had had the size, strength, or intelligence of this one. I didn't doubt her words.

She lifted her head and looked down at Griselda. "Prepare yourself."

The blood drained from Griselda's cheeks. I'd never seen her afraid before.

"What shall I do?" Florizel asked, and stepped closer to Rowan. "The potion lady took a moment to stitch me, and plastered this goo on my wound." She twisted her neck back to look at the white paste that had dried over her flank in a lumpy mess. "It's quite itchy, but my strength is returning. I can help."

"Come with us," I said. "Fetch Morea first, ask for more of her potion, then come to where the new bodies are resting."

My magic welled up again, eager to work in spite of the pain it would cause me.

I stalked out of camp before I could change my mind. Rowan walked beside me, seeming lost in thought. She'd be considering ways to help, I knew. I wished she'd stay back, but knew better.

"Whatever you decide to do," I said, "don't overuse your magic. We need you."

She gave me a nervous glance. "No danger of that. But I can help."

"I have no doubt."

~

THE BODIES STOOD where we'd left them. The fat man had tipped over and lay face-down in the dirt, but my unspoken command got him back on his feet.

"So it's waking them that requires the effort?" Rowan asked.

"I think so. We'll see what happens when I try to get them moving farther from me." I commanded one to walk toward the Despair. He did so without hesitation. "All we need is for them to march."

And to not fall apart on the road, or get away from me. And that's only the beginning of the challenge.

I shook off the melancholy that threatened to overcome me. The most insidious thing about the Despair was how the apathy and hopelessness seemed to come from within. It had almost caught me again. "We'll start now, and send Florizel back to let everyone know when we're ready. This could take some time."

Florizel stepped toward the body closest to her, a thin young man whose head rested on his own shoulder. She sniffed, shuddered, and stepped back. "I'll stay close by, but I hope you'll forgive me if I don't watch."

She disappeared into the bushes behind us.

My father was more confident about the gods' lack of involvement than I was. I'd had the audacity to beg them to save Rowan once, and I couldn't say for certain that they hadn't. And now, this. *Forgive me*, I thought. I didn't know who I might be offending with my actions, but I hoped they were listening.

My magic had recovered fully after I raised the last body, and the next came easier. Still, it took all of my focus and concentration to make the muscular woman move, rise, and walk toward the others. The illness came back in a flood, as though I'd never walked away. My magic levels dipped and stayed low as I forced another to its feet, as though something in me was reluctant to draw more so close to the Despair. The loss was followed by a deep ache in my left shoulder that mirrored the missing arm of the body that now stood gaping at me, slack-jawed and empty-eyed.

That's absolutely perfect. I sipped from Morea's bottle and hoped she'd be bringing more of her potion soon. Something stronger, perhaps. My magic recovered, bringing with it a fresh wave of unease and uncertainty from the land around me.

I hesitated before the next one, a small-framed woman with deep gashes sliced into her face and neck. *We need all of them*, I reminded myself, and silently ordered her to rise. The pain began immediately, slashing across my throat from left to right, digging deep until I choked on it, then tearing at my cheek. It faded as soon as she was standing and the connection between myself and the body lessened, but it left me gasping from the echoes of agony.

Rowan ran to me and placed her hands on my arm. "Aren, what?"

"Just a little faint," I said through gritted teeth. The pain disappeared completely as the corpse walked to stand with the others at my command. "It passes."

I wrapped my fingers around my throat, not trusting that I hadn't actually taken on some injury. Everything was intact, at least for the time being. I'd just have to press on through each one, and hope they didn't get worse.

I felt a hint of warmth in my arm, flowing through my body like a faint stream of light. It took me a moment to shake off my own concerns and realize that it was Rowan's magic.

I pulled away.

"What?" she asked.

"Your magic. It's trying to build me up again, filling the gap before I replenish." I licked my lips, which suddenly felt dry.

She stepped back. "I don't mind, if it helps."

I didn't answer. I knew she would help me, and gladly. But I couldn't let her do that. The danger of me taking too much from her would increase as I used more of my own power, and I didn't like the thought of this death-effect pushing into her if she helped me. There was too much we didn't know.

It was unfortunate, though. The Despair felt so much farther away when she touched me.

The next body rose, and another, each sending its projected pain into my body. A muscular fellow missing most of his head proved to be a challenge, but he soon joined the others. Each time, the effort cost me in magic and physical energy, and the pain became more real. An itching sensation crept through my muscles and over my skin, like my own flesh was rotting in the heat of the sun.

I recognized some of these people. I hadn't spoken to them, except in passing at a meal while we all lived in the rebel village, but it made my task more difficult. They weren't just bodies.

They were people. Some had families. I was certain the blonde woman with her throat ripped out had children.

They chose to fight with Goff, I reminded myself. *They knew they might die.*

They hadn't known about this. I could only hope they wouldn't object, wherever they were now.

More bodies, and more. The pain approached anything Severn had thrown at me, occasionally blotting the world out and making me forget what I was supposed to be doing, but I continued each time I recovered. We needed their numbers. Every arrow taken by one of these bodies, every magical attack wasted on them, would be one less living person who would suffer their fate.

And a larger army meant a better chance of me getting into the city and finishing my business with my brother.

I let the world outside of the bodies go, and lost myself in my work. Each wound that I felt became a communion with the dead, an act of remembrance for a stranger. There was no Rowan, and even the Despair vanished. There was only the pain, and the weight of dead flesh that desired only to return to the earth.

And then they were finished. When I opened my eyes, every broken, tangled puppet stood on his or her own feet.

Almost every one. I remembered that there was another, set off to the side. I moved toward the mountain of armored flesh that the others had so considerately placed behind a pair of fallen trees.

Wardrel. My brother, and my tormenter for so many years.

I didn't hesitate. To pause would have given the Despair an opportunity to enter and re-open old wounds. My magic moved more slowly now, as though it shared my exhaustion. But the power was there, and it obeyed my commands as I gathered it to call up the last body. I was vaguely aware of the sound of Rowan's footsteps following me, but ignored them. I couldn't imagine how this all looked to her, but she hadn't stepped in.

I trust you, she'd said to me, more than once. I wondered whether she trusted me enough to let me destroy myself.

I couldn't help hating him, though I tried to remain impassive and treat this as I had the other bodies. Couldn't help considering this revenge, and almost hoping he knew what was happening. I hoped Wardrel's body would end up filled with arrows, or destroyed by magic stronger than any he'd ever wielded. I gritted my teeth, and I let the magic flow.

The deep pain that stabbed under my left arm came as no surprise, but the swirling darkness that immediately surrounded me did. I gasped. Cold fingers of fear danced through my chest and clutched my heart, and something like laughter echoed through my mind.

I blinked hard, but the darkness remained, blinding me. I tried to let go, and couldn't. The body drew on my magic, and I felt it sit up, as though it were my own half-dead muscles obeying my commands. I pushed the fear aside, replacing it with hate and rage that pushed my magic further and harder. The heaviness in my body reflected the weight of his as I hauled him to his feet. *He won't escape this.*

The darkness turned to blackness, thick and all-consuming and lifeless.

I suddenly felt myself teetering on the brink of a dark and cold chasm, and didn't know how to pull myself back. *Too far,* I thought. *Much too far.* Coherent thought slipped away as the blackness reached up to cover me and draw me in.

Light appeared behind me, pale and gentle. The cold hesitated, then continued its slow creep. The light grew, coursing warm through my body, bringing my awareness back. *Rowan's magic.* I reached out and felt her standing behind me. She pressed herself against my back, holding me tight, letting her magic battle something she didn't understand any more than I did.

The darkness that had clouded my mind disappeared, and I stood in the forest again. I closed myself off to Rowan's magic, and she let go. I didn't have time to reflect on what she'd done, or on what she'd risked. Wardrel's body rested somewhere just beyond my control, collapsed back into a pathetic heap.

I decided to try again, without letting my emotions carry me. The brother who had enjoyed my pain and that of so many others was no more. There was only this flesh, which would no doubt strike fear into Severn if he saw it. I ignored my memories and made him stand and join the others, then waited for the pain to fade.

I still felt Rowan's magic in me, soothing my heart as the Despair's doubts crept back in, restoring my body as that deathly feeling faded far more slowly than I'd have liked.

I looked over the group of standing corpses as I drained the rest of Morea's potion. A boy who might have been a year older than Patience stepped toward me and stumbled as his broken leg buckled under him. He landed hard, cracking his head against a boulder. The nausea that filled me then had nothing to do with my magic. I released him, and he lay still.

Horrifying as the sight of the bodies was, I couldn't push away the surge of pride that swelled in me. It had cost me much, but I had finished it.

No one has done this before. Unprecedented power.

But I hadn't done it alone.

I turned to thank Rowan, and froze. Her eyes stared off into the distance, and her arms hung slack at her sides.

"Rowan?"

She slumped to the ground.

46

ROWAN

I lifted my hand to push away whoever was patting my face. Sleeping seemed like such a nice idea, and they were making it difficult.

"Rowan, wake up."

Aren. I couldn't think what he was doing there, or why I'd be lying on such hard, rocky ground. At least, not until Morea lifted my eyelids and I saw the corpses standing behind her. A monstrous, armored form stumbled into view behind her. I gasped and pushed myself back, though my legs weren't strong enough to get me far.

"Did I faint?"

Aren stepped into view. "Thank the gods that's all it was. I thought you'd left me again. Florizel went for help as soon as you fell."

I sat up and brushed the dead pine needles from my hair. "Everything was fine, but then..." I shuddered. I couldn't explain what I'd felt. My magic had left me, pulling Aren back from whatever had its claws in him, holding him frozen. As it left, a cold and deathly feeling had coursed through me, replacing the magic I'd lost.

If Aren had felt anything like that as he worked, I didn't know how he was still standing.

"I'm all right now," I concluded, and spat on the ground. My mouth tasted of decay.

Aren still looked concerned. "You didn't use up your stores?"

"You didn't take that much, really." More than I was comfortable with, but I'd have given it all to stop whatever was hurting him.

Aren nodded, still frowning. "Morea, is everyone else ready to go?"

"They are. Ruby and Griselda left, and should have begun their portion of the attack by now."

Aren sat on the ground next to me. "We should move, then."

I really looked at him then. Dark circles had appeared under his eyes, and he looked flat, drained in a way he hadn't been even when his magic had failed him in Darmid. I imagined I didn't look much better, but I hoped my skin didn't have that odd greenish cast.

Morea offered me a flask of water, and I drank. It tasted sweet and sharp, and whatever she had put in there warmed me and eased the chill of death that had crept into my bones. My magic burned a little brighter. "Something new for you," she said. "Possibly an improvement. I have one for you as well, Aren, though it looks like the hard work is done."

"Thank you," I said, and wondered whether a Potioner ever really got the thanks she deserved. Sorcerers seemed to hog all the glory, but as far as I could tell, we'd be long past doomed without Nox and Morea.

Florizel nudged me with her nose, and let me use her strong neck to get to my feet.

"Let's go." Aren stood and walked through the crowd of standing bodies. They followed, jostling and bumping into each other until they'd all spread out and found their own space. We reached the edge of the tree cover, and he let them walk ahead. The bodies had seemed like a crowd in the woods. Standing there at the edge of the barrens, they were a sorry excuse for a line of defense.

Aren obviously thought the same. "It won't be enough," he said. "We need to intimidate the soldiers when the first arrows don't take our troops down, to inspire fear and awe when they realize what they're facing. This group looks defeatable. We need... more. And I can't do it."

"I can," I said softly.

I closed my eyes, shutting out the world. We had the framework of our defenses, but if we spread them out too much it would be easy for Severn's forces to cut through and reach the living behind them. What we really wanted was a solid wall of bodies—literal bodies, shambling and frightening and unwilling to die again—to lead the advance and draw arrow fire. Or at least the appearance of one.

I still have enough magic. I can do this.

You will fail, the Despair murmured. *Best not to try.*

You are wrong, I answered. *This is who I am. This is my destiny, and I will accept it on my terms.*

My magic responded. Even depleted, it felt strong and ready, lifting me up and filling me with light.

When I opened my eyes, I was surprised to find the incredible glow I felt within me didn't radiate visibly from my skin. It felt so solid, more real and more a part of me than it ever had before, bringing back the life and strength that had been drained from me.

I breathed deep, steeled myself against the Despair's lingering effects, and moved to stand beside Aren, looking toward the bodies as they moved awkwardly along the tree line toward the road where the living would be waiting.

Warmth enveloped me as I envisioned my illusion.

Another body appeared. Not a significant addition to the army, but it was something. More than that, it was strong. Clear. More convincing than anything I'd created before.

I bit my lip hard to return my focus to my work instead of the excitement that lifted me.

Another appeared, and another, each an exact replica of the real bodies, right down to the timing of their lurching, stumbling footsteps. I placed them well away from the originals. They all shuffled away, and I followed as I added more. Aren kept pace beside me, keeping silent as I worked.

My magic lessened, and I fought back a surge of panic.

I'd have to be more careful. I turned to creating replicas of replicas. They would be less convincing close-up, but at a distance they would work well enough to inspire fear, and they would cost me less of my diminishing magic stores.

The warm glow faded as my magic left me. *Keep the flame of magic burning bright enough that it will come back,* I reminded myself, remembering words from a book in the Belleisle school library. *If the flame is too low, it will go out...*

And if the dead army looks too small, we will fail to protect the living. My magic had come back once after it had been nearly gone. Aren's had too, after being dangerously low. It would be fine. It had to be.

The army filled out, expanding to the appearance of being hundreds strong. They would equal our living troops, at least in appearance, and give the archers on the wall a huge target they would fail to bring down. I added more. Only when I began to feel faint again did I stop. If I lost consciousness they would disappear, and it would all be for nothing. I leaned against Florizel and kept walking.

Aren reached for my hand. "Thank you," he said, and released me again. "It's incredible."

"Mine won't have any strength if you're hoping to have the dead bash the gates in."

"That won't be a problem if Ruby and Griselda are successful," Morea noted, and handed a bottle to Aren. He sipped, nodded his thanks, and kept walking.

Aren quickened his pace as we approached the road, and Morea, Florizel, and I followed. We passed the still-moving bodies, passing them on the forest side of the group. Aren turned back to stop them, and we kept on.

Ulric sat astride the fine war horse that he'd claimed after our escape from Ardare, and held the bridle of another strong beast in need of a rider, both carrying a few weapons and nothing else that might slow them down. The king looked well, if pale and still far older than he had before his fight with Severn. His hair remained white, and deep lines creased the corners of his eyes.

"Well?" he asked.

Aren looked up at his father. "Everything you didn't want to happen is ready. You have a moving shield waiting in the woods, should you choose to use it."

Ulric's jaw tightened. "Show me."

Aren closed his eyes. Moments later, the dead army shambled out of the woods.

Ulric drew a sharp breath as a body near the front released its innards onto the ground. At the same moment, every illusion and copy of an illusion based on that body did the same, coating the earth at their feet in gore. "It's horrible."

"It's our only chance," Aren answered. He nodded over Ulric's shoulder, where low voices drifted toward us from out of sight and up the hill. "At least, it's theirs."

Albion rode toward us. "Are we ready?"

Ulric's gaze remained stuck on the bodies. "I will never be ready for this. But I suppose the deed is done, and we'll use the tools available to us. We'll deal with the consequences later." His jaw clenched tight. "Well done, Aren."

The old king looked to me, and his eyes narrowed. "Your illusions?"

I lifted my chin and met his gaze. "They are."

He looked over them again. "Impressive." He handed me a bow and a quiver full of arrows. They felt heavier in my hands than they should have, as though already weighed down by blood. "We should move now. I haven't had word of Severn's troops returning yet, but they'll come. Best to go while we're only fighting a war on one front."

Albion turned his horse and rode away.

"Aren, your troops will lead," Ulric said. "The others have already been warned, but it will still be a shock to them. I'd advise against paying attention to any reactions."

"Won't be the first time I've repulsed people," Aren replied without any trace of self-pity. "This time it's at least more interesting."

Ulric grunted. "You have to ride with them?"

Aren swung up into the saddle of the other horse. "It will be easier to maintain control that way."

Ulric's lips narrowed. "Stay back if you can. They'll be taking most of the early damage."

Aren's half-smile was rueful. "I'll try to stay out of trouble. Rowan, your illusions will follow the bodies even if you stay back, correct?"

I nodded. "I think so. My magic is maintaining them, but they're connected to their sources."

Florizel head-butted my back. "Up you get, then. We'll keep as far out of the fray as we can when things get rough."

Ulric rode away through the forest.

"Be careful out there," I told Aren as I climbed onto a fallen tree and from there onto Florizel's back. "Don't… I mean…" I twisted my fingers into the coarse hairs of Florizel's mane and squeezed them tight in frustration. There was so much I wanted to say, but nothing that was appropriate.

And who cares anymore if it's not?

I nudged Florizel, and she stepped up beside Aren's horse. I grabbed the front of his shirt, pulled myself closer, and kissed him. His lips were frigid. I pulled back. His magic had changed, too. It had always been dark and cold, but now carried something deeper and danker in it.

"What's happening to you?"

"It will be fine," he said, and finished what remained of Morea's potion. "My magic is as strong as it's ever been."

"It's not the strength I'm worried about."

Morea reached up and took the bottle back from him. "I'll be following with the other healers, if you need anything else."

"Thank you," Aren said, but his attention was focused on the bodies. Morea hurried away.

He took a deep breath. "Shall we?"

A chill passed over me, but I nodded. "Ready whenever you are."

∽

WE REACHED the road at the bottom of the hill, where everyone waited in the last shelter of the trees, still hidden from anyone looking out from the city. I spotted Xaven with his people, who marched on foot and bristled with weapons that seemed out of place with their simple armor. Albion had rejoined the people of Belleisle. It was impossible to tell who among them was a Sorcerer and who was not, as they wore the same coppery-colored armor and all rode the horses that had carried them from the island. It made for an impressive show of bodies. *People,* I corrected myself. *We have the bodies behind us.*

Aren halted the corpses at the tree line.

Ulric nodded, and Aren brought them out. He had the least-mangled bodies to the front of the group, but a few of the gorier illusions remained standing near them.

The crowd was silent, save for the sound of a helmet hitting the ground and someone retching. No one else moved, even when Aren directed the bodies onto the road. They bumped each other and shuffled forward, lacking formation or discipline, all displaying their mortal wounds. They looked like any reasonable human's worst nightmare come halfway to life, a grim reminder of the price of battle.

Armor clanked as several living troops turned and left quietly. *At least they didn't bother with speeches,* I thought.

"Very well," Ulric said. "Aren, if you're ready."

I rode beside him, and tried to ignore the glares and disgusted looks from some of the troops. They had been raised believing this was wrong. We were probably lucky they hadn't all bolted.

And they'll get over it, surely. These bodies are going to keep them from meeting the same fate.

Gods willing.

As we left the cover of the forest and stepped onto the road, I noticed that Aren's breathing had become shallow. His skin had taken on a grayish cast, and his feet dragged over the ground.

"What's wrong?" I asked.

"Nothing," he said quietly, his voice rough as the stones beneath the horses' hooves.

Liar.

Nothing had changed, aside from him. The bodies trudged on as Aren's shoulders slumped, his face lost its expression, and his eyes filled with pain.

"Aren?"

"Don't worry about me," he said. "They're taking a lot out of me, but my magic is stronger. It's healing me as quickly as they're killing me."

"They're what?"

He didn't answer.

The living troops had already covered a good portion of the distance from camp before they met us, but we still had a ways to go before we would reach the city gates. The plain stretched out before us, and the city beyond, locked behind its wall. To our left sat the Despair, which I had no desire to look more closely at. I turned instead to the right, where the plain met the sparkling ocean.

I squinted.

"Aren? Should there be ships out there?"

He turned. "Gods damn it all. No. That will be Severn's troops coming in. They'll land in the outer harbour and be on us before we reach the gate."

My heart jumped into my throat. "What do we do?"

"Keep going and pray for a miracle, if you're so inclined. If we turn back now, they'll follow."

I took a deep breath. "I'll find you later."

Before he could answer, we were gone. Florizel turned and raced away from the bodies, leaping into the air as soon as she'd picked up enough speed. Ulric and Xaven had obviously seen the ships, and wore grim expressions as their troops pressed on. Behind them, Albion and his people had their attention trained on the ocean.

"To the water," I called to Florizel, and she turned.

Six ships, all black with white sails, approached the harbour. They were still a good ways out, though the distance closed with every moment that passed. The bodies and our troops might make it to the gate.

Maybe.

I called to my magic, ready to use the ocean's water to push back against the ships, but hadn't yet recovered from the illusions. I wouldn't be able to do more than splash the hulls.

Farther out and to the east, something massive moved under the water. As it approached, it became a collection of lighter flecks just beneath the surface. Florizel stayed well away from the ships as we looped behind them and back toward land. "What is that?" I called, and pointed. She flew closer.

A gray tail breached the surface, and my breath caught in my throat. My people would have mistaken them for hundreds of dolphins.

I knew better.

Ulric had been as wrong about the merfolk as he was about Albion and the people of Belleisle. We were not alone.

"Closer to the ships," I called, and Florizel obeyed. I'd learned my lesson the last time I'd acted as a distraction, and didn't order her too close. Still, someone on the ships saw us. A shout sounded from one, and moments later the soldiers had lined up on deck, eyes on us. Arrows flew, and all fell short. We circled back, darting closer and falling back, holding their attention as below us the merfolk passed beneath the ships under the clear ocean waves.

An arrow larger than the others shot past us. "Rowan?" Florizel called over her shoulder. "I think they have magic down there."

Another arrow came. I nearly tumbled off Florizel's back as she shied to avoid being hit. "I think you may be right. Fall back."

A chorus of creaking noises filled the air as the six ships shuddered to a halt and the soldiers on board stumbled. Though the wind still filled their sails, the ships sat dead in the water. Ominous clunking noises rose from beneath the waves. Someone called out an order, and soldiers beneath us headed below decks.

I wouldn't be any more help there. I patted Florizel's neck, and we flew back toward land.

The battle was about to begin.

The bodies approached the city, and arrows rained down on them. Severn's soldiers in their red and silver armor held their positions atop the wall and below it, where they waited on the outside with the gates locked tight behind them. There seemed to be hundreds of them.

At least they're not at the palace, I thought, but my stomach turned at the idea of our people fighting them.

My illusions had held up while I was gone, but seemed to be less robust than I'd have liked. I opened myself to the magic in the land, willed it to fill me, and waited.

Nothing happened. Aren had said that his was coming back to restore him, but mine still refused. I had overcome my own limitations, but it seemed I was still no match for whatever damage my own people had done to me in prison.

I let go of my focus on the illusions. They'd have to be enough as they were. *If I lost all of my magic now—*

An arrow shot past us. "A little higher," I called, but Florizel was already climbing.

"What now?" she called back.

"I don't know."

We circled over our people. The arrows from the wall stopped as the soldiers below marched forward. The bodies fell before them. Though Aren had kept them moving in spite of the arrows that protruded from their eyes, their faces, and their bodies, they couldn't stand against swordsmen hacking at their legs and torsos. As they collapsed, so did the illusions that matched them, multiplying the effectiveness of every successful enemy attack.

I searched the crowd for Aren. He wasn't retreating as the bodies fell. Rather, he held his horse still and focused on the soldiers that approached him. Though he held a sword in his hand, he didn't raise it. He just sat like a statue.

I held back a scream as a red-clad soldier raised an ax to strike at him.

The soldier stopped, then turned. He roared, and rushed back at another of Severn's men, striking him in the side of his head and dropping him to the ground. Another joined him in turning against his fellow soldiers, and another, creating a knot of confusion.

I breathed again.

Behind Aren, the rest of the troops joined the battle. The noise of it was horrible, all clashing metal and grunts and cries and bellowed orders. Florizel shivered beneath me, and we looped away from the city, toward where the Sorcerers from Belleisle charged into battle, working whatever magic they possessed as they went.

My arrows would be useless now, unless I wanted to risk injuring the wrong people. I hugged my left leg to Florizel's side, and she turned. We flew high over the wall.

Beyond it, the city had erupted into chaos. Whatever plans Severn and his people may have had for an orderly battle had been thrown out. While the area directly behind the wall was still clear of anyone aside from soldiers, the streets to the east teemed with people in fine clothing, all of them running as fast as they could, many of them yelling or crying, clutching prized possessions to their chests.

"Looks like Ruby got in," Florizel observed, and flew harder toward the area everyone else was fleeing.

We passed over streets and intersections, over tall buildings and tiny shops and an open marketplace where people cowered in their covered stalls. Fine homes with tiny green yards appeared beneath us, well-kept and beautiful... at least, the ones that weren't on fire.

The streets teemed with people who had not yet escaped, and with soldiers rushing in from the north and south.

A flash of red caught my eye. Ruby roared, and every hair on my body stood on end at the fearsome sound. Florizel alighted on a flat roof to catch her breath, and we watched as Ruby pinned a soldier to the ground, one long claw puncturing the armor that covered his chest. Another soldier drove a lance into her side, catching the soft flesh behind a foreleg. Blood poured out, darker red than her scales, flooding the cobblestone street beneath her. She turned and snapped, taking her attacker's head off in a neat bite.

Florizel let out a shuddering whinny. "We have to help her!"

"We can't," I told her. "And this is what she wanted." The great dragon swallowed half of a smaller soldier and roared again.

"Head for the gates, and keep your eyes open. Watch for Griselda."

We flew over the streets, and I watched for a flash of gold hair among the rich fabrics and done-up hairstyles, but saw no sign of Griselda. If she had made it away from the east end, she was either at the gate or staying hidden.

Florizel pulled up as we approached the gates. A dark-hooded figure crept along the inside of the wall, sticking to the shadows, head down.

"Go back! I think I saw her."

A moment later we'd landed on top of a building with a gently-sloping roof across the street from the triple gates. Florizel's hooves scrambled over the copper roof, and I dismounted before she pushed off into the air. I pulled an arrow from my quiver, nocked it to the bow, and crouched.

Griselda was nearly invisible in the shadows, but a gate guard spotted her as she passed. I couldn't hear him over the noise from the other side of the wall, but she didn't respond to whatever he yelled at her. He drew his sword, and she moved farther away.

I released my arrow. He moved at the last moment, and it only caught him in the arm. The next shot was luckier, and he went down as he tried to pull the shaft from his throat. Griselda didn't look up, but kept on toward the gate. I covered her until she'd reached the now-empty stall next to the small pedestrian gate to the left. My magic held steady, though I felt it helping me make my shots.

Promising. A little more recovery would be lovely, though.

The heavy wood behind the gates swung slowly inward, leaving the ornate iron gates closed. A series of locking mechanisms moved, slipping vertically and horizontally in a complex pattern on the rear of the gates, changing the design as they unlocked.

Without Griselda's knowledge, we'd never have opened them. I imagined her smile as she remembered the tricks of the process, as the gates released and our soldiers on the other side pushed them open and flooded the street.

Florizel landed for long enough for me to mount again, and we took off.

Xaven's people and Albion's pushed through the crowds of soldiers and freshly-gathered nobles that met them inside. I couldn't see Aren, Ulric, or anyone I recognized. They had dismounted, and blended in with everyone else.

An arrow whizzed by Florizel's head, and I decided we should take to the streets, as well. She landed, narrowly missing an older woman who looked like she'd been in the middle of having her hair styled when Ruby attacked. Half of her silver hair twisted up into a horn on one side of her head, while the other flowed in stiff waves over her shoulder. She darted away.

"Are you staying here?" Florizel asked as I slid to the ground.

"I should find Aren. Why?"

"Did you hear the horses screaming back near the big buildings? I have to go there. "

I hadn't. I looked in the direction she'd indicated with a nod of her head, and saw what had to be the palace towering over the buildings in front of it. "Do you need me to come?"

She shook her head. "I suspect I can break down the doors myself. Go find Aren, save the country for your kind. I'll take care of mine."

She was gone before I could reply. I spotted Aren, looking somewhat recovered, and fought my way past a few nobles who seemed to be trying to attach themselves to him and his father. I grabbed his arm and he spun, dagger in hand.

"Rowan!" He lowered his weapon.

"Are the bodies all down?" I hollered. I barely heard myself over the noise, but he nodded and stepped closer.

"They did their job. Are you all right?"

A roar echoed through the streets. Someone screamed, and the crowd parted as Ruby's massive form stumbled toward us, walking on three legs as the fourth dragged behind. Blood dripped from what looked like a hundred mortal wounds, and the webbed skin on one wing had been torn to tatters. And yet she still came, snapping at people and harming none of them.

"Ruby!" I cried. "Aren, go. I'll be right behind you."

He looked from me to the dragon. "You should stay out here with her. You've done enough."

"The hell I will," I said. "You're not going to finish this without me."

He stepped out to block a soldier charging at Ulric, and I ran to Ruby.

"You're alive."

The whites of her eyes showed, and she breathed in great, hot, wheezing breaths. "It seems so. But I think not for long, though all that delicious armor fortifies me. I believe I've had a change of heart, little human."

"Have you?"

She raised her nose to sniff at the air, and kicked her good leg out at a soldier, sending him crashing into a brick wall and the back end of her body to the ground. She winced. "I'd like to see more of this life. Another year or two. Perhaps a hundred, I can't say. What do you think of that?"

"I think I'd like it very much. Find yourself an alley to rest in for now. I'll send Morea back when it's safe, and whoever else will come. Would jewels help?"

"They wouldn't hurt. No need for healers, though." She reached back to fold a flap of skin into place. It flopped down again, oozing blood. "Hmm. Perhaps a stitch or two might not hurt." She looked up the street, where Aren and Ulric had disappeared among the people of the city. "You don't need me?"

"No, you've done plenty, thank you." I resisted the urge to hug her.

She dragged herself down a side street and disappeared. A scream echoed out and a balding man fled, waving his arms over his head.

There was hope for her. Hope for all of us. We'd passed the gates, and most of the city's guards were busy with the attackers still at the wall. The crowds I now fought my way through were all regular people, afraid and confused, but at least unarmed.

But that didn't mean the fight was over.

When I reached the palace, Ulric was speaking to someone

through the gate—an old man in a red uniform with a deep scar down one side of his face. I crept closer.

The guard frowned at him. "I didn't think you'd return this time," he said.

"It's not that easy to be rid of me."

The guard's lip lifted in a crooked smile. "A fact that your son would have done well to consider. Welcome back."

A wrought iron gate large enough only to admit foot traffic opened, and Ulric and Aren entered the shaded grounds beyond, weapons ready.

I raced after them.

S creams drifted up to the windows, but I couldn't see anything except confusion in the streets beyond the empty little courtyard. I grabbed the wine bottle, drank deeply, and retreated to the shadows of the room.

The blistered skin on my legs stretched as I settled back into the plush chair in the corner, and I bit back a groan as nauseating pain washed over me. I reminded myself that the pain was temporary, and forced my trembling muscles to relax. I sipped again from the wine bottle and sighed. Severn liked his drink strong, it seemed. I'd have to be cautious if I wanted to keep my wits about me.

But it felt so good to let go.

I added my potion to the remaining wine and swirled the contents gently with a rotation of the dark bottle.

If I could get him to take just a taste of the wine, if I could earn his trust for even a moment, I would have him. Not a perfect plan, certainly. It wouldn't finish him, and if he realized what was happening, it might be the end of me. A small price to pay. With Ulric dead, my purpose for being in the city was gone. *And without Kel to return to...*

The lock clicked, and every muscle in my body tensed. Severn strode into the room, sword drawn, and locked the door behind him. He opened a panel on the door frame and drew out a short, thick chain that he hooked onto the door to keep it closed.

If only I'd known about that.

"Get up," he ordered. He scanned the room for new threats, as though I might have managed to piece together a weapon from the inkpot and quill in the drawer.

I didn't move. He needed to think I was too drunk and weak to be a threat. I blinked hard, hoping he was still only half right. "Can't. This is good wine. I'm surprised you're still here. Why don't you do that... whatever you do to escape situations like this?"

His lip lifted in distaste and he turned to face the door. "I can only return home that way, at least so far. Attempting anything more right now would be quite dangerous." He adjusted his grip on his weapon.

I sipped at his wine again, which was now graced with my potion's bittersweet flavor. He needed to think it was safe, and I was beyond caring what the poisons within might do to me. "I hope you don't mind, I started your victory celebration without you."

He spun toward me. "Don't mock me. The rules haven't changed. I only need my father and brother dead, and the throne is still mine. And then the traitors who've opened the palace doors will die. Them and all the others who have failed in their loyalty."

"Oh, I know. I'm not mocking you. Care for a drink?"

He sneered again, and looked away. *Can't blame a girl for trying,* I thought. Something else in his words niggled at my brain, but I couldn't make my thoughts line up.

I struggled to my feet, hoping it was the strong wine that caused my disorientation. If my injuries were worse than I'd realized, or if the potion was poisoning me more quickly than I'd anticipated, I'd be no help to anyone.

Severn kept a wary eye on me. I spread my empty hand out to the side as I stumbled toward him, still holding the bottle in the other. "I want you to know, I've reconsidered."

"Sit down."

"No. I think your wine helped me see more clearly. See, Ulric is weak. I—" The thought clicked into place. "Wait, you say you need him dead? I thought you killed him already." My stomach clenched. Hearing he was alive was the best possible news, aside from hearing that Aren was with him. But if they burst in here with Severn waiting, with Aren no better than a weapon created for Severn's use and Ulric without his full strength...

My heart raced.

Severn held his sword steady. "I may have overestimated there, as I just spotted him outside. But it won't be long."

I struggled to hold onto the story I'd concocted while he was gone, to not let my true reactions show. I could still gain his trust. I had to. "He can't beat you, though. And you said yourself that Aren can't. This is a minor—" I hiccuped, and forced a laugh. "You know. That."

He frowned. "I don't know what you're up to, but you can stop. It's too late to beg for mercy."

"Perhaps. This wine, though. You should relax with me. It's lovely." The room swam. *Focus, Nox.*

"You know, I looked through your papers." I waggled a finger at him. "You weren't completely honest about the Darmid thing, were you?" Darmid came out *Drrmud.* "I mean, you're right about the danger, and good for you for spotting that. But you could take another decade to figure it out, couldn't you, without ruining all? You just wanted to prove yourself, to show you could face a threat your father wouldn't. If people knew about that, or how you got rid of him... But you've kept it all secret so well."

"Sit," he ordered.

I sat on the edge of the bed and slipped on the smooth blanket. My legs cried out, but I pushed myself up. Severn continued to watch me, wary. I needed to seem more pathetic, less threatening. I thought back to my husband's more emotional nights in the bottle, and pouted. "No need to be nasty. I think it was terribly clever of you. Take charge. Get it done while you have the support of the... you know. The guys with the power. You're doing things no one else dares."

His fingers flexed by his side. He appeared to be trying not to smack me.

Too late to stop my babbling mouth now. Either this would work, or it wouldn't. The wine made me feel as though it hardly mattered, but I would press on.

"I think I told you before that I wanted the advantages of living in Luid," I said. "I long to be aligned with greatness, even if only for a moment."

He frowned. "Then you chose your cause poorly, didn't you?"

"I did choose wrong. Wrongly." I shook my head, letting my hair fall over my face. "I didn't understand until I met you. Until I felt this... this connection. You felt it, didn't you? You said you did." I stood and stepped forward, and what was left of my skirt caught under the pointed toe of my boot and ripped to the top of my thigh. "Oops."

"How much of that wine did you drink?"

I pouted and held up the half-empty bottle. "You left me for so long. I slept in your bed. It smells like you."

The room spun. I had indulged too much. I stumbled again, and he caught me in his free arm. I pressed my body against his, and hoped he interpreted my shudder as a shiver.

"Relax," I whispered, and offered the bottle. "Drink with me. They'll never get in here. Even if they do, you might as well have a few happy moments first."

His eyes narrowed. "If I wanted to die happy, I suspect I could do better than a little wine. It doesn't affect me as it does you."

That's it, then. He's not going to drink. I steeled myself for what would have to come next. Kel would understand.

I raised the bottle slowly to take another sip, then dropped it and reached up to brush his hair away from his face.

Gods help me.

Never had I been so revolted by such a perfectly attractive person. At least that meant the dragon's egg potion might still be blocking his effect on me. I leaned against him, chest to chest, and stroked his cheek. "Is Sara coming back?"

He chuckled, and my blood chilled. "Why, are you interested in applying for her positions if she doesn't?"

"Maybe temporarily." I stood on my toes, put my arms around his neck, and pressed my lips against his. *Sloppy*, I reminded myself.

I only wished I were drunk enough that I would forget this later, if later ever came.

He dropped his sword and reached behind him. A moment later the point of his dagger dug into my ribs. His lips pressed harder against mine. I tried to pull back. He wouldn't let me. His tongue pushed into my mouth and his teeth drew blood from my lower lip before he shoved me away.

"We don't play nice around here," he said, and wiped his mouth on his sleeve. He froze, staring at the faint blue stain his lips left on the fabric. "What is this?"

I didn't have to feign fear. "I don't know what you're talking about."

Someone knocked at the door. Severn's eyes didn't leave me. "What did you do?" he bellowed, and leaped at me. He pushed me onto the bed and pressed the tip of his dagger to my throat.

His eyes glazed over, then cleared. He stepped back and held a hand out. A flame danced on his palm, strong and hot enough that I recoiled from it.

My work was only half-done. The taste of potion might keep him from replenishing his magic, but he still had significant stores within him. That would have to go. No turning back now.

I gritted my teeth, prepared for his attack. "I didn't do anything you didn't deserve, you deceitful, murderous son of a whore."

He raised his hand, then stopped. The flame disappeared as he reached for the front of my dress and pulled me up. The back of his hand caught me across my left cheek, hard enough that bright spots accompanied the flood of pain.

Something broke inside of me as he dropped me and the shock drove out the effects of the wine. Tears flowed down my cheeks that had nothing to do with physical pain. I sobbed as emptiness returned. He hit me again.

"Tell me what you've done!"

I looked up into a room blurred by tears. Severn seemed far

less fearsome now. My work was nearly done, and there was nothing left for him to take away from me. "Why, so you can have Sara fix it for you? Will she be keen to help you after you locked her away?"

He grabbed me by the throat and shook me, snapping my teeth together. "You have no idea what you're talking about. She's more faithful to me than a witch like you will ever understand."

"Then what are you waiting for?" I gasped. I could breathe, but just barely. "Kill me."

He dropped me. I lay on my back, wishing the black spots at the edges of my vision would take me away.

"Kill you?" he scoffed. "So you can take your secrets to the grave with you? I think not."

I struggled to sit up again. "Kill me like you did Myk. Like you thought you killed your father. Like you did..." I couldn't say his name. Not in front of Severn. "Like you did the mer. How's that curse working out for you?"

Severn roared. I waited for the magical attack that would weaken him. Instead, he lunged. For a moment, I felt nothing but heavy pressure in my side, though I understood perfectly that he'd changed his mind about ending me. I sucked in a ragged breath and pushed at him. He pressed harder, slid the dagger deeper. He leaned in closer. "I'd say about as well as it's working out for you. Don't die yet. I still need you."

He pulled the blade free, and sharp pain washed over me. I pressed my hands to my side, where blood spurted out from beneath my ribs.

Another knock at the door, light but frantic.

Severn stepped away and pointed the dagger at me. "Don't go anywhere. We're not done."

I couldn't answer. A new pain gripped my stomach. The beginning of the poison's effects.

He went to the door. "Who is it?"

"Sara." Her voice cracked and quavered. "Please. I didn't know where else to go. Severn, let me in."

He hesitated, though it was obviously her voice. He opened the door as far as the chain would allow. "Sara," he breathed as one terrified eye and a lock of gold hair appeared in the opening. "Are you alone?"

She nodded.

"Get in here. I need you." He closed the door tight and unhooked the chain, then stepped back, dagger ready, unable to trust even her.

The door swung open, and Sara stepped in. She looked wrong, pale and bleary-eyed. She looked around the room as though she'd never seen it before.

"Close the door behind you," Severn ordered.

"I—" Her eyes brightened. "I can't. Severn, you have to—" Her own sharp intake of breath cut her off, and her eyes glazed over again.

Severn leaped forward and grabbed Sara's arm. He pulled her forward and tried to close the door, but he was too late. Aren met him on the other side and pushed back.

Fresh tears filled my eyes, this time from relief. Severn wouldn't win. Not now.

Sara's eyes cleared again, and she moved away from the door. In a quick glance she took in the sight of me on the bed, burned and bleeding, then darted to a corner of the room on the far side of the bed.

Another push from the other side of the door sent Severn stumbling back.

Aren strode into the room, looking half-dead but ready for a fight.

The air pulsed with magic, and Aren dropped to the floor.

ROWAN

F inding Sara in her room had been a stroke of brilliance on Aren's part, but I wished he'd waited for his father before grabbing hold of her mind and forcing her to join us. Ulric had wanted his guards, who his faithful man at the gate promised would be his as soon as they learned he was still alive. They'd gone off together, and I wanted to wait.

Aren had no patience for that. I'd followed him to Sara's room and watched as he blasted through the door lock. Her expression had gone slack as he grabbed hold of her mind, then cleared and composed itself into a calm mask. Tension showed around her eyes as she fought back, but she was powerless. She'd moved quickly and with certainty through the hallway toward the king's chambers.

I tried not to feel sorry for her, but it was impossible. This was the Aren who not so long ago had earned the fear of two nations through his blind use of his power, who I had been so terrified of when we met. His purpose had changed, but that didn't make his actions more palatable.

And yet I couldn't say it wasn't necessary.

Ulric still had not caught up with us when we passed through a dark sitting room. I was about to mention the fact to Aren, to suggest that we should wait, when Sara raised her fist and knocked.

"Aren, what about—"

"Shh."

He stood aside and waited. Nothing happened, and she knocked again. Aren stayed out of sight as Sara spoke to Severn, focused entirely on controlling her. It seemed she fought back harder than most. Severn had probably trained her well.

Aren glanced quickly at me as the door opened and Severn pulled Sara in. He shoved at the door, and met resistance. When I moved closer to help, he held up a hand, indicating that I should stay back.

I stepped toward a pair of chairs set next to a cold fireplace as he rammed the door again with his shoulder. He stepped into the room.

Ulric, where are you? He wouldn't be much help with his magic, not with what he'd just been through. But his sword would help, and perhaps his men.

I tried to hang back, but my feet carried me forward. Though my magic felt like it was finally recovering, I couldn't afford to use any more—not if I wanted to have any left at all when the dust settled. But I couldn't let Aren fight alone.

The first thing I saw when I entered the room was Nox, lying on the bed, hands clutched to her side, covered in bright blood that had soaked into her white apron.

The second was Aren, face contorted with pain, struggling to his feet, sword gripped tight. His jaw clenched hard as he continued toward Severn in slow, halting steps.

The air grew heavy with magic as Severn continued his attack and Aren fought against him. He was doing it, keeping the pain at bay, but it wasn't enough.

Gods help me.

I drew on my diminished magic stores and threw an illusion out, one straight from my imagination. A copy of Sara ran at Severn, arms outstretched and hands hooked into claws. It wasn't perfect, but it was enough. Severn's focus broke, and Aren recovered. He sent a blast of flame at Severn.

An empty ache deeper than I'd felt earlier spread through me. I calmed myself, and felt my power replenish the slightest bit. Not enough by far, but some.

"Rowan," Nox called weakly. I ran to her and grabbed the blanket from the end of the bed to press against her side. I couldn't see much of the wound, but the blood flowing from it told me it was deep. Maybe fatal.

"Hold on," I whispered, and applied as much pressure as I could. "We'll get you out of here. Help is coming."

She grunted. "Not fast enough. Listen. Severn will burn out. Keep him fighting."

I turned back to the fight. Severn had shot back with flames, hot and hard enough that Aren backed away. The carpet next to the door burst into flames and the door swung shut, apparently of its own accord. Severn grinned, then froze. His expression turned sour as his shoulders stiffened and he raised his hands. He glared at Nox.

"You."

One word, carrying with it a heavier threat than a thousand more could have conveyed.

The air filled with smoke and the thick scent of burning wool as the fire in the carpet spread, and Nox groaned between the coughs that racked her body.

Someone hit the door from the other side. It flew open, but Severn wasn't finished. The flames at the door blasted higher as it swung open, and whoever was on the other side of the bright blaze shouted over the crackling of the flames and retreated.

Ulric.

Aren turned to the fire and held his free hand up, fighting back. The flames flickered and wavered, but continued their approach. The curtains at the window ignited as Severn picked up his sword. Aren spun to face him, abandoning his attempt at magical control. He swung and Severn defended, firelight flashing off their blades.

My magic gathered within me. A smaller amount than I'd had the last time I had to use it this way, to be sure, but one I now felt certain I could control.

I closed my eyes against the smoke that burned them and tried to focus my attention elsewhere. There was water nearby, but aside from what was in the pitcher on the table beside the bed, none of it was easily accessible. It flowed through a system of pipes in the walls that led to an underground cistern, it rested in wells outside, and bubbled in the great fountain we'd passed in the square and several large ponds in the gardens. Though I'd never explored the palace or its grounds, I sensed every place I could draw from.

The water lifted out of the pitcher and hurtled toward the flames, making no impact.

More.

I tried to draw from Severn, and found I no longer hesitated over using my magic against my enemy. It would be the closest source, would kill him if he didn't have enough magic to fight back. I reached, and felt the absolute blackness of what remained of his magic pushing against me, protecting him. It was costing him, but not enough.

The flames continued to spread, a greater threat to any of us than Severn himself.

I abandoned the attempt and turned my attention back to the water around me, behind the thick stone walls and far outside the palace.

This is it. This will cost everything.

My breath caught in my throat.

So be it.

I called the water. My teeth ground together as every muscle in my body tensed as though lifting the water with their own strength. A moment passed, and nothing happened.

Harder. More.

The walls rumbled, and cracked. Water spurted from shattered pipes overhead as shards of stone crashed to the floor. I threw myself over Nox to shield her as I drew harder, calling to the element of my gift, sending out every bit of my magic I had fought so hard to gain control over.

The big window shattered as a wave crashed through, drawn from the fountain outside and carried in by magic and its own momentum. It combined with the water from the pipes to wash over the room, dousing flames and drenching everything, crushing and pummeling like the punishing pressure of a water-fall. Though my body trembled, I didn't let myself collapse. When familiar white spots crowded my vision, I shook them off.

Not again. We're not done. I held myself steady over Nox as the deluge from above tapered to a trickle, and tried to ignore the hollow feeling blossoming within me.

Someone coughed as the water receded. I pushed myself onto my knees and looked around.

The water had washed Aren and Severn's feet from beneath them and torn their weapons from their hands. Aren stood first, and Severn raised a hand as though to throw a blast of magic.

Nothing happened.

Aren looked from Severn to Nox, who nodded. An expression of terrifying delight came over his his face. "Severn. What's happened to your magic?"

Severn screamed. It was a sound I imagined a dragon might make as it died. The sound of a heart breaking. He climbed to his feet in jerky, puppet-like motions, trembling as he fought Aren's control.

Ulric dashed into the room, and I called him over. "Take this," I told him, and handed him the blanket that held back the flow of Nox's blood. "It's bad. But I can't—"

Chills gripped me, and I stumbled back from the bed. I hit the wall shoulder-first, and sank to the floor. I searched within me for the spark of my magic.

There was nothing. Not a candle-flame, not a pinprick of light. My stomach clenched.

No. Please.

Ulric watched me, but Aren's attention was still fixed on Severn. The fire and flood had been minor distractions, and now he was back to the hunt.

Severn stooped, slow and stiff, fighting every movement, to pick up his knife from where it lay on the floor, then darted to the corner and hauled Sara up by one arm. She cried out as he spun her around and pushed her against the wall next to the bookshelves, trapping her with his arm. A moment later his knife, dripping with blood and water, was at her throat.

Severn laughed hysterically, then snarled. "Are you enjoying this, brother?"

Aren moved closer. "I think I owe you far more than this."

Severn was aware of what he was doing. Aren had left him in control of his thoughts, but not his actions.

I looked to Sara. She was under no one's control now. Not Aren's, and not whatever influence Severn might have had when his magic was strong. Her hands clawed at his, drawing blood, but he held her tight. Tears coursed over her cheeks.

"Aren," I croaked.

He shot me a sharp look that stopped me from saying more. He looked insane, wild-eyed and savoring every moment of this.

"Don't tell me to stop," he said in a low, calm voice. "I told you not to expect to witness mercy here. My brother taught me better than that." He turned back to Severn. "I can never repay the physical pain he's caused me, or the mental anguish. But this... this I can share. How does it feel, Severn, to hold a loved one's life in your hands and know you have no choice about what comes next?"

The knife twitched, and a thin stream of blood flowed down Sara's throat.

Severn laughed again, but his eyes shone as though he held back tears. "Do it." He pressed his quivering lips together. "Make me kill her. Show me how well you've learned your lessons."

"Please, no," Sara whimpered.

No one moved for several seconds. Aren looked to the bed where Nox lay, holding back silent sobs. Not, I thought, tears of physical pain, but the agony of the realization of what had to have happened to bring Aren to that point.

She whispered a question to Ulric. He looked away, and nodded.

Aren turned to me.

I could have told him to stop, to be the better person and to not let another life be lost. But I didn't. I was done trying to control him, to change him to better fit what I wanted or needed.

"Do what you think is right," I said.

For a moment, nothing happened. Then Aren snarled, and Seven's arm that held Sara pinned to the wall dropped. She raced back to her corner and crouched beneath a dripping tapestry, quaking.

"May I move now?" Severn asked. "If I promise to be a good little boy and not attack? I don't have magic to fight you with." He seemed to be listening for something. "Gods, how do people live like this?"

A wave of terror hit me as I wondered the same, myself. Even with my magic bound, I'd always had it in me. With it gone, I felt truly alone. Empty. Hopeless. The Despair was nothing compared to this.

"You may find out yet what it means to live without it," Ulric said.

Aren turned to his father, eyes wide. "You would let him live?"

Ulric frowned. "You would kill him now? This is still a challenge, Aren. Severn made sure from the beginning that it wouldn't be cleanly fought, but you might still finish it properly. You've disarmed him. He's lost. It's over."

"I didn't disarm him," Aren said. "I think Nox did that."

"Not for long," Nox said, though the words came out breathy and faint. "The potion won't last forever. He'll need a cell like at the prison in Ardare. And more potion. Much more." She coughed, and Ulric pressed harder against her wound. "You can't let him live."

"There will have to be a trial," Ulric said. "According to the law."

Severn snorted. "At last, your playing by the rules works in my favor. Gods, you're a pathetic excuse for—" His jaw snapped shut, and Aren smiled.

"He might become burned out completely in time," I suggested, and was surprised at the flat, hollow tone of my voice. I didn't sound right. "It can happen."

Ulric turned to me, understanding written across the lines of his face.

"What?" Aren looked at me. "What's wrong?"

"I think mine is gone," I said. I choked back a sob. "Small price to pay, right?"

Aren blinked, as though waking from a trance. He stepped closer. "You said this wouldn't happen."

I tried to smile, and failed. "I'll be fine. Just different, I guess. A bit like I was before we met, but—"

Behind Aren, Severn sidestepped toward his sword.

"Aren, watch out!"

Nox gasped and sat up straight. She pushed herself to her feet and launched herself at Severn as Ulric reached for her and missed.

The next few seconds unfolded slowly, as though reality had drawn itself out to a dream pace.

Nox raced at Severn, stumbling, dripping crimson onto the floor as her wound opened. Aren spun, but instead of raising his sword, he reached for Nox. Severn crossed in front of the window and had almost reached his weapon when Nox hit him hard with her shoulder, sending him stumbling.

I screamed as they teetered and tipped out the window.

Aren grabbed the back of Nox's dress and hauled her back, and she fought against him as he drew her farther into the room.

Severn grabbed onto the window frame with both hands. Blood dripped from his hands where broken glass punctured his skin, but he held on, leaning back, one foot braced against the lower part of the window, the other hanging behind.

"Let me go!" Nox screamed. Aren held her tight around her waist, hand pressed against her side. She kicked back at him. "We haven't won yet!"

Ulric came to a halt in front of the window, where Severn remained still as a statue save for the violent tremble in his arms.

"Aren, are you holding him there?"

"I am."

"Release him."

Severn laughed. "Still looking for a fair fight, father? Gods, you're pathetic. This country deserves better, deserves a king who will—"

I didn't feel the magic moving through the air, but the room shook as it had when the pipes burst. The stone around the window casing cracked and crumbled beneath Ulric's power. My heart leapt into my throat as I caught a glimpse of Severn's eyes widening, and then he was gone.

Ulric turned back to us and rested his hands on his knees while he caught his breath. When he looked up, he seemed to have aged again, but his eyes burned with life.

"There," he said. "Fairly finished."

"And by magic," Aren added. "No one can question who the crown belongs to. He challenged you in the woods, and you accepted."

Nox slumped forward, and he laid her on the floor. "Finished," she echoed. "Aren, is Kel gone?"

"Completely."

She took a shuddering breath, and coughed. A fine spray of blood settled on her lips. "At least there's that." Her eyes closed.

"I can help," Sara said. "Please."

Aren looked at her. She stiffened as he intruded on her mind, but didn't back away. "Take her," he said as the scar-faced guard entered the room and looked at the mess.

"About time," Ulric grunted. He pushed himself to stand straight. "Greely, take Nox to the infirmary, then find Xaven's daughter Morea to help." He turned to Sara. "Save her."

The guard collected Nox gently in his arms and followed Sara out.

Ulric paused at the door. "I'm sorry, Rowan," he said. "But I thank you." He left us, intent on keeping an eye on his wounded daughter.

I pulled my knees to my chest and buried my face in my arms as sorrow overtook me. We'd all lost so much, and others had paid a greater price for our victory. I willed the tears to stop, but no sense of peace followed. All I felt was empty and numb.

Aren sank to the floor beside me and put his arms around my shoulders. I leaned into him and breathed in the damp, smoky scent of his clothes. There was little comfort there, but resting was good.

"Aren't you going after Nox?" I asked.

"No. Ulric will keep an eye on Sara, but I don't think she'll try anything. She's probably as much a victim in this as anyone. There's nothing I can do there, anyway. Besides, I'd rather be with you."

He didn't ask whether I was all right, a fact which I appreciated. I was not, and doubted I ever would be.

"Can you take mine?" he asked. He lifted my chin and kissed me. Though it was deep and passionate and almost woke something in me, I felt nothing of his magic. No darkness, no cold, no power that would fill me and lift me and make me whole again.

"We'll find a way to fix this," he said, and tried to brush my hair back. His fingers tangled in the bright red strands that mocked me with the reminder of what I no longer was.

He got to his feet and lifted me, then placed me on the soaked bed. I curled up in his arms and listened to the water that continued to drip from the magic-shattered pipes overhead.

W arm. Floating. Cradled. I drifted in a golden haze, and felt no pain.

I'd have stayed there forever if I could. I sensed there was loss elsewhere, and pain. Unfinished business that could never be completed, because the other half of something was missing and could never be returned.

No, I decided. *Better to drift.*

Pain caught up with me. Not heartbreak, but a deep ache in my side. Irritating at first, but it expanded until I couldn't help letting out a groan. Someone smoothed my hair back from my forehead. Cool hands. Small. Not the ones I wanted.

I squeezed my eyes closed tighter, and warm tears rolled down my temples.

"Oh, no." Rowan's voice, soft and soothing. "Don't cry, please. Nox, you're alive."

As if that were good news.

I opened my eyes. Rowan leaned over me, bright red hair plaited and pulled forward over one shoulder, filling my vision.

She leaned back, and I looked around the room. Sunlight streamed in the windows, and gauzy, white curtains billowed in a soft breeze. All was quiet, but familiar faces filled the room. Aren sat beside the bed, though he slept with his chin resting against his chest. Ulric stood in the corner, looking anxious as a father awaiting the birth of a child. I supposed that wasn't too far off, though I wondered whether his expression had more to do with concern for a daughter or for the Potioner he might still need to save him.

Morea stood nearby, an array of potions and clean dressings handy. "Welcome back," she said.

I shifted my weight and winced. "Thank you. You stitched me up?"

She nodded. "Sara helped. She's quite incredible with healing."

"Where is she?"

"Locked up, awaiting trial," Ulric said. "Her help in this matter will not likely factor into things, but the question of Severn's influence will, if we ever discover the truth of that. You shouldn't worry about her for now, but we may have questions later."

I thought back to the experiments outlined in Sara's books, the ingredients on her shelves, and the excitement in her voice when she explained her theories. I doubted she could blame Severn for all of that, no matter what subtle magical skills he had used to keep her under his power.

Deep and heavy pain surged through my body again, radiating from the wound under my ribs. Anything else—my burned legs, my bruised face—seemed inconsequential next to it, but they would certainly make themselves heard soon.

"Morea, might you have something a little stronger for the pain?" I asked.

She nodded and hurried out.

I sighed and leaned back on the pillows that Rowan arranged behind me. I nodded toward Aren, and Rowan smiled. "He's been awake for two days," she said. "When he's not helping get things in order and hunting down traitors, he's here waiting for you. Seems a shame to wake him now that he's finally getting some rest."

His dark eyes snapped open. "This is worth waking for." He leaned over the bed and hugged me gently, careful to avoid touching my injuries. "Well done, sister."

"You should rest," Rowan said. "Both of you." She turned to Ulric. "All of you."

"Forget about that," I said. "I'm awake now. Tell me what's happened."

It didn't take long. Ulric had defeated Severn. It hadn't played out exactly by the rules of a challenge to a ruler, but that paled in comparison to the lies and schemes that surrounded Severn's rise to power. It was all coming to light now as people's loyalties shifted back to Ulric, as they insisted that they'd had no intention of betraying him, that they'd thought he was dead.

It sounded like Aren had a large part to play in digging the truth out from among the self-serving lies. Whether he was happy about using his skills that way, I couldn't tell.

"And your magic?" I asked Ulric. "Has Morea been helping with that?"

He looked like she had. The once and current king wore clean, evergreen-colored garments, and looked to be in better physical condition than I'd seen him in since we'd met. Handsome, strong, appearing hardly even middle-aged.

He nodded. "I'm not at full strength yet, not pushing it too much, but she's helping. She was quite impressed with the supply cupboards here." He lowered his voice. "No one thus far has figured out that I might not be as powerful as I once was, but hearing that you were successful in your self-appointed mission here would be most welcome news."

I made myself smile, and pushed my blankets back. "I was. I'll have you stronger than ever in no time."

"Not yet," Ulric said before I could try to sit up. His habitually hard expression softened. "I won't see my daughter run herself into the grave for my sake. We can keep this quiet until you're ready."

"Thank you."

"Thank *you*, Nox." The corners of his eyes creased. "We wouldn't be here without you. May I say that I'm proud of you?"

I considered that for a moment. "Only if you promise not to have me hanged for disobedience and desertion."

He smiled. "Fair enough. If you'll excuse me, I need to speak to Morea."

After he left, I turned to Rowan. "What about your magic?" I'd nearly forgotten about her sacrifice, but as the pain cleared the wool from my mind, it all came back.

She looked at her feet. "It's as good as gone. I've been taking what Morea's made up for me, but it's... I don't feel much. A little, sometimes, or a feeling like it *should* be there. But it's not growing. Maybe I'm imagining it."

Aren's brow creased, but he said nothing.

"Let me try to bring it back," I said. "You have the capacity to channel magic. It was there once. I refuse to believe there's no way to make it happen again."

Rowan glanced at Aren, then down at her hands.

"Unless you want something else," I added, speaking more quietly. "Have the two of you talked about this?"

"Not much," Rowan said softly. "We've been busy. Hardly seen each other, really. He's been with your father, I've been with Ruby and the merfolk."

"The merfolk?"

She smiled. "They came after they heard about Kel. Saved us, really. They kept six ships of soldiers from reaching land and joining the battle. Ruined the hulls of some fine boats, but…" She trailed off.

My gut clenched at the sound of Kel's name.

"You really think you can help her?" Aren asked.

I shook off thoughts of Kel and the merfolk. There would be time for that later. "Maybe. Can you feel her magic at all right now?"

"Not from here."

I bit back an exasperated sigh. "Kiss her, you dummy." I closed my eyes as Rowan stood and her weight lifted from the bed.

A long moment later, he said, "It's there, but it's weak. Smaller even than it was when she woke up on Belleisle. Emalda brought it back then, though, and you're as good as she is. Better, even."

I opened my eyes and studied Rowan. Hope mixed with

uncertainty on her face. "Probably. Let me get back on my feet, get myself fixed up, take care of Ulric. Then we'll see."

Aren frowned. "Can it wait that long?"

"I don't know," I said. "Griselda might, though. Have you spoken to her?"

"She's returned to Belleisle with the others," Rowan said. "And so has Ernis Albion, and the others."

"He was here?"

Rowan smiled. "You missed a lot when you took off. No one had much advice to offer before they went. Seems like everyone appreciates what I did, but they think I'm done this time."

"Everyone but me, then," I said. "Let me try. If it's stable for now, we should have time."

Rowan met my eyes, and she was obviously considering her options. If we left things as they stood, there should be no reason for her and Aren to not be together, even if their future would be complicated. If I succeeded, she would take back the magic that had obviously ripped a hole in her spirit when it left her, but she would lose him.

I didn't envy her the decision, but I would make sure it was hers to make.

"Thank you," she said softly.

"I'll get everyone fixed up. Nothing else to do, right?" I tried to keep the pain out of my voice, but failed miserably.

"Nox, I'm sorry," Aren said. "Do you want to talk about it? About him?"

I made myself smile to reassure him. He didn't look ready to have that conversation, but I appreciated his willingness to suggest it. "I'm fine," I said. "I just need rest, that's all. And some time."

He didn't look like he believed me, but he stood and followed Rowan to the door.

I motioned for her to come back, and she nodded to Aren to tell him to go on without her.

"Would a week give you time to decide?" I asked.

Her shoulders slumped, and I saw how much of her calm and pleasant demeanor was a show for the others. Something in her had shattered. "Do you think less of me for needing time to think about it?" When I didn't answer, she twisted the ends of her braided hair between her fingers and continued. "I've been trying to see the good in this for the past few days, trying to adjust to the idea. I mean, I could be with Aren. Ulric has been kinder to me and has let me help with so many things that he wouldn't have trusted me with a week ago. In a sense I have what I've wanted, but…"

"But you've lost yourself," I finished. "And the greatest love in the world can't fix that."

She nodded. "I want him. I love him. But I can't be the person he deserves if I'm not whole. I've never felt this empty, not even when I stood next to the Despair. It's like I'm cut off from everything. I'm going through the motions of being alive, but I'm no better off than one of the bodies that Aren raised to storm the gates."

"The what?"

She smiled, but there was no heart in it. "You should have seen it. Another thing I'll tell you all about when you're ready." The smile faded. "So yes, I want my magic back, more than I can say. But if it means losing Aren, I don't know if I can take that, either. He's everything I—well, everything I never wanted but didn't know I needed, I suppose. How can I turn my back on that?"

A few weeks before, I would have thought less of her for her indecision, for not grabbing at the incredible power she could so easily possess. But as I lay there in the soft infirmary bed, wishing I could go back in time and do whatever it took for me to be with Kel, I couldn't. I'd have sacrificed everything I had and was for one more day with him. Would have given up my gifts and potential renown for a little house by the sea. It shamed me, but it was the truth. I could hardly expect more from her.

"I understand," I said, and she reached out to squeeze my fingers.

"Is there anything I can do for you?" she asked as Morea entered the room.

"No, thank you."

She nodded, and left.

I rolled onto my side and winced at the pain that shot through me. Morea left a cup on the table beside the bed and followed Rowan out. I sat up enough to drink, then rested my head on the pillow. The pain lessened, and I drifted. In that half-dreaming place between sleep and wakefulness I felt a warm body lying behind me, his shape molded to mine, arm draped over my waist.

A whisper came to me again, the soft crashing of waves, and I let myself be swept away.

50

AREN

"Make it quick," Ulric ordered as he stalked out of the large audience chamber.

The gallery was packed with spectators, as it had been for every day of trials all week. The king didn't so much as look at them, or at the thin, unremarkable prisoner the guards dragged out of the room.

"Aren!" Dan called, and the crowd fell silent. The guards paused, but didn't let him look back. "You know what he was like! You know how he forced you!"

I turned away and followed my father out of the room.

Dan wasn't wrong. Had things gone differently, I would have been in his position. Though our magic granted us a measure of protection from his influence, I had allowed Severn to use me just as Dan had. Though I'd had no part in the plot to bring Ulric down, I'd done my share to support my oldest brother. Yes, I felt some sympathy for Dan, and I understood that he thought he'd had no choice. I'd thought the same, once.

But we all have a choice. The course of my life was not predestined, nor was Dan's. Fate or the gods may have played a role, but in the end the consequences were ours to bear. Dan would lose his head for betraying Ulric.

And I would lose my freedom for obeying him.

Ulric went to the basin in the corner of the small, wood-paneled office behind the audience chamber and splashed water on his face.

"Not an easy one," I said, and sank into a leather-upholstered chair.

"Sentencing one's child to death never is, I suspect." He took a seat next to me. "You've done well this week."

"As have you." His recovery had been remarkable. In the six days since Nox had awoken, she'd shared her time between sleep and her potions. Ulric had been her first challenge, and she'd barely paused to eat while she worked. And she'd done it. He was as healthy as I'd ever seen him, appearing younger and stronger than he had before his capture. The air around him vibrated with power that he was able to use without any consequences.

There are always consequences, a voice whispered. I smiled. I couldn't tell whose voice it sounded most like anymore, Phelun's or my grandfather's or the mer elders. The voice was right. Rowan and I had both learned something about those consequences during the battle for the throne.

As of yet, only one of us had recovered. Morea had returned home, but Nox had taken over fussing over me, not satisfied until the last of the ill-effects of my work with the dead were gone. The other effects of that—the people's knowledge of what I'd done, the rumors and the judgements—would linger far longer, but they were hardly her business.

"Did you speak to Nox this morning?" I asked.

He snorted. "I did. She accepted the position as head Potioner, but on a temporary basis. Then she told all of the others they were free to go home. Most went, and she sent them with enough compensation to keep them and their villages happy for a good while."

"Were you angry?"

He smiled and leaned back in his chair. "No. In spite of my many mistakes, I think two of my children turned out just fine. How's the dragon today?"

"Well, I think. Recovering, and not complaining too much

about not being allowed more soldiers to eat. You'd have to ask Rowan, though. She's been taking care of the animals."

He rubbed a hand over his face. "And what of her? Is she adjusting well to her new situation?"

"I don't know," I said. "She's trying. She's suffered as great a loss as any of us, and I think it's changed her. Whether that's permanent, I can't say." I didn't mention Nox's idea. Ulric seemed to accept that Rowan was no longer a threat, and didn't object to us being together in what little time we had available. If her magic returned, that would all change.

No need to tell him, especially if it might not work.

"She made a great sacrifice," he said. "I won't forget it."

We'll see. "I'm sure she'll appreciate that."

He stood and moved to the big desk by the window. "Who's next?"

It took me a moment to realize he'd gone back to work. "That's all for today. I've spoken to a few more witnesses regarding Hamel Darsin, so we'll be seeing him tomorrow. He says he didn't betray you, that if he'd known you were alive he would have supported your return."

"Do you believe him?"

"He believes it, I'm sure. And no one has indicated otherwise." Not even those without magic who knew him, his servants and family—and I'd know if they'd lied to me. "I'd keep an eye on him, but he's not a threat to you now that you're back in power." Like most of them. Ulric was accepting oaths of renewed loyalty from anyone who had thought him dead when they supported Severn. Things weren't going so well for anyone I found had known otherwise.

"Very good," he said. "Are you doing more questioning tonight?"

"No. As a matter of fact, I need to leave after supper. With your permission, of course."

He narrowed his eyes, though without any of the suspicion or anger he'd have shown even a week before. "Going somewhere with Rowan?"

"Sort of. Will you be working?"

"All night."

He waved me off, then turned his attention to the papers that littered his desk—the ones we'd recovered from Severn's room which listed every bit of evidence against Darmid, as well as the names of people who had supported him in his quest for answers and power. Ulric had been over all the information a hundred times already, and had to have known it all by heart.

I closed the door gently behind me. It seemed there was so much still to be said, so many questions I wanted to ask him about his past and my future, about my mother and Severn and everything I'd taken for granted for so many years.

But all of that would wait. Other, more important things needed my attention.

At twilight that evening a small group left the city and crossed the plain, headed for the forest beyond. Florizel and Murad walked with us, but weren't asked to carry anyone. Their work was done. Her wound was healing, as was his mind. They'd been inseparable since their reunion, and had spent their time enjoying their freedom, soaring together over the forests and the ocean, sleeping beneath the stars outside the city walls, avoiding the palace and the turmoil of the city.

I envied them that freedom. Overseeing the proper burial of the bodies I'd raised and those who had fallen after hadn't been pleasant, but I'd owed them that. Investigation into upcoming trials had followed, and would be my unpleasant—if interesting —duty for some time to come. I suspected that as soon as the trials were finished, I'd be required to make amends with the wealthy nobles whose support my father still needed. They'd fared well under Severn, and we had destroyed many of their homes in our attempt to save the rest of the world from him.

If I was ever to gain the favor of my father's people, I had a lot of work ahead of me.

For tonight, though, I was as free as I suspected I would ever be.

Rowan rode beside me on Clover, a horse she'd been forced to abandon on our first journey away from Darmid. She'd been pleased to find the piebald mare safe in the stables, no doubt taken from the cabin on the lake by one of Severn's men.

We'd abandoned her when Kel warned us of Severn's approach and went against his elders' wishes to take us to the safety of the Grotto. My stomach clenched at the memory. Dangerous times, but I wished I could go back to them, to sit and laugh with him again. That wound had not yet closed, and a part of me hoped it never would. I didn't want to forget.

Rowan's aunt Victoria came next, passing the time in quiet conversation with Patience, who rode beside her on a pretty white pony. Both the girl and the Sorceress were finding it hard to settle in at the palace, and had become close. Victoria was acting as a surrogate mother of sorts to the girl. I suspected that when the family was reunited, Ches would have no objection to the arrangement.

Nox brought up the rear, riding alone on a large, gray gelding.

We left the land-bound horses a good distance away from our destination and reached the clearing on foot as the stars appeared one by one in the darkening sky. The pond Rowan had created remained. A stream flowed from one end of it, tracing a silver path through the woods and down the hill toward Luid. No other sign of the fight with Severn remained save for a fallen tree. To a casual observer it would be nothing but a pretty clearing.

But not to us.

Murad shied as he entered the clearing, perhaps remembering the fight, or the brief moment of clarity he'd been teased with at the end of it. Florizel nuzzled his cheek, and he quieted.

Victoria spoke softly to Nox, who stared at the water, expressionless save for the tightness in her lips and a slight tremble in her chin. Victoria handed her a seedling with its roots wrapped in burlap, then scattered other seeds as Nox chose a spot near a dead oak, close to the water.

A slight breeze rippled the leaves overhead, but the air in the clearing remained still.

Victoria pulled a silver spade from her bag and dug a hole, stirring up the heavy scents of moss and soil. Nox placed the root ball gently into the wide space. Victoria filled the hole in, and both stepped back.

Nox joined us on the other side of the pond. I put my arm around her shoulders and pulled my sister closer. She leaned her head against me.

"Ready?" Victoria asked.

Nox nodded, and the garden came to life.

Victoria smiled as her magic flowed. The tiny seedling grew, sending out thorny tendrils that climbed the tree. Soon the barren wood was covered with broad leaves. Blue-green buds appeared and blossomed into massive roses with deep-blue petal edges and glowing, sea-green centers.

Violets, snowdrops, and a dozen varieties of blooms I'd never be able to identify carpeted the ground where Victoria had scattered her seeds, taking root in the thin soil and springing up from among the moss and leaf litter.

Nox sighed. "I wish Kel could see this. He'd have loved it."

Victoria studied her work. "Do you want me to tame them?"

Nox wiped her eyes with a white handkerchief. "No. He liked things wild. It's perfect." She stepped toward the rose-covered tree and rubbed a petal between her thumb and forefinger, then bent to inhale its sweet fragrance. "Thank you, Victoria."

"My pleasure. Truly."

Patience interrupted with a flurry of questions about magic and what had just happened, and Victoria led her a short distance away so they could talk. Nox leaned in to rub her face against a rose, and came back to us. She pulled a crystal vial from her bag and handed it to Rowan.

I caught myself holding my breath as Rowan took it.

"It's not dissimilar to what I made for... to what I made when I first arrived at the palace," Nox said, "but I tweaked it for you. Made it stronger, taught it to reach deeper to find your spark, and I think I've come up with something that will open up the channels for your magic to replenish itself when you send it out. I feel like we might only get one shot at getting this started. That's why it took so long, but I think this is your best chance."

Rowan accepted the vial, pulled the stopper, and sniffed. "So it's really going to work?" She didn't seem as excited as I'd have expected her to be at the prospect of her magic returning.

"Yes." Nox tilted her head to one side, contemplating something. "Your tiny flame will be a blazing conflagration again, if that's what you want."

Rowan nodded, but didn't drink.

My stomach tightened. "What's wrong?" I asked. I suspected that I knew why she was hesitating, but hoped I was wrong. *She wouldn't.*

"We should talk about this, first," Rowan said. She rolled the vial between her fingers, and the deep pink liquid inside shimmered with gold flecks and twisting purple shadows. "Aren, the thing is, I love you."

"Likewise."

"And I want to be with you." She paused. "Is that still what you want?"

"Of course. With everything in me. But I hope you're not thinking of making your sacrifice permanent so that can happen." The idea that she wouldn't jump at the chance to be healed, that a life with me might mean as much to her as her power, chilled me to my core.

"Of course I'm thinking about it," she said, and wrapped her fingers around the vial, holding in its warm light. "I suppose we don't know what will happen either way, really."

"I do," Nox said. "I've been familiarizing myself with the library, doing some reading while I've waited for batches to settle. If you don't get treatment soon, your magic will die completely, as everyone else seems to think it already has. There will be no chance of bringing it back. You'll be the normal, average person you used to think you were. There would be nothing to keep you two apart, even with Aren being next in line for the throne, and especially with you having proven your loyalty to Tyrea." Her brow furrowed. "You'll age normally. There's no reason you two shouldn't be able to have children together, and given your past, there's obviously power in your family line that they'll carry on. You'll die a lot sooner, but you can still have a good life. Kind of like the one you used to expect."

My heart stilled.

Rowan swallowed hard. "Or you can save my magic, and I lose Aren." She squeezed her eyes closed, as though fighting off physical pain. "Gods, I can't face either consequence. What am I supposed to do?"

I took her hand, and she looked up at me. "You need to do whatever is going to make you happy," I said. "But if I might state a case..."

"Go ahead," she said, and wiped her sleeve across her eyes. "Please."

"I want you."

She looked up at me, eyebrows pulled together. "So you think I should give up my magic?" No judgement, no disbelief. Just curiosity.

I smiled and brushed her wild hair back from her face. "No. You're a Sorceress. Your magic is part of who you are. I first loved you before it was free, and I'll continue to do so if you decide to give it up, for as long as you live. I will do everything in my power to make you happy." I paused, half wanting to leave it at that. Having her as my queen would make everything so much better. I could bear captivity if I had her with me.

But when I looked into her eyes and saw the loss and the sorrow she carried with her, I knew I couldn't accept that sacrifice. Asking her to refuse her magic would be to imprison her even as it granted me a measure of freedom.

I cleared my throat. "But if I have a choice in the matter, I don't just want you for just a few years. I want you in my life two hundred years from now, assuming we manage to stay out of trouble and live that long. I want the Rowan I fell in love with, not the shell I fear you'd become without your magic." A lump formed in my throat. I ignored it. "The world is a better place with you and your magic in it, even if you can't truly belong to me. And if there's a way you can, I swear I'll find it."

Rowan hugged me. "Thank you," she whispered in my ear. "I'll always be yours, no matter where I have to go or what happens to me. I love you. Nothing will change that."

Nox smiled sadly as Rowan released me. "Time to get it done, if you're going to."

Rowan hesitated for a long moment. Tears filled her eyes as she looked at me again, then lifted the vial and drank. A shudder shook her body. Her expression filled with joy and life as magic flowed back into her, strong enough that I felt its power washing over me before she pulled it back.

Rowan laughed, and I realized I hadn't heard that sound for far too long. She'd made the right choice, no matter what it cost us. I ignored the heaviness in my heart, and reminded myself that I hadn't lost her yet.

Nox took the vial back. "Congratulations, Sorceress," she said. "Did you make the right decision?"

"I believe I did," she said, though not without a hint of sadness. "Thank you, Nox. For everything." She threw her arms around Nox, who returned the gesture without hesitation.

Footsteps crunched through the woods, and we turned as Ulric entered the clearing.

"You said you were working tonight," I said.

He nodded. "I was, but I heard there was something happening here. Am I late?"

"Depends on what you came for," Nox said. She slipped the vial into her pocket.

Ulric looked at the garden. The roses still glowed, though darkness had covered the forest. Lightning bugs flitted between the trees and among the flowers, and the sound of the stream trickling downhill brought a tranquil mood to the place. "I wanted to pay my respects," he said. "I hope you don't mind."

Nox's smile widened. "Not at all." She took her father's arm and led him to the roses.

Rowan threw her arms around my neck and kissed me hard. "Quick, let's run away before he notices my magic," she whispered. I sensed she was only half joking.

I held her tight. "No more running. We'll figure this out. I don't intend to lose you again."

Ulric spoke to Nox and Victoria, but I couldn't hear what he said. He crouched to speak to Patience, who nodded solemnly and shook his hand before he stood again.

And then he came back to us.

"So," he said. "You've recovered, Rowan."

"Mostly," she said as she turned to him. "Are you going to be cruel to me again?"

The corners of his mouth turned down. "No. I wish I could blame my behavior entirely on my illness, but I'm afraid I can't. I did and said what I thought was in the best interests of my family and my country." He held out a hand, and she shook it hesitantly. "I don't do this often," he continued, "but I owe you an apology. You showed great bravery during the battle, and you made a great sacrifice to save us and ensure our victory. You've showed your loyalty to Tyrea and to my family. I will see that you have public recognition for this. I was wrong about you. Wrong about a lot of things, in fact, and I will do what I can to make it right."

Even in the low light, the blush in her cheeks was obvious as she pulled her hand back. "Thank you, sir. I can't say it was my pleasure, but I'm happy to have helped."

Ulric nodded. "I'm pleased to see that your magic is recovering. You're powerful, and a great asset to Tyrea. That said, you need training. A lot of it, if you're going to reach your full potential. With things as they are, I certainly can't oversee that myself, or spare any of my people to give you the attention you obviously require."

She lowered her head. "I understand, of course."

"Before he left," he continued. "Ernis Albion told me you would be most welcome back at his school. He and I have had our differences over the years, but I can't say you'll find a better instructor anywhere. We'll send you as soon as possible."

Still dumbstruck over my father admitting he was wrong about something, it took me a moment to process what he was saying. "You can't send her away," I said. "You just said—"

Rowan squeezed my hand hard. "Let him finish."

Ulric's expression turned serious. "We need to speak about your future too, Aren. I've asked Pilfanthe to take the position as my Second."

A good choice, if he felt I wasn't ready. The old Sorceress had been a member of his council before. We'd discovered her in the prisons, where Severn had sent her after she figured out what had happened to Ulric. Once she recovered her physical strength, she would be a wise, loyal, and level-headed Second.

A far better one than I'd have been. A flutter of hope awakened in me.

My father cleared his throat before he continued, and seemed to be struggling to keep an neutral expression. "Now, I'll need you here as we finish hearings, get the city back in order, and try to fix Severn's mess. But after that, I'm considering the idea of sending you elsewhere as an ambassador. Severn wasn't wrong about everything. We have been too insulated, and I've been less diligent about relations with other countries than I should have been."

"Darmid?" I asked.

He allowed himself a small smile . "No, I won't be sending you there yet, though we need to start making progress there one way or another, and soon. I was thinking of Belleisle, actually. Not permanently. But I think you'd be welcome there from time to time if we approached them more diplomatically than you managed before. It's time to open ourselves to potential allies, and you're our best door to that."

Rowan squeaked and squeezed my hand again, so hard the bones in my fingers ground together. My skin prickled with excitement.

Ulric crossed his arms and narrowed his eyes at me. "This doesn't change anything. I'll want you here frequently. I won't be around forever, and you have much to learn before you take your place as king."

My stomach turned at the thought, but I nodded.

"But there's time for that later. I feel strong, and should the Goddess smile on me I'll have decades left to rule." His gaze flicked to Rowan, and he tightened his lips to hold back a smile as he looked back to me. "For now, I'll just tell you to give my regards to your grandfather when you see him, and offer you no other advice on what to do with yourself during your free hours when you go to Belleisle."

Rowan released my hand and flew at the king, wrapped her arms around his neck, and planted a loud kiss on his cheek. He chuckled softly, then reached around her to shake my hand. She released him and stepped back, eyes glowing.

He smoothed the wrinkles in his shirt. "This is not permission for anything more. The laws will not change for you any more than they have for anyone before you. If you choose to ignore them, you'll face the consequences. I can't say I'm entirely comfortable with this situation, either. Gods willing, I'll be dead by the time the kingdom has to face the consequences of your affection. But if anyone can find a way to make it work, it will be the two of you." He smiled ever so slightly. "I should get back to the city."

He turned and left without another word.

My legs grew weak, and I sank to the ground. "Did he just say he wasn't going to stand in our way if—"

"Yep."

"And we have time to—"

"Uh-huh."

"Even if we can't actually—"

"Right."

Nox came over, with Patience and Victoria close behind. "Are you two ready to go?"

Rowan offered a hand and pulled me to my feet. "We are."

Nox hung back as the rest of us went to gather the horses. I watched as she plucked a fat rose blossom from the tree and set it adrift on the pond. A soft breeze rippled the surface, fracturing the moonlight that shone on the surface. Her black hair fell over her face as she leaned closer to the water, adding her tears to the spring.

I turned away, leaving Nox alone with her loss.

She seemed more at peace when she joined us again, but her sorrow still surrounded her like a black fog, heavy enough that I felt it even when I tried not to. She would survive. We all would.

But there were some things that neither potions nor magic could fix.

"I wish Cassia were here," she said as we rode back toward the city. We'd let the others ride ahead, and the pair of flying horses soared above, chasing each other through the dark sky.

"She'll be back soon," I said. The mers had all left almost immediately after the battle, barely staying to speak with Ulric. "Mariana and Arnav agreed to allow more communication and cooperation between their people and ours until the Darmid situation is sorted out, and she'll be our go-between. We can bring her out to say goodbye when she arrives."

Nox thought that over. "Do you think she'll stay for a while?"

"Maybe. Are you planning to?"

She glanced down at her hands and tugged her sleeves further down over them. "I'm still considering Ulric's offer. All I've ever wanted was to have my gifts used and appreciated. I now have everything I dreamed of when I first learned who I was. But I don't know. All of my dreams seem wrong. I need to find new ones." The corners of her lips turned down. "I should have died, you know. I wanted to, after I knew for certain that Kel was gone."

"I know. I'm happy you didn't."

She nodded. "Me, too. Much as I want to be with him again, Kel would want me to be to live and be happy. I just need to decide what that means. It will take time, but I'll try. For him."

"Whoa. You plan to be happy?" I leaned over to feel her forehead, and she slapped my hand away.

"I know, it's not like me. But I got a taste of it. Besides, I think I'm out of people to exact vengeance on." She sighed. "It was a short list."

"So the old man is forgiven?"

"I suppose." She shrugged one shoulder. "I probably won't poison him or anything."

"I'm glad we found you, Nox."

She sat up straighter and took a deep breath, filling herself with the fresh evening breeze. "I am, too. And as much as this hurts, I'm thankful that I had the time with Kel that I did. I wouldn't trade any of it." She swallowed hard and forced a smile. "The future's a big place, right? Anything could happen. Maybe even happiness."

I looked over the group riding ahead of us and felt truly at peace for the first time. "You just never know."

51

ROWAN

U lric gave me a few weeks to finish my business in Tyrea —visiting with Cassia when she arrived, sending Ruby off to find a new place for herself where she'd cause less panic among local humans, making my own travel arrangements.

Victoria's, too. She and Patience were on their way back to the border, escorted and well-protected by some of Ulric's people, to make an offer of employment to Ches. Ulric was certainly not done with Darmid, and he required the services of someone who knew his history, his magic hunters, and his king. The rest of the family would be invited to join them, and well cared-for as they settled into their new life, should they choose to come.

Florizel and Murad left with them, headed for the mountains and their herd—or, if the leadmare would not take Florizel back, they planned to start their own. My feathery friend seemed horrified at the thought of being in charge of a family, but I suspected she'd do just fine.

I didn't see much of Nox. Without Ulric's potion or mine to keep her busy, she'd set herself up in the library, gorging herself on the knowledge she'd been denied for so long. She slept too much and smiled too little, but if anyone could rise from the ashes and begin again, I believed it was her.

It wasn't the resolution I'd hoped for, with eternal peace and happiness and joyous reunions for all. We had lost so much, and so many things remained unknown. But that's the way of things. Though we may wish for happy endings, life is an adventure that doesn't end. Each resolution is a new beginning, and not every road ends where we might want it to.

On the morning before I left for Belleisle, Aren and I rode again to Kel's garden. We'd have to say goodbye to each other soon, but I wasn't ready to let go. We'd come to a strange place in our relationship. Elated to be together, deliriously grateful for the thought that we might have decades before his responsibilities truly descended on him, but shadowed by the knowledge that he couldn't escape those expectations for his future.

He'd have to choose a queen some day. The thought carved deep claw-marks into my heart even as it made me cling tighter to what we were allowed to have.

The morning sun filtered through thick green foliage, leaving bright patches on the path we were slowly wearing through the forest with our regular visits. We left our horses in the usual place and made our way to the pool.

I sat beside the water and trailed my fingers over the surface. "Think it'll ever dry up?"

"No." He watched the little stream flowing down the hill. "You found a fine spring there."

I let my hand sink into the cool, clear water. "I feel closer to him here."

"Me, too. It's a good place for remembering. Peaceful."

I tried to remember Kel as he'd been when I first met him, and before the end. Kind, wise, funny, and full of love he'd so wanted to share with someone. He'd found that, and had been happy even though their future had been uncertain. I would try to do the same.

"Goodbye, Kel," I whispered, and drew my hand from the pond.

Aren sat behind me, legs stretched out on either side of mine. "Did I tell you I saw a unicorn?"

"No." I wanted to ask him a hundred questions—what it had looked like, what he'd felt in its presence, whether it was truly the most beautiful thing in the world. But when I turned to him, something in his eyes stopped me. Instead, I looked back at the sun sparkling on the pond and said, "That's wonderful."

He laughed softly and moved my hair aside so he could brush his lips over the back of my neck. I shivered.

"Hey," I said. "Kel might be watching."

"I hope so. He'd be pleased." He rested his chin on my shoulder, and I felt his heartbeat pounding against my back as he pulled me closer. Racing.

"You all right?" I asked.

"No. I'm terrified. I'm about to do something terribly foolish." He leaned back, and a moment later he'd reached around so his hand was cupped in front of me. A silver ring with a pale blue gem set into the band glittered in his open palm. The stone captured the sunlight and multiplied it.

My heart skipped. "Aren?"

"This is the custom where you come from, isn't it?"

"It is." I touched the ring, but didn't take it. My hands trembled. I twisted around to face him again, and my heart swelled at the sight of his smile, warm and unreserved—the one that reached his eyes, the one I'd fallen in love with. "But we can't. It's not allowed, unless you're leaving your family again."

"No. I know that I can't run from that future anymore." His expression became more serious, but the smile didn't leave his eyes. "I meant it when I said that Tyrea would do well to have you as its queen. It won't happen soon. It might not look the way you once thought a marriage should, or the way either of us expect now. But if you'll have me, I promise that I will do everything in my power to be with you. No sneaking around. No hiding. No more pretending I don't adore you. Whatever comes, I want you by my side. This is worth fighting for."

"But what about the laws?"

His smile widened again. "I've already angered the king,

offended the gods, and broken the law with you by my side. Why stop now? We'll find a way. I promise."

I couldn't speak around the lump in my throat as he got to his feet and helped me to mine. He held my hands in his. "So," he said, and a faint flush came into his cheeks. "Rowan, will you marry me?"

"Of course!" I threw myself at him and pulled him into a kiss that left us both breathless, and he slipped the ring onto my finger. "Your father's not going to be happy."

"I don't think your mother will be turning cartwheels in the streets, either." He put his arms around me and held me close.

"Think we'll be able to make it a few hundred years without driving each other completely crazy?"

He chuckled. "I think that's unavoidable. But I'm learning to enjoy your kind of crazy."

I breathed in the flower-scented air. Somewhere in the distance, a bird chirped. Another answered, and another, and then the woods were alive with a chorus of sweet music.

We sat next to the pond again, and Aren set a rose adrift on the water, as we did each time we came. "I do hope Kel can see this," he said. "He's probably laughing at me right now."

"And feeling quite smug, I imagine," I added. We sat without speaking for a few minutes, enjoying the warmth of the forest and the fact that for once we had no immediate need to fight for our lives or our future.

I leaned my head against his shoulder. "Aren, is this it?"

"Is this what?"

"Is this happily ever after?"

He kissed me again, softly and slowly. "Not yet. Something tells me this is only the beginning."

The End

AUTHOR'S NOTE

Thank you for joining me again on this journey, for seeing it through to the end, and especially for all of your support along the way. Whether it was through your purchases, your reviews, or your recommendations to other readers, you have expanded this story's world in ways I never thought possible. Writing can be a lonely profession, but the reading community makes it all so worthwhile.

I hope you'll join me for future books. I'm not done with this world yet, and I have many others in the works for you to explore.

In the meantime, remember this: You have the ability to take words and turn them into reality in your mind. Your love and attention makes stories blossom. You are full of magic, and you are amazing.

-Kate

ACKNOWLEDGMENTS

If it takes a village to raise a child, it takes a metropolis to bring a book into the world. I wish I could thank everyone who supported me through the writing of this book, but I should try not to add too much to the page count.

Krista Walsh, KL Schwengel, and Shannon Andrews receive the first thanks, for being the first readers. Early drafts can be rough going, but you all helped so much.

Joshua Essoe is next. Ripping stories apart so that they can heal and grow into something far better than they once were can't be an easy career, but I'm glad you chose it. I couldn't have asked for a better editor for these books…And I apologize for the horrible faces I made at you while I read through your notes. On every book. Really sorry.

I had a crack team of beta readers on this one, and they all deserve thanks: Annette Flick, Scott Holley, Kathy Dunlavey, and Katelyn Lowden. Every one of you added a unique perspective. I'm so fortunate to have you.

I'm not sure how exactly to thank my cover designer, Ravven. Your professionalism is exceeded only by your mind-blowing talent, and perhaps your patience. Thank you for creating the beautiful covers that persuaded so many people to give this story a chance.

Thanks to everyone else who has supported me as I sweated and cried over this book: My husband and my kids for getting me through not only the writing, but all of the obstacles that stood in the way. Whether it was moving, mental or physical health issues, or just me being a zoned-out weirdo, you took it all in stride. My parents and parents-in-law for your love and encouragement. All of the friends who live in my computer and who talked me down when things got crazy. I wouldn't have made it without you.

And to my readers... I'm supposed to be good with words, but they're failing me now. Your support has meant so much to me, and it's been a delight to get to know some of you over the past few years. I'll try to thank you the only way I know how—by creating more worlds, more characters, and more stories for you to love.

ABOUT THE AUTHOR

Kate Sparkes lives in Newfoundland, which is an island so magical it has its own (tiny) time zone. She's responsible for several humans, a few dogs and cats, and several worlds full of fictional people. It's enough to drive a person a little crazy... fortunately, that's an advantage in her line of work.

You can find Kate on many social media sites, including Facebook, Instagram, Twitter, and anywhere else that catches her passing fancy. The best places to find her, though, are her website (linked below) and her blog, Disregard the Prologue (www.disregardtheprologue.com).

www.katesparkes.com

ALSO BY KATE SPARKES

The Bound Trilogy

Bound

Torn

Sworn

❧

Into Elurien

❧

Bound Trilogy Prequels*

At Any Cost

The Binding

*Available as free downloads to newsletter subscribers. Visit www.katesparkes.com for details on these and upcoming titles~